SAMARIA

BOOK 1: THE DREAM MACHINE

To, Jane.

With compliments.

STEVE SUWALI

Copyright © 2013 SILVER DRAGON FILM ASSOCIATES LTD.

All rights reserved. No part of this book may be reproduced, stored, or transmitted by any means—whether auditory, graphic, mechanical, or electronic—without written permission of both publisher and author, except in the case of brief excerpts used in critical articles and reviews. Unauthorized reproduction of any part of this work is illegal and is punishable by law.

ISBN: 978-1-4834-0096-9 (sc)
ISBN: 978-1-4834-0098-3 (hc)
ISBN: 978-1-4834-0097-6 (e)

Library of Congress Control Number: 2013909611

Because of the dynamic nature of the Internet, any web addresses or links contained in this book may have changed since publication and may no longer be valid. The views expressed in this work are solely those of the author and do not necessarily reflect the views of the publisher, and the publisher hereby disclaims any responsibility for them.

Any people depicted in stock imagery provided by Thinkstock are models, and such images are being used for illustrative purposes only. Certain stock imagery © Thinkstock.

Lulu Publishing Services rev. date: 06/27/2013

DEDICATION

This book is dedicated to my beloved daughter—Lauren Sophia Suwali.

For all that you are, and all that you've yet to be.

Your forever loving father,

Steve Suwali.

ACKNOWLEDGEMENTS

Writing this novel has been a protracted, unwieldy task, something I could not have achieved without the help and support of certain people. I would like to thank the following for their kind advice and support along the journey. Firstly, I must thank my daughter, Lauren, for never once doubting that I would finish what I had started, even though it took nearly a decade! Then there's Sole Ferrer, my wonderful personal partner whose enthusiasm was second to none, and who laboured for countless months, for no reward, editing and proof reading the manuscript. Godfrey Morgan gave me invaluable advice from start to finish and continues to prove to be a priceless asset to the book's owner in all matters legal. Max Giammello: thank you for always believing I had it in me to finish this novel, your faith in me has, I hope, been well founded. My father, Mr Chanan Suwali, always a pillar of strength for all the family and the founding father of the Suwali family in Great Britian, is the source of my strength, enabling me to overcome huge obstacles by following his example. Last, but not least, a massive debt of gratitude is owed to my best friend Zeek for being my greatest counselor in all things.

The publication of this book by Silver Dragon Film Associates is testimony to the enduring love I have for you all. Again, thank you!

CHAPTER ONE

THE DREAM MACHINE

Thomas' fingers curled tightly around the steel mesh of the fence. It was painful, but he could not take his eyes of the menacing shape hurtling towards him. He could feel the knot in his stomach tightening, his eyes bulging as he watched it rapidly closing on him. It was roaring so loudly it made his head spin, but he kept his gaze firmly fixed upon it. With a screaming howl it lifted from the ground, seeming to hang suspended in the air for a split second, before climbing effortlessly up and away into the blue summer sky. He realised he had been holding his breath for ages and exhaled slowly, feeling the adrenaline ebb away as his pulse slowed. It was always the same—that heady rush as he watched the fighter jets launch into the air. He watched until the aircraft disappeared into a bushy white cloud, several of which where passing overhead. The screaming jet engines still boomed in his ears and he knew that if he waited, he would see the fighter again between the clouds. But as much as he loved watching the planes taking off whilst daydreaming of flying himself one day, Thomas turned and began to run home. Today was no ordinary day because his cousin Zowie was coming over to stay for part of the school break. Unlike most other girls, she wanted to fly too.

He jogged steadily over the clumpy grass verges, taking care not to be too close to the roadside or to twist his ankle in a pothole. Thomas cherished the countryside in which he lived. The lush green meadows and golden fields all around him had been a joy to grow up in, providing endless opportunities for exploration and adventure.

It was a good half of a mile from the RAF airbase to Thomas' home where he, his parents, and sister—Lauren, lived in a charming old farmhouse. He had been born in that very farmhouse a day short of fourteen years ago. It was his birthday tomorrow and he would be fourteen years old. His sister was his junior by a year. They spent a lot of time together.

Thomas shot around the last corner and onto the long bumpy drive leading up to the house. The tall privet hedges on either side were now shielding him a little from the sun. His dark hair was wet and plastered to his head from running so far in the summer heat. The salty sweat trickled down and made his eyes sting. A white cotton shirt stuck uncomfortably to his body and thick gravel crunched noisily under his feet as he reached the front door. A quick glance showed no signs of Zowie's dad's car. Oh well, all that running for nothing. She would arrive soon enough, but now it was time for a long, refreshing cold drink.

Zowie sat quietly in the front passenger seat of her father's brand new car. They had been chatting all the way from the city but now she felt a little tired. Her mother and father had divorced when she was only three years old. Her birthday fell on the exact same date as her cousin Thomas', but she was a year older and they took turns at spending their birthdays at each others' house. They were not actually real cousins, not as in 'related' cousins. Thomas' father and Zowie's dad were the best of friends, 'Brothers' they called each other after a couple of drinks at parties, and that is how Thomas and Lauren Shortwater had become 'cousins' to Zowie Kantell.

The car cruised almost silently towards the Shortwaters' with the only real sound being the steady thrumming of the tyres against the road surface. The leather seats felt comfy, cosseting her in the serene air-conditioned interior. She had preferred the sporty BMW her father had owned previous to the current Rolls-Royce, but he had said he was too old to be sporty these days. In truth, she knew he was simply dieing to show Thomas and Lauren's father—Jack, his new toy. Tonight it would be THE over-dinner conversation.

"How boring", she thought, "at least Lauren and Thomas would be more fun." The three of them always had a great time together, discussing their hopes of flying one day, and charging about in the open fields. Her own home was a large modern house on the outskirts of the city, which she loved dearly. She also enjoyed the Shortwaters' home very much. The rambling old farmhouse was situated in the middle of nowhere and held a wonderful rustic charm, a warm characterful appeal that the average modern building could never hope to match. Jack—Thomas and Lauren's father, had wanted to modernise it (her own father's idea she was sure), but his wife—Lilly, had threatened to take the kids and leave him if he did. "*Good for her!*" thought Zowie, who adored historical buildings. The farmhouse remained un-modernised.

Her father was always engrossed in modern 'hi-tech' gadgets. He was wealthy enough to have what he wanted and if it was 'cutting edge', he usually wanted it. He was not spoilt or greedy, on the contrary, he was very intelligent and had worked very hard to reach the position he had achieved. Her dad happened to be a scientific genius and had invented lots of very useful stuff. Some fun things too. His business was based around new inventions using the latest technologies, "but that is not for me," Zowie told herself. She and the Shortwaters were going to learn how to fly, they just had not quite worked out how yet.

She could not wait to go exploring again with the Shortwaters. They had acres of land that had been left entirely to nature. It had overgrown with all sorts of plants and trees over the years. There were different flowers everywhere you looked, and the sound of a bird singing was ever-present, even in winter. The three of them had built a den inside a tree-house far from the house. It really was a baking hot day and Zowie sat patiently in the car as it wafted along, wiggling her toes in anticipation.

IN ANOTHER PLACE, AND ANOTHER TIME

Lord Tamarin, his black cloak rippling in the gentle breeze, looked out from the white marble balcony. He rested his palms on the cool smooth surface of the stone balustrade. Samaria, his beloved realm, shimmered in the scorching heat from both of the midday suns. Never before during his reign had the kingdom faced the threat of peril that it did now. For far to the west of that world, it was said that the forces of darkness and dread were gathering once more. Ogiin, sworn enemy of Samaria, and once the most evil warlord of the vanquished Dark Lands, had been heard of once more. Of the three brave scouts that had left to bring back reliable information, rather than rumours, only one had returned, wild-eyed and almost mad with fear. Samarians were not easily made afraid.

Countless years ago the Samarian armies and their allies had driven the evil Venomeen forces from that world. But Tamarin had always felt they would return as long as Ogiin held sway over them. Did Ogiin still have the power to summon his monstrous legions? If so, their only goal would be to destroy the Essence Of Love. Should this darkness rise again, it would have to be crushed once more, and, this time, forever.

A feather-light touch stirred him from his thoughts and he turned to see Lady Meekhi standing before him. As ever, he was taken aback by her beauty, her piercing yet gentle green eyes, held his gaze tenderly, the bright Samarian sunlight danced and sparkled on her raven-black hair, the silken locks cascading down to her waist, her olive skin glowed, radiant beneath her emerald-green sleeveless robe. Her tresses were perfumed with honey and rose oil, and it was that intoxicating scent that stirred him from his reverie. Taking his beloved gently by the hand, he strode back into the royal palace, the silver dragon emblazoned on his cloak a bedazzling glow of light.

Despite Meekhi's presence at his side, Tamarin's mind was still elsewhere. If The Essence of Love were destroyed it would mean the destruction of love in all its forms, in all worlds. A blanket of darkness would unfold, full of such horrors as the likes of which had never been seen before, a black veil so cold and empty, so heartless in its intent, that all life would become no more than a nightmare, and none would dare to dream again. This must never come to pass. It would *not* come to pass! As long as he had breath in him, he would defend a world free of such tyranny, a world in which his queen could abide in safety, happy, and without cause for distress or alarm.

They had wandered into the great hall, and, standing there, he looked about him. In the centre of this cavernous marble chamber stood The Talking Table, an ancient table of thick, solid oak, in which was carved a wise old face. It was said that The Talking Table was formed from ancient war shields. Shields recovered from fallen comrades an eon ago after the defeat of Ogiin and his accursed Venomeen armies. The table ran in the same direction as the hall and it was here that Tamarin would sit at counsel with fellow lords, and Meekhi. In matters of truly great importance it was said that the table could indeed offer its own advice. He had yet to experience this and prayed such a need would never arise.

The cool ivory coloured walls, and the high vaulted ceiling, provided an atmosphere of peace and tranquillity. Tall arched windows along one long wall added an airy and honest feel to the room whilst the square windows on the opposing wall allowed a view of the serenely calm, deep blue sea below, basking in the heat from the two gloriously red suns. The palace sat astride a range of low rocky cliffs. Too low to be mountains and too high to be hills, they formed a natural defensive barrier along the Samarian coastline. If one tired of admiring the tranquillity of the ocean, then one had only to walk around The Talking Table to the other side of the great hall, and through these windows you could now see the bustling city of Sitivia down below. The seaward face of the palace sat in the centre of a natural, horseshoe-shaped, harbour, formed by the wall of *'hilly mountain cliffs,'* as Meekhi laughingly called them. As the sea warmed in the morning sunshine it would change colour from a deep dark blue to, by midday, a lustrous aquamarine that lasted until both the suns left to rest in the evening. Tamarin and Meekhi often took a stroll in the surf and the cool green water soothed their feet as it lapped easily against the golden sandy beach. He looked at the circular war shields and three bladed swords that adorned the walls of the great hall. Upon the dias at the far end of the room, stood the giant, intricately carved statue of The Silver Dragon, the most revered of all Samarian spirits. When, once before, love had been threatened by hate, The Essence of Love had been in the care of The Dragons of Light from the faraway lands of Dragonia. These dragon spirits had protected and guarded love since love had first warmed the hearts of living things. All had been well for much of history, then, the cold, evil race of Venomeens had come into existence. Incapable of love and devoid of compassion, they were bent only on the cruel domination of all other life. Knowing they could never know such a reign as long as love existed, they set about to destroy it. Love was, and, *still is*, but a small light. Yet a small light can hold back so much darkness. The Essence of Love is a shimmering handful of light consisting of all possible colours, a tiny portion of which the dragons had contained inside a small crystal vial. Everyone, *everything*, that knows love, has the exact same light glowing in their hearts.

During the terrible war against Ogiin and his Venomeens so many ages ago, all of the wonderful Dragons of Light had been destroyed, or injured so badly they could no longer protect Love. Darcinian (the then Samarian King) and his armies, had stood shoulder-to-shoulder alongside the beautiful dragons against the cruel, heartless Venomeens. When finally the Venomeen armies had been defeated, when their shattered ranks scattered into the far reaches of the universe having caused so much unnecessary pain and bloodshed, the great dragon overlord—The Silver Dragon, had given Tamarin, then only a young prince, this task: To forever protect The Essence of Love. He had placed the small crystal vial in Tamarin's hand and said in his deep, rich, flame-red voice; "Love feeds on love. If love knows love, it will always endure. For where love is found, hope can flourish. Young prince, one day to be King of Samaria, it is now your turn to know the price of such love. The burden is heavy, but yours to bear. Keep it safe, Tamarin, keep it close to your heart."

With that the terribly wounded dragon—once the most powerful of all The Dragons of Light, loped off into the distance to die in peace, his body glowing with all the colourful lights within him, lights which would soon fade and become dark. Tamarin had looked at the miniature bottle in the palm of his hand, his strong young fingers curling around it, already sensing that the tiny, near-weightless vial carried such a huge weight of responsibility. Tears trickled down his handsome sun-bronzed face as his watery eyes watched the land about him burn to black ash.

Samarians were blessed, unless taken by unnatural causes they could live for nigh on two thousand years, physically aging only at the very end of their incredible life spans. Yet when the time had come for Darcinian—the old king, to pass on, Tamarin had wept for days on end. The time of his father's reign had become known as The Age of All Ages. A time when Samarians had known both peace and war, abundance and shortage. But always the love in their hearts, their sacred bond of honour, and the path of truth, had carried them ever onward, safe in the knowledge that the justness of their existence left no place for fears or regrets.

Tamarin had carried that little bottle the silver dragon had given him close to his heart every day, until, by chance, he met his beloved Meekhi. Many years after he had been crowned King of Samaria, he had been out hunting with other lords when in the distance they had sighted a slave wagon train. There are no slaves in Samaria and Samarians cannot abide such injustice. He and his lords had spurred their horses into a gallop, their three bladed swords already drawn. The slavers, as always, fought ferociously to keep their "catch", but did not stand a chance. Before they even knew what had really happened, they lay dead, or mortally wounded. When Tamarin had freed the captives from the filthy wagons, he had found Meekhi. She was amongst the others, bound in chains, her ankles shackled, dirty and half starved. Tamarin had almost wretched at the evil stench of death and decay rising from within the slaver's wagons. Two unfortunate souls had not survived their capture but their rotting corpses still sat chained amongst the others, a truly macabre and sickening discovery. They had no doubt been headed for the slave markets of Dizbaar, a dirty pirate-filled land on the southern borders of Samaria. Its self appointed ruler, a grotesque little dwarf called Nazmeer, allowed many atrocities to be committed there as long as he gained his share of the spoils. Tamarin loathed the toad-like Nazmeer, but Samarians did not normally get involved in the internal affairs of other lands. These slavers, however, had been on *Samarian* soil, and had met with swift local justice.

Meekhi was a princess of the Land of Flowers, snatched by raiders whilst out walking amongst the dazzling array of flora for which her land was so very famous. Tamarin had fallen in love with her on sight. She had eyed her handsome liberator carefully. His long black hair hung straight over his strong sun kissed shoulders. He was tall with a handsome, innocent looking face, his big brown almond-shaped eyes sparkling and honest. She had also noted the skill and speed with which he had despatched several slavers using his tribladed sword, a weapon she had not ever seen before. She thought it very fearsome and whilst easily captivated by his boyish charm, she reserved judgement on the true nature of this deadly swordsman.

Tamarin released the captives from their shackles. Most set out to return to their various homelands and some chose to stay, settling in Samaria. He had taken the liberated princess to his palace atop the city of Sitivia and sent word to her father—Langorr, King of the Land Of Flowers.

Meekhi had been no more than nineteen years of age at the time. She adored the Samarians and their simple, honest ways. Tamarin, in particular, fascinated the young princess. She had never seen such a people, nor such a king. They lived a plain but happy life, wanting no more than was needed, and giving each other any surplus so all had enough. Even Tamarin's royal palace was left open to the whole populace to come and go as they pleased. But despite the open doors and gracious hospitality, his subjects rarely intruded upon his privacy. When her father had finally arranged for her safe return home, Meekhi had elected to stay in Samaria. Langorr was not displeased. His people were great allies of the Samarians and vice versa. Although his own nation was sworn to peace and had no standing army whereas Samaria was a land of warriors, he had known and loved the old Samarian King—Darcinian. Darcinian's then heir—Tamarin, had also found much favour with the ageing Langorr.

Meekhi was offered sumptuous chambers within the palace above the capital. She felt need for nothing and mingled well with the local people. The young princess learned the ways of the Samarians, finding much joy in the learning. Tamarin, though deeply in love with her, said not a word of his affections, nor once suggested, or, implied, they should be wed, in fact he hid his feelings from her as best he could, fearing she may well not feel the same for him.

He escorted Meekhi all over his lands, and she loved every second of each journey. It was not long before she knew she had fallen deeply in love with this tall, young king. They often went riding together on imposing, winged Samarian horses. These horses were the largest most powerful animals she had could have ever imagined. They towered over her, their gleaming black flanks warm under scarlet wings. Such magnificent animals were not for riding under normal circumstances, but an exception was often made for Tamarin and the woman he loved. Indeed, it had been on one of these riding forays whilst crossing the Emerald River that Meekhi had brought her horse to a stop neck deep in midstream, the beast snorting heavily as the cool liquid emerald flowed right under its nose. Tamarin had already crossed to the other bank and she had shouted across to him that if he did not marry her soon, she would jump into the river and drown herself. He had replied, with mock sincerity, that he could not allow such a beautiful river to be so horribly spoiled by having a drowned princess floating about in it, so yes—to save the river, he would marry her!

He had turned his horse and ridden back to her through the fast moving emerald that flowed in this magical river, and they had kissed for the very first time. Tamarin was overwhelmed by his love for Meekhi the moment their lips met, at least up to the point where she suddenly pushed him off his mount, sending him sailing into the gushing torrent and thus beating him back to the opposite bank. He had emerged from the water coughing and spluttering, the sweet emerald dripping from both him and his steed. Laughing out loud, he then whispered to his horse; "We will have to watch her, my good friend, she has fire in her blood."

The horse replied, "My lord, you do indeed look somewhat sodden and uncomfortable, but I must say—I rather enjoyed the whole thing!"

Shortly after Tamarin's impromptu dunking, amidst grand celebrations, not only in Sitivia, but throughout all of Samaria, he and Meekhi were wed.

On the night of the marriage, when sitting quietly together by candlelight in their royal chamber, Tamarin had given his beautiful new bride and queen, a gift, a tiny crystal bottle full of moving colours. She had worn this gift around her slender neck ever since that night. For Tamarin, Meekhi truly was his heart. So he had done exactly as the Great Dragon had asked of him many years ago—he had kept The Essence of Love close to his heart.

Zowie saw Jack spring from the house as her father brought the car to a silent, super-smooth, stop at the top of the drive. Jack was praising the handmade vehicle even before he was within earshot.

"Fantastic! She really is a beauty, Douglas. Nice one, mate!" he spouted enthusiastically whilst trotting over to the car with eyes the size of saucers.

Zowie's father—Douglas, or "Dug" as he was more often referred to, had stepped out of the car, leaving the door open so that his good friend Jack could sit inside and inspect his latest gadget. Jack gave Zowie a polite, "Hello sweetheart, the kids are indoors." As he and Dug immediately began discussing the merits of combining British craftsmanship and German engineering. Time, thought Zowie, to get indoors, *sharpish*!

She slipped out of her seat and walked briskly over to the house across the chunky gravel. She loved the dark reed of the thatched roof and the not-quite-straight creamy walls. The ivy that covered most of them was unkempt, roaming skywards as it pleased. Big Georgian windows graced the front wall and the view within was warm and welcoming. It was a large building, but very much a home rather than a house. The front door had once been painted a deep and lustrous dark green, but time and the infamous British weather had left only a hint of its former glory. It was still solid enough and Zowie had to give it a firm push to open it.

Lauren heard the door creak and ran from the conservatory to the entrance lobby. Zowie had just stepped inside and she gave her a big hug. The girls were very close friends and often spent ages on the phone chatting to each other. Zowie explained that their fathers were having 'the usual talk' in the driveway.

"How utterly drab," Lauren was not impressed, "*come on*! Let's go and find Tom. He's gagging for any news."

They found him reading a book in his bedroom. It was a really lovely room with bare oak beams marching across the ceiling and a low window seat which afforded views of peaceful fields bordered by woodland. The walls were awash with pictures of aircraft, hot air balloons, and zeppelins. Model aeroplanes hung from the ceiling beams on string, dog fighting in the breeze. Sunlight streamed in through the open window casting a natural spotlight on his large collection of books on aviation and flight. He greeted Zowie with a cheery "Hi". But his eyes said so much more than that. In fact, they were all staring at each other intently, their eyes ablaze with excitement.

"Has he finished it?" chimed the Shortwaters in unison.

Zowie beamed at her friends winningly. "Yes," she told them, "it's finished. At last!".

Jack spent ages looking around the Rolls Royce. "Marvellous!" He would say to no one in particular as he examined some part of the car, and then, "Incredible," as he moved to another part.

"Fancy a go in her then, old mate?" asked Dug, knowing his best friend was bursting to get behind the wheel. He had always enjoyed Jack's genuine enthusiasm.

"Don't mind if I do, Dug." Jack replied, as expected.

He then ran inside the house to let Lilly know he was popping out with Dug in the new 'Rolls'.

"*I'm* driving it." He told her proudly, as if he had won the National Lottery.

Driving around the beautiful countryside Jack noticed that Dug was not as involved in the conversation about cars as he usually would be. So he asked his good friend, what, exactly, was on his mind?

"I've finished it, Jack." Dug told him excitedly. "The Dream Machine is finally a reality. Ten years of hard work completed, my life's ambition fulfilled. I have tested it and I'm certain it works just fine. Imagine it—you plug yourself in by putting on the headgear, programme in the theme of your chosen dream, and close your eyes. Within minutes you will be having the dream of your choosing for a predetermined time. It will be a worldwide success, Jack! Of course I have built in plenty of safeguards to prevent the wrong type of people misusing it. But imagine the sort of relief it can bring to those in pain, those that are sad, or have lost loved ones, and it's just plain fun for everybody! Want to go over tomorrow, to see it?"

"Wild horses couldn't stop me, old mate. Well done, I always knew you would do it, you egghead." Jack laughed boyishly and Dug joined in. Chuckling like a pair of naughty schoolboys they pointed the car in a homeward direction, flooring the gas pedal and revelling in the sudden surge of acceleration.

Thomas and Lauren sat in Thomas' bedroom on his bed, listening to Zowie tell of her father's new invention—'The Dream Machine'. She sat on the floor before them, barely able to contain herself. Zowie had watched her father slave over this project for so many years. He had thought she was sound asleep, safely tucked up in her cosy bed, when in fact she had be sitting on the stairs, secretly listening to him, watching him working late in his study. She had willed that machine into completion just as hard as her father had worked at it, knowing just how much it meant to him. She had kept Lauren and Thomas informed of its progress on an almost daily basis. A *Dream* Machine, and oh! How they all wanted to fly so badly! They weren't fools, and knew perfectly well that people cannot fly of their own accord, but it was their number one fantasy-adventure wish. Now, with her father's amazing new invention, their wish could become as true as was humanly possible.

She explained to the Shortwaters that her father had built the machine so that a maximum of five people could share the same dream. "Wow!" exclaimed Thomas and Lauren.

She then told her friends how he had already tested it for safety and it was perfectly ok. She said he must be totally dedicated to creating new inventions because he had only just perfected the Dream Machine, and to test it he had programmed it so that he would dream about some new inventions called 'supermodels'. He tested the machine on himself with a colleague present so if there were any problems it was he that would be taking any risk. After thirty minutes of artificially induced dreaming he awoke slightly shaken, to say the machine worked perfectly but he would most definitely restrict some of its capabilities before it was released on general sale to the public. When Zowie had asked if he had dreamed of inventing the new 'supermodels' that he had mentioned earlier, he had replied; "Quite so, yes, amazing capabilities, beyond belief in fact, I must install the 'prevention of misuse security software', then, she's ready to rock. This machine, my lovely Zowie, will be a rip-roaring success. Now, I need a very large Scotch. Strewth!"

As it was nearly her birthday, her father, (now that he was absolutely sure that his machine was *completely* safe to use), had suggested what better present for her and the Shortwater children than to be the first people in the world to share a dream of their own choosing. Sitting there in Thomas' bedroom one day before the big event, they could not agree more.

That night the two families celebrated Dug's new invention, and the children's forthcoming birthdays, over dinner. Lilly served up a delicious, wholesome meal, including jam roly-poly with custard for desert as it was the children's favourite. For the adults, Jack opened a special bottle of wine he had been saving for just this occasion. Tomorrow was Saturday and the children went to bed early so as not to be tired in the morning.

Two riders from the Western Worlds had arrived in Sitivia the previous night. Their tidings had served only to worry Tamarin further. The most westerly worlds were many days of hard riding from Samaria, but the news they had brought with them was truly of great concern. The Westonians were highly respected lords in their own lands—Lord Bestwin, and, Lord Lumarr, swarthy fair-haired warriors wearing thick leather tunics for protection, and furs for warmth in the colder climes of their homeland. Neither was known for his flights of fancy, yet the tale of their journey seemed to stem from some dark nightmare.

The tower guards had spotted the two horses thundering along amidst clouds of dust well before the snorting, sweating beasts had been hauled to a noisy stop at the city gates. Their foam flecked flanks and bulging eyes told of their weariness every bit as much as the weariness was apparent in the dirt encrusted riders sat astride them. Tamarin had ordered the gates be opened and this sorry looking pair be led in. After gulping down so much water that Tamarin felt they might drown themselves, the pair dunked their heads in the water buckets. Shaking out their great shaggy manes and wiping water away from their bloodshot eyes, they turned and faced him. Only after they had shaken loose the thick matted mess on their heads had he recognised them fully. Meekhi had immediately asked stable boys to care of the horses as Tamarin had led these savage looking, but deeply trusted, friends into the palace. They had to ascend many steps to reach the cliff top palace and the climb was obviously quite an ordeal for the worn out Westonians.

They wanted to talk to Tamarin urgently and at first refused his offer of hot food and a bath. But he insisted they eat a bite and clean up a little—as one thought more clearly with good food in one's belly and fresh clothing on one's back. Also, in truth, they had both smelled far worse than their hot sweaty horses and he did not want Meekhi to have to suffer that dubious odour during their counsel.

They had grinned at Tamarin knowingly as they had been led to the baths, and later to the palace's considerable kitchens. They had been seated in a small comfortable room but a short while when Tamarin and Meekhi joined them. There was several seconds silence, which Tamarin broke first, "My lords, Bestwin and Lumarr. I am honoured that you grace us with your presence. You will forgive me if I dispense with court etiquette and get straight to the point. I have heard talk of the return of darkness to the shores of our worlds. Scouts were dispatched so that they may dispel such stories, but it has not been so. Only one of my scouts returned, his mind now not his own, whispering of strange happenings and dark powers of which I could not make any sense at all. Tell me, my trusted friends, has that which we have all feared might come one dark day, come at last?"

Bestwin nodded his head in consent and Lumarr sighed deeply. "My lord, Tamarin, it is so, and worse yet—I do believe this resurrection of evil is not limited to merely the lower echelons of hell, but perhaps their grand master too." Bestwin's gruff westerly voice commanded attention. His voice seemed even gruffer because of the thick golden beard that covered his face, almost as if his voice must have a beard of its own. Of course all Westonian men had thick beards to protect them from their harsh weather and Lumarr had a beard twice as thick as Bestwin's, though his was liberally streaked with the silvery white of age.

Bestwin continued. "The sea bubbles at night, turning pitch black, and as thick as treacle. From it issues the foulest of smells."

"Even worse than we smelled earlier." Lumarr smiled at Meekhi as he saw her grip Tamarin's arm suddenly, alarm rising at Bestwin's statement.

She smiled politely at his rather weak attempt at humour and he shuffled awkwardly in his chair feeling a little silly, before continuing, "Tamarin, we have ridden for nigh over a week. Our

King—Dorinn, cannot see that which lies before him. He feels all will pass soon enough and continues his endless cavorting and dancing. Our army now consists of a few drunken rabble. Parasites they are, feeding brazenly on Dorinn's weakness. The people remain unaware of the danger, but the *sea*, the sea churns and roils as if it were boiling in the largest cauldron of the most evil of witches. Out in the distance, strange menacing shapes billow and blow on the dark horizon. A penetrating chill emanates from them and needles our very marrow. Despite the most urgent pleas, Dorinn is lost to wine and song, wasting precious days in pursuit of the pleasures of the flesh. He will not ride to the shores and look with his own eyes. I believe his spine is as yellow as his drunkard's eyes. We fear that since Queen Yasmina rightfully left him, and disappeared, Dorinn has lost any ability to rule and unknowingly rushes us all to an early grave. He will not confront this threat, my lord. On our journey here we travelled by day and stayed well hidden at night. The forces of darkness are indeed awakening, and on the move. We glimpsed lumbering Rock-Trolls, Wispy Witches—with their tall smoky bodies drifting, Hell-Hounds with heads the size of your war shields, and Hoary Hags—their spiky forms chilling the air as they passed us by. Only Ogiin could summon such creatures unto him so quickly and commandingly. His dark spirit stirs once more in the deep I am sure. In the cold darkness of the ocean he gathers himself once more, and will, in due course, again attempt to destroy all that is good and pure in our worlds." Lumarr's eyes narrowed, focusing on the small glass vial resting neatly at the base of Meekhi's throat, the eternal colours mesmerizing him as they swirled within.

"I had hoped that this day would never come, but… of course, it has." Tamarin stated in a subdued voice, "But if it be our destiny to deal with that evil, this filth that lurks in the darkness, then, by my sword! We will be rid of Ogiin and his foul scourge forever, or, together, take our last sweet breaths of freedom in the trying!"

Lumarr fixed his wise old eyes on the young king, then onto the more experienced Lord Bestwin. "We elders," he began, "know only too well of the black dawn breaking on our horizon, bringing with it the promise of dark days. It is a challenge we have faced before and will face again, but it is on you, our young, brave, new lords, that the weight of our destiny bears. Tamarin, I knew and loved your father, the great king Darcinian. I was by his side often, both in battle and in peace. But now he is gone, as are so many of our allies from the past. I think this old enemy will take new measures to overcome it. I suggest we gather our remaining allies and, if you would permit us, consult at The Talking Table."

Tamarin saw the wisdom in the advice Lumarr had offered, "Agreed".

It had been several days since Tamarin had received the awful news from his Westonian friends. Since then the city of Sitivia had been a hive of activity below the presiding palace. Riders left the city to call allies to arms, fearsome warriors wearing all manner of battledress arrived daily in drips and drabs, answering the call to arms from Samaria.

The city itself was sheltered from the sea by the cliffs upon which the palace stood. The people had built wide streets, made of cobbles interlaced with mortar, they ran neatly between dwellings of white stone or whitewashed brickwork. A marketplace was set in the central square. A place to barter or trade, somewhere where friends would often meet for a jar of mead, a keg of beer, and perhaps some freshly baked bread from one of the many brightly coloured stalls. The protective cliffs were in fact a hollow labyrinth of tunnels linking many rooms and chambers between them. This is where Tamarin's most loyal soldiers were stationed—The Royal Guards.

This elite formation consisted of warriors that had volunteered to serve their king and homeland without question or hesitation. Pledging their lives to serve forever was their greatest wish, and once that pledge was made and accepted, they found great honour in fulfilling their vows. Each aspired to one day be offered a chance to join the 'Ranin' and wear the rare blue cloak bearing the silver dragon. All longed for that honour except for Ramulet, the Captain of the Royal Guardsmen. To become a Ranin one had to serve faultlessly for many years (and we must remember—Samarians can live for a very long time). The lengthy term of service moulded not only Samaria's most formidable warriors, but also some of the wisest. Yet to be a Ranin was a lonely existence, for each Ranin had to ride away from Samaria alone, travelling other lands as a Samarian Knight, defending the weak, protecting the innocent, and opposing tyrants and pain-makers, this was the lot of a Ranin. Each one was given a gift of a horse, but no ordinary horse. He was given a Mercerin. A stunning, lean and muscular creature of snow white colour, a gleaming blue horn protruding from its noble head, and a mane, tail, and hooves the blue of which matched that of its fearsome spike. These steeds though not capable of actual speech, were totally in tune with their Ranin rider. The pair thought and moved as one, and, in battle, they were nothing short of devastating, each would give his life for the other, it was a pairing unto death. In the past the Ranin would, on occasion, be summoned back to the home fires of their beloved Samaria by the Dragons of Light to attend some great festival, or some other such auspicious occasion. But the days of the dragons were lost to history and any Ranin that now left Samaria knew they would never be summoned home again. Yet still, very few declined the offer of the promotion. To wander the world with a view to helping it be a better place for all was a great honour and privilege, so most accepted the challenge without any qualms. No ill was thought of those that declined and Ramulet was such a one. His love for his king, and his fearlessness, were unquestionable. He loved Lady Meekhi for the joy she brought to Tamarin's life and also because she and he had become great friends. Ramulet knew if he were to leave Samaria as a Ranin he would not be able to aid his friends if the need arose. So, despite the powerful lure of unexplored lands and many great adventures, he remained.

Tamarin felt perplexed. Why now? Why at all? What had caused that which had been already defeated, to rise once more? All Samarians knew of the great battles of the past, and of how Ogiin and Chjandi (for that was the name of the Great Dragon) had fought relentlessly in the skies above the oceans for what seemed an eternity, until, finally, the Great Dragon had blasted Ogiin with such a storm of dragon flame that the shattered warlord had plummeted like a stone into the waiting depths, sinking into the abyss, never to be seen again. He pondered the possibility that maybe this current danger was something new, something unrelated, something less deadly. But even as he thought this, he knew he was but hoping against the odds. In his heart he sensed the evil that lived once more in the deep. The small hairs on the back of his neck prickled again and he gave a slight shudder before turning his mind back to the developments in Sitivia.

Meekhi sat in her chambers also pondering the strange and worrying turn of events which burdened not only Tamarin, but also weighed heavily upon herself. As the news spread through the land it troubled all those that valued freedom and justice. She was well known amongst the Samarians and their allies as both warm, and generous, but also as a fearsome warrior in her own right. Many years had passed since her miraculous rescue from the slavers, and in that time she had studied and mastered many of the martial ways. Lethal with her sword, Meekhi was also well versed in hand-to-hand combat, blade throwing, and a dab hand with a spear. Though she could not handle a tribladed sword mostly due to the sheer size and weight of such a weapon, she was the best horsewoman in the land, fearless to the last, and utterly devoted to her husband. Meekhi was adored by all her subjects, but most, of course, by Tamarin. She loved to dance to the wonderfully hypnotic, entrancing music of Samaria, and her dancing was the eagerly anticipated highlight of any party or festival. People would travel from near and far to see their queen dancing under the stars. Dignitaries from far off lands left stunned, forever captivated by the beauty of her form and the strength of her spirit. Those that offered Tamarin a trade for her soon found themselves expelled from the realm or staring down the wrong end of a very large triblade. The king caused neither harm nor injury as their desire for her was a compliment to his queen, but the offer to barter for her as if she were a mere possession was an insult to her honour that he would not tolerate. Meekhi was as free as he was. In fact, on the odd occasion when perhaps a visiting lord, or ambassador, had said a little too much, Meekhi, *herself,* had challenged the unfortunate individual to a duel. Needless to say, those particular individuals left Samaria feeling very sorry for themselves. This occurred extremely rarely as most that called upon the royal couple were of strong moral fibre and good, honourable people. She had never forgotten her birthright as a Princess of the Land of Flowers, and though she was as Samarian now as any Samarian could ever be, she retained a particular gentleness about her, a deep rooted tenderness inherent in the people of her father's kingdom.

She was asking herself the same questions as Tamarin had been doing when he walked into their private chambers. She smiled as he strode over to her and embraced her. Meekhi knew of all the questions and worries on his mind and yet she was taken aback by the sheer intensity of the love he had for her gleaming in his eyes. She felt she would like nothing more than to just melt away into those two glistening pools of warmth and safety, to forever swim in his heart and never again wish for anything else. She hugged him tightly to herself, the strength of her youthful body pinning him to her. He, too, held her firmly, then more firmly still, then more… and more. It was a game they played, and soon Meekhi could feel her breath being slowly but inexorably forced from her lungs as Tamarin's immensely powerful arms began closing the vicelike clamp they had formed about her. She knew he was too strong for her to break free, and he would keep squeezing her tighter and tighter until she admitted defeat and agreed to a penalty of having to bathe him, massage him, or such like. But Meekhi was not one to be beaten so easily. She slipped her arms under his and began to tickle him. Instantly Tamarin's grip broke and he tried to back away but she tripped him to the floor and began tickling him all over. He roared with laughter, his deep musical chuckling infectious, and soon, she, too, began giggling girlishly as she continued to torture her lord, and king. Tears of mirth streaming down from his eyes, Tamarin managed to wriggle free of her and stood up. Meekhi, being no one's fool, immediately recognised the sly grin on his face and that mischievous look in his eyes. She knew it was time to run, now! The raven-haired beauty bolted out of the nearest door and charged headlong down a corridor, laughing uncontrollably. Tamarin was far fleeter of foot than his muscular frame suggested, and he pursued her at high speed, calling out all the penances she would be made to agree to serve when he caught her and showed her what being tickled was *really* like!

Laughing like crazed maniacs the royal pair raced up wooden stairs and down paved hallways until, exhausted, they burst into the great hall. Meekhi darted behind the colossal silver dragon, whilst Tamarin stood on the other side, plotting on how to corner her. They were both still giggling like children. Tamarin was busy telling her of how he would make her promise to wash him daily, anointing him with oils every evening for a week, when a deep mystical voice, ancient and earthy, stopped him mid sentence.

"You resemble your father, Tamarin." The Voice caused a slight echo in the vastness of the great hall. Tamarin spun around sharply, had he imagined it? His gaze returned to Meekhi and he saw that her emerald green eyes were the size of saucers, glued to something behind him. Her mouth hung open and she stood rigid, as if frozen. He could not help thinking of how strikingly beautiful she looked when The Voice came again. "Ah, yes, truly the son of Darcinian, one that sees his truelove before he sees all else. You have grown well, young Tamarin. Well enough, let us hope, to put right the imbalance that now exists."

CHAPTER TWO

THE TALKING TABLE

Zowie had awoken very early. She had been too excited about forthcoming events to sleep for very long. Unable to even doze, she decided to sneak downstairs at the break of day and have a cup of tea whilst waiting for the rest of the household to stir. So she had let out a little scream as she eased open the kitchen door to see Thomas and Lauren already sitting there. They were tucking eagerly into two big bowls of Crunchy Nut Cornflakes, each bowl flanked on one side by a big steaming mug of tea. The three giggled at her little screech and Lauren made her a tea as Zowie poured herself some of the same breakfast cereal. They looked at each other, laughing, and said, "It's gotta be Kellogg's!" Together, they began munching.

It was not too long before the adults were also up. Lilly and Jack were treated to a glorious full English breakfast cooked by Zowie's father. The children looked enviously at the sizzling bacon and eggs and wished they had not eaten so much cereal. By eight thirty am everyone was ready to make the journey to the Kantell home. Dug and Jack travelled in the Rolls and the children followed with Lilly in her ancient, more than a little decrepit, Land Rover, that she had named 'Beanstalk' as it was green, and Jack was always climbing all over it to fix it. The four occupants travelling in Beanstalk were jolted and bumped about constantly with the wind that was blowing in through the ill-fitting windows creating havoc with their hair and making their eyes stream, but they had fun all the same. The children jokingly mimicked their fathers coasting along ahead, congratulating Lilly on the quality of the rust on the dashboard and mock-swooning at the thought of the sheer level of effort it must have taken to get real moss to grow at the base of the windows, and, surely, the big dead spider stuck in the air vent must be such a costly option to have installed? Beanstalk chugged along, creaking and rattling as it followed the Rolls Royce, the occupants of which were engrossed in conversation about the wonderful quality of the stitching in the Nappa leather seats, and the attention to detail that had been paid in creating the steering wheel. Dug was convinced it was the roundest steering wheel he had ever seen.

Zowie found the journey back to her home took considerably longer than the one to the Shortwaters' home had taken. This was because Beanstalk could barely manage forty five miles per hour and of course her father waited patiently in the newer car, keeping his speed low so as to match that of the Land Rover. But, the young trio agreed, the journey was far less boring in Beanstalk despite the extra travelling time. They were just so excited to be having this great opportunity, and their enthusiasm was so infectious even level-headed Lilly was discussing dreams she would like to have by the time they turned onto the Kantell's driveway. More like a *motorway,* Thomas had once commented. Indeed the drive up to the house through its private grounds was considerably long for a domestic home. Even more so given that the house and grounds sat on the fringes of the city where land came at a very high premium.

As she sat in the car Zowie reflected on the past, when her mother and father had still been together, she had been very young but remembered the times clearly enough. Her mother had been so very career orientated, sparing little or no time to either Zowie, or her own husband. Her work and business matters always came first despite the fact that she was not particularly good at them. Her mother had eventually complained that her father was lazy and did nothing much in the way of making money, though in fact he had paid half of everything, and often more. Zowie knew her mother loved her, she just happened to love her job and money more. Zowie accepted that. The ability to have that acceptance without bitterness or resentment came from having such a brilliant father. She truly was the apple of his eyes and after her mother walked away from them both, her dad had devoted himself to raising his young daughter the very best he could. She had absolutely no complaints.

The perfectly manicured lawns and immaculate gardens slipped past the rattling car window and Zowie suddenly felt her heart swell with pride for her father. It was when Thomas asked; "What are you grinning so stupidly about, Zee?"

That Zowie (nicknamed Zee by family and friends) realised that she actually *was* grinning very stupidly!

Fortunately she did not have to answer Thomas because both the cars were then coming to a stop on the tarmac at the front of the house. The large circular expanse of rubbery black was bordered by the lush green of the lawns. The seam, where black met green, was stitched at regular intervals by tall poplar trees that marched each side of the drive all the way from the house to the gate, in the centre of the circle stood a truly stunning creation, a glorious fountain. A tall silver dragon, its wings half encircling lithe bronze maidens that bathed in the water cascading down from its mouth. With the clever use of fibre optics and hidden lighting the water pouring from the dragon's mouth gave the illusion of being real flames, flames within which the bronze women played quite happily. The children, and the adults too for that matter, adored the extravagant fountain, and having gotten out of the cars, they had walked over to it to spend half a minute being mesmerised by the colours swirling and flowing around the nubile bronze ladies. Before leaving Beanstalk both the girls and Lilly had given 'him' a kiss on the bonnet for having had made the journey in one piece at his ripe old age.

The Kantell home was at the opposite end of the spectrum when compared to the old farmhouse from which they had just arrived. Dug had had it custom built and it was all glass, chrome, and wood, with natural light flooding in everywhere from enormous windows. In fact you could say that there were not any real exterior walls at all, and the whole building consisted of enormous glass panes with the odd wooden beam linking them here and there. It was a striking looking home and very well thought out. Dug pressed a button on a small remote control and the front door swished open. Inside the house, 'floating' stairways, and, open plan, were the order of the day. The ambience was as Lauren had once said, "Definitely more Mozart than Motorhead." She was right too. The place was a symphony of colours and fluid architecture. Not to mention every conceivable gadget adorning each room as required. Jack and Lilly enjoyed the very large spacious rooms, though Lilly said she would not fancy keeping all that glasswork clean and polished! She was joking of course, knowing full well that Dug had the house cleaned professionally every week. The floors were either ceramic, wooden, or a mixture of both. The building was three storeys high, with an additional level underground—used solely for Dug's work and experiments.

The Shortwater's were delighted to visit the Kantell's home. Just as Zowie revelled in the cosy unorganised organisation of Lauren and Thomas' home, they, in turn, were always taken aback by the amount of gadgets and modern fun stuff there was to enjoy at her place. She had been too young to physically influence the design of her home when it was built, but her father had managed to somehow incorporate *her* character into the building too. She was indelibly etched into the overall mood of the place and you could feel her in every square foot of it. This was particularly the case in the gardens, where she had been given a reasonably free rein. Beyond the perfect lawns and well kempt rose bushes, Zowie had her own patch of land which she, just as the Shortwaters, had left to nature, and it was buzzing with life. Trees and plants, and all sorts flora abounded, providing a perfect habitat for a wide variety of local wildlife. Naturally, the three children had built a den in there too, hidden deep amongst the thick foliage and dense bracken.

Dug led them inside and it was that agreed that a nice, hot, refreshing cup of tea was in order. So Lilly kindly filled the kettle and began to boil the water. The parents were so excited for the children but portrayed a calm and ordinary mood to string out the day a little, letting the youngster's excitement ferment yet further.

Once the mugs of tea were ready, the adults decided to drink theirs in the large conservatory at the back of the house, so Zowie and her cousins went up to her room to wait, and pass time. Whenever they climbed up the two levels of 'floating' stairs (which had no rail or banister at one side) Thomas *always* said he did not like them and felt he would one day fall over the side, and the girls *always* remarked on how he wanted to fly but could not handle climbing those stairs.

Zowie's bedroom was the largest room in the house. When she had first seen it, Lauren had fallen in love with it immediately, and Thomas, with his predictable wit, had asked; "Wembley Stadium! What time is kick-off?"

The girls had laughed quite genuinely at his jest because the room was of truly of mammoth proportions, occupying the entire third floor. The glass roof was pitched unequally, with a forty/sixty bias. The shorter slope was a dark, but still transparent, blue as it was covered on the outside by large solar panels, and the other slope was crystal clear, light blue, glass, so Zowie could sleep snugly at night under the watchful eyes of the stars. If they were not available, or, more likely, it was raining, then a flick of a switch covered the entire ceiling with a black, one-piece, blind, adorned with luminous silvery moons, glowing planets, and tiny pinpoints of light. Large windows gave a panoramic view to the rear of the house in the direction of the children's den. Privacy was achieved in an instant by the pressing of more buttons and the swift closing of dark blue satin blinds. Zowie absolutely adored her bedroom. Not because it was so extravagant, though she appreciated that it was, but because she knew her father had taken more time to design her room than any other in the house. She had made her own personal mark on it over the years and books on aviation and paraphernalia similar to that in Thomas' room lay scattered about everywhere. Other tomes filled with epic adventures and magical journeys were littered about all over the place, their bookcase accusingly empty. The girls were most definitely *not* as tidy as Thomas. Fresh flowers and all manner of quaint or fascinating objects sat everywhere. The children, being careful to not spill their mugs of piping hot tea, climbed onto the spacious bed and began talking of the day ahead. The time was now coming up to twelve noon. At thirty minutes past one exactly, Dug called upstairs to them. "It's time guys! Come down now, please."

The trio on the bed stared at each other without a word. Each had expected much cheering and clapping from the other two when the time came. But now they became aware of the slight trepidation that they all felt. It was, after all, only a dream that they were going to share, an artificially induced joint dream, and one that could perhaps prove to be such an anti-climax. But still, each of them could not wait to experience it, and with eager smiles on their faces they headed downstairs.

Their parents were waiting at the bottom and appeared as filled with anticipation as the children. Zowie noticed her dad in particular was beaming at her and she felt extra special today. He led them through the house towards the rear of the building where his study and upper workshops were situated. A pair of thick sturdy glass doors opened onto a large workspace, subdivided into two sections. One area was dominated by a massive antique writing desk, many computers, books, files, and various other such items. In the other half stood what appeared to be a gigantic glass globe. It contained five white seats. "*Dentist's* chairs." Thomas immediately commented. Each seat had a pair of what looked like headphones resting on it. Entry to this strange spherical room was gained via a door that, had it not been made of the same glassy substance, would not have looked amiss on board a submarine. Even the big locking wheel was constructed of the same material as the 'walls'. The entire structure was seamless and so did not really have any individual walls as such, or maybe it was all one big wall. Its surface was super-smooth and uninterrupted bar the outline of the door, which itself left no edge or lip on the oversized glass ball. The interior floor was of a mirror-black finish and curved concavely in line with the rest of the machine. A flat, white, second floor was somehow suspended above the black one.

The room fell silent as they gawped at this curious device. Zowie had been tempted so many times to sneak in and take a peek at what her dad was creating, but she had never done so as she knew one day he would finish it and get so much pleasure from revealing it to all of them, but especially to her. Now she was so very glad she had resisted those temptations as she saw the look of pride on her father's face.

Thomas broke the staring session by crying out, "Blimey! Uncle Dug is going to make us fly by firing us out of a giant cannon! Got the ball, but where's the cannon, then?"

His predictable outburst brought about laughter from the young girls, and then from the adults too. It also instigated activity.

Douglas eased the glass wheel clockwise through two full rotations, and the door popped out an inch with a light hiss. It then glided silently to the left leaving clear entry to the sphere. He began to explain. "As we all know, we can sometimes sleep for five minutes and dream a dream that lasts for hours, days, or even years. This applies to the Dream Machine. If the theme of the data I programme into the machine is simple, such as 'flying without fright, fear, or injury,' the occupants will be gently but swiftly lulled to sleep by the machine's secret resonances, and then share a dream based on the input data. They will sleep for five minutes because I will programme the machine to arouse them from sleep mode after five minutes. The dream they will have shared may have lasted far longer in 'dream time'. Today I will programme the machine so the dream, even in dream time, does not last longer than one hour, because I would imagine one might feel more than a little wobbly on one's legs if one awakes after having been flying for more than that. I will programme it so they will dream of flying by themselves without the need for planes, wings, or, in Thomas' case, rocket thrusters or cannons."

Thomas grinned at this as Douglas continued. "The machine brings the senses of the dreamers back to normality before the session is ended, so the occupants remain in their seats until the beeper sounds, and at that point they can remove the headphones, or *Inducer Pods* as I call them, and leave the *Dream Pod*, as I have named the sphere."

It was blatantly obvious that Douglas was very much enjoying showing off his new invention, and everyone thought he had every right to do just that. What an invention! Knowing the children were aching to start the machine, he continued to drag things out and elaborate on his handiwork. "For me, the greatest feature of this overgrown birthday present is its ability to create Black Light."

At this point five jaws dropped and Jack asked his friend what he meant?

Douglas straightened himself out, standing a little taller, and carried on. "I couldn't perfect this blasted machine for years. It was impossible to control dream patterns, electrical brain pulses, and all sorts of other technical stuff. But one night I was working late and I thought I'd just nip upstairs and make sure Zee was ok, and sleeping well. I crept into her room and found her sound asleep. But as I left her room she stirred, and just whispered, "night-night, daddy." Douglas took a deep breath, then continued, "It was only then that I truly realised why my machine would not work. It really is down to Zowie that I found the answer! She sleeps, ergo she dreams. But in order to create a dream, she *must* sleep. So for my machine to create a dream, it *too* must sleep! So I invented, for the first time in history I might add, Black Light. True Black Light actually. Not a name for an existing light that isn't black, but *real* black light. The globe fills with artificial black light and the machine creates the dream within that darkness, sharing it with its occupants. The human eye can't see black light so those inside the Dream Pod see everything as normal. But those of us outside the pod see it go completely dark inside, all normal procedure my dears, and no need to worry about anything, any questions?"

"YES!" Came three eager young voices, "When can we start the dream!"

Tamarin turned slowly, his hand resting ready on his ornate sword grip. His eyes were drawn immediately to the silvery red mist that danced and twinkled on the surface of The Talking Table. Meekhi slipped hastily from behind the towering dragon and took his hand. She felt a slight tremor in him and gripped harder until the tremor ceased. He glanced at her briefly, his eyes meeting hers, and bade her stand still and wait whilst he approached the strange glow alone.

"Are you afraid?" Again that voice came.

"No." He replied resolutely, "It is only that I have often longed to have heard you speak, yet now I fear I have reason to no longer have any doubts about that which gives you cause to speak. Forgive me, ancient spirit, I am young and do not have the wisdom of my forefathers, but I know you to be a friend of Samaria."

Meekhi, having listened very carefully to Tamarin's instruction that she should stay well back, walked up alongside him, and he was glad she did. The pair watched as the strange blinking specks of light settled on the table making it appear like a dark sky full of silver and red stars, tiny dots that winked and twinkled quite brightly. But none alighted on the wise face at the centre. The face itself began to soften a little, the edgy contours of the carving became softer, more cohesive. Then, with a screechy creaking that made Meekhi wince, the entire visage started moving around as if trying to stop itself from sneezing. The nose moved from left to right and back and forth, whilst the lips moved in the opposite direction. Meekhi peeked from one eye and Tamarin stood dead still, gob-smacked, until suddenly the contortions stopped. The dark oak eyes moved, focusing on the young couple. "So serene and wise those eyes," were Meekhi's first thoughts. The mouth seemed to struggle to open, as if glued shut, but then, with some obvious difficulty, the lips parted, and that voice spoke again to mutter, "Beeswax! THAT is what I need!"

"Yes, of course, my lord." Tamarin spluttered, and hurried to call an aid to fetch some beeswax, but the voice stopped him.

"Time enough for wax later, I hope."

Tamarin hastened back alongside Meekhi. The Talking Table began to speak in earnest. "Samarians know full well that all life is governed by the laws of The Source. Freewill, free thinking, the right to choose your own path, are all rights governed by The Source. You have the right to dream, to follow or discard your dreams, but your dreams remain *your* dreams. The power to dream, to aspire, to have faith in that which you cannot see, or touch, is your gift, your blessing. Now, in the faraway world of man and his mechanisations, an imbalance exists. The imbalance must be put to rights and resolved before nightmares prevail over dreams. All life exists in balance, if one has the power to create dreams for another, then yet another must also have the power to create nightmares. Look to the source of all dreams. There, you will discover the Guilty Innocents."

Before either Meekhi or Tamarin could blink, The Talking Table had returned to its former solid, inert state—a wise face hewn from ancient oak. Tamarin took a deep breath and stood staring eye-to-eye with Meekhi. The shock of the table talking faded away and each whispered to the other, "The Pink Mountain."

That evening they gathered many noble lords to be seated at The Talking Table to discuss what had happened, and what to do next. Meekhi and other female warriors attended such counsels too. Samarians did not see either male or female as having greater authority and, in fact, if anything, women were held in the slightly higher estimation. Lords attending that counsel from other lands were of the same vein of thought. All there present knew of the Pink Mountain, a towering peak similar in appearance, size, and shape to a volcano. Only its soaring heights were not ashen and grey, or blackened with soot, but rather were formed of a crystal the colour of coral, and whereas you would normally see smoke, or a lava crust, inside of the crater, within the pink mountain swirled a mist, a thick, glowing, dark green mist, that was the source of all the dreams of mankind throughout the universe. No one knew how the mist had come to be, but it had existed longer than memory served. Somehow it contained the power of dreams, and it was not to be interfered with, ever. At one point along the rim of the crater there was a protrusion, almost a spout, and from this gushed a roaring torrent of bright green water. The glittering liquid emerald crashed down to earth from hundreds of feet above, forming a small lake which, in turn, formed the Emerald River which cut a shimmering swathe across Samaria. It culminated in a glorious waterfall on the coast far away, roaring majestically into the ocean below, the pure emerald green quickly diluting into the briny blues of the waves pounding against the cliffs.

Tamarin, seated at the head of the table, was speaking. "The wisdom of the ancients has called out to us. Alas, we do not yet know of what we have been informed, but it seems obvious we must despatch riders to the Pink Mountain. Something must be amiss there and I am resolved to ascertain what it is. However, there is much to do here in Sitivia too, so I will entrust the city to my lady, and I shall make haste to the far-east to investigate these warnings."

Meekhi was not impressed, and said so openly, "My lord, we know not what we face either to the west, or in the east. Samaria will be looking to you, and our allies here seated, to rally our joined people for whatever may, or may not, lie ahead. My understanding is that in the east we are to try and find something The Talking Table referred to as 'Guilty Innocents'. Whatever this may mean, I feel it does not require the king of Samaria to investigate it. So *I* shall go with any that care to join me, any, *other* than you, Tamarin."

She winked at him cheekily as she had used his name at counsel, a breach of protocol unheard of before that did not ruffle the gathering unduly as Meekhi was well known for her frequent breaches. The warriors seated at the table stood to their feet in unison amidst a clattering of swords, everyone offering to accompany her on her quest. They had all risen except for Tamarin, who remained seated, rubbing his chin. He knew that Meekhi was right, and he had to stay behind. He also knew that everyone else knew that she was right and so he had to agree to her plan, but he had a condition to impose upon that plan. The condition was; that as everyone wanted to escort her, it was most fair that he choose the riders that were to accompany her. No one held any objections to this idea and so he chose Ramulet—Captain of The Royal Guards, and Lady Mercy—the best archer in the land and a fearsome warrior, blessed with both wisdom and, if needed, guile. Her flowing golden mane and angelic countenance, underlined by her name, belied the skill and passion with which she could despatch an opponent. Mercy by name certainly, but most definitely not by nature should one cross swords with her.

The Counsel discussed the news that Bestwin and Lumarr had imparted earlier to Tamarin and Meekhi. It was agreed that the Westonians, along with a handful of Samarians, would form a small posse and travel west, to see what developments had further taken place in their homelands. The trio of Meekhi, Ramulet, and Mercy, would travel east to the Pink Mountain. Tamarin would organise his forces in Sitivia, so that were his army needed, it would be ready and waiting.

Meekhi's journey would take her far to the east, passing along Iret—a treacherous desert full of illusions and deceit, then onto Soledad—The Silent City. Soledad was once a great city full of joy and happiness, but during the course of the old war against Ogiin, it had fallen foul of a fiendish curse imposed upon it by Ogiin and the Venomeens. All life within its beautiful walls had become black marble and its laughter and gaiety silenced in one fell swoop. It was said that the marble faces of its residents still smiled, as if laughing at the wicked irony of the cruel joke played upon their own happiness. Neither man nor beast ventured there, for the sheer sadness that enveloped that once joyous place could, it was said, break even the stoutest of hearts. The Samarians left the Silent City well alone from a sense of respect for their ancient kindred spirits that were forever entombed there within the black stone. Beyond Soledad lay the Pink Mountain, Meekhi's final destination. Upon her return Tamarin would ride west to join with Bestwin and Lumarr to see for himself what fate had in store for them.

The evening was spent with warriors and lords alike clustered into small groups, each wondering what was to happen next, and indeed, what was already happening? Could Ogiin really have returned? *How*? Why? Questions poured from many lips, but not a single answer could yet be found. The information from Bestwin and Lumarr could be treated as absolutely accurate. There was no doubt that things were very sorely amiss in the west. But, was *Ogiin* the cause? Everyone standing in the vast hall felt apprehensive and confused, secretly wishing it was all going to pass over very soon, with current fears being quickly dispelled, and a sense of normality restored.

Tamarin arranged for the three best horses to be made ready for the morning. The horses approved of this wholeheartedly as they were given rich, sugary, man-made meals, which were warm, and a lovely treat from the usual grazing on grass. Despite these horses being of the uniquely Samarian winged variety, they never flew with a rider on their backs as that could prove very dangerous for both rider and horse alike. So the horses knew they had a long journey ahead of them on foot, or on hooves, as it happened to be in this case. Tamarin spent the evening at Meekhi's side discussing the route she was planning to take, the provisions they were to carry, and of how careful she must be. She knew he was worried for her wellbeing and assured him all would be well. After all, how dangerous could 'Guilty Innocents' really be?

An early night was in order so the soon-to-be travellers would be well rested before their long journey began. Tamarin held Meekhi close throughout the night and she slept soundly, secure in the warmth and comfort of his loving arms. She awoke to find he had already slipped away from their chamber. Having readied herself swiftly after a quick bath, she donned clothing suitable for such a journey, being sure to pack her sword and shield, along with other items intended for unpleasant purposes. Her black cloak trailing behind her, she hurried to the stables in the heart of the city far below the palace. Meekhi was happily munching on a thick piece of bread wrapped around a lump of cheese when she arrived.

Mercy was standing there on the straw covered paving. She looked at once beautiful, and menacing, clad from head to foot in black leather, her tunic straining to conceal her ample cleavage. A cloak identical to that of Meekhi's draped her shoulders and her golden locks seemed to glow in contrast. She had a bow and quiver over her shoulders and a sword by her side, and she was eyeing Meekhi's bread hungrily as she had not yet eaten. Meekhi laughed and passed her the still substantial loaf. They walked into the stables to see Tamarin, Ramulet, and the horses, standing directly ahead. A small crowd was gathered around them. The horses were heavily laden with all that was deemed necessary. Each of the gathering bowed to greet the ladies. Though capable of speech, Samarian horses rarely spoke as human speech was not their natural tongue and they only used it if they felt like it. To them, human speech was like a foreign language, to be used as and when required.

Tamarin stood barechested and unkempt, sweating and mucky from making preparations for Meekhi and her escorts. Ramulet looked ready to start a small war all by himself. He was wearing full battledress made up of chain mail over leather, and carrying more weapons than one could imagine possible. A sleek black plait was pointing straight down his back, almost touching his waist. Mercy eyed him up and down slowly. The impression he made on her was very favourable, as it always had been. She had found him favourable for some time, but he, as ever, was so focused on his duties she assumed he was not aware of her keen interest. Meekhi, however, was very aware of Mercy's feelings and approved wholeheartedly. The queen was a close friend of Ramulet and could not imagine a better source of happiness and joy for him, and what better man for Mercy than the illustrious Captain of The Royal Guards. Unlike Mercy, Meekhi had noticed the brief, sidelong glances Ramulet often made in the direction of Mercy. But Meekhi never said a word. She knew better than to meddle in the affairs of other hearts. She loved Tamarin more than life itself, and he loved her as much in return. Her own heart was both full, and content.

Tamarin gave Meekhi a look she recognised immediately and she joined him just out of earshot of the others. He looked down into the two emerald pools that stared back at him with such emotion and he knew he must not allow her, even for one second, to see or sense the unease and trepidation that he felt in letting her and his beloved friends to make this journey without him. His heart ached to be beside her every step of the way, but, as Lord of Samaria, he knew his duty and would not fail his people. Meekhi knew exactly what he must be feeling and thinking as she moved close to him and held him close. The heat from his bare chest was such that she felt it through her tunic and she longed to turn back time, so the journey ahead would not have cause to exist. But of course, this was not possible. She felt the small damp curls on his chest brushing her cheek, and his scent, his wonderful, unique scent, gave her strength, calming her anxious anticipation of whatever may lie ahead. She raised her face to him further, tossing her hair to one side so it could not block her view of him. "I will be back before you know it, my lord, and these 'Guilty Innocents' will pay the price for causing me to have to leave your side." She toyed with her sword grip as she spoke. Tamarin beheld his woman with an even greater respect. She had never before had reason to be involved in matters of a martial kind, but now she had that reason, and he did not find her wanting. Meekhi had always been his heart's truelove, but now, for the first time, he truly saw her in her other role—as the warrior-queen of Samaria. This thought comforted him much, and, after a final firm hug, he released his arms from about her, "My lady, travel swiftly and hearken unto Ramulet for he knows the ways of the wilds, avoid The Silent City as a smile as warm as yours should not fall upon souls so wretched as those that haunt that accursed place, for surely, the sight of you would steal the final spark of life from those stone hearts that yearn to be freed. Go now, I am always with you."

With this he strode directly over to Ramulet, exchanged a few words, and hugged his long standing friend. Then a hug and a light kiss for Mercy, before turning on his heel and heading back to the palace to fulfil his duties as king.

Ramulet beckoned to the women, and the three of them mounted their awaiting horses. He knew that each of them was a mighty warrior in her own right, and he could not have asked for more reliable and loyal companions on this voyage into the unknown. It was also a perfect opportunity to spend time with Mercy. He did not know what lay ahead of them, but he knew he would play his part without hesitation or regret. Tamarin—his great friend, was in need, and Ramulet would not fail him. As for Mercy, Ramulet had longed to join with her for many years. He sensed her affection for him but the opportunity to explore any possibilities had not yet arisen, perhaps now it would.

A long, slim mirror (for adjusting armour and fixings) hung askew on the wall beside him and the captain caught his own reflection. He cut a dashing figure with his cloak swishing about him in the early morning breeze. Though he would readily deny it, Ramulet was the desired catch of many a woman, and was well worthy of those desires. He glanced again at Mercy, and thought—why not? He was neither unattractive nor deceitful, and he would love and cherish her as only a Samarian man truly can. Mercy was only a handful of years older than the queen and he, himself, was only a hundred years older than Mercy, so there should be no great worry over the compatibility of their age. (We must remember one hundred years to a Samarian is negligible when we take into account their immense life spans). Ramulet felt Meekhi poke him in his ribs, and he spun his horse towards the city, heading for the main gates.

Meekhi led the trio of thundering horses as they shot out from below the palace onto the compressed dirt road. The riders carried a look of excitement and determination on their faces, and with the dragons flying on the breeze behind them, they hammered through Sitivia, their knee's tucked under the scarlet wings of their mighty mounts. The people watched with pride as their queen and her escorts raced through the city streets. Many cheered, and some even bowed. Samarian horns (incredibly long, thin, instruments making a loud blaring sound) saluted the departing riders from both the hilltop palace, and the city wall. The suns shone brightly, sparkling on the swords and shields of the three figures streaking through the city streets as if blessing these riders with kisses of light to brighten their journey into the unknown. The towering wooden gates to the city slowly grumbled open as big-muscled men turned a large wheel, and the horses catapulted out of Sitivia and out into the open desert. Meekhi glanced back and saw her friends smiling at her. She turned and looked forwards again, narrowing her eyes, locking them onto the horizon. The adventure had begun and was upon them, and she was ready for whatever fate had in store.

Tamarin watched his beloved Meekhi exit the city. His hands had been resting on the balustrade of the balcony adjacent to the royal chambers. Now they were clenched into fists of steel. He watched the dragon on Meekhi's back occasionally glinting under the suns until she was out of sight. Looking at his hands he saw his fists were balled so tight that his knuckles appeared almost white, stark against his dark complexion. He unclenched his hands and again rested them on the white marble, leaning forward so his palms supported his weight. "If any harm comes to her," he thought to himself, "I will lay waste any foe, any empire, to find the cause of that harm, and destroy it. These 'Guilty Innocents' had better know whom it is they are dealing with".

"OK! OK!" Dug laughed out loud because the children were all chiming at him in a perfect chorus; "*Please*!"

"So then," he began, "shoes off please, and step inside the sphere. One chair each. Seat yourselves comfortably, and I will rig you up."

Zowie led the others inside, sitting in the central chair with Lauren and Thomas sat one on each side of her. Lauren was impressed by the comfort of the chairs, "They're nothing like dentist's chairs, Tom! They're so comfy, I could easily fall asleep in these."

She then realised what she had said, and what exactly she was sitting inside of, and everybody had a giggle at the unintended pun. Then Dug stated the obvious, "I certainly hope so!"

So everyone started chuckling again.

The three would-be dreamers waited eagerly in their seats as Dug fastened a loose fitting belt at their waists. Small bracelets, similar to hospital identity bracelets, were fitted to the children's left wrists, and a wire from each bracelet disappeared neatly into the floor. Each of them had the very light and extremely comfortable Inducer-Pods placed on their heads, with the small earpieces fitting snugly. Dug activated a tiny switch on each Inducer-Pod and the children heard a hollow sound very similar to the sound of the ocean when one listens to a sea shell.

"I can hear the sea." whispered Thomas.

"Don't be daft!" Lauren told him, "We're going flying, not scuba diving!"

Zowie smiled at them both in turn, feeling every bit as excited as they were, and revelling in the sense of camaraderie the three of them had always shared.

Dug affectionately ruffled the hair of the Shortwater children in turn, and gave Zowie a loving kiss on her forehead. Then, with a wink and a smile, he exited the Dream-Pod. They heard the almost inaudible hiss as the door slid back into place and Dug slowly turned the wheel to lock and seal it. Instantly, all external sound was blocked out from the strange little chamber. They could hear only their own excited breathing. A light metallic click, then Dug's voice; "Ok kids, just relax and leave it to me. I'm going to activate the Black Light Generator in a second, and you might feel a very brief, mild, vibration. It's quite normal so don't worry. Then you will fade from our sight, but you will still be able to see us. After that, you will fall asleep, begin dreaming, and start to fly! Have fun, love you all!"

That click again, then silence. A slight vibration momentarily tingled through the seats and the children could see their parents starting to peer, straining their eyes as if trying to see into the rapidly darkening globe.

"Flipping heck, we must be in Black Light!" Lauren exclaimed.

This inspired Thomas to yell out loud, "UP, up and away!"

Zowie's eyes remained glued to those of her father, and, under her breath, she whispered, "Thanks so much, dad, love you tons."

The children were lulled to sleep quickly and easily by the Dream Machine, not even noticing that they were doing so. Their parents watched over them even though they were now lost from view, wrapped in that dense mantle of Black Light.

Lauren felt a little cold although she knew she was in fact quite warm. Her body felt weightless as if floating, but she could not yet open her eyes and all she could 'see' was a luminous green glow.

"Maybe I haven't started the dream yet?" She thought. But then she heard Zowie and Thomas calling out. Their voices echoed, seeming faint and distant. She raised her hands to her face and found she could see them clearly. So she was not asleep in the Dream-Pod as her hands, inside the machine, had wires attached to the wrists. She certainly felt as if she was flying, or at least *hovering*! But what was all this green fog, and what on earth was going on? Suddenly, Zowie's face loomed up in front of her out of the mist,

"Holy crap, Zowie, you scared the life out of me! Are we flying? Where's Thomas? Where are we? Is this the dream? Should we know we are dreaming when we're in the dream?"

Before Zowie could tell her that she was no wiser than she was, Thomas appeared into view, his excitement obvious from his beaming smile. The trio held hands like a group of skydivers, floating helplessly in the green mist for a few seconds before Thomas decided to share his carefully calculated evaluation of the situation. "I think," He told them, "That uncle Dug forgot to programme the weather! It's like pea soup here. The echo is probably caused by the Inducer-pods on the ears of our sleeping bodies. But I'm sure we are flying, wherever we are, though I didn't expect to know we are dreaming whilst we are in the dream."

Zowie's face lacked the humour of Thomas'. She knew her father well, better than anyone else, and she knew he did not easily make mistakes. He would never allow herself and the Shortwaters to experience anything that was not planned and perfected in every minute detail. She had to be honest and share her concerns with the others immediately, "Well...we *are* flying, and, despite the green fog, we may as well enjoy it, because I'm sure something has gone wrong. We shouldn't know we're in a dream, and we shouldn't be flying in Thomas' pea soup. Guys, I think we might really be in a muddle, but don't worry, dad will sort it out, no sweat."

They looked at each other only a little apprehensively. Each had complete faith in Dug, and they *were* flying, or floating, somewhere other than in the Dream-Pod, so they knew they were not physically wherever they seemed to be. It was still an adventure that no one else had ever had, so why not enjoy it while it lasted?

CHAPTER THREE

A GRASS TROLL

Lumarr needed to rest. Bestwin was five hundred years his junior and did not tire as quickly. The half dozen guardsmen that accompanied him and his friend did not seem to tire at all! Westonians did not normally have the gift of such long lives such as the Samarians did. However, a very few Westonians, including himself and Bestwin, had been granted such extended longevity by Chjandi—the Great Dragon, towards the end of that last great war. They had received this honour for their loyalty, and their many fearless deeds during that dark time. But as Lumarr, huffing and puffing, reined in his horse, he wondered—how did the more leanly built Samarians possess such seemingly endless stamina! He could see Bestwin's face and it showed obvious signs of relief at this break in their journey west. The guardsmen on the other hand, had already slipped from their saddles and begun gathering wood to build a fire for cooking.

The hard-charging party had stopped in a clearing amidst a small wooded grove. The wood was just small enough to ride straight through but would have wasted time and further tired the horses had they ridden around it. They had been riding solidly for a very long time and were in dire need of water and something to eat. The horses, too, were in need of replenishment and were tethered at one side of the clearing, upwind of the opposing side so that smoke from the fire there would not impede their ravenous grazing on the lush moist grass surrounding them. The men had removed their saddles to allow the beasts some respite from that temporarily unnecessary burden.

At the other end of the clearing the guardsmen had dug a shallow pit in which to make the fire. They built a small wooden frame over it and hung a large pot there to boil the water in. Very soon, kindling and dry tree roots were hissing and cracking in the hollow. Flames began reaching up to heat and blacken the pot. Vegetables were produced from saddlebags, mainly potatoes, and dropped into the boiling water. A large piece of ham was expertly sliced, and someone produced a flagon of diluted wine. It was approaching noon, this being the coolest time of day in Samaria when the two suns eclipsed and one blotted out the heat of the other. But of course it was still a bright sunny day during this period of eclipse, and it was much easier to see your shadow when there was only one source of light.

The clearing in the middle of the grove was of a good size and full of long green grass that felt soft and springy underfoot. It was an oval shaped area and the woodland that surrounded it, though not sizeable in acreage, was populated by tall trees with thick trunks covered in deep knotty bark. The tops of the trees fanned out and touched each other forming a tight green canopy that hid the undergrowth from above. The blazing suns were intense enough to penetrate through the foliage of the trees to cast a strangely beautiful, calming green light throughout the woods. The green-glowing woods surrounding the clearing gave it a mellow, cool, and relaxing atmosphere for which the hot and sweating travellers were truly grateful. The air was clean and held that touch of moisture that only air amidst trees can have, a hint of lavender graced this quiet place adding its soothing scent to the overall mood. A wonderful place if one had the time and presence of mind to appreciate it.

There were some small hillocks of dry grass near the tree line and also close to the fire, so the men placed their cloaks over these so they could sit reasonably comfortably as they ate and rested their weary limbs. They were experienced riders and knew only too well how quickly a damp posterior can become chaffed and sore in the saddle—not a welcome thought. Bestwin had seasoned the boiling water with a little strong Westonian ale and two large pinches of salt. The resulting aroma from the bubbling pot was causing a few stomachs to rumble in response. Thin wooden plates were unwrapped from a saddle roll and hot steaming vegetables and cold meats were soon served up equally amongst the men. They sat on their cloaks atop the grass mounds, some shedding their triblades for better comfort as they used their daggers to eat. The Westonian daggers had simple, smooth, wooden handles, and the Samarians carried weapons with handles that were also made of wood, but into each grip was set an ivory dragon. These dragons were carved from ivory taken from wild boars—a common source of meat in Samaria. The men ate quickly, drinking water or wine frequently to soothe their dry throats. The many hours of riding had spawned large appetites and the duel suns did nothing to help quench one's long thirst.

Initially the men ate in silence, aside from the occasional muted burp. The only sounds were of metal daggers scraping on wooden plates, men chewing, men gulping, chinking of chain mail, horses grazing, and the occasional stab of birdsong from within the woodland. Then Imo—the shortest of the Samarians by far, looked up at the Westonians and asked them; "My lords, Bestwin and Lumarr—what do you think we will encounter when we reach our destination? I am the youngest here, and though I have heard many of the old tales, I'd like to know what we may face? It is not through fear that I ask, though I cannot deny a degree of apprehension, but knowledge is what I seek, for it is a gift that is always welcome."

The Westonians looked up from their plates and exchanged short, knowing glances, before turning to Imo. Bestwin, in deference to the age and wisdom of Lumarr, waited for him to reply to the question. Lumarr appreciated the respect Bestwin had showed him, and reciprocated by telling the assembly, "I will go and water the horses whilst my good friend, Bestwin, enlightens you as best he, or I, can."

With that, he stood up, and swatting crumbs away from his shaggy beard, he walked off in the direction of the horses, carrying a large skin full of water as if it were weightless.

Bestwin cleared his throat, took a long swig of wine, and settled himself more comfortably into the thick cloak beneath him. Storytelling, fact or fiction, short or long, was a great art in the Western Worlds, and the storyteller always did his utmost to tell his tale as well as possible. Reaching forward from his elevated position on the grassy hump, he carefully placed his empty plate on the ground before him. He leaned back and stretched his entire body before again leaning forward to be within earshot of all those seated about him. The men had their eyes locked on him, and so he began; "Samaria and our own Western Worlds have long been allies. This friendship began in a time of peace, a time long before Ogiin and his Venomeens. Though Lumarr and I have seen many kings and queens come and go, many generations born and others fade, I must remind you that most Westonians know their lifetimes only for what most of mankind would say was a normal term, not the extended ones with which Lumarr and I have been blessed with by the Great Dragon for our service during dark times past. Now, in this current time, there are but a handful of us Westonians that remember the great Samarian King—Darcinian, and, for that matter, the rising of Ogiin and his Venomeens. Our own King—Dorinn, knows of the past only as history and myth. Westonians, as a rule, have never seen or experienced the evil of Ogiin, or the magnificence of The Dragons of Light. Most believe the stories of the past and hold true to our alliance with Samaria. But, sadly, some do not, and I fear our king is one of these. Children are precious to all races of good men, and being Samarian, you, *above all*, appreciate this fact, because you live only a mere twinkling of your lives as children, perhaps fifteen to twenty years, but then you spend thousands of years trying not to forget the wonder and awe of childhood, the joy of innocence, the mystery of life, and the intrigue the world once held."

At this statement the Samarians gave each other knowing looks, nodding their heads sagely in agreement.

Bestwin continued, "Ogiin stands for all that we find abhorrent. The innocence of children, the very thought of new life born free, curdles his twisted soul. His sinister gaze can leave womenfolk, even *your* warrior women, infertile. His wish, his plan, his vile ambition during the Great War was not only to enslave the free people of our worlds, but also to prevent forever another free voice being born. I cannot tell you what we may discover or face on our quest, my dear Imo. But, if the loathsome vermin that Lumarr and I have already seen are indeed associated with a return of Ogiin, then rest assured that there is only darkness on the horizon. The sea has turned black, and, as we all know, the poisonous heart of Ogiin, if he doth possess a heart at all, lies deep somewhere in those cold depths. He was seen to fall, fatally wounded we all hoped, to his miserable end all those many years ago. But with the sea as it is becoming, and the filth that wanders these lands again, I fear the worst. I suggest we all sleep lightly, and keep our swords close to hand."

Imo found himself hastily picking up his sword-belt and fastening it about his waste, the others quickly following suit. They stood up and shook out their arms and legs, as if shaking off any worries that might have entered their minds as Bestwin had told his tale. He spoke again, "I regret that I cannot answer your question in greater detail than this as yet, master Imo."

Imo's response was very direct. "My lord, you have given me detail enough! Brrr!"

At this the burly warriors laughed heartily, and the darkening mood was lifted somewhat. They began gathering up the utensils and fire-making tools. The eclipse was nearly over and soon both suns would again be beating harshly on the back of any would-be traveller. Riding by night had been suggested back in Sitivia but Lumarr had reminded everyone of the strange evil creatures that were afoot in the dark, and it had been agreed that it was better to deal with the heat than to encounter something so horrible. Besides, a chance encounter could possibly alarm the enemy of the investigations being made by this group on behalf of Tamarin.

Lumarr was the last to start packing his saddle roll as he had to walk back after having tended to the horses' thirst. As he arrived back amidst the group of busy men, he stuck his large curved scimitar into a mound so that he may have use of both hands to pack his kit.

Everyone jumped when a long, low moan, reverberated across the clearing. It made the ground tremble slightly. They all stared at each other questioningly, then their eyes darted everywhere, looking for the source of that deep, pained, sound. Nothing could be seen to stir. Then it came again, a low mournful groan that lasted many seconds, perhaps quarter of a minute. Swords drawn, and shields readied, the group formed a circle. Facing out, this circle began to cover the clearing, eyes peering into the dull green hue amidst the trees for any clue as to the origin of this strange, but not yet threatening, wailing. If anything, it sounded as if the source were in shock, a sound of suffering, childlike in its innocence, but very low and full of bass. Then the ground at one end of the clearing began to heave and move. Lumarr saw his sword still standing upright in the grass and made to recover it, but a strong hand grabbed his wrist.

"Leave it be, my lord." barked the guardsman, "It seems we have disturbed a sleeping Grass Troll."

The men formed a line and backed away from the shaking, shuddering, ground. They stood near the horses (which seemed entirely unperturbed by this new and noisy event) and watched as, at first, the grassy humps and hillocks at the far side of the clearing began to writhe around, and then started growing taller. Soon an entire quarter of the clearing appeared to be rising, as if a very thick layer of grass turf was being lifted up and away from the ground. As this sizeable piece of 'ground' rose higher, one could see that it vaguely resembled the shape of a man, but without any real angles to define the form, it was altogether far more rounded. It stood twenty five feet high and had no neck to speak of. The entire body was covered in long, green, grassy fur, a green giant with three toes on each foot and only two digits per hand, its head really was only a large bump between the two shoulders, and from this bump stared two green eyes speckled with golden flecks. Huge, childishly innocent eyes, that instantly told the armed men that this creature meant them no harm. The Grass Troll slowly looked around, its eyes made up of segments with a big dark pupil in the centre. It seemed that the Grass Troll had been sleeping on its front, as they often do to avoid sunlight glaring in their eyes. The men had been sitting on the poor creature unaware of its presence due to its natural camouflage. It had been unaware of *their* presence, until Lumarr had stuck his sword into one of the cheeks of the troll's backside. No wonder it had moaned so woefully.

The troll fumbled about, trying to remove the offending sword from its rear. It no doubt felt like a large painful splinter to the poor creature. The Samarians explained to the Westonians that Grass Trolls were a harmless, wonderful, breed. They tended the forests, fells, and knolls, of Samaria. The rain watered them and the sun warmed them. They were at one with nature. The troll was literally chasing its tail, albeit slowly, as it tried futilely to remove the offending blade with its clumsy paw, and Imo, seeing its plight, deftly manoeuvred past the creature, plucking the scimitar from its buttock as he passed. Instantly a large curved cavity opened below the huge glowing eyes and all recognised it as a smile. Lumarr felt terrible at his mistakenly causing this poor simple creature to suffer so. He wanted to apologise, but of course he did not know how to. Bestwin could see the regret on Lumarr's face and passed a large sack of potatoes to his friend. Lumarr swung the sack carefully round and around his head, then, taking great aim, he hurled the sack up into the troll's mouth. At first it seemed puzzled, its great big friendly eyes now looked confused as it seemed to be trying to peer down to see its own mouth. It stuck out its lower jaw revealing one great big molar tooth right in the centre, matched by another one in the upper jaw. Both teeth were heavily stained green and brown. The men watched dumbstruck as the towering hairy green troll tottered about as it strained to push its lower jaw further out to see what was in its mouth. Then it made a 'hummm' sound, and the potato sack, now empty, was blown very gently from its mouth and wafted down to the ground below. A guardsman snatched it up as to litter such a place was unthinkable. The troll began to chew the potatoes between its two gigantic teeth, its wide smile and glowing eyes showing obvious signs of delight. It looked down at the men and horses, and making a low sound akin to a cow mooing, it lumbered off into the woods stroking at its sore backside, its grassy shape soon becoming invisible in the green glow amidst the trees.

"Well, that's not something you see every day!" Lumarr exclaimed.

"I liked that creature." Bestwin quietly told no one in particular.

There was no more to be said really, and so the horses were made ready quickly. Swinging into their saddles, the riders rode swiftly through the remainder of the woods. Once out on the other side, a lush green valley stretched out before them, undulating gently as it sprawled away between low hills. A tall range of mountain peaks could be seen in the far distance. "We need to be camped by nightfall." Lumarr told them.

The horses set off at a half gallop, the small line of warriors streaking across the soft ground with a fresh brisk breeze reviving their senses after their brief sojourn. The Western Worlds were still a long way off, and time was of the essence.

Tamarin was ill at ease. It was not in his nature to be idly passing time whilst others may be facing any manner of danger in order to bring him news. Sitivia had now filled beyond the cities limited capacity with warriors from neighbouring townships and other lands. So much so, that there were many large tents and marquees pitched up outside of the city wall to accommodate the surplus. Most were unsure of what the reason was for their presence here and rumours abounded. The residents of the capital kept them all well fed and watered, so there were no complaints on that score. Samarians, given their unique life spans, had quickly learned that patience is truly a great virtue. They had great faith not only in their king, but also in Meekhi. Tamarin, since being crowned Lord of Samaria, had earned the love and respect of his people. Darcinian was missed by all those who had known him, and loved by all including those that had not known him, but Tamarin had gained a deep respect from his people on his own merits. Whilst it was true that he had learned much from his father as a young boy, he had also brought his own blend of youth and charisma to the Samarian Throne. He ruled by not really ruling at all. He enforced the principle laws of the land, of course, but they are just and fair laws, so no one resented this in the least. Tamarin loved his kingdom and ensured her borders were kept safe and her people as happy as any, and most surely happier than most. He did not lust after the trappings of kingship such as ornate cloths, rare jewels, and the power of the sword. Instead, he was at one with the people. Often, when travelling across the land, he would call at a simple family home not for vittals or wine, but out of genuine concern as to how those people were faring, and to ask if anything further was required on that particular homestead. He would openly discuss affairs of state with any layperson in the street, even asking their opinions on his kingship, and of ways in which he could be of better service to his people. Native women conceived a child extremely rarely (or over population would have become a serious problem rather quickly), so when a child was born, the Lord and Lady of the land were invited to a special ceremony when the child was exactly three days old. Tamarin and Meekhi always tried to attend these rare and joyous occasions. If they could not attend together, one would attend singly. If that was also not possible, then senior lords and ladies would attend from the palace in Sitivia. The kind and generous nature of Tamarin, paired with his true and honest character, was known to all his people. But also they never forgot that his veins carried the same bloodline as that of Darcinian. A bloodline that dated back to before records began. A line of kings so wise, noble, and distinguished, so versed in the martial ways, that any man, even a fool, would know better than to cross swords with them.

Tamarin sat back in his chair. He was sitting in the great hall staring at the wooden face that had spoken to him not so long ago, pondering this puzzle of Ogiin. Ogiin was not a man, but a dark creature nurtured in the womb of hell, fathered by the darkest thoughts in the minds of the most wretched and evil of men. Tamarin had only been a very young prince but he remembered only too well that Ogiin was no fool, and had in fact outwitted his own father on several occasions. He knew that The Source created all life in perfect balance—up and down, left and right, wet and dry, hot and cold. Thus, if love existed, so must hate. Each defined the other. If there was light there must be dark. If something or someone stood for all that was good in the world, then there must be the counterpart of all that was bad. But Ogiin had tipped this delicate balance because he had sought to destroy all that is good and commence a reign of pure darkness. The status quo had been broken. The Dragons of Light knew there must be a balance in all things and so refused to allow Ogiin to destroy that which they held so dear—The Essence of Love. So, Chjandi, and all the beautiful dragons, were now lost, lost in that awful war. Tamarin had seen the Great Dragon suffer horrendous wounds, and had been told by his own father of how that noblest of noble spirits had disappeared into history, but what of Ogiin? Until now he was presumed dead, his fish-eaten corpse rotting at the bottom of the sea. But did he really die? They knew of the fearsome battle in the sky between Chjandi and Ogiin, but had that vilest of spirits somehow survived the devastating blast of dragon's flame? Had the cold western sea extinguished his blazing body before life was fully snuffed out? The more he thought about it, the more he realised that there had never been any proof of Ogiin's physical death, it had merely been *assumed* that he had died. He wracked his memory but could not remember any mention of Chjandi stating Ogiin had been killed. Dragons never lie, and if Chjandi had stated Ogiin was no more, then Tamarin could have breathed easier. He looked up from the table and stared at the tall silver dragon staring back at him from across the hall. Its intense ruby eyes were devoid of life and he wished he could but ask Chjandi this one vital question. But the lifeless statue just continued to stare blankly back at him.

A trancelike stupor descended upon the king's mind and he became mesmerised by the those two, diamond-shaped, ruby eyes, each of the many facets of luxuriant deep red absorbing him, overwhelming his senses, sucking him in. Several minutes must have passed before he snapped out of it very suddenly, and made a decision. He must check the records to see what had actually been said by Chjandi to his father. Glad to be finally doing something productive, Tamarin moved quickly through the palace and was soon in the Hall of History. His heart sank when he realised just how much of that Great War was documented here. Literally thousands of scrolls were neatly placed on row-upon-row of shelves that reached up to the high ceiling. The room was a giant honeycomb of shelves, shelves, and more shelves. He turned about and stepped back into the corridor, he was going to need help. He shouted for guards, and preceded by the instant sound of running feet, a handful of guardsmen came charging headlong towards him, swords drawn and ready. He raised his hand and they slowed their pace, sheathing their weapons when it became apparent there was no call for them. He told them they were going to aid him in looking for information related to Ogiin's alleged demise. In particular, as to whether or not *Chjandi* had stated if Ogiin was dead, or not. The men removed their helmets, swords, and cloaks. Then they and their king began to clamber all over the Hall of History.

They had been riding hard for two days now and Meekhi could feel her horse was tiring. Though they had rested by night as had been agreed in Sitivia, they had seen nothing of the dark creatures of which the Westonians had spoken. Perhaps, thought Meekhi, these events were more related to the Western Worlds than to Samaria? Of course Samaria would stand by her great ally if needs be, but, as yet, all seemed as she had always known it to be. There again, Meekhi knew she was heading east and it had been said that trouble was brewing in the west. Besides, there was no telling what kind of threat these 'Guilty Innocents' might yet pose. The ground they had covered so far had been desert terrain and very hard going. Her companions had begun to look as weary as she was beginning to feel, and the horses must be worn out too. The heat and lack of humidity made one feel very light headed, as if one was inhaling the scorching sunlight itself. In the far distance she could see the vague outline of a city. "Soledad." She thought, sombrely.

Easing her mount to a standstill, she took a deep lungful of the hot, dry air. Her mouth was parched and she reached for her water skin as Mercy and Ramulet pulled up beside her. They dismounted and filled wooden bowls for the horses before drinking from the bottlenecks themselves. Ramulet noticed they were low on water and that the horses would require more than a small bowlful to keep them going in that sweltering heat. He produced a map from within his tunic and as one of the horses had sat down, he spread the map across its back.

"We have three choices," he advised the women also examining his map, "directly ahead, maybe three hours ride, lies The Silent City. There, there is fresh water and supplies, but also a sadness to break any heart. We have sworn to not venture there and I say we stand with our oaths. To the left, thus avoiding Soledad, we can continue on terrain such as we have travelled these past two days. This course will lengthen our journey by at least a further two days as water will be scarce and we would barely have enough food, not to mention finding sustenance for our winged friends. This is the longest but safest route I feel, because to the right lies the Desert of Iret—the land of lies, illusions, and deceit. Many have entered that treacherous place and none have returned to tell the tale. Even the Ranin, outbound from Sitivia, give that accursed wasteland a wide berth. My lady, Meekhi, our course is yours to command, what thought have you on the matter?"

He left the map spread out on the horse's back and stepped away, allowing them to scrutinize it more closely. He had brought with him some salted bread (essential for such a journey) and wiping it liberally with a rich, honey-coloured olive oil, he handed a piece to each of his companions, and all three chewed on this as they studied the map. Mercy continued to examine it as Meekhi removed a heavy bag from one of the other horses. Mercy had ordered that this bag accompany them. It was full of a mash made from sweet oats and golden maize, a favourite man-made meal amongst Samaria's flying horses. Some of these horses said it was best consumed with a large bowl of the beverage men called beer, though both men and horses, alike, agreed that a horse should never attempt to fly after drinking beer. Meekhi and Mercy served up the very welcome food. They exchanged smiles as the horses ate as if starving. "They appear," Mercy chuckled, "to be as hungry as a horse, or, even, as three horses."

Ramulet was watching Mercy as she fed their four legged friends. He observed her tall graceful figure bending and reaching. He would have helped her but he knew she would have been insulted if he offered. Mercy was proud, but well shy of arrogance, a woman of great independence and ability, yet despite her enviable reputation on the battlefield, she also had a gentler, more tender, and very considerate side to her character, as clearly illustrated by her bringing of the special treat for the horses. He was, in a strange way, glad of these events that had thrown Mercy and himself together on this quest to the Pink Mountain. He assured himself that when this new threat from the west was dealt with, he would ask for her hand in marriage. He was busy admiring the curve of her slender neck as she tossed her long tresses to one side, when Meekhi's teasing voice interrupted his romantic musings.

"Not all the views from this point are so desolate, eh, Ramulet?"

"Quite so, my lady." came his reply in a very matter of fact voice. Meekhi grinned cheekily like a little girl, and Mercy saw her, "What's amusing you, then?" She asked.

Meekhi just smiled at her friends and pointed at the map, noting that those two friends were standing closer together then they ever had before. "We have no idea what lies ahead of Bestwin and Lumarr," Meekhi pointed out, "but we know it will take them at least a week to reach the Western Worlds, and as much again to return. That is two weeks that my lord will have had no news from them, I cannot leave him with such a conundrum on his mind for so long with nothing from either party. Also, I wish to resolve this puzzle of 'Guilty Innocents' as soon as possible, so I am able to assist him in whatever course he may choose to take. Whilst I agree that we should not enter Soledad, I am not convinced we can afford to lose two days by avoiding the Desert of Iret. My friends, what is your counsel?"

"I agree with you," Mercy told her, "we don't know who or what these Guilty Innocents are, and any delay in our arrival at the Pink Mountain may have serious consequences for everyone. I also agree we should avoid the Silent City and its ancient ghosts. Two days is too much time to lose. The Desert of Iret may well be full of illusions and treachery, but I know these falsehoods can never cause me to doubt my faith. My heart is true and my spirit pure. I do not claim to be a Ranin, but I do not fear Iret or its treacherous nature. If you will venture there, my lady, I will ride beside you."

Ramulet exhaled a long, slow, breath. He was hesitant to accede to this new fast evolving plan, but he knew his place was to serve, and serve he would. The suns were now half eclipsed and already one could feel some relief from the heat. He knew there was a watering hole en route to Iret and so he took the last big water skin and poured refreshing cold water over Mercy's head, then over Meekhi's too. The women happily used the impromptu shower to rinse sand and dust from their grimy faces whilst, lastly, Ramulet dowsed his own baking scalp. He then gave the remaining water, more than half a skin full, to the horses. Two of them accepted it in bowls and the third (that went by the name of Rorrdor) asked for his share to be poured over his head and stroked through as it looked so pleasurable when Meekhi and Mercy did it. Ramulet obliged him and Rorrdor immediately wished he had drank the water instead, commenting, "I don't know what all the fuss is about, and it's gone down my ears, I can't hear a thing!"

Ramulet stood leaning against an un-amused Rorrdor. Around them the barren land spread out in all directions with the odd piece of brush or gorse allowing some degree of distance to be gauged. The sand felt hot underfoot, even through his boots, and the horses gleamed, wet with the heat. The riders found their hair to be no longer wet. The air being so devoid of any moisture, their throats felt akin to dry cracked leather. It was very quiet. Not a single bird braved the blazing skies. He knew the other two were still waiting on his opinion, so, finally, he spoke up. "My ladies, I cannot say what lies in wait for us within the filthy folds of Iret. As none that entered have returned from within that poisonous pit of a place, we can rely only upon folklore and myth. But once upon a time that small stretch of land was a glorious utopia only a fast morning's ride from Soledad, a virtual garden of Eden amidst this searing heat. I will not now waste our precious time with lessons in history, but I know an act of utter betrayal, a breaking of oaths and committing of high treason, reduced that oasis of paradise to what it is now. These foul acts were committed by a former Lady of the Royal Court. It is said that her spirit, with its foul and treacherous nature, are now as one with that land. As Tamarin's true friend and Captain of the Royal Guards, I cannot approve of either of you venturing into that place, a place so soiled that a pure heart may recoil in shock at its putrid nature. It is my duty, and forgive my saying it—to not only serve, but also to *protect,* you. I suggest you both take the longer but safer route. I will break right and pass through Iret alone and make for our goal, and if I am not already heading back to you, I will be awaiting you at the Pink Mountain—having solved the riddle of the Guilty Innocents."

He was ill at ease having just said what he had said. These women were skilled warriors and he hoped they would not be offended that he felt that he alone should face whatever dangers Iret had to offer. Fortunately for the captain, they did not take offence. Meekhi gave him her opinion on his offer. "Ramulet, I'm sure Mercy is as appreciative as I for your concerns as to our wellbeing. You are truly an honourable man and no one is more worthy of the high post you hold. But, alas, now is not a time for chivalry, though under normal circumstances it is such a pleasing trait in a man. My lord awaits news from me and I will keep him waiting not one second more than needs be. I too have heard, though not in any detail, of the witch that by subterfuge and seduction did find a position in our royal court, albeit before my time." At the end of this sentence Meekhi gripped her sword firmly, her knuckles whitening, "Had this occurred in my time I assure you, her stuffed head would adorn a wall in the great hall of Sitivia. I say, indeed... I *insist*, that I will take the most direct route to the Pink Mountain whilst avoiding Soledad. So, I mean to travel through Iret. Mercy has already stated her position, and you, my nervous looking Ramulet, need not state yours. I know you will lead us into this place, and, I have good faith, that you will lead us out."

Ramulet stood tall. She was right, of course. The suns were once again starting to combine their efforts in roasting this arid stretch of land and the trio made ready to continue their journey. Meekhi noted Ramulet and Mercy's horses seemed to be weighed down far more so than her own. When she asked them why, they lifted their saddle rolls to reveal a hoard of weapons that even *she* was quite taken aback by, she saw them exchanging smiles, seeing and recognising the mindset of the other as a mirror image of their own. Rordorr, Ramulet's horse, just groaned. "I see, first I'm a map-reading table, and now I'm a pack mule with his ears full of water. That seems about right."

The trio set off at a more leisurely pace in the direction of the Desert of Iret, each of them wondering what might lie ahead. Meekhi secretly wished to come face-to-face with this ancient witch's spirit and she stroked the hilt of her sword lovingly, trying to repress her sudden hankering for the witch's head.

They travelled slowly, but only because water supplies were now very low and they did not want the horses spent before they reached the watering hole. As they trotted along with hooves thud-thudding on the hard packed sand, they veered to the right. The turrets, onion towers and domes of Soledad could be seen more clearly now—albeit still a long way off. The black stone structures, ablaze with colour in history, pointed accusingly at the sky and one could easily see that Soledad was once a great, thriving city. It was unbearable to try and imagine just how many souls lay ensnared in stone within that tragic place. The riders felt a deep sense of loss at that distant skyline, married to a sudden surge of furious anger at Ogiin for his heartless deed. When they came to the point that brought them closest to the city, just before they veered further to the right, each of them felt an ice cold wave of sadness wash over them. It penetrated deep into their hearts like a slimy black virus and Mercy felt her senses recoiling at the thought of such horror. Ramulet reached across and gripped her arm. "Come," He urged her, "let us be on our way with haste. The forlorn cries of the dead should not be heard by those yet living."

"By the sword, yes!" came Rordorr's voice, "I have never imagined such anguish as I feel now, and I have no desire to feel it further."

With that, the horse began to gather speed, and the others followed quickly. Meekhi looked back at the Silent City once more over her shoulder and thought she saw a twinkle of light amongst the dark shapes. She strained her eyes but could not see anything to warrant further interest. The riders and the horses felt wretched, suffocated by that awful wave of suffering emanating from Soledad. The suns had long since passed their zenith and were leaving these upper worlds to shed light on the those elsewhere. A small, low, semi-sphere glowed in both the east and the west, casting long strange shadows from the trio in opposite directions. To the east they could see a tiny point of pink glowing in the centre of the horizon. It was the peak of the Pink Mountain, and whilst they felt relieved to see it, its tiny size alarmed them, revealing just how far they had yet to travel. The riders had unknowingly slung their war shields onto their left arms as if to protect them from Soledad's chilling aura, and as the diminishing sunlight offered up its last warming rays of the day to the silver dragons on each shield they seemed to turn red, appearing to be staring back defiantly into the darkness of The Silent City. Night began to overpower the fast fading light and the horses packed closer together so as to not lose one another. In the gathering dusk the Samarians plodded relentlessly onwards, their eyes scanning ahead for signs of when they would enter the serpent's lair that was Iret.

It was another two hours of dogged riding before Ramulet called a halt. He had noticed that the ground was no longer visible, but rather, covered in a fine thin mist, the colour of sand. Its colour had stopped the horses noticing it, and it was only because of its sifting motion that he had eventually become aware of it. He pointed it out to the others and all of them carefully dismounted. The mist swirled around their booted feet. Mercy reached down and tentatively moved her fingers through it. "It's warm." she told the others.

They looked at each other puzzled, though in fact each of them knew exactly what they were standing in. Meekhi recalled an ancient verse she had once read in the Hall of History, back home in the cliff top palace. She recited it out aloud:

> "When the land becomes a sea of sand
> And the midnight hour is close at hand
> Your sword and shield will aid you not
> For now reality must be forgot!
> Tread no further lest the dreams you share
> are no longer dreams, but your worst nightmare."

The three warriors shuddered as an icy finger of foreboding ran down their spines, each hiding their sudden alarm from the other two. Mercy and Ramulet also knew of these ancient writings. The trio and the horses (which, I do believe, also knew of this verse), stood staring ahead into the land before them. Darkness now had the last remaining remnants of the day by the throat and was firmly throttling the life out of them.

Ramulet stood in the middle of the other two and placed a strong hand on each of their shoulders. The women were glad of that feeling of strength and solidarity, the friendship that bound them together. Meekhi stepped forward and turned around, drawing her sword which managed to still somehow gleam in the dark. She held her blade aloft and spoke out as only a true warrior-queen can. "Mercy, loyal Captain. I am Meekhi, sworn queen of Samaria, and the honoured wife of the great king—Tamarin. I have never known fear, and now, finally, it makes itself known to me. But I shall defy it in the name of Chjandi—The Great Dragon. I shall defy it in the name of my lord—Tamarin, and I shall defy it in the name of our beloved Samaria and her people. Whatever lies ahead of us now, we will endure and survive. The king is awaiting our news, will we disappoint him? Will I fail the man I love so dearly? I say, NEVER!"

Ramulet and Mercy had never seen her like this, it seemed as if a silver light from deep within her was shining all around her form, the halo of her pure soul resisting the darkness. At this very moment, like never before, they understood more than ever why Tamarin had chosen her as his queen. She truly was a queen above all queens. Raising their swords in unison and saluting her, they cried, "Samaria, and The King!"

Swinging smoothly up into their saddles, invigorated by Meekhi's staunch words, they stepped forward, three abreast, into the Desert of Iret.

"Cor blimey, girls! it's all very well being in a dream and knowing it's a dream," Thomas was shouting a little too loudly, "but it feels more like *floating* than flying because of this horrible green mist!"

He had voiced what all of them were thinking. Surely this was not what Douglas had planned? Zowie did not like the idea that her father's amazing invention was not living up to expectations, so she had an idea and shared it with her cousins. "Maybe," she began, "we can't feel we're flying because were not actually going anywhere. I mean, we can fly around in this mist ok, so, possibly… we're flying too *low*, like in a cloud, or perhaps a fog, should we fly higher with our hands linked together, and see what we can find above us, guys?"

"I'm definitely up for that!" Lauren agreed, "Have you noticed that this mist we're breathing in tastes deliciously sweet?"

Thomas thought so too, "Yeah, it's sort of like a toffee taste, I think. Hey! We have in-flight refreshment!"

The girls looked at each other disparagingly.

Having linked their hands together, they simply thought of flying higher, and they began to ascend. The thickness of the mist began to thin quite quickly and that sweet taste became less and less. Soon they could see the green thinning out and getting paler as they climbed higher and higher through it. Upon seeing the lighter hue above closing fast, they realised just how fast they were travelling—very fast indeed. Each of them thought of slowing down but of course each slowed by a different degree, and this caused them to lose their grip on one another's hands. Thomas had slowed the least and so was the first to shoot out of the mist. He was rapidly followed by the girls. They found there was a bright, clear blue sky above them, and they were heading towards it at high speed. "This is more like it!" Zowie called out excitedly.

As they shot skywards, they realised they were flying out of a large volcanic type of mountain. The inner walls of the crater were of a deep pink colour, and made up of some form of crystal. The green mist was massed below them, swirling deep within the crater itself. They had not yet exited the crater mouth when they realised their speed was reducing very quickly, far too quickly, in fact. Then Thomas slowed down completely, and seemed for a split second to just hang in the air, before he began plummeting back towards the mist at breakneck speed. Looking completely bewildered, he passed the girls on his way down, but they did not have time to worry for him as their own brief flights had also came to an abrupt end, and they, too, were diving head first back to earth. Their hysterical screams were replaced by giggles as all three crashed into the mist and found it had transformed into a super-soft cushion of sorts, like a giant bouncy castle made of marshmallow. They lay atop it, laughing and chuckling, "What a rush!" giggled Lauren, "I love this dream! Isn't this just the best thing ever!"

Zowie realised that for some reason they had not been able to fly out of this strange pink mountain. "Maybe," she thought, "there was some sort of magnetic force that had pulled them back. After all, anything is possible in a dream". She told the others and they formed the view that Dug had cunningly built an adventure into their dream to make it more fun. They decided to walk across the mist to the rough, easily scaleable, walls that encircled them, and to then climb up out of this crater. Then they could fly about in the heavenly blue sky that loomed high above them, free of the magnetic pull of the mountain. It looked very warm out there and the three of them walked (with some difficulty I might add, as it's not easy walking on a giant green marshmallow) to the crater's inner face and began to carefully climb up it. The climbing was quite easy and the children attributed this to Dug making it so—as the dream was meant to be fun.

The pink crystal rock face fascinated the children and Lauren put a small shard in her pocket, it could not be called stealing in a dream could it, because she would not have it when she woke up in the Dream-Pod. They had been climbing for a while and stopped for a break halfway to the top. Lauren commented that it was a good thing that Zowie and herself were wearing leggings and not dresses or skirts to climb in, though they still had to be careful where they put their feet as that crystal was very sharp in places. Thomas was wearing jeans which enabled him to climb a little faster, though he too was mindful of the sharp outcrops and his sock-clad feet. He noticed his watch had stopped and the girls' watches had done the same. They figured this was due to what Dug had explained about time in 'dream time' having no connection to 'real' time. It seemed to make sense and after their short breather, they continued to climb. As they approached the upper lip of the crater they could feel the heat of a tremendously hot day outside. Now it was clear that the sky was not a pale blue as it normally should be, but more a rich, velvety, navy blue. They could hear the occasional sound of a bird singing, though it was birdsong far more beautiful than any they had ever heard before. The excitement rising within them was almost unbearable and they scrambled up the last few feet, scrabbling out over the lip of the crater.

Zowie let out a low, long, whistle. The view was nothing short of breathtaking. They were sitting, quite comfortably, at the peak of a pink volcanic mountain. Despite the green mist inside it did not appear to be active and there were no clouds of horrible black flies everywhere, which is the normal way of things with volcanoes as they are drawn to the foul smelling sulphur. In fact the air smelled wonderful—of roses mingled with exotic spices. Beneath them, as far as they could see, lay a land way beyond their wildest imaginings. They could see a lake far below. A green river snaked away from them, shimmering as it flowed along. Strange looking trees dotted the landscape, some of them perhaps half as tall as the peak upon which the children were perched. The volcano itself was perhaps fifteen hundred feet high. Beautiful birds covered in a dazzling array of multi-coloured feathers, darted across the luxuriant blue sky, moving from tree top to tree top, and most glorious of all—a pair of blood red suns blazed in the heavens, each rising from the opposite direction to the other. The children were stunned, amazed at this unexpected turn of events. Sitting happy and safe at the mountain top, they just stared out at that vast, surreal landscape. An emerald green lake, exotic birds, and trees lush with foliage, in the middle of what appeared to be a desert, an impossible combination back in 'reality'.

"It seems," Zowie chanced a guess, "that either dad has sneakily arranged an adventure for us as a surprise in our dream, or something has gone very wrong, because sitting here on top of this weird volcano—we are most definitely NOT flying. I think it's an adventure, as that is just what he would do for us on our birthdays. This place looks *amazing*! Shall we just sit here for now and plan our next move?"

The Shortwaters thought this an excellent idea.

CHAPTER FOUR

OGIIN AWAKES

One of the guardsmen called out, "I HAVE IT!"
He held up an old scroll made from parchment and bound in gilded silk ribbon. Tamarin and the others clambered down like elegant apes from various ceiling-high shelves, and the guardsman passed him the scroll. He eyed the red ribbon and saw it was clearly marked: 'The Fall of Ogiin'. The young king felt a small hard knot forming in the pit of his stomach as he recognised the flowing script as the hand of his beloved father—Darcinian.

The scroll was carefully placed upon a wooden table and very gently unravelled. Within it he discovered a smaller scroll bound tightly with a black silk ribbon. This ribbon held silver writings, again in Darcinian's hand. Placing the smaller scroll, which did not bear any clue as to its content, to one side, he sat down and began to read the ancient wording. The guardsmen crowded around him, reading the scroll over his shoulder. All knowledge from The Hall of History is freely available to each and every Samarian so this posed no problem for Tamarin. He read and read. The content of the text within the scroll was extremely well detailed, and documented those historic events almost by the second. He recalled his father's painstaking attention to detail in all he did, and again came that emptiness in his stomach as he remembered the strong hand of Darcinian resting firmly on his shoulder. Two hours of reading, and they took a break for food and water. Two further hours and the lengthy scroll had been examined word by word, but no relevant clue had been found, no fact stated, as to the actual final fate of Ogiin. His elbow resting on the table and his hand stroking his unshaven chin, Tamarin ran his gaze around The Hall of History. Here, contained within these cool, white marble, walls, was the history of Samaria since the realm came into existence. Yet no mention of the true fate of Ogiin after the most terrible, but ultimately victorious, war, Samarians had ever seen and endured. His heart sank and as he went to rise his eyes fell on the smaller, black-ribboned parchment. Again he sat down, and with much curiosity opened this little scroll to determine its purpose. He unbound the ribbon with great care so as to not damage the fragile parchment, and when he started to read it a slight tremor rippled through his strong young hands as his heart began to beat faster. He felt his face flushing. The writing of his father read: *"For my dear beloved son, Tamarin, from your loving father."*

The guardsmen could see the king's welling emotion and quietly left the hall, the last to leave giving his shoulder a reassuring squeeze before departing. Tamarin's mind was suddenly filled with memories of his childhood. A time so long ago, so far away, and so very cherished. Vivid images flooded his mind with a clarity so shocking that it almost made him reel. He remembered play fights with wooden triblades, learning to ride a horse, splashing water in the Emerald River, chasing his father with a furiously wriggling eel. Most of all he remembered the hugs and kisses with which his father had always showered him. He longed to again look into his eyes and see there the love that only a son can see in his father. Tamarin's handsome young face was full with the heat of memory. He regained himself quickly, he was no longer a child. Childhood was a brief blessing he had savoured without measure, but now he was a man, not only a man, but king of this wonderful realm. His people looked to him to lead, and lead he would. Laying the little scroll carefully on top of the larger one, he began to read, unable to prevent a tear or two of love for his father from brimming in his big brown eyes. The scroll read:

"My beloved son, if you must inquire into the fall of Ogiin then evil must again be striking out against us, and now, you, my son, must be the shield of Samaria, a shield that will refuse to splinter under any onslaught. You are the greatest of my accomplishments and you are this by merit of your own deeds not mine. I loved you from the second you were conceived, and I love you still, from afar. I know not what dire events have caused you to seek out these scrolls, my dear heart, but you must follow your royal instinct. You are my blood. Your eldest child will rule after you. Remember your heritage, and that the wisdom of that lineage courses through your veins. Use that wisdom, Tamarin. Keep faith with the tutelage of the Great Dragon. Discount nothing! Suspect everything! Be sure that time is not spent on idle guesswork. It is the deeds of great Kings that make these Kings great, not their titles, nor any amount of material wealth. My beloved son, we are an ancient people and have spilled much of our precious blood for the sake of freedom and justice. This blood was not spilt in vain. You are not alone. Follow The Dragon, Tamarin, follow your true heart. I am always with you.

Your loving father,
Darcinian."

Tamarin was struck dumb, strangely numbed by this cherished voice from beyond the grave. To hear from his father so very long after his passing was beyond any dream coming true. Yet, still, there was no sign of Ogiin's final fate, no words of guidance from the late king. However, he *had* received words of love, and he felt a warmth envelope him as if Darcinian's strong arms were embracing him once more. The tears welled up again, and, this time, spilled over, trickling slowly down his cheeks, clinging to the tip of his stubbly chin as if wanting to stay and console this young king, before falling silently onto the scroll. He heard the odd plop of his emotion landing on the parchment and looked down through his watery eyes. The tears had caused his vision to become unfocused and bleary. He stared hard at the scroll and noticed that in the bottom left corner was engraved a rampant silver dragon. His hazy vision caused the dragon to seem in motion, as if it were rearing up and staring at him with its dark red eyes blazing. Gripping the little scroll firmly, he stood up so suddenly that he sent the table clattering away from him across the floor. He thumped a nearby pillar. By the sword! His father had not deserted him in his hour of need after all. Tamarin believed Ogiin to be once more somehow infesting these worlds, and he would stand by this belief because it was born of his royal instinct. At once he recalled the dragon on Meekhi's back reflecting the sun as she had disappeared from view. Follow the dragon, Darcinian had said. He would follow the dragon, and his heart, exactly as his learned father advised, for his true heart was, even now, riding hard to the Pink Mountain.

Snatching up his cloak he dabbed dry his eyes. He touched the scroll to his forehead and thanked his father for the wisdom of the past that had now blessed him in the present. He was acutely aware of how fortunate he had been to have known such unconditional love for so long. *Ramulet*, alas, had not been blessed with such good fortune, his own father having disappeared without a trace, depriving him of his love, and leaving his son un-reconciled as to his whereabouts or fate. Both had great fathers then, but only one had great memories. Tamarin would not make much of Darcinian's still-tender love in Ramulet's presence. He strode boldly from the Hall of History, a definite course of action in hand at last.

In the great hall many lords had gathered at Tamarin's behest and he told them of his intentions. He could not desert the brave posse riding to the Western Worlds headed by Bestwin and Lumarr, so he would send a column of one hundred horsemen after them to aid or escort them as needs be. Corsellius, his old and wise adviser, was to prepare the men gathered in Sitivia for any eventuality, any threat from either the west, or the east, Tamarin would take a dozen volunteers and make haste to join up with Meekhi. He explained to the others that he felt his presence was more sorely needed there and his motive was not purely his queen. None doubted him and many volunteered to join his pursuit of the trio headed east. He made his selection of companions quickly. As provisions and suchlike were prepared in the lower levels of the palace, men were sent to corrals sited outside of Sitivia where the warhorses were kept. These were not the enormous, winged, Samarian horses, but immensely powerful chargers that were well trained as battle steeds. The corralled areas contained warm and comfortable stabling, so the animals were never neglected or without safe shelter.

Buried deep below the palace in the rocky heart of the cliffs, was a network of tunnels and caves. The guardsmen knew them as well as they knew their own homes but the underground maze would completely baffle any stranger. Within this subterranean labyrinth were stored Sitivia's weapons of war. The big cold chambers, silent for so long, now buzzed with the sound of tramping feet and barked commands. Swords, shields, daggers, maces, axes, lances, and all manner of deadly items were being moved out into the cities central square. Guardsmen filled their water skins to the brim, many tying smaller ones of wine to their belts. They unsheathed their angry looking triblades and ran pumice stones over them to hone the six cutting edges. The long central blades gleamed intermittently in the flickering light of the burning oil lamps, the pair of much shorter, thinner blades (for ensnaring and snapping an opponent's weapon) leaving no doubt about the deadly capability of this wholly Samarian weapon.

The suns were bidding their farewells to Sitivia, was the encroaching darkness a sign of things to come? City folk watched as the heavy gates groaned noisily before squealing open, and over a hundred war horses poured in, expertly herded by experienced guardsmen cajoling and guiding the beasts into the central square. The horses stamped their hooves, snorting indignantly at this sudden furore as stable hands rushed from all directions and lashed saddles and equipment onto them. People watched in awe as one hundred Royal Guardsmen in full battledress marched down from the palace in two long columns. The dragons on their shields brought an overwhelming sense of pride to the onlookers and the whole city began to cheer. Shouts of 'Tamarin, and Meekhi!' and, 'Samaria!' drowned out the sound of marching feet. With faultless precision the men swung up into the one hundred waiting saddles, and then formed up. Those watching felt relieved upon seeing action being taken at last. The city had been waiting with baited breath upon the king's ponderings and the massed exhalation of held breaths brought with it a strange sense of direction, a setting of a course, the first steps of a journey which, once started, held no retreat. Something was actually happening and the drawn out waiting of the past two days was at an end. Many had wished that their king had accompanied their queen on her endeavours from the beginning, and, now, he would indeed be in swift pursuit of her. This pleased everyone, and none more so than the king, himself.

A sudden hush seized the cheering crowds and stamping horses. The men soothed their steeds and patted their necks, everyone's eyes were looking up, fixed upon a tall figure approaching the square from the palace. It was Tamarin. He was wearing, for the first time, his father's battledress, a gleaming black breastplate over silver chain mail, with a blazing silver dragon at its centre. His sword marched alongside him like a well trained dog. He moved precisely, one might even say elegantly, but he bore an air about him that left no illusions as to his status, and his abilities. The grace with which he, a man of some size, descended the many steps from the palace made one immediately aware of his hidden agility. His dark locks lofted fitfully in the sporadic sea breeze that cooled the incoming night. Halfway down the steps he stopped and faced his people. Placing his hands on the low wall in front of him, he addressed them, "Samarians! I leave you now so I may follow my heart! For without our hearts, what are we? I will return with your queen, or I will not return. Hearken unto Corsellius for he is wise beyond my own meagre understanding, and a pupil of Chjandi, Himself! Be alert, my people, my friends, my Samarians! This city is your city. Keep her safe, may the Great Dragon watch over you all."

Tamarin covered the remaining half of the descent quickly, and was soon amongst his guardsmen. He looked at Etep—the man that would captain the column heading west—and nodded to him with a tight smile.

Etep—a giant of a man, roared in his booming voice, "MAKE READY!"

The horsemen formed up behind him, rich black cloaks covering the rear of their mounts, triblades all hanging neatly to the left. The fearsome warriors tugged and pulled at reins, trimming the column as the horses jostled for space within the confines of the square. Their muscles bulged as they held onto the impatient horses. Then, a long-unheard sound wafted down from the cliff tops, sending an electric shiver of pride down every single Samarian spine, adding a shot of confidence to all present. It was the sound of the Samarian war horns being blown in salute to Tamarin and his Royal Guards. Unlike the instruments that had accompanied Meekhi's departure, these were *war* horns, the melodious, yet menacing, notes floating down from above. At first a light, shrill sound with a gradually expanding bass filled their ears, it grew in intensity and power until the air was alive with a sound no one could mistake for anything but a battle cry, a raw defiant call overflowing with the irrepressible spirit of the Samarian soul. Many a tear wetted many an eye as Etep, his black charger rearing up, raised his sword, and pointing it at the gates he bellowed, "Tamarin, and, the Great Dragon!"

With his voice still resonating throughout the square, he spurred his horse into a gallop and everyone watched that train of horses storming out of the city, a mass of pounding hooves and jangling armour. They poured through the gates, surging out across the open ground before them with dragon-bedecked banners held high with pride, and, before anyone could have believed it, in a cloud of dust and blessings, they were out of Sitivia and bound for Lumarr, Bestwin, Imo, and the Western Worlds.

Tamarin did not wait for the dust of their parting to settle. Sitting astride an incredibly beautiful pure white charger (Meekhi's own horse, in fact), he saluted his people, and with them cheering and applauding him, he, too, thundered out of his beloved city with his fellow riders right behind him. The cries of the crowds diminished quickly, and soon fell silent. The sounding horns could be heard for some minutes longer, until they also faded into the gathering gloom of night. The riders struck due east, and rode on.

He could not remember when exactly he had opened his eyes, nor did he know *why* they had opened so suddenly. But he knew that they were open at last, despite the fact that all he could see was an inky blackness surrounding him. Those dull-red orbs strained to pierce the darkness but were as yet too weak, though there was no mistaking the pure evil that smouldered so intensely deep within them. The sheer hatred that raged therein was unmatched anywhere.

Ogiin did not, *could not*, feel the icy cold of the deep ocean. His broken body lay at the bottom of a deep ravine that had been gouged into the sea bed in antiquity. Arms and legs were twisted into a cruel mockery of what once resembled a coldly handsome man-creature. His torso was burned so horribly that scorched bones were exposed, and so much flesh had been blasted from his skull that no mouth, as such, existed, and flesh clung in little charred clumps to that big white bony head. The lipless mouth exposed long cruel teeth which resembled interlocking daggers. Thick short stumps of bone protruded from his back where his enormous wings had once been. He remembered only too well the searing pain as the dragon had sank its teeth into his back and torn them away before sending him plummeting down into the darkness of the abyss amidst an inferno of enveloping flame. He knew he would never again have the power of flight, for such a recovery was nigh impossible, even for one such as he. But no creature of these black watery depths had dared to touch his grisly form despite its shattered state. Even the least of these ocean dwellers had somehow known that this meal was poisonous, that somewhere, deep inside this broken puppet of a corpse, pure evil still lurked, still living, still hating.

Ogiin knew he needed to regain his former strength, his true form, his full spirit. He needed to feed his barely flickering black soul with the blazing heartbeats of others. Lying there these many centuries at the foot of that freezing wet grave, he had drawn out and devoured the spirit of any passing sea creature, his evil soul sucking the life energy from his victims to fuel his own regeneration. Sea urchins, crabs, fish, sharks, and giant squid, were just a few of the countless thousands that had fallen prey to his ravenous craving. The ravine was littered with the bones of his victims, but such low forms of life did not have the strength of spirit he required, serving only to allow him to totter on the brink of death, able only to rage within himself at this cruel hand that fate had dealt him, a living death, buried alive deep beneath the ocean.

He had realised only very slowly that he could actually see again. Once those inhuman eyes had opened, his memory had started to return to him, his last image being that of that accursed silver dragon—Chjandi, blasting white hot flame into his chest. Ogiin's macabre face twisted into a frown and those eyes glowed a fraction brighter as he thought of the terrible vengeance he would wreak upon the world above, and, in particular, on those pathetic dragon-loving Samarians. This time there would be no Dragons of Light to shield them from his hatred, or from his loyal Venomeens. He had seen the deep, fatal, wounds that he, himself, had inflicted upon Chjandi. Darcinian must now be dead, and good riddance, but his Samarians would still exist somewhere above. He would tear out the souls of their women and feast upon the still beating hearts of their men. Love and light had had their final day. None can love if there is nought left to love.

He could feel his own seething anger eating at him like an unchecked cancer and the effort of vengeful thought drained him. He must feed! Concentrating his mind, he called upon the last vestige of strength left in his foul soul, and began to summon to him all the vile servants of darkness that had paid him homage in times past. His spirit, brimming with evil and lusting for retribution, began to filter out into the sea, and then onto the land. All those of his nature, his *creed*, would hear his relentless calling and be drawn to him without exception. No creature of a dark soul could resist him. Worthless carrion these minions were, he thought, but they would serve as a source of sustenance until he was again himself. He would feed on his own kind to regain his strength. They would rejoice in his calling and he would feast on their souls. Then there would be no need of such creatures as he once again gathered his Venomeens and enslaved the unsuspecting so called 'free worlds'. For, surely, none could yet know of his awakening.

CHAPTER FIVE

HELLHOUNDS

The hard-charging riders had made good ground and were nearing the mountains that had seemed so far away after encountering the Grass Troll. It was agreed to call a halt and make camp for the night. The foothills of the range ahead were only a morning's ride away and that challenge could be tackled on the morrow. They were all thoroughly exhausted, everyone that is, except Imo, no sooner had they stopped and he had slipped from his saddle and was already darting about looking for firewood, and small boughs from which to form the cooking cradle, the man's energy was boundless. Tents were soon erected and again the cooking pot was brought into service. The day was fast fading and stars began to appear, watching over the darkening lands as the suns became barely visible to the men unravelling food and preparing their camp.

They had pitched up on soft, springy grass, allowing the horses to graze close to the tents. A clean stream, burbling nearby, provided welcome fresh water for men and beasts alike. Crickets had begun their evening song in chorus with the frogs from the stream and birds could be heard nesting down for the evening. A solitary owl hooted now and again, bidding a fond goodnight to the animals of the day as he prepared to welcome the creatures of the night, some of whom would fall prey to his nocturnal hunting. It was a typically warm, balmy, evening, and the stars watched on patiently, the silent sentinels of the skies curious as to how this new drama would unfold.

The men were grimy, encrusted in dirt having ridden so hard, and for so long, across the dry desert surrounding Sitivia and then through mile upon mile of grasslands. The Samarians shook out their long dusty capes and Bestwin produced a big chunky piece of pork he had procured from the palace kitchens. He and Lumarr proceeded to season it with various spices and herbs before it went into the pot with the plentiful vegetables. Whilst the meat gradually tenderised in the boiling water, absorbing the spicy flavour of the herbs, one man was posted as sentry in the encampment and all the others went across to the stream. It flowed quite rapidly despite its narrow girth, and the men stripped off. They waded in, splashing noisily through the delightfully refreshing water, washing away the encrusted dirt and rinsing out their long hair. It was the perfect tonic after such a gruelling day in the saddle.

The sole sentry kept a watchful eye over the campsite, patiently awaiting his turn to wash and refresh himself. The others were just out of sight but he could hear them laughing and throwing water at each other. Smiling, he stirred the pot regularly so that the large lump of pork broke up and the contents of the pot began to quickly resemble a delicious stew.

Some two hundred yards from the tents were some sparsely populated woods. They marked the beginning of the ascent into the mountains. The travellers would have to spend a whole morning negotiating their way through these before they reached the peaks proper. Although there was plenty of space between the trees, it was difficult to see deeper into the woods due to the fast closing night. The dutiful sentry turned around to cast a watchful eye over the horses, and, in so doing, he failed to spot two pairs of pale yellow eyes watching him from those very woods. The tight yellow slits followed him as he checked the horses were comfortable and at ease. Then they watched him return to the centre of the camp and again stir the big pot merrily bubbling away over the fire. The aroma of the cooking meat wafted teasingly into the woods and two monstrous mouths, crammed full of fangs, drooled in secret.

The hellhounds were bound for the Western Worlds. The sound of many hooves thundering their way had caused them to leap into the woods and take cover. The incessant calling of Ogiin's spirit tormented their black souls. A calling so intense, so commanding, that it was impossible to resist. Not that the hellhounds would have resisted had they had a choice. Huge brutes that they were, they enjoyed nothing more than tearing apart their living victims and feasting on warm, fresh blood, before devouring the remaining flesh and bone in but a few gory gulps. Despite being the size of a small horse they were possessed of a predatory guile that allowed them to stalk their prey almost undetected. This pair moved stealthily through the woods, weighing up the men and horses nearby. Their oversized paws, long cruel claws exposed, made little sound on the moist earth as they padded softly past the tents to gain sight of the men bathing in the stream. The trees and bushes provided plenty of cover for them to camouflage their dark, mahogany furred bodies, and the pair lay very still, their eyes fixed on the men noisily splashing water at each other in the stream. Ogiin's spirit summoning them felt like a thousand needles being driven into their tiny minds, but their bloodlust was way past denial now and even He must wait whilst that hunger was fed. There were still too many men to attack. However, the horses would provide a sizeable meal, very filling, if not as satisfying, as human flesh.

    The men, refreshed and invigorated by their bathing, dressed themselves quickly, and still fastening their sword belts, they walked back to the camp. Strangely, the horses seemed a little uneasy despite being so very tired. They whinnied, tugging at their tethers nervously. Imo sat with them and soothed them until they quietened down whilst the others finished preparing the food. The hellhounds slavered impatiently as they watched the horses regain the protection of the guardsmen. At long last the lone sentry was able to go to the stream for his eagerly awaited wash. He felt stale and unclean after such an arduous journey and could not wait to rinse away the smell of horse sweat from his skin. Leaving the others to serve up the stew, he made for the water's edge. When the food was ready, the men gathered around the fire and began to eat, saving an equal share for the man now bathing.

The guardsman felt so relieved to finally wade into the cool waters of the stream. His clothes and weapons lay on the grass nearby and he gratefully scooped up big handfuls of water and washed his face. Then, bending over, he pushed his head underwater, the cold permeating his overheated scalp simply marvellous after so long under the glaring heat of the suns. His muscular, sun-bronzed frame ached from maintaining such a sustained pace, and to relieve his aches he sat down in the stream with his legs stretched out downstream in front of him. It felt so good that he leaned back, supporting himself on his elbows as he lay in the water. It had been another gruelling day and the aroma of the cooked pork drifting over to him across the water made him feel ravenous. "Just two minutes more in the water," he thought, then, he would go and eat. He could hear the others serving up the hot meal, just one more minute…

The lead brute, poised in the woods, eased its monstrous head through some bushes with the silent precision of a panther. It, too, had a hot meal on its mind, and there was only one man now in the stream. Its nostrils plucked scents from the air and it recognised what it smelled—Samarian! It had not tasted such flesh for so long. The second beast crept up alongside, also recognising the unique nature of the bathing man. The pair lay watching him, salivating in anticipation of the feast soon to come.

The guardsman eased his head back into the current, allowing the flow to lift away the dust and heat of the day. He stared up at the sky as the flurry of water cascaded over his head and onto his shoulders. The stars seemed very fixed, not winking as they so often appear to be doing. "Perhaps they did not care to wink at recent events," he thought, "Perhaps Ogiin had indeed returned, and they were unhappy in noting his evil presence?" The thought of Ogiin prompted the man to end his bathing and return to his comrades. As he arose from the stream with water pouring from his head, he heard a sound from the trees on the opposite bank. Had he imagined it? He strained his eyes and ears, but saw and heard nothing in the dark to alarm him. Then it came again, a snapping sound, like a twig breaking under weight. The hair on the back of his neck prickled up and he felt suddenly very vulnerable and exposed standing naked in the middle of the stream. His eyes glued to the tree line on the far bank, he began to back away towards his clothing, and his triblade. The bed of the stream was stony and the wet pebbles, covered in moss and weed, were smooth and very slippery. He used his toes to keep a firm grip as he had no desire to fall at this particular moment. Raising the alarm came to mind, but as yet there was nothing to be alarmed about. He gave a wry smile as he imagined what his friends would say if he came screaming naked into the camp having been frightened by a wild boar or suchlike!

Step-by-step the guardsman reached the grassy bank behind him and was grateful to feel solid ground under his feet again. A sense of relief washed over him, but he kept one eye on the woods as he quickly dressed. He was a Royal Guardsman, and he refused to be panicked by noises in the dark. When, at last, he was fully clothed, he found that he could relax, the thin layers of fabric somehow making him feel safe, less vulnerable, and taking a deep breath he turned to rejoin his companions. It was only when he turned his back on the woods that his blood turned to ice. A great crashing sound made him spin around to see a brace of dark red devil dogs bursting out of the woods and hurtling towards him. They were enormous, their yellow eyes locked on him, the gaping jaws revealing double rows of fangs that resembled shards of broken glass. There was no doubting their horrible intent and the guardsman doubled forward for his sword, but just as his hand gripped the butt he was brought to his knees by a hellish sound. The man-eaters were almost upon him now, and from their mouths came the sound that had shocked him to the ground. No bark, growl, or even a roar, came from these dogs of darkness. Instead, a scream like that of a tortured woman emanated from them. It was so high-pitched it was agonising to the ears. They were only a few feet away from him and he had just the presence of mind to raise his shield as the frontrunner of the two sprang into the air, leaping the stream, its forepaws smashing into the wooden shield that bore the metal crest of the silver dragon. The shield cracked under such a massive blow but the metalwork kept it in one piece. The guardsman was thrown onto his back and felt a terrible thump as his head hit a rock. He staggered to his feet but found he could not summon the strength to alert the others. His head was swimming and it was hard to focus his eyes in the dark. But, by the grace of The Dragon! He had kept hold of his sword when he fell. The stinking breath of the creature that had jumped him guided him, and he tottered about, pointing his blade in the direction of that disgusting smell. He knew his blurred vision could not yet be trusted and he had to gain precious moments to clear his head.

He became aware that his head was bleeding profusely, but hopefully he would soon regain his voice so as to warn the others. Through the dark he saw a shape looming menacingly towards him, and again he could see those merciless yellow eyes. With a speed that surprised the creature bearing down on him, the guardsman swung his sword out through a powerful arc, slicing through the beast's nose from top to bottom. Another awful scream shrilled from its mouth before it sank its monstrous teeth into the Samarian's sword arm. The guardsman was well trained and kept his wits about him as the searing pain flooded up his trapped limb, threatening to overwhelm him. He pummelled ferociously at that terrible face with the edge of his shield. Blow upon blow rained down onto its ruined nose but it kept his arm locked in its powerful jaws. The Samarian was desperately trying to retrieve his dagger from his belt when he saw the second hound from hell standing right beside him. Its cold heartless eyes seemed to smile cruelly and it paused for a split second to return his stare before its teeth sliced deep into his thigh. He felt the razor-like fangs open up his flesh as a hot knife opens butter before his leg shattered under that immense pressure. Blood sprayed hotly from the horrendous wound, spurting into the mouth of the hellhound. It made a low, gratified, growling sound at the taste of it.

The pork was exceptionally well cooked and deliciously tender, and the men were tucking into it heartily when that gut-wrenching screeching of the hellhounds ripped open the quiet of the night.

They leapt to their feet, and leaving a pair of sentries to watch the encampment, the remainder charged off in the direction of the stream with their swords drawn. Panicked by the horrific sounds, the horses broke free and bolted in the opposite direction. From a hundred feet away the men could see the hellhounds trying to tear their friend apart. Bestwin retrieved his axe as he ran and hurled it at one of the beasts. It yelped as the heavy weapon sank deep into its flank, causing it to release its grip on its victim's arm. The second creature shook the hapless guardsman like a rag doll and tossed him to one side. The broken man fell limply by the water's edge and, mercifully, passed out immediately. The slavering hounds slowly turned to face the approaching men. Their yellow eyes were filled with an unrelenting thirst for more of the wondrous red fluid that shone such a bright crimson on their fangs, mauling the lone guardsman had driven their bloodlust to an insatiable, frenzied state.

Mouths frothing, the brutes bounded towards the men and leapt amongst them. A storm of snarling fangs and slashing claws engulfed the warriors but their discipline held strong and they kept their nerve. They saw the cleft nose of one and made concerted efforts to do more harm there. The hellhound squealed as time after time the triblades of the Samarians and the curved scimitars of the Westonians wreaked havoc upon its face. Imo was locked in a battle of wills with the other creature. They circled each other eye-to-eye, fangs to triblade. He had a fellow guardsman at his back but insisted he wanted the guts of this particular beast for himself. The man bleeding and battered by the edge of the stream was his drinking partner of many long years and owed him much coin from gambling with cards and dice. He feinted a couple of thrusts at the animal's face and it dodged his sword easily, its eyes blazing at him as it curled its lips even higher to fully reveal the horrifying size of its teeth. Round and around the two combatants circled each other in the dark of the night next to the stream, each keeping a wary eye on the other battle raging right next to them.

Imo squared up to the crouching monster before him and roared, "Creatures from hell! You seek to taste Samarian flesh, but will feast only upon samarian steel! We—the people of the Great Dragon, fear neither you, nor your master. Come hither, doggy, Imo will give you a juicy bone the likes of which you have yet never tasted."

As his words distracted the hellhound, his sword flashed through the night air, severing an ear from the foul creature's enormous head. It howled that horribly female, shrieking howl, and leapt at Imo, who rolled sharply to one side as that powerful body sailed past him through the air. His fellow guardsman saw the opportunity and opened a long gaping gash down its length, exposing several ribs. Despite its wounds the hellhound fought on ferociously and Imo and his comrade engaged it in a savage battle to the death.

"By the sword of Darcinian!" boomed Bestwin, "do these fiends not know the meaning of defeat!"

He had good cause for making such a statement. He and his comrades had inflicted terrible injuries upon the raging monsters, yet they continued to fight as if possessed by the dark soul of Ogiin, Himself. They twisted and turned, slashed and snapped, as if they had not been hurt at all. The men were tiring from prolonged use of their weapons and were desperate to end this before the tide turned in favour of the tireless hellhounds. One of the snarling jaws found a firm grip on the throat of a guardsman, and even as he repeatedly drove his dagger home into that brutal face, the sharp teeth sank easily through his soft flesh, slashing through arteries and crushing bone. Neck broken, the dead man lolled limply in the creature's mouth. Lumarr saw his chance as the animal could not use its deadly jaws for a second, and he drove his long curved blade into its belly, it emitted a long high-pitched scream and turned on him, its eyes murderous. He stood his ground, feet firmly planted a foot apart. He had seen his Samarian ally die a needless death. A lifetime normally so protracted should never have been cut down so prematurely, or so needlessly. He could see Imo and the other guardsman were also struggling in their efforts to defeat this grim foe. It was time, he thought, to cleave open the thick skull of this vile scum. The hellhound dropped its kill and faced him whilst constantly watching Bestwin as he tried to circle it and attack it from the rear. The hellhound stood snarling, its claws and fangs covered in blood and its eyes livid pools of evil fury.

The sudden 'WHOOSH' made the men instinctively drop flat to the ground. Lumarr and Bestwin watched as their deadly foe reared up on its hind legs, ready to pounce on either of them, but its eyes appeared to have seen something further beyond. A thick wooden spear, its deadly tip an angry silver dragon, whizzed over the men at immeasurable speed. It drilled through the chest of the rearing monster so deeply that the dragon could be seen protruding from its back. The animal made no sound, the spear having severed its spine it simply keeled over, dead. The Westonians were on their feet in an instant, running to add the weight of their scimitars to the triblades already railed against the second hellhound. The remaining beast did not seem to notice or care at the loss of its own kind, it saw only a larger feast of flesh for itself.

The sentries left on duty at the camp had seen no point in guarding the tents any longer when the horses had bolted upon hearing that awful howling. Thanks be to The Dragon that Imo had completely unburdened the horses, as, amidst the usual trappings of travelling guardsmen, it is highly likely you will find 'The Wrath of Amaris'. Named after a Samarian Lord from history, this weapon could pierce any armour. It consisted of an incredibly powerful crossbow that propelled the lethal dragon-tipped spear. The sentries had had the presence of mind to snatch up this particular item as they had raced to find their friends.

The sight confronting them had stopped them in their tracks, but their training held firm. Even as their feet were skidding to a slippery stop on the grass, their jaws agape with shock, their hands were already preparing 'The Wrath of Amaris' for its deadly purpose. Within seconds the weapon was armed, and with deadly precision that silver dragon was streaking through the air to plunge itself through the black heart of its snarling target. When they saw the beast fall, the pair raced to the fallen hound and worked furiously to extract the spear from the corpse. The dragon protruding from the creature's back was as sharp as a triblade and the men gripped it as carefully as they could, given the urgency of the situation. Their hands cut and bloodied, they managed to pull the stinking spear from the animal and rearm the bow. A single cloud had strayed in above them and was restricting the faint light from the stars, giving further advantage to the remaining hound.

Imo had jumped onto the brute's back, but in doing so he had dropped his weapons, and so, hanging on for dear life to the scruff of its neck, he was pounding its head with a clenched fist, shouting obscenities that should never be put into print. The hellhound completely ignored the warrior perched so precariously on its back. It barely felt his hammering fists and was far more concerned with the four sword wielding men that were circling it so menacingly. The dark fur of the beast was dripping with its own reeking black blood, yet it seemed to not even be labouring for breath. At first it charged for Lumarr, but turned so quickly, that its jaws caught a guardsman unawares by his midriff. His soft human frame offered no resistance to those vicelike jaws and the savage animal ripped away a large portion of flesh. The men stood aghast as the triumphant hellhound reared up on its hindquarters and gulped down the morsel of fresh meat with blood dripping from its mouth. As the mortally wounded man hit the ground with a sickeningly soft thud, there again came that now welcome 'whoosh'. The Wrath of Amaris punched straight through the animal's left eye, and almost through Imo's too, as that small silver dragon claimed its second kill of the night, protruding three feet out of the back of the hellhound's head. Just in time Imo jumped clear of the falling brute and it crashed heavily onto its side, there was no slow abating of breath, or any final snarl of defiance. It lay dead still on the grass as if it had never known animation, only the blood dripping from its jaws gave any indication of its savage actions mere moments before. The men stood staring at each other for a split second, and then dashed to attend to the wounded. Alas, two were dead and the man by the stream was in a very poor way. His wounds were cleaned and he was tended to as best as was possible. They were all completely exhausted and collapsed to the ground to catch their breath and gather their thoughts. Each of them kept a wary eye in all directions.

It was some hours later when the first long fingers of sunlight began to poke and prod the world awake, that the men stirred. One by one they ventured into the stream to wash away the blood, fur, and gore from themselves and their weapons. They were very shaken by the ordeal and terribly overcome by the sudden loss of two brave companions and a third so grievously wounded. Yet each found it in himself to remember to thank the two sentries for their fast thinking and lightening reactions. They had surely saved more lives from being lost.

The horses were nowhere to be seen and Imo clambered up the tallest tree to try and locate them, but could not see any sign of them anywhere. The men worked diligently and with great care, building a funeral pyre for their fallen comrades. These were Samarian dead and there was no need for long solemn prayers to unknown gods. The Samarians carried the symbol of the dragon as tribute to a great friend and teacher, not as worship of a god or other form of deity. The fallen were placed on top of the pyre with full weapons and battledress. The Westonians held heavy hearts, sad that these brave Samarians had given their lives to ensure that this quest would succeed, a quest that, they, themselves, had brought to the Samarian door. The remaining guardsmen greaved for their loss in silence, making not a sound to betray the grief and fury clawing at their hearts.

Bestwin lit a long torch and moved forward to the pyre. He turned, and looking at the trio standing before him, he offered up the simple Samarian farewell. "The Source sees all."

With that, he pushed the blazing torch into the base of the pyre. They had doused it with pitch from the camp, and, with a great rush of air, flames engulfed the departed as a tall plume of black smoke rose steadily up towards the heavens.

The five of them formed a stretcher for the sixth, seriously injured, man. They made good use of tent poles and the fabric of the tents themselves. The Westonians showed Imo and the others how to build the rig in such a manner that not only was it most comfortable for the injured party, but it could be drawn more easily by two men. The guardsmen volunteered for this duty as Imo was now in command of them. Backpacks were stuffed to overflowing with as many supplies as possible from the campsite. 'The Wrath of Amaris', though heavy and cumbersome, was deemed absolutely necessary, and Bestwin and Lumarr would carry it in turn. Imo would lead the way, hacking a path for the stretcher through the woodland undergrowth. It was agreed that they needed to get clear of the woods as soon as possible. They were in an ideal place to get ambushed, and a difficult place in which to defend their position. The obstacle of trees might even render the lethal crossbow useless.

The unexpected attack by the hellhounds had been an unnerving experience for everyone. Those monstrous devil dogs were not normally to be found on Samarian soil, for, normally, they would be slaughtered on sight. They must have come from further a field, perhaps from the no man's land on the border with Dizbaar. If this was the case, Lumarr suggested, then, whatever was drawing them towards the Western Worlds was certainly sending its summons far and wide. This made the need for haste even more pressing because whatever loathsome plot was hatching, it must never reach fruition.

The man on the stretcher had sunk into a deep coma and the others feared for his life. The hellhounds had almost torn the small posse apart and no one could be spared to take the wounded man back to Sitivia. His best hope for recovery was for the remainder of the party to endeavour to reach the Western Worlds and their capital city of Dorinndale, there he would receive the very best care possible.

The short, stocky warrior began their journey with caution. The trees were not thickly grouped or bunched together, but there were enough of them to hide anyone of malicious intent amongst them. It would take all morning, if not a little longer with the stretcher in tow, to carve a path on foot through the woods and onto the base slopes of the mountains ahead. The ground amongst the trees was thick with leaf litter and woodland debris, forcing the men to wade through as best they could. The mountain range—known as The Dragon's Breath, was a mystical place. Each peak held its own character and beauty, not to mention pitfalls and hazards. One summit could be shrouded in snow whilst her neighbour could be lush with foliage and covered in trees. The range was named after the dense blue neon-bright mists that often swirled through the mountain passes at higher altitudes. Imo decided it would be easier to tow the stretcher on a snowy surface—thus making better time. He had not before seen the likes of those that had ripped and torn at his friends the previous night. Now, he, too, sensed the immense evil they all faced. But he was not afraid, in fact quite the opposite, he was determined to get to Dorinndale without further losses, and also to return to Sitivia with all the information his king needed to form his plans.

The suns were climbing quickly and their warming glow helped ease the minds of the men a little. Many worshippers of the dark hated sunlight, though most would tolerate it if easy pickings were at hand. "Only The Dragon knew," thought Imo, "what other ghoulish fiends were headed in the same direction as themselves, or, worse still, had amassed before them already." His triblade was far too big and valuable a weapon to use for hacking through undergrowth, so he used a machete scavenged from their former camp. As they slowly worked their way through the woodland, he calmly absorbed the beauty of this land that outlanders called Samaria, and that he was proud to call 'home'. Flowers of every variety littered the ground about him, tall flowers, short flowers, big flowers and small flowers. Some were of a single, strikingly vibrant, colour, whilst others were a myriad of hues. Many of these blooms absorbed so much heat during the hot days that they would rid themselves of it by night by glowing like the most exquisitely formed lanterns, thus, many such native woodlands had a fairylike air about them at night, and were often frequented by young lovers. "Older ones, too," he thought, grinning to himself. Birds had begun their joyful chorus somewhat hesitantly today. It was as if they did not want their happy trilling to offend these men still grieving over recent losses. But over the course of the next hour or two, the woods gradually became alive with their own music, and the travellers were, in fact, grateful of it, its chirpy fervour and energy lifting their thoughts away from the funeral pyre still smouldering behind them. Beautiful birds of all shapes and sizes moved from tree-to-tree to ground, and then off to somewhere known only to themselves. Now and again the odd rabbit came into view, darting for cover before Bestwin or Lumarr could aim an arrow. Samarian rabbits can never be accused of stupidity. Deer also frequented such woodlands but the warriors would not claim such a kill this day. Such a quantity of meat could not be consumed at one sitting and they were not equipped to carry so much extra weight. To kill such an animal for a single, hurried meal would be a waste of its life, and a detriment to their own. The deer were no doubt grateful for the noble beliefs held by the warriors forging through their woodland home. Dragonflies of the most amazing colours fluttered erratically amongst the flowers, hovering briefly, before darting off to hover over another drink of nectar. It was not easy to resist the tranquillity of this place. However, the stern discipline of the men kept them on their highest vigil, their eyes constantly scanning about them, as well as into the treetops and the shadowy places where denser undergrowth could harbour any manner of threat.

The 'scrape-scrape' of the stretcher was the predominant sound and another long hour was passed trudging along without incident. A halt was called for rest and food, but no one wanted to linger too long, so lumps of bread and hard cheese were the order of the day. They had a quiet chuckle when Bestwin commented that it was food fit for a queen. This was a polite jest at Meekhi's habit of walking around the palace munching on exactly such a meal, a simple but delicious combination of food that she was well known for having a penchant for.

During their break Lumarr lit a wonderful Westonian pipe filled with an aromatic leaf that not only did not harm you (as it can do so grievously in our own world), it invigorated the senses and smelled absolutely fabulous. The pipe had a very long stem, was carved from a dense white wood, and had a heavy brass lid.

One could easily see it was very old. The brief pause gave them a chance to check on the condition of the wounded man on the stretcher. He was still lost within a coma, perhaps mercifully as his wounds were without doubt excruciatingly painful. It was obvious by the pallor of his skin and the cold sweat on his brow that if he was not attended to by a skilled physician soon, his life would slip away from him. They made him as comfortable as possible and changed the blood-soaked dressings.

Lumarr tapped out the grey ash from his pipe, making sure not a spark remained within it to start a fire in the dry leaf litter. The fragrant smoke lingered about them for a minute before being snatched up by a small gust of wind and carried away. The powerfully built Westonians hauled the straps of the stretcher onto their broad shoulders as the others also made ready to recommence their trek to the mountains, and beyond.

Imo took care to not move too quickly despite his desire to be free of these damnable woods. He had to pace himself so the stretcher bearers could keep up whilst his remaining guardsmen brought up the rear. The suns were fast approaching their hottest point—just before they began the eclipse, and the atmosphere was becoming stale and stifling. The light breeze fought valiantly to drive cooling air into the heart of the woodland but the savage suns emitted so much heat that it offered very little respite. The Westonians, accustomed to far cooler climes, began to sweat in earnest. Their heavy Westonian attire was taking its toll, and coupled with the burden of the stretcher, they found it took strenuous effort to maintain even Imo's deliberately reduced pace.

With the suns converging rapidly on each other it became easier to differentiate between shadow and light amidst the trees. All shadows began to fall in the same direction. Imo had noted this after they had been moving forward for some time. He was hoping to break free of the woodland within an hour or so, and he looked back at his comrades to be sure they were keeping up. It was now that he noticed the tall, dark, shadow, some way off through the trees. Its shape was too well defined to be ignored, so he called a halt as he screwed up his eyes and peered into the woods. Bestwin saw the direction of his interest and also stared hard between the trees. He could see the shadowy shape, but was not sure what it was. Then, in a hushed tone, came Lumarr's voice, "It is a Shadow. We must make more haste, for we are not alone amidst these trees."

Imo asked in a whisper, "I can see it, my lord, Lumarr, but it is the shadow of *what*, exactly?"

Lumarr replied in an obviously anxious tone, "It is worryingly exactly what it appears to be—a Shadow, Imo. I have not seen the like since Ogiin fell. Look at its shape, my good friend—does it not resemble a man? a man in a hooded robe, perhaps? It has no physical form and exists only as a shadow. In times past, a clan of monks made a pact with Ogiin and agreed to serve him in return for a promise of immortality. They have their immortality, Imo, but only as that dark shape you see now. They abide in the deepest wells and darkest weirs, and are most dangerous at night when one can see only their soulless eyes. Be on your guard, all of you! For if that Shadow should spread itself over you, it will fall, devouring your very soul and leaving only the dried husk of your frame behind. These deadly ghouls rarely attack alone so there will be others nearby for certain. Only light can be used to defend ourselves against them, light, and fire. Imo! We must break free of these accursed trees so we can at least see what lurks about us!"

Despite the advice of Lumarr stating that weapons were useless against these phantom figures, the entire group (*including* Lumarr,) instinctively drew their swords. Imo squeezed between the Westonians and also took a firm grip of the stretcher and the party began to move at a much swifter pace whilst maintaining alert for any close threat of danger. The faster going jolted and bounced the stretcher quite roughly but there was nothing that could be done to prevent that. Imo fully understood all that Lumarr had said, and was very aware that the sunlight would reduce greatly during the eclipse, after which it would fade into night all too quickly.

There was no time to waste clearing a path through the undergrowth so the stretcher-bearers just crashed headlong through the woods as fast as possible with the rearguard following right on their heels. Everyone had their eyes peeled for any signs of trouble. It was very hard going, clothing would frequently snag on branches, and several times the stretcher nearly overturned when it hit a large, unseen, rock, or tree root. But they pressed on regardless, sensing the growing presence of darkness around them and occasionally glimpsing dark fur, or, tall smoky shapes, keeping apace with them through the woods. None of the men commented on what he was seeing as each knew that the others, too, must already see the same. Soon it became quite obvious that they were not only being followed, but were being flanked on each side. Whatever they were that was following them, they were matching the pace of the fast-tiring men.

Imo needed to get to open ground fast, he felt sure that the creatures flanking his party would attack them at some point, and he wanted to be free to use his sword when that time came. Bestwin and Lumarr had grim, determined expressions on their faces. He noted that they each stared straight ahead as they hauled mightily on the heavily laden stretcher, and he surmised they were of the same opinion, wanting to be able to fight if the need arose. He knew these two had great experience in these matters and the wisest course of action would be to follow their lead.

As is often the case with a large wood, the undergrowth became denser and more abundant (due to the more readily available sunlight) as they came closer and closer to breaking free of the trees. This hampered their pace further and they were dripping in sweat as they smashed and crashed their way through these thicker, taller, bushes and thickets. Stinging nettles constantly whipped at the man on the stretcher, but they were the least of his worries. The eclipse had just begun when they saw the trees beginning to peter out a little way ahead. Beyond them they could make out a grassy hill ascending away from the tree line. Spurred into one final, heaving effort, they stumbled and staggered towards that open ground just as one sun slipped wholly behind her sister. The instant drop in temperature was welcome, but the reduced light was not. Lumarr noticed the temperature had dropped considerably lower than it should have, and sure enough, the men found goose bumps appearing on their arms. The Westonians warned the others quickly—a Hoary Hag was close by. Hideous skeletal crones, these witches were a repulsive sight. Their naked wart-encrusted bodies were made of black ice and freezing mist, with deep empty hollows where eyes should have been. One touch from them and a man would become no more than a frozen statue. One more touch and that icy effigy would melt into nothingness. Lumarr was huffing and puffing as he told the others that these disgusting but deadly wretches could be despatched only by decapitation. Any other kind of injury would heal itself in seconds, and even a severed limb would re-grow in minutes.

"Well, this just gets better and better, doesn't it." spouted Imo as they were only five minutes away from the edge of the woods.

The low hill to the front could be clearly seen at last. It climbed slowly away at first, but then began to incline more steeply. Boulders and rocks of all shapes and sizes littered the grass, having fallen randomly from the mountain range above. The suns remained fully eclipsed as the weary warriors finally burst free from the claustrophobic woods and onto the pale, coarse grass. They gulped down huge lungfuls of the lighter air as they stopped for a minute to get their bearings and to give their burning muscles a few short seconds of respite. Their legs were trembling from their sustained efforts and a water skin was passed quickly from hand to hand as they scanned first the tree line for any signs of trouble, then the hill they now had to climb.

They spun around to face the trees when a sudden mixture of sounds made them jump. Some of the sounds, though worrying, were easily recognised as that of litter being trampled underfoot by many racing through it, intermingled with these unexpected but natural sounds, were noises that they (except, perhaps, the Westonians) did not recognize, sounds that were most definitely *not* natural. Strange hissings, cold cackles, low, guttural growls, and sinister giggling, made them grab hold of the stretcher again, ready to get up the grass slope as fast as possible. Then came that spine chilling shrieking, the same sound they had heard the previous night. They could not possibly outrun hellhounds up this hill, and no one wanted to have their back turned to those devil dogs. They eyed each other quizzically, knowing they could never get up that hill safely with their wounded comrade on the stretcher. Decision made without recourse to debate, they did what any honourable men would have done—they laid the stretcher behind them and formed a line between it and the woods, ready to face whatever would issue from amongst those trees.

What actually did appear from the woods was not what they had expected at all, it was far, far, worse. All along the tree line, vile, hideous looking, creatures, began to emerge, staying in shadow but not afraid of being seen by the handful of men facing them. There were at least half a dozen Hoary Hags staring at them, the air condensing and forming a mist around their revolting shapes. It made them appear to be floating rather than standing. Hellhounds were crouched just inside the woods, their dead yellow eyes fixed on them. Their long, thick, black tongues lolled wetly as they drooled in anticipation. What appeared on first sight to be thin columns of smoke dotted amongst the trees turned out not to be smoke at all. These were Wispy Witches made up entirely of putrid fumes, the disgusting stench of which already assailed the nostrils of the men watching them. These hags fed by sucking out the life-breath of their victims. They would lock their rancid mouth over that of their prey, and literally suck their life from them. A little deeper inside the woods the men could see the Shadows they had noticed before, the phantoms standing dead still with their heads bowed, facing the warriors on the hill. But worst of all, spaced out evenly along the trees and numbering maybe a score, stood Venomeens. These fiends curdled the blood the most, because eons past they too had been of the race of men, but had chosen the way of Ogiin. Their perverse minds, and greedy hearts, had had cravings beyond the most wicked of imaginings and Ogiin had promised to not only satisfy their ghastly desires, but to give them the whole world to devour, plunder, and pillage as they pleased—under his supreme command. Since the demise of the tyrant these bloodsuckers had disappeared, until now. This was truly a bad omen.

The men stared in disbelief at the Venomeens, and the Venomeens stared back with their dull lifeless eyes. They snarled at the warriors, revealing the long, cruel, snow white, fangs with which they savaged their victims, slurping at the fresh blood to maintain whatever vestige of life still lingered within their tortured souls. That is to say, if any mortal soul remained at all.

Bestwin turned to his good friend Lumarr, "So, there we have it, Ogiin must surely be afoot, or this vermin would not dare reveal itself to us so brazenly. Alas, I fear we are outnumbered by a considerable margin."

It was true, the small group was vastly outnumbered as two, maybe three, score of Ogiin's creed faced them in a ragged line. There was perhaps only three hundred yards separating them. The suns were in such a position that they caused the tallest trees to throw a long fuzzy shadow onto the hillside. It fell to within thirty feet of the warriors. Imo asked the more experienced Westonians, "Why don't they charge us? What are they waiting for?"

Before he had had any reply from the long bearded lords, the row of menacing figures moved towards them. Slowly at first, then it moved rapidly away from the trees before coming to an abrupt stop where the shadow of the trees met sunlit grass. Now only twenty feet away but still in the vale cast by the woods, Ogiin's creed seethed and hissed at them. The bare witches beckoned at them with bony, crooked fingers. In response to this, Imo raised his battledress and exposed his backside to them. He taunted them by slapping his own buttocks, showing no hint of fear. The hags wailed at him and the hellhounds bared their monstrous teeth, but the Venomeens held their positions near the trees, keeping their eyes locked on the little group up on the hill. Shadows floated in the darker areas, avoiding the patchy light and hovering just above the grass, biding their time. Bestwin turned suddenly to Lumarr; "They are waiting for full sunset, Lumarr, trying to hold our attentions so as to distract us from the closing eve. We must make the most of the prevailing light. The Venomeens can tolerate the sun, but this other filth are pained by it. A handful of Venomeens cannot match us, but, massed together, they would overwhelm us for sure. We must get to the top of the hill and find a safe haven, or, at least, a defendable position. Yet if we turn our backs who can say what might happen. I note some of the Venomeen scum are carrying bows."

The two sides stood facing each other. The breeze that had ebbed and flowed amidst the woods refused to witness whatever may come next and faded away, the very air becoming still and motionless. Still the two suns remained as one. The birds of the woodland fell silent and not a sound was heard other than that of the taunts being spat at the men. The sole visible sun was shining directly into their faces, making it more difficult to see what was happening closer to the trees ahead.

Imo decided to take the initiative, "You two," he told the guardsmen, "take the stretcher and make for high ground. The three of us will guard your rear and follow in due course. We will meet on the heights above, may The Dragon be with us all."

The guardsmen nodded, and as Imo and the Westonians formed a small defensive knot, they made ready to haul the stretcher. But when they turned to lift it, they were shocked to see their injured comrade standing on his feet before them, albeit very unsteadily. His face the colour of sand from blood loss, he had managed to take a grip on his triblade. Its blade speared into the grass, he was using it to support himself whilst eyeing his friends, a river of emotions flowing in his gaze. Blood could be seen dripping freely from the cuff of his tunic, running down along his blade and pooling dark on the grass. Despite his horrific injuries and weakened state, his eyes still blazed with that inner flame that only Samarians have within them. It is an integral part of their spirit, born of the Great Dragon. Looking at Imo he spoke in a low voice that was racked with pain, but more so, heavy with the weight of duty. "Imo, you will not make it to the heights with a burden such as I. With me, you are all doomed. One must stay so five may live. That one is I, my friends. I have but a handful of hours left in me at best. I feel it, I *know* it! I am here to do my duty, for my king, my queen, and for Samaria, but most of all, for you, my brothers, for *you*! You will fulfil our quest and return to Sitivia. Tell my lord of my love for him and my queen, and that when Samaria called for my sword, I was not found wanting! You must now concede, Imo, my gambling debt to you is paid in full. Now go, my brothers, and make haste, we will meet again one day... amidst the stars."

The others stared at him in disbelief. What honour! What courage! They knew he spoke the truth, their mission, especially since the appearance of the Venomeens, was more important than any one man's life, or, indeed, *all* of their lives. None wished to leave their heroic, wonderful friend, at the shadow's edge, but each knew this must be done. There were no more words to be said, but the bond of honour they all shared wrapped about them like a warm blanket, shielding them from woe and staving off regret.

The suns seemed not to care much for each others' company, every day they would dawdle in their rising, as if reluctant to greet each other as they eclipsed, more so, after passing each other, they would hasten away far more quickly than they had arisen. The men standing on the hill were acutely aware of this fact.

The wounded guardsman hugged and kissed his friends with great affection tempered by haste. Imo told him, "You, my brother, you will be remembered long after we are forgotten. I will make sure of this. It is *you* that adds the flame to the dragon on your cloak. May the Great Dragon guide your sword arm and should you fall, His spirit will carry you aloft to a land of infinite colours, joy without limit, and everlasting peace. Fare thee well, my noble friend."

With this, five weary warriors, laden with woe and seething with frustration, began to climb up the hill, taking with them their weapons and supplies. They did not look back, that which would take place behind them was inevitable and they did not wish to bear witness to it. Perhaps the departed breeze had seen the future of that brave solitary guardsman and could not tolerate the thought of it.

Ranician, the wounded guard, rubbed at his eyes with one hand whilst supporting himself on his sword with the other. He felt hardly any pain now as he had lost too much blood. Light headed and dreamy, the sunlight in his eyes made him want to just lie down and sleep, but he was a Royal Guardsman and he did not lie down, nor did he sleep. From within the folds of his cherished cloak he produced a flat piece of stone and began, with some difficulty, to edge his blade. Though his shield lay close by, he did not retrieve it, dead men had no need of such things. Awkwardly, he briefly turned his head to ensure his fellow guardsmen, and friends, were making good their escape, which they were. He could see them slogging against the rising incline, the sun shone on their backs and three silver dragons blazed at him, filling his soul with light and his heart with courage. His grip tightening on his sword butt, he turned back again to face the vermin that were awaiting their chance. He removed his dagger from its sheath and tucked it into his sword belt. His strength was fast fading, but he had a duty to fulfil and could not afford to pass out, thus failing his friends. Staggering over to where he had discarded his shield, the dieing man reached down and picked up a clay jar. He had to buy as much time for his companions as he could. He would not wait to be killed in a massed attack, "I shall choose when this fight starts," he thought, "despite my leg being splinted amidst two spear poles."

A little smile broke his pained expression.

Ranician knew his life was fast ebbing from him. Deftly, he fastened a light cord to the neck of the jar. Keeping the cord several feet long he began to spin the jar around his head. The suns had had enough of each other and were beginning to part at last. The whirling jar made a rhythmic thrumming sound as it circled his head. 'WHOOO, WHOOO,' sang the jar, forcing the climbing men to look down below them. They watched as the jar circled faster and faster. Then, taking careful aim, Ranician released his improvised slingshot. A Hoary Hag was cackling at him through a toothless smile when the jar, travelling at incredible speed, smashed into her head. Her ugly face exploded into smithereens and many of her cohorts squealed in shock, jumping back away from her. Her headless body staggered about amongst her panicked kin for a few brief seconds before collapsing into a stinking wet puddle on the grass.

A tear slipped from Imo's eye, "*That*... is my best friend, Ranician, a true Samarian, and a man one should be careful not to upset."

The men continued to make ground up the hill though the going was more difficult now as more and more rocks lay strewn everywhere. Underfoot, loose screed and shale offered very little grip and the climbers hunched forwards, doubled over and using their hands to support themselves, they scrabbled up the incline with grim determination.

Ranician watched with great satisfaction when the witch's icy head disappeared in a million pieces. "A chilling sight," he thought, his own humour making him laugh despite his injuries, and, this, in turn, making him ache terribly, which made him laugh even the more. The sudden unexpected demise of one of their own had enraged the long line of vermin at the woods' end, many surged forward to the very edge of the shadowline in front of Ranician, cursing and spitting at him vehemently. He fiented a stagger, and as one Venomeens ran a little too close, his tri-blade carved through the air, its deadly tip slicing open the neck of his enemy. The creature fell gurgling to the ground, clutching at its ruined throat, it died in a mass of thrashing limbs and a disgusting drowning sound. The suns were setting fast now.

CHAPTER SIX

THE HIDDEN CAVE

The climbers had reached the very top of the incline and were now clambering over very rocky ground. Darkness was looming and the gaggle of gargoyles below would soon be coming their way, unhindered by sunlight. They needed to find somewhere to hide up until dawn.

Ranician could barely stand. He could see the pair of red orbs far away in the sky, parting from these worlds as he would, himself, soon do. But he would not wait for this pack of vermin to engulf him. Calling upon every ounce of strength left in his torn and broken body, he stumbled forward into the midst of his enemy. From above, his friends could see his triblade raining down a furious storm of blows upon the shrieking, frenzied mob, several of which he killed. But then the throng surrounding him backed away as darkness became almost complete. A Shadow emerged ominously from the woods and floated towards the lone, battered Samarian. The ghostly figure moved towards him without a sound, and, seeing it approaching, he withdrew his dagger with the dragon motif inlaid in its handle, "You filth," he thought, "Will not lay claim to this soul." He placed the tip of the weapon to his chest and drove the blade through his own heart, feeling no pain. As he fell silently to his knees he saw, just above the tree line, in the distance, some beautiful lights. They were multicoloured and twinkled in the darkness, he felt sure they resembled the shape of a dragon, and were heading directly towards him. Ranician died content, with a smile upon his face. The Shadow, robbed of its victim, and precious sustenance, stopped still in its tracks, its head bowed even further. Others joined it, until they numbered five.

Lumarr pointed uphill to indicate a narrow path leading up into the mountains, from below it had been obscured by the larger boulders. Beginning only a short distance away, the men reached it quickly. It was almost night time now, and it was not easy to see in which direction the path led, but it led away from the closing ranks of the enemy for sure, and this had to be a good thing. The loose surface (used for centuries by travellers to and from Samaria) was littered with small stones, large rocks, and all sorts of debris from the heights above. It would be very easy to slip, or twist an ankle, trying to negotiate such terrain in the dark. Bestwin warned that the screed would prove very noisy underfoot and would give away their position, and direction of travel, to their pursuers. They knew that finding safe shelter must be the priority now. Ranician had given his life to give them more time to reach the mountains. They could not afford to be caught out in the open in the dark. It was agreed that should the unholy host below catch up with them, then one of the guardsmen, being the swiftest on foot, would press on with their mission whilst the others remained to hold up the enemy.

A sheer, smooth rock face, climbed up and out of view on their left. To their right, at the edge of the path, was a drop of several feet. But as they trudged wearily uphill it soon became apparent that the path led up the side of a mountain, so the drop to the right would become more and more perilous as they climbed.

Finally the full blackness of night arrived, stars speckled the sky, and a cool night breeze had picked up, as it so often did in these parts. Their cloaks rustled in the wind, occasionally flapping back and forth, causing them to grab at them to silence them. Exhausted from travelling, their hearts heavy with sorrow for their fallen comrades, they trudged doggedly up the mountain. Their left hands skimmed along the mountainside to ensure that, in the darkness, they did not wander too close to the sheer, ever increasing, danger, on their right.

They had been hauling their weary bodies up the steep path for some minutes when they became alarmed by noises to their rear.

The now familiar sounds put them in no doubt as to the source. Swords drawn, they had no choice but to continue to forge ahead with the rearmost pair walking backwards to better sight anything following them. Bestwin led the way, with all of them constantly looking back to be sure the last two were keeping up, and also because it's completely natural to look over one's shoulder when one knows something menacing is stalking you. Thus, it was as Bestwin looked over his right shoulder that he failed to notice the large crevice in the rock face on his left. He had been leaning quite heavily on the rock due to exhaustion, so when this opening suddenly appeared in the mountainside, he simply disappeared, falling headlong through the gap. He did not yell out only because it happened so fast that he did not have time to react. Landing with a loud thump he sat up and peered about him. It was pitch black and he could only see the starlit sky beyond the gap through which he had fallen. That gap was soon full of worried-looking faces quietly calling out his name. He crawled towards it and whispered, "I'm in here! Quick, get in here! It's some sort of cave, I think."

The others quickly squeezed through the narrow aperture and entered the small natural cave in a far more dignified manner than its first occupant.

Being seasoned warriors there was no need for talk or discussion, boulders and branches were gathered from the path outside and interwoven to form a makeshift barrier across the mouth so they would, hopefully, not be seen hiding inside. A torch was lit briefly to make a quick assessment of where they were, it was simply a small cave with no other exits, tall enough to stand in comfortably, and large enough to hold perhaps fifteen men. The entrance was very small in width but higher than the tallest of them. It was much more than they could have ever hoped for and it was decided they would hide out here until daybreak. If they were discovered, they had a fighting chance of holding back Ogiin's creed at the cave mouth as numbers counted for nothing in such a confined space. The men had made their decision and they unburdened themselves of supplies. With one of them taking up station as sentry, food and water were passed around. They needed that vital energy in such a dangerous predicament, one is not efficient if hungry and starved, a fire was out of the question of course, but was sorely missed in the cold dark cave. Nervously the men chewed quickly on tough ham, taking the occasional swig of water, no one had any appetite, but each knew strength meant survival.

The sentry was to be relieved every hour. They were all so tired that no one could be expected to stay on watch and remain fully alert any longer than that. Whilst one guarded the entrance to the cave, the others would try and sleep to gain some much needed rest. A row of torches was laid out ready to be lit in an instant by means of flints, as fire would be a useful weapon as well as aiding vision within the dark confines of their makeshift fort. A hoard of dry branches, having fallen from the heights above, was stockpiled inside the cave. Imo took first watch as the others sat, or laid down, on the cold, but dry, floor, and closed their eyes with swords close to hand. 'The Wrath of Amaris' lay primed and armed next to them.

Imo stood to one side of the barrier, out of sight from the path, hidden behind the improvised wall of boulders, vines, and branches, his whole body ached from the toils of that very long day, and he thought of the valiant Ranician, his hand tightening on his sword hilt. All his life he had wanted to taste adventure, to test his constant training in open combat, perhaps, one day, he may even be offered the honour of joining the Ranin, but the enemy they now faced was not what he had envisaged any future opponent to be, not the testing of mettle he had wished for. Still, he was not afraid. Not afraid of the enemy, no, but, yes, afraid of not fulfilling his mission, of failing his king. He looked down at his strong sinewy arms, and vowed that as long as he could lift his sword, he would not fail. Time passed slowly. He glanced over at the others sleeping, he had never known such weariness, his eyes so heavy he could barely keep them open. Resting his shoulder on the cold surface of the cave, he peered through the little gaps in the barrier, keeping his ears pinned back for the slightest sound.

The light, refreshing breeze, blew into the cave in fitful bursts, and he cursed it for causing the greenery in the barrier to rustle.

Samaria

In the distance he could hear an owl hooting, and the odd call of a night bird nestling in the woods down below. He isolated these sounds so as to pick up anything that was different, unusual, or out of the ordinary. Through the mesh of the barrier he could see the clear sky and a myriad of Samarian stars. Under different circumstances this would be a beautiful night. Then Bestwin's voice whispered gently in his ear. "Rest now, Imo. I will take the next watch."

Silently, Imo slipped away from the wall and took the Westonian's place on the ground. The hard earth had been warmed a little by Bestwin lieing upon it, and as soon as he laid his head on his arm, he was asleep.

Bestwin now stood exactly where Imo had previously positioned himself. He had rested but an hour yet he felt so much better for it. He, too, glanced occasionally at his sleeping friends. He picked up a handful of pebbles and kept hold of them. He knew of old that Lumarr was prone to snoring quite loudly, and should he begin his nocturnal racket, Bestwin would aim a pebble or two at him to stop him from betraying their hideout. The Westonian watched the three Samarians wrapped in their jet black capes, the silver dragons even now somehow glowing as they watched over the men that bore them with such reverence. He, a proud Westonian, knew nothing but honour and respect for his Samarian allies. He knew they would never desert him or the Western Worlds. To a man, each would readily give his life in service of King Tamarin. How wonderful it must be—thought Lord Bestwin, to have such a kind, honourable, and just, king. Dorinn, his own king, made his blood boil. He and Lumarr would have proudly led the Westonian army against the evil that troubled their shores, but that was not to be, it had fallen to these brave *Samarians* to heed the call of the Western Worlds. He felt sad, embarrassed of Dorinn. Although his eyes were scanning the area outside the cave like those of a hawk, and his ears were as alert as those of a bat, it was his nose that warned him something was amiss. An awful smell was starting to fill the cave. He took a step toward the men to see if any of them, too relaxed in his sleep, was responsible. But no, the smell seemed to be concentrated near the barrier, but was spreading into the cave. The sickening stench almost made him wretch out loud. He tossed his handful of stones at the others and they immediately sprang to their feet amidst the clattering pebbles, sleep filled eyes shooting questioning glances in all directions. The foul odour began to saturate the confined space and it was all the men could do to stop themselves from coughing and spluttering. "Look!" warned a guardsman, pointing to the foot of the barrier. In the faint light at the mouth of the cave they could see a dirty green vapour pouring in along the ground. It spread across the cave floor, and seemed to be pooling close to one of the walls, "Torches!" came the cry from both the Westonians, followed by Lumarr shouting, "We are discovered! It's a witch!"

Bestwin held his position at the mouth of the cave and a guardsman joined him. The others frantically struck flints until a torch burst into flame and was used to light others. In the flickering firelight they could see the rancid vapour had now pooled into a misty puddle opposite them. Their own shadows danced eerily on the cave walls as the mist began to rise and take shape. A sinister cackle issued from within it as it started to resemble the form of an old hag. Bestwin, knowing there was no need of stealth now, shouted to the others, "Deal with the crone! It's merely a distraction, we must hold the barrier, or we are doomed!"

The Wispy Witch was almost fully formed. Her smoky, emaciated arms were raised high over her head, as if ready to pounce as soon as she was able. They could distinguish the deep hollows where eyes should have been. Her revolting silhouette was easily recognisable for what it was. Cold, evil laughter poured from her grinning mouth, filling the cave with its maniacal sound as her misty form began floating around the cave, almost dancing with delight. Her chilling wails echoed all the more louder within the tight confines of the cave, sending shivers up the spines of the men facing her.

It was so dark outside that Bestwin could not see beyond the barrier. He felt sure he had seen several pairs of dull red eyes just outside the cave, though he could not attribute them to any particular fiend. However, he felt confident, having seen such things before, that they were the eyes of Shadows, Shadows waiting to envelope himself and his comrades in their ghastly shrouds of death. Lumarr tossed him a pair of burning torches and he and the guardsman set about lighting the barrier, setting it ablaze. The flames licked at the wood, scrambling between the stones and rocks and igniting the branches that were interwoven between them. The cracking and spitting of the fire added further confusion within the cave, but it at least formed a formidable deterrent to anything else wanting to enter. The men at the barrier continued to feed its flames with stockpiled fuel as the other three circled the seemingly demented hag in the dull, torch lit gloom of the cave.

Lumarr and Imo probed the witch with their swords, and although she evaded those deadly blades as best she could, she seemed impervious to harm from their weapons. Lumarr called over to the guardsmen, "The oil! Pitch! Douse the stinking bitch!"

The men lunged for the big jar of pitch, and as Imo and Lumarr poked and prodded at her darting body, they threw a large splash of black oil over her. Instantly, Lumarr put his torch to her chest, and she began to burn. The flames raced up her body and engulfed her, now wailing, head. Then she began to burn along her entire length. Little gritty red sparks shot from her as she raced around the cave, screaming agonisingly as the sheets of flame ravaged her body. Many times she tried to escape but the blazing barrier was more than she could bear. Imo chased her around the cave, hacking pointlessly at her and shouting; "DIE! Die you evil hag! DIE! DIE!"

After half a minute of leading him round and around the cave, the hag finally fell to her knees, succumbing at last to the hungry flames. Her sinister face seethed despite being contorted in pain. Even in her final seconds she hissed at them, "Ogiin will crush your bones! We will suck out your souls!"

One of the guardsmen stepped up to the shrieking crone, telling her in a flat voice, "suck on this." With that, he rammed a burning torch into her gaping mouth. The hag's scorched body went up in a tremendous gush of purple flame, and, then, in a blinding flash, disappeared completely, leaving the cave filled with the most horrendous stench. The men gathered together at the blazing barrier. Clothing held over their mouths and noses, they looked at each other for answers. Fortunately they had piled enough fuel to keep the fire burning for some time, but the cave was slowly filling with smoke which would become a serious problem soon enough. They could see tentacles of smoke trying to enter under the barrier but these would shrink back from the intense heat, their withdrawal accompanied by horrible shrieking. The chaotic cacophony of excited witches could be easily heard through the crackling flames. These high pitched sounds were soon accompanied by the deep, bass rumble of hellhounds growling. Venomeens were flittering about outside, but it was impossible to see exactly what they were doing. Further away along the path, the men would catch the odd glimpse of red pupil-less eyes floating in the blackness.

They found nooks and crannies in the walls in which to affix their burning torches. Fresh torches were placed near the cave mouth ready for instant use. Mounting the torches thus allowed each man use of both his hands. Imo was held aloft by the Westonians to peek out over the top of the barrier. He could see that a large group of the enemy had crowded around the cave. The creatures of the dark seemed to be disorganised, milling about in a grotesque throng, perhaps waiting for the fire to die away. The Venomeens, however, seemed to be doing something more co-ordinated. He could not quite see what it was, so Imo craned his neck to get a better picture of their plan. It seemed as if they were scurrying about picking up the largest branches and logs that they could find. Luckily, the men inside the cave had rapidly cleared the immediate area of large pieces of wood for their own purposes. Imo jumped down from the shoulders of his friends. Smoke had started to cover the ceiling of the cave and he coughed violently, water streaming from his eyes before he spoke, "We are truly trapped my friends, there's too many for us to attempt a breakout. I think the Venomeen scum are going to try and build a battering ram of sorts—to destroy our fire. Furthermore, I'm not at all happy to report that there two hellhounds sitting directly opposite us.

Needless to say, *Shadows* await us also. *A pretty pickle we find ourselves in then*, what say you?"

The Samarians looked to the Westonians. Bestwin and Lumarr not only had first hand experience of these matters, but also outranked the Samarians there present. It was only a matter of time before the fire had to eventually burn out. Only fire and light could be used against the Wispy Witches and those phantom Shadows, light without fire was many long hours away as yet, whatever plan they conceived, the enemy simply could not be allowed to breach the barrier and gain access to the cave.

Each man wracked his brains for some means by which to gain a fighting chance, some advantage. No one actually expected to find any such plan, but Bestwin thought he had an idea, and he outlined his thoughts quickly to the others. Low, in the middle of the barrier, they removed some of the smaller rocks forming their defence. Those outside could not see their actions through the fire and smoke. 'The Wrath of Amaris' was brought into play, mounted on the hard ground and pointing out of the cave. It remained unseen by the enemy, ready to be fired through the hole they had created. They soaked its long, purposeful shaft and deadly tip in pitch, doing the same to many of their arrows. Having placed a good supply of these by the barrier, Imo climbed onto Lumarr's shoulders, from his elevated position he had a clear shot at the closest hellhound. The creature was far too big to get into the cave, but it was their plan to purely enrage it rather than kill it. He fired a burning missile at the brute and it buried itself into the mammoth jaw of his target. The hellhound let loose an ear piercing shriek and charged for the cave mouth, trampling a Venomeen that stood in its way. It began scrabbling in the dirt, digging away at the small recess in the rock which led to the defenders of the cave. Its gaping jaws snapped and snarled with fury through the narrow gap as its yellow eyes tried to gain sight of its prey. The gigantic beast, furious at having been attacked, managed to force its powerful frame firmly into the crevice, its nose but inches from the barrier when Bestwin released the 'Wrath of Amaris'. The mighty spear ripped through the heart of the hellhound and it shrieked hysterically once more, groaning woefully before dieing where it stood. The spear being soaked in pitch had burst into flames as it tore through the barrier. It had erupted from the beast's back and, still blazing furiously, had arced high into the night sky and out of view. Simultaneously, Imo had smashed a jar of pitch onto the hellhound's head, soaking its rough black fur, and the hellhound was now a grotesque bonfire. As Imo had doused the hound, the others (except Lumarr, as Imo was standing on his shoulders) had picked Wispy Witches as targets through small gaps in the barrier, and a volley of pitch-soaked arrows had burst into flame as they exited the barrier and found their marks. Burning Witches ran amok outside the little cave, scattering Venomeens in all directions. The Shadows moved quickly away from the flaming hags. The men whooped and cheered inside the cave, they even each took a quick, big swig from a wine skin. It felt good to kill this enemy that had been responsible for the loss of many true friends.

Bestwin humbly pointed out that the exit was now blocked by a burning hellhound, so the Venomeens would have no use of a battering ram. If they came to try and drag the burning brute away they would come under fire from within the cave, and Venomeens were not immune to such weapons. The men had gained a little time and slapped Bestwin on the back, congratulating him on his most excellent of plans. But he merely smiled uneasily, and, in a tone far less confident, told them. "Whilst *they* are held at bay for now, *we* are still trapped within this cave. I'm afraid this is not a stalemate my friends, it is a siege, and, measuring our remaining resources, the odds are stacked against us, still."

CHAPTER SEVEN

THE DESERT OF IRET

Tamarin and his escorts had been riding hard for a long time and the horses were weary, as were the riders. It was getting dark and a halt was called. The men tended to their steeds and took some refreshments, as well as taking the opportunity to wash the ingrained sand from their faces. In the distance they could vaguely see the skyline of Soledad. Tamarin was eager to catch up with Meekhi and kept their break short, so within half an hour of stopping they were again heaving themselves up into their saddles. He knew Meekhi would not have ventured into Soledad, and the Desert of Iret was not to be trifled with lightly. Legend told that it had been the undoing of Lord Amaris, now often referred to as the 'Lost Lord'. Tamarin had no intention of getting lost when his lady may have need of him. He and his men veered away from both Soledad and that treacherous desert, taking the longer but safest route to the Pink Mountain. The horses pounded along the sandy road in the dark of the night with a clear sky full of stars above them. The only other sounds being that of their creaking harness, the jangling of weapons, and their own heavy, intermittent, breathing. The forced pace to the Pink Mountain had reduced their journey time considerably, and with any luck, coupled with the very short break, they must surely overtake Meekhi soon.

Meekhi was leading the way forward, albeit gingerly. The other two rode abreast of her, a little astern. The shallow mist into which they had ridden seemed to be getting deeper. They kept a watchful eye on it, and, sure enough, they could see the horses' legs became less and less visible as the strange vapour began to rise up them. The air about them felt warmer, very soothing, and it was difficult to not relax one's guard. Mercy suggested they sling a rope between the three horses to prevent them losing each other in the rising fog. It was a good idea and the riders bunched much closer together. Before long the tall horses were belly deep in this strange sifting mystery, and it became apparent to everyone that if the mist continued to rise at this rate they would soon lose all sense of direction as they would not be able to see more than a few yards ahead. It also occurred to each of them to turn about, but when they looked back they were shocked to see a wall of mist had risen up behind them. A wall so high, it appeared to disappear into the night sky. Meekhi turned to the others. "I chose this path as it served us a faster route to our ultimate goal—the Pink Mountain. Perhaps if we make haste we can get clear of this rising haze that threatens to engulf us."

She urged her horse to set a brisker pace, and the others followed suit. But the mist was rising faster and faster, and very soon the riders could not see their own legs. It seemed very odd riding along watching only each other's upper torso bobbing along on the fog. Ramulet warned them, "*Beware*, my ladies, soon we will lose sight of each other, perhaps even of reality. Remember, this is a land of falsehoods, stay close together, and trust *only* in The Dragon."

The trio gritted their teeth and continued to move forward with the impenetrable wall of vapour so close behind them that the horses' tails were no longer visible. Shortly after, only three heads could be seen moving along on the surface of a sand coloured fog. The horses were now completely submerged and had no sense of direction at all. Then, the 'floating' heads, too, were gone from view, and the desert of lies had consumed the queen and her companions.

Once it had fully closed about them, they were pleasantly surprised to see that the fog was not the colour of sand at all, it was of a sparklingly golden hue, and, somehow, it was very bright inside it. Little bursts of gold, green, and yellow, twinkled in the mist like crisp sparks, the diaphanous haze a marvel to the eye. They could see each other clearly at last, and it felt reassuringly safe in this place, as if this strange, unnatural, phenomenon, would shield them from prying eyes. The warriors eyed each other in bewilderment, confused by their surroundings, annoyed at the calm they instilled. Meekhi broke the silence, "Don't rest your guard, my friends, this must be an illusion. We did not see this bizarre spectacle from outside of this place, it cannot be real, all within Iret is poisonous lies."

Rordorr decided that now was the time for him to have his say, "I'm of the same mind as you, my lady, but mores' the pity. Look at the ground underfoot—I have never seen such lush and tempting grass. It looks so delicious and moist, and because it does, I know it cannot be real, because I have never had any such good luck in the whole of my life."

Ramulet could not resist teasing this big, powerful horse, "It's true nature meant that horses should whine, but you, my good friend, never stop whining. However, your whinging has the ring of truth to it. Such grass cannot exist here, in a desert."

Rordorr tossed his mane, "That's easy for you to say, Ramulet, but us horses have much to whine about. For one thing, we can not make beer, and for another thing…"

"Shhhhh!," Came Mercy's voice, "can you hear that?"

They did not have to strain their ears. The sound of pan pipes and eerie fairy music seemed to be emanating from the mist. It did not come from any particular direction, but rather from this golden haze itself, the haunting melody partnered the colourful sparks well, and, coupled with the sense of wellbeing proffered by the surrounding fog, the atmosphere within Iret felt calm, relaxing, and very safe. Mercy was not convinced—"*Very unlikely,*" she thought to herself, "nothing in Iret could *ever* be at peace."

The riders slipped from their mounts, not realising that in doing so the rope that bound them together would fall to the ground. They stood there surrounded by the bright golden haze, blinking at each other as the horses waited on them. Meekhi seemed to be thinking hard, and the others allowed her a minute to her thoughts undisturbed. After some deep consideration she looked up. "My friends, this is all an illusion. We know the Desert of Iret is full of lies and false images, treachery, and deceit. I confess that although I cannot see the way forward towards our goal, I do believe that I can *feel* the way. I should have never ventured into Iret, no good will come of my mistake I'm sure, but the spirit of The Dragon will guide us, he will not abandon his own to such a filthy place. I will lead, and we will continue our journey. Let us not lose sight of one another in this deceiving mist. We must trust only in each other. My winged friends, perhaps one of you can rise above this fog of lies that blinds us so, and gain us an honest heading?

Rordorr immediately extended his enormous red wings. He attempted to rise from the ground, but very quickly found he could not, his wings feeling as if they were cast from heavy bronze. The horse strained and heaved, but to no avail. He reared up on his hind quarters, almost falling from his efforts. It was no good and he looked at Meekhi dejectedly, "It would appear, my lady, that I cannot fly in this infernal mist, I do most humbly apologise."

"It is not of your doing, dear friend," she told the embarrassed horse in a soothing voice, "it is this accursed place. It means for us to be trapped here forever, as many have been in the past—legend tells us. Iret is filled with the ghosts of the men it has consumed. But our true hearts will overcome this untrue place. We shall yet prove to be the antidote to the poison of Iret. Let us move onwards, the truth is our shield."

Each rider held on to their horse by the reins, and the whole group began walking. They had taken only a few steps when they could hear their own voices being whispered all around them. A thousand voices called to them from within the golden glow. Low, husky feminine whispers and deep masculine bass called to each of them. Adult voices and childlike voices, familiar voices and strange voices, voices nearby and voices far away, each chased by a faint echo. The Samarians ignored them and continued to walk. Then the voices seemed to change, to fuse together and mould into one. Suddenly, they replicated the sound of Mercy's voice exactly. They cooed and whispered at Ramulet sensuously, erotically, tantalisingly telling him of hidden love and passionate desires. He maintained a stone-like visage, but Mercy was very obviously embarrassed by these base utterances. The voices seemed to know her innermost feelings, and were betraying those deep, dear emotions, for all to hear. She could not look at the others as they walked along. Inside her she already felt a white-hot hatred growing for this place, but then, the voices changed and seemed to disappear momentarily, to return a few seconds later as the voice of Ramulet, wooing Mercy and making vulgar suggestions to her. Ramulet's face was bright red and seething, he ignored the crass taunting, but he, too, could not look at the others. Meekhi felt the suffering and outrage of her friends. She had never imagined such things would happen to them and felt terribly guilty at having brought them to this awful place, so she resolved herself to getting them out of it. The guilt stopped her from looking about herself, and she stared straight ahead.

The embarrassing voices had stopped them from watching each other and maintaining communication. Even the horses, out of respect for the victims of these awful whispers, hung their heads low as they plodded on. It was not long before they realised they had drifted apart from one another, and Ramulet called for them to stop. The women were closer together, whereas he was some distance away. They could see him standing there clearly enough in the shimmering golden light, and he waved to them. Then, in a split second, hundreds more 'Ramulets' appeared, followed by as many more 'Mercys' and 'Meekhis'. It was impossible to tell the real Samarians from the multitude of perfect impostors that crowded into the sparkling glow everywhere. Oddly, there was no replication of the horses.

Whenever any of the trio spoke they were immediately mimicked precisely by countless images of themselves, their voices echoing softly away into the mist. It was as if a thousand mirrors were reflecting the images of the three warriors. The horses did not know whom to trust and backed away a little to see what happened next. Whenever one of them approached a false image it would call upon the other two Samarians for help, claiming that it was in fact the real Samarian. A deep sense of unease straddled them as they eyed the countless images and tried to determine friend from foe.

Ramulet kept his eyes firmly trained on the area where the queen and Mercy had been standing. The sharp thinking captain had quickly spotted how to distinguish between reality and illusion, but as he stepped forward to share his discovery, the ground opened up under his feet, and he slipped down into the treacherous clutches of Iret. Instantly, as the ground closed up again above him, the false images of him vanished from the sight of those left on the surface. None of his comrades had seen him disappear into the ground as their view of him had been obscured by the plethora of false 'Ramulets'. The women turned round and around slowly, swords drawn and eyes peeled. They were eager to cut down these apparitions, but were afraid that they may inadvertently harm their true friend. They were shocked to see all the 'Ramulets' had disappeared, including the genuine one! This was immensely worrying, what had happened to him? They were surprised and pleased to hear Rordorr's solid, reliable, horsy voice call out to them, "My ladies! Look to the cloaks! Look for the dragon."

They spun their heads and instantly saw the reason for his outburst. Whilst the form and clothing of the false images were perfect in their every detail, their cloaks lacked the silver dragon, why had they not noticed this before? Some further bedevilment of Iret, no doubt. Recognising each others' crest-bearing cloak, the women joined each other quickly, standing back-to-back, dragon-to-dragon. The horses, now aware of where their loyalties lay, gathered next to them. The women were glad to be flanked by these loyal, immensely powerful, animals. They were desperate to find Ramulet and do harm to these false images born of Iret, but this was not to be.

Just as suddenly as they had appeared, the remaining replicas disappeared. The Samarians breathed a sigh of relief but remained on the alert. The horses relaxed a great deal more, having been thrown into confusion when it had been impossible to discern twixt friend and foe. They had been completely focused on those illusions and now that they looked about themselves, they found they were once again in a desert. No golden mist, and no haunting music, surrounded them, but there was still no Ramulet. It was dark, and a sinister yellow moon hung overhead, large and looming. Where were they? Samaria had not one, large, leering, yellow moon, but six, small, silver moons. Then a biting wind fetched up, slapping and pinching at their faces in angry fits and bursts. The sand at their feet was as dark as charcoal and no stars brightened the dreary black sky, tall rocky outcrops could be seen jutting out of the desert everywhere in the pale moonlight, and there was no sound save the intermittent whistling of the wind. The barren wasteland extended in all directions without so much as a tree, cactus, or shrub, in sight.

"Forgive me," Meekhi humbly asked of her friend, "In my haste to serve my lord and land I fear I may have brought catastrophe upon our quest, and in so doing I have also lost our beloved Ramulet. I cannot imagine where he may be, or even if he still lives. This land, if it is indeed land and not further illusion, is alien to me. I know not what to do. Ramulet must be found, but the Pink Mountain also awaits us. In my mind, I am lost. What say you, Mercy?"

Mercy did not reply straight away, she stood staring at the pale moon with her hands on her hips. Meekhi stood beside her assuming the same posture, and some slow minutes passed before Mercy placed her mouth close to Meekhi's ear, "My lady, do not blame yourself for the decisions made by others. We are each of us where we have chosen to be at this very moment, even my Ramulet is thus, I do not fear him dead, I feel his heart beating next to mine yet. You know full well of my love for him, he is a fearless warrior, second to none, and, as Captain of the Royal Guards, he would have us continue on our quest without him. I am certain this would be his wish, and to deny it would most surely offend him. Ramulet is not so easily vanquished, as I'm sure this land of illusions will soon discover to its eternal regret. Iret will rue the day it challenged one such as he, and it will suffer for that mistake for all time to come. Samaria needs us to complete the task set for us by Tamarin. I say we endeavour to reach the Pink Mountain.

My heart will remain with Ramulet, but my sword will travel with my queen."

Deep inside, Meekhi wanted to stay and search for her close, and dear, friend. But this was not the Samarian way. In this place of lies Ramulet may just as easily be one of the craggy outcrops protruding from the dirty black sand and she would see only rock. She felt confident that the lies of Iret could not overcome the truth of Ramulet, or any other Samarian for that matter. Her mission was urgent, and many were depending on her to complete it quickly. Ramulet was indeed a deadly warrior, and a wily one at that. Like Mercy, Meekhi felt he would be able to fend for himself. She was saddened by his sudden disappearance, and she was angry with herself for leading them into this predicament. To make matters worse—the horses were still unable to fly.

Rordorr stated that he would stay in the vicinity of where they now stood. He said Ramulet may well have need of someone that did not get lost easily. The women were impressed by his loyalty to his rider and his courage in remaining within a land polluted so heavily with lies and the poison of treachery. Meekhi spoke to those that would move onward with her. "Iret is a truly loathsome place and I should never have ventured here. It is drenched in a lifetime of betrayal, infidelities, and dark deeds. Whatever happens next, whatever we face, we must be agreed that reaching the Pink Mountain is our utmost goal. We are leaving Ramulet to face whatever it is his destiny to face. We remaining four, horses and women alike, must pledge this—should any of us fall, or are lost, the others will press on without them. We must take to Tamarin the news for which he awaits in Sitivia. Are we agreed?"

It was agreed.

A quick, fervent, farewell to Rordorr, and Meekhi set off once more, letting her heart guide her through the dreary wilderness. As they walked, they saw the rock formations around them change shape from time to time and they tried their best to ignore it, but it was very disconcerting. The wind was bitterly cold and the women wrapped their capes about them as the horses covered their flanks with the warm down of their feathered wings. It was a heart breaking trek through the dirty sand—not knowing where they were heading, which direction they had come from, or even where they where, Iret truly was an unholy place and after several hours of trudging along, using the moon to judge their course, they were becoming very tired, the women were more weary than the horses, and the horses very kindly suggested they remount to get some much needed rest for their aching legs. It was an offer both Meekhi and Mercy were happy to accept. As Meekhi was leading the way, her horse agreed to be guided by the reins. This was unheard of ever before in Samaria as these horses were more than capable of reaching wherever they were headed without need for input from any rider. Anyone suggesting use of reins would normally be met by a powerful kick, or, at best, some unsavoury words. But these were exceptional circumstances and as everything they could see may well not even exist, the horse trusted Meekhi's royal instincts more than his own eyes.

Not too far ahead Meekhi could see a taller outcrop of rock. It was considerably larger than the others and she had been watching it for some time to gauge her direction in relation to the moon and it had not changed shape once. It stood directly ahead of them so she decided to reach it before stopping for a brief rest and a little water. Mercy agreed, and they headed straight for it. They were only twenty yards away when a loud clattering noise stopped the horses dead in their tracks. The clattering was coming directly from the tower of rock, and was getting louder. Initially, in the dark of night, it had been difficult to see that the rock *was* in fact moving and subtly changing shape. The horses, startled by it, reared up, and Mercy was thrown from the saddle, landing heavily in the sand. A little dazed, she staggered to her feet to see that the rock was starting to take on a different shape entirely, "By the sword! What sorcery is this!" She exclaimed.

Meekhi had managed to swing her horse around, and she galloped over to Mercy with her arm outstretched. Mercy grabbed hold and was swung up onto Meekhi's horse. The crunching, grating sound was horribly loud now as Mercy leaped from Meekhi's mount to her own saddle. Her head was still spinning from the heavy knock from when she had fallen. They drew their swords with the horses stamping their hooves, agitated and nervous. The strange noise was akin to tons of shingle being poured from a great height onto yet more shingle. The rock was obviously alive, and, when it stood upright, Meekhi called over to Mercy, "IT'S A ROCK TROLL! Tamarin has warned me of them. Man-eaters that often hide within Iret! Mercy, be on your guard!"

Sure enough, it was now easy to see that the moving rock was, in fact, a troll, a huge towering beast, its skin thicker than an elephant's hide and covered in rocky scales the colour of slate. Fishlike, the scales overlapped forming a body-armour of stone. Its single eye sat where a nose should be and as it opened its cavernous mouth, row upon row of teeth could be seen. They appeared to made of jagged flint, sharp, and deadly. The creature was a carnivore and delighted in human flesh. Despised and hunted by Samarians for their allegiance, in history past, with Ogiin, they survived mainly in Dizbaar now, but if they crossed into Samaria they would spend much of their time within the land of lies as it offered them some safe haven from Samarian patrols. Anyone daring to venture into Iret was fair game to them—a chance to feast on such a rare delicacy. The towering grey monster stood twice the height of a man but was immensely more powerful. Its huge rocky paws could easily crush a man's skull with a single squeeze.

The troll's single oval eye roved hungrily over the Samarians. The women, caught by surprise, were momentarily rooted to the spot, a few seconds too long it transpired, because, out of nowhere, a long spiky tail covered in those clattering scales shot out from behind the troll and landed a terrible blow into the left flank of Mercy's horse. Horse and rider were sent tumbling across the sand, swept along by the brute force of that massive tail. Mercy felt her ankle twist agonisingly as she tried to regain her feet, she could see her horse's wing was broken, but he, too, was attempting to stand up. Meekhi immediately charged the troll, her sword flashed many times, but only sparks issued from its stony armour. She wheeled her horse about and it kicked out with both rear legs, landing a crushing blow to the troll's midriff, but the beast did not budge. She knew the horse would be vulnerable with her weighing it down and she jumped from the saddle. Throwing her dark mane to one side, she ran to Mercy's aid. She had just gotten her to her feet when she saw the huge fist bearing down on them. She only just managed to pull Mercy clear when the gigantic curled paw slammed into the ground where Mercy had lain, the ground reverberating under the impact. "I suspect...," Mercy told her in a voice filled with pain, "this bad boy is most probably NOT an illusion."

Meekhi started dragging her away from the clutches of the scaly colossus. It chased after them, its scales moving on each other making that horrible, gravely, scraping sound—chhh chhh chhh. They felt the ground shaking as its massive feet pounded into it. The horses tried to distract the troll by running around its legs but it ignored them, staying focused on the brace of beautiful women that it knew would just taste so good. Mercy managed to get on her feet, but couldn't walk. She stood holding onto Meekhi's shoulder and Meekhi supported her with one hand whilst pointing her sword at the fast approaching troll. Her cloak blowing in the wind and her hair whipping about her face in the hostile wind of Iret, she screamed at it, "Come then, desert dweller! Let us show you that even a heart of stone can feel the fatal touch of samarian steel!"

With that cry on her lips she smiled kindly at the injured Mercy, whispering, "*Move,* my friend. Take the horses and make to the Pink Mountain." Then she leapt forward and again engaged the troll. It was slow moving with its cumbersome fists, but its tail was as fast as lightning. She cut, thrust, and jabbed, at the grey tower of evil, but her sword was ineffective against its impenetrable hide and she was constantly ducking, diving, and jumping, to avoid that lethal tail. The troll finally caught Meekhi a swiping blow with its fist. Fortunately, it just glanced her shoulder, but she was thrown ten feet across the sand, landing awkwardly on that very same shoulder, the shoulder powering her sword arm. She changed her sword hand and chased back towards it as it was closing in on Mercy—who had fallen trying to escape its grasp.

The troll almost had a hold of Mercy's foot when Meekhi leapt onto its rough, craggy back. Standing upright, it tried snatching at her with its great clamp-like paws, but could not quite reach. Then its tail started whipping at its own back, striking time and again all about the flailing Meekhi, who could barely hang on as stone smashed against stone, sparks flying everywhere in the dark as the brave warrior-queen scrabbled for grip, trying to avoid a fatal strike.

Mercy could see her friend was in serious trouble and forced herself back onto her feet again. Her ankle was ablaze with pain and swelling fast. She could not walk, but she could just about hobble. She moved a little closer to the incensed troll and the frantic Meekhi and could see that deadly tail was landing repeatedly within inches of her queen. She could sense that Meekhi was tiring fast, and it was obvious that the troll was immune to the odd sword strike that was being landed against it. The horses were still trying to distract the troll by running about and kicking out at it whenever the opportunity arose. Mercy summoned her horse and it limped towards her woefully slowly. She had no time to tend to him but it seemed quite clear that more than just a wing had been broken. The warrior with the golden mane took her bow from the horse, and resting against him to steady her aim, she let loose three arrows simultaneously. The missiles whistled through the air to strike precisely against the troll's eye. They shattered on impact against the stone surface, having done no harm at all. The troll apparently had a second eyelid it used to protect its monstrous orb when danger threatened. But she had caught its attention once more. It lumbered towards her, arms outstretched, and mouth gaping wide open, its hands opening and closing repeatedly—ready to grab her up and crush her to pulp. Mercy made to escape but yelped out loudly as her ankle screamed in pain, protesting at this abuse and causing her to lose balance and fall. Her strong arms tried to pull her away from the pursuing beast, but not fast enough. Meekhi was raining blows upon its gargantuan head, but it ignored her in its headlong charge for the woman crawling away. Mercy looked up and saw the moon had assumed a twisted, almost lurid, smile on its face. It was horrifying. She grabbed her sword and made ready for what must now surely be her final moments. The troll arrived at her feet. It eyed her up and down as it opened its jaws even wider. Her injured horse, seeing her so helplessly cornered, reared up on its hind legs, matching the height of the troll, and smashed its mighty forehead squarely into the creatures face. The sheer force of the impact made the troll reel, staggering backwards and causing Meekhi to drop her blade. She still rained punches upon its head, blood pouring from her cut hands. The horse also staggered, and, stumbling away a short distance, it keeled over in the sand. "NO!" Mercy cried out, struggling to her feet yet again and brandishing her blade in angry, vengeful outrage.

Meekhi, having lost her sword, grabbed her dagger and stabbed repeatedly at the troll, trying to reach around and penetrate its eye. As her blade again failed to do any harm, she started yelling over to Mercy, "MERCY! Take the able horse and get out of here, NOW!" Then her wrist twisted awkwardly as the troll tried to dislodge her from its shoulders, and her dagger slipped between the slate-grey scales of the beast, sinking into the soft, vulnerable tissue, underneath. The troll reared up suddenly, roaring in pain. The sudden jolting movement threw Meekhi from its back, and she landed face down in the sand with a heavy thud. She jumped to her feet immediately despite the agonising pain in her injured shoulder. Her mouth was full of blood and as she wiped at her face and spat sand, she saw her hand was also covered in fresh blood from her nose. With fury blazing in her emerald eyes she snatched up her sword and raced over to Mercy.

The troll had refocused on Mercy and it was charging directly at her. "I think..." croaked Meekhi from her gritty throat, "our boy here *definitely* prefers a fairer woman."

Mercy grinned at her, "Or, perhaps, my lady, he can see *you* are nothing but trouble!"

They laughed, the way only the pure can laugh when they expect death to come knocking soon. "I need you to shoot between the scales." Meekhi quickly explained, "It's vulnerable there. I'll make our boy bend over, and you let him have it! Be ready, Mercy,

I doubt we'll get a second chance." She stood up and faced the oncoming troll.

Mercy, nursing her swollen ankle, stood beside her, gathering up her bow and arrows. The wind was gusting heavily and the leering moon of Iret waited impatiently, eager to see the Samarians perish. The pair stood their ground, their clothes in tatters and their dirt encrusted locks whipping in the wind like heroic banners proclaiming obstinate defiance. Facing their enemy eye-to-eye, they were ready for whatever hand was to be dealt them next.

The troll was perhaps only twenty feet from them when Meekhi shot forward, ducking through between its legs, she stabbed up with her sword, driving the long single blade deep between the scales on the brute's groin. It howled a terrifying howl of pure agony and its tail slammed into her as she ran to its rear, sending her hard into the sand yet again. It was a savage blow, but this was no ordinary woman that the troll faced. The Samarian Queen, spitting blood and gritting her teeth against the pain, rolled as she hit the sand, leaping back to her feet in an instant.

"You, my ugly friend!" she cursed at it, her eyes seething with the anger and fury that only such a woman can seethe with, "You... in this land of lies, will now know the power of truth, the truth of ice cold steel, and, hot blooded Samarian women!"

Despite her sore, aching body, Meekhi launched a furious attack on the troll, a flurry of sword strikes rained down on it as it swung, grabbed, and roared, at the elusive, nimble-footed, woman that it sought so desperately to devour. Several of her blows had been aimed under the overlapping armour of the troll and they had found their marks, causing the clattering monster's rage to reach such a crescendo that it began pummelling the ground in frustration. "Come on, you cycloptic wretch!," she taunted, "It's time I taught you how to behave in the presence of a lady! Make no mistake, we shall be putting manners on *you* this night!"

Utterly exhausted, Meekhi's body was wracked with pain after suffering those incredible hammer blows from the beast's tail. Her face covered in blood, and her hands bleeding profusely, she used her young limbs and supple frame to dance around the troll. She ran round and around it, changing direction suddenly, stabbing between the scales on its legs. This disgusting creature, she swore to herself, would never lay one loathsome finger on Mercy. Unable to match her speed, the troll began beating down with both massive fists together. It would raise its arms high above its head and slam its fists down, attempting to squash her like a bug. It raised its arms high again as she darted past, and the air was cut by the whizzing of arrows. The troll, with its arms raised so high, had arched its back and the scales on its chest had lifted, separating momentarily. Moments long enough for a master archer, such as Mercy, to release two arrows with pinpoint accuracy. They were now buried deep in its chest, having pierced its heart. It peered down with its one pink eye at the sleek feathered flights protruding from under its thick scales, and then, looked disbelievingly at Mercy. She gave it a friendly wave, though her eyes were as hard as diamonds when she said, "Goodnight, sweet love, we were just not meant to be. I think, maybe, I have broken your heart."

The lumbering leviathan began to totter on its big clumsy legs, and Meekhi wasted no time. In a flash she drove her sword home in the exact same spot as the arrows. The troll fell backwards, dead even before it hit the ground. The ground shook violently with the incredible force of the impact and a dark cloud of dust shot up into the air. For reasons no one will ever know, and no one has ever since explained, Meekhi leapt up onto the dead creature's chest and began jumping up and down on it, hurling insults at it as she stamped her feet and shook her head furiously. Then suddenly she became perfectly calm, and composing herself she jumped from the giant corpse and ran to Mercy's aid. Mercy, though in obvious pain herself, asked her to tend to the injured horse first. In the midst of all the pandemonium, Meekhi had not seen the horse suffer that tremendous blow to its forehead. She raced over to it. The other horse was already there, and they were talking to each other very quietly. Mercy hobbled over as fast as she could, using her sheathed sword as a crutch.

The injured horse lay on its side, unable to stand. Fresh blood flowed freely from its nose and its eyes were pale as the flame of life began to flicker, dancing its last dance before it was to become extinguished. The fast waning horse spoke to the other in a low voice,

"Fulfil our task, cousin, and defend the queen and Mercy. Soon, I shall join with the spirit of the Great Dragon."

At this point, Meekhi, and Mercy shortly after, arrived at his side. Meekhi lifted the head of the mortally wounded animal onto her lap, and stroked his beautiful face. Tears trickled down their faces, and Meekhi, her voice full of love and weighty with emotion, told the horse, "You are the spirit of Samaria, my loyal and courageous friend. You are all that which we aspire to be."

The horse, with some difficulty, momentarily opened his eyes and looked at his three weeping companions, with considerable effort he told them; "I am Samarian, I have served my lord, my queen, my homeland. I am content, I have had all that I wished for and there is no regret within me. Do not grieve, for now I must join with the Great Dragon. Make haste to the Pink Mountain, you must finish what we have started." He gave a long restful sigh, and passed from that life to the next.

The trio stood solemnly around their fallen comrade and, eventually, the one surviving horse broke the silence, "My cousin is with us no more, let us bring action to his words. There can be no funeral pyre, for we have not the means in this evil, unclean, wasteland that is Iret. Take what you need from him, he has carried it this far for your needs, then we must continue to the Pink Mountain. Tamarin still awaits our tidings."

The horse was obviously trying to suppress his anguish at the loss of his friend, but his shaky voice and the horse-sized lump in his throat gave him away. Mercy was crying openly—long drawn out sobs wracked the core of her, and diamond bright tears of love dripped freely from her big, chocolate-brown, eyes. Meekhi also wept, though not so obviously. She was queen of Samaria after all, and in these dire times had to show some strength and fortitude to inspire her people. Sadness welling from their hearts and their bodies filled with pain, the beautiful warrior-women knelt down beside the dead horse and began the ghoulish task of removing much needed supplies from their fallen friend, it was a galling task, but it was what the departed would have wanted. They felt dirty and wrongful, plucking items from the broken body, and they turned their eyes away as often as they could. Mercy subdued her sobbing and croaked, "He died protecting me, I will not leave him to this Iret, this quagmire of poison, this field of filth, if we cannot build a pyre for him, then I shall anoint him with our oil, I shall soothe his wounds with it, and then I shall send him on his way to the Great Dragon in a blaze worthy of such a fearless and noble warrior."

"Yes...yes... every warrior must have his just due." agreed Meekhi, "Make it so, dear Mercy, the touch of Iret cannot be allowed to defile one so pure. Here, let me help you."

Having taken from the horse all that which was needed, they began to gently pour oil over the dead horse. The other horse watched them, deeply touched by this act of kindness for his lost cousin. He knew it would mean much to the departed, and in a voice filled with grief he told them, "Truly the maidens of Samaria are the most honourable maidens of any world. On behalf of all those of my creed, I salute you, gratitude for the deed you do for my kind." The mighty horse bowed its head and bent down to one knee. The women also lowered their heads in acceptance of his respect. They then stood back, and Mercy stepped forward once more, and, having lit a torch in this godforsaken place, she put the flame to the dead horse. There was a lightening-fast flash of flame, then it disappeared, no fire, no pyre. They looked at each other, outraged. Iret would not prevent them from honouring their dead. Meekhi looked up at the moon and it seemed so invasive, almost lecherous in its leering. To her, it felt as if the only reason it gave any light at all to this eerie landscape was to highlight the abject misery of these travellers. She yelled up at it, "I will not forget you, whether you be real, or, an illusion. One day I will join with the stars, and on that day I will seek you out, oh moon of shame, and I shall tear you asunder!"

They poured most of their remaining pitch over the inert lifeless form of the horse, and again put a torch to it. The thick black oil flickered into life, the little fire growing momentarily before flickering weakly, waning, then once more receding into extinction. Beside themselves with anger, time and time again they tried to ignite the oil, with always the same result. Then the horse warned them. "Look! My ladies, look at the sand!"

The ground began to tremble and they leapt back (Mercy falling over) with swords drawn, ready to face any new threat. Mercy landed badly, her ankle was now so swollen she felt her boot might burst open with the pressure. "What new witchcraft is this?" she asked, trying with great difficulty to regain her footing. The ground continued to tremble, more gently now, and they feared another troll or some other dark creature would soon erupt from the cold heart of Iret.

Meekhi noticed it before Mercy, crying out, "By The Dragon! Look at the ground, look to where our tears fell!" The dark grainy sand had tiny, darker spots all over it where the river of sadness cascading from the weeping women had fallen. All over the still horse droplets could still be seen sitting on its jet black fur and crimson wings, but now the tears had begun to sparkle brightly, like diamonds in the dark, they began to twinkle and blink in the cold moonlight. The moon itself seemed to diminish, its deathly pale light fading, as if offended by these tiny shining jewels. The ground stopped shaking and minute silver stems seemed to be growing from the tears, they grew quickly, hundreds of them. Soon the entire area was covered in silver stems tipped with exquisite silvery buds. The trio watched, mesmerised, as the buds burst open to form the most beautiful little flowers, these flourishing in number at an astronomic rate. Meekhi turned to the others. "Though Iret be nothing but treachery, lies, and illusions, I feel this is not of the making of this putrid place, this is something else entirely, something quite wondrous. Stay wary, yes, but we will wait and see what comes from this strange event."

The three of them looked up when they noticed that the light around them had changed. The moon was retreating rapidly, much smaller than it had been, and now radiating an air of cowardice rather than gloating. It was then that they realised this new bright light was being emitted by the flowers themselves, a deep, rich silvery glow, that penetrated each of them to the core and warmed their very hearts. The entire area was now amassed with the beautiful, delicate blooms, and they had entirely covered the fallen horse under a large, glowing mound, of silver.

Mercy was pleasantly surprised to notice that, miraculously, the swelling in her ankle was reducing, and Meekhi, too, felt her aches and bruises being soothed away. They were staring at each other, awed by this strange, magical turn of events, when Meekhi felt the small crystal vial at her throat become burning hot. She loosened her tunic to lift it away from her skin. Free of the garment, the colours in the bottle began to glow brighter and brighter. She could not see the vial under her chin, but Mercy could. She pointed at the ever more intense colours and opened her mouth to say something, but was struck silent by what happened next. A whirling, swirling, stream of multicoloured light swarmed from the vial and covered the mound. Meekhi was rooted to the spot, peering down at what appeared to be a rainbow-coloured stream of light pouring from her throat. Then the vial cooled down again and they watched as the coloured lights danced all over the silver mound. It began to glow with the same colours as the lights moving atop it, and the yellow moon retreated even further into the blackness of the sky.

It seemed to quake, slowly absorbing the twinkling lights that covered it, until it became pure silver again in hue. From it emanated a light so intense that it was too much for the naked eye to bear, and the trio watching averted their eyes as this beacon illuminated the ground and the heavens as far as one could see. Then, in a flash, the dazzling glare was gone. The sudden return of darkness left everyone momentarily blind as they waited for their eyes to adjust. Mercy, screwing hers up, could see the silver flowers quite clearly. The light had completely disappeared and they stood there in the dark, staring at this bizarre spectacle with the cold wind chilling them, the stark surroundings feeling once more alien and hostile. As they looked on, they were amazed to see tiny specks of light start to rise from the flowers. Lights of every colour you could ever possibly imagine, lights so small they were each the size of a grain of sand. Millions of them rose from the mound, climbing steadily towards the heavens. They seemed to form a small shapeless cloud and it drifted ever higher and higher. It stopped midway to the sky and began to take shape. They were gob smacked to see it take the shape of a flying horse. It turned and faced them from above, enshrined within a glowing halo. Pride swelled their hearts to bursting and the nearby horse reared up, whinnying loudly. The figure shining in the sky bowed, and Meekhi and Mercy raised their swords in salute as they watched the tiny lights finally fade completely from view.

They were left speechless and it was a long time before anyone spoke. They just stood staring at the sky, not wanting to miss anything that might yet happen. Meekhi eventually snapped out of her trance and looked at where the horse had lain, quickly alerting the others to what she found there. The silver flowers had changed colour and now boasted so many colours it was impossible to count them. It reminded her of her own homeland—The Land of Flowers. In the midst of the blooms, right in the centre, grew the silver sapling of a tree. It was a very young beginning of a tree, but a tree none the less. She told her friends, "We that live in Samaria now know Samaria, *herself,* abides within us, too. Iret, this loathsome place, should never have existed on Samarian soil. Only through treachery and the deceitful ways of a witch's spirit did it come into being here. But a land of lies can never withstand the onslaught of truth, of honour, and, of faith! I believe Samaria—our beloved realm, has taken our dear friend to her bosom, nourished and tended him, finally sending him aloft to the Great Dragon. She would not allow one so noble, so selfless, and so pure, to be tainted by the poisonous clutches of Iret. So know this, my friends, if *Samaria* is ready to cleanse away this stain of Iret's vile existence, then the time of Iret will soon pass. I beseech the Great Dragon to allow me to be instrumental in the destruction of this accursed place, and that of the spirit of the filthy whore that haunts it."

"I will be by your side when that time comes, my lady." Mercy swore solemnly.

Samaria

"So shall I." added the remaining horse. "Killing is not something I take lightly, yet if I come face-to-face with the witch-spirit of Iret, I shall…well, I shall… I shall do things that it is not polite to say in front of two gracious ladies such as your good selves."

This last comment made those two particular ladies show the hint of a smile, and this lightened their mood a fraction. It was time to take stock of their situation. Their injuries, though not completely healed by the silver light, had been vastly improved by it. Mercy could walk, but was still in pain. The horse was sad, but unhurt. Meekhi's shoulder ached a little, but other than the bloody nose, she was fine. She used a little of their water to wash her face, and Mercy refreshed herself also. They were all woefully tired, but Meekhi (and the horse, too) ordered Mercy to sit in the saddle to rest her ankle. Meekhi was not lacking in her praise of Mercy's marksmanship when shooting at the Rock Troll. Naturally, no one had felt like eating after the tragic loss of their friend, and it was agreed that they must get out of the desert of lies as soon as possible, so, after a quick drink of water, they had set off. Meekhi tracked on her original heading, the horse following with a grateful Mercy resting on his back. They had travelled for only fifteen minutes when Meekhi put forward an idea. "That ugly pile of dung," she said pointing at the dead troll behind them, "must have come into Iret where the boundary of this wretched place lies closest to Dizbaar. We know history tells us that men by the score, women too, have come into Iret, and that none of them have ever left. But we are not men, nor are we the kind of womenfolk you might find in, say, Dizbaar? We are Samarians, and most certainly my winged friend here is not just any common horse! Breaking free of Iret is imperative, and, I think I know how. The troll weighed so much that it must have left footprints in the sand. It was not an illusion, so nor will its footprints be. Let us find them and retrace its track, do you agree?"

They did, wholeheartedly, impressed with her quick thinking, but then Mercy, tipping her face to one side and grinning cheekily at Meekhi, asked, "My queen, my monarch, my dear friend. I have to know—why on earth were you jumping up and down atop that would-be suitor of ours, shaking your head and screaming at it, when it was already dead?"

"Ah, yes… *that*," came the reluctant reply, "I have been known to have a tantrum from time to time, when I am really very angry. Tamarin enjoys them very much, and says I'm so very fetching when I'm having a demented fit. As you have seen for yourself, there is nothing alluring in it at all."

Mercy laughed; "I'm not so sure about that, my queen, I thought you looked absolutely magnificent!"

All of them laughing at the much needed touch of humour, they began to search for the footprints of the troll.

It did not take them long to find a massive imprint of the brute's clumsy foot in the ashen sand. Ramulet was constantly on their minds but their duty to Tamarin and Samaria demanded they press on. They each wished him strength by their blessings and left him to the good graces of the Great Dragon. Keeping an eye out for further trouble, Meekhi led them once more through the Desert of Iret.

CHAPTER EIGHT

THE GUILTY INNOCENTS

Tamarin and his horsemen were finally past Soledad and the Pink Mountain was firmly in their sights. Perhaps another thirty minutes and they would find Meekhi, her escorts, and whomever, or whatever, these Guilty Innocents turned out to be. It was the longest time he and his beloved had ever been apart and his heart ached to have her beside him once more, safe in his warm embrace. He reined in his mount sharply and the men behind came to a sudden halt, almost rear ending him amidst a large cloud of dust. He dismounted, "Ahead lies The Pink Mountain—the mountain of dreams. My lady will be somewhere on those heights and it is there we will find her and her escorts. Be cautious, these Guilty Innocents may well prove to be dangerous. They may be hostile armed warriors, or worse. For now, take water and a minute to rest, because when we remount, we do not stop until Meekhi is found. Do you understand my meaning, my most loyal of subjects?"

"Yes, understood, my lord!"

"Can you see that?" asked Lauren, "Over there, there's a big cloud of dust, I do believe there's *people* down there!"

The others looked and also saw the dust rising, and, although it was distant, there was definitely movement at the base of it.

"It's people! I'm sure it is!" beamed Thomas, "I say, Zee, this must be the most detailed dream anyone could ever have. Awesome! Uncle Dug *totally* rocks!"

Zowie stared long and hard at the small, distant figures, more visible now that the dust cloud was clearing. She had absolutely no idea what was going on, but had a niggling worry that things were about to change for the worse, and turned to the Shortwaters, "This could be a part of the adventure dad has planned out for us, but if they come up here let's stay shtoom about ourselves and about how we got here. Then we'll see what happens next, shall we? I must say, it's all very exciting! How cool is all this!"

They watched as the figures gradually became recognisable as men. Men with dark features, wearing cloaks with silver dragons boldly emblazoned upon them. They were standing by large, fierce looking, horses. Zowie felt responsible for the Shortwaters as it was her father's invention that had brought them to this dream, or place, or whatever it was. She had an idea. "Listen guys, if this is the dream it's supposed to be, then we should be able to fly because that's what dad programmed the Dream Pod for. Maybe we just couldn't fly properly inside this mountain, perhaps there's too much gravity inside there or something? I don't think we should try again until those men have passed us by, or they will see us. Also, if they come here and we end up meeting them, they shouldn't know this is a dream because they should be dream characters created by dad's machine. So don't tell them it's a dream. Oh my word! They're coming this way!"

The men had remounted and were riding hell-for-leather straight towards the Pink Mountain. Tamarin cleared his throat and began calling out at regular intervals; "My lady! Meekhi, it is I, TAMARIN!"

There was no response to his calls and he pressed his horse to a flat out gallop. Birds squawked away from trees as the riders pounded towards the mountain, leaving a trail snaking out behind them in their wake.

The children sensed that they were not going to avoid a meeting with these dangerous looking men on horseback, and Zowie pointed out, "Look, the one at the front seems to be looking for someone called Mickey and they're doing something about his eye tomorrow, that lot look pretty dangerous to me, I say we hide. If

Mickey is around here somewhere he'll answer them, or they will find him, and then, hopefully, they will bugger off."

The plan to hide was readily accepted and they slipped behind a tall piece of pink crystal jutting out of the mountainside. Bunched up, they were invisible to view from below. A little nervous, but so excited to be having this amazing adventure, they huddled close together, grinning at this bizarre predicament and resisting the urge to giggle.

Tamarin slipped from his horse as they reached the foot of the magical mountain. In deference to their special location the entire troop of men, including the king, bowed their heads momentarily to honour this sacred place. Tamarin scanned the towering peak and again his voice boomed out, "MEEKHI! RAMULET! MERCY! It is TAMARIN!"

Thomas whispered, "I think this guy is a bit twisted. He wants this Mickey person badly, and is harping on about omelettes without mercy tomorrow! I'm glad we're hiding, girls. He's a proper nutter! Uncle Dug's crazy humour just cracks me up totally!"

They could no longer refrain from giggling at Dug's surreal adventure game, chortling quietly to themselve's whilst hidden safely behind the outcrop, high up the mountainside.

The Samarians formed a crescent around the base of the mountain and, with great agility, began to climb it methodically. Calls of, "My queen," and, "My lady," filled the air. Only Tamarin called out to Meekhi by name. The children very soon realised that they would eventually be discovered, within half an hour at most.

"Crap!" Zowie hissed, "We're going to get sussed out. If we're hiding they will think we are guilty of something. It's probably best to just face them. It's only a dream after all, and this meeting may be a good thing. Shall we introduce ourselves? I think we should."

The Shortwaters looked far from convinced, but when Lauren finally agreed, Thomas, not wanting to look afraid, was also up for it. Feeling a little nervous, they clambered out from behind their screen and stood in a row, looking down at the men down below who were climbing all over the pink shale surface, calling out as they did so. They were looking left and right, but not too far above them as they would reach those heights in due course. Zowie noticed that one of the men was wearing a very slim band of silver on his head. She correctly assumed this was the leader, and called down to him, "Hey! How are you today? Lovely weather for a ride in the country! Can we come down and stroke your horses?"

Thomas frowned, "Doh! *Stroke your horses??*"

Tamarin's triblade was out in a flash, he stood looking up the mountain at what appeared to be three strangely dressed children staring back down at him. He sheathed the deadly weapon, but kept his hand on the hilt. The guardsmen were now standing upright, also looking up at the children that seemed to have appeared from nowhere. In a hushed voice Tamarin ordered his men to encircle the strangers, and they began to discreetly move up the mountain again. He stood tall and threw his cloak over his shoulder revealing his gleaming breastplate and armour. He tossed his long hair away from his face and took a few big steps up the slope. He was now very clearly visible to the children and they saw him calling to them, "Who are you? How dare you toy with the mountain of dreams," His voice boomed up to them, making them jump and quite afraid, "I am Tamarin, Lord of Samaria. I seek Lady Meekhi and her escorts. I ask you again—who are you? Are you the Guilty Innocents? Speak now, lest we have to encourage you!"

"Oh shit!" The children exclaimed in unison.

Zowie told the others, "Let me handle this, he knows the mountain is in a dream. He called it the mountain of dreams. This may not be a dream we're stuck in, guys! Let's just see what happens."

Lauren was more composed. "*He's* certainly a dream, Zee. Just look at him! He's so properly fit."

Zowie laughed under her breath, agreeing he was very attractive. Thomas was not so impressed. "Typical. We are facing an omelette eating maniac with a three bladed sword, and you two fancy him! *Can we come and stroke your horses??* Oh please. I think this dream is fast becoming a nightmare."

Zowie gathered up every ounce of maturity she could muster in her young voice and hollered back down the mountain, "My name is Zowie, and we don't know anyone called Mickey. We are not guilty of anything, we are innocent of everything! Where exactly are we, anyway?"

Tamarin stopped for a second, allowing his men to gain height above the children and encircle them. They noticed, too late, that they were now surrounded by these handsome, sun-bronzed warriors.

Lauren piped up, "I think we should let them capture us! They have nice faces and I don't think they'll hurt us. I quite fancy being captured by them actually, this really is a brilliant dream."

"Oh my giddy aunt! Give it a rest, sis'." Thomas did not like the look of those big swords at all.

Zowie looked on, waiting for a reply from the tall one standing directly below her.

"Bring them down!" He ordered his men, adding, "Watch them carefully."

He looked up again at these strangely clad youngsters. For certain they had uttered the words 'guilty' and 'innocent', but could these really be that which Meekhi had come in search of? Besides, where on earth was she, and the others too?

The men closed quickly on the children and the girls instinctively clasped their hands over their heads, as prisoners of war might do in our own world. They were trapped—a ring of armed men surrounded them with deadly looking blades pointed directly at them. "Move carefully and slowly down the mountain." One of them told them, "If thou hast touched a single hair upon Lady Meekhi's head, today will be your last, of that I assure you."

Thomas watched the girls standing with their hands on their heads, he was not about to get pushed about by some character from an artificial dream, so he faced the man that had ordered them to move, "Don't you point that big pointy thing at *me*, mate! This is a dream and I can fly away, so tough luck, macho man! Follow me, girls!" Shouting, "Up! up and awaaay!" he leapt up about three feet into the air, hung there for half a second, and then promptly crashed back to earth to begin tumbling down the mountainside towards Tamarin. He could be heard shouting warnings as he rolled, "Don't try to fly! Uff! Ouch! It doesn't work! OUCH!"

Tamarin watched the boy rolling and tumbling directly towards him and stopped him dead, with his leather boot. He lay huffing and puffing with Tamarin's foot on his chest, he was covered from head to foot in pink dust. The girls then began a headlong charge downhill to see if he was ok. The guardsmen pursued them closely, with everyone skidding and slipping on the small, brittle shards of crystal, crunching underfoot.

Tamarin looked down at the wide-eyed boy under his boot. The lad looked so very odd with his hair having been cut short and the strange garments he wore, but he seemed to have an honest, perhaps even honourable-looking, face. Then the girls arrived in a flurry of dust and rocks, nearly trampling the boy as they fought to stop themselves quickly on the steep, slippery slope. They stood staring at him, and he stared back. These were not very young children as he had first thought, they were, in fact, on the cusp of adulthood. The girls had a natural beauty akin to his own native womenfolk. He appraised Zowie first, with her gleaming dark hair and intelligent hazel eyes. The contrast reminded him a little of his Meekhi. Then there was Lauren, her honey coloured curls in disarray, and those dark eyes giving nothing away. But he would have the truth from these strangers, for Meekhi must be found. "Where is my lady? Where is Meekhi? Are you the Guilty Innocents of which the table spoke?"

Thomas groaned, "Flippin' heck! We've got *talking tables* now!" Then, in a louder voice, "Look, mate, take your hefty great boot off me. I think you should know I can cook fantastic omelettes, and, if you treat us properly, I might cook one for you. For your information we don't know any Meekhi or Mickey, or anyone else that sounds like that."

Tamarin was unimpressed. He was not in the habit of being talked to like that by anyone, let alone this strange looking young man. He reached down, and taking Thomas by the scruff of the neck, hoisted him high into the air, "What manner of creature are you? You throw yourself down a mountain to offer me an omelette?? Mind your tongue, lest you find yourself without one!"

At this sudden threat the children became instantly aware that their dream of flying had gone very, *very,* askew. If this was a dream, then it was not one created by Zowie's father, as he would never have allowed Thomas to be threatened with having his tongue removed. Of course Tamarin would never have carried out his threat. Samarians loved children and adored their childish ways for reasons we have heard of earlier in this book. But he was looking for Guilty Innocents, and he had to be sure these three posed no threat to his people or lands before he could lower his guard with them. He had guessed straight away by looking at Thomas that here was someone that was not easily made afraid, and perhaps a little too daring for his own wellbeing. His eyes searched over the two girls looking for signs of character. Finally, his eyes fell fixed on those of Zowie. She held his gaze without challenge or provocation, but also without fear. He spoke to her kindly, but firmly, leaving no doubt as to the truth of his words, "You that call yourself Zowie, who are you? What are you doing here? Why are you at the Pink Mountain? I can see you are not Samarian, yet you have the look of warrior children. Where are you from? Have you seen Lady Meekhi, or her escorts? Do not lie to me, little one, these are pressing matters and I have neither patience, nor time, for falsehoods. Speak."

The children sheepishly swapped glances. They could not believe this was happening, and yet there they were—the three of them in this strange world, stuck on the side of a pink mountain, surrounded by men carrying huge three-bladed swords. Zowie decided it was best to come clean about how they got there. Lauren, watched over by the guardsmen, was busy dusting Thomas down because he looked so garish covered in pink dust. Zowie took a deep breath, she felt it was the deepest breath she had ever taken in her life. Then, being as worried as a young woman of that age, in that situation, could ever be, she began to tell of how she came from another world via the use of a machine invented by her father. She felt quite ridiculous as she told the whole fantastical story. Tamarin kept his eyes locked on hers as she spoke and she felt that if she should trust anyone in this strange world in which they now found themselves, then she must trust this man. He had an air of great integrity about him as well as his obvious physical power. Just the sight of him was enough to convince her of his martial prowess, but his eyes held a twinkle that hinted at a much softer, kinder heart, than that implied by the fearsome weapons he carried. It was taking her ages to tell her story as her mouth had become parched in the baking heat, and she kept stopping, her dry throat forcing her to cough. Tamarin raised his brow, "Water." and a man disappeared up the mountain, returning a few minutes later with a helmet full of emerald green liquid. Tamarin asked of him, "*Water from the source of the Emerald River*? Indeed it is closer than returning to the horses at the foot of the mountain, but this is no ordinary refreshment you are offering here, my friend. These are not Samarians to whom you give such service."

Bowing his head, the man replied; "My lord, if thou wouldst have me fetch water from the horses I would not hesitate to retrieve it, but these strangers, the dark haired maiden in particular, appear *almost* Samarian to me. I felt it would do no harm, and their need is pressing. If I am mistaken, the fault will lie with me."

Tamarin smiled at his fellow countryman, "There will be no fault I'm sure. Womenfolk, be they friend, or, stranger, shall never have cause to fear poor treatment at Samarian hands, I stand corrected, your choice is a wise one."

He passed the upturned helmet to Zowie. "Drink then, if you are truly innocent, little one. But, beware, if you are not. This water is the life blood of our lands. It may not agree with any enemy of Samaria, and certainly will not sit well with the unjust."

She took the water, and with Thomas warning her, "Don't drink it! Its had someone's sweaty head in there!"

She lifted the upturned helmet to her lips and took a drink. The ice cold liquid slipped down her throat as nothing had ever done before. It was odourless and tasted sweet. She could not believe just how refreshed and invigorated it made her feel. "WOW!"

She exclaimed, before gulping down the lot. The Shortwaters looked her up and down, waiting to see what happened next. They thought her eyes looked brighter than ever, and her skin seemed to somehow glow. Thomas turned meekly to Tamarin. "Can I have some, please? I'm gagging for a drink, my sister too."

Tamarin nodded to his men and more went to fetch water as he turned back to Zowie and told her to continue her story.

Zowie felt so alive. The glittering liquid emerald seemed to have made her stronger, braver, and less nervous. She knew her story must sound ridiculously far fetched to these kind of people, but she told it honestly anyway. She had expected the crowned warrior to burst into laughter, and maybe lop off her head, but instead, he just stood there, quite still, massaging the stubble on his chin. His eyes were roving from herself to the Shortwaters, and back again. After a while, he turned on his heels and began to walk back down the mountainside towards the horses. The guardsmen gave the children a nudge and they found themselves following him.

At the foot of the mountain, Tamarin studied the children for ages before speaking. His piercing gaze made them very nervous, as if he was examining their very souls. Birds were squawking above them in the clear blue sky, and they felt that they were being laughed at by these men. Although nothing could have been further from the truth. The one fact that gave them the most comfort and reassurance was that they weren't actually there. This was some problem with the Dream Machine, an unforeseen glitch, and as the timer was set for an hour, they would eventually wake up safe and sound inside that big glass globe. But when Tamarin finally spoke, he did so in such an honest and earnest tone, that the children could not help taking to him. Lauren and Zowie, in particular, were very impressed by this handsome warrior-king.

He began, "Ancient lore tells us of your worlds, little ones. Yours is the world that may well die young due to the apathy of man. Nature herself, legend says, will remove the blight of man from the surface of your world, so that which she created in the beginning may yet endure into the future. The tales tell of mighty machinations wrought from iron and steel. Monsters created to serve man's hunger, his desire to consume everything. But his appetite remains unfulfilled, his avarice not easily assuaged. Yet also…," Tamarin dropped to the sand, kneeling to relieve his aching back before carrying on, "Yet also…ancient scriptures tell of one warrior, one lone spirit, that may one day come and save your world from annihilation." He took a swig of warm water from a gourd, gargled, and spat it out, then continued, "You *are*, truly, the Guilty Innocents. It is you I have come to seek out I am sure, as well as finding my Meekhi."

The children thought to say they had not committed any wrong deeds, but wisely remained silent. Tamarin took a long breath, "All life, in all worlds, lives in balance, in harmony—a status quo. Dreams are not for man to control, nor can any man choose their nature. Your father must surely be a great sorcerer and alchemist to have contrived such a contraption, but his wizardry has upset the natural order of things, an order governed and created by The Source. When this unholy machine was tested by your father, The Source will have felt the anomaly in the fabric of life. When he engaged this machine a second time to do *your* bidding, you have been transported here to see what interfering with nature has produced. You innocent children had a wish for a dream, and it was artificially created for you. In balance, The Source must, by its own laws, allow a being that is not innocent an equal wish. I see now that that violator of innocence would be Ogiin, and his wish would be the opposite of yours. For, without a doubt, that heartless demon would wish not a dream, but, a nightmare!"

A cold chill ran down the spines of the children at the mention of Ogiin. Each was staring at the others—inexplicable panic in their eyes. Finally, Lauren spluttered, "Well, that is as clear as mud I can tell you, Mr Tomatorind, but what does all that mean for *us*?"

Tamarin rose to his feet, "I know not what it means for you, or for any of us, little one. But I do believe you are all innocent of knowingly committing any wrong-doings against my realm, or my people. You may join us if you wish, and if you care not to, then you are free to do as you please. I can offer you safe conduct

back to Sitivia—our first city. But first I must find my lady. Let me make something clear to you now, so we do not make any future mistakes—I am Lord *Tamarin*, and my queen is Lady *Meekhi*. You will refer to us as such in future, or there will be consequences..."
His eyes came to rest on Thomas as he finished his sentence, but his look remained friendly. He turned to his men, "Food and water for these travellers between worlds. Swiftly, my friends, my lady and her escorts are yet to be found. You—Arcadian, you tend to the little ones. The rest of you fan out. We must encircle the mountain to find Meekhi. Make haste, if these little ones have been here for some time as they say they have, and I believe they have, then where is she? She should have arrived here before us, or we should have overtaken her en route. I fear for her wellbeing and want her found, NOW!"

The children welcomed lumps of bread and cheese from a particularly well-muscled man named Arcadian. He seemed friendly enough, but he did not say much. Munching on the delicious, strong flavoured, cheese, they watched the guardsmen start to search the Pink Mountain for their missing queen. It was obvious to them that this Tamarin loved his queen immensely. They weren't sure of what exactly he had tried to explain to them earlier, but it seemed prudent to leave questions until later given his pressing desire to find this Meekhi quickly, and the dexterity with which he handled that monster of a sword was not easily forgotten. The name 'Ogiin' kept playing on each of their minds and it did nothing to calm their nerves. It was a horrible name, and one that they sensed belonged to something as equally horrible, they hated it. Even thinking of it made them feel cold, clammy, and hollow, inside. Wherever they were, and whatever Tamarin had tried to explain to them, they were stuck with it for now, so best just to get on with it, and, as Lauren and Zowie kept reminding each other, Tamarin *was* extremely good looking.

After an hour of exhaustive searching the men came back to the horses, worn out and finally succumbing to the need for water and food. Tamarin had had the presence of mind to bring along extra horses from Sitivia for carrying additional supplies. As the men rested on the warm sun-baked ground and began chomping through their food, Tamarin came and sat with the children. He could see that these young ones meant him, and his, no harm. This father of Zowie's had inadvertently upset the balance of nature, and now these three were here in Samaria. Not of their own choice, but somehow linked to this imbalance, and here all the same. He could not be of any real service to them as yet as there was still the matter of the missing queen to deal with, not to mention the goings on in the Western Worlds. But these little ones were showing remarkable fortitude given their shocking predicament. He decided that whilst the men took their break for vitals, he would try to ease the minds of the young ones somewhat, and also, perhaps gain any information from them that might assist him. He did not know much of these other worlds from whence they had travelled—only the most ancient of writings spoke fleetingly of them. He had been watching them for a while and thought—what an amazing period of time childhood was. But Tamarin was no fool, Ogiin was undoubtedly afoot somewhere and it would not be wise to trust anyone, or anything, on face value. He had to bide his time and allow the matter to unfold.

Sitting opposite the children, he raised a wineskin to his lips (the warm water in the skins had become stale and tasted disgusting, it would no doubt lead to sickness, so wine was the only other option) and took a long haul, gulping down several refreshing mouthfuls of the rich, red beverage. He reached out and offered some to the children, behaviour that was quite normal in Samaria regarding young adults. Zowie gripped the floppy skin at the neck, "When in Rome, do as the Romans do." She said, and took one big gulp of the strong wine. "Oooh! That's very strong stuff, guys." She coughed, wrinkling her face in a very peculiar manner.

The other two laughed at her, Tamarin too. Bracing himself, Thomas took a drink and the others watched his face also creasing up. Lauren took her turn last, the wine was smooth, and a touch spicy, slipping down their throats easily, warming their stomachs. They felt their faces flushing and heard Tamarin say, "Perhaps that is enough wine for now, eh, young travellers?"

They nodded gratefully as the colour of their faces began to slowly return to normal. Tamarin asked questions of their home world, and though they answered him truthfully, he found nothing that helped him find any other reason for the return of Ogiin, he surmised the children were being totally honest with him, they had no reason to lie or make any pretence. The Talking Table had advised him of their presence, so they must yet have a role to play in this new chapter of his kingship. But now, he thought, he simply must find Meekhi. His men were so very tired and he decided two hours rest would have to be allowed. They were riding horses of the non-winged variety and these beautiful animals did not have the strength or endurance of their winged counterparts. Meekhi was not at the Pink Mountain. The children had not seen or heard anyone here so it must be that she had failed to arrive at her destination. Therefore, this must mean something had gone a wry on her journey, and as his group had not come across the missing trio en route to the Pink Mountain, this left three possible options. First, they had disappeared into thin air by some strange magic, possible, but unlikely. Secondly, they had come to harm in Soledad, this was more likely, but as Meekhi had given her word of honour to not venture there, she would not have done so unless forced to by grave circumstances. Thirdly, and most likely he thought, was that they had taken the shorter route through the Desert of Iret to save time, foolhardy, yes, but a brave, and courageous, choice. Yes, this must be the cause of them not showing up at the Pink Mountain.

Tamarin shuddered at the thought of Meekhi lost within Iret, and he felt a cold sweat break out across his back. He knew in depth the dreadful legend of Iret, of the treacherous witch—Teritee, of how she had seduced the heart of Lord Amaris and gained his trust. Amaris had pledged himself to her believing her to be a true Samarian whom he had met, by chance, at a dance. But a million seeds of darkness filled her black heart, and her allegiance lay with Ogiin and his creed. The pair had dwelled in apparent happiness for some many years until her treachery and deceit had come to light. Her false beauty had disappeared in the pure light of truth, and to hide her now sagging chins, her decayed, rotten, body, and her poisonous soul, she had run away from Soledad to evade capture. Many believe she had intended to hide out forever in the Gardens of Paradise that flowered not too far away, a bountiful oasis in the middle of the desert. She planned to continue sustaining her wretched soul by seducing travellers that stopped there to rest, absorbing their spirits to feed her own. But Lord Amaris, upon discovering her betrayal of Samaria, of King Darcinian, and of himself, hunted her down. He caught up with her deep amidst the lavish fruits and lush foliage of the Gardens of Paradise. Legend said her scream was heard as far as Sitivia when the triblade of Amaris cleaved open the witch's skull, severing her into two halves. Since then Amaris had not been seen again, and thus, was now often referred to as the 'Lost Lord'. The severed corpse of Teritee had bled for days. The tortured souls and broken hearts that she had thrived upon for so long had become part of her very being. Her broken body, sliced asunder by Amaris, gushed thick black blood in quantities beyond imagining, she had been that full with the souls of those she had consumed that the air had become saturated in their wailing. King Darcinian had ordered that the Gardens of Paradise be cordoned off as a black slick oozed and belched from the witch, spreading ever wider, killing all it touched like a plague. It soaked deep into the rich fertile soil of the gardens, destroying them. The entire area became devoid of life within days. Over time, tales began to emerge of illusions, false images misleading travellers that ventured through there. Some claimed to have heard a witch's hysterics in the area. Samarians generally gave the place a wide berth, but in memory of the great Lord Amaris the former gardens were not buried under piles of stones. It became known as The Desert of Iret ('Iret' being the Samarian word for 'lies'), and now feared Tamarin, Meekhi was probably lost within its venomous veil.

The wine, coupled with the warm evening, had taken its toll on the children, and they were huddled together, asleep in a semi-sitting position with their backs propped up against a saddle roll. It was an unpleasant surprise for them when they were poked and prodded awake by guardsmen telling them it was time to get underway. Lauren told the others, "This dream is seriously messed up you know. Who sleeps in a dream? I was dreaming I was on a date with Tamarin, and I was just *loving* it, I can I tell you."

"Yeah, in your dreams!" laughed Zowie.

Tamarin was soon on the scene and asking why they were laughing, and of course they apologised because they could not explain themselves. He noticed that the girls were blushing. Thomas watched his sister and Zowie coyly eyeing him up, and said what he felt was needed to be said, "Oh, for god's sake, give it a rest."

CHAPTER NINE

THE WITCH—TERITEE

Ramulet opened his eyes slowly. His head was pounding and he was looking at what appeared to be the ceiling of some sort of cavern. He managed to get to his feet and shook his head to try and clear his blurred vision. Above him there was no indication as to where he had fallen from. A seamless ceiling of red rock lay overhead. The dazed guardsman leaned back against a roughly hewn wall to support himself and gain his bearings. He was in a large underground cavern, and if he had fallen from the ceiling above him, then he had fallen a very long way. He checked his body for any broken bones but, mercifully, there were none. He ached all over from the force of the impact. The floor of the cavern was paved with large, square slabs of stone, they appeared to have been shaped by a skilled mason. The air he was breathing should have been cold and musty, but it was warm and clean. He could smell the unmistakeable scent of a wood fire burning, though such a thing was not in sight. As his senses settled a little after having banged his head so severely, the captain realised that he was not in a deserted cavern, but more in a home, of sorts. There was furniture dotted about, a bench seat covered in hide the colour of which was mottled—patches of black merging with a dark red, a strangely carved wooden table upon which sat assorted decanters and bottles—filled to varying degrees with liquids and potions of differing colours. Directly across from him the ceiling sloped down towards the floor, but stopped six feet shy. In this confined space, between the sloping ceiling and the floor, there stood a large bed. It was crudely constructed from old timbers and covered in shabby looking silks. It gave him the shudders. He unsheathed his mighty sword, just in case. Knowing he could not trust his eyes buried so deep inside the rancid belly of Iret as he was, he took a few seconds to take stock of his situation. Yet, it all looked so very real to him. Exploiting his lifetime of training, he scanned the room carefully, his mind carving the space into sections, absorbing all the detail in each segment before moving on to the next.

The air had a strange fragrance to it, womanly, yes, but by no means feminine or sensual, more a feline kind of scent, mildly seductive and musky, but also beguiling. Truly a mask of a scent that withheld well its true purpose, it was too refined, too concocted, to occur by mere coincidence. The room was well lit with a pale yellow light, but he could not see the source of this illumination.

His senses were tingling and he fought desperately to overcome the grogginess caused by the fall. His back and limbs were tender to the touch and he knew he must be covered in bruises under his garments. In fact it was most likely his chain mail that had saved him from more serious injury. Treading as gingerly as he could with his head still pounding, Ramulet moved quietly into the centre of the cavern. He could see that the cave was the lower loop of a 'U' shaped tunnel. The walls curved away from him to the left and right, with both exits apparently heading in the same direction, parallel to each other. He took a few steps to the left and sniffed at the air, then to the right, tasting the air again. The smell of burning wood was definitely coming from the right. A fire meant someone had to have lit it, and this person, or persons, must know a way up to the daylight. He needed to get back on the surface immediately—his queen and Mercy were in dire need of his sword. His throat was as dry as a discarded desert boot, and he crept up to the strange table littered with bottles. He had hoped to find water, but they smelled really quite revolting and had the air of alcohol and alchemy about them. His wisdom got the better of his thirst and he left the table as he had found it. "Witch's brews, no doubt." he thought to himself, spitting at the collection of bottles and jars. He began cautiously edging out of the subterranean chamber towards the smell of burning wood.

Ramulet crept stealthily along the wall, and the more distance he put between himself and that strange scent the faster his head cleared. Maybe there were fumes rising from those bottles that had exaggerated his headache. Dim, low burning torches, were hung at even intervals along one wall, and as he left the cave into which he had fallen, he found that the tunnel into which he was creeping was far gloomier. The torches struggled to offer any real light at all, and little pools of dirty yellow flickered weakly on the solid rock walls, vaguely punctuating the darkness of the tunnel. It was quite cold here, and the Samarian was grateful for his warm cloak. The floor seemed to be paved just as the previous room had been, and Ramulet was grateful for this as an earthen floor of loose dirt would be far more difficult to negotiate quietly. His sword at the ready, he moved steadily forwards. Ahead, at the end of the tunnel there appeared to be a brighter light, brighter than in the previous room. Daylight! He hoped with all his heart, Meekhi and Mercy on his mind. He smiled, thinking, "So, there really *is* light at the end of the tunnel!"

But Ramulet was to be disappointed. As he approached the end of the tunnel it was clearly not daylight he was seeing. The glow, though constantly bright, ebbed and flowed, and this, coupled with the strong smell reaching him, told him he had found the location of the wood fire. Stepping silently from the adjoining tunnel into the firelight, Ramulet stood still for a few seconds to give his eyes time to adjust. He again took stock of his situation, and what a situation it was. Another cave faced him. It was not as cavernous as the previous one, but it was sizeable none the less. The circular floor was covered from wall to wall in a plush red rug, and a hearty log fire blazed in a hearth carved into the wall opposite. The smoke seemed to be rising away from the logs, being carried up through the dense rock above them. To his left, a large, shabby old wooden chest, stood against the wall. It was covered in dozens of candlesticks, each a different size or shape. All the candles were alight and added their honest brilliance to the warm orange glow of the fire. To his right, a stone shelf had been hewn from the wall, and it was covered in jars, they appeared to be of the sort used to hold wine, or other intoxicating brews. A big, ornate glass jug, filled with water, stood in the centre, and, despite the close atmosphere of this heated cave, that water gave the distinct impression of being icy cold. Directly in front of this, in the centre of the room, was a small, white marble table, and it seemed to somehow not fit in with the rest of the place. It was too small, seemingly lost in the middle of that large red floor. The only thing adorning the table was a small but exquisitely detailed dagger, resting in its sheath on a black ebony stand. It was incredibly beautiful and he felt a strong urge to retrieve it, but held his ground. He could see no other way out from this room, perhaps he should have taken the other tunnel. Tapestries and rugs covered much of the walls, making the smaller cave feel very snug indeed. It had taken him only a few seconds to absorb the general detail of the room, just as it had taken only seconds to see the backless, blue suede couch standing beyond the table, in front of the hearth. Since he had crept into the room he had not taken his eyes off that couch, or off the woman that lay so provocatively upon it.

Ramulet stood spellbound. The woman was nothing short of breathtaking. She was not tall like Samarian women, but neither was she overly short. She lay along the length of the couch, dressed skimpily in vibrant, violet attire. He had never seen such garments in all his days. The purple material was so sheer, entirely transparent. Her clothing consisted of a thin gold torc at her neck and a belt of the same colour and design. Two wisps of material ran from the torc at her throat to the torc at her waist, bracing her firm, ample bosom. Two more lengths ran from the torc at her waist along her shapely legs to her ankles, where they fastened to delicate gold bracelets, nothing was left to the imagination. Fine sandals, adorned with tiny jewels, wrapped her feet. Her skin was pale, and her hair a sea of glossy, russet-and-chestnut, waves. She had a youthful figure, but her eyes spoke of intimate knowledge gained over many, many, years of experience. Big, cold blue eyes, stared back at the Samarian, eyes that gave no hint of surprise or alarm. Ramulet was suddenly consumed by an intense thirst. His throat was bone dry and he desperately eyed the jug of water on the shelf.

"Drink, sweet Ramulet," The woman on the couch cooed at him, "I see you are in sore need of refreshment."

Her voice was like music in his ears, at once seductive, and disarming, tinkling sensually from her pouting lips like droplets of crystal. Slowly, tantalisingly, she slipped her elegant legs from the couch and placed both her feet, side-by-side, on the deep pile rug. "I see you, too, have become trapped beneath the blistering desert. *Drink*, Ramulet, a warrior must keep up his strength, and you really are so wonderfully strong. I have never seen such muscles, such power, and so handsome too! I was warming myself by the fire. Here, come sit with me." She patted the couch beside her irresistibly, "Rest your weary limbs, my beautiful Samarian."

Ramulet found her voice slipping, sliding, oozing down his ears like warm oil of olive, filling his whole head with a sudden calm, a desire to rest. He raised his sword, and pointing it at the lovely stranger, he demanded answers; "Who are you? Where am I, and how do I return to the surface? Are you real, or an illusion? Beware, lady, this blade will dispatch both equally well!"

She rose slowly, keeping her womanly charms in full view of Ramulet who felt himself flush at the sight of her. She was standing facing him directly, her stance warm and welcoming, seductive rather than sinister.

"So, Ramulet," came her voice, warming his gut like mulled wine, "You wish me harm? But we have just met! Why would you bear malice against one so helpless such as I? It is only that I am enthralled by you! Why should this offend you? You are the dashing Captain of the Royal Guards, are you not? Perhaps we could become friends? *Close* friends if you'd like, perhaps more…? I know I would enjoy that very much. You must be so very thirsty, you look parched my mighty warrior?"

Ramulet found himself in a very peculiar and uneasy situation. His thoughts were clear, and yet he could not think clearly. He knew not to trust this irresistibly enticing vision. Just as equally, he knew not to touch anything she offered him, or to believe a word she said. Most of all, he knew his heart belonged to Mercy, and yet he could not deny wanting this slithering nymph clad in violet silks.

Samaria

Every time he tried to say something, or formulate a sensible course of action, his mind became confused. All the right sentences were on the tip of his tongue, but in the wrong sequences. He remained motionless, helplessly staring at the bared beauty displayed before him. Again that silky voice called to him, "Ramulet, please... come sit with me and take some water, for I see your face is so flushed. You *must* rest. Maybe some wine, if you would prefer?"

    She was now standing but an arms length from him, and he could not remember how she had got so close. He couldn't help being drawn in by her bold, brazen, nudity, his eyes unable to resist roving over her fabulous form, and he was becoming intoxicated with that strange musky scent, the fragrance permeating his mind, subduing his will. She reached out and ran a pale, slender finger down his arm, tracing the outline of his bulging muscles. "So strong, my warrior captain," She purred as her hand moved to his face and the other slipped inside his tunic to stroke his powerful chest. "I am very real, I assure you, my beautiful Samarian." She was whispering in his ear as she stroked back his hair, "I am a survivor like you, and I'm so glad you have come to me, my Ramulet. I, too, am trapped here. I have longed for one as pure and noble as you to come so that I may be freed, free to return to Samaria and the sunlight above. You have strength enough to save me, I can feel it in you. The pitiful efforts of a score of lesser men have failed to release me from these wretched caves, but now I know *you* will be my true saviour. Come sit by the fire and allow me to serve you some refreshment, be at ease but for a few minutes, do I look as if I could harm you? Look upon my person well. Make close investigation and see I carry no weapons, dearest Ramulet." With that, the mysterious woman took him by the hand and began leading him to the couch by the fire.

    Ramulet's head was spinning. He couldn't help trusting this ravishing beauty, and besides, it could very well be true that this stunning young woman was trapped beneath Iret like himself. If this was so, then of course he would lead her to the surface, freeing her from this accursed cave. His eyes wondered aimlessly, almost drunkenly, about the room, and when they fell once more upon the beautiful little dagger, he blurted out, "How do you know my name, and rank?"

For a split second he thought he saw a glimmer of panic in her face, but then she answered him smoothly, confidently, keeping her eyes locked onto his, "My sweet boy, you wear the regalia of the Royal Guards of Samaria, and your mighty sword is set with the insignia of Captain. The Captain of the Royal Guards is much vaunted, and rightly so. He is the right arm, it is said, of the king himself. His name is Ramulet. Who would *not* know you on sight?"

Her answer could so easily be true, and was totally convincing to Ramulet. He breathed a small sigh of relief. The logs continued to blaze in the hearth, and he could feel the heat from the countless candles. The couch looked so comfortable and inviting, surely ten minutes to clear his head would not go amiss. The musky scent fuelled his thirst further, and just as they reached the seat, he made a request, "Water."

Her eyes beaming at him, she skipped daintily over to the array of bottles. She lifted the large jug of water as if it was weightless and poured into a large golden goblet. He watched her strut back to him, her comeliness burning deep into his masculine gut.

Ramulet found himself lying on his side along the couch, facing the hearth. He sipped at the water, which tasted sweet and was as cold as he had imagined it to be. It was such a relief to drink. In fact it tasted so good he gulped it all down and passed the goblet back to the smiling beauty sitting beside him and massaging his head, teasing out his long black hair from their restraining plait. She clapped her hands gleefully like a child and slinked across the room to fetch more water. The flames in the hearth were dancing to some strange, silent melody, hypnotising him, and he stared into them as if he might see some wonder within. He was bemused by the fact that the burning logs hissed but never cracked. Meekhi and Mercy seemed a distant memory, so far away and almost forgotten. The couch was even more comfortable than it had looked and the gorgeous creature next to him was moving her strong, soothing hands inside his tunic, kneading his aching back and running her long nails tantalisingly over his chest and stomach. "A good enough situation," he thought, "just another thirty minutes and I'll get up." His fellow prisoner, also imprisoned beneath Iret, had gained his trust, and his unreserved attention.

It did not occur to Ramulet to ask this woman her name, or how she came to be where she was. Nor did he ask how long she had been there. It was now clear to him that she was not only harmless, but she was, in fact, a blessing. Why shouldn't he enjoy this brief respite? After all, did he not do enough every single day of his life for others! Her soft, sweet caresses felt divine on his bruised body. He lay sipping the sweet water, being stroked and kneaded into an almost mindless state whereupon his own independent thoughts sailed in and out of his head without once finding anchor. That sweet heady scent became heavier as time passed, but it also seemed much more appealing, at once erotic, and exotic, giving rise to almost irrepressible stirrings within him. The hearth had been carved very deep into the rock face and the fire burned hotly in the recess, causing the heat from it to be projected directly onto the couch. The mission to the Pink Mountain was lost to Ramulet's befogged mind, as were his queen and Mercy. The couch felt soft and svelte, and he eased onto his back, allowing his sword to fall to one side. Closing his eyes he felt the warm nimble fingers of this lithe little nymph soothing his aching frame, her strange perfume lulling him minute-by-minute into a deep sleep.

Mercy felt weary and she knew the horse was also tiring as they had been doggedly making progress for some time now. She suggested a break for a little food. It was her intention to try and walk from now on. Meekhi agreed and the horse had no objections, so they stopped for a rest and some vitals. The women rummaged through a bag and found some ham. It was very dry, and perhaps too dry to chew. There was plenty of oat mash for the horse and three skins of drinkable water. They also discovered a flask of wine. The horse offered to trade some of his oats—so the women could boil them with the ham, in exchange for some wine in his mash. Laughingly the deal was done, and Meekhi lit a small fire. Fortunately she had had the foresight to bring kindling. A traveller's pot heated over the flames and as soon as the water was hot (but before it boiled) Meekhi added the oat mash with plenty of wine. Ten minutes later the horse was lapping up his burgundy coloured mash, enjoying the sensation of his stomach being warmed by the alcoholic beverage. Kneeling in the sand, Meekhi added more water to the empty pot and tossed in the pork with some oats, salt, and pepper. They were ravenous and watched the steaming pot with eager anticipation. But then the fire began to flicker, and die out.

"No! No! No!" Meekhi yelled at it. "We need more wood, quickly!"

They darted about looking for more fuel for the fire. The horse would have helped them, but he felt a little detached and sleepy at that time, the very strong wine and oats were just so tasty. No proper firewood could be found, but small black sticks, and strangely shaped twigs, littered the area, despite there being no trees or brush anywhere in sight. They thought this a little odd, but if the fuel burned, then did it really matter?

Using their cloaks to hurriedly gather up lots of small pieces of wood, they began adding them to the embers of their fading fire. It seemed reluctant at first to accept this new fuel, tiny flames licked at the black sticks, tasting them tentatively, then retreated back into the embers as if the taste was too bitter for them. But the flames returned and licked again, and again. Slowly but surely, the fire began to burn brighter. "YES!" They clapped happily. They nursed the little fire until it reached high enough to start boiling the water in the pot, thus readying their meal. Horribly thick, black smoke poured and spat from the burning sticks, spiralling into the dismal sky in a thin black column. Meekhi slapped a lid onto the pot. The horse was sitting very calmly, talking complete nonsense. Meekhi and Mercy sat down with their backs against his warm flanks, eagerly tearing strips of tender ham whilst spooning up the boiled oats. The horse, a little merry, was telling of how, in fact, he was next in line to the throne. The wine was undoubtedly very strong, and listening to the horse rambling, they very wisely had only a small taste of it.

Rordorr was becoming very concerned for Ramulet's wellbeing as there was still no sign of him, and he was fed up from walking about in this dirty desert with no sense of direction. Whenever he had heard tales of swashbuckling adventures through deserts, there was always somewhere for the horses to eat and drink. But for him? of course not. "Oh no," he thought, "Rordorr not only has to look for Ramulet whilst parched with thirst, but he has to do it with two skins full of water, and a bag of mash, strapped to his back and out of his own reach!"

He could have said it was a cruel twist of fate to make him suffer thus, but he didn't say it. He accepted the situation for what it was, after all if he did not have bad luck, he would have no luck at all! As always, he decided to take the most positive view—if he was going to die in the desert, he would most probably just pass out, feeling no pain when the buzzards ate him alive as he left this world.

The impregnable wall of mist that had prevented their earlier retreat had completely disappeared, and now there was nothing but dreary desert in all directions. Meekhi and Mercy had vanished from view some time ago, leaving supplies for Ramulet with Rordorr. The harsh, lumpy sand, was unpleasant to walk on, it felt dirty, leaving one feeling soiled as one lifted one's foot (or hoof) from it, akin to when one steps into something foul and smelly. Such was the inherent nature of Iret. The air tasted contaminated when breathed in, feeling thick and toxic in the lungs. "No doubt," thought the horse, "I shall contract something quite revolting and intensely painful, to then die here alone, my bare bones the only testament to my existence, how ignominious a death for a flying horse of Samaria, but not unexpected, given *my* luck." He had no idea how long it had been since the women had left and he couldn't even gauge time by the suns, moons, or the stars, as there were none that he could see, and even if there had been such things, he could not know if they were real, or more lies of Iret. Rordorr fervently hoped that Meekhi and Mercy had escaped Iret and reached the Pink Mountain safely. The sand seemed to be getting hotter and hotter, though it was impossible to say if this was due to the heat of the day, or for some other reason.

Samarian horses have hooves far more sensitive than non-Samarian horses. The shoes fitted to Rordorr's hooves were made of a lightweight metal forged by skilled blacksmiths. A Samarian horse had to choose whether or not it wanted to be shod. Some preferred not to be despite their sensitivity, and let nature take its course. Others, such as Rordorr, preferred to be shod. But every Samarian earned their keep (or horseshoes, as the case may be), and a horse wanting shoes to protect its hooves would probably work for the blacksmith for a month or so, to pay for the making of the shoes and the consequent fitting of them.

The ground was definitely getting much hotter and Rordorr could feel it through his shoes. The gritty sand was hard and compacted, so he felt the full weight of his large winged body with every step. He could hear his own breathing was making a strange rasping sound, as if his lungs were made of leather. Looking around, he knew there was no foreseeable respite from this, but he refused to abandon the captain. He started moving slowly in what he believed to be concentric circles. If he did this in ever widening loops, he would cover a large area without missing anything. The horse hoped to catch sight of Ramulet, but deep inside he felt the likelihood of achieving this was very remote. He was a horse of some many years and he had heard enough about this poisonous place to know that survival within Iret could easily test one beyond one's limit of endurance.

Unbeknown to the desperately searching horse, the constant jostling of the supplies tied upon his back was causing something to happen. A long curved knife with a dragon inset into the handle, had come free of its sheath, and was now chaffing back and forth across the main retaining strap in time with the horse's movements. Rordorr nearly stumbled and fell when suddenly the heavy weight bound to him slipped suddenly to the desert sands. The beautiful black horse trotted back to the fallen packs, his eyes falling immediately upon a skin full of water. Placing a big hoof firmly on the neck and using his large square teeth, he pulled out the cork, easing his hoof slowly down the skin, applying just enough pressure to allow the water to flow steadily into his waiting mouth. He was very happy indeed to find that it was still cool enough to drink, slurping and sucking at the bottle neck until it was dry. There was one full skin remaining, but he would save that one for Ramulet, or, for eternity. His aching throat lubricated at last, he looked up, and in the not too far distance he saw a thin finger of black smoke rising up towards the sky.

It was time to make firm decisions, he thought. In this land of lies one could not rely on anything except oneself. The smoke in the distance may not be real, more likely it was a trap to lure him into quicksand where he would rot and fester for days before sinking to a gruesome death, but it was at least something he could physically see, and he could use it to gain a sense of direction. It was his only choice, and he decided to investigate it. Taking the severed strap of the pack in his mouth, he began to make for the thin column, dragging the supplies along with him. He fanned his heated flanks with his enormous red wings as he trotted across the baking sands.

Meekhi and Mercy felt good, their stomachs full, they had nearly dozed off to sleep when the horse yelled out. "OUCH! My ladies, I think one of your weapons is going to pierce me! Please adjust it."

The women were rummaging about themselves looking for the offending item when Meekhi yelped, "EEK! That really hurt!"

"*What* really hurt?" inquired Mercy.

Then the horse leapt up, bowling the women over, and began jumping and bucking as if it was possessed by some awful demonic force.

"No more wine for that horse." Meekhi joked.

But then both women started crying out together, "OUCH! OUCH!!"

The three companions were leaping about thrashing their arms and legs. The area where they had been resting was teeming with what looked like very large cockroaches, hideously large brutes that seemed intent on biting them. Meekhi lanced one with the tip of her sword, and, plucking it from Mercy's thigh, she took a closer look. The disgusting black creature was nearly as long as her hand and resembled a bizarre combination of scarab beetle and cockroach. It had clearly visible bulging black eyes, but, more shockingly, it had a mouth full of equally black and very nasty looking, teeth. She tossed its dead body from the sword.

Several of the squirming bugs had attached themselves to the horse's legs and underbelly, so the women hastened to his aid. Mercy was struggling to run ably as yet, hobbling along as best she could. The fast-burrowing insects were quickly lanced and thrown far from their intended victim. They could see the horse was bleeding from the numerous bites, but, thankfully, the wounds appeared to be only superficial. They had seen that the intention of these horrible bugs was to burrow inside their prey. They were all of them in grave danger. There were hundreds of the little horrors scrambling towards them and already the trio were wholly encircled within the closing tide. Meekhi pointed with her sword; "LOOK!"

They could not believe what they were seeing. The cooking pot was still mounted above the fire, and the flames were still burning. Hundreds of the flesh eating beetles were pouring from it and scrabbling awkwardly across the red hot embers, making directly for the shocked onlookers. "By the sword!," warned Mercy, "We have *eaten* from that pot! Our quest may well be doomed if we are poisoned by Iret, but not whilst we can still breathe... and fight!"

Ignoring her ankle, she hopped around the horse, pouring thick gloopy pitch as she did so. Meekhi saw the plan immediately and set the sticky black trail ablaze. A ring of fire sprang up around the huddled threesome. The beetles could not penetrate this flame despite their fiery origins. They made a terrible din akin to the sound of a thousand rattlesnakes, but balked at crossing the scorching circle. A few of the damnable creatures attempted to scramble through, but they exploded with a loud cracking sound, their burst black bodies pinging off in all directions.

The horse's urgent plea drew the women away from the dangerous, but amusing, spectacle, "Climb onto my back, quickly, bring only your weapons."

Meekhi hurriedly helped the injured Mercy climb up and then swung up behind her. The horse reared up, as if gathering all his Samarian might, and launched himself from within the burning ring with the speed and grace of Pegasus Himself. The clattering rattle around them grew in intensity as his hammering hooves crushed hundreds of the crawling beetles. The horse kept the presence of mind to charge directly through the camp fire, sending the pot flying and trampling the flames as he bolted through. Both rider and pillion hung on desperately as he thundered across the wastelands. Eventually, some minutes later, he turned his head, "My ladies, I must rest. Forgive me, for I am spent."

He came to a stop, and it was only then that they noticed he had at least two dozen of those awful beetles still attached to him, gnawing greedily on his flesh. They immediately went to work removing them from him, each angry and upset to see those evil little insects feeding on their friend—a friend that had surely saved their lives minutes ago. They used their daggers to lance the gruesome creatures, then stamped on them to ensure they posed no more threat. The bugs exploded with a loud wet 'POP' when crushed, and this gave them and the horse a great deal of pleasure as the ground around them became littered with gooey black-and-yellow splats. After the bug-killing frenzy came to an end, Mercy asked, "Have we killed them all?"

No one replied, but everyone looked for more of them and Meekhi felt along the horses frame as Mercy smoothed down his legs. "My gratitude." The horse offered graciously. Of course they told him that it was nothing at all, and that they, in turn, were grateful to him for carrying them both to safety. Pleasantries over, they realised they had escaped the crawling nightmares at the expense of losing the tracks of the Rock Troll. The horse felt he should have stopped sooner, but both Meekhi and Mercy were happy to be as far as possible from that erupting pot. Though none made mention of it, in the back of their minds each was worried about that which Mercy had said earlier—they had each eaten from the pot which had later spewed forth the evil of Iret.

Meekhi squatted, staring blindly into the sand, She could not help feeling responsible for all of this, if only she had taken the safest route around Soledad. She was missing Tamarin so very much, even amidst this land of lies, he would know what to do, he always had a plan, a course of action. She, unfortunately, did not. True, she was a warrior-queen and did not fear Iret or the filth it contained, but should she have put her beloved friends at risk in this desert of lies? She watched Mercy trying to mask her aching ankle, and the brave horse—the legs and underbelly of whom were peppered with bloody teeth marks. The pair of them had suffered a terrible ordeal and she could not expect them to carry on much further without a decent rest. Worse yet, they now had no supplies with them at all. Despite her longing to reach the Pink Mountain, and to be far away from this accursed place—leaving not a trace of herself within it, she decided that they simply must stop awhile. The horse lay with one soft, warm wing spread over the women nestled into his side as they tried to relieve their aching bodies. Meekhi kept one eye open. She had ordered the others to sleep whilst she kept watch.

She found she could not relax at all, despite being so snug under that velvety wing. Mercy had dozed off quickly and the horse was snoring loudly. She did not know if this was down to his prolonged gallop carrying the weight of two, or due to his wine infused mash, earlier. Slipping carefully from under her feathered blanket she stood staring at the grey, bleak emptiness that surrounded them. It was enough to drive one insane not knowing what was real and what was imagined. For all she knew she could even now be standing in blazing sunshine with the Pink Mountain in sight. She was infuriated both with the desert of Iret, and with herself. Iret was merely a pack of lies infested with filth. But *she* was Queen of Samaria. She remembered her wedding day as if it was but a few hours ago. Oh! How happy she had been that day, and every day since. She recalled the moment Tamarin had placed the thin silver wisp of a crown upon her head. It was at that exact moment that she, too, was given the near-immortal lifespan of a born Samarian. This had been a magical blessing given by the Great Dragon to all, non native, kings and queens of this mystical land. If a king, or queen, of Samaria, ever wed a non Samarian for true love, then the newcomer would be granted this incredible gift so they may reign alongside their truelove for many years. During her reign Meekhi had endeared herself to her subjects, and vice versa. Her time as queen had remained unspoilt for as long as she remembered. Then, of late, disturbing rumours had begun to spring up, followed by Bestwin and Lumarr's arrival at the city gates. She had volunteered to undertake this quest, and now here she was, one wonderful companion already departed from this world, Ramulet lost—maybe worse, and her two remaining friends bleeding and hurt whilst they were all entirely lost inside this snake pit known as Iret. A single solitary tear of frustration trickled down her beautiful face. It left a thin streak on her dusty cheek as it tracked a path for itself before dripping onto her tunic. It reminded her of the dead horse and the silver mound, and she found more tears spilling over from her emerald eyes. She watched the tiny teardrops hit the ground, leaving little dark circles in the sand. Wiping at her face with her cloak, she looked again at the ground. Surely she had shed but a few tears of anguish? Yet, more and more black marks were appearing. Raising her sad face, she saw that it had started to rain. It came slowly at first, with drops of water pitter-pattering onto the ground from the steel-grey sky above. But the rain gathered momentum very rapidly.

Mercy and the horse were very quickly on their feet, having managed to have slept for nigh on an hour. The women wrapped their clothing about them tightly but, unfortunately, the poor horse had no choice but to bear the brunt of it. The light rain had become a torrential downpour, then lightening ripped the sky apart and a deluge erupted from it. Raindrops the size of a fist plummeted from above, pummelling the bedraggled trio standing out in the open without any form of shelter. For the women, each gigantic raindrop hitting their faces felt like a harsh slap, and even the horse could be seen wincing as the storm pounded into him. They were at a complete loss, there was nothing they could do to escape the awful weather. The ground quickly became waterlogged. No doubt, thought Meekhi, because Iret could not absorb anything pure or clean. Vision was reduced to no more than an arm's length. Screwing up their eyes, and with their hoods pulled down tight over their faces, the valiant women attempted to scour the area for anything they could possibly use as shelter. It was a thankless task—they had not seen anything before the downpour so it was hardly likely they would see anything now. The horse tried to act as a barrier against the rain for them, but the rain was not to be thwarted and gusted from all directions, lashing them without respite. Already they could feel the cold water beginning to seep into their boots. Meekhi stared down at the muddy black sand. Oh, how she hated Iret! She raised her sword in anger and thrust the blade down into the surface of the desert. An enormous thunderclap sounded out, rolling across the heavens and making them all jump as lightening crackled across the raging skies. The flashes of light strobing across the hilt of Meekhi's sword (a dragon carved from blue azure and hematite) made it appear to be moving, as if alive. It looked so surreal and they stared at it until another bolt of lightening, as powerful as any had ever seen, actually struck the sword as it protruded from Iret. Blue fire poured into the weapon, the dragon glowing neon-bright in the gloom. The blade was alive with the raw energy of the storm and long streaks of electricity could be seen crackling away from it across the boggy ground.

"LOOK!" Meekhi bellowed against the tempest, "What is that?"

The lightening blast hitting the sword had revealed what looked to be a dark hole in the sand, not very far away.

"We didn't see that before, my lady! Beware of illusions." Mercy hollered back.

"We must look at least, Mercy. It may be a small cave or such. COME!"

The rain seemed to be driving directly at them from everywhere as they splashed over to the large depression. "It's just a big puddle." Mercy yelled with obvious disappointment on her face.

But Meekhi was examining the pooled water more carefully, she lowered her hood, and, with the rain blasting her face, she walked right around it. Smiling, she looked up at the other two, "By, The Dragon, we are saved! This is no ordinary puddle we see, it is a troll's footprint, and it's filling with water. Look, there is another over there, and there, too! We have again found our way out of this filth. The troll must have come from this direction."

"Look! Look!" Squealed Mercy in delight, as more and more footprints became visible as they filled.

They began walking once more, flanking the horse on each side. Hope replenished, and the thought of escaping Iret filling their hearts, they struggled on against the fury of the storm. The wind picked up even further. It howled like a banshee, hurling big heavy gusts at them, trying to drive them back. No wind born of nature could change so quickly. In under a minute the high wind had become a full blown gale. Stinging sand and mud were slung at the Samarians mercilessly. The two women had to call on every iota of strength they had left to stop themselves being bowled over. The storm slammed into them with shattering violence, forcing them to a snail's pace. "This is no ordinary wind," yelled Meekhi at the top of her lungs, "this is Iret trying to prevent our escape! Remain strong, my friends—the pure heart will always prevail!"

Meekhi and Mercy were forced to pull their hoods so tight about their faces they left just a tiny slit to peep out from. Without the hoods it would have been impossible to breathe in those conditions. At last, as if exhausted, the rain eased off, leaving the troll's footprints easily visible in the sand, but the wind had reached such a frenzy that they found themselves trapped in the middle of an angry desert storm. Sand forced itself everywhere and they did not dare open their eyes more than a fraction or they would be blinded in an instant. Their clothes were caked in mud and sand, becoming heavy and slowing them even further. Meekhi emptied Mercy's quiver and stored the arrows inside her tunic. She opened the mouth of it and managed to make a makeshift shroud for the horse's snout to stop him inhaling sand. He looked quite ridiculous, but it was an effective measure. Before it was fitted he managed to say, "A pity we can not get Rordorr to wear one of these, from time to time!."

The roaring wind screamed across the wilderness, ripping into the three lonely figures battling so stoically against it. Thick mud clung to their boots and their waterlogged cloaks felt as if they were made of lead. The noise of the wind was deafening and there was no point in trying to speak. In any case, they had their hoods firmly wrapped around their faces with just their eyes peeking out and the horse had to be led by Meekhi as he could not see at all. But the trail of watery footprints was not difficult to track, and, doubled over, they plodded relentlessly in the opposite direction to where the footprints had been heading.

Was he dreaming? Ramulet sighed with pleasure, his mind in a constant state of euphoria under the ministrations of his new, nubile young friend. She was lieing beside him but he could not for the life of him recall her doing it. Besides, what did it matter? She was unarmed, and such a loving, caring creature, posed no threat. Surely he had rested only a few minutes, so a few more would not be of any consequence. She writhed against him in a manner he had never dreamed a woman to be capable of. It was as if her entire body had no joints at all, enabling her to move in an almost completely fluid manner. All his manly bumps seemed to mould perfectly into her womanly hollows and Ramulet was convinced he had never felt more comfortable in his entire life.

It vaguely dawned on him that the heady scent that filled the room came not only from this woman, but also from the logs burning so brightly in that glorious fire. She was feeding him grapes, though he could not remember her fetching them. But what grapes! Blood red and full bodied, with a translucent skin that caused the juice within to twinkle in the firelight. These tantalizing little baubles were lowered into his mouth one at a time and he could not believe how wonderful they tasted as he bit into them, their delicious nectar exploding into his mouth and drenching his tongue.

Lieing on his back, he was hypnotised by the woman's eyes. The pale blue of hers never left the deep brown of his. Her body moved on his, her hands fed and stroked him, but her *eyes* held him captivated with their bewitching allure. He looked up at the ceiling of this marvellous room. It had been carved using the very best of craftsmanship. Figures of warriors—men and women, mighty centaurs, and a flying horse, adorned the entire expanse of rock above him. The quality of the work was beyond belief and he had never seen such intricately detailed faces anywhere before. Between the figures the ceiling itself seemed to be in constant motion, so he could not see it in any real detail—an unremarkable backdrop to the truly remarkable carvings. It was rumoured, Ramulet mused to himself, that the statues within the walls of Soledad held such fine and precise detail. The thought of Soledad stirred him a little from his pleasant reverie and he made to rise to a sitting position, but a soft pale hand held him firmly on the couch. "Not yet, my wonderful warrior, you are not fully rested. Here, let me nourish those big muscles further. You can rescue me when you are stronger, and we will leave this place together. Eat now, we will need all your strength soon enough." The nymph was insistent.

Ramulet lay back once again, it was impossible to resist her voice, or her charms. She produced a large, polished red apple out of nowhere, urging him to enjoy it. It was a very big fruit and gleamed in the candlelight. He took it and held it firmly, it was such a size he could not clasp his hand around it. Staring at the enormous apple he decided he would share it with his generous host, so he sat up to carve it. She was eager to have him lie down again but he insisted on sharing the fruit. He reached around for his own knife but remembered he had let his belt slip over the side of the couch. Sitting up so suddenly had made him feel a little light headed and he shook his head to clear it. It was then that he saw the candlelight reflecting on the dagger that sat on the white marble table. The light was shining on a small silver dragon inlaid into the ivory handle. A *Samarian* dagger! It was perfect for halving the apple with, and despite his being only half dressed ("how had that happened?" he thought), Ramulet stood up, quickly fastening his garments about him. The woman leapt up from the couch, placing herself between him and the table, her sultry voice again filling his ears. "Here, sit, my Ramulet, I shall carve the fruit for us, do not trouble yourself. I...I mean... *we*, will have need of your strength later. Sit, and I shall tend to all thy needs."

But Ramulet, even in his confused state of mind, was not one to be waited on hand and foot. On the contrary, it was his Samarian nature to wait on womenfolk, not the other way around. Now that he was sitting up on the edge of the couch, he found the thick heavy odour from the fire, and from that woman, quite nauseous. His eyes narrowed, focusing on the dragon inlaid into the grip of the dagger in the middle of the room. It drew him like a powerful magnet and the sight of the silver dragon began to lift the mist from his mind—unclogging his thinking and releasing the shackles from his own freewill.

A little unsteady on his feet, he stood up, looking directly at the white marble table sitting squarely in front of him, "Lady, I know not whom you are, or how you may believe me to be. But I would have you know—I am Ramulet, Captain of the Royal Guards, loyal friend, and willing subject, of the great king, Tamarin. My sword belongs to the crown of Samaria and my heart to her that makes the blazing suns seem pale in comparison—Lady Mercy."

Hearing his own strong, but, still gentle, voice, rallied Ramulet's thoughts further towards clarity, and he felt himself suddenly awakening within. Stretching his mighty muscles he rested his hand on his sword to ensure it was again where it should always have been, then, he turned to the woman to find that she was crying. Tiny tears ran down her pale white face. "How had he not noticed her pasty bleakness of pallor before," he wondered. She was a deathly shade of white indeed. He towered before her as her watery eyes looked up at him so longingly. She seemed incredibly sad and helpless when she opened her mouth to speak, "But... but, my lord, I wish only to tend to your needs and serve you. I cannot harm you, as you can plainly see! I can give you so much pleasure, such succour, bliss beyond measure! There is no reason to be alarmed. Please, I beseech you, sit with me by the fire and tell me your wishes. I am most certain I can fulfil any desire you may have. Pray tell, what is it that you wish for?"

"I wish," He replied in a stern tone, "to take a closer look at the dagger that adorns your table! It is of my people's making, and bears the royal crest. How did you come by it, and... who exactly *are* you, my lady?"

His instincts were sharpening by the second and his fingers hovered over the grip of his blade. The 'Lady' blocked his path to the table and continued to woo him, cajoling him into sitting down and allowing her to please him.

The dragon on the dagger twinkled, winking at Ramulet in the candlelight, beckoning him, and he could not resist its calling for its lure was far greater than that of the would-be seductress standing before him. He took a step towards the table and the woman grabbed his hand, thrusting it beneath the gossamer-thin layer of silk that covered her bosom. He was firstly taken aback by the sheer strength of her grip, but also shocked by the sudden vulgarity of her actions, he had never seen such effrontery. He withdrew his hand as quick as lightening, but not before his mind had registered the fact that her body had felt ice cold to the touch. With a strong shove he sent her crashing onto the couch as he strode over to the stable. She was as agile as a cat and vaulted over the seat as she hit it, landing crouched in front of the fire, facing the Samarian, the couch now separating them. He watched her carefully as she began to prowl stealthily around it towards him. Her manner was so feline he sensed a predatory cat was facing him rather than a beautiful woman. The fire hissed and blazed behind her, casting eerie shadows that danced on the walls. Ramulet was about to pick up the dagger when to his absolute astonishment he saw the approaching woman unclip the golden torcs at her neck, waist, and ankles, revealing herself to him in total nudity as her silks floated to the ground. He froze, shocked, and yet he was still drawn by her beauty. She picked up the apple that he had dropped before and sent it sailing through the air, into the fire.

It landed amidst the smoking logs with a resounding thud and a great whoosh of bright purple and yellow flame shot up from the glowing hearth. The fire seemed to burn brighter and the room was filled with a scent not dissimilar to before, but more pungent, much more powerful. She continued to creep towards him, her crimson red lips smiling evocatively, and her eyes burning with the promise of unknown pleasures.

Ramulet would surely have stood motionless—rooted to the spot, had he not seen something flickering on the wall above the hearth, a small, bright, silver star of a light. It was the reflection from the dagger. The thought of it, of the dragon, and of his beloved Samaria, broke his hypnotic state and he barked harshly at the approaching nymph,

"Hold your distance, WENCH! What obscenity is this?! How dare you trifle with a Royal Guardsman, *Gather your garments, woman*! You insult me!"

"Ramulet," She purred at him, "why are you so angry? Have I hurt or offended you in some way? Do you not like me? Am I not pleasing to your hungry eyes?"

She raised herself so she was kneeling upright and held out her pale slender arms to the reluctant guardsman, beckoning with her hands.

"Do you like this, captain? Does mighty Ramulet prefer to fondle old relics, or, *young maidens*? Forget that ageing blade and come here to me, I shall show you pleasures you will never forget."

He had to forcibly peel his eyes from her and her obvious assets. Taking a step backwards, he looked down again at the small knife. For some strange reason he was thrilled by it and he knew he had to pick it up. Turning to the woman, who had now risen to her feet, he told her, "Do not come any closer I implore you, for I am not beyond severing that beautiful head from that delicate neck of yours. I must inspect this Samarian-forged weapon. Then we can discuss how we are to escape this accursed rat run in which we find ourselves imprisoned."

He could never have imagined what transpired next. She began to spit like some monstrous feline. Her body moved more as a cat than any woman. "You fool!" She hissed at him venomously, "You pathetic Samarians! You call yourself men, but have more interest in rusty trinkets than a beautiful woman such as I! I have known and destroyed dozens like you. Yes, Ramulet, *some even more powerful than you*! You gutless Samarians are but seasoning for my spirit!"

He was stunned to see two vertical black slits appear in her blue eyes, just like those of a cat. She growled at him in that half-purr, half-growl, that only a feline can manage. His senses reeled as he watched her perfectly manicured nails extend into long cruel claws and her teeth became as deadly as that of any big cat. Her ears became elongated, stretching to a point, and her lithe, sensual form, was now covered in a furry down the colour of rust. She was coiling her body like a spring and he could see the tension building in her legs as she readied to pounce. Spittle spotted the corners of her mouth as her lips curled back to snarl at him. "Ramulet, give me your offspring and I shall spare your life. Deny me, and you shall rot alongside the countless others I have destroyed. I assure you, you shall never lay a hand on that trinket you so admire."

Ramulet braced himself, ready for when she pounced at him. He had already drawn his triblade halfway and he had no qualms about cleaving this evil creature in two should she attempt to attack him. But she did not attack him, not directly. As quick and graceful as a gazelle, she leapt to the right of the surprised guardsman and landed on the wall. Like a giant cat-spider, she ran up to, and along, the ceiling, towards the centre of the room, positioning herself upside down, directly above him. His fighting instincts rose to the occasion and instead of wasting time unsheathing his sword, he grabbed the dagger from its mount in front of him and swiped at her with it. The second his hand clasped firmly around it, the creature on the ceiling rasped at him, "Now, you, too, shall die, Samarian! That blade is mine! Put it down!."

But it was not only that chilling threat that Ramulet experienced when he gripped the butt of the dagger. Flashes of his childhood raced through his mind at the speed of light. An image of a face assailed his senses over and over, a beautiful, wise face, a kind and loving face. A face he had not seen since he was but a very young child. It was the face of his father. Simultaneously, he felt a warm wave of love, and a deep longing, wash over him. He could feel that warmth right down to his toes and the sensation was very welcome. Pointing his sword at the freakish monstrosity above him, he slowly unravelled his fingers from the dagger until he could see the motif clearly—a silver dragon holding an hourglass, with an equal balance of sand in each vial. It was his father's seal, The seal of a Samarian Lord. Not *the* royal seal, but the mark of nobility, of the Royal House, none the less. Ramulet knew the seal so well because it was the mark of Lord Amaris—the lost lord.

"Aahh!" the spidery catwoman spat at him, "I see the truth is finally beginning to dawn on that dim-witted brain of yours! You understand now, Ramulet. Your pathetic excuse of a father thought he had destroyed me. The ancient fool thought that one as potent as I could love one so disgustingly pure and devoted as him. You—his son, should now know that I broke his heart and froze his soul! My lord—Ogiin, shall feast upon it soon enough, and now yours too, my handsome warrior."

Like some giant serpent, her forked tongue flickered in and out of her mouth, even the blue of her eyes had changed to become completely white so the black slits were all the more galling.

Ramulet felt a fury rising in him from the pit of his stomach, a raging hurricane of vengeance begging to be unleashed. His eyes blazing with hatred, he locked his steely gaze onto the creature perched upside down above him, "TERITEE!" He roared, "I have come to finish that which my honourable father began. But at *my* hands your death will be neither quick, nor painless. It is possible, you filthy stinking whore, that you did indeed somehow freeze my father's soul. But rest assured, his devoted son shall tear *yours* apart!"

The witch cackled maniacally at his threat. She flicked her revoltingly long tongue at him, scuttling away along the ceiling in her terrifying insect-like manner, before flopping onto the floor opposite him. The table stood between them. Her eyes were as white as the marble it was made from. Ramulet raised his sword, and, to clear a path to this repugnant witch, he brought the blade scything down through the air. Teritee howled, "Nooo!" As she watched the steel smash into it and shatter it to smithereens. Most of the candles extinguished in that instant, with only a handful remaining to still flicker nervously at the duelling pair. The fire in the hearth shrank back to a dull glow and the most incredible stench imaginable filled the room in the even-eerier half-light. If a witch can weep, then Teritee was weeping through her murderous eyes. Ramulet watched as she began to age right before him. Within seconds the striking young nymph was gone, and that which stood before him almost made him wretch. The long chestnut tresses were now stalks of grey straw, her face sagged heavily, forming many chins, her eyes were buried under countless wrinkles, and appeared to be infested with big, fat, brown maggots. Thick dark veins could be seen all over her, bulging through her flaccid, paper thin, skin. Her firm, ample breasts now resembled the drooping dugs of an old crone and many of her teeth were missing, leaving a distinct buck-toothed impression. She appeared so utterly repulsive that Ramulet wanted to look away, but he dare not. Approaching her with great care, he pointed his sword directly in her face. "It would seem, my, *oh-so-beautiful,* Teritee, that my father did a very praiseworthy job in teaching you some manners!" He laughed a loud, intentionally offensive, laugh, ridiculing the witch in her true, natural form. He wanted to hurt her, to torture the creature that had betrayed his father's love. "Now, allow me," he fumed at her, "to remove your ugly head, so never again will you have to face the grotesque horror of your own filthy reflection!"

She moved much faster than anyone could imagine such a raggedy old crone to do, and managed to get the couch between herself and that very dangerous sword. "Like your impotent father, Ramulet, your ambition far outweighs your ability. That table kept me still young—'tis true, but there are many magic tables to be found in as many worlds, and I will acquire another easily enough. Amaris—my former lover destroyed my body, my beautiful body!

But, as you can see, my spirit lives on, and as my lord—Ogiin, regenerates and grows stronger, so do I! It is time for your father and his son to be reunited. Did you really think, you stupid oaf of a Samarian, that I was *alone* in these caves?"

She backed further away from him, but he noticed her covert glances at the ceiling.

Ramulet raised his head expecting to see the carvings, but what he actually saw made his blood run cold. Surely, he thought, when he had fallen through the sands above, he had fallen straight into hell itself. The ceiling now revealed its stark, stomach churning truth. The former figures were actually corpses, dry, mummified husks of what were once men and women. The life spirit having been sucked from them, and they remained as the witch's trophies, buried deep within Iret. At least a score of them adorned the roof of her cave, staring down with their lifeless eyes, their ghastly faces contorted forever in agony, and what had before seemed a misty blur between them now had Ramulet's senses electrified, because, like so many pale, oversized bats, Venomeens were glaring at him from above. Backs to the ceiling and their mouths drooling, they had their cold red eyes affixed on him in united hatred.

"You see?" The witch hissed at him, "When Venomeens feast on fresh blood their strength increases, and this empowers Ogiin further. He is joined with every single Venomeen. Their spirits feed him just as yours shall soon feed them! I but wanted your aid in bearing a child of noble lineage. But you have made your choices, and, like your fool of a father, you will now serve only to adorn this lair with your rotting hide! As the Venomeens begin to consume your pathetic nation, Ogiin will draw such power from them that he will become more omnipotent than ever before, and remember, my beautiful warrior, you Samarians have no pet dragons to call to your aid now, do you!"

The Witch broke into a fit of hysterics, her skeletal finger pointing tauntingly at the sword wielding guardsman standing in the middle of the room. Ramulet's mind was racing. The odds were against him, and who knew what other tricks this toothless whore had up her sleeve alongside these previously hidden ghouls.

She was still pointing at him with her big bony digit as she enjoyed the insults she had taunted him with.

"Wrinkly witch," He told her, "one day I shall take your ugly head into the sunlight without your moth-eaten body, but, for now, I will settle for your hand!"

The triblade carved through the air as Ramulet brought it down in a flash. Teritee screeched and retracted her outstretched hand, but not before the blade had neatly sliced off the ring and little fingers of her left hand. Instantly, Ramulet was over the couch and about to decapitate the cowering crone when he heard the soft thumps landing behind him. A powerful, well-aimed kick from the Samarian caught her square in the jaw and she was sent flying, spitting shattered yellow teeth as she smashed into the stone wall next to the fire. His blade scythed the air again as he spun around to face the new threat. Four Venomeens faced him, though one had his sword buried deep in its head. A twist of the grip by the Samarian, and the Venomeen looked completely confused upon seeing the top of his own skull fall to his feet. The creature crumpled to the floor, but the others drew their swords. Short stubby blades, forged without skill or finesse, the dull, clumsy weapons were still very capable of doing plenty of harm.

He knew the longer he dallied the slighter his chances of survival, and he was adamant these bloodsuckers would not taste his lifeblood for the sustenance of Ogiin this day. Beyond the Venomeens facing him was the dimly lit tunnel along which he had stumbled earlier. More of the scum were looking poised to drop from the ceiling so he had to act now! In a blur of speed the Venomeens could never hope to match, he used the flat of his blade to knock the remaining candles onto the thick red rug. He did not know what was contained in those vials and jars upon the shelf but he recalled the distinct odour of alcohol, so they were sent smashing amongst the still flickering candles. Flames rippled across the floor and he leapt through them, muscling the Venomeens apart as he did so, and racing off down the tunnel, grabbing a burning torch as he passed it. The room behind him was ablaze, the fire covering the entire floor in an instant. He could hear the witch screaming something but could not decipher her ranting. It sounded as if she was shrilling orders to the Venomeens. He could hear screams that came from too high up to be from anything he had confronted thus far, so the fire must have been roasting the rest of the fiends still lurking on the ceiling. Excellent!

The steady clump-clump-clump of running feet warned Ramulet he was being pursued and as he raced down the tunnel, extinguishing each torch as he passed by. Being fleet of foot, the Samarian was gaining a good lead on his pursuers whilst leaving them to give chase through darkness. When he arrived in the place where he had originally started, he was struggling for breath from both, his exertions, and the grogginess caused by the witch's concoctions. Sucking in a huge lungful of air, his canny mind searched the room for a means of escape, but there was nothing. Moving to what he had assumed was a bed, he used his torch to set it ablaze. "That treacherous whore will take no more souls here!" He thought. The sound of footsteps was very close and soon the Venomeens would be upon him. Nerves tingling, Ramulet remained calm nonetheless, sniffing at the nearby jars and vials. Again, the strong heady smell of intoxicants assailed his nostrils. "This bitch certainly likes her drink!" He thought, disgusted even further by the witch. One by one, he hurled the bottles in all directions, aiming half a dozen into the tunnel from whence he had just come. Angry grunts and groans indicated that the missiles had found their marks. He took the blazing covers from the bed and dragged them around, igniting the entire place. The blaze had just taken a good hold when a pair of pale, snarling faces appeared. Ramulet stood firm and faced them as they edged towards him, their lust for his flesh evident in their eyes. The cavern was an inferno and as hot as hell. Another pair of Venomeens burst into the room from the tunnel, but these two must have been hit by the flying bottles because they burst into flames upon contact with the burning floor. They ran screaming back into the tunnel, and as the remaining pair watched them leave, shocked at the sudden combustion of their comrades, Ramulet leapt forward, thrusting his triblade deep into the heart of one of them. The Venomeen screamed a shrill, inhuman scream, but did not die immediately. Much to Ramulet's chagrin the creature began trying to slash at him with its own weapon whilst still impaled upon his blade. The other was trying to get to the rear of him and Ramulet used the Venomeen stuck on his sword to maintain a barrier between them. Round and around the guardsman swung the dieing creature, its arms becoming weaker and its slashing less frenzied. Time was of the essence, more bloodsuckers could arrive any minute and that crawling crone was still alive somewhere in these buried caves.

Despite the desperate need for haste, Ramulet bided his time, wiping rivers of sweat from his face with his cloak as he formed a plan. The fire had climbed high up the cave walls and in the resulting light he could see that this ceiling, too, was another gory tapestry of corpses. Some still fully dressed, but all of them male. The scorching heat within the blazing cavern was not what boiled the blood in his veins. It was the witch's cruel and heartless acts of evil that filled him with pain as he struggled to imagine the suffering of these lost souls. Waiting until the Venomeens were in alignment of one another, he pushed forward with the force of a charging bull. His sword punched right through his first victim, the primary blade burying itself deep into the second. The secondary blades punctured lungs and shattered ribs as they were driven fully home. The Venomeens died standing on their feet and Ramulet used his boot to hold them down as he removed his weapon from them. The heat had become unbearable, but he had no desire to re-enter the tunnel he had just come from, so he turned and sped away from that burning hell into the other one. This tunnel had no torches to guide him, but the blazing cave behind gave some measure of light.

Ahead of him, Ramulet could see a bright orange glow. He raced towards it, the suns perhaps? But sadly his hopes were quickly dashed. The tunnel ended back inside the room where he had met the, then beautiful, witch. Pushing a long hanging drape aside, he took stock. It seemed the tunnels did not form a 'U' shape as he had initially thought, but rather formed an oval—linking the two caverns together. That room, surely the devil's own private chamber, was an inferno, and he could hear that now familiar clump-clump of the pursuing Venomeens closing behind him. The lone Samarian had no choice and stepped back into the cave he had tried so hard to escape. The stench was shockingly unbearable and he looked up to see the corpses on the ceiling burning furiously, the bodies disintegrating, their ashen embers drifting to earth. They all seemed to share the same grotesque smile, as if the pain of flame was a small price to pay to be finally released from the clutches of the witch. Ramulet looked away from those poor wretches, what was he to do? Then he noticed some movement near a wall, behind tall, searing hot, sheets of fire. It was Teritee, her eyes livid, seething at him through the inferno. He could contain himself no longer. "You filthy scum!," He roared at her, watching her wince under the onslaught of his words, "You whore of Ogiin! You betrayed my father, his king, and our homeland. You have tried to seduce me with your lies and false promises. I—Ramulet—son of Amaris, and Captain of The Royal Guards, will return for your head, and be assured, you poxy diseased whore! I shall take that for which I have returned! You have my word of honour on this! I shall burn your infested remains without ceremony or dignity, I shall soak your festering carcass with forever-burning fusions so you may spend eternity roasting in a hell of my making. What is more, I shall line up all your kin, screaming in agony, beside you. But time is short, and you look so very old and revoltingly ugly, that I must now take my leave."

With a brilliant smile for Teritee's benefit, Ramulet leapt straight into the fire that was still glowing in the hearth.

Despite his sturdy boots, the heat from the smouldering wood began to burn his feet almost instantly. The thick acrid smoke choked him and he pulled his cloak over his mouth and nose. As he had suspected the fire vented via a chimney chiselled out through the rock, and he began heaving himself up the sooty black shaft. It was a tight squeeze and his weapons snagged frequently as his fingers and toes sought purchase in the charred uneven walls. His strong young muscles did not fail him and he made swift progress, expecting that at any moment the witch would grab his ankle, or a

Venomeen arrow would find him out in the dark. But she did not grab him, and no weapon or Venomeen touched him. Seeing bright light above, true, honest, sunlight, he scrambled up with ever more speed until, at last, he found himself peering out from the middle of a low stone mound, into a sunlit desert. Covered in soot and choking from inhaling the thick smoke, he tumbled down the mound and landed, sprawled, in the warm sand. His feet, though not actually burned, were very sore from their brief toasting in the fires below. He had to squint to see as the light was so intense and his eyes had grown accustomed to the twilight of the caves. His immediate thought was to block the chimney to prevent those ghouls climbing up after him, then he had to find his queen, and his beloved Mercy. "Only," he thought, "The Dragon knew what had become of them." Apprehension filled him as he wondered if they were somewhere in the subterranean labyrinth that lay hidden far below. When he made to get to his feet, his legs buckled under him through fatigue. Sword in hand, he knew he must take a few minutes rest before standing up. If only he had a drink of water in this terrible heat. His eyes were red, stinging, and his throat was parched. The sand felt warm and comfortable under him and within seconds of sitting down, Ramulet was fast asleep. He did not hear the steady clump-clump-clump coming towards him.

Rordorr could not believe his eyes. Upon reaching the source of the smoky column he had seen earlier, he had discovered this! *Another* false Ramulet, sleeping in the sand as if it had not a care in the world, what sheer audacity! He was livid, this Ramulet was even the wrong colour! Black face, black hands, and no silver dragon on his cloak, how was this mockery supposed to fool anyone? Halfway to the column the true Samarian sunlight had suddenly burst through the dreary veil of Iret, and the land now appeared to be normal desert, "More of Iret's skullduggery, no doubt," He thought, "but what to do with this terrible, ever so ugly replica of the good captain?" He cautiously nudged at the dozing figure. It was solid enough he thought, so it *could* be killed, and *would* be killed as one of the enemy. His sense of honour (because

Samarian horses are very honourable indeed) would not allow him to simply trample the impostor to death. He decided to wake it up before he kicked it into oblivion. He felt the real Ramulet would wholeheartedly approve of this plan. "Wake up! Wake up and face death, you black serpent. You dare to mock the great Ramulet!? Wake up you dark devil! Wake and face Samarian justice you stinking fiend."

The still figure did not stir despite the noisy tirade of abuse from the horse, so Rordorr began nudging it harshly with his muzzle whilst still insulting and taunting it. He wanted this poor facsimile of the captain on its feet when he disposed of it. Then it occurred to him that this abomination may know, or at least have a clue, as to the whereabouts of the true Ramulet. He would awaken and interrogate this sleeping pig. Torturing it was a very real and appealing option if it was not forthcoming with the information he required. He was about to take the black Ramulet by the hair with his teeth and drag it around to wake it up when he heard scraping sounds from the top of the stone pile from which the smoke was rising. He decided to investigate, after all it could be the real Ramulet struggling to reach the surface!

Craning his long neck and taking a deep breath to avoid choking, he stared down into the dark shaft. What he saw were pale angry faces with bared teeth climbing up towards him. Venomeens! The fast thinking horse retracted his head and backed up to the pile of rocks. If this filth lay below the surface, then what cruel fate had befallen Ramulet? He feared for the lost captain, and, with a furious kick, sent a whole bank of stone crashing down into the hole. He heard shrieking, and with a satisfied grin (a horse's grin really is a grin worth seeing) he calmly walked around to the other side and sent the remainder of the mound tumbling down the hole. No shrieks this time, but the smoke fizzled into nothingness.

The rocks crashing and banging down the shaft awoke Ramulet. Was he dreaming, or was this another illusion born of the witch's ways? Clear as daylight he could see Rordorr staring down at him, but the horse looked far from friendly. "So!" The enraged animal told him, "The Venomeen scum thrive below and you apparitions roam the surface. Where is Ramulet—Captain of the Royal Guards? Tell me now, and I shall kill you quickly, lie, and I shall break every bone in your body and leave you to rot in the sun. Speak up, you black fiend!"

"Rordorr, you great big whining beast, it is I—Ramulet." Ramulet replied warily as this horse could well be an illusion.

"Fiend!" came Rordorr's deep horsy voice, "Are you so stupid to think me a fool? *At least try and be the same colour as Ramulet*! I see I'm wasting my time and my breath. It is time for you to go back to the hell from whence you came. What would you have me break first? Shall it be arms, or legs? Or should I simply crush your fat ugly face and be done with it!"

"WAIT!" Ramulet barked through his smoke laden throat, "Look, you big winged lump!"

He used his cloak to wipe the soot from his hands and face then showed the glaring horse. "Humph!" Came the obstinate response, "I see you are as cunning as a fox, you filthy miscreant. You seek to deceive me, and, when my back is turned, I'm sure that nasty looking sword will be at my throat. I have seen that you of Ogiin's creed cannot bear the mark of the Great Dragon, and you, you denizen of darkness, carry no such mark on your cloak."

Ramulet stood up very slowly and removed his blackened cloak. After a vigorous shake the silver dragon could be seen again, glowing through in the bright sunlight.

"My lord, Ramulet, I feared you dead, but I see it really is you. Forgive my suspicions but this accursed place, until but an hour ago, was full with only deceit and false images."

"Rordorr, be at peace." Ramulet assured him as he dusted off the soot from himself. "You have good reason to be cautious, old friend. That mother of all whores, the witch—Teritee, yet lives beneath us in an underground lair so gruesome, so grotesque in its nature, I care not to divulge that which I have witnessed there. She has survived these long ages on the spirits of straying Samarians and other unwary travellers. Venomeens also lurk below in the dark. Your face, Rordorr, is an uplifting sight for these sore eyes."

The horse carried the bag of supplies and water over to Ramulet, who drank deeply of the clean water, gargling Teritee out from his mouth and spitting her into the sand. He quizzed the horse as to the whereabouts of the women and Rordorr told him all he knew. The witch, he told the horse with some great pleasure, was now minus two fingers and in a very much worsened condition than he had met her in. The two companions were agreed that he had probably weakened her evil powers, for now at least, and this explained how the pure, true sunlight had penetrated the Desert of Iret, restoring the place, it seemed, to a landscape without illusions.

It was hot and the sky completely clear. Rordorr having the greater height scanned the horizon and spotted the coral coloured tip of a peak in the distance. With the captain taking a well earned rest on his back, the mighty horse set off towards the Pink Mountain. Ramulet had fallen asleep atop him and Rordorr was very happy to have found him alive and safe. He trotted gently towards his destination but kept a wary eye open, for, no doubt, he would walk straight into the middle of a bottomless bog and kill them both.

They couldn't believe it, the storm had stopped in an instant, the whirlwind of sand settling in the blink of an eye. Meekhi stared questioningly at Mercy and the horse as the day became drenched in brilliant sunlight and the temperature soared. The cold, bitter mood of Iret dissipated to be replaced by the joyous air of Samaria. Surely this must be the doing of Ramulet. They had kept faith that, wherever he was, and whatever he faced, he would overcome any obstacle. Meekhi hastily removed the quiver from the horse's snout as it was now stifling him in the sudden heat. It was just so hot! Their heavy mud-covered garments became unbearably warm and they found the temperature rising to a point where almost any clothing at all was intolerable. They removed everything except their underclothes and weapons, storing them into makeshift sacks formed from their cloaks. The horse very kindly offered to carry these across his back.

The Pink Mountain could now be seen clearly, looming up not too distant ahead. The trio filled with joy at the sight of it and found renewed vigour surging through them. They set their sights on a direct course for their original destination. There was a light balmy breeze blowing, and even dressed only in their thin undergarments, the women were grateful of it. The horse tried yet again to fly, and he managed to hover briefly, but, unfortunately, it seemed he had still to recover his full potential.

CHAPTER TEN

WE STRIKE THROUGH SOLEDAD

Secretly Tamarin was quite impressed that these children from another world could ride so very well. The horses were much larger than they had ridden before they had told him, but they handled them well. Lauren had explained to him that she lived in the countryside and that her family kept horses, but he did not understand what 'countryside' meant. He led the party heading away from the Pink Mountain, with the children riding three abreast behind him. He was careful to not hasten the pace unduly because he did not want any of the young ones taking a nasty fall. Heading back the way they had come, he kept his ears attuned to the conversation taking place just behind him.

The children were chatting, more at ease in their surroundings now than when they had met Tamarin for the first time. Zowie was trying to work out if this was a reality as Tamarin had explained, or a glitch in the Dream Machine.

"It really is very strange," she whispered not quietly enough, "this obviously isn't *our* reality, but it certainly *feels* like a reality... of sorts. I've never had a dream as deep, or as detailed, as this. Could we genuinely be in a different world? I mean a completely different *universe*? Guys, I'm confused!"

Lauren was not convinced that it was a dream at all. She said that everything that Tamarin had said made perfect sense and surely this place must be real. Then Thomas interrupted her. "It IS a dream! It's definitely a dream! I can see the truth guys, and it's a brilliant, fantastic, stunner of a truth!"

Zowie looked at him as if he was demented, "Tom, what the heck are you talking about, you plonker?"

"It *is* a dream!" He was adamant. "LOOK! Over there! You don't get women like *that* in reality. They're just too drop-dead gorgeous. This has to be a dream, and uncle Dug is a flippin' god! Oh! Thank you Dug, thank you!"

The girls, confused, looked in the direction of Thomas' finger. In the middle distance they could clearly see a pair of beautiful, scantily clad women, and a huge horse, trudging through the sand under the blazing suns. One was dark and the other fair. "By my blade!" Tamarin cried out, "My lady and her escort! Guards, follow me!" He raced off at tremendous speed with is men. They tore across the sands towards the labouring trio. The children could barely hold their horses still as the others shot past on all sides. Soon, all they could see amidst the clouds of dust were dazzling dragons disappearing into the distance. Thomas was crestfallen, "I saw them first, hope Tamarin remembers that! Finder's keepers, and all that."

"Yeah...ok. Well, good luck with that, Tom." Zowie told the dejected boy, "But remember, this Ogiin fellow is meant to be about here somewhere."

Three more horses instantly joined the race to meet Meekhi and her escorts, the children rinsing every drop of speed from their mounts lest Ogiin suddenly appeared. Being so much lighter than the well-built warriors ahead, they soon found themselves at first catching the charging horsemen, then overtaking them. Now they were leading even Tamarin, and though none of them had any intention of slowing down, equally none of them had any idea what to do or say when they reached the threesome ahead.

The loud hammering of hooves caused Meekhi and Mercy to turn their attention in the direction of the fast approaching sound. The banner—a silver dragon on a black pendant, was unmistakeable—Tamarin accompanied by his Standard Bearer. The noise grew louder by the second and a cloud of dust came charging at them from ahead.

"Tamarin, I knew you would come." It was all Meekhi could say through her sore, blistered lips. She flopped down in the sand with Mercy. The horse remained standing as he thought that was most befitting the arrival of the king. Mercy, her own voice as dry as aged oak, told Meekhi, "My lady, you are now in safe hands, and you, my dear friend," she croaked, turning to the horse, "will be well taken care of. But I, after gathering supplies, must take my leave and return to find Ramulet. I cannot abandon him to the cesspit that is Iret."

Meekhi smiled at her warmly. "Be at peace, Mercy. None are abandoned that live with honour, you know this well. We shall return together to Iret to find our beloved Captain. But first, you, and our friend here, will be tended to."

Mercy peered into the storm of dust and horses bearing down on them, the heat haze attempting to obstruct her view. She saw that Tamarin and his men were in fact chasing down three small strangers dressed in bizarre attire, "On your guard, my lady! It would seem the king is not alone."

Meekhi staggered to her aching feet. Upon seeing the children riding towards her hell-for-leather, she barked, "To arms!"

Mercy had the sack of weapons open in an instant and the pair stood ready, awaiting these strange looking strangers. The horse moved forward so as to fend off any sudden attack. The children were almost on top of the Samarian queen when Zowie saw her sword catch the sunlight, "BIG SWORD! There's a big sword!" She warned the others, but they had also seen the weapons being wielded ahead and were reining in their mounts, fast. The gigantic horse ahead moved forward, and to their absolute astonishment, it spread out a pair of massive crimson red wings, blocking their view of the warrior-women behind it. They sat atop their mounts, jaws hanging, staring in awe at this amazing, wondrous animal. When he actually spoke, Lauren fell out of her saddle.

"You will not approach Lady Meekhi or her escort. You will not dismount, *those of you that are still seated that is*, and you will await the arrival of the king. Do not test my warning, strange riders."

The horse's stern face allowed for no misunderstanding of his words. His magnificent wings retracted suddenly to nestle on his black flanks. Zowie just had to speak to him. "You are just so beautiful Mr Horse. We mean no one any harm. We are...lost... and Tamar...and *Lord* Tamarin is helping us. He will be here any second now. We'll just sit here and wait. It's cool with us."

"Cool??" Asked the horse, "How anyone can be cool in heat such as this is beyond me. Perhaps you have sunstroke? I see the king has arrived, be still."

Thomas couldn't help staring at Meekhi and Mercy. True enough—such beauty, born of purity and honour, was indeed a very rare sight in his own world, but also it was easy to see these women possessed a power, an inner strength, that was so much more than skin deep and made their physical beauty nothing short of astonishing. He found them simply enchanting, and thinking out aloud, he muttered, "Wow, you two are just too good to be true. *Angels*, that's what you are. I must have died in the Dreampod and gone to heaven! Death is great, and I'm happy to be dead. Really, I don't know why I didn't think to die years ago."

He noticed everyone was staring at him as he talked to himself.

"*Heaven*, Tom?" Lauren poked fun at him, "For heaven's sake, more like! Put your eyes back in your head and give it a rest will you."

Embarrassed, he managed a just retort, "Because you weren't ogling Tamarin at all, *were you?*"

Zowie silenced them with a curt, "Now is NOT the time, you two."

Meekhi quickly realised that these riders were in fact no real threat, but rather just children barely approaching adulthood, strangers with outlandishly cut hair and wearing ridiculous attire of unknown origin, circus performers perhaps. Tamarin was moments away, and, winking slyly at Mercy, she moved forward to address the new arrivals, "You may dismount, I can see you are not armed." She turned to Thomas, "We are not angels I assure you, but we thank you for your gracious comments. Take care what you say within earshot of the king, young stranger, for I am his queen and such comments are not well advised in Samaria."

Zowie slipped from her saddle and stood beside Lauren who was rubbing her backside after falling from her horse. They whispered to each other about the striking beauty of these fearsome looking women and the unbelievable appearance of a winged horse. Thomas remained seated in his saddle and Zowie asked him to come down and join them.

"I can't," he moaned, "this horse is really wide and I've got cramp, I can't move my legs."

The girls reached up and took his hand, yanking him down from his perch. He lurched about on the sand like a crab, yelping, "Oooh, aah! Ouch!"

Then Tamarin arrived. He gave the hobbling bow-legged boy a strange look as he sprang from his horse to Meekhi's side. "My lady, are you hurt? What ill has befallen you?"

"I am well and unharmed, my love." She told him, "Please tend to our friends."

"Mercy," Tamarin faced her whilst one arm still embraced Meekhi, "you are injured. You know Arcadian is a physician of high order, please allow him to help you". He told his others, "Men! Look to our four legged friend."

The children further warmed to the nature of the Samarians as they watched them all hurriedly darting about to help their own. Tamarin and his queen stood locked in each others arms. They could not quite catch what they were saying, but Thomas thought Tamarin was asking her something about where she had lost the omelettes and raw boar. Lauren suggested that maybe eggs and pork were the staple diet, and that perhaps Meekhi had lost their supplies. This seemed perfectly feasible given Tamarin's previous eagerness to find omelettes at the Pink Mountain. The girls emphatically stated that they would refuse to eat raw meat, be it Samarian or otherwise. But they *were* quite peckish and actually would not mind an omelette right now. Thomas was of the opinion that if those women could handle raw boar then he would trust their judgement and tuck into whatever was on the menu. One thing they all finally agreed on at last—this was no dream, or at least no dream as they knew dreams to be. Somehow they had been transported to this lovely, if a little scary, world. Possibly when the timer Dug had set on the Dream Machine timed out, they would return to their own world. Certainly if they did not, then their parents would move heaven and earth to retrieve them, or follow them to this strange place. Oddly, they felt neither panicked, or afraid. Nor were they aware that the king and queen were listening to their conversations. Tamarin and Meekhi were not in the habit of eavesdropping, but in these dangerous times they had to be sure of whom they allowed in their midst.

Meekhi had told Tamarin of the events that had occurred since she and her companions had left Sitivia. He had held her gently at arms length so that he may gaze upon her entirety with pride, overwhelmed with relief at her wellbeing. Although he was not happy about her risking herself through Iret, he understood why she had done so. He would most likely have done the same thing himself. He was grateful to have her and Mercy returned without any real harm having befallen them. Mercy, a little bumped and bruised, seemed to not have any serious or long lasting injuries, and the horse would be fine after a good rest and the application of some special balms back home in Sitivia.

The children struggled to get to grips with the sight of the winged horse having a discreet conversation with the king and queen. They were finding this magical new world hard to take in, to accept, and just stood staring about themselves, absorbing a striking landscape that was completely alien to them. It was still very warm but a light breeze fanned them just enough to stop it becoming unbearable. Looking back in the direction they had come from they could see the Pink Mountain towering up behind scattered groups of incredibly tall trees. The sound of a waterfall from that direction was barely audible, but could definitely be heard if one strained one's ears. The direction that Meekhi and her friends had come from appeared to be bare golden desert, blistering in the sun, a shimmering haze preventing any more revealing a view.

"That's it!" Zowie decided. "Dream or no dream, we're here in the middle of it anyway. As long as we are, I intend to make the most of it. Can't say I much fancy this Ogiin bloke, so, if they'll have me, I'm going to hook up with this Samarian lot until either I'm back in the Dreampod, or dad turns up, or I'm dead, like Tom, hehehe. That's that sorted. What about you two?"

"I'm in." Lauren was not going to be the last to decide.

Thomas was of the same mind, "Me too, Zee. This is going to be a mega blast, I can just feel it."

They could see that the winged horse had left the group of people chatting with each other, and was slowly trotting over to them.

"Oh my word," whispered Zowie, "If that horse talks to us I shall simply die! Wouldn't it be the most totally fab thing ever!"

Her rhetorical question was answered by the horse himself as he sidled up to them and said in a deep, weary voice, "So, you are the Guilty Innocents of whom The Talking Table spoke. Humph, you don't look much to me, but time will tell. I am Faradorr, a native of Samaria, and I heard you talking earlier. Mind you remember our names well here, for it is not wise to upset those such as the people of this land."

Zowie was bursting with excitement, thrilled at conversing with a horse. She just could not contain herself. "Faradorr, it is our honour and pleasure to meet you, and we think you are just so beautiful. I am Zowie, this is Lauren, and this is her brother—Thomas. We won't forget your name, I promise."

"It is not *my* name I was thinking of, little ones. Zowie, you have a look about you that I feel I can trust, a familiarity, so here is some advice—I have heard Toe Mess often mention omelettes. You have misheard the king. The word you seek is 'Ramulet', NOT 'omelette'. Ram-u-let. It is the name of the Captain of the Royal Guards, and his triblade is as fast as any in the land, so beware."

"Toe Mess?" laughed Thomas. "Well, that's just charming that is. I'm sorry, Faradorr, if I've misheard Lord Tamarin. I won't forget again. I didn't mean to be rude, old chap. My name is Thomas. Thom—as, not Toe Mess."

Faradorr was grinning, his big horsy teeth on display. "Certainly Thomas, I will not forget your name again, but I would also like to add that not one of the present company has any interest in raw boar. What a disgusting thought! My king was asking of *Rordorr*, a Samarian horse like myself, and, I am proud to say—my *brother*. He is lost with Ramulet."

The girls were almost jumping with joy. "Can Rordorr talk human talk as well as you, Faradorr?"

The horse looked down at the three young people staring up at him.

"Oh yes," he replied, almost laughing now, "Rordorr can certainly talk, very much so, most definitely much more than I can."

They liked this talking horse very much, they had only really spoken to Tamarin in this weird world, and he was a *King*, so it was quite relaxing to talk to a normal person, if a talking horse really is a normal person. Faradorr talked to them on an equal level they thought, and so did not intimidate them at all. Tamarin saw all honourable people as equal, and certainly did not consider himself to be better than the children in any way. But, after all, he was a King, and kingship creates a certain air of authority which can appear quite intimidating to the unfamiliar. The children and Faradorr were laughing about Thomas' raw boar when they heard Mercy shouting out over everyone else, "My lord, Look yonder!" She had jumped to her feet, and despite her weak ankle began running back towards the wasteland from whence she had emerged not so long ago. Faradorr looked into the desert of Iret, and before setting off after her, he told them, "It would seem you are about to meet The Captain of the Royal Guards, and... my brother."

Zowie and the Shortwaters strained against the suns to see into Iret. There, appearing from the shimmering heat, were Ramulet and Rordorr. Even from this distance it was easy to see that Rordorr was even bigger than Faradorr. The man walking alongside him was tall and of a similar appearance to Tamarin, perhaps a few years the king's elder. Only Ramulet had his long hair pulled back in a ponytail, did not wear any crown, and looked very much the worse for wear.

They watched on as Mercy, charging headlong through the sand, was swooped onto horseback by Tamarin's extended arm as he passed her before reaching the captain of his guardsmen. Others of his party soon joined him and Ramulet was helped up into a fresh saddle. After he and Rordorr had taken a long drink of cool water, they rode back to where the children stood. Rordorr was immediately tended to by experienced horsemen, but he maintained that the poisonous air of Iret had ruined his once powerful lungs so their kind efforts would ultimately prove futile, thus, they shouldn't worry too much about him, he was most likely already doomed. The children could see that Rordorr was in fact in much better shape than his brother. Faradorr approached him and the two bowed heads to each other in the traditional Samarian horse-greeting.

"My brother, you have found Ramulet." Faradorr congratulated him. "I knew you would not fail him. The Great Dragon be praised, you appear to be unharmed, are you well?"

"As well as my poisoned lungs allow. Ramulet escaped from fires burning deep beneath Iret. But less of me, my dear brother you are wounded! Have you suffered many swords and spears? Have you also been poisoned? Were you tortured? Buried alive? Set on fire?!? Did some dastardly fiend hang you by your tail! Tell me everything, I feared for your life, Faradorr. The queen and Mercy, they are well? Where is our cousin—Blackstorm?"

With a sad look in his eyes, Faradorr told him his story, and of the loss of Blackstorm in the battle with the Rock Troll. Rordorr lowered his head in sorrow. "He left as he always lived, setting a standard for others to follow. He is with the spirit of the Great Dragon now, I am sure of this, and this world is lessened by his absence."

Ramulet had been talking with the others and some of them had helped Mercy in cleaning him up. A fire was lit and food was cooked. Everyone including the children sat around it at a distance as the day was already so hot, and the reunited friends and lovers told each other their tales. Mercy was jubilant at Ramulet not only surviving Iret and rejoining her, but also because he had dealt a nasty blow to the witch—Teritee, whom all had thought dead long ago. Her witch's craft appeared to have been considerably weakened by the destruction of her subterranean lair, and of course the severing of her fingers could not have done her any good either. Ramulet, although happy to be free of Iret was a little melancholy as he toyed with his father's dagger. He believed Lord Amaris to be still alive somewhere because the witch had not once mentioned his death. Surely had that been the case then Teritee would have delighted in taunting him with it, especially as her own demonic father had been destroyed by the Dragons of Light, consumed forever by the blue flame of truth when her base treachery had been revealed. It was rumoured that his screams rang out above all others in the Underworld, and would continue to do so until his daughter's surpassed his own.

The captain bided his time, trifling with his food until he found the opportunity to hold brief counsel with Tamarin in private. He kept the horrifying details of the monstrous evils he had seen to himself. There was no need for the womenfolk to know of such awful things, but, at some stage, he would have to tell Mercy of Teritee's attempted seduction of him. She had a right to know that he had been almost too weak to resist the witch. He explained to the king that there were many Venomeens thriving beneath Iret, that each spirit they fed upon also empowered Ogiin, and that the witch had told him of Ogiin's imminent return. The king listened carefully to all the captain had to say. He had always been aware of the stark contrast between his own joyous childhood, constantly showered with his father's affections, and Ramulet's sudden loss when Amaris disappeared. He swore that after these current pressing affairs were put to rest he would aid Ramulet in finally settling the matter of the lost lord by bringing the full weight of his crown to bear upon any quest Ramulet embarked upon. The captain was grateful of this, knowing the king to be as good as his word.

Tamarin was resolute in his decision that Ogiin was to be the focus of their attention. Venomeens, deadly dangerous as they were, posed no cohesive threat without leadership. Without Ogiin they remained fragmented and afraid, surviving on carrion in the most remote and unpopulated parts of the world. Their re-emergence on Samarian soil was a telling fact in the question about Ogiin's return. He gave his orders—they would return to Sitivia armed with the knowledge gained by Ramulet, and the children would go with them if they so wished, they were not prisoners by any means. They must have some part to play yet, or The Talking Table would not have mentioned them. Whenever they stopped for a break they would be trained in combat by Ramulet and Mercy, because whilst he would endeavour to protect them, much evil was now afoot in Samaria and his priority was his beloved realm. He could say this openly before his queen because she knew, understood, and accepted this, before they had wed. It was Tamarin's first duty to defend his people against any threat.

Arcadian had done a marvellous job of soothing and strapping Mercy's ankle, and when she saw the children flinch at Tamarin's words of combat training, she went and sat with them, telling them it was not as hard as it sounded and she thought there would most likely be no need for its use anyway. Comforted by this and her bright honest eyes, they actually started looking forward to this training. So much so that Thomas exclaimed, "I hope that flippin' Dreampod doesn't pull us out of here just yet! I'm going to be a full-on Ninja by the time we get back girls, awesome!"

The teenagers made fun of it, making chopping movements with their hands whilst crying out in a mock Japanese manner. Mercy watched them, noting just how innocent they truly were, and wondering how much of that innocence would remain untainted if Ramulet's warnings of Ogiin's return bore fruit.

Tamarin had a lot of thinking to do. He was more worried than he had allowed the others to see. Meekhi had told him of the pot erupting with the evil of Iret, the very same pot from which she had eaten along with Mercy and Faradorr. Would this have some awful effect yet to manifest itself? He did not possess the wisdom to know the answer but he knew he must have that answer soon as any delay may have dire consequences. Though Ramulet had caused the Desert of Iret to become weakened, apparently losing its ability to create illusions, it was still a dangerous place. The witch remained at large, and Rock Trolls wandered there freely. Returning to Sitivia and seeking learned counsel was of the essence, but they would not tempt fate twice through Iret, nor would they take the longest route for time was short. Soledad was still a Samarian city. Yes, its streets and halls were now home only to black statues and the mantle of dust upon them, but the city was still alive with Samarian souls. Cruelly caged within their individual tombs of marble, surely these ancients could bear no malice to their fellow countrymen? True, it was said—the sorrow and grief that echoed through that city was enough to break one's very heart, but he would lose his heart anyway if Meekhi came to harm. The choice was made and he made it known to his company. "Mount up! We must return to Sitivia at once. We cannot afford the luxury of returning the way we came and we cannot chance our luck through the desert that is Iret, so, we will strike through Soledad. Any that feel they can not bear her loneliness and torment may take the longer route. There will be no judgements made upon you for your choice. We are born with freewill and by it we must live, and die. Do any fear Soledad's curse?"

"I'm afraid we probably do." Zowie piped up, her hand raised in the air as if in a classroom, "We've heard a lot about witches and curses and this Freddy Kruger type—Ogiin, but we don't have these things in our world, so we know nothing of them. My cousins and I have decided we are on your side—you *Samarians* I mean, but you should know now that we're just kids and probably not of much use to you. But if you're going to this Soledad place, then we'll come with you and see what happens next, trust me, we are having a very strange day."

Tamarin looked at her, he respected her bold honesty, "Those that can recognise their own fear can often conquer it, little one. Those that can not see it often live in its shadow, unable to look into the dark. We all know there is peril ahead, but it is you that has had the strength to voice her fears so openly. This shows courage and a true heart. We are honoured that you and your brave kinsmen will ride with us this day.

As for these things not being in your world, little one, I would not be so certain. Perhaps when we have settled matters here, in our world, I can assist you in dealing with the tyrant in your world—this Freddy Kruger."

Zowie smiled back at him and mounted up, there was nothing she could say to that really. Lauren did the same, coming alongside and telling her, "Creep! Talk about teacher's pet."

They pulled faces at each other whilst Thomas, still suffering from the after effects of cramp, very carefully mounted his horse.

Tamarin boomed out the command; "Standard Bearer, raise the Standard! We are bound for The Silent City!"

The horses headed off into the sandy distance. The children, despite their fears, felt an extraordinary excitement fast growing within them. All about them there were black capes whipping about, trailing out behind hunched riders, the silver dragons so lavishly applied upon them making them feel warm and safe inside. They had wanted to fly in a dream, but had somehow flown into a reality that was better than any dream they could possibly have imagined. Soledad lay ahead, but before then their combat training would commence. Thomas admired these warrior people with their three-bladed swords and long dark hair. "I can be like that," he thought. Zowie and Lauren measured the situation quite differently. If training was being given, then there must be a strong possibility they were going to have need of it, but a need against what? They had never seen a troll of course, and had absolutely no desire to meet any witches. Lauren admitted she was not sure if she could actually fight anything properly—as in *really* fight someone. Zowie, on the other hand, said that she quite fancied the idea, and that she thought she could be 'quite tasty' with one of those single bladed swords that Meekhi carried. Thomas approved of her 'have a go' attitude, whereas Lauren frowned at her, "There's something very seriously wrong with you, Zee. Do you have any idea of just how much therapy you need?"

Zowie remained undaunted, "A lot, a lot of therapy, and probably some head chemicals too, because... I've always wanted to kick the crap out of someone that deserved it!"

They headed west towards Soledad with the silver dragon held aloft. It was snapping back and forth wildly, as if to warn the Silent City of their approach.

He was impervious to the cold now and he felt stronger, able to move his limbs, though the movements were still clumsy, mechanical, and vague. In his mind's eye, Ogiin could see the stormy shores of the Western Worlds. He could see his minions of every evil ilk arriving at the shoreline, gathering at the waters edge to greet him. Fools! Even as they bent their knees and bowed their heads to pay him homage, his spirit reached out and sucked the very life out of them, there was no escape, he bound them all to his will. Their decaying husks lay dotted everywhere on the stony, windswept beach. He could see his Venomeens too, though they were yet sparse in number. Shadows also loitered in the dark of the night, but there was little point in draining their life—they had so little to offer, but left unmolested, could provide him so much by their feeding on others.

He had felt the burning pain of Ramulet's sword slicing through Teritee's gnarled hand. The ugly old witch was useful and he did not wish to see her demise... as yet. Had she succeeded in securing an offspring in her rotten, disease-ridden, womb? "Unlikely," he thought, "hers was a well trodden path, most likely incapable of sustaining life." He wanted a puppet ruler for Samaria, preferably sired from noble lineage so as to lay 'authentic' claim to that position. The current Samarian King and his followers would soon be no more than livestock for his Venomeens. He would take for himself a bride from amongst the Samarian womenfolk. They were renowned for their beauty and strength of spirit, and their famed longevity would allow him his pound of flesh again and again. If the witch had failed, then he would sire a servile king himself with a woman of suitable position. His cruel face cracked into a twisted death's head of a smile—the woman would have no choice in the matter. He would need many puppets in many worlds as his empire expanded. Nothing could stop him now that Chjandi—the silver dragon, was no more. Master of the entire universe, this was his undeniable destiny!

He enjoyed the thrill of feeling his limbs moving, the power slowly returning to long-dormant muscles, sensation tingling in nerves that had been but frozen in the gloom of these icy depths. He felt the pain again in his back where his ruined wings had once been. Slowly, with terrified sea creatures scattering away in all directions, he managed to stand upright on the sea bed. A large predatory shark came close, its dark eyes roving over him, then, suddenly, it rolled, its powerful tail propelling it far far away from this evil personified. It disappeared into the grey-blue darkness, grateful to yet know life. It was time to leave this watery grave to which he had been condemned for so long, and raising his arms high above him, Ogiin called out with his spirit to all the creatures of darkness to join him. Even the sea, such an immoveable natural mass, began to swirl slowly above him as he whipped the deep into a whirlpool the likes of which had never been seen before.

CHAPTER ELEVEN

THE CALL OF COMRADES

Etep raised his hand, bringing his hard charging horsemen to a stop. One hundred strong, this company of guardsmen had less need for caution than the Westonian lords it was pursuing. It would be madness for any small group of enemy to attack such a force of fully armed men, so stealth was not a priority. Etep had maintained a very rapid pace up to this point, but now the horses were at their limit and the riders were sorely in need of rest. They had just ridden hard through a deep rich grassy valley flanked on each side by gentle green hills, and ahead of them lay a large, well populated wood, beyond which a range of mountains could be seen. There was a cool fast flowing stream nearby so this seemed the ideal place to camp for the night, and from where to make a fresh clean start at sun up. The men busied themselves with the kind of efficiency only the very best of training exhibits. Tents were springing up everywhere and horses were unburdened of heavy saddles and weapons.

Etep was looking up at the darkening sky as he discussed tomorrow's journey with fellow guardsmen, when the smell of burnt wood and charcoal caught his nose. Further investigation revealed, close by, the burned out remains of a funeral pyre, a *Samarian* funeral pyre. He did not know which poor soul had departed that world but the sight of the pyre both saddened, and alarmed, him. Word spread quickly through the encampment that danger was afoot. The number of sentries was doubled and the horses were corralled to be made safe. Etep considered Imo a good friend, and had done so for many years, so naturally he feared for his safety and that of the Westonians, but it would be folly to try and continue his journey with tired men and weary horses in the dark, through woods, and over mountains that were known to be treacherous. He would have to be patient and kerb his concerns until sun up. As he wondered what unlucky fate had befallen the Samarians of the pyre, a cold foreboding washed over him despite the warm evening, and he wished he had some inkling as to the state of progress of Imo's party.

He and two others (these two being skilled scouts and excellent trackers) were looking out over the woods towards the mountains when a small flash of light appeared far away, up high and way beyond the trees. It must have originated somewhere in the mountains. A long burning torch soared up into the dark sky and arced through the black vastness, before heading directly to where he stood. He stood firm with his eyes glued to the mysterious bolt of fire descending upon him from the heavens. It soon became apparent by its trajectory that the fiery streak, whatever it may be, would fall a safe distance away from him and his men, so he and his comrades waited for it to land. It arrived very suddenly, a burning spear from a Wrath of Amaris ramming itself into the ground some fifty feet away from the surprised onlookers. "Well now, I didn't expect to be seeing that this evening." joked Etep, his face devoid of even the slightest trace of humour.

Moving forward they saw the spear was soaked in oily black pitch. Using his cloak to protect his hands from the piping hot, still smoking, shaft, Etep heaved the spear from the ground. Sure enough the tip was a snarling dragon, but more to the point—there were pieces of bloody pulp and dark fur still trapped in its deadly jaws. He was a highly experienced guardsman and examined the shaft of the spear closely. The solid Samarian oak, though blackened, was barely touched by the flames. Looking back over the trees he used the treetops as reference points and soon had a very accurate picture of where the spear had originated from. It was going to be dangerous navigating through woods and mountains in the dark, but he knew he now had no choice, and no time to waste. Imo and his company were, at best, in deep trouble. He had given his word to Tamarin to find and protect Imo's party, he would do all within his power to keep true to that promise.

The alarm was sounded with small horns blaring loudly and the men began running about gathering up weapons that had not long ago been discarded for the night. They donned uniforms that had barely had a chance to dry having being rinsed clean in the stream. Etep split his force in half, he and the first half would be mounted on horseback and the rest would follow on foot. Horses could easily become a liability amongst trees, and nothing is really more effective in a confined space than a well armed foot soldier with his wits about him. Someone had deployed the Wrath of Amaris against a foe fearsome enough to merit its use. Such an enemy may well require the power and speed of cavalry to challenge and defeat it. He was only guessing at what they may face and wanted to try and cover all eventualities. Armed to the teeth, his formidable force was a sight to worry even the most battle hardened adversary, and he began leading them into the woods. That dark sense of foreboding still pricked uncomfortably at his mood and he looked up through the trees, using the stars to maintain his bearing. Even as they penetrated the very edge of the woods his unease began to grow, and he asked himself—how many of them would survive to see these same stars a week hence from now?

It was quiet amongst the trees save for the odd hoot of an owl, and one sudden crash of bushes as a large deer leapt away from the marching men. In fact, thought Etep, the woods were too quiet, so quiet, in fact, it was as if they had either witnessed some dreadful deeds and been sworn to silence, or they remained mute because they wanted no part of whatever was afoot. The entire troop had their hands on the hilts of their weapons, their nerves tingly, the atmosphere taut, and edgy. Their eyes darted everywhere, drilling into the darkness between the trunks of the trees, searching for the slightest movement, but they saw and heard nothing that gave cause for concern. Etep decided that were his friends still alive then they should know help was close at hand. He summoned the special horn be brought to him. The instrument, known as—The Call of Comrades, was carried by all large units of guardsmen. It was used to announce your impending arrival to friends, and to prevent them filling you with arrows as an enemy.

The horn was passed along the riders until he took a firm grip on it. Raising it to his lips he blew into it gently to clear any debris that might stifle its call of friendship. Then he coughed, and spat, clearing his throat before filling his large powerful chest with air, raising the mouthpiece to his lips, and blowing with all his might. The silent night was suddenly torn asunder by the unmistakeably militaristic blaring that issued forth. Birds took immediate flight, or settled even closer on their young ones. The sound of clattering wings and panicked squawking filled the air, amidst the undergrowth unseen animals grunted in annoyance and shuffled away, snorting in indignation at their rude awakening. The sounding horn infused the guardsmen with a greater sense of urgency, and despite the hindering trees and blinding darkness, they quickened their pace to the point where no more speed could be gained without hitting an obstacle in the poor light. The men running behind had little difficulty in keeping up given the terrain the horses were having to bulldoze through. Those on foot could hear the horses up ahead smashing through bushes, crushing thickets as they powered forward, creating a reasonably clear, flat, trail, in their wake for those following.

They looked at each other in stunned surprise, was that the Call of Comrades they had just heard? It certainly sounded like that most Samarian of horns, but where could it be sounding from, and who might be sounding it? The occupants of the cave had not dared to even think of a rescue party. The air inside had become thick with smoke and they had been lieing flat on the ground to try and gain some vital oxygen. Each was aware that the fire would not last forever, and that daylight was their best hope. Whilst keeping a wary eye on the mouth of the cave they had seen Venomeens fanning the flames so as to blow the smoke deeper into the cave, there was little to be done about that, but it did nothing to lift their spirits. Then they thought they heard the horn sounding. Listening carefully, they heard it twice more. Now they were certain, and

Imo was beside himself with excitement. "Now they're going to get it!" He beamed at his friends, "We will cut their heads off! We will burn them alive! I *know*... we will *impale* them, yes, *impaling is good*! I say we impale them, there is samarian steel on their menu tonight, my friends, and I volunteer to be the cook. Or...*should we roast them*?? Roasting is also good! I think I'll dice them first..."

The wise and experienced Lumarr erred on the side of caution, not as excitable as Imo, he pointed out that there was no telling the size of the rescue party, if indeed there was a rescue party. The vermin outside could be faking a Samarian horn to draw them out into the open, or, the horn may well be sounded by Samarians, but for the attention of someone else, worse still, the horn-sounding party could be very small in number and unaware of the presence, or, size, of the ghastly gathering outside the cave. These sobering revelations dimmed the initial fervour of the cave's occupants, but it did not stop Imo from telling them, "If any fellow Samarian comes along that path, I am going through that fire to join him, we are a united nation, united in honour, united in faith, and we stand, or fall, thus."

Etep could see the end of the woods ahead and urged his horse forward faster still until he burst from the low, overhanging foliage of the trees, onto a grassy slope that banked up and away towards the mountains. It was not long before his men were amassed along the tree line in full strength. The peaceful night gave a clear view of the incline ahead. He could easily make out the large boulders dotted about on its surface and it was not difficult to note that the slope became much steeper after about halfway up. The burning spear must have come from somewhere on the heights above.

Looking about him he saw a shape that made his heart sink. Spurring his horse over to it, he saw the still form of Ranician lieing there on the desolate mountainside. He had known Ranician as a brave and loyal guardsman, Imo and the others would never have left him here if in any way it could have been prevented. The fact that they were not present implied they had escaped Ranician's fate and could well be alive yet.

He ordered a makeshift pyre be erected quickly to send their fallen friend on to the Great Dragon in dignity, with due honour. This was done, and very soon the pyre was in place. After a brief salute and sombre farewells a torch was shoved into the base of the structure and for the second time that night a Samarian funeral illuminated the sky. The first gush of flame lit up the surrounding area and by its light some of the men spotted a small path winding away from the top of the hill, beyond some larger boulders. If not for the pyre it might have taken them much precious time to find that path in the dark. Etep silently thanked Ranician for this final contribution from his sacrifice, and began to organise his men. Again he sounded the Call of Comrades.

There was absolutely no mistaking it, it was a genuine Samarian horn they could hear, and by the way the creatures of the night outside the cave were behaving, it was being sounded by real Samarians, for sure. Taking a deep breath, Imo had stood up on Lumarr's shoulders and could see that they looked panicked. The Venomeens were running about in all directions, they made strange clucking noises in between their incessant hissing and Imo correctly assumed they were communicating with each other. The fanning of the smoke into the cave ceased, and whilst the occupants were grateful for this, the fire, itself, had robbed their refuge of much oxygen, causing breathing to become a heavy, laboured affair.

The Westonians—highest in rank, and, thus, justifiably expected to lead, were quizzed as to what they proposed by way of action. Lumarr's creased his brow in contemplation, weighing up their options. They were standing up now that the air was not quite so heavily laden with smoke, their long shadows dancing on the cave wall in the firelight. Weary from guarding the cave without sleep, and from fighting for breath, they waited on Lumarr for their next move. Finally, he spoke. "We must break free of the cave, this is certain. We are hopelessly outnumbered and darkness brings its own dread of phantoms upon us. I fear events dictating our course will transpire long before daylight touches this mountain. Something Samarian comes our way and we must give warning of the horde that lies in wait. One of us must escape this cave unseen. Once made aware, and thus prepared, the approaching men will tackle the enemy with a sudden, unexpected, strike, thus reversing the advantage of surprise that this scum currently have," he stopped to cough hoarsely through his stinging throat, spitting phlegm on the wall before continuing, "then, when the battle is upon us, the rest of us shall join the fray and take our vengeance on the pack of wolves currently prowling at our door. What say ye?"

"I will go." Imo volunteered. "I'm the smallest here, and the least likely to be seen. If we can reach through that fire and remove some of the hellhound's fur, I can use it to mask my scent and hide myself in the dark. It is the most sensible option, though I do not mean to undermine any plan you may have, my lord."

"So be it." Lumarr agreed, "I salute your courage Imo, and may the Great Dragon bless you with speed and stealth."

"To be honest," laughed the wily guardsman, "I don't need the Great Dragon for *that*!"

The men smirked at his true joke as they started work immediately. Pieces of the barrier were very quietly and carefully removed. Twice, parts of the burning barrier collapsed into ash, but mercifully those outside did not notice, being preoccupied with the sound of the fast approaching horn. Bestwin watched over them with his eagle eyes. They were looking back down the track to see what was coming their way. Imo and another guardsman began the grisly task of cutting away a large sheet of charred flesh and scorched fur from the dead beast still smouldering beyond the fire. The stench was horrendous and both of them fought their urge to vomit as their daggers hacked away at the warm, steaming corpse. Some minutes later Imo held up a sheet, nearly three feet square, of bloodied fur. He seemed pleased with his new acquisition and grinned at the others. "Do you think the colour suits me?"

Bestwin gave him a friendly clip around his head and warned him, "Take care, my friend, these devils know not the meaning of the word mercy."

"When it comes to such as they, I know it not either." He replied coldly, swinging the soggy sheet of flesh around himself, and onto his back.

"I will see you all soon." Were his last words as he began to wriggle and writhe beneath the flames, heading out of the asphyxiating atmosphere of the cave.

It was a gut churning experience for him, bitter bile rising at the back of his throat, not only was he constantly expecting a Venomeen blade to pin him to the ground at any second, but also he had to squeeze past the stinking, half-cooked and skinned, body of the hellhound. He edged forward a few inches at a time on his front, using his elbows to support himself and his toes to inch him out of the cave. It took him at least ten minutes crawling at a snail's pace before he got his first whiff of fresh air. It was one the most wonderful things he had ever tasted, he thought, after hours of inhaling the smoky stench of burnt flesh and dead, incinerated hag. He could feel the warm weight of the hellhound pressing against him and he tried desperately to ignore the feel of the slimy skin wrapped about him.

Imo neared the path at last, and could see from their grouped feet that many of the Venomeens were standing bunched together, probably debating the imminent arrival of whomever had blown that horn. He could also see several pairs of bony, big-knuckled, feet with horrendously long, filthy, black nails. These were wondering about in no apparent order, but what worried him most was gigantic, enormously fanged, hellhound, lieing directly opposite him and the cave. He poked his face out a fraction further and under the light of the stars he could see some of those ghost-like Shadows hovering in a straight line—blocking his intended route back down the mountain. The dark robes just hung there, barely skimming the ground, their heads bent. He could not allow the horn bearing party to walk directly into such a ghoulish ambush. But how was he to get past them? Plainly, he had no chance of retreating down the path he had travelled up earlier that night. So, there remained but one choice, and although he did not much fancy his chances, he would have to take it.

He lay perfectly still for two or three minutes, filling, and refilling his lungs many times over with that sweet fresh air to regain his strength and clear his head of any smoky confusion. Pulling the foul, sticky, wreaking fur around himself even tighter, he waited until he felt none of the vermin were looking his way, then, he shot across the path and crouched right next to the mighty monster sitting opposite him. It had looked to be dozing, and now he knew for sure it was asleep. He could hear its deep rumbling breathing, its revolting breath doing nothing to help his growing nausea. He thought of how these hellhounds must be burning hot inside because, despite the warm night, he could clearly see its breath forming in the air as it exhaled. He would have dearly liked to cease that breathing forever, but now was not the time. The stout little guardsman could feel his heart pounding furiously as he crouched, frozen. The beast beside him wrinkled its nose but did not stir. His grisly cloak of fleshy fur had served to camouflage his presence well. It seemed to take an eternity to creep to the very edge of the track and the sanctuary of darkness. He eased himself over the precipice until he was dangling by his fingertips, the heavy, wet and slimy skin on his back slipping from him and falling quickly away into the inky blackness below, he was glad of its loss, its sheer weight had been a great strain on his already tenuous grip. Now he was able to feel for small outcrops and shallow crevices where he could find safe purchase and moved slowly along the rock face. He froze every time a stone or pebble became dislodged and clattered earthwards. There was quite a distance to clamber along the mountainside to pass by the Shadows, before he could then endeavour to climb back up and go in search of whoever was sounding the Call of Comrades. Those wraiths—the Shadows, must not see him emerge, or he was doomed. Steeling himself, he breathed deeply of the night air, and began swinging like a monkey from ledge-to-lip-to-crevice.

Etep began to organise his men in readiness for proceeding to, and along, the narrow pass up above. Observing that rocky trail from the foot of the hill he had decided that horses were pointless up there on the heights, whilst a brave and loyal comrade in open battle, up on the tight track a horse would only prove to be a hindrance, even a danger, to his men. He would proceed along the mountain with foot soldiers, leaving a large compliment of men behind in reserve with the horses. A signal by horn would soon bring up reinforcements if required. He had no idea how far the Westonians had progressed and it could mean his own force becoming strung out over a long distance—leaving them thinned out and vulnerable to attack. As the soaring spear had proven, the party under Imo's watchful eye had faced a formidable challenge not so long ago, but what had it been, and how many of 'it' were there?

Shields held edge-to-edge formed a solid barrier across the five leading men as they began moving up into the mountains. Triblades were drawn and ready, eyes were peeled, and ears pinned back. The second row of men carried blazing torches and the third row, again, carried their swords and so on and so forth. The column lit up the mountainside and the woods below seemed to move and sway in the flickering glow. In the dead of the night, fire and steel marched fearlessly in search of friend and foe.

They had not been moving for more than fifteen minutes when they heard heavy, laboured breathing, somewhere just ahead. It was the unmistakeable sound of someone breathing deeply, but trying to do it quietly, as if wanting to conceal themselves. Concentrating his senses after coming to a stop, Etep determined the direction of the sound—it was coming from over the edge of the track to his right, and it was definitely heading down towards them. He and a dozen men tentatively approached that side of the path whilst the remainder remained vigilant. The starlit sky gave excellent visibility now that they were well above the woods, and Etep knelt with his head hanging out over the blackness, two strong men hanging onto him by his sword belt. His eyes tried to search along the mountainside below, but he could not see too far ahead at that oblique angle. His ears, however, functioned perfectly. Standing up, and dusting off his knees, he announced, "By The Dragon! Our old friend—Imo, comes this way."

One of the guardsmen urged caution, "How can you know it is Imo? Voices can be imitated and this could easily be some sort of trap, no?"

Etep looked the man in the eyes, "I have known Imo many long years, no one, and I do *mean* no one, can swear, curse, or spew forth profanities as strongly or as quickly, as that little maniac. Imo approaches for sure. I'd wager my cloak on it."

No guardsman would ever risk losing his cherished cloak, so he was taken at his word. Some of them peered over the edge, and, sure enough, a pair of big amber eyes appeared into view, staring from beneath a nest of matted hair. First, Imo's round, friendly, face became visible, then his familiar voice growled up to them, "Are you going to squat there gawking all night, hoping for a kiss, or give me a hand up?"

Many powerful arms reached down and took a firm grip, hoisting him up amidst his friends. Immediately, the men gathered around him clamped their cloaks over their noses, attempting to hold at bay the appalling stench rising from him. "By the sword!" coughed Etep through many folds of cloth, "You smell worse than a festering swine, my friend. What on earth have you been eating!?!"

There was a short, hushed burst of laughter at his old soldier's joke, his delight in seeing his friend alive and well, if somewhat sticky and smelly, was obvious, and the relief showed on his face. Imo would have hugged him closely were it not for himself being in such a disgusting state.

Even as Imo told Etep of the ghastly gathering that lay in wait further up the mountain, men brought up water and soap for him, and after a good scrubbing and rub down, he was clean, and dressed in fresh garb. The guardsmen listened carefully, stunned by his description of the enemy facing them. It was the Shadows that seemed most daunting, how did one kill something that was to all accounts and purposes already dead? Etep told Imo of his discovery of the departed Ranician, and his consequent building of the funeral pyre. Imo was very grateful of this.

There was no time to waste as their friends were still trapped within the cave. Etep and Imo headed the column together as they tramped up the narrow ledge to try and rescue them. When they rounded a particularly long curve their hearts leapt for joy. In the far distance they could see the faintest pencil line of light. Dawn! It was still some ways off as yet and if they waited for the sunrise proper, their comrades may well be lost. They pushed on.

Etep grabbed Imo's arm and they skidded to a halt on the loose shale that littered the mountain trail, hovering directly in front of them, stood Shadows. They were fanned out, blocking the way ahead. In the darkness they appeared all the more terrifying, just hovering there, vacant hooded robes that would have seemed empty if not for those dreadful dead eyes staring out from them. Swords would be of no avail here and torchbearers from the rear raced up to the front, shoving the flames at the near-motionless ghosts before them. Behind the Shadows lay a long stretch of track and an almost spent fire could be seen dwindling in a cleft in the mountainside. Directly in front of the fast fading flames all manner of hideous creatures could be seen screeching and clucking at each other. Etep having never seen a Shadow before, looked to Imo for guidance, but, alas, other the tiny snippets gained from the Westonians, he also had no knowledge of such things. But he did know this had to be his decision, he holding the senior rank. With his sword in one hand and a fiercely blazing torch in the other, he roared up the mountain, "Westonians! Hold fast! It is Imo, we are coming!" He then charged uphill and began trying to set alight the Shadows, his fellow torchbearers following his lead and doing the same.

Bestwin and Lumarr heard his battle cry and with a nod to each other and the remaining guardsmen, they began to tear down the smouldering barrier that had bought them so much valuable time. Outside the cave, the Venomeens and witches gathered close together to prevent their escape. The Shadows seemed impervious to the flames being stabbed and jabbed at them further downhill, but they by no means liked it. Their silent, motionless hovering of before had hidden an incredible turn of speed and as any guardsman tried to make contact with a torch, he would find the Shadow was now behind him, or perhaps five feet away. They moved in the blink of an eye and it was near impossible to make contact. However, the relentless harassment by the fire-wielding warriors distracted them enough for some men to slip past and race to reinforce the Westonians, and it was one of these frontrunners that first fell prey to those awful apparitions. He had not looked to his rear as he had passed them, and was, instead, looking as to what might lie ahead. A Shadow disappeared from its position and immediately reappeared hovering directly above him, it fell on him like a semi-transparent veil. The spectre wrapped itself around him tightly as if to cocoon him, and then within seconds it again arose to retake its earlier appearance. The guardsman lay dead, his appearance that of an ancient mummy, dry as dust, already crumbling away from view. His comrades were outraged, sickened by the awful sight. "STAY IN GROUPS!" bellowed Etep, "Do not be singled out! Stick together! Form hedgehogs!"

His men did not need to be told twice, and, seasoned veterans that they were, they instantly formed groups of three, six, or nine, depending on how many men could band together quickly without anyone being left vulnerable. These groups then bristled with blades and torches, thus forming 'hedgehogs'. Each group was too big for any single Shadow to envelope and so at least some form of protection from these ghouls could be achieved. Rotating as they moved, the hedgehogs continued to press on up the mountain. They sighted the Venomeens some minutes later, the bloodsuckers heading downhill towards them, snarling and growling as they came. They waddled rather than ran, their clumsy flat feet ungainly and wayward, always keeping their eyes fixed on the Samarians ahead. Their translucent skin, pale, and sagging in many large folds over their entire bodies, appeared luminous, glowing eerily against the contrasting backdrop of night. The men braced themselves—ready to tackle the red-eyed devils coming on at them. But they could not see what lay beyond the closing Venomeens.

Crouching low, its long, thick, black tongue lolling to one side, the hellhound moved stealthily towards the men coming up the hill.

It remained undetected, well hidden behind the bloodsuckers and the Shadows. Its nostrils were flared wide at the scent of so much human flesh. The creature could barely contain itself at the thought of the feast just some yards ahead and its huge powerful legs trembled uncontrollably with excitement. Behind the creeping hound, witches and hags were shrieking to each other up and down the mountain. They had strict instructions from the Venomeens to guard the mouth of the cave, but were acutely aware that one their very own had been roasted alive inside that same cave not so long ago. Without the Venomeens their earlier bravado had taken absence.

Imo knew of the presence of the hellhound and tried desperately to sight it. He could not see it anywhere and was worried as to where the damnable creature was hiding. He called back to the rear,

"Bring forth the Wrath of Amaris!" Then, after very brief consideration, he bellowed, "Bring forth *all* the Wrath of Amaris that you can muster! The scum have a hellhound hiding here, somewhere."

But the animal, by pure chance, chose to attack before the deadly crossbows could be brought to bear upon it. It leapt over the waddling Venomeens and landed squarely amidst the Samarian hedgehogs. The tight little mountain path quickly became a savage battleground with Shadows loitering menacingly in the background, waiting on the sidelines for a lone soul to become detached from his comrades and fall victim to their shrouds of death. The men knew they had to maintain their small, close formations, even whilst defending themselves against the Venomeens. The hellhound growled—a terrifyingly deep and sinister sound that sent a ripple of fear through many a brave heart. It slashed out at them, turning and turning again amidst the soldiers that were trying to bring it down in the dark, its natural night camouflage making their task that much more difficult. Its deadly jaw snapped up and down relentlessly, threatening to tear flesh from bone in an instant. Men were sent careering off the mountainside by the enraged brute as it slammed into them wildly, rearing up and swiping at others with its lethal claws as it did so. There was a great crash of steel-on-steel when the Venomeens smashed into the front ranks of the Samarians. Each man was ducking, jumping, stabbing, and slashing, moving in every direction whilst always remaining mindful of the menace of those hovering Shadows. To break from one's group would most likely cost one's life, but to stay in formation, whilst being savaged by a hellhound, and fighting off Venomeens in such a restricted space, on a precarious ledge, in the dark, was near impossible. At least the pandemonium on the mountainside allowed more reserves from the foot of the track to squeeze past and get up the hill to help, their greater numbers and far greater swordsmanship eventually beginning to tell. Decapitated Venomeens began to stain the rubble with their stinking blood. But the hellhound continued to wreak havoc amongst Etep's men. Shadows prevented anyone from breaking rank to try and set up the Wrath of Amaris, and despite the many wounds to its monstrous body, the demonic hound had barely slowed in its frenzied attack.

The Westonians could see the Wispy Witches and Hoary Hags waiting for them to exit the cave. They had enough presence of mind, and desire for self preservation, to light fiercely burning torches before kicking out the remnants of the fire, emerging sooty, and bleary-eyed, into the open, the fresh, clean air, filling their lungs at last. The sudden intake of oxygen made them feel briefly light-headed and unstable on their feet, but this giddiness passed quickly and they recovered their senses before the enemy could seize any advantage. They had heard Etep's earlier orders to his men, and, so, they, themselves, formed into a small, tight, hedgehog. In fact there were no Shadows in their vicinity, but the defensive formation provided excellent all-round visibility for each of them. Unfortunately, the *view* they gained was far from excellent, they could see that their immediate problem was the witches attempting to encircle them. The icy air condensing around the Hoary Hags chilled them even the more because it had been so hot inside the cave. They slashed at them wildly whilst trying to torch the Wispy Witches. A little further downhill, they could see the Venomeens fighting against a strong force of guardsmen. The familiar uniform was in evidence right down the track as far as they could see. The Venomeens, fighting ferociously with their cruel fangs bared at the men, seemed to be suffering the greater casualties. Beyond this melee they could see that hound from hell tearing into the Samarians without restraint.

Lumarr and Bestwin, being old hands, understood the picture clearly. Whilst initially the men seemed to have the upper hand, this was clearly a battle of attrition, and this vile vermin had yet to deploy their most deadly element—the Shadows. If that damned hellhound kept tearing at the men as it was, it may well cause the hedgehog formations to become broken, and this would be a devastating blow to their rescuers as the Shadows would show no mercy. Lumarr turned to Bestwin, "We must get down to where I can see horses and heavy weapons, that hound must die soon, or we will be lost."

Bestwin agreed; "Yes, we must. I have a plan to aid us, but have your shield to hand."

The four continued to fend off the death-dealing crones as Bestwin bellowed for all he was worth, "Men below! Bring down fire and flame upon us, directly onto us, NOW!"

His booming cry was heard by the embattled men fighting for their lives on the narrow track, and his wish was barked from man to man until it reached those waiting helplessly at the bottom. Immediately a group of archers moved into position and fires were lit for igniting pitch-soaked arrows. The night sky was slowly brightening but was still dark enough to provide a stark backdrop to the volley of burning missiles that began to rain down on the mountainside outside the cave. The men fighting there raised their shields over their heads just in time as scores of arrows screamed down, many slamming into their raised shields. The archers, deadly in their art, continued their onslaught, and exactly as Bestwin had hoped, it was not long before a Wispy Witch was hit—directly on the top of her head. At first she looked puzzled, as if unaware of her imminent fate she stood still with the burning shaft pointing straight up at the sky like some bizarre totem, then, she burst into flames—screaming that same scream they had heard earlier in the cave, she began running amok, grabbing at her ugly sisters in blind panic. They, in turn, ran screeching in all directions, trying to evade her dieing clutches as she desperately sought their aid. She finally managed to grab another of her kind in her fearful frenzy, and she, too, became engulfed.

"It seems there's a spark left in the old girls yet!" Laughed one of the guardsmen, but his good humour was lost on the grave faced Westonians.

The blazing witches were creating chaos amongst their own and giving the archers below much needed illumination up on the heights, allowing them to target them without endangering their friends. The rain of fire ceased, but a rain of death commenced. The Hoary Hags were impervious to the arrows but the sheer panic of the Wispy Witches forced them to, on occasion, get close to the sword swinging men, resulting in a pair of frosty heads thawing at the men's feet. "One cube or two?" the same Samarian tried another stab at humour, and received the same stern looks for his efforts. There had been a handful of Venomeens amongst the witches, but when the barrage of arrows began pelting the mountainside they had sought refuge inside the cave. Their frustrated, smouldering red eyes could be seen staring out from the smoky gloom within, livid at being thus thwarted so far. Lumarr told the guardsmen, "Friends, you must join with the nearest of your countrymen, Bestwin and I shall deal with that rampaging brute of a hellhound."

Using their shields as a battering ram, the Westonians charged downhill side by side, closely followed by the guardsmen. They ploughed into the rear of the Venomeens fighting Etep's troop, and smashed their way through, thrusting their heavy curved blades into the enemy as they passed. The Samarians were quick to join the fray amongst their fellow countrymen and watched Lumarr and Bestwin forging through, the men immediately giving way to the Westonians.

The lower levels of the path were jam packed with horses and men that simply could not get to join battle higher up, though Imo had shouted for heavy weapons, those that had heard him had themselves been too busy and unable to relay the command downhill. He had seen the Westonians making for the foot of the mountain, and, guessing their intentions, he disentangled himself from the vicious fighting and followed them, killing the hellhound would turn the tide much faster, with far less causalities to his own. Nimbly, he stormed off downhill, ever watchful of those silent Shadows.

The sound of clashing blades filled the twilight of the coming dawn. Birds refused to fill the hills with their chorus of new life whilst Old Man Death took his fill, and more, on the heights. The Samarians, greater in number and infinitely superior fighters, did not possess the inhuman strength and stamina of the Venomeens. The men fighting at the front began to tire but it was impossible to bring up the fresh reserves along that dangerously narrow strip. The Venomeens had the advantage of never tiring, and, being inescapably linked to Ogiin's spirit, they starved for human blood, hungering for the life-giving power it held, craving the living spirit their master needed so desperately to resurrect himself. The men fought on with every last ounce of strength remaining in them, using centuries of training and experience to their utmost, but it was impossible to land a decisive blow against this medley of monsters with the hellhound raging in their midst. The Shadows continued to watch on, unmoving and silent.

At the foot of the mountain they had heard the Westonians and Imo shouting at them minutes before they had finally arrived, sweating, with two covered in smoky soot. The horsemen had not failed them and half a dozen of the deadly crossbows sat armed and ready on the grass. Imo turned to the Westonians, "My lords—kill the hound."

He left them at the first bow and ran to the second one, "Men! Bring me pitch!"

Lumarr and Bestwin set about sighting their weapon, using a large boulder as a prop to gain the required elevation. Guardsmen brought many able hands to the task and Imo aimed a second spear onto the heights before he sprinted over to a third, and soon, that, too, was staring up the mountain with its dragon eyes. He bolted back to his first crossbow and securely bound clay jars of pitch to its shaft. The others would take longer to ensure precise targeting as their target—the hellhound, was constantly moving. He began soaking the second spear with oil. He affixed more jars of oil to yet a third spear. However, it was the *Westonians* that fired their weapon first. The great 'whoosh' made everyone up on the heights look down as the whistling spear caught the hellhound totally unawares in its hind quarters. A great cheer went up from the men fighting the beast as it let out an ear-piercing, high pitched scream that curdled the blood of those that had not heard such a sound before, but it was not finished by any means. The long range had caused the Wrath of Amaris to lose some of its potency and it had not drilled through its target as previous spears had done earlier against similar victims. With the projectile buried deep in its flesh, the creature went completely berserk. It seemed not to care for its own safety at all as it pounced on a guardsman and savaged him with its monstrous jaws. Etep leapt to the fore, causing several gaping wounds to that huge, demonic head, but it kept its teeth locked onto the soldier's midriff. The dark blood gushing from the man's mouth told the others that he would very soon pass from that life, his vital organs torn and ruptured. Etep retrieved a lost triblade and launched a furious attack on the screaming hound using two swords. A master swordsman, the weapons moved as one in his experienced hands and the hellhound was forced to drop its victim to confront this new threat. Etep twisted the spear embedded in the beast and it screamed in agony, its eyes blazing a hellstorm of fury at him.

Bestwin and Lumarr had not wasted any time in re-arming their weapon, but this time, as they fired a second spear, they heard another 'twang' and 'whoosh' as Imo also fired a bolt onto the heights. Lumarr was dead on target this time, and the Wrath of Amaris not only rammed into the hellhound's neck, but it almost decapitated the snarling brute. Imo's shot seemed to disappear into the side of the mountain itself, followed by the unmistakeable sound of pottery shattering. The Westonians could see that the shortest of the guardsmen was also certainly one of the most cunning. He had fired directly into the cave, soaking its interior in the highly flammable oil, and now his second bolt—already alight, was heading for the same destination. It took incredible marksmanship, but Imo *had* that credential, and the Wrath of Amaris delivered the torch of death to the drenched cave.

A massive fireball erupted from the cave mouth, followed by burning Venomeens running out, wailing pitifully as the flames engulfed them. Etep ran forward with both triblades spinning in his hands. He began making short work of the bloodsuckers as others finished off the screaming half-headless hellhound. What witches and Venomeens remained, saw that this battle was lost and began backing away up the mountain, putting distance between themselves and the angry faced warriors following them. Etep's triblade had just parted another Venomeen's head from its neck and he looked back proudly at his men as they walked up towards him. They were to be the last sight he would see, because, having broken away from them, he had been spotted by the Shadows, and now, once more, that grey blanket of death fell from above. Etep was no more.

The Westonians and Imo had returned, standing helpless as the sinister grey shape on the ground rose up, once more becoming a sombre shroud, hovering before them, barefaced and unrepentant. The sight it left behind was too hideous for words. The mountainside was quiet now and Imo, his heart bleeding for his lost friends, thundered, "Loose the third Wrath!"

A loud twang, and another spear, ablaze and laden with pitch, soared up from below as he had planned, smashing into the rock face just past the cave. The ensuing ball of flame tore along the mountainside, engulfing witches and Venomeens alike. When the firestorm subsided, they could not only see the death and carnage that had been wrought upon Ogiin's creed, but also the chilling fact that the Shadows still remained, entirely unharmed.

The Westonians cast a glance at each other, sad regret in their eyes, and then at Imo, who was about to attack the Shadow hovering by Etep. Bestwin spoke gently to the fuming little Samarian, "Imo, we offer our deepest regrets at the losses you and yours have suffered this terrible night. Etep was a great warrior and the master of our salvation. We cannot risk more losses against the ghouls that hover thus before us. They will not attack us as amassed as we now stand, and you, my brave friend, must temper your vengeance with patience. All scores will be settled in time. Peace, Imo. We must continue our journey to the Western Worlds and relay what we find there to Tamarin."

Upon hearing his king's name, Imo calmed a little from his fury over the death of his friend Etep. First Ranician, and, now, Etep. Ogiin's creed owed him a hefty debt and there would be no respite until the balance was fully paid. The blood lust settled temporarily, the red mist cleared from his welling eyes. He turned to Bestwin, "My lords, you who have fought alongside my countrymen today as brothers, must know this—I will never stop pursuing these ghouls until I see each and every one of them destroyed. Etep was by far the best of us here and had served my king, even the great king—Darcinian, with record unblemished. He and I will dance with The Dragon amongst the stars one day, but until that day comes, I shall pursue Ogiin's filthy vermin whilst breath..."

A mighty thunderclap cut him short, but there were no black clouds in sight, no pitter-patter of rain, no sudden drop of temperature, nothing. The men crowded along the path looked up, confused. Exhausted from battle, and weary of loss, not one of them fancied taking on some new nightmarish adversary so soon. Lumarr noticed the Shadows had begun flitting about, unable to stand still for a second. It seemed as if the devils were nervous, agitated. Then Bestwin pointed a big thick finger, "There!" Sure enough, they could see the day beginning to peel back the blanket of night on the horizon, no longer a wafer thin line of light, the distant sky to both east and west was changing. It was only then that they noticed that it was not nearly as dark as it had been, and they could see each other quite clearly. The dawn had crept up on them unseen and now they could even make out the men and horses down below. They glared at the Shadows, which began to move away from them, their grey robes edging soundlessly up the track. It was obvious they feared daybreak and the scorching anger of the blazing suns. They had to head up into the mountains and find refuge from the approaching dawn, or descend to the awaiting men and their torches. The men felt confident that the spectres were somehow in a weakened state as morning approached, and thus, perhaps, vulnerable to fire.

The Shadows began retreating faster and faster, backwards up the hill. Their cold, evil eyes, continued to stare emotionlessly from under those grey cowls, but they lacked the arrogance and confidence of the earlier hours. The guardsmen (particularly Imo) made ready to give chase, but the burly Lumarr blocked their way. He stood with his arms spread wide, and, when the men had steadied, he raised one finger to his lips in the universal sign of 'Shhh'. He had his back to the Shadows when he did this, but turning sharply, he pointed to the top of the mountain upon which they stood. At the peak, a mist was gathering very quickly, swirling around the mountain top at ever increasing speed. It was of a bright blue colour and twinkled with sudden flashes. The Dragon's Breath was forming.

The warriors, worn to the marrow, began pursuing the Shadows up the mountain as the dawn allowed them to see what lay ahead. They could see the peak was now completely shrouded in the Dragon's Breath. The strange, blue fog, seemed to be circling at a phenomenal rate, and then, suddenly, it disappeared out of sight, as if sucked away by some unseen vacuum. Having lost sight of it, they refocused on the Shadows which had put more distance between them while they had been distracted by the Dragon's Breath. But now the saddened, angry men, had only one subject on their minds, one single sense of purpose—the destruction of the grey phantoms trying to escape up into the mountains.

Imo ordered torchbearers to the fore, and then they began following the Shadows, trying to close the gap to the point whereupon they could bring their flames into effect, and determine whether or not they served good purpose against the ghostly shrouds. The path ahead curved sharply to the left and he urged caution as the Shadows were out of sight around the bend. He did not want anyone walking into an ambush. But when they rounded the bend the sight that met their eyes was the last thing they had expected to see. Those harbingers of death—the Shadows, were hurtling back towards them at breakneck speed, their dark gowns billowing out behind them. The warriors facing them immediately sensed that this was no sudden counter attack, but rather, fully fledged flight. The reason for this became apparent when the men looked further up the mountain and saw the Dragon's Breath barrelling down towards them. Daylight had just barely kissed the strange blue mist, but already it was alive with raw energy. The light moved from spark to spark within it and it crackled as it gathered momentum. It was truly breathtaking, an electrical storm raging within the fog.

The men braced themselves for when those ghastly ghouls would impact on their shields, and burning torches formed a blazing barrier. But their flames would never test the mettle of the Shadows. The hooded demons, floating like death, itself, down the mountain, were engulfed by the Dragon's Breath. It rolled over them as it continued downhill and the onlookers cheered as it lofted the grey robes up high into its centre. Blinding flashes of light and energy struck mercilessly at the silent Shadows as they hung helpless in the air, suspended in the transparent mist. Not a single sound was heard from them, but their acute suffering was plain to see, and a joy to behold for the cheering men. The fast moving cloud rolled over *them*, too, as they stood bemused by this marvellous spectacle. But to them, it felt as fresh as a spring breeze wafting over a dewy meadow at daybreak, reviving and invigorating their senses. The Shadows, however, danced like puppets on strings within the Dragon's Breath, buffeted and bowled in all directions. The mist continued down the mountain and broke up on the big boulders below. It rolled more gently over the grass and dissipated into the woods, leaving the hillside wet and lush in its wake.

Bestwin walked a short distance up the path. Lieing there were the remains of what must have once been the Shadows. Whilst no physical body could be seen due to the all enveloping shrouds, the men could now see what had once resembled a face under the hood.

The small shrivelled corpses appeared to be made of ash and the terribly tortured faces beneath the cowls made even the boldest of them shiver. The faces seemed to have been dredged up from the depths of hell, such was their ghastly appearance. Molten flesh and eyes filled with terror gave testament to the agony of their final moments. A light mountain wind was beginning to peck at the fallen Shadows and soon they were all but dust, carried away by the blustering breeze and a bright new dawn.

Imo trudged, limp-shouldered, back to the fallen Etep. Gently he lifted his now near-weightless friend in both arms, and carried him down the mountain. Guardsmen searched through brush and bush, finding out other comrades that had fallen from the heights. Yet more were brought down that had died in battle above. Much to the sadness and dismay of the Westonians, more Samarian funeral pyres sent smoky sorrows up to the heavens.

The suns were rising in earnest now and the men at the foot of the mountain were grateful for their offering of warmth on their backs. Injuries were attended to, and many a man slapped another on the back to congratulate him on his brave deeds that night. Imo was the toast of the morning and it would be fair to say he was deserving of it. The Westonians thanked the horsemen for their bravery and sacrifice, then they sat on a small boulder with Imo to discuss the next move whilst sipping at hot herbal tea, laced with cherry rum.

Bestwin began. "I'm more certain now than ever before that that most despotic of tyrants—Ogiin, blights these worlds once more. The vermin we have so narrowly defeated today would never be so brazen were they not filled with some new confidence, some new calling. I fear we have dealt with but the least of our problems. We can neither linger nor tarry. Time, I feel, is not on our side. We must make, without further delay, double quick time, to our homeland."

Imo's voice, heavy with sorrow, betrayed his complete exhaustion, "My lords, I am your loyal escort, as are my fellow guardsmen. I agree we must make extreme haste to the Western

Worlds, for my liege awaits our news. Whatever your plan, our swords ride with you."

Lumarr lit his pipe with great care and attention, just as he had done the previous evening, the fragrant smoke trickling into the air and masking the unpleasant odour of the smouldering funeral pyres. He puffed on it repeatedly to get it going well, then he leaned back against Bestwin's shoulder, closing his eyes for a few seconds, opening them again before taking a long haul on that aromatic leaf. He exhaled slowly, deliberately, and the others waited patiently. He obviously had something to say, and when Lord Lumarr had something to say—only a fool failed to hearken unto his words. "I have lived," he began, "to see all manner of events transpire over these many long years. I have seen kingships fade and kingships rise. I have seen queens disappear and princes appear. I have watched as entire nations died whilst a single infant was born. Suffice to say—I have gained some experience of how the natural order of life should be. If Ogiin is returned, and I agree with *you*, Bestwin, that he has, then something entirely unnatural, and new to me, has occurred. I saw that foul demon fall from the sky in a blaze of dragon's flame, to be lost to the deepest depths. I saw this with my own eyes. How is it then that he has returned, and more importantly—*why*?"

He paused to take another long, slow, puff on his pipe, and with his finger gently tapping at the warm bowl to make it smoke more smoothly, he continued. "This mountain path is long and torturous and we are now too many to travel quickly and remain discreet. I therefore suggest that we reduce our number to one score. The remainder must return to Sitivia with the wounded so they may receive the care they need, and also to inform Tamarin of what we now know is afoot in his realm. Those of us remaining will forge through these mountains and on to the Western Worlds with all speed. If we do not encounter any more of Ogiin's creed on route, the journey can be completed in short order. I have no doubt our own homeland is, itself, under threat, if not already weathering this black tide. If this be so, then either Bestwin, or I, must remain there to rally what is left of our armies and defend our shores. The other will return to Sitivia with this escort to summon our staunchest ally to our aid. This is the only option I believe us to have. If any have a differing view, I would hear it now." He tapped out the burnt embers from his pipe, and after cleaning out the bowl with the tip of his dagger, he refilled it with fresh leaf.

Neither Imo nor Bestwin had anything to say. His words held the ring of truth. Bestwin rummaged in his tunic and produced a shorter, stubbier, version, of his friend's pipe. He filled it with leaf passed to him by Lumarr and put flame to it. The Westonians moved and sat upright, back-to-back on the grass, puffing easily on their pipes in the morning sunshine as if relaxing at a village fete. Imo watched the grey-blue smoke rising from their little ceramic bowls. The Samarian could not help wondering how on earth those fragile pipes managed to survive the heat and violence of battle. He knew the Westonians were showing him much respect, despite their outranking him, they were leaving it to him to organise the guardsmen surrounding them on the foothills. It was a mark of gratitude for his service and he was grateful to them for it. Imo would decide who stayed, and who returned to the capital. He rose to his feet and bowed his head, "My lords, I shall organise our escort, and return."

The Westonians, sitting back-to-back as they were, could now talk without fear of being overheard. Lumarr broke the short silence first, "Bestwin, many a brave warrior has departed this life for our sakes, and each a Samarian. These are the people of The Dragon and I beseech the spirits of the ancient dragons to keep their people safe, for I fear we will not see our homes without further molestation by Ogiin's creed. You and I, my old friend, must try and protect these brave young guardsmen as best we can, even as *they* seek to protect *us*."

Bestwin was of the same vein. "You have spoken the very thoughts that filled my mind. My heart bleeds to see so many brave souls lost at the calling of the Western Worlds. Had King Dorinn not lost his way, had he even one tenth of the heart of one of these bold guardsmen, then perhaps these pyres would not be darkening both mood and sky here today. That fool owes a hefty debt to

Tamarin and his noble warriors. I would see that debt fully paid in due course, with Dorinn's own pathetic hide!."

"Mind your thoughts, Bestwin," whispered Lumarr, "Dorinn is the *rightful* king. But he is not the *right* king—I agree. It is not for the likes of you or I to crown kings, nor to dethrone them. Nature was born of The Source and she has a way of balancing everything. Have faith my Westonian warrior, this chapter in our history is yet but within its first paragraph."

They saw Imo approaching and curbed their concerns so as not to worry the wily little guardsman heading towards them. He had organised the men well. Already horses were being fitted with stretchers for the injured and the bulk of the troop was forming up, ready to re-enter the woods at the foot of the hill, and make for Sitivia. A smaller group of fearsome looking men stayed closer to the Westonians, and would now form the escort for the westbound party. Imo had chosen wisely and these particular warriors were renowned for their fighting skills and courage.

The start of the journey had been a brisk affair. Those going east had been saddened at not having the opportunity to head west and face whatever threatened Samaria from those shores. Lumarr had assured them that the battle the previous night was but an inkling of things to come and this cheered their fearless hearts no end. The horses jostled each other impatiently, eager to leave this place where the thick, sickly sweet, smell of death still clung tenaciously to the morning air. The Westonians were at the head of their small column and with hands raised in farewell, they watched the larger party enter the woods. Bestwin turned to Imo, "It is time." He then moved forward with Lumarr at his side and eighteen guardsmen to the rear. The tight rock-strewn track leading up into the mountains was littered with the detritus of battle, yet seemed completely different in the bright morning sunlight, making it almost impossible to imagine the atrocities that had occurred there only hours before. This was most surely a blessing. The road ahead would hold many new challenges, but every rider present was prepared to meet them, whatever fate they may hold in store for him.

CHAPTER TWELVE

THE SILENT CITY

Tamarin signalled his riders to stop. A biting chill in the air partnered the sighting of the ominous silhouette of Soledad's skyline, her sombre towers and domes edging into view. They had travelled at a reduced pace for the last leg of the journey. Meekhi was still suffering from her bruises, and Mercy needed respite for her ankle to heal fully. Thus the journey had taken far longer than expected, but that was a price Tamarin was happy to pay to ensure the wellbeing of the injured women. The little strangers also appeared to be waning, but Ramulet was holding up well. "Remarkable, considering his recent ordeal," he thought. In fact, at half distance, Ramulet had dropped back to engage the young ones in conversation. Thomas had pleaded ceaselessly to be trained by him in combat. Tamarin heard him say, "As you're the Captain of the Royal Guards, I reckon you must be really hot at all this."

Ramulet had agreed that he was very hot indeed, but yes—he would train Thomas if he so wished in such a sweltering heat. The boy had given the captain a firm handshake and was now grinning from ear to ear. Tamarin had a confusing, but not unpleasant, take on Zowie. There was something very Samarian about her, but he could not put his finger on it. "Time," he thought, "will, no doubt, reveal all." It was mid evening and the usual long shadows were being cast by the setting suns. Everyone could feel the sad, eerie loneliness of Soledad reaching out to them. It was a truly horrible sensation, a forlorn emptiness that swamped one's soul and threatened to engulf one's heart. Turning about, Tamarin faced his people. "We have reached Soledad and will shortly feel her cold embrace. For so many years this mighty city has known only the sheer loneliness and horror forced upon her so long ago. But do not fear her, my friends. She is a Samarian city, and I say she is our friend and ally. One day Soledad shall be released from her enforced role as a stone cold prison for souls. We will enter and leave the city not in fear as others would have us do, but with our heads held high in acknowledgement of the blood ties we share with our brethren so cruelly ensnared there by Ogiin's curse. Let us now see that which has not been seen before by any of us here. The drumming of our beating hearts shall break the silence of the Silent City!"

He leaned across and took the hand of his beloved Meekhi. She had reached out for his, and he held hers for a few brief seconds, their eyes locked together in that wordless, voiceless communication, that only those truly in love can ever experience. Her long slender fingers slipped from his grip as finally he took hold the reins of his horse and started the final leg to Soledad.

Meekhi watched the man she loved as he rode so confidently into an unknown that others had not dared to tread for time beyond memory. She noticed his warm, beautiful, eyes—fixed unerringly on the high walls in the distance. She knew the strength in his lean muscles and the power of his pure heart. The cloak on his back proudly boasted his faith in the Great Dragon. She found her own heart was pounding furiously within her breast, not with fear at the imminent arrival in Soledad, but rather it was overflowing with the love and adoration she had for him. She had made a mistake at the Desert of Iret, and she swore to herself—this would not happen in Soledad.

Mercy's mood was a little low, her spirit muted. She had been overjoyed at the safe return of Ramulet, but since that return he seemed vague and distant to her, almost evasive. She had hoped he would feel the same joy upon seeing her that she had felt for him, but if he did, he was keeping it well hidden. Mercy was not one for being kept in the dark, or kept waiting. Sidling up beside him, she overheard him explaining to Thomas that he had no idea what 'Ninjitsu' was. She politely interrupted the conversation and

Ramulet seemed grateful for an excuse to break away from the pestering young stranger. He and Mercy trotted along together a tad slower than the rest of the party, until they were at the tail of it, then they attached themselves to the rear.

Riding close beside him she reached out just as her queen had done earlier, and her hand, too, was enclosed in a loving grip. She wasted no time. "My lord, since you escaped from the claws of Iret, I have been saddened by your absence from my side. Have I offended you in some manner? Or perhaps you are still not fully recovered from your terrible ordeal? Tell me, what ails you?"

Ramulet had not planned on exactly this moment in which to explain the happenings within that miserable cave, but the moment was now thrust upon him and he would serve Mercy no morsel other than the truth. Holding her hand firmly as they trotted along, he, without hesitation, explained of his shame at his own weakness, of how he had been biding his time to talk to her and explain to her the sickness he had suffered within Iret. She did not say a word, or interrupt even once, listening patiently to every single detail. He told her everything, squeezing out from himself the pus of Iret as one would lance a boil, omitting nothing, unburdening his conscience completely. Step by step he told his whole torrid tale, and this took some considerable time in the telling. When he had finally finished he fell silent, awaiting a response. It was only then that he noticed that he was no longer holding Mercy's hand, *she* was holding his.

Mercy never had, and never would, doubt her Ramulet, her most honourable captain. She faced him, holding his gaze and gripping his big powerful hand more firmly, "My lord. Your shame flatters me unduly for there is nothing to be ashamed of, yet you feel this shame because you would not offend my heart. Iret is a place of poison. Any man that ventures there will become infected with its filth. You were bereft of your senses whilst within that subterranean horror. But still, whilst intoxicated by the witch's fumes you had the heart to break free of her—destroying her lair in the process. Yes, I am proud of you, yes, I admire you—big, bold *Captain of The Royal Guards* that you are, but let me tell you something new that I hope will lift your melancholy mood," she leaned over so her face was right next to his, her lips nuzzling his ear, he catching a light kiss of her sweet perfume, "Ramulet, Mercy loves you with all her heart and has always done so!"

Statement made, she spurred her horse to catch up with Meekhi and Tamarin. Ramulet only managed to blurt out, "My heart is..." before she was already three horse lengths away, so he cleared his throat quickly, booming out, "MY HEART IS YOURS TOO, AND ALWAYS HAS BEEN!"

Everyone except Mercy spun around to look back at him, and he suddenly felt he must search deep inside his cloak for some reason. The guardsmen nodded to each other approvingly and Tamarin and Meekhi winked knowingly at Mercy. Zowie and Lauren thought it just so wonderfully romantic and Thomas became less confident in the chances of Ramulet being a true Ninja. Ramulet, however, was pleased to at last let the woman of his dreams know of his feelings for her, loving her all the more for her instant understanding of his earlier predicament. He nudged his horse to catch up with hers and she gave him a sugar-sweet smile that caused him to blush. Rordorr turned his face to Faradorr, "As if we don't have enough to deal with right now, my brother. What with Ogiin and Teritee creating havoc in the realm, we now have young lovers courting in the midst of these terrible upheavals. By The Dragon! They will bewanting to be wed in Soledad next, and then, no doubt, we will *all* be peering out of black marble eyes."

His brother turned his head to face him, "But brother, are those not tears of joyful emotion that I see welling up in your eyes even now?"

"Humph!" Rordorr snorted, "I have sand in my eyes. It will probably leave me blind."

Faradorr smiled fondly at him, and the two mighty horses continued to trot alongside the small column with Rordorr averting his eyes from his laughing brother.

The long hours in the saddle were beginning to take their toll on Tamarin. He and his men had ridden from Sitivia to the Pink Mountain and back to Soledad with barely a pause. The horses would soon need a lengthy break and some proper nourishment or they would collapse from exhaustion. As the sunlight began to diminish at last, the dark outline of Soledad sat starkly against the lighter hue of the heavens. Whilst still half an hour's ride away, it was easy to distinguish onion domed buildings from those with square towers or sloping roofs. A high wall encircled the city completely, punctuated with watchtowers where sentries from the garrison would have once stood. No birds circled the sky above and no sound came from this former metropolis. Only the eerie echo of silence could be heard. The very blackness of the city shocked everyone. Everything they could see was black—black stone, black marble, black memories.

Tamarin began to organise his men. Ramulet (despite his stiff protests) would remain at the city gates to protect Meekhi and Mercy. They caused quite a furore about this ruling but he insisted, and that was that. It was of course very chivalrous of the king, but these two were a feisty pair and did not appreciate being 'nursed' in that manner. The children, as free agents, and not subjects of the crown, could do as they pleased. The Samarians were surprised to hear that the young ones would enter The Silent City alongside them. Initially Thomas had suggested he stay with Ramulet to help guard the women, but a severe twist of his ear by his sister had changed his mind very quickly. They had received some basic training en route to Soledad, learning how to hold and manoeuvre a sword correctly through some simple basic strokes. They could hardly be considered competent, but Ramulet and Mercy agreed that now, at least, they were unlikely to cut off their own ears. They remained unarmed as the weighty triblades were well beyond their size and ability, and the lighter, single-bladed, weapons numbered but two—Meekhi's and Mercy's.

Despite the understandable nerves, the children were actually quite excited by the thought of entering a deserted city of stone. They had heard many of their riding party talking of the history of the place—of how beautiful it had once been, and of the awful curse that now held it bound in blackness. They thought it terribly sad, and Zowie told the others, "If I see a stone baby I'm going to break down, I just know I am, it would be just too horrible for words."

The Shortwaters had not considered such a possibility and Lauren winced at the thought, "That Ogiin really is a very nasty piece of work, and this Teritee doesn't sound any better. She's a proper old slapper if you ask me—seducing guys all over the shop to get what she wants. I'm so glad we hooked up with these Samarians, they really are a lovely lot. Good call, Zowie."

"I think," suggested Thomas, "that our adventures are only now about to begin. What's more, I'm not afraid of wherever we are, or whatever we may face. You know what? I think the air and water here make me feel stronger, *you know*...braver..."

"I think you're right, Tom," Zowie agreed, "I feel like we're different people here. I mean...I'd never have dreamed I would enjoy handling a sword, but I'm really into it!"

"You certainly are!" Lauren quipped, "I saw your eyes when Mercy was teaching us, and you were only *totally* loving it."

Zowie's killed the conversation with, "Hope we don't have need of it then hey, guys..."

Tamarin had noticed how for some time now the sound of the horse's hooves falling in the sand had been changing. Rather than the dull, flat, thud-thud of before, there was now a definite clatter to their footfalls. He stopped and swung out of his saddle with Ramulet joining him in an instant. They used their hands to brush away the surface sand and revealed large stone slabs beneath it. "My lord, it is the old road to Soledad." Ramulet told him.

Tamarin looked ahead and could see the great gates of the city, firmly sealed as expected. Looking back, he could make out the faint outline of a wide road, long hidden beneath the sifting sands. "In ages past," he told Ramulet, "how many feet did sing and dance upon this road, my friend? How many blazing torches lit this ancient path during the Festival of Light when maidens brought forth the sparkling water from the Emerald River, fireworks lit the night sky, the sound of drums, merry songs and cheers of joy held sway over the sands, buried right under our feet, Ramulet, is the glory of our fathers' time—The Age of All Ages".

Placing a hand on Tamarin's shoulder, Ramulet turned to the solemn gates that lay yonder, and the high wall amid which they sat.

"My lord, we should not linger outside the walls. There is far more than fond memories beneath these sands, as I have had the misfortune to discover at first hand."

"You are right, captain," Sighed Tamarin, "let us be away to the sanctuary of the city."

The cities aura of loneliness was almost unbearable and bit into the Samarians like a harsh arctic wind. They stood at the gates and a silent screaming tore through their hearts, flooding them with torment and anguish. The Silent City wretched up its mute suffering upon the warriors gathered at her door and the tormented cries of the entombed ancients were heard in the mind far louder than any sound any ear could ever withstand. The riders felt as if they were drowning under that tidal wave of misery as the hidden ghosts of Soledad whispered relentlessly, agonisingly, "Save us! *We suffer so*! Save us! Save us!"

Forlorn for centuries, desolate Soledad begged for release from her age-long lament, again and again the haunting voices assailed the hearts and minds of the living. Tamarin flinched upon seeing the look of sheer misery on the faces of Meekhi and Mercy, no one could bear such infinite sadness for long without madness taking hold of their mind, even his own heart felt weighed down to the pit of his stomach, these ancient spirits, cursed though they may be, were *his* people still, *his* subjects, and they must surely be looking to him to put right the ghastly wrong done unto them. He was relieved to see the young ones from the other worlds, at least, were unaffected by the incessant pleading.

It was twilight when he and Ramulet stood before the enormous gates. Once made from tough Samarian oak, their surface now had the smooth sheen of polished stone. They saw the formidable looking lock that sealed them, and with faces sad enough to break any heart, they lifted it up. From its feel and weight they knew that it, too, was made of stone. Tamarin scraped away centuries of dirt and dust to reveal an inscription that made him lock onto Ramulet's misty eyes. It read:

> *Since the crystal bells of Soledad did ring their final peel*
> *These blackened stone portals forever I did seal.*
> *Stone bells know only silence and never again will ring.*
> *Thus in the name of compassion, and that of my King,*
> *I tell you do not enter here, Soledad nought but tears doth bring.*
>
> Lord Amaris,
> In the name and service of:
> King Darcinian.

Ramulet froze rigid when he saw what Tamarin had just read. Tamarin, too, was overwhelmed upon seeing the mention of his own father by the father of Ramulet. Both King and Captain eyed each other with an even more binding respect. A bond of brotherly love existed between them just as it had between their fathers. The inscription had reminded them of the history their two bloodlines shared, and had shared for so very long. Again Tamarin felt a pang of pain for his beloved friend, pain for the disappearance of his father, a question as yet still unresolved. He could not imagine the burden of misery that must bear down upon Ramulet's shoulders every day. Most surely he would have moved heaven and earth to find Ramulet's father if he had known he might yet live. The witch had unknowingly given Ramulet hope, and he would fan the flames of that hope as soon as he was able. Tamarin took a deep breath, disguising his emotion from the many eyes watching from behind, for a king cannot be as free as others with the troubles of his heart, duty demands he serve the needs of his nation before his own. The pair locked forearms in the manner of Samarian brothers, then Ramulet stood back. Only a king could undo the bidding of a king, and he raised his triblade high over his head. His entire body radiated the power that coursed through his veins, a strength of spirit handed down from father to son since Samaria was born. He whispered a barely audible, "Forgive me, father." Then his sword struck the lock, smashing it to a million pieces. There was a very loud 'CRACK' when the lock shattered under the force of his blow, making the young ones jump.

The children were well aware of the history relating to the current, cursed state of Soledad, but they could not understand why suddenly everyone had become so drenched in misery at the gates. The spirits entrapped within the city had called out to fellow Samarians only, and this was why the children could not hear their heartbreaking appeals. They had been raised with good manners and were polite enough to not inquire as to why the others felt so awful. They could sense the tension mounting quickly in this amazing adventure of theirs, but Soledad made them jittery and gave them the creeps.

The riders had dismounted at the gates with the girls standing beside Meekhi and Mercy. They found themselves hugging the two women as they watched Ramulet and Tamarin. The accompanying guardsmen were faring no better against Soledad's ghosts but they stayed close to the king, ready to do his bidding. He was examining the large stone rings mounted into the centre of each gate. He and Ramulet pulled hard on them but they would not budge an inch. Tamarin beckoned the others to join him, and as the children approached, they could quite clearly see, even in the fast-fading light, a rampant dragon had been embossed on one gate, and a very ornate triblade on the other. These symbols were now as black as the gates themselves, but they still sent a shudder down the children's spines. Not an unpleasant shudder, but rather one of those electric tingles you get when you are excited momentarily by something you can't explain, a warm, pleasant, tickly kind of a shudder.

Guardsmen joined the king, taking hold of the heavy rings hanging like outsize door knockers on the gates, together they heaved and hauled, their booted feet slipping in the sand, but to no avail, entry to the city remained strictly forbidden. The children watched their futile efforts as night began to take a firm grip of the land. Zowie asked Meekhi why the horses were not used to pull the gates open, and she replied that the horses were close to collapsing as it was, any further strain may well mean the death of them.

"What about the winged horses?" The girl persisted.

"Zowie, no Samarian would dream of asking a flying horse to perform such a menial task! If one of them was to *offer* his services, well, that would be an entirely different matter."

The winged brothers were sitting dozing in the sand, unaware of the stubborn reluctance of Soledad to open her doors.

"*I'm* not Samarian, so couldn't *I* ask those two for help?" Zowie suggested.

Mercy saw no harm in this. "We need those gates opened, and opened quickly, so I can't see why not."

Zowie ambled off in the direction of the beautiful black horses, looking as if she was about to commit a serious crime. She walked around so as to come face to face with them, and the city, strolling up to the pair as if out for a leisurely Sunday walk. "Err... excuse me. I really hope I'm not interrupting anything important, but..." she stared down at her feet and faltered a little, before asking, "could you please help Tamarin open the gates? Because they are stuck shut. All the men are pulling but nothing's happening, and it's getting dark now, if that's ok with you, of course?"

The horses turned their heads and took a sidelong glance at the men still heaving and prying at the hefty portals. Rordorr told Faradorr, "Little brother, you have injuries still and I've no doubt they will ultimately prove fatal. Stay and rest whilst I aid the king. You would think they would have asked me sooner. Should the gates crash down upon my back and I am crushed into the sand, as will most likely happen, then tell my beloved wife—*Eronell,* that whilst I died in the service of my king, it was she that was foremost on my mind."

Faradorr shook his head and returned to his light sleep as his brother rose and stretched his mighty frame, fully extending his spectacular wings as he did so. Zowie jumped back, shocked again by the glorious sight of those crimson marvels. He lowered his big head so he was looking her straight in the eyes, and spoke to her conspiratorially, "You, little Zowie, are the one with the sense and wisdom to ask of my services. This shows quick thinking and an understanding of simple truths. I believe you and I could have been friends were I not doomed to be buried under the black gates of Soledad."

Zowie was thrilled beyond imagining at the thought of having a *talking horse* as a friend, but she had picked up on various snatches of conversation that day and was beginning to understand this gigantic animal and his strange, dreary ways.

"Yes, Rordorr, I think we could have been really great friends if you were not going to be buried alive under the gates. But I think a part of that high wall will come away too, and as I'm going to help you pull on those gates, I am sure I will be crushed alongside you, an all too brief friendship then, but one that will hold true to the very agonising end."

"At last," sighed the horse as he headed for the obstinate gates, "a friend that truly understands me and my positive way of thinking."

Zowie and her new-found friend approached the men whose efforts were still being thwarted by the dead weight of stone they were trying to move. Rordorr caught Tamarin's eye, and, sweating profusely, the king accepted his kind offer of assistance. A strong harness of thick rope was formed and strapped onto the horse. Rordorr took up the slack and the lines became as taut as bow strings, he shuffled about to gain a secure footing then began hauling for all he was worth. Men raced to add their weight to his efforts. Zowie stood by his head with the Shortwaters—offering encouragement. Mighty muscles bulged all over his heaving frame and the stone rings were creakily lifted from where they had rested for so long as the ropes attached to them began to sing with the sheer energy being poured through them. Everyone was sweating heavily with the effort but it was Rordorr that bore the brunt of the strain. Twice his hooves slipped, and he nearly fell, only to regain his balance just in time. The harness was digging into him quite painfully and he began to fan his flanks with his wings to minimise the burning of the ropes biting into his flesh. As he beat his wings he found himself hovering over the sand, a few seconds at a time. Then, suddenly letting the ropes go slack, he turned his head and told all of them to let go. The night air was much cooler now and he took some long, deep breaths. His eyes met Zowie's, "Stand back, Zowie, and move your fellow travellers with you. I am a foolish horse to say the least. I could not make use of my wings within the clammy clutches of Iret, but I am not in that dung ridden snake pit now."

The stunning black animal spread his beautiful red wings and began to beat the night air with them. The silence of the desert was suddenly filled with the sound of those wings flapping faster and faster. They watched in awe as he lifted easily into the air. Tethered as he was to the gates, he made a spectacular sight as he hung there in the air, silhouetted against the sky, his gigantic wings trying to bear him further skywards as the ropes stretched to the limit and began humming under the enormous strain. His powerful legs pumped his hooves up and down as if he were trying to ascend some invisible staircase and his nostrils flared wide with the incredible effort. The laboured huffing and puffing was heard by all below.

Gathered below, they could do nothing but look on helplessly as Rordorr's flanks started to lather up. Lauren swore she could actually hear his heart pumping furiously. The harness was cutting into his softer underbelly and a thin, bright red, line of blood could be seen staining it. "Oh! Rordorr! Please stop!" Zowie shouted up to the enormous horse suspended in the air above her, "You will hurt yourself very seriously!"

His big rolling eyes, bloodshot from his efforts, peered briefly at the young lady pleading with him to desist. "Of that I have no doubt, my friend," he told her, "I will probably crush you too when I fall dead from the sky."

He began to beat his wings so fast that it appeared as if he was galloping on the air flanked by two, bright red, starbursts.

Mercy and Ramulet stood together and Tamarin wrapped an arm around Meekhi's shoulders. "All that we are, my lady," he whispered in her ear, "all that Samaria aspires to be, all that the Great Dragon has taught us in his infinite wisdom, hangs in the air before us, in that horse." Meekhi raised her hand and held Tamarin's, her eyes remaining locked on Rordorr.

Finally, to everyone's surprise, the great gates of Soledad finally shuddered, a fine dust beginning to fall from them. With an awful creaking and the grating of stone on stone, Soledad broke her long silence and they scraped open. Rordorr landed immediately but was too weak to stand. His trembling legs gave way and he fell forward onto his knees. Men and the children ran to his aid. A sore, bleeding red welt could be seen running across his belly where the rope had bitten quite deeply into his flesh. It would heal, but was smarting badly. His pain was obvious in his face. Zowie and Lauren were stroking him when Tamarin arrived next to them. He vowed to the horse; "You have done us a great service. I can, for now, but offer you my gratitude, but rest assured I will see you are amply rewarded in the days yet to come."

"Alas, my lord, king," he replied hoarsely, "The service of which you speak was nothing in itself—I am forever your humble subject, but I sense the wound to my stomach, though insignificant to the eye, will become infected, and, most likely, I will not see any future in which to receive such reward. But still, you have my deepest gratitude, the sentiment is well received, Sire."

Tamarin had to bite his lip to prevent himself from laughing at this wonderful, oh-so-miserable, horse. "Rordorr," he told him as earnestly as he could, "as your demise is so close to hand, I assure you your family will be cared for in your absence, and should your ordeal become too great to bear as the infection spreads, I shall see to it that your suffering ends swiftly."

He was tapping the tip of his sword grip as he teased the horse—a gesture not unnoticed by Rordorr, who replied, "It would be a merciful end, my lord. I am most grateful for your kind considerations."

As Tamarin walked back to Meekhi and the others to make plans, Zowie frowned angrily at Rordorr. "You really are a grumpy old trump of a horse, aren't you, Rordorr!" she scolded him, "of course you're not going to die, and fancy giving Tamarin consent to lop off your head. I have never heard such a crazy thing in all my life. Now you get yourself sorted out and back on your feet, you depressing big lump. I'm going to see what the next step is."

She trotted off in the direction of Tamarin and Meekhi and he looked at Lauren and Thomas with big sad eyes, whispering to them in a resigned tone, "Desert Fever. That is what ails young Zowie. I have heard of it striking down many foreign travellers. Enjoy her friendship while you can, little ones, I don't expect her to last more than two-to-three days."

They stared at him in disbelief as the men tended to him. "Yeah right, of course." Lauren told him as they went off to join Zowie before he could see they were pulling his leg.

Tamarin and a handful of others stood staring, behind them were the children, and only a little further back was the trio of Meekhi, Ramulet, and Mercy. The sight before them was unlike anything they could have ever possibly imagined. A vast, sprawling city lay ahead. The streets were still surfaced in their original sandstone, but everything else visible to the eye was of black stone. What was truly surprising was that it all seemed to be in perfect condition, as if it had been swept and cleaned daily. Small, humble dwellings, sat snugly amidst soaring domed structures and lofty towers crowned with battlements. The curse of stone did not seem to have affected materials such as fabric, so bright coloured silks and satins hung in many a window, giving stark contrast to the cities sombre black buildings. But what really had everyone rooted to the spot were the stone statues. A city at war against Ogiin and his creed had been instantly frozen in time. There were perfectly detailed, but somehow terrifying, figures everywhere, motionless, but alive. Samarian warriors had been transformed as they ran about their duties. They could see a pair of black marble figures looking out from the top of a tower, some archers had knelt to put arrow to bow, and others had yet to taste the food that was still an inch from their open mouths. Fortunately for Zowie, there were no stone infants in sight.

Tamarin noticed that the statues were well dressed and that none of their clothing had been turned to stone, nor had it perished in any way. Thus preserved, it gave them a gaudy, almost macabre, appearance, their black skin and bright garb creating the look of a circus. He dropped to one knee at the gates of the city. When, solemnly, he spoke, the others also bent a leg. "Soledad, oh people of my father's time, forgive my intrusion. I am Tamarin—son of Darcinian, Lord of Samaria. I have breached your gates as Samaria has need of this, her most ancient city. As a young boy I saw your mighty walls from afar, but dwelled safe in the lap of Sitivia, sister to Soledad. Your plight tears at my heart and I would have you know this—one day I will undo this evil that has been done unto you. You have my royal pledge, my vow of honour."

Standing up and peering into the dark, brooding streets, he changed his earlier decision—his queen would most definitely be safest at his side *inside* the city. He sent for Meekhi and Mercy and they were with him in a flash. Taking a long, deep breath, they stepped forward into Soledad.

The children felt so sad for the Samarians, they could see how distraught they all were. Many hid their faces, attempting to disguise their suffering at this insufferable lament, and others were actually struggling to walk, as if some terrible cramps had them buckling up in pain. They were so grateful that they could not hear or feel whatever the others were suffering from. Zowie whispered, "This place is just so spooky. I feel as if every statue is staring at us, and I daren't look up into some of the darker windows because something really scary could be standing there looking back! To be honest, guys, Soledad gives me the heebie jeebies. I mean *my god*! Just look at those statues, they are still *alive*. Oh my word, it's just so awful. I hope Tamarin gives Ogiin a proper pasting when he catches up with him!"

"I know what you mean," Thomas whispered back under his breath, "This place is massive and those statues will be everywhere. But let's look on the bright side, it's not as awful as daytime TV and we're having such an awesome time here, we've just got to remember that the timer will time out on the Dream Machine eventually and we'll be back home, safe and sound. So there's nothing for us to really worry about is there, might as well enjoy it while we can."

"I'd love to believe that, Tom." His sister told him, "But everyone says if you peg it in a dream, then you never wake up in reality. That's why people don't die in dreams, because if they do, they're not around to tell anyone afterwards! I say if anything dodgy comes our way we make the most of our new fighting skills. I've no intention of kicking the bucket here. I'm sure Zee is up for that?"

Zowie nodded. "Bring it on, I say. But let's be careful not to get ourselves hurt. Imagine how dad, Jack, or Lilly would feel if we pegged it in the Dreampod or ..."

She cut short her rambling when she saw what the others were gawping at. They had been slowly walking along what was most likely the main route through the city, with smaller streets branching off at various intervals. It was down one of these side streets that the reason for their sudden stop stood. Five gigantic winged horses, their wings spread ready for flight, were reared up high on their haunches with their forelegs pawing the air. On their backs sat fearsome warriors with swords drawn and faces upturned to the skies, ready to do battle for all that is Samaria. But they had been turned to stone an instant before leaving the ground. Magnificent still to the eye, their brave hearts and fearless determination had not saved them. They had stood frozen in time for these many long years, still challenging a long-gone enemy that had damned the city without ever once showing them his face.

Tamarin and Meekhi ran up the street, quickly followed by the others. Rordorr and Faradorr remained on the main road with their heads hung low. They had seen the horrible sight from afar and had no wish to examine it further, winged horses were already few in number, and to see five of their own unique kind so cruelly deprived of Samaria's rolling plains and blazing skies was a terrible blow for the two brothers.

Tamarin was appalled at the sight, "My lady, tonight we will rest here and allow the horses to regain their strength. Tomorrow we leave at daybreak. We should make Sitivia by sunset via this most direct route. I have no desire to linger within Soledad. This was once our great capital—until silenced in stone. Her mood is so oppressive it stifles my breath and I feel her pain as a dagger through my own heart. Let us find the great hall, and rest there. Perhaps the lost souls will, in reverence to the Great Dragon, appear more muted within those hallowed walls. If only it were in my power to aid them, what would I not do to put end to their diabolical incarceration. Let us swiftly move on."

"My darling," Meekhi took hold of his arm, "I agree the great hall would best serve our needs, but I am not sure how long we can continue to endure the beseeching cries of these ancient Samarians. The pain of their loneliness crashes through my mind like a river of ice, chilling my very soul. May the Great Dragon bring respite to these tortured souls, for surely none do merit it more than they. Let us hasten to find our lodgings for this night, and be free of Soledad at sunrise as you suggest."

Ramulet politely interrupted them, "My lord, I remember my father telling me when I was but knee high that the great hall of Soledad had a dome the size of a moon. Whilst that is highly unlikely, I suggest we make for the biggest dome we can find, such as the one that to stands proud before us in the core of the city."

They were about to set off again from the main street when Lauren yelped, clutching at her foot.

"What's up?" cried Thomas.

"I've got a wicked blister on my foot." She replied grimacing.

Mercy and Meekhi rushed to the girl's aid, examining her foot.

"My lord, why do these young ones travel in stockinged feet?" Meekhi asked Tamarin, "This girl is sorely in need of suitable attire, boots too."

"I had not really thought of it, my lady." He replied before turning to the children and asking them; "Why are you wearing stockings on your feet? Is your climate so much hotter than ours that you do not need footwear? Surely the ground cannot be so kind? Little ones, you will need appropriate boots in these lands or your feet will be as minced as meat."

Zowie was about to explain to them about having to take off their shoes in order to use the Dream Machine, but she thought better of it. She did not know quite what to say really, but was let off the hook when Thomas piped up, "We kicked off our shoes to climb up out of the Pink Mountain." It was a plausible, harmless white lie, and it saved having to try and explain the inexplicable, so the girls hastily nodded their agreement. Meekhi examined Lauren's foot through her shredded sock, her eyes wandering over the equally scruffy looking feet of the other two.

"Once within the great hall I will find suitable clothing for them." She told Tamarin, "They will not travel much further as they are. I'm surprised they have made it this far on horseback bare footed, with no protection." She ruffled Lauren's hair, and with a kind smile, she scooped her up off the road and placed her atop Rordorr's back. Zowie would have been envious if Mercy had not then placed *her* atop Faradorr. The girls beamed as if every Christmas and every birthday had arrived all at once whilst Thomas backed away from Meekhi a little, stating in his most manly voice, "I'm fine. No problems here. I will walk with the other men." He had no intention of being swooped up in some big hairy guardsman's arms like a helpless toddler and being placed atop a horse with these lovely ladies watching. "I," he thought to himself, "am representing the men of our own world here, and I'm as much a man as anyone else present, us earthlings are tougher than we look!"

They conceded to his wish but could not fail in hearing him let escape the occasional 'Eek', 'Ouch!', or 'Crap!' as he found the stone surface far harsher on his sore feet than the desert had been.

Despite the eeriness of the city the onset of night brought a welcome blanket of darkness to the travellers. Now that it was fully dark, Soledad seemed more normal with her shadowy buildings and spooky spires. The sky was awash with stars and they lit the road well enough to walk in reasonable safety. The six moons made an appearance only once every forty five days, and this was not one of those breathtaking occasions. Occasionally the starlight would twinkle in the eyes of a statue as if it was winking at the new visitors and this did nothing to calm their jittery nerves. For the children, everything they had experienced since entering the Dreampod had been completely surreal, so Soledad did not bother them too much as it was only an extension of this unreal reality, another vision conjured up within this bizarre fantasy. It is not that they were unafraid, more that they hadn't really come to grips with it all yet and the very real risk of coming to harm was perhaps too alarming a concept to accept so readily. The Samarians noticed how deadly quiet their former capital was. They knew the city was devoid of normal human life but not a mouse made a sound and they could not hear a single insect. The night sky should have been aflutter with the sight of bats feasting on fat, sun-roasted, insects, and buzzing fireflies, but none dared to trespass here. The only sounds were those of their own regretful making as they made their way to the great hall. Silence, loneliness, and grief, manifested themselves deep inside their marrow, one or two of the guardsmen stopping to wretch violently at the roadside. Soledad was exacting a high price for their intrusion. There were dark doorways everywhere—single doors and double doors, archways and alleyways, low doors and tall doors, doors wide open and others shut tight. Some doorways even had statues just entering or leaving a building, frozen mid step, poised on a timeless threshold, never in, and never out, always aware. The air in the city did not move, not a rustle of a leaf or the hint of a scent. Only in the very tallest buildings, high above, was there any motion, with warm coloured yarns billowing occasionally from cold, empty windows.

 The road led directly into the heart of the city. When they arrived there, they encountered wide stone steps leading up to a pair of enormous doors, one of which was ajar. The structure held an air of solemnity, an echo of authority as would a temple, or maybe a church. Tamarin led the way, and soon all of them stood inside a vast hall. It was pitch black inside and men felt along the walls to find the torches that should have been mounted there. These were taken outside and soaked in fresh pitch. After centuries of absence, light reigned once more in the great hall of Soledad. Meekhi ordered *all* the torches be lit, and when they were, the full former grandeur of the place became wholly evident. The high vaulted ceiling was immense, and beautifully carved from stone there were mythical figures happily sharing space with magical dragons and legendary kings. At the far end of the hall a stairway ran up to other chambers that lay beyond view. Wooden chairs and tables were dotted about irregularly, as if the occupants had left in a hurry. Strangely there were no statues to be found in the great hall. None, except the one that had dominated the place well before Ogiin's evil curse took hold of the city. A black marble dragon towered up into the domed ceiling, its mighty paws resting near the foot of the stairs. The stone hide could not detract from its nobility, its magnificence, or its sheer weight of presence. It cast its constant gaze over the entire hall with ruby-red eyes, eyes that had remained untouched by Ogiin's poison.

The Samarians moved to just in front of the statue and dropped to one knee, heads bowed. The children did likewise immediately, sensing the huge significance of the act. Tamarin, alone, raised his head, "Chjandi—greatest of the Dragons of Light, I am Tamarin—Lord of Samaria and your most humble servant. Here..." he placed a hand on Meekhi's shoulder, "Is my love, and my queen—Meekhi. We are but a handful of your people, yet we will seek to undo the dark deed done unto Soledad. We have with us travellers from worlds afar. I ask that you watch over us and these young ones as we seek to unravel this mystery now assailing the shores of our worlds, for we are in no doubt that that foulest fiend—Ogiin, knocks once more at the portal of peace, bent on havoc and dark deeds."

As they stood up the children felt a warm, fuzzy shiver run through them. Zowie put her face close to the others and whispered, "I'm totally into this, it's so cool, these people are just so right in everything they do, we could use the likes of Tamarin back home, he'd make one helluva Prime Minister! I hope we stay here for a very long time. If not for missing dad, I could live here forever, I think."

"I know what you mean," agreed Thomas, "I feel completely at home with the Samarians, like we're all, sort of, you know… like a family."

"Me too." added Lauren, "It's as if I'd known them all my life! But we've to come across this dodgy Ogiin guy yet, him and all his motley crew that we've heard so much gruesome stuff about. Bet that won't be any fun if it happens, look what he did to Soledad!"

Meekhi turned to Tamarin. "My lord, Soledad is, as ever she was, a *Samarian* citadel, and you are as King here as you are in Sitivia or any of your lands. All that you survey is yours. The great king—Darcinian, built this city, and now it falls to you to not only free the spirits trapped within, but to show gracious hospitality to visitors from afar, visitors that have come in friendship." She nodded her head towards the children.

"Ah, yes!" He beamed at them, "Welcome to Soledad, little ones. Do not fear her sombre dress, for this is a false mask not of her own choosing, and one which we will one day remove with great joy. Beneath it lies a heart full of music and dancing, of learning, knowledge, honour, and beauty! I can see you are not privy to the callings of her entombed souls and for this I am grateful to the Great Dragon. Guards! Bring forth the rations, we will prepare food and drink and raise our glasses, because tonight, Samarians once again walk the streets of Soledad!"

The children did not really know what to say to this, so they said, "Thank you very much, we're glad to be here."

The men began busying themselves bringing in food and water from the horses tethered outside. Rordorr and his brother had spied a large patch of green grass, nourished from a black stone fountain resembling a sunflower. The grass appeared untouched by the curse and they decided to eat their fill there. Faradorr had no further desire for human food or wine, and Rordorr was still very sore from the wounds to his belly. However, he was sure he would again soon be able to fly. The flying horses were looking forward to adding the string of their own specialised talent to Tamarin's bow.

Ramulet and Mercy were standing very close together, away from everyone else. They were having the sweet conversations that they had hoped to have with each other for so long. No one disturbed them, they had more than earned a little time together in peace. Tamarin had his arms wrapped firmly around Meekhi and her head rested on his chest, he having pulled his cloak about her so that she would not feel the cold. He would not be apart from her again. In his heart, he could not believe how close he had come to losing her. He felt her warmth against him and held her tighter as if to pull her into himself completely, thus protecting her from the evil now prowling throughout his kingdom. She allowed herself this brief indulgence. She needed to, if only for a minute or two. Tamarin was wearing his armoured breastplate but she could feel his strong young heart beating so powerfully beneath it. She revelled in the snug security of his muscled arms folded about her, the scent of the perfumed oil in his hair reminding her of better times when she would bathe and anoint him as they laughed and splashed together in the palace baths. But she was not the only one with needs that night and she lifted her face to look into his eyes, "My love, these young ones have dire need of more suitable clothing. Look, they are shivering, come, let us tend to their attire, The Talking Table led us to them, who knows where *they* may lead us?"

He gave her forehead a gentle kiss. Her unselfish nature and caring ways always created a pleasant little knot in his stomach, he knew he could not have found a better queen for his people had he searched for eternity. Reluctantly easing away from her, he called over to the children, "Little ones, come with us. It is time you were suitably attired and equipped for the road ahead."

They could not hide their excitement, especially the girls. They had been admiring Mercy and Meekhi ever since they had met them. Trotting over, they each took hold of one of Meekhi's hands. Thomas, walking beside Tamarin, found himself having to half run as the long-legged king strode across the great hall.

At the foot of the stairs they looked back. Arcadian had lit a fire indoors, situated at the tip of the dragon's tail. He had produced from his bag a clutch of green celery-like stems, and used these amidst the kindling to start the fire. These particular stems were well known to Samarians—once alight they could burn brightly for days if not tampered with. They were a sought after rarity, but no one was surprised that Arcadian should happen to have such a thing in his possession. He was famed for having many strange and rare commodities about his person at any given time. The men were preparing the evening meal and this reminded Meekhi of the other pot earlier, brimming over with those disgusting beetles. She was about to remind Tamarin of her concerns not only for herself, but also for Mercy and Faradorr, when he placed a finger tenderly on her lips and whispered in her ear, "My lady, do you think a matter of such great importance could ever slip my mind?"

She knew he was right—he would never forget, that was enough.

Tamarin vaulted up the stairs two at a time and the others had to chase hard to keep apace with him. The night had dampened the haunting pleas of the city enough to allow them to think more clearly, but still the men below kept their cloaks wrapped about them as if to shield them from that ever present veil of sorrow.

At the top of the stairs the children found themselves on a landing that ran the width of the great hall. Tamarin and Meekhi had brought a pair of blazing torches with them, and using these they examined the various doors that led off from the landing. The voices below were greatly amplified by the vast dome above, and could be heard clearly upstairs. There was a low stone wall, waist high and a foot thick, preventing anyone from falling to the rock hard floor below. Tamarin leaned out over it, "Ramulet! We need pitch."

Stepping carefully up to it and peering over, they saw Ramulet pick up a corked jar. He swung his arm a couple of times and then, with a perfectly smooth underarm action, he sent it sailing up to Tamarin who caught it equally smoothly and without mishap.

"We could use Ramulet and Tamarin in the England Cricket Team." Thomas quipped to no one in particular, and for his efforts Lauren jabbed her elbow into his ribs. "Behave yourself!"

Torches taken from the walls were soaked in fresh oil and lit before being passed, one each, to the children. The flames hissed and spat, producing thick black smoke as if to blend in with the sombre state of Soledad. Tamarin finally found the door he was looking for—the door to the arsenal, and eyed the children with a very serious look on his face. "Do not wander astray, little ones. This city has not known the footfall of man these many long years. The spirits of our people are here with us and mean us no harm I am certain, but I cannot say what else may lurk in her darkest corners. I believe this doorway should lead us deep down into the bowels of the city. Stick together, and mind your step."

He pushed open the big, heavy, door. When it was fully ajar, a rush of stale, stagnant air, escaped from it, making a ghastly, ghostly, gasping sound. The girls gripped Meekhi's hands a little tighter and Thomas gritted his teeth just in case they started chattering. For a few brief seconds they stared at the tall dark doorway, and then Tamarin stepped through with the children following and Meekhi bringing up the rear. Holding their torches aloft, they looked about themselves. They were at the top of a wide stairwell that ran directly down from them to another small landing, where it descended to the left and another small landing. This pattern repeated over and over so no one could see how far down it spiralled into what was, essentially, a very deep shaft at the rear of the great hall. Up high above them was a flat ceiling, it housed a large trapdoor which appeared to have been sealed for centuries.

Whilst the city had, for some inexplicable reason, remained scrupulously clean on first impressions, this hidden area was thick with dust, the air smelling old and unclean. The steps were covered in a heavy layer of dirt and were quite dangerous because of it. Tamarin was about to start the descent when he stopped and knelt down. Bringing his torch to bear, he looked carefully at the thick layer of dust. Meekhi peered over his shoulder with the children trying in vain to do the same. Sure enough, there were footprints in the dirt. They appeared to be human but were the same size as those of a large toddler. Zowie caught a glimpse of them. "They're baby footprints! Surely there can't be a baby living down here, can there?"

Tamarin straightened his back, "These," he told them, "are not the footprints of a young child, similar in size, yes, but as strong as a man, naughty as a pixie, and as cunning as a fox. They are the footprints of a Benijay, a form of tiny elf. Generally, they are no threat to man, and usually a friend to Samarians. But be on your guard everyone, these footprints are fresh and were made recently, so it is quite likely we are not alone in Soledad. If any of you see anything at all, you must alert me immediately."

The torch held out high above him, he began his journey down. The flames threw wavy shadows onto the walls around them and the children were sure to stay close to the leader. Meekhi followed keeping her eyes on them to be sure they did not slip and fall over the side. The stairs had no rail to aid the less cautious or the clumsy, and without anything to hang on to the descent was a dangerous venture the children were not relishing at all. Meekhi was at once enthralled, and heartbroken, by Soledad. It had been the capital of Samaria before her time and she had only ever known Sitivia and Rosameer (a great fortress of a city near the border with Dizbaar) as the two foremost cities within her realm. But the spectre of Soledad had always loomed nearby, not so far from Sitivia. The Desert of Iret lay like a pool of stinking waste where the Gardens of Paradise had once flourished, and Soledad stood a little further beyond, like an enormous black tomb, housing the undead. She ached to see this great city breathe freely once more and the all-enveloping curse of stone be lifted from her forever.

The children were very careful to stay away from the edge of the slippery steps and kept focused on the silver dragon on Tamarin's back as it shone in their torchlight. The flickering flames made it appear to move and the sight of it infused them with much needed courage inside that dark tunnel, a tunnel which seemed to go down forever. The thick layer of dust muffled the sound of their ginger footfalls and Tamarin kept them all in good cheer with a running commentary. He was proud of this city, a city that had sacrificed itself during the Great War of old. His father had built Soledad with guidance from Chjandi, Himself. Tamarin had never set foot in The Silent City since her gates had been sealed by Amaris when he was but a babe-in-arms, but he knew much about her from the tales his father had told him. He knew there were many secret passages and tunnels, somewhere there was an underground lake— once used for great celebrations, and parties by the water's edge. The grand statue built in honour of the Great Dragon was the first of its kind in all Samaria. Myth told that buried deep within it, was beating a heart of real flame, a flame placed there, it was said, by the Great Dragon, Himself. All these facts and fables he explained to the children and Meekhi as he stepped deeper and deeper into the depths of the city. They were lost within his tales of the reign of his father—King Darcinian. The pride in his voice was impossible to disguise and he had no intention of hiding it, he really was so extremely proud of his heritage.

They had been heading down the stairwell for a quite a while now and the light from the torches could no longer stretch to the ceiling above. It was very cold and the children's teeth were chattering. Meekhi could hear them clattering away noisily and her heart went out to these young ones—so far away from their own homes, and indeed, their own world. At last Tamarin called out. "We have reached the bottom. Careful now, everyone step down gently. We need to find the stores, and the arsenal. To be honest, I have no idea in which direction they will be. Sitivia was built, more or less, as a replica of Soledad, so I'm hoping my instincts are true and we won't have too much of a problem finding what we need. Patience, little ones, we will calm those restless teeth as yet."

The children laughed and clamped their mouths firmly shut, embarrassed by their jiggling jaws.

They were standing at one end of a long narrow passage that was punctuated by doors to the left and right. The limp light fell short of the far end, thus giving no clue as to its full span. It really was bitterly cold down here, and a strange, fetid, unidentifiable odour tinged the air. Covered in thick dust like the steps, the floor appeared unused for centuries and Meekhi stooped down to examined it further. "It seems," she said, looking up at the others, "our little elf was here too, but some time ago. These footprints must be at least two days old."

"Actually," suggested Thomas, "they could be far more recent. You see the moisture down here would cause them to diminish more quickly. Just a thought…"

"You're right, Mr Forensics." Lauren applauded him, "Good for you!"

"You're a proper scientist you are, Tom!" Zowie was also impressed.

Tamarin and Meekhi raised their eyebrows at each other, surprised at the unexpected wisdom of these young ones.

"I stand corrected, Thomas," Meekhi gave his shoulder a squeeze, "You, it seems, are a useful fellow to have in such a situation."

He beamed at her, "No problem, anytime. Anything you need, just shout. I'll give you my mobile number when we get back upstairs."

The girls scowled at him scornfully. "Tom! are you crazy!"

"A *mobile* number, eh," Tamarin was both curious, and puzzled, "and you would give it to my queen? Mmm, a number that is mobile? How so? Are not all numbers mobile—issuing from, and, resulting in, equations of allsorts? a unit of measurement perhaps? I do not claim to be a mathematician but are not all numbers mobile? Forever flexible in that by addition, or subtraction, or other such manipulation, they can always change? Have you through some great wizardry discovered one that moves only at your command? Explain this, for I am greatly intrigued."

Thomas was about to go into the details of cellular communication, and of how he could get Meekhi a really good pay-as-you-go deal with Vodafone, maybe even a free handset, when his sister saved the day, "Sorry, Tamarin. Thomas banged his head quite severely inside the Pink Mountain, and ever since then he's been talking some very peculiar rubbish. Just ignore him, please. He'll be better in a few hours I'm sure."

"It is true, he has truly talked much nonsense ever since we met. I hope you recover soon, young Thomas."

Meekhi, concerned, knelt down on one knee in front of him. "You are very brave, Thomas. To suffer such a blow and make no mention or issue of it is very noble of you, a truly Samarian trait. Perhaps you have the makings of a Samarian Knight! I shall tend to your injuries when we return to the great hall."

"Perfect. It is actually *very* painful." came his apparently heartfelt reply as he discreetly stuck his tongue out at the girls. His horrible facial expressions were returned without hesitation, they thought it funny to see him so smitten.

The passageway was quite narrow and barely wide enough for three people to walk side by side, so Tamarin led the way followed closely by the girls. Thomas walked with Meekhi, quietly discussing what he needed to know and do to become a Samarian Knight.

They would stop at every door and wipe away the thick layer of dirt from its smooth surface to try and ascertain what lay behind it. Half a dozen had been passed when they reached one secured by particularly heavy doors and a rusting lock with chain. Tamarin wiped at it and found the symbol he was looking for. On initial examination the lock appeared very rusty and long neglected, but further investigation showed it had traces of fresh oil around the keyhole. He told the others to keep a very wary eye as he rummaged inside a pouch on his belt and produced a hairpin. With this pin he made short work of the lock, picking it in seconds. The doors were heavy but swung open smoothly, *too* smoothly for his tastes.

Torches were thrust through the doorway and even the Samarians gasped at the splendour and wealth that greeted their eyes. With the torchlight illuminating only the foreground it was still easy to see that this was an enormous chamber. Leather mannequins stood on single, wooden peg legs bedecked in the most dazzling armour. Others wore garments of chiffon and satin, leather and lace, or men's tunics, gorgeously detailed, and perfectly stitched at every seam. Swords, shields, and numerous other weapons were neatly stacked on stands and tables. The most striking triblades they had ever seen were mounted on the walls, the hilts inlaid with diamonds, rubies, amber, and emeralds. Ancient war shields ran along another wall. All of these had been edged in gold gilt, snarling silver dragons with sapphire eyes boldly embossed upon their faces.

"Behold the ancient splendour of eternal Soledad." Tamarin's voice was low and reverent. He was looking back through time at a snapshot of his father's reign, at a time before he was old enough to fully appreciate the glory of it. The magnificence of it all forced him to take a slow, deep breath, long forgotten memories beginning to stir in his mind.

Meekhi tugged at his arm, whispering in his ear, "So clean, and kept in pristine order, my lord. This... *is not how it should be.*"

Now he placed his lips close to her ear, shielding his voice by covertly cupping one hand, "Indeed so, my lady, and the lock was well oiled recently. The great hall, indeed the entire city that we have seen thus far, is too well kept, but by whom, or what? Let us not tarry here. We will take what we need and return to the others. Then I think a counsel with Mercy and Ramulet is in order. Also, I am getting hungry! You guide the girls through this treasure trove and I shall advise our future knight."

He and Thomas paired up and began sifting through the room with Meekhi and the girls doing likewise. Incredibly detailed tapestries depicting scenes of hunts and battles covered the walls almost entirely and the children could not resist the lure of the various images portrayed there. They told so much of Samaria and its history that they could sense that that legacy was just as alive today, in the king and queen, as it had ever been in the past. The girls had no idea what to look for so Meekhi chose for them. They were to be dressed in battledress created especially for female warriors, and, much to their delight, they were given cloaks bearing the mark of the dragon. Lauren also took a liking to a particular bow. It was made from a very dark wood, perhaps ebony, and it gleamed as if made of glass. Meekhi fastened a quiver over Lauren's shoulder, and the bow was hers, Zowie found a sword that was just perfect for her, and each of them were also given a dagger and shield. Tamarin and Meekhi took a pair of shields and rapped on them firmly with their knuckles. Finding them to be of the absolute finest craftsmanship, they each slung one over their shoulders and Meekhi took another two for Ramulet and Mercy. Tamarin had to climb up a tapestry to reach a duo of triblades that hung side by side some way away from the other swords. They had caught his eye as soon as he had entered and he brought them down very carefully. Meekhi barely touched the blade of one of them and it caused a tiny cut to her finger. She stood sucking it to stop it bleeding.

"Still razor sharp, after all these years." Tamarin muttered in amazement, "We yet have much to learn from the ancients."

Taking her hand he sucked at the tiny cut, and, tasting no blood, he told her, "I think you have survived this deadly encounter, but, I implore you, let caution reign in such matters, I would not have you injured through chance or otherwise."

Smiling back sweetly, she squeezed a pin prick of blood and wiped it on the tip of his nose.

The swords were exquisite in detail and flawless in workmanship, but each was very different from the other. One had a centre blade that was made of a material similar to that of Lauren's bow, a black, glassy type of substance. The flanking blades were the usual bright steel. Along that centre blade was inscribed:

"I will endure where others may fall, to serve my king that is my all."

Meekhi lifted the hefty-looking weapon and was surprised at how light it felt, a masterpiece of design, but unfortunately its proportions were too big for her. Lauren looked it over, "That sword has got Ramulet's name written all over it."

"*Really*, by The Dragon! This is an amazing discovery! Where?" Tamarin was astonished and began examining it for his friend's moniker.

"I'm not talking literally, Tamarin." Lauren blushed, "It's just how we talk in our world. I meant it's perfect for Ramulet. Don't you think so?"

He laughed at his mistake and agreed with her. Then he held up the other sword. The craftsmanship used to forge and detail this weapon was truly beyond belief. The hilt was carved into a dragon so realistic that it appeared alive whichever angle it was viewed from. When he gripped it he felt as if the sword was holding *him*! The long central blade was of a metal he had never seen before. It was most definitely a metal of some sort, but it was feather light, and a dark metallic blue in colour. The secondary blades were of a rich burgundy. The dragon was sculpted from the purest silver with the same red, ruby eyes that adorned the statue in the great hall. It was so light even the girls could lift it easily. He tapped at the blade matter of factly. "This sword is so beautiful, so unique I fear it may be meant for decorative purposes only. Stand back and I shall test its metal."

They stood well back and he found a thick, solid wood, table, to try the metal upon. Meekhi held his torch for him, and raising the triblade up high, he brought it down onto the table in one lightening fast strike. It was sliced neatly in half, but it was not the sharpness of the blade that had them all spellbound. As the sword had commenced its journey to the table, a flame had appeared right along the central blade and the fiery weapon had lit up the whole room. Tamarin stepped away from the ruined table and manoeuvred the sword through several strokes, but no further flames appeared. Then when he went to strike a mannequin, the blade burst once more into a blinding, bright blue flame. He laid it down very carefully on a nearby chest. The blade was still very hot and the light from the glowing metal revealed that this sword, too, had an inscription etched ever so delicately upon it. The writing glowed blue on the red hot blade, it read:

A dragon's flame burns within,
and when that flame makes my heart sing,
then you shall know why I was made,
and your darkest foe shall soon lay slain.

Meekhi was watching Tamarin staring at that rapidly cooling blade, and its mysterious message. "My lord," she told him, "My sweet love, this one has *your* name written all over it."

They shared a moments mirth as he pretended to search for his name, then he hefted the mighty sword once more, fitting it to his belt with a big grin on his handsome young face, "Yes, I do believe it does."

Suddenly, they heard a rustling from behind one of the long, hanging drapes, followed by a series of rapid footsteps at the dark rear of the room. Mirth and mystery were forgotten in an instant and Meekhi immediately pulled the children behind her, drawing her deadly new sword. Tamarin gripped the fire breathing triblade at his side and called out, "Who goes there! Know this—I am Tamarin, Lord of Samaria, and all here by me are under my royal protection! Show yourself, whether you be friend or foe. If friend, then I bid you welcome to our great city of Soledad, but if you be foe, I tell you now your future is short lived and you shall know the taste of samarian steel this night."

CHAPTER THIRTEEN

THE BENIJAYS

The guardsmen had been busy and had built a big blazing fire inside the great hall of Soledad. Many lay resting on their backs using saddle rolls as cushions for their heads, whilst others grouped together pondering current events, and the next most likely course. For the first time in so many years the delicious aromas of cooking food wafted into the streets of the Silent City. The walls of the great hall seemed to form an effective barrier against the cold embrace of that accursed place, and some of the men, though still prickled by the voices of those entombed in stone, were trying to lighten the mood by telling jokes and discussing this new adventure, just as soldiers have done the world over since soldiering first began. Arcadian and one other had ventured outside to tend to the horses and to see if they could do anything further for Rordorr, or his brother. The flying horses were at peace and wanting of nothing more than rest.

Ramulet lay with his head in Mercy's lap. They were talking quietly as she stroked his face, running her strong, yet slender, fingers through his thick long hair. He looked up into those warm, hazel brown eyes, eyes so deep and filled with emotion. Reaching up he caressed her cheek with the back of his hand, telling her of how he could not wait for Samaria to be safe and at peace again so they could be wed and he could shower upon her all the happiness and joy she so richly deserved. Smiling at her handsome captain, Mercy could think of nothing that would make her happier than to be his wife. Startling her, he suddenly sat bolt upright, alarm written all over his face, barking, "Guards, to arms!" Then he sprang to his feet, drawing his sword.

Mercy was up like a shot and standing right next to him. "What is it?!"

"That foul odour, can you smell it? Sickly sweet fumes dripping thick with poison, the same stench that bewitched me in the caves below Iret, it is the disgusting scent of Teritee. The witch is somewhere nearby, I can smell her!"

Everyone began sniffing the air, and, sure enough, there was a horrible smell beginning to pervade the hall. It had been masked till now by the burning wood and the cooking food, but it was getting stronger by the second.

All eyes were turned on Ramulet, as captain it was his duty to take charge in the absence of the king and queen. He ordered the horses, both talking and otherwise, be brought into the hall for their safety. Once this was done he gathered Mercy and Arcadian close, "Wherever that stinking most repugnant of whores may be lurking, she may or may not be aware that us Samarians again walk within Soledad's great walls. If she is not aware of our presence then perhaps we can give her a nasty surprise, but if she knows we are here, and our giveaway beacon of a fire would suggest she does, then, does she know that the king and queen are not with the main body? We must find Tamarin and the others quickly, but quietly, so as to not alert her of our intent or their absence. You, Arcadian, must organise the men and take charge here, Mercy will come with me in search of the others, they must be warned."

He rallied the men, and told them that should they come face to face with the witch, or or any of Ogiin's creed, they were to show no mercy, and give no quarter. At the foot of the stairs he turned back to them and gave them an unmistakeable reminder of his orders, "Kill them all. Spare no one, kill all of them!"

When Tamarin and Meekhi had drawn their swords the children had instinctively followed suit. Now they stood waving them about awkwardly as if participating in a poorly rehearsed school play. The gravity of their situation began to dawn on them clearly at last—the Samarians were at war against evil, merciless horrors led by a demonic warlord, and as they had allied themselves with them, so those same dreadful creatures must now be at war with *them*, too. Standing in that big cold chamber, buried deep beneath the city with weapons in their hands, they realised that they may actually have to fight to survive, and that was a truly shocking thought. Even Thomas with his penchant for humour had a deadly serious, worried expression on his face. Tamarin glanced back for an instant, then whispered, "Wait here by the door, I will try and corner whatever lurks within these four walls. I will endeavour to flush it out, and if it breaks for the door you are to capture it. If it resists…well, you know what to do. Little ones, do not be afraid, protect yourselves, and each other. Be worthy of the dragon now draping your shoulders."

He started creeping further into the room towards the tapestry from where the sounds had come. Zowie did not like standing with her back to an open doorway leading to an unlit corridor, so, shaking like leaf, she began to move forward in tandem with Tamarin to form a pincer movement. Meekhi would have stopped her, but remained still so as to protect the other two. Lauren hissed at Zowie in despair, "Zee, are you nuts! *Get back here*, NOW!" Her words fell on deaf ears and Zowie continued to move forward, her sword wobbling terribly in her hands.

Tamarin, despite his height and muscular frame, proved to be far more nimble than Zowie, gliding from table to table, holding his torch up high to illuminate his path. Zowie found she just could not keep up, and to compensate, she made a very thorough search of everything she passed. Her inexperience with the sword was telling and she couldn't stop it banging and clattering against everything. Forgetting Tamarin's warning to be on guard, she sheathed the weapon, finding it much easier to move forward stealthily now that she had the use of both hands for balance. The Shortwaters had their eyes locked on her, they admired her courage, but had no intention of following her reckless example. There was definitely someone, or something, scurrying about at the rear of the room. Sometimes the sound would come from low down, then it would come from high up—from behind the furthermost tapestries as if something had run up the wall. Meekhi reached for a longbow and raised it quietly, standing with an arrow primed and ready for anything that posed a threat to Tamarin or her friends. Lauren was so impressed by the warrior-queen's fearless fighting spirit, it inspired her into aiming her own recently acquired bow and she was astonished at just how easily it fell to hand, and at how comfortable she was using it. She felt confident she could hit anything she aimed for because she was the best archer in her local archery club. Jack and Lilly encouraged outdoor activities rather than the latest fad for video games, computers, and being glued to a mobile telephone. Thomas attended karate classes in the city with Zowie. The three of them often went sailing together—taking Dug's beautiful wooden yacht out on nearby broads. An adult always accompanied them, and she could not help thinking that the adults would certainly wish they had accompanied them on *this* particular adventure.

Tamarin eased himself up onto a sturdy looking bench at the back of the room and beckoned to Zowie. He pointed to a large bump protruding from under the rearmost tapestry. It was moving very slowly and the resulting bulge in the fabric was easy to trace. Passing her his torch, he launched himself off the bench and managed to engulf the lump within the fabric before king, tapestry, and lump, came crashing to the floor, sending artefacts and armour flying in all directions. Meekhi and the others ran forward as Zowie held up the two torches to find Tamarin. She could only just about see him because he was completely entangled in the heavy material and frantically grabbing at something. That 'something' was making strange muffled sounds that sounded very like speech; "No you don't!" The bump squeaked in a cute, childlike voice, "You ain't getting me, you big oaf. Get oorf me!"

Then there was a chuckling sound and a little giggle, followed by Tamarin calling out, "Curses! I've lost it! Slam shut the doors!"

Meekhi raced back, and just as she heaved the second door shut, something slammed into her legs, sending her sprawling. She managed to keep hold of her torch and just caught a glimpse of the 'lump' as it disappeared again under a table. "I saw it!" She called to the others, "It's small, with big ears and blue fur. I don't think it's dangerous. I think it's afraid of *us*!"

"There! There!" Lauren and Thomas cried out as they saw two tiny blue feet moving from under one table to the next.

Tamarin joined Meekhi at the doorway. The children stood alongside, their eyes roving left and right. Tamarin was a mite flustered having been wrestling with a very heavy, extremely dusty, tapestry. He pointed his sword into the room and in a voice becoming of his kingship he bellowed, "Come out! NOW! Whoever, or whatever, you are, you will come to no harm if you bear no ill will towards Samaria or her people. If you *do* mean harm, then come and face me! I give you my word—I shall face you one to one. Show yourself now to the King of Samaria. Remain in hiding and we will first empty the contents of this chamber into the passage behind us to find you out, then empty your guts onto the floor."

There were small wet sniffles and tiny little grunts from the rear of the room, and everyone at the door found themselves leaning forward to try and hear what was being said in that strange, childlike voice. It came again, this time definitely discernible as speech. "Empty my guts, huh? Why would you want to do that? My guts are always empty anyway! Some king you are, humph! Your girlfriend's very pretty I do say that, unlike you! Why you want to hurt poor little Solipop! Horrible big people, big people always making me trouble for me little people. Alright, alright, no point moving all the furniture about and making the huge noises, here I come..."

A pair of big furry ears started to slowly rise from behind a pile of clothing at the back of the room. It was quite dark there, and they moved a little closer still to shed light into that area. A small round face appeared, with enormous oval eyes. It could have been mistaken as a human with panda bear ears and huge eyes, except that it had whiskers. When the creature was fully standing, it was no taller than a three year old child. Its body—naked bar a loin cloth type of affair, was covered in a soft light blue down.

Apart from the fur and those gigantic ears, it did actually resemble a human child, but one could not fail to see that that little body was, despite its diminutive size, endowed with disproportionately powerful muscles. The strange creature looked Tamarin straight in the eyes, and pointing an accusing finger it told him, "You don't look like no king to me. Coming in here and nicking, and pinching, and stealing, and taking, and pilfering all that stuff. You're going to be in a LOT of trouble you are. *Oh yes, you are.* When Babel finds out you've pinched them there swords and stuff, she's gonna sort you right out! Don't you worry, I'm gonna tell her all your thieving grabbing ways! Now put everything back you pilfering pilferers, and bugger off. Making all them noises you been making, you will have that scary witch woman down here in a flash. Then we'll be in a proper muddle of trouble, won't we. Come on! Put all the stuff back, oh you horrible, thieving, lot."

Tamarin was so shocked at being called a thief—a thief that stole his own belongings, that he was momentarily stuck for words. The children (especially the girls) thought the little creature the cutest thing they had ever seen and stood staring at it, muttering, "Aah, ooh, it's just so *cuddly*."

Meekhi also thought it cute, but knew not to trust anything other than her own people unless it was *known* to be trustworthy. She looked at the little blue face again, noting the bizarre-looking creature had an enormously long tail. "Who are you? What are you doing here, and what do you know of witches here in Soledad?"

It chose not to answer her questions, but Tamarin did, "*That*, my lady, is a Benijay—a type of Elf. I suspect its mother is nearby as all the young call their mothers 'Babel'."

"Aren't you just the smarty-pants then," The elf chided him, "Studied hard with a tutor, did we? Teacher's pet, were we? Bribed our teachers with big juicy goodies from...."

Its babbling was cut short when Tamarin glared down at him, booming with a voice that would have stopped a runaway train, "ENOUGH! I *am* Tamarin—Lord of Samaria. Stop your senseless waffling and answer my lady's questions! Why are you here? I was not aware that anyone or anything still lived within this city. You do not strike me as foe, but, by the Dragon! I would know your intentions, and I would know them NOW!"

They could see that the elf was squirming behind that pile of clothing. It seemed unsure of what to do, or what to believe. Then, quite suddenly, it stepped out from behind its cover and started walking towards them, "Ok, ok, I'll be believing you, for now," it piped in its baby voice, "but if you kill me, I will never speak to you again, because I don't like being killed I'm sure. I am Solipop. Me Babel gave me the name because we should have gone straight past this horrible Soledad place, but me, because I'm smart I is, thinks I will have a look in there 'cause cities is full of tasty grub, so I pops in for a look about and Babel follows me, so I doesn't get lost. There was a rope over the wall you see, then the rope was gone you see, and me and Babel is stuck here for some days, see. So because I popped into Soledad, Babel is calling me Solipop. I like the name, I've never had one before you see, what do you think of it?"

They could not believe the audacity of this little blue elf. What did they think of his *name*?? Like a flash, Tamarin's hand shot out and caught him by surprise. He lifted him by the scruff of his neck, hoisting him up high with a sword at his throat. "I tell you this, little Solipop—your name suits you. My name, as I have told you *already,* is Tamarin, or, to you—*Lord Tamarin.* I see innocence in your eyes and no malice there present, so I do not consider you foe. But speak quickly now, little elf, tell us all you know of Soledad and of this witch. We are allies, you and I."

He placed Solipop back on the ground and released him. The elf rolled his big oval eyes as he gathered himself and fluffed up his suddenly wilted ears. He had never dealt with humans before and they appeared considerably more amicable than the witch he had seen earlier. However, he wished his Babel would turn up soon, there were far too many people waving swords about for his liking. He told the humans how he had been crossing the desert with his Babel when he had seen a rope dangling over the wall, and after climbing up that rope into Soledad, he had gone looking for food and found some fruit growing in an overgrown garden. Babel had pursued him, threatening to tie his tail in a knot for entering the Silent City. They had gathered a stash of food, but when they had returned to the rope with their horde, they had seen many ugly, dangerous looking people removing the rope. These pale demons had been trying to heave the witch up over the wall and into Soledad, but as soon as her face appeared at the top, she would fall back to the desert having lost her grip. Solipop had noticed that she had two fingers missing from one hand. That witch really was the ugliest, most revolting thing anyone could ever imagine he told them, wrinkling up his nose in disgust. The hissing things that had entered the city had no hair and evil eyes. Their mouths were crammed with yellow teeth and they carried nasty grey weapons. The Benijays had followed them and found them holed up in a dwelling far from the main gate. Babel had insisted that they somehow pay for the fruit she and Solipop were taking because it belonged to the king, so she had gone on a secret cleaning mission—tidying up the streets and statues (Benijays are obsessed with paying for anything received as well as with keeping things clean and tidy). When she returned they would try and find a rooftop from which they could throw a rope over the wall and get as far away as possible from those awful, yellow fanged, bald people. He had wanted to take a last look at the big beastie dragon in the great hall whilst Babel moved through the first quarter of the city at whirlwind speed, cleaning and dusting everything she saw. She was due to return soon, and she would not be happy at *all* that the humans were taking so many lovely things away without paying for them! Solipop was quite indignant about this last fact and Meekhi knelt down to face him. "Solipop," she told him, "everything in this city belongs to Tamarin. This, standing right here in front of you, *is* Tamarin. Anything we take is ours already, and we have sore need of it. Little elf, I like your honesty, and, I admire your courage. You must stay with us until your Babel joins us. This witch you saw is very dangerous indeed and I am sure those nasty bald people you saw are called 'Venomeens'. Here, this is Zowie and Lauren, they are warriors from another world and they will protect you until Babel arrives. Meanwhile, eat this."

She fished about in a pouch and gave him a dried date which he began chewing on with great relish as he weighed up the humans, his big eyes rolling round and around so quickly it made everyone quite dizzy.

The girls thought him utterly gorgeous, each taking hold of one of his tiny hands. Thomas smiled at him and ruffled the fur atop his head, which seemed to annoy him. But Tamarin's face remained grave. "We must hasten back to the others," he told them, "they must be made aware that Venomeens have installed themselves in this, our most sacred of cities. The witch, and from Ramulet's earlier account we can be sure this is Teritee, may also have breached the wall by now, and even if she has not, we have inadvertently left the gates wide open for her."

They gathered up their belongings quickly, including their new weapons. Meekhi had found Thomas a small, light triblade, of which he was enormously proud. Each of the children also carried a shield picked from the ancient armoury. Torches held high they left the room to darkness, stepping back out into the narrow passage leading to the winding stairs.

The children felt wonderfully warm and snug in their samarian clothing and plush new capes. Solipop had made an instant hit with them and he seemed to enjoy their attention very much, but he kept tugging at Meekhi's cloak with his palm upturned and outstretched. "Our new friend is hungry." she told Tamarin.

"Unfortunately, that, my lady," he replied, "appears to be the least of our concerns right now. The men will have something for him, I'm sure."

They reached the foot of the stairs in minutes, but the ascent would have to be made far more cautiously than their recent descent now that they knew that danger threatened from far more than just slippery footing. They had been climbing for a fair way when a tiny speck of intermittent light appeared high above them. Tamarin signalled the others to move as quietly as possible, keeping a wary eye on the wavering glow so far above. As they got higher, it became apparent that the light was descending towards them, and that it was being emitted by a torch such as their own. Then they heard Ramulet's voice calling down to them, "My lord! Is that you? Who goes there in the darkness below?"

"It is I, old friend," Tamarin hollered back up, "and I am happy to hear your voice."

"My lord, the witch—Teritee, is afoot here in the city I am certain. Beware!" Ramulet's voice was a little clearer now as he came closer.

"She is not alone," Tamarin warned his friend in turn, "Venomeens seem to have infested this city also. An infestation we must eradicate immediately. We are coming up to you, wait for us at...WAIT!"

He froze halfway up the stairwell, spotting movement between himself and Ramulet. There was a hushed silence as the party above and the party below stared into the murky middle distance between them, they had all seen something moving there for sure. Suddenly, the cold gloomy shaft was filled with tension and the sound of controlled, shallow breathing, as they tried to catch sight of whatever was lurking so secretively on the black steps. It felt colder than it had before and the children wrapped their warm clothing about them, turning white at the thought of encountering a dangerous witch.

Ramulet, straining his eyes, could see the small cluster of torches burning many levels below. He lit another torch and let it fall over the side, illuminating the various levels as it plummeted down past them. The group below saw the light sailing their way and watched the stairs carefully as it passed by. "THERE!" Meekhi pointed to a landing about six levels above, she had seen something trying to hide from the light as the torch sailed past. Now that area was again in complete darkness and Tamarin called up once more, "Captain, something lingers two thirds the distance down from you. We will meet you there."

He drew his sword and the children prayed fervently that the movement above was a mouse or a bat, and more from instinct than bravery, they also drew their weapons. Meekhi would ascend last, walking backwards and guarding the rear. Solipop stayed close to her. It was a precarious undertaking with the stairs having no barrier to prevent a fall from either side and the flickering light from the smoky flames too unsteady to give a clear, stable view. Tamarin, slightly hunched to hold both torch and blade, moved much faster than Meekhi could possibly hope to do backwards. The children stayed close to him and did not notice her and Solipop starting to trail behind. The elf was trembling, his great big eyes not daring to look too deeply into the darkness of the tunnel for fear of what may be looking back at him. His fur was standing on end and his tail was coiled tightly around one leg.

Ramulet could see the lights below climbing steadily towards him and he and Mercy began to climb down to meet them. Tamarin sensed movement around the next corner, but even as he rounded it slowly and with caution, something squealed out loudly and launched itself at his chest. Dropping his torch he grappled with his assailant in the dark, but lost his footing in the inch-deep dirt. He just managed to get a weak grip on the lip of the small landing when his body slipped over the side. Hanging there in the darkness by his fingertips, he waited for his attacker to appear and finish him off. He clawed at the loose dusty surface, but his hands were slipping and he realised he had only seconds before he disappeared over the side. Then the panicked faces of the children appeared above him, they placed their torches on the landing as they reached past his head and grabbed at his tunic and cloak, trying to pull him back up. He could hear Meekhi racing up the stairs and the sound of Ramulet and Mercy jumping from landing to landing in an effort to reach him. Aware that whatever had jumped him in the dark was still lurking somewhere nearby, he strained to speak, warning the children, "Release me, little ones, danger still abides in the dark. Look about you! Defend yourselves."

Leaning out over the edge, gripping his cloak, they were not so easily dissuaded. Zowie told him, "No way, Jose."

They redoubled their efforts to rescue him but Tamarin was no lightweight. Lauren leant out a little too far and found herself diving head first into the void. Tamarin reached out in a flash and caught her by the forearm, but was himself left with only one hand clawing desperately at the ledge. The muscles in his arms were screaming in pain as she dangled helplessly in his grip, his blade now swinging by its thong from his thumb. Beads of sweat began breaking out all over his forehead and he groaned in pain as he strained to haul her up, but he simply could not swing her back onto the landing with such a tenuous grip on it himself.

The situation was beyond hope and he could feel his fingers beginning to numb. It would not be long before he lost all purchase. Zowie and Thomas wrapped the folds of his cloak around their arms and heaved for all they were worth. Meekhi arrived just in time to see Tamarin and the children disappear over the edge into darkness. The silence of the deep dark shaft was broken by their screams, and Tamarin's fading cry of, "Look about yooou…"

She was rendered speechless by the shock, peering out over the edge she watched on impotently as the one and only great love of her life disappeared from view. Ramulet and Mercy were seconds away, but too late. Then she noticed Solipop talking to someone right behind her. She could hear him clearly enough.

"Babel, this is not the nasty people with the horrible teeths, is my new friends gives me nice grub too. Babel, my friends are all called Tamarin."

Spinning around she saw Solipop talking to a considerably larger version of himself. This second Benijay—obviously Babel, leapt from the landing and began pouncing down from level to level into the darkness. Meekhi and the others raced down as fast as they could in pursuit, but they could not catch up with Babel. They saw the adult she-elf leap from a landing into what appeared to be nowhere at first, but then the torches revealed a long wooden lever protruding from the far wall. They had not seen it earlier, but then, no one had been looking for it at that time. She landed on the lever with such force that she depressed it. The sound of heavy clanking chains and creaking wheels filled the stairwell, the screeching of rusty metal on rusty metal painful to the ears. It was joined simultaneously by a deep rumbling vibration that caused centuries of dust to fall about them like rain, clogging the air and causing them to cough violently. This was followed by an almighty 'BOOM!'. The whole shaft shook violently and the falling dust rose back up in thick choking clouds, causing everyone to wave their arms about frantically in order to try and see through it. Babel jumped from the lever back to the landing, and in an instant she was beside Solipop—scolding him.

"I told you to wait in the big room. I even locked the door! What are you doing with a king? Which one is a king? Have you been taking food from strangers! How many times have I told you not to! Show me your tail, I will tie such a knot in it—you'll be fiddling for a week to unravel it! Then I'll tie it again. You really are a very naughty elf. I... err..."

Babel found herself looking down the wrong end of Meekhi's sword and she had a look on her face that did not bode well for the elf.

Meekhi's voice—as hard as any sword steel, drilled into Babel's big fluffy ears, causing them to wilt visibly.

"The one that is *king*, Babel, is the one you have just thrown over the side along with three of our new-found friends! Tamarin—whom you have sent tumbling to his doom, is my husband and my very reason for breathing. *Your* breathing however, should my lord not survive your unprovoked attack, will cease shortly. SPEAK! *Why did you attack us*? Talk as we go down to find him and the little ones. Do not try and escape."

Babel, having made certain her offspring was unharmed, turned to her.

"If you are wife to Tamarin, then you are Lady Meekhi?"

"I am she."

"I am Babel, mother to Solipop, whom you have already met. I saw only that my little one was surrounded by weapons and I am first and foremost a mother. I meant the king, nor any of you, any harm, my lady. Let us go down and see what has happened."

The elf's voice was soft and honest, holding the unmistakeable ring of truth. Meekhi kept her weapon drawn but she could see why a mother would react as Babel had, but her immediate concern was for those that had disappeared into the darkness, and they headed downstairs as fast as was safely possible.

Upon reaching the passage at the bottom they began looking about for the others. Surely they must be seriously injured, or worse. But there was no sign of them. All except the elves hunted high and low, thrusting their torches into every nook and cranny, but they found no one. "Curses!" Meekhi was beside herself, "Where can they be? Had they managed to grab hold of anything we would have seen them, they should be *here*! We did not pass them on the way down did we? Can anyone see anything at all?"

Mercy was as confounded as her queen. "They seem to have disappeared into thin air, this is truly an impossibility is it not."

Ramulet held his torch up high so as to illuminate the elves. Babel had Solipop's tail wrapped around her wrist to prevent him wandering off. She was tap-tapping one of her little feet and staring at the bewildered humans. He strode over to her, looking directly at the pair of Benijays, "I know of your kind, you have no axe to grind with us. History tells us we and the elves have always shared a bond of friendship. I heard you tell my lady—Meekhi, why you attacked the king. But what did you do after that? What is the purpose of that lever, and what was the noise that followed?"

Babel looked up at the towering guardsman. "I saw that lever yesterday and read the instruction above it. It opens the ground we are now standing on, and a great lake lies far below. Scrolls I found in the city speak of how people would dive from these steps into the lake below to swim for their pleasure, I cannot see any pleasure in that at all, but you are *human* after all, I think the floor opened up when I pulled the lever and your friends fell straight through here, into the lake below, if it is still there."

"Still *there*?" Mercy ranted, astonished, "and if it is not, they have fallen further than they would have!"

"And if it is still there," Babel replied meeting her eyes, "then I have probably saved their lives by the only means possible."

Ramulet and Mercy were surprised when Meekhi spoke. Given that Tamarin and the children could well be dead, her calm manner was completely unexpected. "Babel, your quick thinking may well have saved the king and our comrades from certain death. For this, I am grateful to you. I can see why you were concerned for the wellbeing of Solipop, he is your offspring and your behaviour is as nature intended. Rest assured we mean neither of you any harm. The witch and her evil allies however, mean all of us plenty of harm, let us remember who is the real enemy here and not bicker over what is already unwittingly done and past. I will remain on the last step. *You*—Babel, must climb up and again activate that lever. When the ground opens, I shall jump into whatever lies beneath us and find at once my husband, and your king."

"I shall join you, my lady." Mercy immediately stepped alongside her. Ramulet was about to echo Mercy's sentiment but Meekhi put up her hand to silence him. "Ramulet, our soldiers and horses must have a leader in our absence, and that leader is to be you. I will not hear otherwise. Mercy and I will search for Tamarin and the little ones, you shall galvanise the Royal Guards. Babel, you can do as you please, but I suggest you and your young stay close to Ramulet. There is much evil afoot here in Soledad."

So it was arranged as Meekhi commanded. She and Mercy made ready to dive headlong into whatever they may find. Ramulet stood behind them holding up torches as high as he could. Babel bounded up the stairs till she was level with the lever protruding from the wall. It was too far to activate by hand or tail, and in the past it must have been released by cord-and-pulley from the landing. The cord had long since perished in the damp atmosphere of the stairwell. Ramulet called up to Babel, "She-elf! We are ready when you are!"

The elf sprang away from the stairs and landed on the lever, which promptly snapped in half. Her yelp was heard by the others as she plummeted down towards them—her huge eyes now doubled in size with fear. Meekhi raced up several flights and leaned out, Ramulet anchoring her by her cloak. It was an impossible angle and her booted feet rested on the very edge of the step. Solipop was trembling, his face covered by both his hands. Then, without any dramatics and hardly any sound at all, the elf flopped limply into Meekhi's outstretched arms. Ramulet and Mercy heaved them both back to the steps, and even before Babel had both feet firmly on the ground Solipop had leapt up into her arms, the pair standing rolling their eyes at each other with their tails entwined.

The scene, charming as it was, could not distract the Samarians from Tamarin and the children. They raced back up the stairs to the site of the lever. It had broken off flush to the wall and could not be activated again. Meekhi was thinking fast. "We must return to the great hall. It seems that other than the lake below and the positioning of the palace, the city of Soledad is built akin to Sitivia. Indeed, I believe Sitivia was mostly modelled on this former citadel, so there must be a Hall of History here somewhere. There we will find maps of the city, and our path to Tamarin. Only The Dragon knows what condition he and the little ones are in, we must make haste."

They started the long climb back up, and, as they did so, Babel touched Meekhi's hand, telling her in her small soft voice, "Thank you, my lady, for saving my life so my Solipop would not be orphaned so young."

Meekhi returned her gesture with a friendly squeeze of her little hand and Solipop beamed at her, still hugging his mother dearly.

CHAPTER FOURTEEN

SOLENIA

As his scrabbling fingers had slipped away from the cold stone Tamarin's first thought had been of Meekhi, and of how he needed to survive the fall in order to protect her from the rank evil now at large in his realm. He also thought of the valiant little ones now hurtling to their doom beside him. Their bravery and loyalty astonished him, but, alas, he would most likely never have the opportunity to repay them. His warrior-blood had not given up on the prospect of life just yet, but he knew full well of the hard, cold stone, awaiting them below, and his eyes, searching desperately, could see nothing in the pitch blackness that might be used to save any of them. He still held that special sword and thought of how he would have preferred to have died wielding such a weapon in combat, rather than from falling down the stairs.

The children were calling to each other as they tumbled head over heels through the air, and cries of, "Must be the end of the dream, time to wake up!," or, "This is really gonna hurt," filled the air. But then they heard a terrible squealing, scraping sound, accompanied by a loud rumbling. They could just make out the stone floor below them as they sped terrifyingly towards it, only now it seemed to be moving away from them.

"The ground, it's opening up! It's opening up!" Zowie shouted out. Sure enough, the entire floor at the foot of the stairs was parting like a gigantic trapdoor, and even as this thought registered, the four of them shot through the gaping square hole. Looking back up as they continued to plummet, they saw two heavy slabs of masonry rise, slamming back into place with a resounding

'BOOM'. They continued their descent, hitting deep water some seconds later. The force of the impact knocked them breathless and the children were struggling to stay afloat, laden down as they were with their weapons and cloaks. Tamarin's powerful muscles had no such problems, and wherever they had fallen to he could see about him quite clearly, the water was as still as a pond and tepid to the touch. He could see a thick, rusting steel chain, was suspended across it. It spanned the water only a foot or two above the surface, and swimming over to his young companions he helped them get their arms over it to prevent them from drowning. He then did the same and they bobbed about on the surface, regaining their breath and allowing their hearts to settle after that incredible plunge from above.

They were in a vast underground cave (features Samaria is famous for having many of) that housed a large lake. It was far too big to be a pool and 'lake' was definitely the best description. The water formed an oval and the two longer shores had beaches—*real* beaches, of soft, white, powdery sand. Beyond these, the cavern walls rose up to form a giant dome, in the middle of which they could just about recognise the square shape of the enormous trapdoor through which they had fallen. No way out was obvious at first glance and Lauren turned to Zowie, her hair plastered to her face, asking in a depressed voice, "Why? Tell me, just when we get some lovely new clothes and are all geared up for action, do we fall off the stairs into what is probably the sewer of Soledad?"

"This is no sewer," Zowie told her, "this is clean, fresh water, but I haven't a clue where we are. How would I have? Shame about our posh new gear though, we looked so lush ...for a little while." She ended her sentence spouting water from her mouth.

Thomas was laughing quietly to himself at the state of the bedraggled girls when Tamarin told them, "This chain must have been used for pulling a ferry, or other craft, across the water. By The Dragon!, you are saved only by its presence. Follow me, we must reach the shore and assess our situation. The water is calm enough, but who can say what lies beneath its still surface?"

This last part of his sentence motivated the children into clambering along the chain at unbelievable speed. Hand-over-hand they raced along and Tamarin could barely keep up. Weighed down with weapons and shields as they were, they still reached land in record time.

Standing dripping on the sand with gloomy faces, they looked about themselves, and out across the water. They had not forgotten Ramulet's recent harrowing underground experience and their senses were electrified, on high alert for signs of trouble. Looking up they saw tiny lights glowing in their thousands on the ceiling, like a sky laden with diamonds. "WOW." The children exclaimed.

"Yes, wow indeed." said Tamarin quietly, "this must be Solenia—the fabled lake of Soledad, one of the many wonders of this once great city. My mother and father were wed on these very shores, though I have no memory of it for I was as yet not conceived."

"That's it," sighed Zowie wistfully, "if I ever get married, it just has to be here. How cool is this place!"

"Frankly," replied Tamarin removing his cloak, "I do not think it very cool. In fact, I'm rather hot. It's very humid down here. But know this, little ones, you fell from above in your efforts to save me. A truly brave and unselfish act one that I shall never forget, I will not doubt your loyalty or intentions again. Let us deal with Ogiin and those of his creed, then, we shall talk further on this matter. but I tell you this upon my oath; You, Thomas, will be knighted a Knight of The Realm, and you two—Zowie and Lauren, will be Ladies of the Royal Court. But for now, our most pressing need is to keep our wits about us and find a way out of here and rejoin with the others. Stay sharp and remember of what, and of whom, Solipop told us."

Soaked through to the skin and squelching along in their soggy clothing, they began searching for any telltale signs of escape.

Running up and down the long flight of stairs in such poor visibility had exhausted Meekhi and the others, with the exception of the Benijays, both of whom seemed tireless. Gasping as if she had just run a marathon at top speed, she turned to Ramulet and passed him the triblade they had secured for him below. "Tamarin wishes for you to have this. I am sure it will serve you well."

Ramulet bowed his head, and after briefly examining the deadly looking weapon with the glossy black blade, he fitted it to his belt. Looking down into the hall from above, all seemed to be as they had left it. The cooking pot was bubbling away merrily, but none were eating as yet. The men were waiting for the king and queen to return before they dined, as was the correct thing to do. Standing in little groups and chatting amongst themselves, they spotted Meekhi and the others re-emerging at the top of the steps. Running down toward them, Ramulet was barking orders as he moved—telling them of what had happened since he left them not so long ago. They immediately began forming search parties to find the king. Meekhi's small group was only halfway down the steps when the doors of the great hall slammed open. The torches burning brightly along the walls made it easy to see the cause—Venomeens had invaded that sacred place.

A half score had burst into the room brandishing their crude grey weapons. They leered at the men and women facing them, their cruel smiles revealing row upon row of those savage interlocking fangs. There was a low hissing sound coming from them and it could be just about distinguished as "Sssamarians must die!"

The men didn't hesitate, running forward and attacking the foul fiends daring to trespass in a place born of such reverence. The sound of steel-on-steel filled the room and sparks flew as triblades clashed with Venomeen swords everywhere. Rordorr had been standing with his rear to the door and a powerful, well aimed kick deprived a Venomeen of his head. The hideous, decapitated body began running about in a crazy zigzag until Ramulet, leaping down from the staircase above, sliced it into half from neck to groin with one strike of his sword, a terrible stench filled the hall as the creature's green-and-yellow guts poured out, flopping slimily onto the floor and slithering about like so many huge worms.

Faradorr found it impossible to kick out due to his injuries. His brother however, despite being wounded himself, was doing a stoic job of protecting him. Mercy and Meekhi found themselves back-to-back and fighting for their lives. Their blades moved as fast as lightening, the air singing as they scythed through it. But this new enemy was not slow and ponderous like the troll had been earlier, the Venomeens moved quickly enough to prove a deadly challenge, but still they lacked the fighting skills of a warrior race such as the Samarians. Unfortunately this lack of swordsmanship was compensated for by weight of numbers and more of them kept appearing at the door. Soon the Samarians were outnumbered three to one and were struggling to keep the pale-skinned bloodsuckers at bay.

Ramulet fought like an enraged tiger. He moved so fluidly one could see only a blur of swirling cloak and flashing blade. He knew the enemy numbers would soon tire his men. There was no doubting that each one of them, to a man, would stand to the last in defence of their queen, but the odds were against them unless somehow the tide was turned. He gave commands as he fought, "This is the scum I met beneath Iret, beware, the witch could be close by anywhere. Cut them down, men! Slaughter them for the filth they are! In the name of the Great Dragon, and the King! Kill them all!"

Their captain's words spurred the guardsmen into even greater efforts but the Venomeen numbers were simply too great and the Samarians found themselves being forced to form a thin defensive line as they retreated slowly towards the statue of the dragon, and the steps next to it.

Babel was midway on the steps with Solipop close behind her, he was peeping out at the mayhem, his big eyes rolling around fast enough to make anyone looking at them feel quite giddy. His fur sat flat all over him. Babel knew she had to act—this swarming evil would show her kind no more mercy than it would her newfound friends, but getting involved in battle was not in her nature, nor that of her people. She could see Meekhi and Mercy had become separated, each holding her own amidst the embattled guardsmen. She called down to Meekhi, "My lady! My lady! If you could but mind my Solipop, perhaps I can be of assistance!"

Meekhi shot a glance at her whilst driving her sword deep into the chest of the Venomeen directly in front. She could not see what the tiny elf could possibly do to help, but she knew her handful of guardsmen would eventually lose this battle unless something new was brought into the equation. Elves were well known for their great wisdom and vast knowledge.

The once silent Great Hall of Soledad smarted from the sounds of clashing steel and splintering shields. It was not intended to witness such gory violence and agonising death. The torches continued to smoke and burn on their mounts, illuminating the bloody havoc being wrought all around them. Outside, the Silent City sat quietly in the dark of night, unaware that the war that had frozen her heart so long ago had returned to her once more, blighting her again in blood.

Meekhi made her decision—in a fast twisting motion she ducked under a sword aimed at her head, and sliced into the legs of her assailant. Continuing her spin she extracted herself from the battle and somersaulted backwards to the steps—which she leapt up three at a time to join the Benijays. Perspiration dripping from her brow and her hair plastered to her flushed face, she told Babel, "You had better make this good, and quick. My people need my sword down there."

Babel looked up at her. "My lady, us elves are sworn not to kill, but perhaps we can help others to do that which we can not. I entrust Solipop to you."

The she-elf placed Solipop's tail on Meekhi's wrist and jumped from the stairs onto the head of the stone dragon. The statue towered above them, and Meekhi was taken aback by the power the elf must possess to leap such a great distance, a remarkable feat of both strength, and agility. She watched, astonished, as the little blue elf, her tail waving high in the air, disappeared into the dragon's mouth. Shortly after, she emerged from the tip of the tail, close to the cooking pot. The elf grabbed at Arcadian's fire sticks still burning under the cauldron, plucking out several pieces of the special wood that does not extinguish easily. The red hot embers began singeing her furry little hands and the pain was obvious on her face as she began pouncing back to the stairs, weaving in and out of the combatants in her path. Back by her offspring, Babel dropped the burning wood at Meekhi's feet and pointed at the quiver hanging on Mercy's back. Meekhi needed no further urging and called to Mercy, "Mercy! Your bow! We have need of you, now!"

With some difficulty, Mercy extricated herself from the confusion of battle as Solipop examined his mother's injured hands, big sloppy wet drops falling from his dewy eyes and splashing onto the stone at his feet. Even amidst this chaos Meekhi could not but help being touched by a child's love for its mother. Even as Mercy arrived by her side, Meekhi was kneeling, tearing a strip from her own undergarment and placing a makeshift bandage on the she-elf's singed hands. There was no time for long speeches of gratitude and she nodded her head in acknowledgement to Babel, then, removed the arrows from Mercy's quiver. The golden haired woman took up position on the steps and Meekhi passed her the burning arrows one by one.

The hard pressed guardsmen could not have been more grateful when they saw the missiles begin drilling death into their opponents. The Venomeens, further enraged by this unexpected development, looked up, clucking furiously at the women raining down fiery death down so efficiently.

It quickly became apparent that Mercy's supply of arrows was insufficient to stem the growing tide of Venomeens as still more were waddling in to join the fray. Many pale, saggy-skinned corpses lay butchered already, but more just kept on appearing. The influx had slowed it was true, but the steady trickle of new arrivals remained a worrying concern to the Samarians. They could not fight on at this pace forever and had no idea of exactly what number they faced. Meekhi warned Mercy, "We need more arrows, or we are undone."

The pair searched around the hall and spotted two guardsmen fighting ferociously with bulging quivers on their backs. Mercy could see that Rordorr had backed his brother into a far corner to the rear of the Venomeens, and was fighting as if possessed to defend him. The scum must have sensed the frailty in the younger horse and Faradorr, himself, could not have looked more angry, frustrated at his own hapless situation, but he was wise enough to know that to get involved would only endanger further those trying to protect him. Killing a flying horse was considered a great victory for those most favoured by Ogiin—the Venomeens. To taste the blood of such a one was as tasting the sweetest nectar to these waddling demons, and the taking of such a noble spirit would do much to serve their master's needs. Rordorr had already lost one of his kin to the Desert of Iret and he would die himself, without qualm, before he allowed any more of his kind to pass from that world at the hands of darkness. He would continue to defend his brother till the battle was won. Then, he would die from his own many terrible wounds, which he had yet to receive. "This must surely be his fate," he thought.

Meekhi made ready to fight her way through to those much needed arrows, but little Solipop, upon seeing the pain his Babel had endured in aiding the Samarians, broke free from his mother and followed her earlier example by leaping up onto the head of the stone dragon. The women and Babel were mortified, calling out, "No! Solipop! No!" But it was too late. The infant elf scrambled down the statue, and, to their horror, he leapt into the heart of the battle. With incredible skill and courage, the tiny elf jumped from shoulder to shoulder of Samarian and Venomeen alike. As he headed for the arrows his tail, with amazing dexterity, plucked raised swords from the grasp of the startled enemy, leaving them defenceless against a three-bladed death. On the steps, they could barely breathe as they watched him grab the arrows from both quivers and begin his return journey. Mercy cleared his path with what remaining shafts she had left and he returned unharmed with the fresh ammunition. They were speechless as he stood on the stairway with his arms outstretched—his strong little hands full of arrows and another clutch of missiles gripped within a tight coil of his tail. His mother stared harshly at her brave little one, scolding him in a tone that gave away her complete lack of anger, "If you *ever* do that again, I will put TWO knots in that mischievous tail of yours!"

"A third will be tied very tightly indeed by *us,* young Solipop! However, we are grateful for your brave deed." Whilst Meekhi admonished him, Mercy winked and he stood rolling those big irresistible eyes, looking rather smug.

Meekhi, armed with her fresh cache, began lighting them and passing them to Mercy, who in turn fired deadly volley after volley into the enemy. The missiles began to take their toll and the guardsmen seemed to be gaining the upper hand despite having lost two of their own. The Venomeens refused to tire at all. Each one was fighting now with the same savage ferocity with which they had started. Flashing those terrible teeth and snapping at the Samarians by extending their necks, their limitless stamina was wearing down the exhausted men. However, Meekhi, Mercy, and the elves, had made victory a real possibility and each man present saw this opportunity to turn the tables. Ramulet led a charge forward, supported by the deadly archer on the steps. Babel and Solipop stood behind the two women, looking away from the carnage being wreaked below.

The retreating men closed ranks, formed an offensive line, and pushed the bloodsuckers back towards the open doors, close to where Rordorr was standing. His assailants had left him to reinforce the others as they had been driven back. To his complete frustration, he could not attack them in their rear because he could not leave the equally frustrated Faradorr exposed to threat. Meekhi passed the remaining arrows to Babel and asked her to light them for Mercy, she then ran downstairs to join her people in crushing the Venomeens. Only Ramulet had seen the likes of them before and she had never encountered such cold, heartless creatures, in her life. She could almost *feel* their craving for her blood. They glared at the Samarians with such dead, emotionless eyes, red and yellow pools of blood lust, the force of their hatred slamming into her like a mailed fist. Such evil could not be allowed within the borders of her realm, not now, not ever.

Meekhi was hurrying past the steaming cauldron when it began to boil over violently, the contents frothing up and pouring over the sides, hissing as they dripped into the flames below. She stopped

Samaria

in her tracks sensing something was very amiss here. The fire still burned but the water had turned a muddy green colour and the smell of aromatic herbs had been replaced by a strange nauseous odour, assailing her nostrils and making her gag. The men had their backs to her and were completely occupied with the blood thirsty Venomeens. Mercy was concentrating on her own deadly art and even Babel was otherwise engaged. Meekhi stood dead still, somehow knowing not to move as she watched the foaming fluid. To her horror, a head started rising from the middle of the scalding hot water. The withered face of an old woman began appearing into view, flat, wiry strands of white hair dotted the pock marked, mostly bald, scalp. The skin on her face and many chins was so loose and saggy it seemed as if the water had boiled her half molten. The sunken eyes were buried so far into her head it was impossible to tell whether she had any eyeballs at all, only a pair of fleshy pits being visible. She seemed to have recently burned her face as it was scorched and raw. Deliberately slowly the gruesome countenance cracked into a wicked grin, exposing awful blackened teeth and a purple tongue. The head kept rising from the steam until two hands emerged, reaching up out of the boiling brew and take hold of the rim. One of them had two fingers missing. Teritee!

Meekhi froze, transfixed, gripped by the hideous apparition materialising right before her very eyes. The witch continued rising, scalding water, pieces of meat, and various vegetables falling from her until she stood upright, the green brew bubbling and boiling about her bony, bowed knees. The fierce heat didn't seem to bother her at all. The crone was wearing not a jot of clothing and her obscenity disgusted Meekhi to the core. She had been motionless for only a few seconds but in that time the witch had somehow managed to perch herself atop the cauldron. Her clawed feet gripped the pot behind, and her fingers gripped the rim in front. She sat hunched over the boiling water, grinning at the queen like some monstrously deformed toad. Meekhi tossed her long dark hair to one side and glared back at the witch, her initial shock overcome and her wits keen once more. Standing tall, and summoning up all the fighting spirit of a true queen such as she was, she leapt forward with her sword drawn. But the witch was quick, flopping to the ground and avoiding that flashing blade. Meekhi kept her eyes on the crablike figure on the floor. "You, Teritee," she told her, "have seen better days!, but all your days are now at an end. Losing some weight would improve your appearance greatly, here, allow me to help you, by removing your head!" Again she tried to attack the witch but again the creature's form belied her speed and she evaded the sword repeatedly seeking her neck, cackling sinisterly at the beautiful young queen, "Meeekhi...we are *joined* you and I, but I shall live, and you shall die, heeheehee..."

Conscious of what Ramulet had explained earlier, Meekhi pursued the witch cautiously around the cauldron. The ugly hag seemed to prefer being on all fours, but even as she watched in disbelief, a second pair of legs began emerging from under the witch's arms! The flabby rotten flesh burst open, spilling bright yellow pus and thick green mucus onto her bulbous belly. A pair of gnarled feet erupted out of her armpits and continued to grow until she had six limbs. The pair—both witch and queen, chased around the fire, but Meekhi could not quite catch the mutating creature. Soon the witch resembled more a spider than anything even remotely human. Meekhi never saw how the witch had gained hold of a Venomeen sword, but she was certainly holding one now. When their blades met, Meekhi was shocked at the sheer strength of the witch, her savage blows forcing her to stagger back under the onslaught. Fending off the deadly blows, she thought, "The bitch must gain such strength from some dark magic."

The great hall of Soledad continued to echo with the sounds and cries of pitched battle as the beautiful young warrior and the repugnant old witch fought with a ferocity that one would not imagine possible from one so decrepit, or one so pleasing to the eye. Again and again, sparks flying, they clashed against each other. The witch was extremely dextrous, swapping her sword between limbs often to distract and confuse. Meekhi, however, was an experienced swordswoman, and though the six-limbed monstrosity was unnerving at times, her own superior skills and youthful agility had the upper hand. Several times the tip of her blade managed to nick Teritee's sagging skin. When, suddenly, half a dozen false images of the witch appeared, each moving independently of the others, Meekhi was livid at the cowardly ploy. More lies! More deceit! More treachery! Her mind raced—this was a repeat of the trickery in Iret, but which image was real? There was no way of telling and she had no choice but to fight them all. Using everything in her own arsenal, she backed up her swordsmanship with kicks and punches designed to unbalance the creature, hopefully creating an opportunity for a fatal blow to be dealt. But it was impossible to kill an illusion and she had already driven her blade into three false hearts when her sixth sense told her she had made a serious mistake in her judgement. The real witch pounced from behind, knocking her onto her back by the statue's tail. Teritee was on her in a flash and she was pinned down with the grinning hag sitting astride her chest. She fought to dislodge the slimy creature, but her supernatural strength and enormous weight were too much to overcome.

The witch lowered her wrinkly face and a forked tongue of revolting proportions snaked out, licking slowly over Meekhi's face and lapping at her chest. It changed colour as it slithered about her flesh, changing from purple to green and back again. It felt rough through its slimy coating and Meekhi could sense the witch tasting her. Every fibre in her body repulsed at this perverse invasion, she heaved with all her might to escape Teritee's clutches, but her effort was in vain. She could feel her limbs tiring from the effort, but she would not relent.

"M...M...Meekhi," the crone crooned as she slavered over her neck, "your soul will taste so good, better yet than your flesh, yes, so pure, so strong. Ogiin will linger upon the savouring of you, yes he will take his time with you for sure, my pretty."

Meekhi repeatedly strained to break free with all the power of her strong young muscles, but the intense effort served only to be weakening her further. She turned her face away from the slobbering witch to avoid her drooling on her mouth. Her breath smelled awful, and she thought she would vomit. As she turned her face away, she saw a blue flash fly from the dragon's tail, but she could not identify it. There was a loud 'TWANG!' And the witch rolled off and away from her. Meekhi could see Solipop standing there, just a few feet away, with a gigantic frying pan held high in his long, powerful tail. "I panned her." He stated, quite literally. She leapt up and grabbed him just in time, the witch's sword smashing into the ground where he had stood only a second before. She threw the little elf onto the back of the towering dragon, out of harm's way. The witch seethed at the small, furry blue figure scampering back up to its mother, "I will have your soul for this! Elf!"

Solipop paused, and looking back at her, he chortled in his giggly, childlike voice; "Out of the cooking pot, into the frying pan!" Then he made a hasty retreat back to Babel.

The young elf had distracted Teritee for but a few scant seconds, but a few seconds was all that Meekhi needed, and her gleaming blade sliced through the air, severing the witch's left ear from her head. She shrieked so loudly that everyone in the great hall turned and stared at her, at last aware of her presence. Teritee glared at Meekhi with a hatred beyond belief, her eyes betraying her agony, and, perhaps, her envy. But whatever was on her mind, she did not have the chance to act upon it, because a burning arrow had buried itself deep into her bulging belly. Shocked, and in agony, she looked down at the shaft burning between the folds of flab that made up her midriff. She began backing away from Meekhi whilst keeping an eye on the flaxen haired archer on the steps, an archer already aiming another shot. She turned her head to the right and saw Ramulet coming at her from across the hall. "We are not done yet, Samarian Queen. One day, I will suck out your soul!" Her threat made, the witch kicked over the boiling pot and dived head first into the steaming pool. She seemed to become as one with the green liquid, dissolving herself, almost instantly, into the thick green bog of her own making. She was nowhere to be seen. The puddle, still bubbling and popping, seeped into the mortar between the paving. Ramulet tried to take a torch from the wall and put flame to it, but the torch would not come away. He pulled harder, but instead of coming away it made a loud click, and rotated down as a lever would do, "More wizardry by the ancients!" He thought. The great dome above them began to part, opening up to reveal the beautiful star-spangled night sky. Meekhi smashed a jar of pitch onto the mess created by the witch and Mercy sent a fiery arrow to ignite it. The area near the upturned pot began to burn, but much of the sludge had trickled down through the ground already.

The Venomeens became ever more agitated, making loud clucking sounds when they saw Teritee disappear. They began glancing over their shoulders at the open door and Rordorr moved a little closer to it, so they knew he would be waiting.

Her supply of arrows reduced to nothing, Mercy joined Meekhi amongst the others. The Samarians faced the nervous looking Venomeens with renewed confidence. Meekhi was furious, "You sons of hell have dared to soil this sacred place with your foul presence, your master feeds on the souls of others, so now we shall send him a feast of his own kind. Tell him we defy him! And now, you must pay the costly price of your trespass!"

They charged what enemy remained with the speed of lightening, triblades flashed, and Venomeens fell. When their numbers reduced enough to no longer threaten Faradorr, Rordorr joined the battle with a vengeance—his terrifying hooves shattering the enemy, crushing them into the ground like dust. Together, they made short work of those unscathed by Mercy's arrows, and soon silence again reigned in the great hall, bar the odd thud when a guardsman aimed a solid, self satisfying kick at a dead, or dieing, Venomeen.

The men sat down where they stood—exhausted from the exertions of such close quarter combat. Arcadian moved from corpse to corpse, chopping off any heads that still remained attached. "No point in taking chances," he thought. Meekhi rested at the foot of the stairs, her elbows on her knees and her head in her hands. Her hair hung straight down, masking her face from view. She was distraught. If an enemy force of this magnitude had entered Soledad, then how, if they still lived, could Tamarin and the young ones survive any such threat, it was imperative they find them immediately, she had to know what had befallen her beloved without further delay.

Mercy came and sat beside her, aware of what must be on her mind. She placed an arm around Meekhi's shoulders and soothed her. "My lady, we shall find Tamarin, and the young ones, soon. Have no fears, this will happen. But were it not for one, small blue person, there may well not have been a queen to search for her king." Her eyes settled on Solipop, who was still halfway up the stairs with Babel. She continued, "Meekhi, it was the little elf that saw you fall. He alerted me to your situation before he disappeared into the dragon's mouth. I couldn't get a clean shot whilst you were entangled with that loathsome bitch—Teritee, but he did for her as best he could. You should be made aware of this fact, I think."

"Indeed I should," Meekhi replied, "and thank you for reminding me of his gallant behaviour."

The close friends smiled warmly at each other as Meekhi rose to her full height, and looking up at Solipop, called over to him, "You! Little blue person, come here, I'd like a word with you."

Solipop crept sheepishly down the steps towards her. He stood just out of reach, staring down at his feet with his big fluffy ears pinned back on his head. Meekhi gave Babel a sly wink and knelt down in front him. "Solipop," she told him in her gentlest, kindest, voice, "today you have most surely saved my life. You put yourself in harm's way for one that is but a stranger to you. This will not be forgotten, consider yourself a citizen of Soledad, your Babel also. When this city one day returns to the light, all within her walls will be yours to enjoy as you both please."

The young elf beamed as Meekhi stood up and Mercy ruffled his big ears, which were now standing proudly erect. Before turning to the more serious matters in hand, Meekhi detached the pouch from her belt and handed it to him. It was full of dried dates.

Ramulet approached them, and having made certain of their well-being, he told Meekhi, "My lady, these hellish ghouls must be those from the tunnels below Iret. They and the witch must have sought refuge here after their underground lair became an inferno. Measuring their numbers and assuming these *are* the same vile filth, I would say we have slain most, if not all, of them. But we cannot rest our guard, I suggest we focus on finding the king, there is no telling where that rancid whore has disappeared to."

Meekhi, dejected, and fearful of Tamarin's fate, looked up at him. "Yes, we will form two squads and try to find a way beneath the great hall. I shall take the guards, you and Mercy will form the other squad. But first let us extinguish this seemingly tireless fire so as not to chance the burning down of the city."

"Guards, bring water." Mercy summoned men to extinguish the flames.

"It seems," muttered Faradorr philosophically, "cooking pots are best left alone until we know why such poison stems from them so often."

Rordorr, far more enthusiastic, suggested, "I feel that all those that have eaten from such caustic cauldrons are doomed. We should find Tamarin before people start dropping down dead all around us."

Everyone glared at him in a very unamused manner and the big horse looked down at his forelegs as if he had suddenly found something of great interest there. Then Babel surprised everyone by raising her voice.

"My lady, I overheard that loathsome witch talking to you, and now you are all talking of *pots*, rather than a single pot? Have you experienced a pot brimming over with evil before? Please, tell me all."

Meekhi turned to the She-elf, "Babel, we are grateful for all you and your Solipop have done for us and our cause, but now is not the time for the telling of tales, we must find the king. I will tell you what you ask after he is found."

"You must tell me *now*, my lady." The she-elf insisted.

"Why now? Little friend."

"Because... us elves know things that humans possibly do not. I believe the witch when she says you and she are somehow joined. I assume this is a pairing you would prefer to sever?"

Meekhi looked into the knowing eyes of Babel and saw in them a deep and ancient wisdom that she could not claim to either recognise or understand, but it was a wisdom she instantly respected, "Very well, then." Placing her hand on the elf's shoulder, she told her story (and that of Mercy and Faradorr too) as briefly as she could. The elf listened patiently, occasionally muttering "Mmm", or, "Aaah, yes—I see".

When Meekhi had finished talking, Babel stood rubbing at her fluffy little chin with both hands whilst scratching at her big blue ears with her tail, before she spoke. "I would say this—those that have eaten from the pot that is now upturned before us need have no worries, with the exception of Ramulet, Mercy, and your ladyship. Mr Faradorr, too, should not sleep easy as yet."

Rordorr whispered to his brother, "I knew it! You are truly undone, my brother. I shall miss you."

At this, Faradorr gave him a gentle push, shoving him away from the proceedings. Babel continued, "The wood you used as fuel in Iret was not wood born of nature, it would be the charred bones of men that have fallen victim to Teritee, Iret absorbing the discarded carcass's into itself over time. Teritee and Iret are as one, one born of the other, each full of the poison of the witch. This is the connection between those of you that I have named, and Teritee. You have cooked using the dead as fuel for your fire, and *you*, captain, have willingly eaten from the witch's own hand."

There was a shocked gasp from everyone and Mercy moved hastily to a far wall, fearing she might vomit. Ramulet stood in stunned silence wondering how this elf knew of his seduction beneath Iret when none had uttered a word of it in her presence. "These elves were wily characters indeed." he thought, his estimation of their kind far greater now. Meekhi controlled her own desire to gag at the horrifying news and asked the sad looking elf of how they could break so evil and insidious a tie to Teritee. Babel looked pityingly upon the disturbed expressions of the Samarians, their senses jarred at these awful revelations.

She told them, "The flame of the Great Dragon could perhaps cure you, but the Dragons of Light are no more. It is possible that a magical elixir wrought from that rarest of plants—Wartywart, infused with essence of Lozzwozz, could do the trick. Do we have any such medicinal gems to hand?"

Ramulet picked up on her train of thought, "Wartywart and Lozzwozz were common in these parts many years ago, but alas, now such magical herbs and vines are a scarce find, but find them we will! The most likely place to find such things is the herb garden in the palace of Rosameer. I shall set forth for that city right now, by your consent, my lady?"

Meekhi answered the chivalrous captain firmly. "You shall do no such thing. First, we find Tamarin. The king *is* Samaria and he must be found without delay. Then all decisions will fall to his wisdom. You Benijays, you will accompany Ramulet and Mercy in our hunt, for your own safe keeping, and because Samaria has need of your vast wisdom."

The men, women, horses, and elves within the great hall formed up as instructed by their queen. Torches and swords in hand, they began their search for Tamarin and the children, Meekhi's first port of call being the Hall of History.

CHAPTER FIFTEEN

THE HOST OF OGIIN'S CURSE

They had had no luck in finding a way out from the underground lake. The hundreds of bright sparkling lights high above them on the ceiling gave ample illumination despite the incredible size of the cavern, and it was easy to see where the walls had been worked smooth by the toils of long forgotten masons. They were covered in the most exquisitely detailed illustrations. Dragons, warriors, and exotic maidens still haunted this vast space, their presence in ink almost tangible. Strangely, it was not cold this far underground and everyone found their clothing drying very quickly. Thomas was quick to notice this, "Tamarin, I mean... *lord* Tamarin, our clothes are drying fast. This Samarian gear dries faster than my jeans would have anyway, but there must be a breeze, an air flow of some kind. I can't feel anything, but there must be fresh air, a vent of sorts, or it would be a lot more humid down here with the warm water and no ventilation."

"Just '*Tamarin*' will suffice, Thomas. No need for titles amongst friends, eh. We will save such formal pleasantries for when we are attending at court. But yes, I was thinking exactly the same thing. This air is breathable, not laden with moisture. Most surely it must enter here from somewhere."

Zowie had been watching them standing, talking. Nonchalantly she wandered over to Thomas, striking suddenly and plucking a long hair from his head, ignoring the expected "OW!" She walked to the water's edge with the others watching her curiously. Lifting the single hair up high, she released it. It was blown back to her, floating down to the sand at her feet. Tamarin saw her reasoning immediately and plucked several more hairs from Thomas' head before joining her. Thomas scowled at them and rubbed at his irritated scalp. Tamarin raised his arm, dropping the hairs one at a time, watching them all drift gently back to the sandy beach. "By the sword!" he exclaimed, "You little ones have much wisdom for such tender years. The problem, as I see it, is that the draft is blowing towards us. This means it enters this once great aquatic arena from the opposite side to where we now stand. The two shortest sides of the lake seem to melt into the rock and I do not think it wise to dive in to try and see where the water goes to, or comes from. The walls are too smooth and too steep to attempt to climb them. So... little ones, we must cross the lake."

"Oh, great..." The Shortwaters mumbled unhappily, "trust us to end up on the wrong flippin' beach."

Tamarin could see that despite their mock misery, these three tended to take a humorous outlook on even the most dire of predicaments, this pleased him immensely, they seemed blessed with irrepressible spirits, always showing courage in the face of adversity. A man could not ask for better companions in such a situation.

Everyone stripped off their heavy outerwear and made sacks from their cloaks in which to transport their clothing and weapons. The crossing would involve moving slowly hand-over-hand along the long rusty chain that snaked out across the lake. No one was keen on crossing the unknown depths of Solenia but there appeared to be no choice but to take the plunge. The children were grateful for the myriad of lights twinkling above them, crossing the water in the dark may well have proved too much for them. Their surprising show of resilience thus far had its limits.

They were busy securing the makeshift sacks and Tamarin decided to make sure that the chain was anchored securely enough to withstand their combined weight bearing down on it. He crossed the beach and over to the wall in front of him—following the chain. It was attached to a substantial steel ring, fixed solidly into the rock. He wanted to be sure the children would be safe and so he took a firm hold of the ring and started pulling on it. It did not move back or forth at all, but it did seem to turn a little, clockwise. Bringing the full force of his broad shoulders to bear, he turned the ring until it had turned a full half circle. A crunching sound issued from just behind it and he jumped back, expecting the anchor to fall away from the wall. But it did not. Instead, the entire cavern was instantly filled with a loud whirring sound that echoed loudly out across the water. The children hurriedly opened the sacks they had tied shut so carefully, redressing even before Tamarin had returned to them. He also scrabbled back into his armour and the four of them stood gripping their swords, looking around the cave, wondering what was making so much mechanical noise. A large section of wall, to the left of the steel ring, recessed itself into the surface of the rock, sliding back to reveal a spacious, previously hidden chamber. Tamarin herded the children behind him to protect them from anything dangerous that might emerge from the darkened space beyond. A grating sound made them spin around, and they could just about make out movement on the other side of the lake. Another sliding door, exactly opposite the first one, had also slid open. "What did you do?" Thomas asked.

"In truth—I do not know, but I do know that in antiquity, us Samarians used many cunning mechanical devices when building cities and erecting fortress's. I think I have just activated one of those ingenious devices."

"Just like ancient Egyptians." Zowie was impressed, "I've always wanted to travel through time and see how on earth they managed to create what they did, and to explore the fascinating mystery that surrounds them. Now I've travelled through a dream to Samaria, and this place really puts the mockers on Egypt. Trapdoors, secret chambers, emerald rivers, flying horses! And this isn't myth, it's flippin' real! I wish I'd brought a camera...I can see me now, hosting a show... on Discovery Channel..."

Thomas couldn't believe what he was hearing, "And you say *I'm* bad? You should hear yourself! I prefer National Geographic anyway." Even as he was speaking, a deep grating rumble shook the cave, and, looking at the shorter sides of the oval lake, they were amazed to see whole sections of wall move away from the main body, the gigantic slabs of stone forming the staggered patterns of diving platforms at varying heights, linked together by a network of stone stairways, loud crashes shook the cavern as these fell into place one after another, the still surface of Solenia dancing when peppered with pebbles and tiny fragments of rock,

"My friends!" Tamarin cheered proudly, "Marvel at my father's work and the ingenuity of Chjandi—the Great Dragon. Soledad truly was a city above all others, an oasis of innovation! Sadly, those stairs do but reach only halfway to the door through which we fell. But what magnificent parties must have taken place here. What merriment! What *fun*! How exhilarating to leap from those heights and dive into those warm, welcoming waters. There would be music, entertainment…"

"I don't mean to be rude, Tamarin," Zowie interrupted his torrent of praise for his father, "but I think we should stay focused and alert right now. What is behind that wall in front of us?"

"Yes, of course." He regained his composure, a little embarrassed at his outburst, "Come, I will lead."

Followed closely by his young companions, he crossed the soft white sand and stood in the doorway revealed by the sliding wall. It was, most definitely, a room. There was no visible exit from it other than the one in which they stood. The ceiling was littered with tiny sparkling lights, just like the main cavern. In the middle of the room stood something none of them had dared to hope for—a marine vessel. It was a handsome craft, hewn from rich red mahogany. The bench seats were covered in soft black suede. Fitted to the port side were two looped ropes—for running the chain through. There was a clever pulley system, so by cranking a lever in the middle of the boat the craft would move smoothly along the chain. Tamarin entered cautiously. The walls in here were also adorned with painted scenes of high order, but having been protected from the warm moisture of the lake by the thick rock wall, they had been preserved perfectly. Bright, vivid colours blended with subtler pastel shades, leaping out at you with an alarming sense of reality, the images mind boggling. Mid height along the walls ran a thick, dark oak, shelf, atop which sat countless small bottles, decanters, and vials carved from crystal. Some had been painstakingly formed from precious stones, such as rubies and emeralds. Below the shelf were much larger jars made of coloured glass, together with pottery of clay. These, too, were incredibly ornate, the end result of many hours of loving labour.

Tamarin walked the length of the boat slowly—his fingers stroking tenderly along its sleek rails. He was only too aware of the urgency of their situation, but he could not help being enthralled at discovering these glories from Samaria's past. The children entered the room and began looking over the various items on the shelf, being careful not to disturb anything. Tamarin was philosophical. "The deeds of our forefathers and the wisdom of dragons past, bless us still today. This craft is as firm today as when she was built, she will carry us across the water without mishap. Truly my father—the great Darcinian, was a king forever beyond my own meagre measure. However, I *am* his son, and Lord of Samaria. These gifts from the past will aid his line even now in the present, and unto the future."

The children looked up from the dazzling array of glittering vials and smiled kindly at him, respect in their eyes. They loved the way in which he so openly revered his departed father. Sentiments often felt back in their own world, but certainly not often portrayed so unshackled. Thomas cocked his head to one side, "Shhh! Can you hear that?"

"Hear *what*?" The girls asked him.

"Yes, Thomas," Tamarin whispered, "I can hear it too. From where does it stem?"

"*Hear what*??" The girls asked again.

They strained their ears to listen, and sure enough a small insect-like buzzing could be heard. Their eyes shot about in all directions trying to locate the source of the strange noise, then, Zowie spotted it, a tiny spark of light, darting around the room. It whizzed past between the four people trying desperately to see what it was, and shot off again. Tamarin tried to catch it between cupped hands, but it evaded him easily.

The prow of the boat was decorated with a wooden dragon's head lavishly coated in silver gilt, and the flashing light, its strobe effect mesmerising, came to rest atop it. The tiny beacon was so bright, it was impossible to see its source. Then, it went out completely.

Necks craned, they crept forward towards the bow, approaching that proud-looking dragon's head with great care. From there came a tiny, squeaking little voice, as clear as crystal, and of a definitely female nature. "Are you The King? Are you *really* Tamarin? Has a Samarian Lord returned to Soledad at last? Are you really, really, *really*, He? Please, please, be the real king."

Tamarin still could not see where the minute little voice was coming from, so he told 'it', "I am Tamarin—son of Darcinian, and Lord of Samaria. King I am, by birthright, and the will of the Great Dragon. If it is the true king of Samaria that you seek, then you have found him. Reveal yourself to me."

The air was filled with jubilant squeaks and the strange, tiny sound of miniscule hands clapping, then the brilliant light reappeared on the dragon's head. It started to zigzag around the room, darting about as if demented. The petite voice was crystal clear, clear as polished glass, and it could be heard squeaking, "It's Tamarin! It's Tamarin! At last! It's the king!"

Finally, the dazzling glow settled on Zowie's shoulder, hovering there for a second before disappearing from sight. Lauren and Thomas peered closer, then, jumped back, yelling, "Oh! crap!"

Zowie tried to twist her neck around and look down her own face to see what was on her own shoulder, she saw something small and silvery below her ear, but couldn't say what it was. Tamarin came over quickly, staring down at her shoulder in complete puzzlement. A little figure stood there, a miniature female figure no more than two inches tall, with long silver hair and golden wings so fine that they could easily have been spun from spider's silk, she had the prettiest face, with bright scarlet lips and a porcelain complexion, and she was wearing clothing that glittered like multi-coloured diamonds, it was so intensely bright, it was impossible for anyone to keep their eyes focused on her. She stood on there looking directly back at Tamarin. "So, who might you be?" He asked.

"I, by birthright, and, *by the will of the Great Dragon*," giggled the miniature girl—imitating Tamarin rather well, "am Hi-Light—a fairy princess. Very nice to meet you, King Tamarin, and it's about time too! Soledad has slept for far too long."

He slowly held out his upturned palm, and the little fairy leapt onto his hand with the grace of a ballerina. Zowie stared in disbelief as he held his hand in front of him for all to see, but he remained wary, "So, your name is Hi-Light, and your parents would be...whom?"

"My father is King Burin—Lord of all Samarian fairy folk. My mother is Queen Burina—of the same fairy folk, of course. You are a rude king, my lord, a king that returns the gracious greeting of a royal princess with such questions."

Tamarin apologised for his bad form. "Forgive me, little princess Hi-Light. Much evil now lurks in this kingdom of mine. Caution must be our byword. How do you come to be here, and what is your purpose?"

She took a deep breath, "I have been here since Ogiin cursed the city to stone. A seed of his evil plays host to his curse deep under those waters outside of this boathouse. That seed anchors the curse in Soledad. When the city became stone, my people fell asleep. Why I was spared I do not know. Those shining lights you see above you are sleeping fairy folk, lost to slumber as long as this wicked enchantment holds sway. They will awaken only when Ogiin's curse is broken. When his evil no longer has a willing host here under the city, Soledad will begin to resuscitate. I have hidden behind that door for so very long, and I have been so alone these many years. I used to keep the city spick and span in eager anticipation of a royal arrival, but recently I saw an elf of the Benijay breed cleaning statues and thought I would leave her to it, after all... I deserve a break! What is your plan, my lord? How are you this side of the lake when the only way in, or out, is opposite you, on the other side?"

Tamarin's instincts told him Hi-Light was genuine enough, but he chose to err on the side of caution and not reveal too much of his situation, or that of the others now in the city. He told her, "Little princess, we need to reach that far door and return to the surface. We intend to use this beautiful craft for the purpose for which it was intended. You say there is something evil lurking beneath these calm, peaceful waters?"

"Yes, my lord," the little fairy piped up in her wee voice, "a curse so powerful as the one that grips Soledad must have an anchor, somewhere where it can be firmly rooted. Someone, or something, that bends to Ogiin's will, willingly had the curse placed in its black heart by accepting his spirit therein also. This creature has then remained here under the water ever since, the power of the curse rising from it and enveloping the city."

"This creature of which you speak," he pressed her, "what manner of creature is this? Be there only the one, or are there many? Can you help us in any way? I know your people were once great allies of my father."

"Alas," she sighed squeakily, "the power of my people is generated collectively, and as my entire nation sleeps, my sole contribution is worth nothing." She sighed again, the great sadness in her voice apparent despite her diminutive stature, "I have never seen that which lurks below the surface of the water, having always remained as far from it as possible. But I know it is there. I feel it like a cold wet hand slithering under my garments. I am sure it knows I fear it. I think it relishes my fear, my lord. I believe it thrives on instilling terror in others."

Tamarin passed the little fairy to Zowie, who was still staring, transfixed on the near-weightless figure standing in the palm of her hand. He pondered the situation for a few moments. The Shortwaters were as mesmerized as Zowie by the miniature women. They were still standing, spellbound, when he declared his intentions. "This creature, whatever it may be, shall see no fear in the eyes of a Samarian King. The lake must be crossed and the boat is the only means with which to accomplish this task. I cannot ask you young ones to take such a risk with me. I suggest you remain here with Hi-Light, I can send men back to take you across the lake under escort."

Zowie spoke for all of them. "We're going with you. Better to cross with you then to be left stuck here with something nasty hiding in that black water. Also we have no supplies with us, and there's no telling how long any rescue might take to arrive. I only wish we had had more time to train with the weapons you gave us. I'm not sure we will be of any help if a giant octopus or a mutant crocodile attacks us."

Lauren and Thomas nodded in consent whilst still remaining unable to take their bulging eyes off of Hi-Light, who seemed to be enjoying the attention and appeared to be performing pirouettes in Zowie's palm. Tamarin was about to speak, but suddenly Hi-Light again became a flashing spark of light and flew onto his shoulder, trilling in his ear, "I can help! I can help your friends! Follow me."

She flew up into the air and shot across the room, landing on the most breathtaking item in the room—a bottle. It was a hand's length tall, made of gold, emeralds, and pink crystal, with a solid sapphire stopper the size of a walnut, and a thick amethyst base. The fairy princess beckoned the others closer so they could hear her. "This vial," she informed them excitedly, "is a Wishing Well. My father—the Fairy King, presented it as a gift to the people of Soledad for their generous hospitality in allowing our people to live here by the lake after we were forced to move away from the borders of Dizbaar due to the unpleasant types settling there. Solenia was a lake of such beauty and many Samarians leapt from great heights to swim and bathe here. But some could not swim, *which I thought was quite funny*, but others thought otherwise—some people have no humour. So my father and other powerful fairies created this Wishing Well potion. They would take a tiny sip each and wish that they could swim as well as anyone else could, and, then, they *could*! It's Samarian fairy magic, my lord, the very best kind of magic. No disrespect to the Dragons of Light intended, of course. I am sure the potion would work for any mortal ability as well as for swimming. The effect of the potion lasts for months, sometimes even years."

Tamarin's eyes wandered from Zowie to Thomas, then to Lauren, before returning to settle on Zowie. "This must be of your own choosing." He told them. They each gave the same answer, "I'm in!"

Hi-Light fluttered elegantly back onto Tamarin's shoulder and sat with her legs dangling as he lifted the weighty bottle. It shone, sparkling in the bright effervescent glow being generated by the fairies sleeping above them. The stopper unscrewed without effort and the wonderfully fresh smell of elderflower, exotic blooms, and honeysuckle, filled the room. It was irresistible and Zowie stepped up eagerly. "I'll go first." She stood with her mouth wide open and head tipped back. Tamarin gently eased the bottle over until a single solitary drop of transparent orange fluid slowly formed on the spout, plopping onto her tongue a second later. She swallowed, saying in her most solemn voice, "I wish I could fight, and use my weapons, as well as any."

The Shortwaters repeated the short ritual in turn. Then they stood watching each other, waiting, looking for any change in anyone. Tamarin couldn't detect anything, "Do you feel any different?"

"No." The disappointment in their voices was obvious.

"Maybe," suggested Thomas, "it has gone off? I mean it's been here for ages, and it must be way past its 'sell by' date."

"My father's magic does not age." Hi-Light told them indignantly, "Try your weapons."

With the exception of Hi-Light, everyone stepped outside of the hidden chamber and onto the beach. Zowie was the first to draw her sword and the weapon felt alive in her hands, as if it were an extension of her own limbs, perhaps even her spirit. She danced around on the beach with the blade spinning, slicing, and jabbing, as if wielded by a master swordswoman. The Shortwaters wasted no time in joining in, and soon Tamarin and Hi-Light were treated to a truly talented display of weapon craft. The children were whooping and cheering, thoroughly excited and so very pleased with their new skills. Tamarin asked Hi-Light, "Will you be joining us on the crossing, little princess? The magical gift you have bestowed upon my good friends is not one they will easily forget, and I am sure it will serve them in good stead. It would seem your sole contribution has been one of great substance and import after all, my gratitude to you, and to your kin."

"I will remain here with my people." She told him, "Together we shall await your return, and the awakening of all Soledad along with her smallest inhabitants. I will be safe enough behind the wall. Simply turn the ring again and the door will seal once more. A king of Samaria has spoken to me in the Silent City today, my prayers are answered, my hope and faith renewed."

The children came running back shouting, "WOW" to Tamarin, and, "Thank you so much!" to Hi-Light. The fairy princess bowed, smiling, "A friend of Samaria is a friend of her fairy folk, I hope your newfound talent allows you to bring to justice those that mutilated your hair."

Tamarin hauled the gleaming boat down onto the beach, a task normally performed by six strong men. On each side of her gleaming bows was the proud inscription—'Swan of Solenia'. Hi-Light had tears streaming down her face as she stood on top of the Wishing Well, waving to the others as the thick stone wall closed, sealing the chamber, and possibly her fate, once more. The girls wiped at their eyes, and even the normally perky Thomas looked sad. "She is just lovely," Zowie had really taken to the fairy, "we are going to sort out this horrid Ogiin and wake up her people so she can see her mum and dad again."

The Shortwaters liked the idea and Tamarin hitched the boat to the long chain stretching out across the dark forbidding water. Now that they knew something of Ogiin's creed lurked hidden below the surface, the calm, flat expanse of water, looked twice as broad and thrice as deep.

The children nervously boarded the boat and Tamarin heaved it into the shallows. He told them, "I will take us across. Keep your eyes peeled, my friends. Alert me of absolutely *anything* that moves. We will not talk as we cross unless it be a matter of urgency, let us not awaken this host of Ogiin's seed needlessly, may the Great Dragon be with us."

An occasional metallic rattling from the chain was all that could be heard as the craft moved slowly across Solenia, but even that muted chink-chink-chink sounded alarmingly loud. The water remained near silent as the bow of the boat sliced smoothly through its dark surface, sending large ripples ebbing gently away. Above them, hundreds, perhaps thousands, of fairy folk slept their long sleep, oblivious to this new drama unfolding below. Zowie and Lauren sat on a seat that ran across the stern. They kept looking over their shoulders as if they expected some demon to rise up behind them from the depths, devouring them where they sat. Thomas sat in the bows, his eyes scanning the surface of the water for the slightest hint of movement. Tamarin, upright in the centre, was cranking a lever back and forth effortlessly, every push and every pull taking them closer to the land opposite, and a hasty exit from this curse ridden cavern. He could not help making comparisons to Ramulet's experiences trapped beneath Iret, and his own current predicament beneath Soledad. Always under our very feet, this filth! Was Samaria built upon the bulging brow of hell itself, how could such nightmares exist so close to this, the birthplace of dreams. When the scourge of Ogiin had been dealt with, he would have most of the underground caves filled in, or destroyed, they harboured evil too easily for his liking. The children fingered their weapons, but not with fear of attack. It was with the alert readiness of seasoned veterans that they prepared themselves. The tiny fairy had truly given them the one gift they were in need of most in this incredible faraway land.

The Swan of Solenia was only five minutes away from the shore when Lauren pointed to the wall near the square stone arch that led to the way out. Something moved there. Tamarin ceased his pumping of the lever and everyone peered keenly from the bows. Her discovery was not to be a pleasant one. There were three reptilian creatures crawling about on the wall around the archway. But these were no ordinary lizards, like chameleons their skin mirrored the grey wall they occupied. Each was as long as Tamarin was tall. Scaly skin covered their bodies and the four legs were too long, giving them the appearance of squatting on the wall like a praying mantis might do with its high-raised knees and elbows. Long tails furled and unfurled, doubling their body length and revealing a solid, spiked ball, at the tip. But it was the other end of the lizards that gave the biggest cause for concern. Their heads ran transversely to the body like that of a hammerhead shark. The wide, shallow heads had many eyes tapering from each end to the centre, the orbs growing in size as they neared the middle. The actual entire centre of the face was a mouth, a mouth filled with teeth like daggers and a curling blue tongue. All three of them had their rows of eyes fixed on the approaching boat as their tongues darted in and out expectantly between those dreadful jaws. The hammer headed lizards moved easily on the wall, keeping The Swan of Solenia in their sights all of the time by turning their long necks through the most impossible of angles.

The small craft bobbed about on the dark water. Everyone had their weapons drawn. Zowie spoke just as Tamarin was about to say something himself, "We're sitting ducks here, I thought Hi-Light meant there was only one host for Ogiin's curse. We can't go back either, there may be tons of these things under us right now. We have to get onto that beach ahead of us, if we have to fight, it must be on dry land, there's no other choice. Time to test the Wishing Well, I suppose…"

Tamarin was impressed, "There is truly the spirit of the warrior in you, and in your kin, too. There is no more to be said. You have chosen our only course of action. Be fleet of foot, but mind you do not stumble and fall, I can see the fiends ahead will offer no reprieve should you do so. Use your shields well in defence, but remember, and remember well, a shield can crush a skull as well as any other weapon, its purpose is not purely for defence. Your cloaks are an excellent tool for causing distraction. In the name of the Great Dragon, and for Samaria, we move to do battle."

As the boat began to creep forwards, the enormous lizards scrambled down to the beach to greet it. When their hammerheads came fully into view the children suddenly realised just how dangerous the landing would really be. The wonder and wistful romance of their adventure thus far dissipated into thin air, and the reality of those incredibly wide jaws sunk in. They barely recognised each other's appearance, wearing battle garb and brandishing weapons, each seemed older and somehow more grown up. They were as one with the Samarians in spirit, but not as yet tested, or bloodied, in combat. Thomas told the girls, "Look, you two hold back. Let Tamarin and I go first. If I'm to be a knight, then you've gotta allow me to be chivalrous. Anyway, I'm a *Ninja* now!"

The girls were touched by his attempt to disguise his concern for them. "We'll be right behind you, then, Tom."

The gigantic reptiles were pacing up and down along the beach, eager to taste the approaching fresh meat. Raising their tails like a scorpion, the spiky balls hanging menacingly in the air above them, they waited to set about the occupants of the craft. Their eyes alternated in intensity as they ran down each side of the face. They were of differing colours and lit up one after another like a row of lights might do, strobing from end to centre and then repeating the sequence. The effect was hypnotic, and, no doubt, was meant to be exactly that. They could see in all directions ahead of them and two of them had reached the point where the boat would beach. Swishing their long tails they had only to wait for their meal to arrive.

Seconds before the grating of hull on sand was to be heard, Tamarin shot the others a quick, final glance. "Happy hunting." He encouraged as he jumped from the boat to find two pairs of snapping jaws lunging at him. Using his shield to protect himself he splashed through the shallows to gain better footing on dry land. Thomas hesitated for a split second, then, he, too, leapt from the boat, and was pursued along the sand by the third creature. The girls saw him drawing the lizard away from them and they jumped from the craft, wading quickly through the water and onto the white sand. Tamarin had his hands full fending off the pair of hammer-headed horrors attacking him. The girls could hear the crack-crack of blows against his shield as he repeatedly blocked those teeth and tails from finding flesh and bone. Thomas—running flat out, had lost his footing and fallen, now defending himself against a mace of a tail that was trying to batter him to death. It was difficult for him to regain his feet in the soft sand whilst being hammered by that deadly club. He could not avoid injury much longer. Lauren stormed up the beach, bellowing for all she was worth. "HEY! Fish Face! Get your ugly mug away from my brother! If you fancy a go, have a go at me, you fly-eyed mongrel!" Without really thinking of how she was doing it she somersaulted through the air, landing a heavy strike to the middle of the creature's tail. It spun around with murder in its eyes. "Way to go!" cheered Zowie as she cart wheeled past and landed next to Thomas. The lizard turned once more to the boy and he landed a savage kick to its face. The children caught a fleeting glimpse of each others' excited eyes. The amazing transformation created by the Wishing Well was only now fully dawning on them, and they were revelling in their newfound fighting skills. They charged the single snapping reptile in unison. Ducking and diving to avoid its lethal tail and jaws, they managed to land many a blow with their blades, but its natural armour served it well, deflecting most of their efforts. Some, however, found their mark, and long thin wounds appeared on the surface of its skin. Lauren, having tripped on her cloak, managed to raise her shield just in time before the spiked ball smashed into it. The samarian steel held firm and she rolled to one side, recovering her feet and rejoining the fray. Zowie managed to step past the jaws and drove her blade deep into its back. Snarling, it twisted free, leaving her barely enough time to extract her blade. Dark green blood oozed from the wound, soaking quickly into the white sand. But the enraged brute was far from done, whipping about in the sand so fast it was impossible to tell where it would strike next. Thomas could see Tamarin dancing nimbly between the other two, slashing and stabbing at their hides in turn. He caught Thomas' eye and shouted; "The head! Remove the head! The neck has little protection!" Even as he tried to help the young ones, he jumped onto the back of one of the giant lizards and brought his sword down upon the other one's neck—severing the head from the body. The jaws continued to snap as the head rolled end-over-end down the beach, leaving a dark green blood trail in its wake. The decapitated body jerked and jolted in its death spasms, thrashing about with ever-slowing convulsions as life quickly faded. The other opened its jaws wider than ever before and snarled at him, the sound filling the cave. They circled each other, looking for the opportunity to make a kill.

Thomas and Lauren were trying desperately to get a blade past those ferocious jaws, but every time they neared that horrible, multi-eyed, face, the tail would rain down like a sledgehammer, pummelling the sand flat within inches of their feet. Then Zowie remembered Tamarin's earlier advice and began waving her cloak out to her left. She taunted the lizard like a skilled matador, minding to keep a safe distance. It became focused on her frantic display, paying far less attention to the Shortwaters who were discreetly working their way to its rear. Its tail was up high, ready to lash out at Zowie, but that was not to be. The Shortwaters landed perfectly choreographed strikes to the middle of it, neatly cutting it in half. The big spiky ball forming the tip fell heavily onto its previous owner's head before rolling away in the sand. The brute seemed confused by having been hit on the head by its own tail, and Zowie saw her chance, her sword sliced cleanly through the softer flesh of its more vulnerable neck and it began its spasmodic dance of death just as one of its brethren had done earlier at Tamarin's hands.

The children raced back up the beach to help Tamarin finish off the one remaining lizard, but he seemed to have matters well in hand. He had managed to get astride the writhing reptile's back, and take a firm grip at each end of its wide hammerhead. His legs were locked around its midriff and his muscles bulged enormously as he applied incredible pressure. The children dared not use their swords as he and Ogiin's beast rolled back and forth in the sand. Then there was a sudden 'CRACK!' And the creature went limp.

"Bet he thinks you're a real pain in the neck." Thomas smiled thinly.

"I am sure he does, young Thomas, and he's right." Tamarin replied getting to his feet and dusting himself off.

"Cor," Lauren whistled, "I'm so knackered. But that wasn't *too* bad I suppose. The way Hi-Light was talking earlier, I was expecting a lot worse. Well done, everyone! But Zowie, please, don't talk up any more mutant crocodiles!"

Zowie, curious, asked Tamarin, "Why didn't you use that special sword? Why keep it strapped to your back when all this was going on?"

He unsheathed the beautiful weapon and held it up high, "This is no ordinary sword," he told her, "of that much I am certain. The lowly dim-witted vermin we have just vanquished did not merit the use of such a weapon, I am sure there are challenges yet to come that will prove more worthy of this precious blade."

He was standing with his back to the lake, and Zowie was facing him when she said, "I think…, those worthy challenges may have just arrived."

Swinging around, he could now see what the children had just seen. The water at the centre of the lake was beginning to churn angrily, surging out to the beach as it began to foam. Steam started rising from it, the water swirling faster and faster, huge bubbles forming and bursting in their hundreds on its surface. They stood staring, wondering and worrying at the cause. Tamarin warned the children, "We know not what lies through the doorway at our backs, but we cannot venture there until we know nothing threatens our unguarded rear. We must wait to see what is revealed here. Something of the purest evil rises before us—I feel it in my very marrow, I cannot leave such a presence unchecked to threaten my people."

The children could sense it too, goose bumps immediately covering their arms and Thomas noticing a nervous tick start up just above his left eye. The centre of the lake was in terrible turmoil as if some gigantic, underwater volcano, was erupting violently beneath its surface. Enormous plumes of water sprayed in all directions, some almost dousing the fairies sleeping high above. To their horror, amidst the spray, a large, sinister figure, started rising from the depths. Black leathery skin covered a smooth head with long pointed ears. It had not one single hair upon it and lidless eyes glared at them with red pupils as it arose. The hooked nose was long, sitting above a mouth of crimson gums and the longest, most terrifying teeth anyone could imagine—row upon row of cruel, curved, interlocking fangs, behind which snaked a thick, blue tongue. Thin tight lips of the same blue curled back in an evil grin of a smile. There was no neck to speak of and long, sinewy arms finished in deadly talons. From the waist to the wrist, webbed, heavily veined wings, flapped wildly as the host of Ogiin's curse rose steadily from the lake, revealing thin wiry legs that trailed thrice the length of any man's. These terminated in potent claws, black, hooked, and deadly. Water poured off it as it made its presence known. The nightmare stood twice Tamarin's height. It rose above the water and hovered there, fanning its bat-wings with an unnerving thrumming. The eyes knew nothing of emotion or compassion, perhaps not even capable of thinking beyond its purpose. This demon, moulded within the darkest corner of Ogiin's mind, was born to delight only in the killing of the people of The Dragon, to scream in ecstasy as it wrought agony and terror upon its victims, and to serve its master without question. Evil incarnate had them in its sights. "OH! My god!" was all the children could muster as they staggered back from the water's edge.

Tamarin was, himself, in shock, "May the Great Dragon preserve us."

He raised his sword in defence of his young friends, "If gods do truly exist, then they have abandoned this city long ago, my friends. But The Dragon knows his own. His spirit stands forever strong by the righteous. Honour will prevail, but I cannot say if this day is to be the day of that just, and final, victory."

The winged demon started gaining height over the water, moving so it was facing Tamarin and his companions. It hovered there, flapping its rubbery wings. "Young ones," Tamarin told them, "this vile creature may well be beyond your prowess. There is no cowardice in wise decision and you have proved yourselves warriors worthy of the name. Escape now, through that archway. Find my lady and tell her of what you have seen here. Leave, NOW!"

They hesitated, it was a very tempting option. But since they had met the Samarians they had become immersed in the Samarian way. The Dreampod, and life in their own world, seemed a million years ago. They *felt* Samarian, and *thought* Samarian. They would not desert someone whom they not only accepted as a true friend, but also as *their* king.

"Sorry, Tamarin," Zowie told him, "we stand together. All for one, and one for all! as 'The Three Musketeers' would say."

"I would like to meet your friends—The Three Musketeers," He told them out of the corner of his mouth, remaining focused on the hideous harpy hovering before him, "they are obviously of noble blood."

"Yeah," replied Thomas, "Box Office blood. There are four of them anyway, but it's a long story. Besides, that thing over there will soon be over here, and we'd better be ready for it. What's the plan?"

The creature began to open its jaws and the foursome on the beach had no choice but to stare as that former slit of a mouth opened up so wide, the face was almost obscured by it. Smoky fumes poured from the gaping cavity as that obscene tongue slowly protruded out at them, curling in and out as if tasting the air. They found themselves suddenly diving for cover when two streams of thick green fluid jetted from between those monstrous fangs, missing them by inches. The revolting goo splattered the shore, beginning to fizz and sizzle immediately. The sand melted away in front of their eyes. "It's some form of acid!" warned Lauren in alarm.

Thomas remained unmoved. "It's that puking thing out of The Exorcist!"

"Is it? I have never seen the like before." Tamarin was keen to understand the nature of his enemy, "What is The Exorcist? Why does it harbour such evil as this? Is this a devil you have vanquished before, reincarnated? How so? Quickly, time is short!"

No one had a chance to admonish Thomas because the flying nightmare began streaking down towards them at lightening speed. They became split and paired. Thomas and Zowie rolled to one side, and the other two went the other way as the beast shot through between them, its talons raking the sand where they had stood. It landed further up the beach and stood upright like a man. But this was as far removed from anything human as was possible. That revolting blue tongue at first moved slowly along the splintered fangs as if testing their keenness, then down to its chin, before slithering right down to its waist, the tip rising and pointing like the head of an angered cobra. It retracted in the blink of an eye, disappearing behind that wall of teeth. The creature seemed to be savouring the human scent that came from just ahead. The children in their worst nightmares could not have conjured up such a thing, and even Tamarin knew that this was something before unseen in his lands. He knew Ogiin would entrust something so valuable as the curse over Soledad only to the most powerful and loyal of his minions. The eyes blazed with intent, with but one desire, only one purpose, the pinpoints of red in their centres piercing the foursome like long, thin knives. The green acid squirted from its mouth once more and again everyone dived for cover. The creature raised its head skywards, letting out a blood curdling scream that echoed over and over throughout the cavern. Then it lowered its gaze, refocusing on its intended prey.

The children could feel knots the size of grapefruits in their stomachs and Tamarin's mind raced as to how to tackle such an airborne foe. Whilst his thoughts were far from calm, his sword hand remained rock steady with nary a twitch, nor tremor, from the Samarian.

Using its elongated birdlike legs, the demonic harpy launched itself in the air, flying straight at Zowie and Thomas—claws outstretched and ready to tear flesh from bone. Zowie managed to avoid its grasp as it whooshed past but Thomas was not as lucky, receiving a gash to his shield arm. It began to bleed, and before Tamarin could stop her, Lauren went running to the aid of her brother. Zowie was already by his side, sword readied as the awful creature circled for another attack upon the injured boy. Tamarin made for the trio, but too late. Lauren—desperate to reach her brother, was not looking behind her. Ogiin's fiend snatched her up in its claws and flew off to above the centre of the lake. Zowie and Thomas were panicked. "No!"

"Curse you, demon!" Tamarin roared at the winged gargoyle hovering above the water like an enormous, horribly grotesque insect. Lauren screamed, struggling frantically to break loose from its death-grip, but it held her too firmly. The leathery abomination raised its head again, laughing so wickedly that the sound chilled them to the bone as it again echoed around the cavern. Then it hurled her into the water with such incredible force that the stricken young girl ploughed straight beneath the surface and disappeared from view entirely, reappearing seconds later, flapping wildly with just her head visible from shore.

"TOM!" Zowie told him, "Quickly, take the boat and save her, you can't fight with your arm injured like that, GO! GO! GO!"

Nursing his arm, Thomas sprinted for the Swan of Solenia. Tamarin stood by Zowie's side when she bawled angrily at the creature flapping its wings so noisily over the lake, "Oi! Bat's breath! Come and get some!"

Half courageous and half livid, she stood brandishing her weapon, challenging the brute by wildly waving her shield, trying to buy time for Thomas to get to Lauren, who could be heard thrashing about in the deep water with ever less vigour.

Thomas lay hidden close to the boat, desperate for a chance to make his move. His sister could not stay afloat much longer. The devil that had snatched her rocketed past him towards the others and he jumped in, reversed the mechanism, and began pumping the lever as furiously as he could with his one good arm. It was not enough, and he brought his injured arm into play, ignoring the pain searing through his shoulder and the blood dripping at his elbow. The Swan of Solenia began to make rapid progress towards the lake centre, and Lauren's position.

Tamarin weighed up his next move, "I will tackle this flying fiend first. Let us see how it deals with a more seasoned adversary. Have faith, little one, I will have this creature's head this day."

He stood ready on the beach, legs apart and knees slightly bent, holding his sword up high, enabling a more flexible, fluid strike.

His shield was mounted firmly on his other arm and he gripped the leather strap in a vicelike grip. Zowie, a quick learner, took up a similar stance just to his rear. She watched the creature diving at them, its head pinned back and its arms swept along its sides, the eyes bulged, those awful teeth openly displayed with relish. She hoped beyond hope that the king would have his wish of this demon's head, for she sensed, as Hi-Light had done, that this thing was revelling in her undeniable fear. Tamarin, true to his word, was determined to decapitate it, but when it was only yards from him it released yet more jets of deadly acid from its mouth and he was forced to raise his shield, his vision obscured when it slammed into it and sent him sprawling in the powdery sand. He rolled over and over, springing back up to his feet to find that it had landed just past him and was slashing frantically back and forth at Zowie with those razor sharp claws. Its teeth snapped repeatedly, lunging for her again and again over the top of the shield. Burning acid squirted repeatedly but Zowie was moving like a professional soldier. She was using her shield well to protect herself and the venom did not appear to have any noticeable effect on the samarian steel. In fact, twice, she managed to slam the shield into its face, causing it to scream. She screamed back at it equally loudly, "DIE! Die! Die, you scumbag!"

The demon from the depths was, however, too nimble for Zowie to bring her sword to bear. To survive, she was forced to focus on merely defending herself against the onslaught, desperate to avoid injury, particularly from that burning spray. Tamarin, running flat out to her aid, could see she could avoid that frenzy of claws only for a few seconds more. There were deep gleaming gouges in her shield where it had been raked down to the bare metal, and it was smeared with thick green venom. The raging creature saw Tamarin just in time to move and his sword missed its head by an inch. Turning in an instant, it faced him without fear. "Ogiin's curse will stand, you will fall, Samarian. Fall, and die." Its voice seemed to hail from far, far away, from somewhere where evil reigned supreme and light dared not to tread. Tamarin wasted no energy on words. He began slashing at it with every stroke and thrust he knew. He could feel his heart pounding like a hammer within his chest and sweat streamed from his brow as he brought a lifetime's training to bear down upon this enemy. But the contest was well matched and not easily settled. Zowie, having fallen under her shield after that punishing assault, sprang back to her feet and hovered behind him, poised to strike if the opportunity presented itself.

Thomas was only a few feet from the drowning Lauren. He stopped pumping the lever and rushed to her aid. Hanging far over the side of the boat, he called out, "Sis'! I'm over here, it's Tom, *Grab my hand*, quick!"

She was thrashing about in the water—unable to make headway weighed down as she was by weapons and cloak. Breathless, she spluttered, "Tom, stay in the boat! There could be more things in the water, stay in the boat Tom!"

Her brother—never a big fan of water, removed any heavy items and dived headfirst into the black stillness of Solenia. He could see something flashing just below the surface as he raced to his sister's side. When he reached her he realised, with overwhelming relief, that it was her sword he had seen earlier, it was reflecting the fairy lights above. They hugged for a very brief second, and then, with Thomas' help, Lauren made her way to the safety of the vessel. She clambered aboard first, Thomas helping heave her up into the boat. She could see him struggling to get aboard himself and she had to pull him with all her might until, finally, he, too, flopped over the side, and to safety. It was then that she noticed the gash to his arm was soaked in blood. He looked pale and weak, sitting numbly in the bottom of the boat. She could see the others on the beach struggling to keep that crazed brute at bay, and she knew if they failed in their efforts, it would be mere seconds before she and her brother also succumbed to a terrible fate. Her eyes met his and she could see he was in pain, "Tom, if we get killed in Samaria, you know mum and dad will never talk to us again!"

He gave a weak smile, laughing a small hollow laugh. Realising exactly what she had said, she chuckled unconvincingly as she took up the lever and launched the craft back towards land. Having expended all her energy trying to stay afloat her arms felt so awfully heavy and numb, as if she had carried a great load over a vast distance, but she knew they had to get out of the water where they were so vulnerable.

Tamarin had forced the creature to retreat under a flurry of blows, but then it grabbed his wrist and twisted, forcing him to lose his grip and drop his weapon. Empty handed, he launched himself at it, slamming his forehead into its nose as his fists pummelled its head. It reeled for a second, momentarily stunned by the speed and savagery of the attack, then, it tossed him across the sand like one might swat a fly. Zowie saw the second sword fall from his back as he sailed through the air. She grabbed it up and threw it back to him, shouting,

"Now might be a really good time to use this, Tamarin."

Whilst he crawled out of the shallows spitting sand and mud, Zowie stood face-to-face with the host of Ogiin's curse. Her blade moved deftly in her hands and she managed to twice slash across the creature's chest. Two gaping wounds opened up, revealing what appeared to be a mass of black maggots writhing within. But then, to her horror, and consternation, the cuts healed up again in an instant as if they had never been there. Shocked at the revolting sight, she was caught unawares, yelping out loud when a clenched, big-knuckled fist, caught her square in the stomach, completely knocking the wind out of her. As if pole-axed she fell on her back, unable to move, watching helplessly as this apparently invincible servant of Ogiin raced towards her on its long gangly legs, arms outstretched, fangs bared ready to bite deep into her tender young flesh. She could see the boat was fast approaching the shore and prayed Lauren was unharmed. Bravely, she braced herself for when those vicious talons would draw blood, but then she heard Tamarin's voice in a tone she had not heard from him before, a voice of absolute authority, the voice of a true, warrior-king.

"Creature from the depths of hell, stand back from our comrade, your time in this world, and, any other world, is done. You who dare to infest my realm, the realm of the people of the Great Dragon, will now go the way your master will soon follow. Turn and face me, dark seed of Ogiin. Face me, and know there will be no mercy for you on this day. No quarter will be given, and none is expected. Face me now and you will see that a true Samarian is never afraid of the dark. Filth! This day is your last!"

Turning quickly away from Zowie it faced him, catching sight of the sword he held in his hands. Raising its face up high, it again filled the cavern with its chilling, maniacal laughter, trilling its elongated tongue revoltingly, before dropping its head and fixing its cold eyes on him. It rasped in its dull, black, leathery voice, 'The Flame of Dragonia', GIVE IT TO ME!"

Stunned, Tamarin looked his weapon up and down. 'The Flame of Dragonia' had always been deemed a myth, a legendary sword given to the first king of Samaria by Chjandi—the Great Dragon. Forged in Dragonia by the dragons themselves, it was reputed to carry the spiritual essence of the Dragons of Light within its perfectly crafted blades. He eyed up the demon standing so confidently before him, "You *shall* receive this sword this day, creature of Ogiin. But not as you would wish it. For now 'The Flame of Dragonia' again sits safe in the hands of a Samarian King. Prepare to return to the black swamp of Ogiin's soul from whence you were spawned." Strangely, now that he knew exactly *which* sword he had, by chance, discovered, he found himself instantly bonding with this mythical weapon of fables and lore. It seemed to absorb him and flood right through him, all at the same time, not feeling like a sword composed of steel and stones anymore. It felt not only like an extension of himself, but an extension of his faith, his entire being, his very soul. Within its super light, immensely strong, core, was embodied the spirit by which his ancestors had reigned over this wondrous land since memory began, and beyond. He felt at once exalted, and humbled, by the legendary triblade. Knowing it had been once handled by the dragons sent his pulse racing with excitement.

As he and the spawn of Ogiin approached each other, Lauren quietly beached the boat and helped Thomas ashore. Weary beyond belief, they slumped in the sand on their knees and watched Zowie taking up station close to Tamarin.

Tamarin was as nimble as a black panther. Springing from his feet, he launched himself at his enemy, but it sprayed scorching venom at him and he was forced to twist in mid air to put his shield between himself and that torrent of death. Even as he landed and rolled, the creature stamped towards him cackling wickedly, its claws grabbing for his prized weapon. A fierce side swipe from Tamarin's shield caught the harpy on the side of its head as it reached out for the blade. It stumbled clumsily from the brutal blow, losing balance, almost falling, but a sudden flapping of leathery wings saved it, instead launching it up into the air. It circled quickly, tightly, coming at him again in a steep dive. Lauren could not get up, her legs still shaking, but she managed to put a shaft to her gleaming new bow. The shot pierced the creature through the head from ear to ear, and, with complete puzzlement etched across its face it fell to the lake, sinking quickly from view. The lake returned to its former placid state, "Cracking shot! Way to go, Lauren!" Zowie cheered as she ran to hug her, and to see to Thomas' wound. She did not hear Tamarin's warning of, "ZOWIE! Behind you! Beware!"

Their relentless foe had risen from the water, and hovering in the air, it had torn the arrow from its head. The fiend was apparently unharmed, closing fast on Zowie from the rear as she ran to help the Shortwaters. Just as she turned her head and saw those evil eyes so close to her, it extended its long arms and grabbed her at the waist. It lost no momentum at all, arcing around to again make for the centre of the lake. Zowie knew exactly what had happened to Lauren, and with a feeling that made her sick to the stomach, she wrapped her legs around the creature's reeking midriff, crossing her ankles and locking it between her thighs. She placed her head close to the flapping monster's ear to avoid any venom it might have in mind for her. The overwhelming stench from its slimy hide made her stomach turn over, but she hung on for dear life. It could not use its claws as it was flapping its wings, and when it tried to release her over the water, she grimly hung on. There came a zipping sound as another arrow from Lauren's bow narrowly missed its target, the creature growling in anger and turning once more for the shore. As soon as she was passing close to the beach Zowie let go, landing softly in the shallows with a small splash.

Tamarin stood between the flying peril and the Shortwaters. The venom spewed forth once more from the creature's mouth, but to his astonishment, a flame appeared in the centre blade of his sword. Not a blazing furnace, it was more like looking at a fire in a mirror. A bright blue flame could be seen dancing within the metal itself, and as he pointed it at the fast approaching streak of death, a bolt of lightening erupted from the tip—meeting the jets of venom head on. The acid seemed to turn to dust as the flame seared through it, striking its source in the mouth. The airborne demon crashed to the sand howling and screaming, flapping wildly as it bowled head-over-heels along the beach. When it stood up, they could see its mouth and lips were badly scorched with angry blisters peppering its face. Its eyes raged hell at Tamarin, who, in turn, roared back his defiance, "In the name of the Great Dragon!" He then charged the creature that had risen so menacingly from the cold depths of Solenia only minutes before. Every time he brought his sword to bear, he could see licks of blue flame running along the length of its deadly centre blade. For the first time they could all see fear in the eyes of the devilish demon, but it was still not defeated. Deprived of its venom, and its mouth ruined, it fought on furiously, slashing and clawing in a savage rage. It punched and kicked, snapping its jaws within a hair's breadth of his face. Then, finally, with a sudden unexpected twist of his wrist, Tamarin defeated its attempts to avoid his blade and 'The Flame of Dragonia' carved deep into its leathery hide. The smell of burnt, rotting flesh, filled the air. But those cold eyes still showed nothing but bloodlust, and it lashed out in desperation. The hooked claws found the Samarian's chest, but failed to penetrate the chain mail under his breastplate. All the same, it was a ferocious blow and he was sent flying backwards by the force of it, his mighty sword slipping from his grip and falling to the sand. As he regained his feet he saw the monstrous harpy making for his fallen weapon, but it was too slow. Zowie grabbed up 'The Flame of Dragonia' and faced the towering demon. Its face, despite its scorched mouth, cracked into a grin, pus trickling from the burns. In a serpent's voice it mocked her, "Only *royal* Samarian blood can wield 'The Flame of Dragonia'. Ogiin will savour your young soul for an eternity, but it is I that shall part your flesh from your bone!"

It charged for her on its awkward legs, but was slowed by the wound caused by Tamarin, a wound, they noticed, that had not healed itself. Zowie realized, in that instant, that she was no longer afraid, the sword in her hands filling her with an energy so powerful, so alive, so eternal, that fear became impossible. With this sudden dawning came renewed courage and a bolder heart. She sidestepped the hobbling harpy and was amazed to see blue flame in the blade when she brought it crashing down onto a leathery black shoulder. The steel sliced cleanly into the fetid flesh and a gaping wound caused her opponent to fall to its knees, its semi-severed limb hanging useless by its side. Tamarin was beside her in an instant and, taking up the sword, he delivered the coup de grace, severing the host of Ogiin's curse in two at the waist. Its remains putrefied in seconds, then turned to dust and collapsed in on themselves. Only a dirty black stain remained to mar the pure white sand. They both flopped heavily to the sand, exhausted.

Tamarin, despite being utterly drained, gathered himself and crawled over to Thomas to examine the wound to his arm. The initial heavy bleeding had subsided and he could see that it was not as serious as it had looked, though it was, no doubt, very painful. He told him, "It would appear I judged well when I promised you a knighthood. You have acted with fearlessness and honour. It has been my privilege to have you by my side in battle, and that goes for you, too, Lauren. Your love of your brother is to be marvelled at. Well done, both of you!"

Next, he turned his attention to Zowie, who sat nursing her aching stomach where the creature had clamped her so tightly in its deadly embrace. "*You*, Zowie, are truly an enigma to me. You fight like a Samarian, yet are not of our world. But more than this, you have wielded the sword of Kings—'The Flame of Dragonia', and it has seen fit to react to you as it would to royalty, truly a miracle beyond my understanding. I still have much to learn on these matters, but, I am a keen student, my friends, the Great Dragon reveals that which we need to know when we need the knowing of it. There will always be much beyond the ken of man, but suffice to say, I am deeply grateful of your intervention."

They had been resting only a few minutes when muffled voices and the sound of running feet stirred them. Grabbing for their weapons they stared into the dark archway leading away from the cavern as the sounds became louder. Then Meekhi and a handful of guardsmen burst onto the beach, Tamarin's eyes met those of his beloved as she ran into his arms, holding him so tight so as to stifle his breath, whispering tenderly in his ear, "My love, I feared the worst. I thought I had lost you forever." Tears of joyful relief stained her beautiful face, clouding those dazzling green eyes. Tamarin hugged her and soothed her, stroking her hair and reassuring her that he was fine and unharmed. He told of the bravery of the young ones, and of how they had fought like the most seasoned of warriors. Meekhi thanked them graciously. Then Ramulet and Mercy appeared, having been drawn by the sounds down below. Babel tended to Thomas' arm with a skill and knowledge that Arcadian was truly impressed by, and eager to learn from. As he was being bandaged up Lauren turned to Zowie, "Any idea as to why that sword reacted as it did to you? There's something special about you, Zee, you just seem to fit in here, in *Samaria* I mean. Hey, at least you got to kick that disgusting thing's arse."

"It deserved it, stinking, puking, exorcist freak. But hey! That was an amazing shot! Right through the head! Quite a talent you've got there, cuz, you'd put Robin Hood to shame. So much for us thinking we wouldn't need to fight, eh. Hi-Light really saved our bacon, probably our lives."

Thomas, obviously in pain, mumbled, "Mmmm, bacon!"

Having seen Tamarin in battle, they all agreed that the Samarians were possessed of a strength and agility unknown in their own world. Given what they had just witnessed, they were very grateful of this fact.

Tamarin and Ramulet exchanged stories about what had happened above and below. They each needed to be aware of everything. Through the arch, a long, dark, stairway of stone, led away from the underground cavern. Slowly they climbed up it, emerging in a small chamber at the rear of the great hall.

Tamarin and the children had never seen Venomeens and could not resist staring at the headless remains littering the floor. Babel's nursing was working wonders for Thomas and he spoke out so all could hear him, "It would seem they all panicked, lost their heads so to speak, ahem." The assembled warriors admired his enduring humour, even if the smiles were a little forced. A few had actually laughed out aloud, but Lauren and Zowie just groaned at his ceaseless one-liners…

Tamarin was concerned about the dreadful news regarding the witch—Teritee, and, her link, through Iret, with Meekhi, Mercy, and Faradorr. He wasted no time in organising his people. Rordorr assured him he was now able to fly well, and Faradorr said that he, too, could once more traverse the skies, albeit in short stints. Tamarin told them, "Go now, my magnificent Samarians, fly to the fortress city of Rosameer and gather there the precious Lozzwozz and Wartywart. Babel and Solipop will travel with you. They are safer with you than in this city of haunting ghosts and submerged demons. Babel can prepare the elixir in Rosameer and Faradorr can benefit by it immediately. Then leave our elfish friends under the care and courtesy of my cousin, Vansivar, Lord of Rosameer, and return with the greatest urgency to Sitivia. There, by the will of The Dragon, we will cure this taint of evil that blights these fair ladies."

Babel and Solipop were far from reluctant to leave Soledad, and after brief farewells and more gratitude from the Samarians, a pair of mighty black horses took to the air with little blue elves perched on their backs. Solipop did not stop waving with his hands and tail until the people below were tiny, barely visible specks.

Tamarin gathered his people and horses. Not one of them had an ounce of energy left in them but all refused the chance of a short break. Certainly none had any desire to partake of food prepared in any cooking pot. They mounted up just as the suns began to hesitantly peek at the world from under the blanket of the horizon. His queen by his side, he led them out of The Silent City and headed towards Sitivia. The children were in high spirits having tasted the heat of battle and sipped from the sweet cup of victory. They felt as one with their new found friends, bonded now in blood, and fused in faith.

Funeral pyres burned in the city gardens where Tamarin and his people had paid tribute to those that had fallen in the great hall. Much further away, near the sewers, another, far blacker, pall of smoke rose skywards where they had unceremoniously dumped and set ablaze the piled corpses of the decapitated Venomeens, crowning the macabre heap with a sack filled with their heads.

Meekhi glanced back over her shoulder, calling to Mercy, "Look! Where the suns are just kissing the top of the great hall the great hall, it looks golden, as it most surely must have been before the curse took Soledad in its grip."

Everyone looked, and it certainly gave that impression. Tamarin stared at it longingly, "If only it were so, my dear heart."

CHAPTER SIXTEEN

BLOOD WARRIORS

Imo lay quietly on his front, peering covertly over the edge of a tall cliff, with Bestwin and Lumarr either side of him. They had left the remainder of their group further back, out of view with the horses. Down below, on the cold stony shores of the Western Worlds, lay a sight to unsteady even the sturdiest of resolves. The sea, once a crisp dark green, appeared as black as the darkest night. It swirled, moving thickly like treacle, forming an immense whirlpool, they could not see what lay below, deep at the epicentre, but none had any doubt—Ogiin lived once more.

The beach was littered with hundreds of corpses. Each one of them had been a creature of darkness, one of Ogiin's own creed, now even more hideous in death as an empty twisted shell, than in life. They had come in droves upon his ceaseless calling, and upon their arrival he had drawn from them their life spirit to regenerate himself. A steady stream of wailing spirits flowed from the shoreline to the centre of the turbulent waters. But many of Ogiin's creed there present still lived, not as yet snatched by his hunger, feeling no sense of loss, no compassion, as their brethren dropped about them like flies. They stood looking out to sea, awaiting the return of their former master. The trio spying from atop the cliff recognised the fiends as being of the same ilk as those they had encountered at the cave in the mountains.

The sea began making a strange sound, an unnatural howl akin to the wailing of the wind. It was so unbecoming and the men watching clenched their fists, tensions rising. The centre of the whirlpool began erupting in big, thick, waves, each rolling away from the core and slopping heavily onto the beach as if already exhausted by their short journey. An eerie cry rose up from the throng below and, from their cover at the foot of the cliffs, Shadows moved into sight.

From their elevated position they could just make out a figure rising in the centre of the tempestuous black sea. A hairless head, covered in skin so white that it glowed in the light. The figure was large, much bigger than any man that any of them had ever seen. It resembled the human form well enough, but was somehow entirely inhuman. From it, chilling waves of pure evil reached out, creeping over them like the cold, stroking hand of death, Himself. Their eyes the size of saucers, they looked at each other with complete disbelief. They had hoped against hope that their worst fears would not be confirmed, but they had hoped in vain. Now Venomeens could be seen hauling a mid-sized Westonian fishing vessel into the water, their unnatural strength moving the dead weight with ease over rolling logs. Bestwin whispered to the others, "Where did that scum get that craft?"

Lumarr's reply was, sadly, predictable, "From its former owners, whom they have drained of spirit, then slaughtered, for sure."

They stared down into the long, sleek vessel that was being launched. There appeared to be many people aboard, and Lumarr fitted two pieces of circular glass into a small, rolled reed mat, one at each end of the cone, looking into the boat with his makeshift telescope, "By all that is sacred! That boat is filled with our maidens, *Westonian* maidens. They mean for that devil-Ogiin, to drain their souls as he ravishes them! By my honour! This must be stopped, NOW!"

Anger rising he made to get up, his hand already unsheathing his sword, but Imo and Bestwin slammed him back to the ground, hard. Bestwin met his friend's fuming eyes with his own.

"Stay your hand, my mighty warrior," He pleaded, "those poor maidens were doomed as soon as they were captured, and we will be too, if we are discovered. We cannot hope to challenge so many of this vermin, and don't forget what rises from that hellhole of water. Countless thousands more innocents will suffer such a fate as those poor souls if this evil is left unchecked. We are but a few, and the purpose of our quest lies elsewhere. We must bide our time Lumarr, only by force of arms can we face such odds. We must..."

"My lords, forgive my intrusion," Imo butted in, "you can see many more of this filth arriving from all directions. It will take Ogiin perhaps two days, at most, to rally his dark hordes. I say we hasten to Dorinndale and see what awaits us there. Then, I am duty bound to make for Samaria, then onto Sitivia. My king awaits my news. It serves no purpose to linger here and bear witness to such pointless tragedy. Better we make good use of what we have learned of this bleak, heartbreaking day, and apply ourselves to resolving the greater issue. What say you?"

"Come Imo," Lumarr resignedly agreed, "we have seen enough here. The day of reckoning has yet to dawn, but the sights below have caused the sun to set in my heart. It may well never fully rise again, for although I know confronting the enemy now would surely be the death of me, rest assured, my friends, leaving those hapless maidens to their terrible fate will kill me anyway, every single day, for the rest of my days."

The Westonians led them in a frantic race to Dorinndale. The landscape was moor-like and the open ground made for rapid progress as the horses thundered across the downy turf. When the centre of the Western Worlds came into view, they began slowing their pace, until it gradually petered out to a full stop. Ahead, the palace tower stood high above all else, atop it a flag flapped wildly in the harsh, blustery western wind. The two golden broadswords crossed over a shield bearing the royal arms, boasting Westonian sovereignty over these windswept lands. It snapped back and forth, cracking loudly in the wind as if pleading urgency to the riders watching it from the crest of a small, moss laden, hill. The air was cool and held the hint of rain as grey clouds sailed briskly across darkening skies.

They eased their tired horses gently down the slope ahead and had not travelled far when the contorted corpse of a woman could be seen lieing abandoned and forlorn amidst the long coarse grass.

"By the sword!" roared Bestwin, spurring his horse forward, the others on his tail.

From horseback they looked down at the unfortunate soul so cruelly robbed of her life. "Are we too late? Has the capital fallen?" asked Imo.

"Perhaps," Lumarr told him, "but I think not. Look, the city gates are sealed from within. I think this miserable wretch was caught alone and wandering by some passing phantom. Let us see what lies within the walls of Dorinndale before we pass judgement."

They pressed their steeds to haste and as they approached the wall Imo blew hard on his Samarian horn—The Call of Comrades. Several times he summoned the city, blowing impatiently until, finally, two small white faces with raggedy beards appeared up high on the battlements. "Who goes there!?" someone shouted down, "Identify yourselves *now*, or our arrows will be sent to greet you!"

Bestwin, angry, cleared his throat and roared up at them, "We are Lords Lumarr and Bestwin, with allies from Samaria. Fire upon us and you will find your quivers mounted in places where quivers should not be! Open these gates, damn your eyes!"

There was some faint discussion heard high above the horsemen, then the gates began to creak open far from smoothly. Bestwin and the others had not the patience for them to part fully. He stormed into the city, dismounting in the central square before the last of his column were past the gates.

Imo looked about him, taking in for the first time the first city of the Western Worlds. These lands were as different from his native Samaria as cheese is to chalk, and Dorinndale came as a complete shock after his beloved Sitivia. The streets, narrow, and paved in dark grey granite, appeared sombre and unwelcoming, buildings were peppered with small square windows holding thick, almost obscure, glass, and there was little in the way of artistic opulence or expression of the soul. "The cold climate dictates this miserable picture, I'm sure," he thought. Sombre walls of black flint and blacker stone supported pitched roofs of grey slate. Lots of tight passages punctuated the facade of every street in sight, giving the impression of a thriving anthill rather than any magnificent citadel. But this *was* the capital, but still he could not see any people. Then a group of dangerous-looking warriors with barrel chests and bulging arms came running up to the new arrivals. Lumarr wanted answers, "What has happened? Where is everyone? Where is Dorinn? Speak up, man! Come on! Spit it out!"

The biggest, swarthiest of the men, answered him. "We began finding people outside the walls. They appeared to…to have the life sucked out of them. My lords, some of us knew of your mission to seek counsel with King Tamarin. We have awaited your return. Many have fled the city. They are in small groups and will be picked off easily by what rises from the sea. Yes…we have seen from the cliffs for ourselves and know what we now face. The army, as such, no longer exists. Our soldiers have deserted their posts, or are lost in drink with that fool—Dorinn. He ordered us to lock and bar the gates, considering this matter to be of Samarian concern only, and has stated he will make a pact of peace with anyone wishing to pass through our lands leaving us unmolested. Dorinn believes Ogiin wishes to exact his revenge upon Samaria alone, as the Samarians revere the dragons that defeated him in history."

Lumarr and Bestwin were furious, beside themselves with rage they seethed at Dorinn. Imo and the rest of the Samarian escort said nothing, but felt the sharp sting of Dorinn's treachery like a lash upon their backs. Lumarr turned to them, iron in his voice, "Come."

Led by the Westonians, they hurried through the cities tight, winding streets until they came to another open square, at the opposite end of which loomed the palace. It matched a Samarian palace in name only. Built from enormous blocks of grey stone, it would be more easily paired with a gothic cathedral. The heavy wooden doors were firmly closed, though many a dull orange glow could be seen glimmering through dozens of small windows. Lumarr and Bestwin hauled open one of the doors, striding into the building with purpose on their minds. The Samarians followed, sensing justice was afoot. The place had the appearance of having been ransacked. Empty wine jars, dirty broken plates, and upturned tables, littered the floor. Half naked women flitted from door to door, giggling as they were chased by drunken men in an equal state of undress. Laughter and merriment could be heard throughout this former bastion of Westonian civilisation. Not a single guard or sentry was in sight and their entry remained unchallenged. The small, still loyal, cadre of men that had been manning the wall had followed Bestwin's party into the palace. Lumarr could contain himself no longer. "BY MY BEARD!" he thundered, "I will not have this debauchery here, in this—the heart of our very foundations! Men," he pointed to the Westonian soldiers, "scour the city. Find those that will still fight under our banner for their families and their homes. Gather the women and children and make ready to leave this place. It will not be long before Dorinndale is overrun by the plague of darkness approaching from the coast. Never in my darkest dreams did I think I would live to see such a thing, to see a king of these lands betray his own people so brazenly. We will save what remains that breathes and lives, the rest we must surrender to the hands of fate, and beseech her, be kind."

He then turned to Imo, barely able to conceal his shame of Dorinn's misdeeds. "My friend, noble Samarians, I would ask that you help us find Dorinn, you will know him if you see him, bring him directly to me, and, if he will not come willingly, you and your men are to *bring* him. No court etiquette will be required or is requested, a cur is but a cur, do you understand my meaning, Imo, do I make myself clear!"

Imo nodded knowingly, "I understand you, as clear as crystal, my lord."

He gathered his guardsmen and disappeared into the bowels of the palace in search of King Dorinn.

Lumarr beckoned Bestwin, "Dorinn will be the undoing of thousands of years of just and honourable existence, unless he is stopped, king he may well be, but *kingly* he is most certainly not. Come, my friend, let us salvage what we can. That clown of a king must be found soon, I only hope the Samarians can stay their well founded anger and refrain from cutting his throat, for now at least."

The pair knew the palace of Dorinndale well, and began a systematic search for the errant old king.

Imo passed from room to room. They were dark confined spaces, numerous, but small compared to the palace in Sitivia, and he longed to once more walk amongst those bright and airy chambers back home. Despite Dorinn allowing the city to so quickly slide into decadence and decay, there was still a firm air of tradition and timeless honour rooted in this place. Dorinn was the last, and least, of a long line of truly remarkable kings, kings that had always held true to their alliance with Samaria. The thought of Dorinn opening the back door to Samaria for Ogiin boiled Imo's blood. "What base treachery," he thought, fingering his sword grip. He and his men navigated through many long, low, corridors, and in doing so, passed numerous statues immortalising the history of the Western Worlds. There was even a magnificent bronze of Lord Amaris, he who had served many years here as Ambassador for Samaria. On numerous occasions drunken women appeared out of nowhere, stumbling blind-eyed out of doorways, grabbing and clutching at the handsome guardsmen racing through the palace. But these intoxicated trollops held no allure for the well-disciplined soldiers and were firmly brushed aside. At one point a man, drunk beyond his senses, bare chested and with a large overhanging pot belly, tried incessantly to make Imo drink with him, shoving a jar of stale ale into the Samarian's face repeatedly. Imo warned him several times to back away, but the drunk paid no heed, so Imo cracked the clay jar over his head and left him to sleep it off. There was no time to waste on such foolery.

They had been trawling through the palace for nearly half an hour when Imo turned the handle to a door, only to find it locked. Thinking Dorinn may be deep in debauchery behind it, he slammed his shoulder into it and it shot open—the lock shattered. But that miscreant Dorinn was nowhere in sight. This particular room, however, stopped the Samarians in their tracks. Warm pastel walls framed a large window overlooking the west of the city, and the sea. Delicately carved furniture adorned the large space which was dominated by a huge four-poster bed. The bed itself was draped in voiles, satins, and silks. A narrow-bladed, dragon-handled sword stood in a matching stand. All the trappings of a true Lady of the Samarian Royal Court were correct and present. Imo backed away from the room respectfully, and so did his men. They sensed to whom this chamber had once belonged—Yasmina, Queen of the Western Worlds, once a Samarian princess by birthright, then a queen that had been driven away by her husband's infidelities and brutal manners. Wrong doings that Samaria still felt uneasy in the forgiving of, but could not judge a land by the deeds of one man, deeds his own people had found abhorrent and had cost him their respect. The Samarians resealed the chamber, and despite the urgency in finding Dorinn, they took their time in ensuring the room was completely secure before they moved on to the next door. This one, too, was locked, but a well aimed kick from a burly guardsman splintered the frame and sent it flying off its hinges. There he was at last—Dorinn, sitting on a high backed wooden rocking chair with a pimply whore on his knee, and a bottle of wine in his hands. He looked old, far older even than his years. His long hair and generous beard had wholly greyed, the light in his eyes extinguished when, to his complete, miserable surprise, the queen had left him. His clothes were dirty and he had a dishevelled look about him. Dirty broken fingernails, scum encrusted hands, eyes rheumy and bloodshot from drinking, did but add to his shameful appearance. The glorious golden crown bearing the royal crest, sat lopsided on the whore's head. "Hello boys," the words stumbled with difficulty from his drunken lips, "here, I do hope you have brought more wine. Yes...that's the ticket! More wine, and more women! That's what we need, lads. Is there any of that honeyed chicken left? These girls give me the appetite of a horse!" He slapped at the girl's backside, his befuddled eyes struggling to identify the intruders.

Imo stared in disbelief at the sorry excuse for a man, let alone a *King*. He snatched the crown from the intoxicated girl's head, telling her in a voice that held no secrets, "WENCH, LEAVE US!"

She gathered her skirts about her and left in a hurry, looking terrified as the room filled with angry looking warriors carrying swords and dressed for battle. Even one of such a lowly position as she, knew of the Royal Guards of Samaria, and the black cloaks now surrounding Dorinn made her heart quiver and quake. Imo again fixed his steely gaze on the slovenly king. "Dorinn, King of the Western Worlds, rise, and follow us. You are arrested. You have failed in your kingship of these honourable lands, and you have sought to betray your true ally in the form of Samaria, and her noble king, Tamarin. You will return with us to Sitivia, and there be judged by what remains of your people. GET UP!"

Dorinn lolled limply in his chair, rocking back and forth as he casually reached for a fresh bottle of wine. His half open eyes rolled in his head as he tried to focus on Imo. "Who are you," he slurred heavily, spittle spraying from his foul smelling mouth and catching in his beard, "to tell *me* what to do? I am King! Don't you know who I am? I will have you impaled for daring to talk to me that way. I will...I will have you hung, sliced, and quartered! Now bring me some more of that stuffed chicken, and send for a fresh wench." He managed to grasp another bottle, "A clean goblet too, it allows one to fully appreciate so invigorating a libation."

Imo eyed him up and down with utter contempt. The man was far too drunk to understand what he was being told. But night would fall soon and bring with it all the perils of darkness. There was no time for courtesy, if, indeed, any were due. He attempted to get him on his feet, but Dorinn struggled, trying to fight him off. Placing the crown safely inside his tunic, Imo grabbed the drunk by the hair at the top of his head and hoisted him to his feet suddenly. Dorinn screamed and moaned, made threats and threw curses, but Imo kept a tight grip on his grey mop. Dorinn was then frog marched back to the palace lobby whilst the others went to find Bestwin and Lumarr. As Imo passed the chamber belonging to Yasmina he could not help but feel even more anger and loathing for Dorinn. The Samarian simply could'nt resist and aimed a firm kick to the old man's backside. This hastened Dorinn's pace considerably.

The Westonians and the others were already waiting when he finally arrived with his staggering 'prisoner'. The revulsion of the Westonians upon seeing and smelling the state of him was plain to see. They did not greet him. Bestwin produced a length of cord and bound his hands and feet. He was already barefoot. "Bind him fast over a mule," Lumarr instructed the men, "strap him on tight. He will face his people in Samaria. Unless my queen returns, the Western Worlds have a vacancy for a true king."

Outside the city a long, thin, strung out line of refugees, could be seen heading for Samaria. Perhaps only two hundred horsemen remained of Dorinndale's former army. But these were worthy men, stout, square-set Westonians, carrying battleaxes, broadswords, and deadly war hammers. Wrapped in heavy leather tunics and thick long furs, they made a formidable sight.

Lumarr spoke in private to Imo. "Imo, Ogiin's creed will sweep through the Western Worlds unchallenged. This horde of horror should have been crushed on our shores long before Ogiin could draw upon their strength. Alas, it is now too late. It grieves me to see our people leaving their homes and fleeing east, I am somewhat consoled in having an honourable and charitable neighbour in Samaria so that they at least have somewhere to flee *to*. These lands will be regained by our people after we have dealt with the devil that has arisen from the depths. Sadly we cannot spare the time to escort this caravan of misery to Sitivia, we must hasten past it to Tamarin and make ready for the slaughter that will most surely ensue, staining the sands there soon enough. I salute you and your brave countrymen for escorting us thus far, we would not have survived otherwise, let us now take what remains of our own garrison and ride for Sitivia as if there were no tomorrow, because, if the black tide is not held in check, there may well not be."

Imo nodded. "My lord, my sword and men are at your command, just give the word."

A mix of riders hammered past the slow moving line of refugees, their backs displaying either rampant dragons or crossed swords. They would not stop until they reached the gates of the Samarian capital. No one could afford to stop. Darkness was fast falling on the Western Worlds, and none wished to remain to greet it.

The horses had slowed to little more than a crawl some time ago, incapable of mustering any more speed. Mercy and Meekhi offered to tend to their needs and they stopped to give the animals some water, and a little maize. Tamarin was busy consulting with Ramulet and Arcadian, the topic of conversation being whether or not Sitivia still stood? Tamarin and Meekhi had encountered Ogiin's creed only deep within the nation's interior. They had been absent from home for some time now and there was no telling what lay ahead on the coast.

Lauren was familiarising herself further with her bow. She was impressed by the skill with which it had been made and could not quite fathom the wood used in its construction. Her brother was with Zowie. His arm was healing faster than he could ever have imagined possible. The poultice applied by Babel was truly working wonders. Zowie was pleased to see him making such a swift recovery, and he asked, "Zee, what do you think is going on? I've heard several people saying there's something very Samarian about you. What do you think it is? I mean, 'The Flame of Dragonia', it responds to you as if you're Samarian royalty! any idea why?"

"I haven't a clue, Tom," she felt a little embarrassed by that strange, inexplicable, event, "I'm as baffled as you are. Anyway, it's the least of our worries right now. I hope Sitivia is ok. I'm simply dieing to see it. It sounds completely amazing."

Mercy, close enough to have overheard, joined the conversation, "Sitivia is even more beautiful than you could ever imagine, seeing truly is believing. We're not far now, you'll see the splendour for yourselves, how is that arm, Thomas?"

Thomas turned to face the tall, fair beauty that was Mercy, raising himself to his full height and puffing out his chest, "Arm? Oh, you mean *this* arm? What do you mean? There's nothing wrong with my arms, merely a scratch earlier. I hadn't noticed it until it was pointed out to me. I'm all set for round two, are *you* ok?"

Mercy smiled at him with genuine affection, noting he did actually look quite impressive in his black cloak, and silver battledress, "I am very well, thank you, Thomas, and more at ease with warriors such as yourself to watch my back." She finished off tending to the horses, and Thomas whispered to Zowie, "You see, there may well be something Samarian about you, but there's definitely something *ninja* about me!" He started making mock-Japanese sounds and chopping his hands at the air again, the pair of them laughing hysterically when Lauren rejoined them. "Mount up!" Tamarin's voice sounded out loud and clear. Everyone jumped up into their saddles as the suns neared their eclipse and once more they began speeding towards Sitivia. The gradual overlapping of the glaring orbs above lowered the baking temperatures a fraction and the weary travellers were grateful of it. This journey in defence of freedom appeared to traverse along a never ending road.

The horses carrying women were fleeter of foot due to their carrying less weight and it was not long before they were stretching out a lead on the men. Zowie and Lauren were enthralled by this particular episode of their fantastic adventure—leading the pack, side by side with Meekhi—Queen of Samaria, the beautiful Lady Mercy just astern, racing to Sitivia not knowing what they would find there. Lauren called out over the noise of the pounding hooves, "I don't care if I'm killed here, Zee! I wouldn't have missed this for the world! Way to go, uncle Dug! I've never so felt so alive before in my life!"

Zowie, was, as ever, pragmatic, "Our parents are *never* going to believe this. More so if you're dead! So let's not let that happen, please, because I'd never be able to explain *that* one, would I."

Inside, she agreed with all Lauren had said. Never before had she, too, felt so exhilarated, so bursting with excitement, so drunk with the desire to feel more, see more, know more, be more. Further back, Thomas had managed to get his horse alongside Ramulet and was asking questions about how to use various weapons, as well as his shield, to better effect. Ramulet, riding flat out, gave time to his many queries, answering them as best he could. The young lad was to be knighted and thus warranted his full and proper attention.

Samaria

The suns were parting company when Meekhi brought her horse to a stop. The other three did the same amidst the rising dust, hauling in their mounts when they saw her pointing ahead. The men caught up a minute later and all eyes followed the direction of Meekhi's finger, Sitivia. The suns, shining as a pair again, made the not too distant city shimmer under their relentless unforgiving glare, the skyline wavering and vague. The palace atop the cliffs, still too small to define precisely, was reflecting the light like a brilliant mirror. Tamarin breathed a sigh of relief, almost home. It was impossible to assess the state of the city from that distance, but once having sighted it, he heeled his horse to such a storming pace that even the women could not keep up as he disappeared into the hazy heat.

He was only minutes from the city when the horns began blaring, welcoming him home, telling him that his beloved Sitivia still sat in Samarian hands. The gates opened wide, and, covered in sand and dirt, he shot through them to much cheering and applause from his people. The others were only moments behind. Parched and panting, they slipped from their saddles as stable hands dashed forward to take care of horses on the point of collapse. They gladly accepted small wooden buckets of ice cold well water. The children, watching them use ladles to pour it over their heads, followed suit, thoroughly enjoying the experience as the water filled their ears and streamed down their backs.

Tamarin and Meekhi made straight for the steep winding steps leading up to the palace to consult with Corsellius, who had been diligently minding the city in their absence. They were surprised to see a handful of high ranking guardsmen hurrying down towards them. Tamarin's brow furrowed and Meekhi gasped when they recognised them as members of Etep's cavalry troop, sent earlier to find and escort the Westonian lords. Tamarin could see the haunted look on their faces, a telltale sign of men that have recently been in combat and suffered heartfelt losses. He raised his hand to silence his approaching soldiers—wishing to talk in private. He hugged each of them briefly before continuing on his intended journey up to the great hall. The men followed with Ramulet and the others also in tow.

The children could not believe the simplistic charm and radiance of Sitivia. It held an air of grace that Soledad could never match, cursed or not. This was undoubtedly the character of Meekhi infused within the bricks and mortar, the wattle and daub, the sand and the stone of which the city was built. The ravishing raven-haired warrior-queen was adored by her people, and her love, tenderness, and caring, gave as much succour to this land as the Emerald River. In fact, many said the sacred river flowed in her eyes, giving them their dazzling green colour.

The Samarians strode briskly through the palace, making for the great hall as fast as they could, but the children fell behind, staring gob-smacked at the riveting scenes portrayed in the murals painted on the ceilings, and the thousands of years of history so lovingly and lavishly depicted on many walls. The girls instantly fell in love with the place but the huffing and puffing Thomas thought an electric elevator service up from the city far below would be a very good idea. When they finally made it to the end of the corridor down which they had seen the others heading, they found themselves in the great hall of Sitivia. Tamarin and others were standing around a large, ancient oak table that had a very grave wizened face carved upon it. There was a map spread out, and a tall, well built guardsman was talking very quickly with Ramulet and the king. The man kept jabbing his finger at various points on the map and moistening eyes betrayed the emotions of both Meekhi, and Mercy, when they learned of the grim deaths of Etep and the others, and the ultimate selfless sacrifice of brave Ranician.

Tamarin feared for the Westonians, but he knew, under the circumstances, that they had a better chance of survival through the mountains with their smaller escort. It was a wise choice that had been made. They were fearsome warriors, and Imo a cunning, capable, and wily fellow. But one could not rely on their wellbeing because of these facts alone. There was as much chance of seeing them again as there was not. Bottling a rising tide of emotion, he thought of how best to tackle what must surely be coming his way.

There was a slim chance the Westonians would muster enough forces in the Western Worlds to deal with the threat before it became beyond their means. But this was unlikely from the facts imparted to him by Bestwin and Lumarr when they had first arrived in Sitivia, and more so given the more recent news from the returned guardsmen. He stood with his fingertips spread out on the map as his mind attempted to absorb so much information and convert it into a positive, viable strategy.

Meekhi looked him up and down as he stood there contemplating his next move. His face was grimy and unshaven, his hair dirty, thick and matted from his travels, and he looked so tired. She thought, "He has searched for, and found, me. In my place he has discovered the Guilty Innocents, and they have aligned with us through the kindness's he has shown them. He has survived a monumental fall to Solenia, where he has fought, and with a little help, destroyed the host of Ogiin's dreadful curse, and even now he is standing before me planning the defence of the realm. Not once during these testing trials has he once uttered a word of complaint, nor has he sought a moments respite for himself. Truly he is the most remarkable man alive, and I am blessed that he is mine." She slipped a loving arm under his cloak, wrapping it warm and lovingly about his waist. He acknowledged the gesture with a fleeting glance, their eyes barely making contact, a split second that spoke volumes.

Tamarin's greatest dilemma was the fact that Sitivia had been rebuilt after Ogiin's fall to the depths. With the villain destroyed, those of his perverse creed had been thought vanquished forever. The new city could withstand any assault, from any army of men. Even without the support of the allies now gathered within her walls, Sitivia had a standing army capable of stopping practically any invader in his tracks. Any invader, that is, apart from a supernatural one. He had never seen a hellhound, but from the descriptions he was sure these ferocious monsters could penetrate the cities defences with ease. Then, what of those Shadows? Or the witches, such as the one that had entered Imo's cave as smoke? No, Sitivia was not the place from which to defend her new people from old enemies. Regardless of what he had already seen there, *Soledad* was more suited to this purpose. She had served his father well against the same foe, and she would serve his son just as well. Having resolved his mind, he spoke his thoughts to everyone. "My lady, friends, brethren, we cannot defend against such an enemy as we face from Sitivia. I am not sure if defence or attack will be our game plan, perhaps neither, but the populace of this city needs to be made safe. The people will start for Soledad *immediately*. Her high stone walls will afford some measure of protection for the very old, or injured. Also, she is our first city. The very first statue in honour of the Great Dragon, Chjandi—Lord of The Dragons of Light, still stands tall, ever watchful, omniscient, in her great hall. Ramulet will lead our people to safety there. Myself, Mercy, a handful of guards, and the queen, must remain here for now."

Many eyebrows were raised at this, and old Corsellius asked what they were all thinking, "My lady will remain?? But, my lord, why risk her wellbeing…"

"Corsellius," Tamarin cut short his old tutor, "Meekhi and I must await the return of the two brothers—Rordorr, and, Faradorr, our winged friends bring something of vital importance to me, for my lady, and for Mercy, we cannot leave Sitivia without first receiving this precious cargo. There is also still the possibility that the Westonians may yet return with our own men, I will give them three days. If the horses have returned by then, we will join you all in Soledad, if they have not, then I shall wait for them here and my lady and the others will leave to join you in the Silent City."

Meekhi tensed visibly and Tamarin noticed her annoyed expression. "My lord," she told him, alarmed, "I will not leave you alone in this city to face, single handed, whatever horrors that may yet walk her streets! You are my husband, and my king, I will stand by you come what may."

"Me too," Mercy chimed in.

"My ladies," he told them in a firm, but kindly tone, "I am King, and my mind is set. Events will unfold as I have stated they will, this matter is not open to debate, I thank you both from the bottom of my heart for your kind concerns."

Looking up from the map, his eyes met all those present in turn and none challenged him further. "Make it so."

The city was galvanised into action. Great quantities of stores were loaded onto mules and donkeys, into large wagons, and piled up on flat carts. The arsenal was stripped bare of arms and these too were loaded up for transportation. Huge wooden barrels filled with fresh water were mounted on wheels to be hauled by teams of six horses apiece. These were not a materialistic people and little thought was given to household possessions, items of so-called wealth, and the like. Only essentials and weapons were to be carried. The Hall of History was emptied of its precious priceless contents. As wise Corsellius told Arcadian as they made history safe, "If you do not know where you have come from, how can you know where you are going?"

The Royal Guards donned full battledress. Their bright silver dragons could be seen dotting the road to Soledad as riders stormed ahead to prepare the old city and provide protection along the way for the fleeing people. Meekhi watched sadly as her beloved Sitivia began to look more and more deserted and forlorn. She bit deeply into her lower lip, battling to stem a flood of mixed emotions. Zowie, standing next to her on a balcony overlooking the square, took her hand, squeezing it to offer a little comfort. Meekhi looked at her in such a way that she withdrew it immediately, thinking she had perhaps overstepped the mark by touching the queen in so casual a manner. But Meekhi smiled at her, retaking her hand, "Come with me."

The queen moved quickly but gracefully through the palace, purpose in her stride, seeming to flow seamlessly as she dodged around the people scurrying about everywhere, removing essentials. The Shortwaters ran along in hot pursuit of Zowie, who, herself, could barely keep up with the long legged Meekhi as she strode through her palatial home. They passed by Mercy who asked, my lady, to where dost thou hasten with such urgency?"

"The Green Room," came Meekhi's unexpected reply.

Mercy sprang up instantly, joining Thomas and Lauren in chasing her through the palace.

Eventually they arrived at a pair of quite striking doors. Pastel green mottled with burnt orange. The tall gilt frames had an air of age and intrigue about them. A heavy looking brass handle, formed in the shape of a horse's head, was mounted in the middle of each. Meekhi glanced over at Mercy, and Mercy raised her eyebrows, shrugging, as if to say, "I haven't a clue what you're doing."

Meekhi lifted and turned one of the handles, pushing against it. The door swung open completely silently. She waved a hand, signalling Zowie to go inside, which she did. The Shortwaters were about to follow her through but Meekhi barred the way with an outstretched arm, telling them in a hushed voice, "Thomas, Lauren, sometimes people just need to be somewhere because that is where they belong at that time. I suspect that is why you are all here from your world. This room is where Zowie should be right now, I think. I just feel it. Let us see what transpires. Please, wait a while here, with me."

Zowie was totally absorbed by the room the second she saw it, she liked it even more than her own bedroom back home. Standing there in the Green Room she felt she *was* in her own world, a place she had not even known existed until she had just walked into it. But now it was as if she had been in this place a thousand times before, it was both magnificent, and, delicate. The typical silks and satins abounded, the overall feel was incredibly feminine but with a strong undercurrent of iron will. A large luxurious bed sat at its centre. Glass panelled doors with frames of pale green wood opened out onto a balcony overlooking the sea. Murals with the most fantastic detailing decorated the walls. The ceiling was a mosaic made up from precious and semi-precious stones, countless thousands of small gems combining to portray a precise map of Samaria. Zowie just stood there soaking up the mood of the room, straining her ears as if she expected to hear it talk to her. She was completely speechless.

A minute or two later the others quietly slipped in behind her. Meekhi placed a hand lightly on her shoulder and she turned her head, startled back to reality by her touch. Meekhi turned her gently—so they stood face to face. "This room contains many possessions that belonged to Yasmina—a princess of Samaria. Later, she became queen of the Western Worlds through wedlock. It was not fated to be a good marriage. Her husband, King Dorinn, was not all he had appeared to be. The décor and furnishings of this chamber are to her tastes and suited to her character, with many of her own belongings being brought here from Soledad, the city where her former residence was located. We know not where she is now, but she has, *always*, a home here in Samaria. Yasmina is of a slighter frame than myself or Mercy. In her memory I had a sword commissioned and placed in this room. I would like you to have it, for now. I know Yasmina would not mind in the least, as, I am sure, in your hands it will serve her motherland well. Should you ever have the good fortune to meet her, you can return it to her. It is truly a very Samarian sword, and as I am sure you are aware, some of us feel there is something very Samarian about *you*. I shall entrust you with the safe keeping of this unique blade until Yasmina requires it."

Zowie was lost for words, stammering, "I…I don't understand…I…oh, ok then, I suppose you know best."

"Hardly," Meekhi dismissed such praise as she walked over to an eye catching black-and-silver silk draped over an upright object, "it is not that I *know* best, young Zowie, it is only what I *feel* is best."

She gripped the fabric and lifted it away from what was revealed as a sword stand. The stand in itself was an ingenious work of art, being formed from a single enormous block of jade, interwoven with strands of gold and silver. But the weapon itself was breath taking, crafted for over two years by a master amongst master sword smiths. A triblade built for a woman's hand and stature, the gleaming blades seeming needle-like even compared to the smaller-than-usual weapon Thomas carried. The hilt was made of solid silver, with a black-and-green leather binding to ensure a firm grip. A raging dragon was etched in red and black along the length of the flawless central blade. It was an eye catching creation and Zowie's hand was shaking when Meekhi passed this gift to her. There were no words she could say to express how she felt, so she said all that there was to be said; "Thank you very much. I'll take really good care of it, and give it back straight away whenever you want it, or if I meet Yasmina."

Mercy and Meekhi clapped their hands, and Thomas said, "You deserve that, Zee. Your dad gave us this amazing adventure and you've been a real rock ever since we arrived. Well done to you!"

"Tom's right," his sister chimed in, "You *do* deserve it, and even *I* am starting to see something Samarian in you, top job, cuz."

Zowie carefully removed her existing weapon and hitched the featherweight triblade to her belt, she looked from Thomas' three bladed sword to Lauren's gleaming black bow, and then back to her own weapon. "Who would recognise us back home now?" She thought.

Tamarin's head suddenly appeared at the door. He saw her wearing the new sword, and looking at Meekhi he nodded his approval. "Come," he told them, "Ramulet is now departing for The Silent City."

They sprinted back through the palace and onto the long flight of steps leading down into the heart of the capital. The atmosphere had been entirely transformed since they had arrived. In the space of a day, Sitivia resembled a ghost town. The cheering crowds were gone, empty doors and windows already pined to once again be full of happy faces and the sound of joyful laughter. The streets felt eerie, devoid of the usual good cheer. The clatter and clamour of everyday life had been silenced in one fell swoop when the inhabitants had set off for the former capital some hours ago. It was the wish and command of the king, none would disobey him. A smattering of horses clattered about on the stone paving near the stables. Ramulet sat tall, mounted on one of these imposing chargers. Upon seeing Mercy approaching, he jumped down from his lofty perch and walked into her outstretched arms. They held each other close and he told her, "Remain vigilant and be sure to take the cure as Babel instructs you. My sword must leave your side for a brief spell but my heart remains here, locked within yours. Make certain you arrive safe and well to The Silent City, lest I have to return to find you."

Mercy, aware of what had transpired earlier in Soledad, was reluctant to not accompany her truelove, but she knew she must be wholly well within herself to serve him fully, so she would await the winged brothers as Tamarin had ordered. Their loving embrace unfolded and reluctant fingers slipped from lover's hands. Thomas gave Ramulet a firm handshake, "Remember, Captain, shield up, chin down, and keep your blade arm fluid!"

It was a very good impersonation and brought light humour to the emotional parting. The girls gave Ramulet a big hug as they had grown very fond of him. Tamarin embraced him firmly, "The Silent City is yours. Keep her safe for my return."

"It will be so, my lord." Ramulet saluted as he reared up his mighty horse, and, pursued by his guardsmen, launched himself towards Soledad with a thundering of hooves and resolute intent.

Dusk bowed out to night, and Sitivia was almost deserted. A few torches burned throughout the city like solitary fireflies dancing nervously, alone in the dark. A dozen guardsmen were all that remained to protect the king and queen. These brave souls walked the ramparts, eyes skinned for anything lurking in the black desert, but also looking anxiously to the skies for sight of the flying horses.

Tamarin sat in a high-backed wooden chair beside The Talking Table, with Mercy opposite him in a similar seat. Meekhi was perched on the armrest of his seat, running her long fingers through his dark locks, massaging his scalp, soothing him, trying to ease the gnawing tension she sensed growing within him. Tension she knew stemmed as much from his worries about her own wellbeing—she having been tainted by Iret, as from the threat from Ogiin and his creed. Thomas sat cross-legged on the floor next to Mercy. They were discussing Samarian history and, in particular, the legendary knights of old—The Ranin. The long lost fabled knights fascinated him, turning his stomach to jelly with the tales of their glorious victories.

The girls were holding hands at the foot of the towering silver dragon that sat silently, almost patiently at the far end of the great hall, its imposing height further elevated by its prominence upon the platform on which it stood, despite the city being empty and the echoey vastness of the hall, they could feel the omnipotent majesty of these revered dragons filling that great space to the rafters, creating a warmth, a solidarity of spirit, a hidden weave that bound the fabric of Samaria into an impenetrable cloth of faith. Lauren whispered, "This dragon, like the one in Soledad, feels like it's alive, don't you think? Just look at those ruby eyes, there's so much emotion in them, so much raw power."

"I think," Zowie replied, saying what she truly felt, "perhaps they *are* alive, in a way. The Samarians believe in them so much that it's as if the dragons had never left. As long as they have their faith, these dragons will live forever—in their hearts. Perhaps that's the only place they ever really need to be."

Lauren didn't get a chance to opinionate on Zowie's deep thinking because a guardsman ran panting into the hall. Gasping for breath, he hastily grabbed a lungful of air before warning them, "My lord! Movement to the west! Something approaches... fast... not the horses, by land!"

Tamarin leapt to his feet, almost knocking Meekhi off her perch and grabbing her just in time, "To arms!" He barked, "Man the wall to the west, but mind to leave lookouts to the other points. Arm the Wraths! Seal the gates! The time of reckoning is upon us! In the name of Chjandi and his host of dragons, we stand, we stand strong!"

Charging out of the palace, along the ramparts, onto the battlements, the children felt their pulses quickening, but not from fear. They could feel the adrenalin starting to race through their bodies, and, once more, the cry for battle was rising within them, flushing their faces and electrifying the senses. Like a powerful drug it overwhelmed all logic and reasoning, scattering common sense to the four winds. They welcomed it, not as fools without fear but as comrades in a united cause. They had seen in Soledad the true nature of the enemy, they knew they were doing the right thing, on the right side, at the right time.

Arcadian had remained behind in Sitivia and he used a telescope to scan the landscape through the darkness. There was something out there in the distance but it was impossible to distinguish its nature. Mercy held out her hand and the barrel-chested guardsman graciously passed her the scope. She leaned out over the parapet and began sighting the land in imaginary grids, exploring it sector by sector so as to not miss an inch. There! She could see dust rising, leaving a barely visible trail in the blackness. Screwing up her eyes, she strained to gain better sight of the cause, and then the light from millions of stars illuminated her hopes, and her fears. The starlight was flashing on silver dragons, Imo and the Westonians were riding as if all hell itself were in pursuit of them, and, perhaps, it was. In the distance, behind the terrified horses, were the telltale shapes of two monstrous hounds, bounding along in hot pursuit of her friends. As she warned the others of her discovery and they began to open the gates, a blood curdling high-pitched wailing slashed open the calm of the night. Tamarin balked momentarily at the sound, it was his first hearing of such a thing and sent a cold shudder through him. He had no time for the luxury of stairs and threw himself off the high wall, followed immediately by Meekhi, each landing easily and rushing to help open the heavy gates. The children ducked when Mercy somersaulted over their heads and also disappeared over the side, plummeting down to the gates below. They eyed each other nervously, unsure, then charged for the edge of the wooden platform upon which they stood. But as they got very close to that lip so high from the ground the Shortwaters thought better of it, skidding to a clumsy stop, arms and legs akimbo. Zowie, just behind, and about to bowl them over, had no choice, she rolled forward, jumped, and sailed over the wall.

"Holy crap!" they peered cautiously over the edge, expecting to see her in a mangled heap, but instead they saw she was unharmed and running flat out to catch up with the others.

"That girl really is weird." Thomas told his sister quite earnestly, "I think we should stay and help these chaps out up here."

Lauren was in complete agreement, on both counts.

Tamarin and his team opened the gates just wide enough to allow the width of a horse and rider through. Soon they could hear the thundering of hooves accompanied by the tortured jangling of tackle in torment. The horses themselves could be heard whinnying loudly, abject fear resonating in every petrified cry. Lumarr was first to blast into the city, the others arriving seconds behind him. They leapt from their horses shouting, "CLOSE THE GATES! To arms! Close the gates!"

Men were already heaving on the large wooden wheels and the gates of Sitivia slammed shut with a dull, resounding 'BOOM'. Tamarin and Meekhi rushed to greet their friends, but there was little time for polite formalities. The riders looked near-dead from their long, furiously paced charge back to the safety of Sitivia. One of their horses staggered awkwardly on its feet, lost its footing, and collapsed from exhaustion, its eyes bulging. Foaming at the mouth, it died quickly where it lay. Imo pointed to the well and told his fellow riders, "Water…go and drink."

He turned to Tamarin as Meekhi rushed to fetch him a drink. "My lord," he panted, exhausted, "The Western Worlds are…for now, lost. Dorinn planned to betray the ancient alliance, make… peace pact with Ogiin. Dorinndale deserted. Her people have fled to Samaria. They were to come here… but we redirected them to Rosameer as Ogiin's creed will…," stopping, he graciously accepted water from Meekhi, gulping it down before continuing, "…Ogiin's minions will no doubt strike for Sitivia first, and here we may not have the capacity to offer sanctuary to so many more. I am sure the people of Dorinndale will escape the path of that which pursues us. Ogiin lives, and rises from the depths. *There*, is Dorinn, breaker of treaties, and traitor to his own people, lashed to the donkey."

Another startling scream ripped through the night and something very large and heavy slammed into the gates. They could hear horrifying snarling and scraping as the great gates shook violently, creaking worryingly under the repeated battering. Mercy pointed out the children to the bedraggled new arrivals, "The Guilty Innocents are in fact these young ones you see before you, they are considered friend to Samaria having proven themselves by the sword to be so."

The weary travellers—worn to the marrow, raised their swords in salute to the children and they returned the gesture though they did not really understand why they deserved a salute from these fierce-looking men.

The gates shook again making the children jump. Lumarr removed his head from a deep bucket of water and shook out his hair. "Tamarin, bring the Wrath of Amaris to bear on that brute at your door. It has proved most effective for us."

The handful of men on the wall needed no urging having sighted the monstrous hellhounds, and a dozen of the deadly crossbows were mounted and readied just above the gate. Tamarin peered over cautiously and saw the demon dog scrabbling away. Its dark fur was on edge and its eyes appeared demented with its hunger for human flesh. Then a second hellhound slammed into the gate alongside it, causing it to buckle momentarily, the adjoining walls rocking violently under the impact.

"By all that is sacred!" roared Tamarin, "Bring down these vile monstrosities, lest they breach the city!"

Silver dragons mounted on the tips of crossbow spears sat waiting patiently, their claws reaching out for the howling, slavering hounds, below, then came the sound of the Wraths being released, followed by the blood curdling screams of the hellhounds as multiple spears pierced their flesh, staking them to the ground on which they stood. They died a fast but agonising death. Everyone, (especially the children), breathed a sigh of relief. Bestwin told Tamarin, "They caught our scent some hours ago and gave pursuit, but it is not Ogiin's main force. The others will arrive at the gate very soon, we can count on that."

"Where is everyone else?" asked Imo, suddenly noticing the deserted city.

"Little ones—explain to Imo." Tamarin asked the children as he climbed back up the many steps to scan the distance to the west.

Zowie explained, in a nutshell, everything they had experienced since arriving at the Pink Mountain.

"So! The king carries 'The Flame of Dragonia'?" He wanted to be sure he had heard correctly.

"Yes."

"Excellent." Imo was impressed. After sticking his head in a bucket of cold water he chased off after Tamarin.

Meekhi asked of the Westonians, "My lords, what has become of the garrison of Dorinndale, and indeed, the great army of the Western Worlds? Does it now align against us? Surely, even that bloated pig—Dorinn, could not sway such honourable a nation to base treason and treachery?"

Bestwin answered, humbled and embarrassed by his discoveries at Dorinndale, "My lady, but a hundred or two warriors remain worthy of the name and loyal to the pact. Many of our finest have drifted away over time, loyal to Yasmina and refusing to serve under such a dog as Dorinn. Others were more easily baited, finding fine wine and loose women too strong a lure when discipline and morale reigned no more in the Western Worlds. What little remains of our forces have elected to escort the people of Dorinndale to your fortress city of Rosameer. Neither Lumarr, nor I, could deny them this duty."

"It is well done, my lord," Meekhi eased the Westonians' unease at bringing no army of their own to face Ogiin's creed, "your fellow countrymen, those that have ridden to Sitivia, are a welcome and valuable compliment to our strength, I am certain they will uphold the honour of your homeland admirably."

The children were staring at the fat bundle of a man strapped across a donkey's back. "Shouldn't someone cut him down and give him a drink?" Lauren asked the small gathering.

Every adult voice around her replied, "NO!"

Then Tamarin hollered down to those below, "Release him! Traitor that he is, he is also a King. Give him water and arm him. Destiny eagerly awaits Dorinn, King of the Western Worlds. Let her decide his fate. Should he survive the approaching holocaust perhaps his people will show mercy, perhaps not. Release him *now*, my friends."

Mercy's sword flashed and the cords holding Dorinn were cut. He fell to the ground like a sack of potatoes, crawling on all fours to the well seeking water. He did not speak, or dare to look at anyone present.

Zowie was repulsed by the cowardly traitor and said so, "Bring back hanging! That's what I say. He's gotta go in the stocks at least! I'm a dab hand with a coconut."

Mercy looked at her incredulously, "*Hanging?* But, why show such mercy to one so dastardly in his deeds. You have too soft a heart, my young warrior."

Zowie beamed back at her, masking her own complete confusion.

The warm night, and a sky bedecked with diamond, ruby, and sapphire, stars, did nothing to ease the minds of the few remaining guardians of Sitivia. Only the children took note of the natural beauty that surrounded them in such abundance. A light and tender breeze wafted in from over the ocean and carried with it the fresh scents of brine and seaweed. Night birds could be heard making their final calls for the evening, sounding as if they too were bidding their farewells before vacating this ghost town. Imo told of how they had used bodies of hellhounds to barricade the mouth of the cave, and that perhaps the dead beasts at the gates would serve a similar purpose, blocking any access pinned to the ground as they were, but Tamarin told him there was no point in trying to hold the city, they were too few to man such a large perimeter. It would be futile against the sort of odds that Imo himself had told of. No, as soon as Rordorr and Faradorr arrived, they would abandon Sitivia and make for Soledad. Bestwin raised a question that all had pondered but none had dared to raise. "What if the two brothers had been intercepted en route to Rosameer, or returning to Sitivia?"

Tamarin had also considered this possibility and was prepared for it; "Should such a tragedy have transpired, then Meekhi will lead you all to Soledad, where you will hold the city come hell or high water. I will make to Rosameer and procure the remedy for my lady, for Mercy too, then rendezvous with you. If the two brothers fail to arrive then this is my final plan, I will not have it questioned." His face was grave, too stern for any to question his authority.

The sentries sounded the alarm once more, there was something moving in the distance. Lumarr observed carefully and told Tamarin, "As Bestwin said, during our race to reach you, we passed a large gathering of Ogiin's creed, the hellhounds lieing dead at your gates were the fleetest of them, staying hot on our tails as you have seen. Yonder approaches the rest of their kind, two more of those demon dogs, and perhaps a score of the Venomeen scum. I imagine they had been west bound to join with their master when they saw us, and gave chase."

"Then they have run themselves to an early grave, Lord Lumarr, you are no longer but a few caught alone in the dark, out there you were exposed and vulnerable, now, here, you are within our walls, and Samaria minds her own. Let us make haste, for they will be upon us in an instant."

The children were unsure of what to do next and Mercy told them to stay close to her. They were very grateful for that comforting advice. Tamarin spoke out loudly and clearly, for all to hear. "We are not here to hold the city, my friends, Sitivia must fall today, so she may rise again tomorrow. We bide our time only in the awaiting of the mighty horses. Ramulet has told us of the ability of the Venomeens to clamber up a sheer wall, even to run upside down on our ceilings, so our high defences offer no barrier to their inhuman ways. We will hold our position from the palace! It is easily reached by those with wings and not easily breached by the serpents approaching. Keep your wits about you and remember to look above you as well as everywhere else. We must slaughter them on sight. Be not afraid, people of The Dragon, truth and honour do stand proudly at our side. Now, make to the palace, and *guards*—ignite the River of Fire!"

They stormed up the long flight of steps leading back to the palace. Imo picked Dorinn up by the belt at his back, and lugged him up the steps like a piece of worthless baggage, his head frequently banging on stone. The children liked the look of Imo, his round friendly face and endearing smile made him appear friendly and approachable. There was something of the lovable rogue about him too, but this only added to his charm.

As the last of them dashed inside, the guardsmen slammed shut the pair of steel-reinforced doors, sealing the palace with an ominous 'CLANG'! Meekhi and Mercy, aided by the children, raced from floor to floor, pulling shut wooden shutters, and locking them. The children noticed the vertical slits cut into the panels for exploitation by archers if the need arose. Next, they hurried to the rear of the beautiful building sitting atop the cliffs and sealed the seaward face of what was now their sole refuge. Returning to the great hall they found the others already there, with Dorinn having been dumped ignominiously in the corner. Guardsmen, along with Tamarin and Imo, were pulling on a steel ring that had been previously concealed beneath the floor. The Westonians kept watch at the windows as the ring creaked noisily under the strain before beginning to rise, bringing with it a large, square-shaped granite slab. Below the slab was a hollow space big enough to hold three men. It revealed a lever on one wall and a wheel mounted on the other. Tamarin jumped into the hole and rotated the large wheel clockwise until it would turn no more. A glug-glug-glug liquid kind of sound could be heard, as if vast quantities of a thick fluid were moving. There was a look of relief on Tamarin's face when he turned around and pulled the lever on the opposing wall. Instantly, a strong smell of potent pitch filled the room. Bestwin stretched out a strong, hairy arm, and heaved him back up out of the hole by the forearm. The gloopy glugging continued and it seemed to be chasing around the outer walls of the palace. Even Meekhi looked puzzled. Tamarin opened a window and poked out his head, and Imo did the same to the rear of the building.

"Let the dragons face their enemy." Tamarin ordered.

Lumarr walked to a wall and removed one of the most ancient wooden war shields. Beneath it was yet another lever, on which the Westonian had to use considerable force before it pulled away from the wall and rotated down. The grating of stone on stone made everyone's teeth on edge and a rumbling vibration shuddered through the building momentarily, causing age-old dust to fall from the ceilings like snow. All around the palace's exterior wall, at irregular intervals, steel dragon's heads began to slide out from hidden sockets, slamming into place noisily. Their angry snarling faces were truly terrifying—with wide open mouths and piercing black eyes. Bestwin then opened yet another secret trapdoor in the floor, and they could see a river of the blackest pitch flowing below it. The Westonian looked over to the king, and he nodded his consent. Bestwin dropped a blazing torch into the river of pitch and slammed shut the stone slab over it. Tamarin retracted his exposed head, closing and sealing the window before turning to the others, "Beneath us," he told them, "is a veritable *lake* of finest pitch. Burning as hot as the fires of hell, it now flows within the outer walls. By the wall, just there, hangs what was until today an innocent sash. Pull upon it now, and the dragons that ring this palace shall rain down a flaming fury upon any impudent enough to be caught in their sights."

"*My lord*," smiled Meekhi, a little taken aback, "Many years are we wed, yet still you hold such secrets from your queen?"

"Ahh, yes, my lady," he laughed, "for you I wanted to save for last the knowledge of... *my bed of fire*."

She blushed in good humour, and, chuckling, the Westonians slapped Tamarin on the back, Bestwin adding, "A bed of fire, eh? Can you still muster the strength to fight this night??"

From their lofty position they had a good view of the city wall, and the unmanned gates at its centre. They saw a pair of hellhounds reach them, their horrible hysterical wails piercing the night as the slobbering brutes discovered two of their own kind lay dead before them. Mercy took Lauren's hand, "Bring your bow."

The two of them went upstairs and took up a position that would allow them to bring down fire on either side of the palace.

Imo asked Thomas, "Young master, will you join me at the main door?"

"Sure, it's as good a place as any, I suppose." Thomas sounded far more confident than he felt, *"Thomas Shortwater*—future Knight of The Realm, and stinking hot Ninja, to the rescue!"

Imo looked him up and down, puzzled. "If you are thirsty then drink now, quickly, for we are short in time. It will ease your being so hot. Sadly none of us are too fresh, but if you are hot, *and* stink, you can bathe once we are in Soledad."

"Err... right, ok," Stammered Thomas feeling embarrassed, following him and a handful of men to the palace gate.

Zowie turned to Meekhi, asking where she should be. Meekhi told her, "You will be where you need to be when you need to be there, Zowie. As it was in the Green Room, so shall it be here, such is the destiny of us all, always. Stay alert."

The hellhounds were being whipped into a crazed frenzy by lash-wielding Venomeens. The bald-headed bloodsuckers were directing the huge hounds to drag the corpses of their own away from the gate. Not an easy task as the Wrath of Amaris had firmly nailed the dead to the desert. They gripped the still warm flesh between their powerful jaws and ripped at it. Their vicelike grip shattered bone and sliced through muscles until the bodies had been completely dismembered and the sand was awash in blood. Dragging the gory chunks away, they left the gate once more exposed and vulnerable. Fortunately for those on the other side of the wall, Ogiin's creed did not know the city had been evacuated. They had no idea what lay in wait for them once the defences were breached, and the Venomeens much preferred that the hellhounds bore the brunt of any Samarian counter attack.

The hellhounds began battering the gateway to Sitivia. The 'BOOM-BOOM' caused by their relentless ramming could be heard clearly in the palace, carried up as it was on the sea breeze in the dead quiet of the desert night. The defenders of the palace moved from point to point trying to see from which direction the attack would come. The seaward face of the building was protected by its natural defences—the cliffs, these fell away steeply to the harbour below and consisted of jagged outcrops covered in thorny gorse and slippery shale, thus Tamarin focused the bulk of his attention inland.

It did not take the Venomeens long to realise that there had been no response to their attempts to breach the gates. One of them crawled up the wall, moving up the sheer surface awkwardly like a crab. Upon seeing the deserted streets it let out a horrible gargling sound—most definitely a laugh of sorts, before it started hissing and clucking its news down to the others.

Lauren could see the creature perched astride the wall and had an arrow aimed directly at its head. She felt Mercy's hair brush against her own, and her soft voice urged her, "Take it, take it *now*!"

She pulled her bowstring fully taught and felt the glassy black bow take the strain, the action powerful but silky smooth. Narrowing her eyes she focused on the Venomeen, its repulsive features filling her vision as she concentrated. Lauren had never killed anything ever before in her own world, but now every atom in her body knew that the pale-skinned bloodsucker sitting on the wall had to die. She felt no remorse as she let loose the deadly shaft gripped between her fingers.

Tamarin saw the missile penetrate the Venomeen's skull precisely between its evil, hateful, eyes. It pitched over the wall and fell dead amongst it own kind. He called up to Mercy, "Good work, my lady!"

To which Mercy shouted down, "Indeed it was! The good work of Lauren!"

Everyone in the palace heard this and Thomas proudly boasted to Imo, "That's my sister's shooting, mate!"

Imo was still confused by Thomas' foreign tongue. "*Who* is your sister's shooting mate? I thought Lauren fired the shot. It was most definitely not Lady Mercy."

Thomas still could not explain, simply shrugging his shoulders at an ever more perplexed Imo.

The defenders saw another white head glow momentarily over the top of the wall, but before anyone could fix their aim the Venomeen had climbed over and scampered down the wall, diappearing off into the city. The distressing sound of the gates opening could be heard. The hellhounds, their lust for human blood barely bearable, burst through and came bounding up the steps to the palace, slamming straight into the reinforced doors, sniffing and howling at the scent from within. It was obvious the doors would give in minutes under such incredible pressure. Arrows rained down and pierced their flesh but were ineffective against their monstrously thick hides. Venomeens were now ducking in and out of shelter, hiding from the archers as they also made their way up to the palace. Zowie, standing close to the silken sash that released the River of Fire, shot a questioning glance at Meekhi. "HOLD! Hold but a few moments longer, we need to destroy as many as possible."

A shower of arrows pelted the wooden shutters of the palace in rapid succession, thud-thudding noisily on impact. No great marksmen the Venomeens, but their arrows could kill as easily as Samarian ones if they found their mark. The defenders could see something else moving a way off behind the Venomeens, something dark and almost transparent. Tamarin shouted at the top of his voice so all within the palace would hear him; "The palace will be breached any second now. These ghoulish fiends appear focused on *us*, so I suspect the horses in the stables down below are as yet unharmed. The guardsmen and Westonian soldiers will form a raiding party. When we let loose the fire it should distract this scum long enough for you men to climb down from the back of the palace, taking that miscreant Dorinn with you, and make your way down to the horses, preparing them for escape. Stealth will be of the essence my friends, these damnable creatures can pick up your scent far too easily. Imo, you shall remain at our side. Those of us left will separate, forcing the Venomeens to do the same. Then their advantage of numbers will be reduced and our advantage of superior skill, familiar terrain, and bold heart, will be increased. Should the odds remain stacked against us and our defence withers, we are all to fall back to the great hall for a final, massed counter attack. Finally, if this also fails, there is a trapdoor in the hollow where I released the pitch. A slower route by which to flee then that taken by our soldiers, but one not easily discovered. You will escape to the horses via this secret tunnel and make for The Silent City. I shall make for Rosameer and meet with you later. Are we all understood!?"

They understood perfectly, and Imo, who had taken a liking to Thomas, cautioned him, "The king speaks the truth, should we have need for stealth as we escape you must take particular care not to be scented by those accursed Venomeens, because you stink."

A small group of Ogiin's cruel creed made a dash for the palace, some of them being picked off by archers, but others managing to reach safety in the lee of the wall—out of sight of the deadly bowmen targeting them. A larger group charged the palace en masse, brandishing their crude weapons above their heads and sounding like giant serpents, hissing as they ran. Tamarin ordered his marksmen to hold their fire, allowing the bloodsuckers to get closer. When they could be heard clattering noisily up the outer walls with their dull blades knocking against the stonework, he barked at Zowie, "NOW!"

She pulled down firmly on the red-and-black silk drape. Feeling resistance at first, she gave it a big tug. Instantly the dark night outside the windows was lit up, the blackness erupting into a blinding glare. Everyone rushed to the windows, and peering out of arrow slits could see torrents of fire gushing down onto the enemy. Burning Venomeens could be heard and seen screaming as they plunged to their deaths below. The hellhounds were ablaze too, their intense wailing almost unbearable. Unfortunately, no Wrath of Amaris could be brought to bear on them because of the impossibly steep angle. They rolled and writhed in agony, whining and howling as the torrent of fire bit deeper and deeper into their hides. In the midst of the chaos outside, Tamarin's guardsmen were lowered out of the seaward windows and made for the stables unnoticed.

The children, located in different parts of the palace, cheered gleefully, "YES!" But a great, crashing, 'THUD' brought their jubilations to an abrupt end. One of the hellhounds had succumbed to its fiery end, but the other, still ablaze, had run amok and smashed through the palace doors. Imo grabbed Thomas' arm and pulled him to safety as the huge burning hound careened into every wall in a frenzy of agony-fuelled hatred. Imo had dealt with this kind before and knew now was not the time to engage the rampaging beast. He and Thomas took the most sensible course of action available—they ran away. They ran like the wind, with the blazing behemoth hot on their tails. The monster was too big to negotiate the corridors of the palace easily and, as such, it scraped past walls and doors, smearing them in burning pitch and causing them to smoulder and catch alight. The whole building would soon be an inferno.

Imo knew that the fire would eventually consume the hellhound chasing after them. There was little point in risking either Thomas or himself in tackling it. He would let the beast chase them until the eager flames stilled its black heart. They continued their deadly game of 'catch'.

The doors torn asunder, Venomeens crept cautiously into the palace. Entering alone or in pairs, heads turning in every direction, they sniffed the air, searching for humans. One of them rasped, "Sssamarian... *females*!"

Another, with a look of pure evil on his face, hissed back, "For Ogiin's pleasure..."

The marauders broke up into small groups and began to search the burning building. As they left the shattered doorway the smoky shapes of Wispy Witches appeared where they had stood, and behind them, hovering silently, biding their time, were Shadows, barely visible against the night at their backs. Only the light from the fires reflected in those red, dead eyes.

Tamarin, Meekhi, the Westonians and Zowie were in the great hall. They continuously scanned the skies, desperate for sight of the flying horses, but there was nothing to be seen save clear night sky and a beautiful tapestry of stars. Tamarin readied for battle. His long black cloak hung down from his broad shoulders—draping his back, and 'The Flame of Dragonia' rested ready at his side. He was looking up into the ruby eyes of the dragon statue.

"Long lost friend," he spoke his thoughts out aloud, "I beseech you, keep safe my lady, my friends, and my countrymen. Guide them to Soledad, and have your breath of truth be their shield to protect them there. Your people, Great Dragon of yesteryear, have sore need of your wisdom now, for I do not know what to do next." He bowed his head as his royal house burned around him, as, soon, would his city.

A strange earthy voice startled them all. Drawing their swords, they began looking about for the source. Then Tamarin recognised the mellow, wooden sound. It was The Talking Table that had spoken. They gathered around it and Zowie was gob-smacked to see the wise, wooden face, moving, wrinkling its nose as if about to sneeze. The face spoke calmly, but with a sense of urgency not to be ignored. "Young King, the invaders are but a few of the many tentacles of their evil master. They seek the blood of the living to rebirth that that was once dead. Defend yourself with the blood of the dead. Tamarin, son of Darcinian! You carry 'The Flame of Dragonia'. This sacred blade can bring death to the living many times over, but life to the dead only once. Ancient shields in history past did split and splinter to hold back the onslaught of the demonic hordes. Soaked in Samarian blood they were, and still they remain stained thus. Even now, the blood remains the same, remains Samarian, remains pledged. A wall of ancient shields and the flame of the Great Dragon, combined, can yet turn the tide, merging past with present. Tamarin, you are *never* alone, for you are a, *Samarian* lord. You may well find my need for beeswax far greater in the days yet to come."

The table fell silent and that lovely gentle face was once again a hard, inert, carving. Tamarin looked to Meekhi, who looked as baffled as he felt. Naturally Zowie didn't have a clue as to what the table was talking about, all she could say was, "Thomas will be gutted that he missed this! It really *is* a talking table. Wow!"

Meekhi, a sudden look of deep concern on her face, asked her, "What do you mean, my youngest knight will be gutted? Gutted by whom? Not whilst I breathe will this gruesome event come to pass! Imo is a fearsome warrior and Thomas, too, has proven himself no slouch in combat. They will not be easily slain. Thomas, brave soul that he be, will stand his ground, and…"

Her words were cut short by cries from the corridor leading to the great hall. Thomas' voice, shouting, cut her off, "CRAP! Craaap! This thing has gone totally mental!"

Imo's voice in the background was urging Thomas to keep running, and to not look back.

The pair burst into the great hall with the blazing hellhound still in tow. Imo skidded across the slippery, polished stone, floor, and Zowie grabbed him just before he lost balance. Thomas also came sliding across their way, slamming into Imo and sending him and Zowie crashing down in a heap. The hellhound, yellow and purple flames dancing excitedly all over its body, smashed into the far wall, keeling over onto its side. The fires of hatred burned far brighter in its eyes than the flames engulfing its ravaged frame. Tamarin and Meekhi were already in motion. Before the smoking black beast could stagger back to its feet, Tamarin drove 'The Flame of Dragonia' into its skull right between its eyes at exactly the same moment as Meekhi thrust her own blade deep into the animal's heart. It moved no more.

Lauren came charging into the room calling for Thomas—having heard his cries of 'craap' as he had passed the chambers where she and Mercy had positioned themselves. They had seen the flaming hellhound and given chase to it, even as it had pursued Imo and Thomas.

Now they were all gathered together in the great hall. The hellhound was making a revolting sound, sloppy wet pops and squelches turned their stomachs as its burning hide boiled its innards at one end of the room. Even the most battle hardened covered their noses and Lumarr ushered Lauren and Zowie away from the reeking mess. Sinister cackles and furious clucking, paired with the sound of tramping feet, could be heard throughout the palace. Doors were being opened and slammed. Crockery, china, stone, and glass, was heard smashing as the Venomeens vandalised all they passed in their search for human blood and the life-giving energy it held for Ogiin. The building was not truly ablaze as yet but small fires had broken out everywhere and would eventually spread, engulfing the entire structure.

The nine remaining occupants of the great hall braced themselves for the inevitable arrival of Ogiin's creed. They stood by The Talking Table, swords drawn and bowstrings half taught. Everyone was watching the doorway at the far end, wondering what form of evil would first arrive to face them. Tamarin stood side by side with his queen. Without taking his eyes off the door, he asked her, "Of which strange riddle did the wise voice speak? I am entirely baffled, yet an answer to this riddle could be our salvation still, this dark night. Can you fathom logic in these words of wisdom? Can we unclasp this mystery?"

"I fear I can not," she replied honestly, "I agree there is hidden purpose in the words of this ancient oracle, but sadly their true meaning eludes me, my lord."

Tamarin frowned in frustration, "I shall share this load with present company, my lady, for many heads are better than two at times like this."

He sought the advice of all present but everyone seemed as lost in this conundrum as he was. No one had time to try and tease the tangles from the tangled advice any further, because a group of Venomeens appeared in the doorway. They stood there, staring at the defenders with their dull lidless eyes. Numbering only four they were easy meat for the Samarians, yet their demeanour was altogether too confident, too assuming, overly smug. The reason for this became apparent soon enough. Behind them many more of their loathsome ilk were waddling along to join them, but worse still, they could see not only a pair of Wispy Witches, but the spectre of Shadows.

Two bowstrings snapped back to their relaxed state as Lauren and Mercy took down the closest Venomeens. Another glared at the archers, hissing, "*Feemales*! Kill them!"

They watched as maybe a full score of pale, saggy skinned ghouls, poured into the room. Tamarin's heart sank as he saw the odds stacking ever higher against his people. The Wispy Witches and Shadows hovered menacingly just behind the Venomeens. Imo grabbed burning torches from the walls and passed them around. "Those hovering harbingers of death," he warned, "swords will have no effect upon them, but they don't like fire. It will not kill them, but it is effective in keeping them at bay. Fire, *will*, however, destroy those ugly crones at the rear!"

Each of his comrades took in this information instantly. It was a matter of life or death. Matters were made much worse knowing that if you should fall victim to Ogiin's creed, your life blood, your very spirit, would be used to make that demon of demons more dangerous than ever to your surviving allies. Survival was not only the obvious option, it was essential if one was not to empower the enemy with one's own strength.

Light pooled around the group of defenders from the flickering torches they held aloft. The glow barely extended across the hall, and in the half-light where torchlight met shadow, the Venomeens looked all the more sinister as they began to spread out, forming a pincer movement towards the Samarians. Meekhi called out to Mercy and Zowie, "*You two*! Watch the left flank! Do not let them encircle us!" Turning to Imo, she barked; "Imo! You, Thomas, and his sister—Hold the right! I will hold the centre with Tamarin and the Westonians."

They took up their positions as commanded. The Westonians remained in reserve at the centre—just behind the king and queen, ready to rush to the aid of any weakening front. Mercy and Lauren managed to get off several more shots before Tamarin and Meekhi locked swords with the Venomeens. Battle broke out all around The Talking Table—which the Samarians had dragged up onto its side, using it as a solid makeshift barrier.

The Samarians and the children fought with supreme skill, their swords flashing far to fast for any eye to track, but enemy numbers were against them. It was nigh on impossible to deal a fatal blow with so many Venomeen blades railed against them. Zowie ducked under a savage swipe to her head and countered with a long arcing slice under the Venomeen's guard. Yasmina's sword claimed its first victim when she severed the creature's legs with deadly precision. It shrieked and fell to the floor thrashing its arms. More replaced it, trampling their wounded in the process, and continuing their assault on the young girl-warrior, who fought back like a wildcat. Thomas saw her make her first kill and shouted across to her, "Hope he's not driving home, the guy's totally legless!"

Zowie and Lauren couldn't help grinning despite the dire situation. Thomas had a winning way with his humour, even at the most inappropriate of times, and such stoicism was always good for boosting morale. The defenders kept a particularly wary eye on the Wispy Witches loitering close by, and even more so—the Shadows. It was imperative no one became isolated from the group, or those ghostly Shadows would not waste such an opportunity. The witches were intermingled with the Venomeens, looking for a gap, a chink in the Samarian defences when they could reach out and touch one of the humans, freezing them until the witch could drain their life-essence. The Shadows kept disappearing, to suddenly reappear somewhere else. They moved in the blink of an eye and it was impossible to keep track of them. They could only barely maintain the perimeter around the table and pray nothing penetrated it. Then Zowie noticed something quite wonderful and cried out to Tamarin, "Tamarin! Your sword, the blade! The flame is alive again!"

He scythed 'The Flame of Dragonia' through several strokes, enabling him to see the flat of the primary blade. Sure enough, the blue flame was dancing within. The sight of such a marvel, something born of Chjandi, spurred him into even greater efforts and soon he brought that fiery blade crashing down upon the head of a Venomeen. Blue flames streaked from the sword as it descended on the bald skull, cleaving it into two. "I am never alone, great lord." He whispered softly to himself.

The sight of the blazing blade panicked Ogiin's rabble and they fell back to regroup. Seizing the brief window of opportunity, Tamarin grabbed Imo and the Westonians, and together they hauled The Talking Table further back, closer to the wall so that a barrier to the front and rear was achieved. Tamarin ordered everyone to take up position behind the table. It was formed from very thick, solid, reworked war shields, and offered a good degree of protection over which he and the others could still inflict grievous harm upon the enemy. From behind the table and with the wall at their backs, Mercy and Lauren could bring their bows into deadly effect again, shooting from either side. This they began to do immediately and to good effect, forcing the Venomeens to shelter behind their own roughly hewn shields. The Wispy Witches and Shadows had no such fear as the arrows passed straight through them.

Tamarin knew it was only a matter of time before the greater weight of numbers the enemy possessed took its toll and his people would begin to fall. It was an impossible situation—trying to fight so many without getting touched by one of the ever present crones, or never knowing if a Shadow would pop up right next to you, claiming your life in a second to empower its Lord against your remaining friends. He could see that the children, despite fighting as well as any Samarian, were tiring fast, their young bodies exhausted of any reserves they may have had left. He raised his voice to be heard over yet another screaming Venomeen that had succumbed to Mercy's deadly shafts, the flight filling its mouth and the tip sticking out of the back of its head, "Listen to me all of you, remember the escape plan. Imo will hold here with myself, when I give the order the rest of you will break for the trapdoor, meet the horses, and make as was planned earlier."

Zowie offered to stay behind with them but was silenced by Tamarin with a raised hand. The Venomeens charged forward again, keeping their shields up as Lauren and Mercy poured volley after volley into them.

Bestwin and Lumarr knew the enemy must be divided to reduce the strain on the Samarian centre. They broke from behind the table and took up position a little way to Tamarin's left. Their deadly curved scimitars at the ready, they forced the enemy to fight on two fronts, relieving a little pressure on their friends. Dorinn's apathy still weighed heavily on their conscience and the honour of the Western Worlds rested in their blades. Lumarr signalled Lauren, "They must turn their backs to face us, fill their yellow spines with steel-tipped death!"

The Samarians rained down a storm of blows upon their enemy from over the table, and whilst more of Ogiin's creed fell under the onslaught, too many did not. Lauren was out of arrows and Mercy kicked a quiver over to her whilst maintaining her own incessant firing. She knelt down to gather up the scattered shafts, and, suddenly, terrifyingly, a Shadow appeared right next to her behind the upturned table. Lauren screamed as it spread out its mantle of death, ready to engulf her. Tamarin heard her panicked scream and spun around in an instant, instinctively driving his crackling blade into the heart of the phantom hovering before him. A great blinding flash ensued, followed by a loud, 'CRACK!'

Scorch marks scarred the floor where the Shadow had been, but the fiend, itself, existed no more, "By the Great Dragon!" He exclaimed, hope revitalised and new found confidence in his voice, "Now, Shadows of darkness—you will taste the burning of light!"

Those black-hearted servants of Ogiin—the Venomeens, fell away quickly from the wall formed by the table, aghast at the sudden combustion of the Shadow. The Samarians watched on helplessly as perhaps as many as half a dozen more Shadows joined with them across the way, seeming to appear from the adjoining passage. Tamarin knew even with the deadly capabilities of 'The Flame of Dragonia' he would lose most, if not all, of his people in the next encounter. "It is time," he thought, "for the women and Thomas to leave." About to give this last command, he bit his lip when Mercy burst out, "My lord! At last I recall the ancient myth, the lore of times long since past! This is the answer to the riddle of The Talking Table! I'm sure of it. Listen:

> *When Dragon's sword is no longer lost, and*
> *wisdom old is found,*
> *The blood that is forever yours will rise from*
> *sacred ground.*
> *If Samarian souls do darkness face,*
> *Look ye then to The Dragon's grace.*

*For when dragon's flame greets the Talking Table
Those long since lost, will become once more able.
Fire to wood, fill the dark with dread.
If thou art true King, awaken the dead!*

It is the old, old prophecy, my lord. I thought it but legend, wistful myth, but by The Dragon's mighty wings! I see now, it is the truth. Here. in the Great Hall of Sitivia we stand on sacred ground! Strike The Talking Table, my king! Strike it now, with the sword of kings!"

The sounds made by the vermin across the room had increased in pitch and pace as Mercy had recited the ancient verse. Ogiin's creed, suddenly overcome by blind panic for some unknown reason, began swarming across the floor in an all out massed attack. Tamarin raised his glowing magical sword up high, and as he brought it crashing down onto the table's edge, he whispered, "Forgive me, old friend."

The blazing blade bit deep, becoming stuck in the thick old oak. He stood tugging at it, trying to wrench it free. The blue fire reached out, licking all over the tabletop before returning to the sword. The wood remained untouched. Mercy and Lauren each released their last arrow, and one more Venomeen fell thrashing to the ground, a silver shaft buried deep in its throat. Strangely, suddenly, the whole charging horde stopped dead in their tracks, even beginning to back away, a little at a time. The defenders were puzzled, as apart from getting stuck and mildly damaging the table, Tamarin's sword seemed to have achieved little else. Meekhi noticed that every single, cold, cruel eye, across the room, was fixed not on her and her comrades, but on the front of The Talking Table. She stepped up onto Tamarin's bent knee and peered down over it. When she stepped back down her face was pale with disbelief. She could barely speak, stammering with considerable difficulty, "It is...it is...it is... *bleeding.*"

Tamarin moved from behind the upturned table, keeping one eye on the Venomeens, and took a quick look. A thick, steady, flow of blood, was pouring from the mouth of the face carved into the table. The crimson tide was spreading out across the stone floor towards their enemies, who appeared mortified at the sight of it. He glanced over at the sweating, blood-soaked, Westonians, standing a few feet away from him, "My lords, I pray thee join with my people, safe away from this new wonder." He then turned to the battle weary fighters still behind the shelter of the table, "Mercy, I believe your quick thinking has born the fruit of our salvation. I, too, now remember the verse of old. All of you, listen, we need not fear this flood of blood. This sacred table was formed from the reworked wood of war shields way back in the depths of history, shields that, in battle, were drenched in the blood of our noble ancestors. A Samarian is *always* a Samarian, holding both our honour and our duty close and dear. From what I know of the fable, we have reawakened fallen friends from the past, so that they may take just retribution against the evil that stole their time from them in this world. It is said they can arise for only one night—to defend The Throne of Samaria. My people! Take heart! We are about to bear witness to something that can occur only once in an eternity, something so noble, so honourable, and, so *Samarian*. We alone, gathered here this night in this sacred hall of Sitivia, shall see the rising of—THE BLOOD WARRIORS!"

As if on cue, the heavy doors of the great hall slammed shut of their own accord with an almighty crash. Venomeens strained in vain to force them open again. They bent their blades with their superhuman strength trying to lever the heavy frames apart, but some mysterious unseen force kept them sealed tightly shut. The burning torches suddenly went out and the vast hall fell into pitch blackness. Even the light from the stars did not dare to intrude into that solemn inkiness. All and sundry fell silent, not even daring to breathe. Then, with a blinding flash, the torches again burst into life, bright blue flames of incredible intensity roaring loudly from the wooden stems, whooshing up as if driven by some enormous invisible bellows. The eerie blue hue filled the entire chamber. The Venomeens cowered near the door, covering their petrified faces with their flabby hands. Shadows flitted about here and there, jittery and nervous. Tamarin guarded his people vigilantly with

'The Flame of Dragonia'. The pool of bright red blood lay like a still crimson lake between them and those that meant them harm. As if pinched by so many invisible fingers, points of this scarlet carpet began to rise up like drapes. They rose until they started to resemble figures. Thousands of lights, the size of pin pricks and of every imaginable colour, danced all over the fast-forming shapes. The figures became larger, taller, fuller as they absorbed the blood from the cold stone floor as a sponge takes up water. The defenders stood dumbstruck as faint flashes of silver could be seen on the glistening cloaks made of blood. Dragons! Silver crests could be seen moving within that sea of red. At last the figures were easily recognised as Royal Guardsmen, though they were entirely formed from blood. Even their weapons were red, fluid, and macabre-looking. One could see right through their bloody bodies and they struck terror into the hearts of Ogiin's creed. Meekhi and Mercy wept openly at the sight of the dead rising, rising to keep their oath of honour to Tamarin, to their king now, and to their kings before. The children, too, filled with emotions too deep to control. Imo and Tamarin raised their blades to their faces in open salute to the spirits of ancient Samaria.

The Blood Warriors formed up in perfect formation and turned with parade ground precision to face their king. Their eternal loyalty, devotion, and valour, could not be masked, or in any way diminished, by their unearthly appearance. They raised their swords to him in salute and he bowed his head with humble respect. A voice spoke, though none could say from whence it came, it was a powerful, masculine voice, "We salute you, Lord of Samaria, but ask that you leave us now, for a cruel vengeance be ours to wreak upon this cringing vermin, a sight of wholesome slaughter unbefitting of our queen and kinsmen. Leave now, dearly beloved, and may the Great Dragon be at your side, always."

They turned about again, raising their swords in unison at the Venomeens huddled and cowering before them. Bright red triblades dripping with well fermented revenge began slicing through the air as they marched on their enemy. A Shadow tried to appear behind them and attempt escape, but a blood-red sword was plunged deep into its dark heart. It disappeared in a smoky red flash. The defenders of the palace watched the wet, bloody capes glistening in the strange light as they moved away and towards Ogiins creed, the silvery red dragons looking back at them with remorseless eyes.

Tamarin's heart was fit to explode, so filled was he with pride and love for his ancient brethren. He knew better than to interfere with the workings of The Dragon's ways and lofted his blade once more in a final salute. "My brothers from beyond the pale, you have my eternal gratitude. You have forever the gratitude of both, this King, and, this land. One day I shall join you in the next life and we will embrace with loving arms in a world free of pain, filled with colour and joy. Fare thee well."

He and Imo jumped down into the square hole in the floor and opened the secret trapdoor. Hysterical screams and tortured cries could already be heard from the vicinity of where Ogiin's creed had stood. Thomas and Lauren covered their ears so as to blot out the grisly sound of flesh and bone being ripped apart, but Zowie felt neither nausea nor revulsion—she only saw the Blood Warriors meeting out justice and held not a jot of sympathy for their victims. They passed quickly through the narrow hatch and into a tight tunnel that wound steadily downwards. The ground was firm and dry but one had to watch ones head from banging on the rough low ceiling. Meekhi was leading carrying a torch and the others followed, with Imo bringing up the rear. No one spoke as they escaped the slaughterhouse above. Each was still lost in thought, shocked and awed at having seen the rising of the Blood Warriors.

After some fifteen minutes of creeping along the narrow passage Meekhi came to a small wooden door, which was locked. Two powerful kicks from her strong legs, and it lay in splinters. They were in the cities central square. Emerging quickly and straightening their backs, they stood looking back up at the palace atop the cliffs. Flames could be seen licking at a few of the windows, but this is not what held their attention. Shredding the night, there came the most tormented, spine tingling, screaming, from behind the shutters of the great hall. The sealed windows were repeatedly illuminated by bright purple and blue flashes from within, and blood red mist seemed to be rising up through the roof. It was as if the most gruesome of tortures were being committed behind those walls with the greatest of relish. The agonised cries made the hair on the back of everyone's neck stand up. Sagely, Lauren muttered to herself, "We reap that which we sow."

Hastily, the brave and battered group made their way towards the gates to rendezvous with the guardsmen and horses. Halfway there, they noticed the palace was silent once more. Tamarin reiterated his plan. He would make for Rosameer alone, whilst the others returned to The Silent City and joined with Ramulet. They left the city a little awkwardly, having to clamber over the shattered ruins of the gates and the half crumbled wall. The night was cooling and each filled his lungs to the full with the clean air, rinsing away the poisonous memory of the events within the palace. The sight of guardsmen and horses—five minutes walk away, could not have been a more welcome sight. Worn out and weary, they walked slowly in the lee of the wall, unaware of the sole pale-skinned figure clambering like a spider along the top of it, wielding a short, stubby sword.

Meekhi was chatting with Mercy about the recent magical reappearance of long lost warriors and the eternal spirit of their people. She was telling her of just how proud she was to be a Samarian, and how lucky she was to have not only met Tamarin, but to have been blessed by his love for her. Since she had first set eyes upon him, she had not once felt worthy of such a man. She told Mercy that, come what may, she would never leave Samaria, or fail the man she loved so deeply. They walked close together as the Venomeen on the wall stretched out its bony arm high above its head to deliver the most devastating blow to the Samarian queen. Zowie saw the movement on the wall too late, too far to intervene, she cried out; "MEEKHI! WATCH OUT!"

Everyone turned quickly and saw the sword beginning its deadly descent. Tamarin's heart nearly stopped as he realised no one could reach the creature in time and Meekhi was never going to be able to avoid the oncoming blade. The royal couple locked eyes for a split second, more being said in that scant second then either could write in a lifetime, an instant exchange of hearts. Then a whooshing gush of air sounded above them and a long blue tail reached down from the sky, plucking the weapon from the Venomeen's grasp. Solipop's giggly little voice could be heard high in the sky, "Nasty beastie things wanting to hurt pretty queen lady woman person, it's not *good* behave, it's *bad* behave. Bad! Bad! Bad!"

The lone Venomeen looked up in shock, searching as to where the sound was coming from, but for its efforts the bloodsucker received a pair of very large hind hooves rammed into its head, shattering its skull like an over ripe plum and causing it to topple off the wall, dead before it hit the ground at Meekhi's feet.

"I will have lost at least *one* of my shoes doing that," Came the voice of Rordorr moving through the night, "no doubt I will break my ankles when we land, all this drama, and I get killed by a lost shoe. It would be just my luck."

Tamarin, Meekhi, and everyone else, burst into fits of grateful laughter as a pair of majestic winged horses smoothly circled the air, swooped down, and landed easily without incident, to then trot up to Tamarin. Each of Rordorr's shoes remained securely attached to his hooves. Meekhi lifted Solipop from the horse's back. "You elves, it seems," she told him, "have a penchant for saving my life. I cannot thank you enough, little Solipop, but know this—anything you ever need of me is yours for but the asking of it."

The small blue elf stood rolling its unbelievably big eyes at her, "Me like them food dates, oh yes! Yum yum yum! Sticky messy gooey juicy! Yes! Solipop likes them sweetie dates plenty much nice sugar dates, lovely!"

"Solipop! Is this how I've raised you to be!" admonished Babel.

Meekhi placated his mother with a gentle wave. She and Mercy, keeping a very wary eye out for any further lingering threat, hurried back to the city and returned with a large sack jam-packed full with fresh, juicy, and *very sticky,* dates. The sack was far larger than Solipop and the little elf was beside himself with joy, shoving his head wholly into the sack and retrieving it with the sticky fruits stuck all over his furry face, his cheeks so full as to make a hamster envious.

Rordorr had a small leather bag hanging around his neck. As Tamarin removed it, the horse told him; "My lord, forgive me, but the elves insisted on returning with us. I have the remedy here, with me. My ladies must each drink half of the elixir contained in the vial that is secured within that bag. It will take immediate effect and at last not even a trace of the filthy witch—Teritee, will remain to stain the pure spirits of our own. Also, my lord, I believe it is starting to rain, we will all have pneumonia by tomorrow, I'm sure of it."

Before Tamarin had finished thanking the winged brothers for returning with the cure, an enormous bolt of lightening crashed into the palace roof, blasting open a gaping hole. Then a thunderous downpour began, the heavens tore apart without warning and sheets of water began drenching the desert. No one had noticed the dark clouds drifting in so quickly from the east and settling directly over the city. Everyone became soaked in the sudden deluge, but Tamarin pointed up to the palace with a big wet grin on his boyish face. The water was streaming in through the ruptured roof. Lightening flashed across the sky—lighting up the city sporadically. "The roof will flood, then," he cheered happily, "the water will move from floor to floor, soaking the walls and killing the fires. The seat of The Throne shall not expire this night." He winked at Meekhi, who began jumping up and down—clapping her hands in glee as she shook her head from side-to-side like crazy. Zowie looked at Mercy incredulously, who simply told her, "Don't worry, she does that."

The elixir, made from the essence of Lozzwozz and Wartywart, was carefully measured into two goblets and the women drained them quickly. Faradorr, having already taken his medicine, pulled a strange horsy face and told them, "My ladies, I envy you not."

Meekhi and Mercy then made faces even stranger than Faradorr's, but managed to keep the medicinal brew down. Rordorr told Tamarin, "Rosameer had heard the call to arms from Sitivia, my lord. Lord Vansivar and the garrison from Rosameer were already headed here when we arrived in the city. Babel prepared the cure and we passed Vansivar and his troops on our return."

Tamarin thought for a second before responding, "My friend, I must again ask of your service, for you and your brother are fleetest amongst us. Vansivar must be told to divert to Soledad. It is my intention to challenge Ogiin's rising tide from that ancient city. It was built with such needs in mind. Her walls tower above those of Sitivia. Will you and your brother do me this service?"

The brothers bowed their heads in assent and Tamarin ordered food and water for them so that they may be fully nourished before they again took to the lonely skies. In fact everyone decided to take advantage of the opportunity to grab a quick, but hearty, meal. Sitivia offered up every type of food and beverage. The children gorged on Samarian fruits, the likes of which they had never seen before. Thomas tried some venison and herb soup and said it was to die for. Many of the dishes were quite spicy, but as both the Kantells and the Shortwaters loved nothing more than a spicy Indian Chicken Madras Curry with rice and a nan bread, this posed no problem at all for them.

The rain was still pouring down by the bucketful when they mounted up. They watched the flying horses disappear up and away into the night sky, melting into the murky blackness in minutes. Solipop sat behind Meekhi, (who had become very impressed by the brave little elf), and Babel sat with Zowie. Soaked to the skin, they turned once more towards Soledad.

Tamarin knew his people must get some sleep soon. They were all on the very brink of collapse through exhaustion. He cast a loving eye over Meekhi as she battled stoically against the hammering rain with her cloak wrapped tight about her. He looked at his posse of riders with deep admiration—the valiant guardsmen conversing with the inimitable Imo through the rain—laughing at soldier's jokes as if sharing a jar at a market stall, the brave young ones that had stood so defiantly in the name of Samaria against Ogiin's creed, Mercy—parted from her beloved Ramulet, her quick thinking having saved their lives in the great hall, Bestwin and Lumarr—like two great bears weary from battle, and, finally, the furry blue elves—a small, wise, innocent breed, that had known only peace until they had entered the world of man, and had since saved both himself and Meekhi—king and queen of the realm. Surely, no matter what Ogiin may yet summon to his perverse cause, a people such as this would not pass so easily into oblivion?

CHAPTER SEVENTEEN

A SUMMONS IN THE SKY

It had been the longest journey of their lives. Stopping briefly only once, for water, their party was finally in sight of The Silent City. Only Soledad was now far from silent. The people of Sitivia could be seen working everywhere and the place was a flurry of activity as they prepared the old capital for a new war against old enemies. The riders sat sagging in their saddles, utterly fatigued, staring at the city looming ahead of them. The horses were worn and ragged, their entire bodies sleek with sweat. The children were practically falling asleep in their seats. Only the elves seemed wide awake and alert. The blistering desert heat and baking sands had taken a serious toll on the entire company. Reddened bleary eyes stared unfocused from under sand-encrusted lids. Bone dry lips had cracked painfully and not a single face was recognisable due to the layer of desert dirt caked upon it. Even the hardy Westonians were on the verge of collapse. Meekhi tried to focus clearly on Soledad. "Oh, to suffer this now—if only it were true," she panted, "this mirage offends me most sorely. Does not The Silent City look as if it has regained some of its former glory and colour? This is truly a cruel trick of this infernal heat."

The aching riders squinted at the city, feeling as the queen felt. Babel diffused their displeasure, "My lady, this is no illusion. The Silent City appears to be awakening from its long, and untimely, slumber."

The horses could not be made to gallop any further as this would almost certainly kill them. The depleted animals trudged on doggedly as their riders slowly absorbed the changes that had occurred to The Silent City. The wall had regained some of its former brilliant—white colour, if only in patches. It looked odd, with the white pock marking the black like the markings on a Dalmatian dog. The towering dome of the great hall was entirely its original gleaming golden self, and a tired and dreary grey flag bearing the remnants of a silver dragon hung limply from a mast at its centre, but still it sat atop walls of black stone. Riders were spotted riding hard towards Tamarin's party. They were led by Ramulet and carried water for humans and horses alike. On arrival, he and his men happily poured water over the heads and faces of their grimy comrades, overjoyed at their safe return. The dry, gritty dirt, clinging to their skin, became as mud, and had to be rinsed off a second time. Tamarin told him of what had transpired in Sitivia, and as Ramulet gently wiped at Mercy's face with a damp cloth, revealing her true self once more, he told of what had been happening in Soledad. The curse of stone was broken at last! This was, no doubt, due to the slaying of the demon that had dwelled for so long in the depths of Solenia, anchoring Ogiin's cruel curse to the city. All over Soledad colour was returning to everything, albeit very slowly. Her native citizens, too, were recovering from their stony state, and some even had a flush returning to their cheeks. But none had as yet recovered fully, and the transformation from cold stone to living flesh-and-bone was going to take a long time. Ramulet warned him that the semi-stone state of the people of Soledad may prove too much for the young ones, but Tamarin said that after the testing of their mettle on the subterranean shores of Solenia, and the recent battle in Sitivia—the young ones were not easily daunted.

Ramulet led the bedraggled riders from Sitivia into Soledad. The towering gates, that had appeared so sombre in black stone, were now almost completely silver, and the dragons embossed upon them stood proud in stark relief. The new arrivals could not believe the speed with which the city was metamorphosing into its former glorious self. Colour and life were creeping into everything. The statues, though still motionless, had a definite air of the living about them, and those terrible pleas for release had been banished to sad memory. Now, Soledad felt so much more like a beautiful thriving city, rather than an old, and haunted, crypt.

After making a brief inspection of Ramulet's preparations, Tamarin told him, "Ramulet, my riders and I must sleep. We have not done so for days and are far from being at our best. I will tell the others to take full rest and will steal a few short hours for myself. Keep up your good work, but seal Solenia, my friend, we know not if anything else of Ogiin's making, or other ill will, lurks there still. Please see to it that someone of compassion tends to these horses, they have served us faithfully and are close to collapse, none of them must see further service in these trying times. I suspect one or two of them may not survive the night as it is. Tell the sentries that Lord Vansivar rides even now to Soledad with the garrison of Rosameer. He is to be admitted immediately and I am to be made aware of his approach the second he is seen. Also warn our archers to beware, Rordorr and Faradorr will most surely arrive before Vansivar, I do not want them shot out of the sky. I shall rejoin you soon."

Dog tired, his thoughts becoming random and disjointed from fatigue, Tamarin joined Meekhi and the others. The children were taken to a room where, almost instantly, they fell asleep on large svelte couch's that were covered in big, luxuriously soft, cushions. The Westonians were lost to a deep, well-earned, slumber, in a room next door to the children, whilst Tamarin and Meekhi dozed in each others arms in a chamber close to the main barracks. They wanted to be certain to hear any sounding of the alarm. Mercy was so tired she could barely keep her eyes open and even walking was an unbalanced and erratic act. Her ankle still pained her annoyingly and she found herself a small room, easing oh-so-gratefully back onto a couch. She was asleep before she had fully laid down and was unaware of Ramulet entering the room an hour later when she was deep in sleep, and with the aid of Babel, removing her boots, bathing her sore feet, and wrapping a bandage of Babel's making around her ankle. The bandage contained another of the she-elf's concoctions that would heal the ankle by the time she awoke. Ramulet had kissed Mercy ever-so-lightly on the lips and left as quietly as he had arrived, closing the door silently behind him. Imo dozed up high on the city wall, dreaming of maidens and mead whilst his comrades patrolled its length.

Soledad had been bathing in the sweltering heat all day, and now the cool of the night coaxed her into releasing some of the warmth she had absorbed from the suns. The air in the streets was dry and slack. The heat and lack of humidity forced a languorous stupor upon the cities newfound inhabitants who were more accustomed to a constant sea breeze. But not so the Royal Guards, each and every one of them on sentry duty remained as sharp as any triblade. There was very little conversation so as to be sure to detect the slightest sound. These soldiers—personally trained by their king and their captain, were well versed in their art. Some closed their eyes so as to familiarise themselves intimately with the sounds of the night, thus sensing instantaneously if something changed, or went amiss. Occasionally a horse whinnied in the stables below, perhaps feeling the impending danger, or the approach of some dark evil.

Ramulet had spotted it himself only a split second before, when an eagle-eyed sentry had sounded the alarm, "RIDERS! To the south, two columns!"

The captain peered, with some difficulty, through a thin, long telescope. The night was not keen to reveal all that was hidden within the folds of her mantle and he had to strain his eyes. Imo had jumped up the second the sentry had called out the alarm and he too was looking desperately through a similar scope, searching the dark, trying to catch any glimpse of movement. Ramulet called to him with urgent orders; "Go and make ready the main gate, but do not open until I give the command. I see banners flying the dragon, but this could be a ruse. However, I believe this to be Lord Vansivar and his garrison from Rosameer."

"Shouldn't we inform the king, as he requested?" asked Imo.

"Tamarin, good Imo," Ramulet whispered in a secretive tone, "is more weary than he will say, and even a king such as he must sleep eventually. I say we let him rest until he is forced to rise. We can receive and refresh Vansivar without need of the king. Indeed,

Imo, you, too, should be sleeping. The time of sleepless nights aplenty fast approaches, let us not welcome them too soon."

Imo smiled, "Captain, gratitude for your concerns, but I am well rested. The shortest sleep for the shortest guardsmen, eh. I will make ready the gates and await your command."

Archers stood poised and ready along the battlements as the city was unexpectedly roused by the sudden activity. The riders that Tamarin had led to Soledad continued to sleep soundly, lost to the deepest depths of sleep that only utter exhaustion can bring.

Ramulet had his eyes firmly fixed on the two columns heading directly for the city. They were closing fast and he was sure he could recognise the shape of Lord Vansivar leading his horsemen across the sands. Vansivar was reasonably easy to recognise in the dark, even at this distance. He was far taller than most and wore his hair in two plaits, very close together, running straight down his back. He rode a black and white horse of incredible size, an animal perfectly matched to his own imposing stature. Vansivar was cousin to Tamarin, and a loyal, devoted subject. Longer than Ramulet could remember, Vansivar had held Rosameer by order of the king. He had held the fortress city honestly, justly, and was a welcome sight to the men in Soledad. The blurry image of him and the garrison of Rosameer continued to expand in Ramulet's telescope.

A furious beating of gigantic wings startled the captain and he looked up to see Rordorr and Faradorr hovering over him. Faradorr called down to him, "The market square below! Make haste Ramulet, and bring the king!"

Ramulet virtually dived off the wall, his cloak streaming up behind him like a reluctant parachute. He charged past Imo, shouting, "Tamarin, to the square, NOW!"

The horses circled elegantly and landed in the square, their hooves slamming into the stone paving and causing a loud clattering that startled many of the sentries, making them stare down at the commotion below. The brothers looked a misery—barely able to breath, and shivering with over exertion. Faradorr hardly raised his head when he warned Ramulet, "Hellhounds...ridden by Venomeens...cutting off Vansivar."

Rordorr forced himself to clear his throat and explained further, "Perhaps twelve of the beasts, probably spying ahead for Ogiin... will hit our riders in the flank. Vansivar is unaware. We saw them from above. We..."

The wounded horse collapsed onto his haunches with his scarlet wings splayed to either side just as Tamarin arrived. He and Ramulet could see the two grey arrow shafts protruding from Rordorr's left flank. Imo had followed the king to the square, and now Tamarin turned to him, his urgency apparent, "Imo, fetch Corsellius, Arcadian, and Babel. No winged brother of mine shall pass from us this night. Ramulet, gather up one hundred horsemen. No more than this number. I will lead them to the aid of Vansivar, and you will remain here, to hold Soledad secure."

"I think not," came Meekhi's voice as she approached them, "Ramulet and I are far better rested than you, my lord. We shall take the troop to aid our comrades. *Tamarin*, we cannot risk The King in a minor, petty, skirmish such as this. Soledad needs you here. Your people, *our* people, need you here. Who else will lead against the full force of Ogiin's evil creed? Nay, my lord, this small duty falls to the queen and her guardsmen."

"To her friends, too," Mercy added, as she stumbled up to them still lacing up her boots.

"Very well." agreed Tamarin reluctantly, hating the fact that Meekhi was right, "so be it." He knew Meekhi's words held the ring of truth and it was his duty to protect Samaria first, all else came after.

Corsellius and the others arrived at the square in minutes and began to tend to Rordorr's wounds. His brother, they soon discovered, also had an arrow embedded deep in his flesh. The Venomeens riding atop the hellhounds had seen the horses before the horses had seen them, some climbing up into the branches of tall trees and hiding there, to then fire their deadly shafts at the two brothers as they passed overhead. Babel and Corsellius tended to the grievously injured horses together, combining their individual skills for best effect. Arcadian left to prepare a shelter for further casualties, for surely they would come. One hundred strong, a troop of the Royal Guards was forming up along the main route out of the city. Ramulet, Meekhi, and Mercy, sat three abreast at the head of the ever lengthening column. Cold stone statues watched on helplessly as the curse of Ogiin thawed far too slowly.

The children, finally roused from their deep slumber by so much raucous activity and shouting, had joined Tamarin up on the ramparts, looking out over the battlements for the approaching riders. Telescopes were no longer necessary to see what was happening in the middle distance. The hellhounds raised an enormous cloud of dust as their gigantic paws thudded along on the sand. Vansivar and his riders had, at last, seen the threat to their flank, turning quickly to face it head on. The Samarians from Rosameer had formed a line in the form of a crescent as they rode, swords drawn, towards the closing hounds, there was no point in trying to break for the city, they would be easily cut off. Tamarin was saddened upon seeing that the distant soldiers had not a single primed Wrath of Amaris at the ready. A handful of them carried the devastating weapon aboard their steeds but were not aware of the true nature of the hellhounds, or their vulnerability to the dragon-tipped spears. He called down to Meekhi from high on the wall, "My lady! The Wrath will prove difficult to deploy whilst you are in motion. Endeavour to lure those devil dogs to within range of the city! Take care to mind yourself and return to me unharmed."

Meekhi waved a gauntlet-clad hand at her husband to reassure him and made ready to burst from the city and tear into the ranks of the enemy.

The children looked down at the long line of silver dragons waiting to join battle, bold and rampant on black. The mighty warhorses, large powerful chargers, were impatient, stamping their hooves in frustration, chomping at the bit, sensing battle in the air and eager to do that which they had been trained to do since they were but suckling foals. Swords and shields flashed intermittently in the starlight giving the assembled warriors a bejewelled appearance, as if about to ride out on parade in peacetime.

The soldiers from Rosameer began gathering pace and were soon hurtling headlong towards the hellhounds at breakneck speed. Tamarin could hear the thundering of their hooves, even the deep baritone of Vansivar roaring above the din. "Use your shields to good effect, men! One bite from those jaws will prove fatal! Aim to kill the riders aboard them, in the name of the king, attack!"

Many of the horsemen were firing from the saddle as they closed with the approaching pack. The Venomeens hid themselves well, protected behind crude but effective shields. The arrows proved useless against the immense beasts being ridden by the Venomeens. Tamarin was about to open the city gates and release the rescue column, when Thomas told him, "You, need a Firewall, Tamarin. Those bloody huge dogs are dangerous enough I know, sodding great things scared the crap oughta me in Sitivia, but I doubt they're very smart. I think a firewall would stop them, stop them dead!"

Tamarin had little time to talk, yet he knew these young warriors were versed in a knowledge beyond his own ken so he forced himself to listen with forced patience; "A wall of fire, Thomas? How do we create this, out there in the desert? We know that fire can kill those monsters. But time is short. Quickly, my friend, tell me your plan."

Thomas took a deep breath, his heart beating like a trip hammer.

"It's not a wall of fire. It is a *'Firewall'*. The British army used it with great effect in Africa. I saw it in the film—'Zulu'. British Army—best army in the world by the way, Tamarin. Anyway, outnumbered by thousands, they took down wave after wave of Zulu warriors. Ask Meekhi to get those hellhounds to chase them back to the city. Leave the gates *open*. Please trust me, we *can* do this!"

Tamarin quickly ran his eyes over the children, scrutinising them for an instant before deciding to risk it, at least Meekhi would return to the city sooner this way, and then he would see the effectiveness of Thomas' plan. The girls knew Thomas well enough to know he would not offer such a thing if he did not think it would work.

Tamarin called down to Meekhi, "My lady, we have a new stratagem, lure Ogiin's creed back, and *into* the city!"

She and Ramulet looked far from convinced but nodded their understanding of his wishes.

Lumarr and Bestwin had awoken only very recently. They were, perhaps, the most weary having travelled the greater journey over the longest period. Ignoring the fatigue weighing on their limbs like bags of sand, they tagged themselves onto the tail of the waiting column. Samaria was not only fighting for her own survival and way of life, she was also the last remaining hope for the resurrection of the Western Worlds. The Westonians felt the very least they could offer Tamarin was their swords for the protection of his beloved Meekhi. They drew their shockingly huge scimitars and sat in silence, ready to do what fate bade them.

Thomas raced up to the gates, bawling; "We will need twenty five Wraths and fifty men, two men per bow to load and reload quickly, plenty of space, with everyone facing the gates, lots of ammunition for the Wraths, and strict discipline—British Army style!"

Tamarin relayed Thomas' commands to the soldiers wondering to himself, "Why on earth he had repeated the words—'British Army style'." Then he told Imo, "Open the gates! Release the column!"

Fireworks, normally used as part of the festivities on grand occasions, were launched up into the sky, illuminating the area beyond the city with a yellowish white glow. They hissed loudly into the darkness and crackled noisily as they fell back to earth. Meekhi's column broke from the city just as Vansivar and his men clashed with Ogiin's creed. Samarians fell heavily as the weighty black hounds ploughed through their charging ranks as if they were never there. The sheer height of them made it near impossible for the horse mounted Samarians to bring their swords into play against the Venomeens that clucked and spat at them from above. The horses, fully spent from their long, fast paced journey from Rosameer, had little hope of out manoeuvring the twisting, snarling hounds, and many a vicelike jaw managed to gain a death grip on the tired animals, throwing the riders violently from their saddles. The dark of the night seemed to favour those of its own hue, their dark fur blending into her and making them more difficult to see. They tore the tired horses apart with great relish, gulping down flesh and bone in huge, bloody, chunks. Vansivar's men were, unsurprisingly, too weary to fight at their best—such a long time at the mercy of the hostile desert had sapped too much vital energy. This could so easily become a bloody massacre for the men of Rosameer.

Ramulet barked commands at his elite guardsmen as they neared the battle raging furiously before them. He gave his orders clearly and precisely; "Do not engage those hounds in close combat, use your bows against the riders, kill the Venomeen scum, it is *they* that drive these goliaths against us. Shoot, and move, *shoot*, and *move*!

He began to arrange his men into such a position so as to run circles around the battle and attempt to pick off the Venomeens. The men fighting for their lives within that ring cheered as they saw the guardsmen arriving to their aid. Mercy had already let loose three silver shafts, all of which had found their marks. The Venomeens didn't fail to notice Samarian women arriving on the scene, their eyes and noses drawn to Ogiin's sweetest, and most desired, morsel.

Meekhi and Ramulet called out to the riders from Rosameer, "Men of Vansivar! Make for Soledad—her gates are open to greet you. Make for Soledad. Break for the city, by command of the king!"

To extricate oneself from such an intense battle is a difficult task and none of the men fighting off the hellhounds wished to leave the fray until Vansivar had done so. Lumarr and Bestwin battled their way through the pandemonium, hacking at the hellhounds mercilessly until they were alongside of him, urging him to withdraw immediately and make for Soledad. The giant of a man finally grasped their meaning over the din of steel-on-steel and the cries of the wounded, bellowing back his acknowledgment of their repeated requests.

Thomas was very busy. He had arranged 'his' men in five rows, five pairs in each. They faced the open gates, leaving enough space for riders to pass on either side. He had instructed them as to how his plan would work and Tamarin had given his consent for Thomas to direct this 'Firewall' of his own making. The girls were nervous and tense, Lauren gnawing at a thumb nail. They knew how much depended on Thomas getting this right.

Vansivar threw a long thin dagger with amazing accuracy and it pierced its intended target through the chest, the Venomeen crashing to the ground from its perch and being trampled in the melee. Then the Lord of Rosameer broke left and charged from the madness at the centre of the battle, towards Soledad. Now his men felt freed of their duty to protect him and were able to follow Meekhi's commands without reservation. They began to disentangle themselves from the fighting and head for the city. But their horses were so worn beyond their limits and the men of Rosameer paid a heavy toll. Venomeen arrows found their backs too easily as their waning mounts staggered slowly away. Once their own men were no longer in their sights, the Royal Guards brought a hellstorm of fire down onto the red-eyed Venomeens, many of their number falling screaming to the sands when the silver shafts drilled into their saggy flesh. The hellhounds almost resembled giant porcupines—so many arrows protruded from their thick hides. Meekhi rode in close to them knowing that the Venomeens would pick up on her scent and pursue her. It was a bold and brave gamble by the queen.

The archers on the wall sat ready, their Wraths primed with burning spears. Below, Thomas and his 'Firewall' waited with baited breath. Tamarin watched as the riders began streaking towards the city, the hairs on the back of his neck standing up as the hellhounds began to scream their ungodly screams, enraged at their feast escaping them. Lauren was on the wall with a taut string and a full quiver whilst Zowie remained below at the gates, Yasmina's unique blade gripped firmly in her hand.

Vansivar was fast approaching, and the guardsmen were shouting directions from the heights above, "Break right!" Or, "Break left!"

He and his men began pouring into the city, breaking left and right as instructed to avoid colliding with Thomas' 'Firewall'. Finally, Meekhi's relief column also began to charge hard for the city, and their horses being fresh, they lost no time in escaping the snarling fury of the snapping fangs pursuing them.

Lauren and the bowmen, rained steel-tipped death onto the Venomeens below and yet more fell to their deaths, or died when the following hellhounds crushed them into the sand, causing their flaccid white bodies to burst open, their blood leaving dark ugly stains on the golden sands. The Samarians were still sending up illuminating flares and the carnage left after the battle could be seen in their glow. The broken bodies of men, beasts, and vermin, lay strewn everywhere. Bestwin and Lumarr brought up the rear of the pre-planned retreat, ensuring every surviving rider was safe with Soledad's embrace before they too followed suit.

Horses raced down the street, passing Thomas on either side, the sound of their hammering hooves almost deafening. A score of hellhounds, some with Venomeens still clinging desperately onto their backs, were headed straight for the doorway to the city. Such a great number was a daunting sight, the hoard pounding on relentlessly in a flurry of fur and fangs. The ground shook under their massed weight and even the mighty wall of Soledad trembled at their approach. Tamarin and Imo manned the battlements, one each side of the gate. Zowie still remained below with Thomas. He had never felt more nervous in his life. If he failed with his 'Firewall,' hellhounds would be free to tear the city apart from within. Many lives depended on his success this night, including his own.

Dozens of blazing spears sailed into the night from the city and a handful of hellhounds shrieked out their nightmarish screams before smashing heavily into the desert sands. Any Venomeens trying to escape the weight of their dead bulk were picked off by marksmen from the cities defences. But still too many of Ogiin's mindless monsters were hurtling headlong towards the city. Imo and Tamarin directed a withering hail of fire at these, but they were too close, and too fast, now for accurate targeting. Zowie was standing firm right next to Thomas. She told him in a very matter-of-fact voice; "I think this might *really* hurt if you get it wrong, so get it *right*, please, Tom."

He did not reply, he was focused on the thunderball of claws, fur, and fangs hurtling towards him. His 'Firewall' stood steadfast in their ranks, ready for his command. Finally, he got the opportunity to do what he had always wanted to do since watching the film 'Zulu'. He barked at the 'Firewall'; "FIRST RANK! FIRE!" A deadly volley of spears, tipped with snarling silver dragons, ripped into the front runners amongst the hellhounds. When the first row of the 'Firewall' knelt to reload, Thomas shouted; "SECOND RANK, FIRE!"

Again, a stream of spears tore into the oncoming wall of death. Hellhounds screamed horribly as he ordered row-after-row of bowmen to fire and reload in turn. By the time the last row had fired, the first row was again ready to loose its reloaded Wraths. But there was no need for further volleys. Some still panting, but mostly dead, black, bloodied bodies littered the gateway to the city. One Venomeen managed to avoid the torrent of arrows and spears and sneaked into the city, creeping along the inner wall. Zowie spotted it, racing around the bowmen to confront the sole invader. She caught it unawares, her blade flashed, and it stared in disbelief at its own disembowelling. The sword swept back, and up, parting head from body. It did not take another step. Guardsmen rushed out to finish off any beast still breathing, and a large cheer went up from the troops for Thomas and his 'Firewall'.

Tamarin jumped down from his elevated position and shook Thomas vigorously by the arm, "By The Dragon," He told him, "what a brilliant idea. You are a captain in the making, my friend. This British Army must truly be a marvel to observe in battle. Perhaps, one day, I will have the honour of meeting its commander?"

Thomas could not really speak for the British Army, so he thought it better to waffle, "I doubt it, Tamarin. They are very different to Samarian armies and swear their allegiance to our queen. They use Jaguars, Tornadoes, and Euro-fighters from the RAF, Harriers from the Royal Navy, Commandoes from the Royal Marines, war ships, and..."

"Amazing," Tamarin interjected, genuinely impressed, "to harness the power of the wind, birds of prey, and that of nature's big cats, to do battle on your behalf. We will talk again of this British Army and its alliance with the elements. But now we must prepare our own forces."

Thomas was grateful to be let off the hook. He had realised as soon as he mentioned Tornadoes he was just digging himself a big hole, but he just couldn't stop himself from carrying on with his babbling. Zowie winked at him as Lauren joined them and gave her brother a huge hug. "Brilliant, Tom, just brilliant. I won't ever complain when you watch those films again, promise."

"Thanks, sis'," he beamed, "all I can say is—Michael Caine, *eat your heart out!*"

The corpses of the hellhounds were liberally doused with pitch and set ablaze. Ramulet did not want them used as gigantic stepping stones by the enemy when trying to climb the wall. The gates were closed and secured. Fresh sentries took over the watch all along the defences, and food and water was served to all.

Rordorr and Faradorr had been taken into the great hall and slept, courtesy of a special potion prepared by the wise old Corsellius. Babel watched over them and Corsellius went to inform Tamarin that the injuries suffered by the two brothers were very serious. Faradorr would recover in time if kept rested and cared for. With Rordorr the situation was far graver as yet another arrow they had not noticed initially, had penetrated one of his lungs. Everyone was doing all that could be done for the winged brothers. Their futures lay in the unpredictable, and often thorny, hands of fate. Meekhi, Mercy, and the children came to look in on the horses. Tamarin remained with his men. He was as concerned about Rordorr and Faradorr as anyone else, but he had to be sure that the city was fully prepared for what was now inevitable.

Vansivar had also been hit by Venomeen arrows, continueing to fight despite numerous wounds. Tamarin was at his elder cousin's side when he died holding his hand. The Lord of Rosameer had not once shown regret for playing his part and had stated he was ready to join with the Great Dragon. He had even smiled as he parted, as if surprised to be greeting an old friend. Tamarin bit his lip, yet again bottling his ever-swelling torrent of emotions. But the furious anger and deep sorrow in his face could not easily find cover. His inner fury was plain to see as he clenched and unclenched his fists. They had lost too many of the garrison from Rosameer. Perhaps only four score had survived the attack to remain fighting fit. Another two dozen had terrible injuries and could not participate in any forthcoming actions against Ogiin. Ogiin—oh how that very name caused him to grip his sword. "But," he thought, "the hour of reckoning will come, that devil has tasted the bitter pill of defeat before, and this time nothing will suffice short of his head on a pike."

He was at least comforted by the information Imo had brought from the Western Worlds. Ogiin was feeding on his own followers to empower himself, thus reducing the size of any army he might gather unto him. "I hope," thought Tamarin, "that, for now, he maintains a ravenous appetite."

The former citizens of Sitivia grieved upon seeing so many funeral pyres burning outside the walls of Soledad. The sacred flame situated at the base of the dragon's tail in the great hall was lit to commemorate the loss of those brave warriors, having given their lives so readily even before they had reached their goal. Their sacrifice, their selfless heroism, meant surviving comrades would fare better against reduced odds in the battles yet to come. Such was the Samarian mentality—duty, even unto death.

The remainder of the contingent from Rosameer was a small but welcome addition to the cities defences. They were bold, capable, soldiers, but it was a simple honest fact that the regular garrison of Rosameer was not of the same calibre as the Royal Guards of

Sitivia. The news that no allied army would be forthcoming from the Western Worlds was a serious cause for concern for the soon-to-be outnumbered defenders of Soledad. Although many individuals had ridden from various foreign lands to answer the call of Samaria, they numbered but a few hundred in total. In history past, Samaria had fought alongside not only the Westonians and other nations against Ogiin's creed, but also she had had the inestimable might of The Dragons of Light fighting beside her. Now, she stood alone in the dark against whatever new nightmares were approaching. Her people braced themselves for battle, but knew not what they faced. Ogiin must surely have some new card to play, a hand of death as yet unseen, a deciding black ace secreted within the folds of his sleeve.

The rest of the night passed without drama, and at last the completely drained Samarians had rested well by the time the suns reluctantly re-entered a world on the brink of war. A simple breakfast of cold gammon, fresh goat's milk, and bread, was eaten by all, with Thomas commenting that the gammon was so good that Samaria should consider exporting to 'Marks & Spencer'. The soft warming caress of sunrays managed to lift everyone's spirit's a fraction after the horrific losses of the previous night. It is far easier to fear the darkness when you are surrounded by it, less so in the revealing light of day. However, they remained acutely aware that as surely as the day had arrived, the night would most certainly follow. Meekhi prepared a rich creamy mash for the horses in the great hall. She, and Mercy, accompanied by the girls, went to spoon feed their poorly friends. Thomas remained with Tamarin as there was to be a counsel of war, and he wouldn't want to miss *that*.

Already the desert was shimmering under a haze of heat. Visibility was good, if a little distorted. Anything on the horizon would be spotted immediately in the blazing light, and this gave the defenders some little consolation. The counsel was held in the former Throne Room. Solitary stone statues stood either side of the pair of thrones, former guardsmen that had kept vigil over the sanctity of that chamber until they had, in an instant, become black stone. Now they seemed somehow undignified in their appearance as colour returned to them in little patches everywhere, causing them to look like badly worn painted dolls. Tamarin could not help wishing for the ancient guards of Soledad to awaken more quickly, lending their venerable blades to the task in hand. The Throne Room was a spacious affair, with high ceilings and large windows, all of which were thrown open to try and ease the stifling heat. Ramulet had already informed him that the former heartbreaking cries of The Silent City had not been heard since he had slain the creature from the lake and Tamarin was immeasurably grateful for this. The days ahead would exact a heavy toll on his people and he did not want those very people tormented by their own ancestors as they fought for their existence, and, maybe, for the existence of all people.

Imo had arrived a few minutes late for the counsel as he had been searching for King Dorinn, a brief search by himself and a handful of men had drawn a blank. Either Dorinn was in hiding, or he had escaped the city during the distraction of last night's fighting. Tamarin could not spare anyone to hunt for him, "Dorinn is currently of no consequence to us. We will deal with that debaucherous dog after we have dealt with Ogiin. Ogiin's creed employed a vessel to reach their master at sea, and this tells us that that devil cannot use the skies as he once did in history old. Legend tells us—the Great Dragon didst blast the wings from that creature's back. Thus, if Ogiin will come in person to Soledad, he will have to come mounted on horseback. I cannot imagine one as cruel as he crossing the sands without causing suffering to another. Lest any of you have any illusions...uh... *where are Lord's Bestwin and Lumarr??* Should they not be with us now at so vital a gathering?"

He was the first to notice the absence of the Westonians from the counsel. Everyone looked around, as if by doing so they could conjure up the Westonians out of thin air. Tamarin gestured at Imo with a well recognised nod, and he left the counsel immediately to find the missing lords. Tamarin turned his attention back to the warriors seated before him, "As I was saying—lest anyone here has any illusions, we are truly on the back foot. We know not the size of our enemy, nor the method by which he intends to attempt to overwhelm us. Whatever his design, we will overcome. We MUST overcome. Look not to the victories of old, for, glorious that they were, they were not accomplished alone. Today we stand alone. But we stand united in honour of our faith, of ourselves, and our homeland. Make ready now for what will be the deciding moment of your lives! Ramulet, you and…"

Imo came crashing back into the Throne Room, "The sentries saw them leave the city on horseback at a breakneck pace, in the early hours."

The War Counsel looked at each other quizzically, puzzled by the Westonians leaving at such a crucial time. A debate began as to where they had gone just as Meekhi, Mercy, and the girls returned, and they joined in.

"I know," suggested Zowie, "they have gone in search of that fat bloater—Dorinn. If he has done a bunk, they will have noticed him missing before anyone else. I'm sure they've been keeping tabs on him, because they wanted to punch his lights out as soon as possible."

Mercy agreed, "Zowie has answered the riddle. This is of course where they have gone. But what is a bunk, and what are tabs? Pray tel, what lights does that pig—Dorinn, carry, that the Westonian lords wish to extinguish with such violent force?"

With a faint smile on his face, Tamarin interjected; "My lady, the young ones' tongue is far removed from our own. We cannot take literally all they say. I have learned this much, and still have much to learn. But yes, Zowie has solved the question of their purpose. The Westonians are free men and may do as they wish. Dorinn's dastardly deeds are to the detriment of his nation and he will have his come-uppance in due course, such is the balanced nature of The Source. *We*, meanwhile, *must prepare for war*."

Lauren whispered in Zowie's ear, "Flippin' heck! *Dorinn's dastardly deeds*, that was worse than 'Susan sells shells on the seashore!' Bet he couldn't say that after a few glasses of that wine, eh!"

"Probably not," Zowie laughed, "Maybe you should try him with—'the sixth sheik's sixth sheep's sick'."

Not to be outdone, Thomas joined in. "Keep it simple—try repeating 'red lorry, yellow lorry,' quickly."

Noticing Tamarin looking at them curiously, they decided to shut up.

An hour later the counsel was over. Every citizen of Sitivia donned battledress and a red cloak not bearing the mark of the silver dragon, that cherished crest being unique to the Royal Guards, an honour not so easily gained. The only thing a guardsman may possibly covet over his own black mantle would be the silver dragon emblazoned on a rich dark *blue* cloak, marking him out as a Ranin Knight.

Not for so very long a time had Soledad seen such activity, soldiers running up, down, and along her perimeter. Massive cauldrons of pitch being kept at near-boiling point, the sound of clattering hooves, as creaking carts laden high with supplies and weapons moved in organised chaos throughout the streets. In the background, the metallic grating of grinding wheels edging sword blades was a constant reminder of the reason for all the preparations. The weathered old flags of Soledad had become dull and frayed over the ages, and new ones were hoisted up with pride. Gleaming dragons once more looked out over the city from her tallest buildings. The Samarians worked with supreme efficiency and the cities defences were bolstered up rapidly. By midday, Tamarin, with a small group in tow, took a short break to visit the flying horses and have a bite to eat, themselves. Rordorr still slept, he was running a dangerously high fever, shivering and sweating where he lay. Babel was doing all that was within her power for him. Faradorr was awake, but in much pain. He acknowledged the arrival of the king with a weak nod of his head, but then fell once more into a troubled half-sleep. Tamarin approached them and placed his hands upon their heads. "You will awaken to a bolder, brighter, Samaria, my brothers. A Samaria you will have helped to shape. May the Great Dragon soothe you in your dreams, and assist you in your great awakening."

Zowie felt sure she saw him wipe a solitary tear from his eye as he took a seat, the others joining him and seating themselves on the cold floor. Men brought food, it was hastily prepared but delicious all the same, and everyone tucked in. They were ravenous after that hectic morning and not even their sadness at the sight of the dozing horses could dampen their appetites. Lauren and Thomas sat together talking amongst themselves and Tamarin and Meekhi did the same. Ramulet was somewhere in the city, forever organising and reorganising his men. Mercy finished her meal and downed a half-jar of wine just as Zowie put her last piece of bread and cheese in her mouth. Mercy winked at her. "Come, let me show you something."

The pair walked over to the end of the dragon's tail. "There," Mercy asked her, pointing, "Do you see the diamond-shaped tip of the dragon's tail? Right there next to the sacred flame? In an age now gone by, ceremonial balls of spectacular design were held here in Soledad. On very special occasions, the Dragons of Light would attend, in person. The Great Dragon, Himself, would breathe fire onto the tip of that tail, igniting the signal—summoning the Ranin back to Samaria from neighbouring lands to celebrate with their brethren. Those close enough to heed the call would return as fast as their mounts could carry them, and, trust me Zowie, a Ranin's steed cannot be matched for pace. They often attended the largest festivals and it was a truly glorious time, you would have loved the parties."

Zowie replied hesitantly, "Errr, I can't see any black diamond-shaped tip, sorry."

"Yes, it's quite dark down there," Mercy agreed, "let me get a torch so you can see more clearly."

The flaxen haired warrior took an unlit torch from the wall. Each torch had a flint fixed near the bowl so one only had to strike a blade against it to spark a flame into life. Mercy used her dagger repeatedly, but no spark issued from the old flint. She was about to try another when Tamarin took the torch and offered to help. He held up 'The Flame of Dragonia', and Mercy asked, "Is that quite big enough to strike a spark!?!"

They were all completely surprised when they saw the sword burst into blazing life as he brought the blade down onto the flint. It sliced cleanly through it, then the wooden handle too, the fiery blade striking the black tip of which Mercy had spoken. The end of the stone dragon's tail glowed momentarily with the white-hot heat from 'The Flame of Dragonia'.

"I can certainly see the black tip now." Zowie laughed cheekily.

But the black stone began to glow deep inside, as if a flame of its own burned within it.

"By The Dragon!" exclaimed Tamarin, "I fear I have mistakenly lit the ancient signal. I did not believe the age old tinder would still burn."

Sure enough, a dull orange glow could be seen travelling up within the tail, along the dragon's body, headed straight towards the head. They stood staring up at the ceiling, opened to the skies by Ramulet when they were in Soledad last. The head lit up glowing a bright red crimson and the whole statue quivered, puffs of smoke belching from its jaws as if it were clearing its throat, then a jet of flame streamed out from its mouth. The erupting flames roared up higher and higher, dancing across the sky, beginning to take shape. The torrent ceased to pour from the dragon in seconds but the sky was a swirling mass, a bright cloud of orange, red, and blue. A small, final, wisp of smoke, floated up lazily from the dragon's mouth leaving the heavens filled with words written in flame, bright, blazing letters with an intense blue border spelled out the ancient call: "RANIN, RIDE HOME."

The fiery script hung high in the sky and did not appear to be diminishing. Tamarin turned to the others, embarrassed. "I am a fool to make such a stupid, clumsy, mistake. This signal will serve only to remind our people of friends long since departed. It will do nothing for morale amongst our warriors, forgive me, it was rash of me to use such a blade for so menial a task."

The others said nothing—it had been an accident after all. The horses were still asleep—resting, and having finished their meal, they left the great hall and returned to their duties amidst the statues of Soledad.

Ramulet greeted Tamarin warmly and asked of the writing in the sky. Tamarin, a little flushed, explained how it had come about. The captain placed a friendly arm around the shoulders of his king. "My lord, we do not have the Ranin in this age of ours, but we have a great and noble king—King Tamarin, son of Darcinian. THIS king will lead us to victory. I feel it in the very core of me. Have faith, my lord, king. You are all your great father could wish you to be, and more."

It had taken some hours for the writing in the sky to finally fade away and disappear, and many a Samarian had wondered what it had meant. To avoid confusion Tamarin had made a brief speech explaining his accidentally lighting the old signal. The scorching suns were just about to meet and the people in Soledad were eager for the eclipse to lower the baking temperature in which they were all labouring so hard. It was just as the pair of blazing orbs began to tentatively 'touch' each other, that the distinctive voice of Imo rang out over all else, "Movement, riders to the southwest!"

Tamarin raced up a ladder to the observation post, and looked out into the desert as Ramulet joined them. Indeed, two small specks could be seen on the horizon, heading directly for Soledad. They were leaving an easily visible trail in their wake. Everyone on the wall strained to identify the possible new menace, but Lauren recognised them first. Frantically, she warned the archers, "It is Bestwin and Lumarr, it's the Westonians! Don't kill them!"

The Westonians were once again riding hell-for-leather to reach the sanctuary of a Samarian city. Ramulet raced down to the gates as Imo and others manned various weapons, ready to deal with anything chasing after their friends. In a matter of minutes Bestwin and Lumarr became clearly recognisable to all as they neared them, but those that were watching felt every second pass as if it were an age, for no one doubted that something very unpleasant was not too far behind.

Ramulet had opened only one of the cities great portals, and the Westonians almost brushed him as they shot past. They stuck their heads inside water barrels—drinking as they were submerged (an act common to hot lands), then threw back their hair, water pouring from their beards and dripping from their noses. Tamarin was fast approaching when Bestwin raised a hand to stall any questions, at least until after he had spoken, "Sire, we checked in on that disgusting bag of gas—Dorinn, last night, and he was gone. We thought we would trace him quickly, but found evidence of him having stolen a horse. Naturally we gave pursuit, we would not want him to miss his own execution, but when we had ridden just beyond yonder horizon, we noticed he was veering to his left towards Rosameer, and then Dizbaar. The dog is trying to get across the desert, over the border, and escape into the badlands."

Bestwin took a breath, and Lumarr picked up the thread. "We wanted him to face justice, but heard harrowing sounds from the west and thought they merited further investigation. My lord, I only wish I had better news. Not so far from where we stood we saw a sight that some would deem too inconceivable to be true. An army, a veritable land armada, approaches this city. There is a vast rolling mass moving this way, still too dense to define, and moving at some speed I might add. There was no sign of that devil—Ogiin, but I have no doubt he is there, hidden amongst his creed, the dark tide has risen high enough to swallow up the sands and will soon be lapping at your door. It will not be long before this storm of evil is crashing against the very pillars of our existence, seeking to decimate our people and carry us into oblivion. We will deal with our absent king in due course, he cannot go unpunished. But for now—brace the gates! Man the wall! Our swords are with you, Tamarin, and let it be known by all that *Westonians*, too, did fight this day, arm-in-arm with their Samarian brothers."

There was nothing more to be said. The gates were closed and braced. The wall was manned. Arrows and swords were stockpiled and the cities devastating catapults were refurbished and prepared. There were plenty of boulders to be used as ammunition, waiting to be used for centuries. Huge compressed hay balls were made ready to be lit and hurled at the enemy. Buckets of pitch were placed at equal distances along the wall to aid the archers. Each knew his place and was in it. The children looked on nervously, excitedly, and perhaps a little fearfully, waiting for events to unfold. The suns were fully eclipsed and the light relief from the heat was gratefully accepted by all. Meekhi told the children sternly, "If the wall is breached we will retreat into the city to then counter attack from the centre—the great hall. Stay close to me, my young friends, you are about to play a part in the making of history."

"Oh, bollocks," Lauren mumbled glumly, "I was always crap at history."

Zowie gave her a cheeky grin, smugly telling her, "Top of the class, me."

Meekhi smiled at them reassuringly, aware that they had no idea as to the full size and magnitude of the evil about to engulf them. In her heart she asked that the Great Dragon take them now and return them safe to their own world, so that they may be gone before the darkness began to bite into the light.

Ramulet's big, bold voice boomed out; "WESTERN HORIZON!"

There was no need for him to give details. It looked as if the troubled sea, itself, had come to Soledad. The entire horizon—where sky met sand, turned black. Like some deadly plague from the deepest depths of the underworld, the thin dark line began to blot out the land as it crept forward towards the ancient Samarian stronghold. Ogiin's creed had arrived.

"By the sacred waters," Tamarin cursed, "how can there be so many! that is not merely an *army*, it is an *ocean of evil*. STAND TO! Make ready, my friends, the waiting is over, the challenge commences."

The children were shocked at how suddenly things went from sitting about waiting, to a frenzy of activity. Ramulet was ceaseless in his organising of the cities defences, running from post to post, adjusting the machinery of war and placing his men in more advantageous positions. Imo spoke with Tamarin, "My lord, they are at their weakest whilst the suns do shine upon us still. Those horrors, the Shadows, will not appear until nightfall. But I fear that when they do, no wall of any city can stop them. They will cause havoc amongst the people and unnerve the men. Those icy bitches—the Hoary Hags, will have suffered in the desert heat and therefore be weakened by it. They will probably wait for the light to reduce at least before they probe our defences. It is the dark that is our greatest enemy. We must look to the light for advantage."

"Thank you, good and wise Imo, then we must capitalise on what hours of daylight remain yet ours, whilst the enemy cannot utilise their full potential. Captain, how are we prepared to strike *first*?"

Ramulet like the idea and was keen, "As ready as we will ever be, my lord, king."

"Be discreet, and open the eastern gate, captain," Tamarin ordered, "We will take two columns of riders, they will split up and ride back around the city to gain the heights to each side of us on the western approach. By the time we gain those heights, the suns will be in the perfect position to blind the enemy to us from both directions. Our riders will remain invisible to them behind the high dunes until we charge them. We will strike into the heart of each flank, cutting them down as each party slices through them and passes the oncoming other, returning to the city by retracing the path of our comrades—who will do exactly the same in the opposite direction. What say ye, can we do this? I say we can."

Ramulet thought it very viable. "It is a bold plan, my king. They will not expect to be attacked so soon, so brazenly, and out in the open beyond our defences."

"I like it," added Imo, "They are vast in number, but perhaps we really can reduce the odds with a first strike, eh? Certainly it will make a shambles of any plan of their own devising, they will need to lick their wounds and this will buy us further time to prepare to repel them. Sire, I think it is a great plan. Let us put it into play, by your leave?"

Meekhi and Mercy agreed, they were enthusiastic about hitting the enemy first, and hitting him hard. They would ride one with each of the raiding parties. The children were to remain behind, protected by the relative safety of the high wall. They would have argued this point, and probably been allowed to join the raiders, but they each knew this was not for them, not their place, not where they needed to be.

The horizon that was the black mass of Ogiin's creed kept seeping across the middle distance like a thick, poisonous flood. Row upon row of Venomeens waddled forward in their thousands. Many of them restrained scrabbling hellhounds on hefty steel chains. Others carried cruel duel-tipped spears, swords, or axes. Maces and hammers, too, were much in evidence. The intention was clear—this army meant to take no prisoners, save, perhaps, a handful of women for Ogiin's delectations.

Most of the jostling horde shielded their faces from the angry red suns, it was clear the light caused them some serious discomfort. Further away, in the far distance, wooden siege towers could be seen—crudely fashioned for the scaling of the cities defences, they where hauled along on enormous wheels by hellhounds and horses. The long stinging whips of the Venomeens driving them knew not the meaning of restraint, the soft hide of the horses was being cut to ribbons. Tamarin noted that, mercifully, there were no enemy catapults in sight. Perhaps this mindless scum had not the intelligence to devise such a contraption, or, perhaps, such things were still too far to see...

Tamarin had timed his plans for the raid to perfection. They sat ready just behind the high brow of two opposing sand dunes, flanking the enemy on each side. He knew neither planning, nor strategy, were his enemy's forte, such mindless minions relied most upon their own savagery, expecting others to fear such a thing, as they feared their own master's vicious displeasure. The most forward elements of Ogiin's force were channelled by the natural landscape between the high sand hills, and in a perfect position to be ambushed. He thanked his father for his vision in planning such a secure location for the city of Soledad. She could not be easily approached unseen. Blinding speed and ceaseless slaughter were to be the order of the day, complete surprise was of the essence and the advantage it gave must be driven home. Samaria had not wished for this war, but now she would offer no quarter, the enemy should expect neither mercy nor compassion, too many lives were already lost, and her people, left bereft of such kindly notions, sought only vengeance. It was his duty to ensure his people, his beloved Meekhi, and his friends, survived this day. He knew in his heart that the only way to win this war was to either greatly decrease the enemy's number, or to increase that of his own. As the latter was impossible, he would concentrate on the former. Their triblades would carve through Venomeen flesh easily enough, but then the night would fall, bringing with it its own witches and phantoms, loathsome ghouls not so easily bested.

The hills behind which the horsemen were hiding petered out as they approached Soledad, and, from a high vantage point in the city, it was possible to see behind them.

The children held their breath, imagining the horses forming up in the hollows behind the crests. One charge was to be led by Tamarin and the other by Meekhi. Imo would ride second to Tamarin, Ramulet to Meekhi. Mercy sat astride her gleaming chestnut charger, just behind Imo. She was keen to spill the black blood of those that served Ogiin, were it not for that black-hearted devil she may even now be attending her own marriage to Ramulet, Ogiin had to pay dearly for causing this non-event.

The king raised his sword up high. The suns were at their backs and in the best position to dazzle the enemy whilst having no detrimental effect on either Samarian column. He looked up at the pair of blazing orbs, thanking them for their assistance. He could just about see over the top of the hill, and he exposed the tip of his sword to Meekhi, causing the light to sparkle upon it. Seeing the corresponding flash opposite, he knew she was as ready as she would ever be. Those still in Soledad saw the duel signals and clenched their fists in apprehensive anticipation.

Tamarin's enormous black hunter stormed up and over the dune, Meekhi's own snow-white steed mirroring his actions. They attacked from both directions in formations shaped to form a tight 'V'. This would enable them to punch a hole through enemy ranks with concentrated force whilst still allowing each rider a clear line of sight, driving a death-dealing wedge deep into the enemy flank.

The king and queen were watched from the city, in the fore, and galloping flat out at the enemy with their swords pointing ahead. Halfway to the massed ranks of startled Venomeens, Tamarin's sword burst into flames, much to the cheering of his own people. Meekhi sat tight to her horse, her sword-arm trailing now, poised, ready to strike. Mercy was already rapid-firing arrows into the panicked Venomeens, wanting to kill as many from a distance as possible before bringing her own blade into deadly effect. Bestwin and Lumarr had opted not to use their curved scimitars in this particular action. Instead, each of them carried enormous war hammers—a dreadfully heavy, cumbersome weapon of Westonian origin, it took tremendously powerful arms to wield it. A truly devastating tool in the right hands, it was capable of shattering skulls with a single blow and smashing bodies by the dozen with each swing. A Westonian rode with each column, his terrifying hammer swinging ready by his side.

The army of Ogiin's creatures approaching Soledad, had, much earlier, found Sitivia deserted. They could not sniff out a single living soul there, and so had not bothered to enter the city. The only booty they sought was the warm life-blood of the living, and the praise from their master when they savoured that thick red nectar in his name, adding to his power with every drop they plundered. The last thing they had expected was to be attacked from both sides in broad daylight. Trapped as they were between the enormous dunes, they were mortified to see Samarian cavalry storming towards them, their banners resplendent on the tips of lowered lances, and hundreds of triblades hell bent on their destruction.

The leading Venomeens, panic stricken, tried desperately to retreat, forcing the centre of their own lines to become compressed, unable to move, and unable to defend themselves when the first horsemen smashed into them, tearing gaping holes into both flanks as they collapsed under the onslaught. They were cut down like grass, the Samarians carving a large swathe right through the centre of them. Triblades could be seen flashing left, right, and centre, from the city, and occasionally 'The Flame of Dragonia' would be spotted raining fiery carnage upon all that stood in its way. A triumphant roar went up from the city when they saw their opposing columns meet, then pass each other, laying to waste all that yet survived in their path. From the battlements they could see the stream of silver dragons breaking free of the battered Venomeen ranks on each side and racing for the safety of the high dunes without hindrance. The men in Soledad began to load and prime the catapults as had been previously planned. The children, armed with telescopes, would help range the weapons for them from their high viewpoint.

Upon his return Tamarin raced to the wall and retook command. He could see a large gap had been created in the enemy lines by his daring raid, the horsemen having punched a big hole straight through the wide column of waddling Venomeens. Those of that vermin that were closest to the city were now cut off from their own kind by the dead and dieing behind them. Silent or screaming, thirty rows deep, the fallen were an obstacle not easily overcome in a hurry. The Samarians had lost not a single soul due to the sheer audacity of their savage first strike. The immediate panic it had caused in Ogiin's followers had been well exploited by his warriors and they had managed to inflict maximum harm with no losses. He was pleased with the results of the efforts of his people, and those very people themselves were now in high spirits. If this kind of mindless creature was the best Ogiin could offer, then by nightfall Tamarin might just about vanquish his entire daylight army.

TWANG! WHOOSH! The enormous catapults of ancient Soledad once more surged into life, gigantic clay pots filled with pitch and equipped with slow-burning fuses sailed high into the clear evening sky. They seemed to hang for a second or two, suspended in the air over the trapped Venomeens as if selecting their prey, before slamming down to earth and exploding into blazing balls of bright orange flame and thick black smoke. The Venomeens tried attempting to scale the steep sand banks on either side, but the waves of oil engulfed them, consuming all in their path. The guardsmen, posted along the wall as they were, punched their fists into the air as many of Ogiin's minions were reduced to little more than ash. The catapults' range would not extend beyond the burning or the dead, so, after another five minutes of heavy barrage, Tamarin called a halt in their actions.

Anyone that could get their hands on a telescope did so, leaning out over the battlements to see what the enemy would do next. The people were filled with renewed confidence after witnessing the victorious raid led by the king and queen. After some few minutes the stench from the roasting Venomeens hit the city, and, despite its stomach-turning smell, it was very welcome, the foul fumes speaking volumes as to the suffering of those caught in the inferno. The Venomeens had formed up again, safe beyond the reach of the catapults, spitting at, and taunting, the soldiers watching them. They hissed so loudly they could be heard in Soledad, and those with telescopes could see their green-black tongues darting in and out of their mouths as they stared with both hatred and hunger at the city. From behind her walls, the desert sounded as if alive with gigantic serpents.

Tamarin congratulated the children on their marvellously precise targeting of the enemy. Lauren confided to him; "We've always wanted to fly, it was our dream, as you know. We have studied the dynamics of flight, and, trust me, that is very deep stuff. When you need flights or distances calculated, we're the ones to ask." She beamed proudly at the tall, dark, and handsome, king.

"I see, I shall bear this most valuable knowledge in mind."

He gave Lauren's shoulder a squeeze of gratitude and she winked at Zowie, wiggling her eyebrows up and down furiously and grinning like a clown.

Lumarr had everyone on high alert again when he bellowed, "Something new comes!" Tamarin's heart missed a beat as the horizon turned completely black yet again. More and more Venomeens were appearing, and in amongst their numbers were slow, lumbering rock trolls, hellhounds beyond the counting, hags of every kind, and in the very far distance, something of the coldest, most heartless evil, was approaching. Even from so far away and over the heads of such a vast demonic horde, a wave of pure black malice gripped the city by the throat, obstructing airways, numbing nerves, silencing voices. Everyone grabbed for their cloaks, the goose bumps on their arms alarming in the heat. Horses shivered in their stables, dogs began howling with fear in the streets, and brave men averted their eyes when they gathered their loved ones close to them. From beyond the grave, Ogiin was coming.

Tamarin, Meekhi, Ramulet, and the Westonians, stood with their heads locked together in desperate discussion. The situation was dire. They could not hope to defeat Ogiin's vast legions in direct combat. The approaching night would undoubtedly bring a silent, gruesome death, to many within the city at the hands of those robed ghouls—the Shadows. Tragic as that would be, it also showed how precarious, how utterly insidious, the situation truly was—not only would their own numbers decrease in the darkness, but every warrior that fell would empower Ogiin further as his life energy was absorbed by him. The killings committed by his unholy host were the most vital source of his own strength, at least until he became wholly himself again.

The Westonians and Imo urged every torch in the city to be lit, indoors and out. More were to be stockpiled, available to hand for everyone. Whilst not deadly to Shadows, fire could hold them at bay, and it would finish a Wispy Witch with certainty. Tamarin knew 'The Flame of Dragonia' could destroy any Shadow, and he assured everyone that this would be much in evidence, if he but got the chance.

The city was well stocked and her walls towered thrice the height of those that ringed Sitivia. If in siege, Soledad could hold for months, and if her water wells remained still clean, then she would hold for maybe a year, perhaps even two. But this was only possible if her population and army remained safe, but, alas, the deadly threat of the Shadows caused her boast of secure refuge to be a hollow one. As if those phantoms of the night were not enough to contend with, they had yet to see what atrocities Ogiin, himself, could, and undoubtedly *would*, wreak upon them. Surely, in comparison to their master, the Shadows were still the minor issue. What to do? Simply waiting behind the walls with idle hands was pointless as darkness was approaching fast. Frustration and anxiety began to gnaw like a disease infested rat at the minds of the king and queen, attempting to infect them with panic, nibbling away at their confidence, trying to thaw their resolve.

Soledad shimmered in the twilight hours of dusk, so many fires and torches burned in the city that it appeared as a mountain of diamonds in the encroaching darkness, a tiny, brilliant beacon of hope standing fast as the floodgates of hell began to part open. Tamarin sat at counsel in the great hall. They had to somehow survive the night, absorb any losses, repel any assault, to then again face the rabid wolves at their door, by day. Defensive nights and offensive days, this plan was workable, but, without more information, could not take into account the power or capabilities of Ogiin. Meekhi gripped her sword so tightly that it made her knuckles crack loudly. "If we could get to that devil, himself, and destroy him, we could turn back the dark tide, and drown it in the sea, I do firmly believe this. But he is surrounded, thousands deep, by his assorted rabble, and I know from my own recent experience—those rock trolls are stubborn in greeting death, regardless of how insistent the invitation may be."

"Indeed, my lady," added Ramulet, "Ogiin is the head. Cut off the head and the rest will succumb to our blades in short order. But, as you say, he is currently beyond our reach, and, I might add, we do not know if we have the means of ending his evil existence once and for all. How *does* one kill him? Tell me, and I will do it!"

"I wish I knew, my captain." Imo was in a dejected mood, more suited to combat than counsel the inactivity was beginning to get to him and he sat toying with a stem of corn in the corner of his mouth.

"Aye, Ramulet," Huffed Bestwin wracking his brains, "that is the key we need to pick this particular lock, how to tear the heart from him that is heartless! A pretty pickle indeed. Darcinian, and I'm sure his son's skill will prove an equal match in battle, was a great warrior. He locked blades with Ogiin and Ogiin almost killed him. This monster is not human, no, not a man, but something that has crawled its way to the surface from the very guts of the underworld. He is not to be underestimated, my friends, we need be certain of any possible weakness before we attempt to exploit it."

"It is true," Lumarr was puffing easily on his pipe. He stroked at his silvered beard, his wise face commanding attention, "Ogiin cannot be bested by bold heart alone. Many knights, brave warriors, even your esteemed Ranin, fell at his hands in the Great War. He tore through them as if they were clay dummies. I know because I saw it with my own eyes, bearing witness to his near-invincibility. Something as evil, as deadly a demon, as Ogiin, can only be defeated by powers as great, or greater, than his own. I do not doubt that every single soul in this city will fight to his last, but without the mystical might of the dragons, we remain ill equipped to face his dark and deviant powers. If only we had the means by which to summon some advanced and potent magic to our own aid, a good, strong, honourable magic, then perhaps we could level the odds a little better in our own favour. Alas, I am no sorcerer, and know of none worthy of the name."

Tamarin was sitting on the marble steps near the statue of Chjandi. He swept back his gleaming black locks and turned to look his friends in the eye. "Perhaps," he ventured, *'The Flame of Dragonia'* can inflict some harm upon that demon. But to be tested I must reach him, I must get within striking distance. Somehow, we must slaughter them in droves. We MUST reduce their countless number so as to create a clear path to their master."

Zowie butted in, "Can I take a look at your fireworks, please?"

Her bizarre request amidst such a serious discussion astonished everyone.

Tamarin raised his eyebrows impatiently, as if to ask, "Why???"

She explained. "We, us *young ones*, we know a fair bit about flight, and that takes some knowledge of *science*. I think you would call it *alchemy*. You must have a special powder you use to propel your fireworks, yes? a black powder? We know this powder as gunpowder, don't ask me why, please, and it can be used in a very nasty way. I think it's time the Samarian army had the use of bazookas! What do you think, *Lauren? Thomas?* Can we do it?"

"Yes, yes, of course we can, awesome thinking!" They replied gleefully.

Meekhi turned to old Corsellius, "Corsellius, I bid thee, take these three to the tower where we prepare the black powder. They are to have all they require. Young ones, I implore you, do not send Soledad skywards."

The children left with Corsellius and Arcadian. Tamarin stood up and addressed the others. "Darkness comes. Darkness comes to extinguish the Samarian flame forever. But we will not go quietly into the abyss with our heads bowed, fading from history as if never born, erasing the great deeds of our forefathers by our own shameful failure. We are alive yet! We are *Samarian*! Thus we are, thus we shall remain. We will endure any onslaught Ogiin may bring to bear upon us, but we *will* remain. There is perhaps another two hours before the night finally steals our thinning shield of light. Prepare the city, each must watch his neighbour, these shadowy spectres can appear anywhere. Post fresh sentries with a keen eye, and change them often. When darkness envelops us—I want flares in the sky at irregular intervals, all night. Shoot at anything you see, be it moving, or not. We must survive tonight so we may deal out death tomorrow. My lady, my friends, I would have no others by my side on this, the darkest night of my life."

Filled with love and admiration the others raised their mighty triblades in salute. Meekhi and Mercy struggled to hold in check their pride in their brave, young king. They knew only too well of how he always endeavoured to live up to his father's legendary reputation, but they also knew Darcinian had ruled for a very long reign, experienced in battle, and a seasoned warrior when the Great War had broken out. In comparison, Tamarin was still but a young boy, his broad shoulders strong, but inexperienced. The great hall emptied as they all left to do their duty. Only Meekhi remained. She and Tamarin stood locked in a close, loving embrace, at the foot of the statue. He was admiring her sultry, smouldering beauty, when he looked down and saw the little vial resting at her throat. The colours within it swirled and glowed as they had always done, and he squeezed his woman even closer to him, whispering soothingly in her ear, "Fear not, 'The Flame of Dragonia' is at your side and at your service. I swear by all that I hold dear, you, my precious Meekhi, my living dream, will come to no harm on this eve of nightmares reborn."

He buried his face in her raven tresses, nestling in close, revelling in her perfume of fresh jasmine and exotic sandalwood. He lost himself in the warmth of her tight-but-tender embrace, the feel of her bosom pressing on him, her slender hands stroking his face. She spoke quietly, almost in a whisper, "Tamarin, you will overcome this scourge that is Ogiin. It is your destiny, just as it was that of your great father. But this time...this time *now* is *your* time, it belongs to the present king, not to memories of old. You have nothing to prove, no measure to achieve. My love, you have only to be yourself, and you will succeed, evidence enough that you are your father's son. I feel the spirit of Samaria within you, her heart beating within yours. You *are* Samaria, and you will not fail our people. I am grateful of your love, your considerations, and protection. But I do not fear for myself. I am your wife, yes, but also, a Samarian queen, and I stand beside you now with complete faith, and will do so for eternity. I fear only for our people—those that must this night face the unleashing of hell's serpents. 'The Flame of Dragonia' will serve you well, but it is you, not your blade, Tamarin, that is the rock upon which the waves of darkness will break, and fade away."

He held her face cupped in his hands, staring deep into those moist green pools that were her dazzling eyes. He kissed her there, the salt of her tears electrifying him, then her forehead, and, finally, he kissed her lips, tenderly, softly, a deep, long, lingering kiss, full of love and admiration. She returned his kisses with equal fervour. Hand-in-hand, they left the great hall to keep watch over their realm, and a great howling rose up in the darkening desert about them.

CHAPTER EIGHTEEN

SHADOWS IN THE DARK

The twilight of sunset began to spread throughout the desert and Soledad sat like a zealously coveted jewel, her fires and torches blazing, waiting to be snatched in the dead of night. Ogiin's army of darkness had stopped advancing just out of range of the archers keeping watch atop the citadel. Not a single bird could be seen or heard, small desert rodents burrowed deeper and deeper into the ground in fear, and even the sands lay perfectly still, as if to avoid the attentions of the evil forces at work upon them. The howls and grunts from outside of the city were largely ignored by those within it. Such sounds, if paid heed, could easily cause one to doubt one's course. The sentries could hear a heavy, ominous pounding, approaching slowly, accompanied by a strange, raucous clatter, as if someone was moving vast quantities of shingle. Meekhi and Mercy knew the sound only too well. They raced to Tamarin who had left the gates only half an hour ago at the behest of the young ones.

Meekhi slammed open the door of the chamber in which the children had been ensconced since they had left the great hall with Corsellius and Arcadian. This particular room had, in the past, been used for the exploration and investigation of alchemy. It was in this very place that past Samarians had discovered the black powder Zowie knew as 'gunpowder'. Mercy almost bowled Meekhi over as she slammed into her from the rear, causing the queen to stumble inside in a most undignified manner, almost falling flat on her face, saved only by Mercy grabbing her long hair.

Red faced, but forgiving, she told her, "Ouch! You can let go of my hair now, you unruly mare!"

Tamarin, biting back a laugh, stood in the middle of the room next to a large trestle, he was holding up a long bamboo tube with a fuse protruding from a hole at one end. The children were obviously proud of this odd-looking tube—it was written all over their faces. Meekhi, having recovered her composure, dashed over to him, urgency ringing in her voice, "Rock trolls—we heard them. They're coming straight at us, the only way Mercy and I managed to overcome such a brute was to get low and close with it, then striking up between its flat stony scales. Our archers will achieve nothing from the heights, even their eyes are impervious to arrows and we dare not open any gate to tackle the grey gargoyles, lest we invite a flood of Ogiin's creed into the city."

"My Love," Tamarin tried calming her, "I understand full well the need to act in haste. Your description of these rock trolls is of grave concern. But dally a minute, I am fascinated by this tube the young ones have engineered. I am informed that it just needs to be pointed at the enemy, and, holding it firmly, one lights the cord, which then launches a highly explosive bum at the target."

"Bomb, *not* bum!" the children shouted as they curled up in hysterics.

"Ah, yes," he agreed, puzzled at their sudden mirth, "an explosive *bomb* destroys the enemy. I wish to see an example of this."

On route to the demonstration, the children politely explained to Meekhi and Mercy why they were giggling so much, and they too had a chuckle at Tamarin's genuine mistake.

In a courtyard below the chamber of alchemy, Zowie very proudly offered the weapon up to the king, who, holding it in a firm grip, aimed it at a large clay water pot, sitting on a heavy wooden table. Zowie and Lauren (the main engineers of the weapon) jointly lit the fuse. Everyone waited in absolute silence. The fuse seemed to burn a very bright purple in the fading evening light, sparks flying from it in all directions. It crackled down to the tube, appearing to fizzle out. Then there was a hollow sounding 'crump,' and just as they saw a flash of flame from the muzzle of the tube, the water pot, along with the entire table, exploded with a thunderous "Bang!"

"Excellent!" cheered Tamarin, "You are sorcerers of the highest order. Wonderful! We will need as many of these as you can possibly make. I will send ten men and they will each do as you do. Well done, my young friends, this service you have done us will prove invaluable."

He turned on his heel and left to try and sight the rock trolls that Meekhi had warned of.

"We have bazookas filled with exploding bums!" A delighted Tamarin told his Captain of the Royal Guards. Ramulet tilted his head, as if to say, "What are you talking about?"

Tamarin explained, and Ramulet was also very impressed by the deadly, flame-belching bums of the children.

Perhaps a mere half hour of the faint remnants of light remained. The old capital threw long shadows across the darkening sands in opposing directions, and even as the dance of day drew to an eerie apprehensive close, the drums of darkness began to beat a very different tune. Trolls became distinguishable, their distinct shapes lumbering towards Soledad, mindless mountains of muscle driven relentlessly on by the will of Ogiin. Venomeens frantically rushed aside for fear of being crushed. The colossal trolls each carried a club that a dozen strong men could never hope to lift. Tamarin asked of his captain, "Why send those mindless giants, Ramulet? The Venomeen scum can scale our walls as easily as a spider might. Why risk the trolls? I mean, after dark, surely those accursed Shadows will penetrate our defences with ease. What be your slant on this?"

"I think...," Ramulet replied after taking a minute to consider such a poignant question, "Ogiin wishes to preserve those Shadows from hell as best he can. They are, after all, his most prized minions. If the trolls can breach our gates then his legions of pale-skinned bloodsuckers will be scaling not only our walls, but swarming all over the city like ants. I feel Ogiin wants not only to wipe out our people, but also any trace of our very existence, to decimate every city, reduce it to dust, and grind that dust into the desert sand so as to leave nothing of what once was. The trolls are his destroyers, they can level the land whereas the Shadows move on the cusp of the physical world, touching only soul and spirit. Neither can be allowed to gain ground on us, for should such a catastrophe come to pass in the dark of night, my king, we would be hard pushed to e'er see a sunrise again."

"Then it will never come to pass, Ramulet." Tamarin told him assuredly, "We will use the weapons of other worlds to halt the monsters in their tracks. You really must see an exploding bum, my good friend, it truly is an awesome sight, although I admit it leaves a terribly unpleasant odour after wreaking its havoc."

Orders were relayed back to the chamber of alchemy and two score of 'bazookas' were brought into service along the wall, being placed at strategic points on the battlements. No more could be made as there was no more black powder.

The light was clinging on desperately by its fingertips, as if not wanting to abandon the defenders of the city to the cold clutches of night. Visibility from the wall had reduced to no more than a hundred feet, beyond this and no one could trust their eyes, the dwindling twilight playing games with their minds. Imo had noted that countless Venomeens were creeping forward behind the trolls that were almost upon the city. The Westonians stood on watch either side of the main gate, high up behind the fortifications. A large force of men was stationed just behind the gates in case any breach occurred. These warriors were also armed with long, sharp pikes, as the most likely causes of any breach would be the trolls, or, the hellhounds. Tamarin and his friends waited—searching the desert every time a flare rocketed skywards, and then fell, illuminating the enemy for a few brief seconds before plummeting suddenly to earth. The ground beneath the flares seemed alive, writhing, wriggling, creeping forward as it slithered along. Thomas had had the idea of fitting 'parachutes' to the flares to allow them to descend slowly, thus achieving better, extended, surveillance. He was busy with Corsellius and Mercy, fitting small, specifically packed squares of cloth, to all of the remaining flares.

The ground shook and the city shuddered as the rock trolls made their first charge at Soledad. Once within range, guardsmen fired a huge volley from the Wraths, but the spears failed to penetrate their thick, rocky hide, trails of sparks showing where the silver dragons scraped the surface before careening off into the darkness, some gaining minor satisfaction by burying themselves into Venomeens. Tamarin stepped forward and aimed one of Zowie's 'bazookas' at the leading monster, Meekhi lit the fuse. The expected 'crump' was heard, but the explosive charge overshot its target by a large margin and landed amidst the Venomeens behind it, blowing them to pieces.

"Great shot, my lord!" Meekhi cheered.

"I was aiming for the troll." Tamarin told her glumly.

The trolls were even closer now and he had to lower his 'bazooka' to take accurate aim. To Zowie and Lauren's horror, the explosive package inside the tube rolled out and down to the sand below, outside of the cities fortifications.

"OH! Crap!" They cried out. Lauren turned to Meekhi, "The tube has got to be kept level, or even pointing up a fraction. As soon as you point it down, the charge will fall out."

Tamarin heard her instructions and called for Ramulet. He and Tamarin, armed with a clutch of 'bazookas', leapt from the wall, as the trolls, only seconds away, approached. The pair knelt and each lit a fuse, pointing the deadly tubes directly at a pair of trolls looming fast out of the darkness with their clubs raised and their teeth bared. The Venomeens and witches hiding behind them were now within range of the bowmen and the archers rained death upon them in torrents. Tamarin and Ramulet shot each other a glance as they knelt together, side-by-side in the dark, waiting for the fizzing fuses to burn down. The ground shook and quivered and they could see the hate-filled faces of the clattering giants bearing down on them, their ravenous eyes testimony to their endless craving for living flesh. A daunting sight, even for the two bold warriors facing them, they were so close now the sound of their heavy breathing, puffing and huffing like enormous bellows, filled the air. Zowie and Meekhi raced down to the gates and opened them just wide enough for the pair outside to retreat once more to the sanctuary of Soledad when the time came. Lauren, meanwhile, remained high above, adding her own blend of skills to those of the other archers.

Just as Meekhi had prised open one of the heavy gates (with some considerable help), she had heard the now familiar 'crump'. She and Zowie stepped outside just in time to see the muzzle flashes to their right, and the oncoming trolls, mere feet away with their scales rattling horribly, exploded in sheets of flame. Chunks of burnt and charred troll rained down all about them and they had to take care not to be hit as the rocky nature of the grisly downpour would most surely cause severe injury, maybe even death.

Zowie grimaced, "How utterly gross."

"Oh how *splendid*!" Meekhi raved jubilantly, delighted at the gruesome sight. She grabbed up a fresh tube and knelt down beside Tamarin, Zowie did likewise, and the four put flame to fuses.

A small group of guardsmen had also left the safety of the city and stood close by with swords drawn, ready to protect king and queen if the need arose. The roar of the soldiers above was almost deafening when they saw four more gargantuan trolls meet such a sudden, brutal death. But now they were too close for anyone to wait for a fuse to burn down. They had only just made it to the relative safety afforded by the slammed and barred gates when the first almighty crash sounded. The rock-encrusted monsters were attempting to smash down the barrier with their enormous clubs. At such close range and with the delay caused by the fuse, the children's improvised weapons were of no more use. The gates, as sturdy as any in the land, would not withstand such a relentless punishment for too much longer. Guardsmen poured pitch over the trolls from above and set them ablaze, but they seemed impervious to the burning oil, appearing even more terrifying completely engulfed in flames as they pounded away unhindered.

Venomeens, their pale skin glowing in the light from the burning trolls, were creeping up to the city, their eyes reflecting the flares soaring skyward from Soledad. Thomas was sending a steady stream of his modified fireworks to the men igniting them, and they seemed to be working rather well, floating down from above gracefully, illuminating large areas of the foreground for much longer than before. Lauren and the bowmen used this to maximum effect by picking off the bloodsuckers as best they could. But there were just too many, and, eventually, they reached the city.

Like giant red-eyed spiders, they began to scale the walls of Soledad, carrying their stubby swords and shields on their backs. The Samarians welcomed them with burning oil and a hail of arrows. But now, from out in the darkness, Ogiin's army of evil struck back, firing thousands of deadly black shafts into the city, aiming particularly at those defending it from the wall. The rate at which these missiles poured into the city was so intense that they obliterated any of Thomas' floating flares drifting into their path. He returned to the others to tell them that he had done all he could do, and the flares served no further purpose whilst the deluge of arrows remained. Men toiled furiously along the battlements, fetching oil, pouring oil, and shooting arrows. A handful of the bloodsuckers made it up to the top, but were quickly cut to ribbons by eager triblades. The entire city was working flat out to protect the perimeter, and, to make matters worse, it was now fully dark.

Tamarin and the others knew that soon Ogiin's foulest fiends would be amongst their midst. The howling wolf was at the front door and his snarling mate would soon be inside the house, gouging at their backs. As the men on the wall slaved relentlessly to hold back the Venomeens, the gates began to show signs of weakening. The thick wooden beams creaked worryingly under the thunderous blows being rained upon them. Steel rivets rattled with each impact, threatening to resign their post at any second. Tamarin ordered even more torches be lit and mounted in the streets, wedged firmly into every nook and cranny they could find, especially in the darkest places. The civilian population—each a formidable warrior in his own right, rushed to obey his commands, aware that a failing in one could lead to the destruction of all.

Ramulet ordered that the entire city form groups in readiness for the grey robes of death that fell from above. The Westonians were still standing above the gates, "Tamarin! These brutes will tear the gates asunder in a few minutes! They are causing the beams to buckle dangerously! We must stop them now, or we are undone!"

Tamarin cursed under his breath. Only close combat and a very precise sword strike could vanquish these gigantic creatures, but to lead an attack into the darkness beyond the city was a death sentence upon anyone foolhardy enough to attempt it. Mercy implored the children in desperation, "Is there no way to use these 'bazookas' without waiting for the fuse to burn down? Can we not shorten the fuse?"

Zowie answered quite emphatically, "No! It could blow up in your hands!"

But *Thomas* had other ideas. "Actually, there may be another way, guys. You girls know more than me about flight and propulsion, but I know a bit about soldiering. British Army, Tamarin, best in the world it is, even if I do say so again. Well..., that does include the Royal Navy, Royal Marines, and Royal Air Force, but, *best in the world*, for sure. Anyway, what we need are sticky bombs."

"Sticky bums?" Tamarin was intrigued, "Is a sticky bum more devastating than a bazooka bum?"

"*Bomb*s not bums." the children were forced to corrected him yet again.

"Bombs, yes," Tamarin was in a hurry, "can we make them? How do they work?"

Thomas sounded confident, "We remove the explosive from the remaining tubes, err... bazookas. We fit a fuse directly to each charge and then cover the charge in something very sticky, so it will stick to anything it is slammed onto. The fuse is lit, the charge is stuck onto a troll, and then we leg it before it explodes."

"Remarkable idea, Thomas, do it, please. Also, tell me—how does one 'leg' a troll? Is this part of the plan? Is a leg as powerful as a bum?" Tamarin needed every weapon he could lay his hands on and if the bums were running out, then he wanted to get his hands on as many legs as possible. Thomas nodded in the negative whilst his sister and Zowie began to very carefully disassemble the bazookas. Arcadian went to fetch a big bucket of thick, sticky, tar.

They had to be extremely careful moving about through the city as the rainstorm of Venomeen arrows was relentless, not letting up for a second, the sound of their whizzing through the air becoming the backdrop to the activities within Soledad. Ramulet gave Tamarin his opinion on the plan to use sticky bombs, "Sire, the young ones may well have devised another potent weapon to be put at our disposal, but still—these sticky bums must be affixed directly onto those minions of darkness pounding at our door. I cannot see the trolls consenting easily to this of their own freewill. Thus, Sire, I volunteer for this mission."

"My good, fine, captain," Tamarin told him with genuine affection, "not ever have I, or would I, doubt your courage, or your loyalty. But it is I that invited the Guilty Innocents—as we knew them formerly to be, to join our ranks. Thus it is I that will take their sticky bums and slap them onto our enemies. Gratitude for your kind offer, there is none more valiant in the land."

The pair joined the men high up on the wall, adding their strength and experience to the efforts being made to stem the plague of Venomeens attempting to breach the city. Every single occupant of Soledad was aware that the Shadows could now appear anywhere, at anytime.

Completing the sticky, explosive bundles, had not taken the children long, and they stood up, stepping away sore-backed from their messy handiwork. They had only wanted to fly together in an artificial dream, and now here they were in the black of night, helping the Samarians battle against the evil forces of Ogiin in a faraway world. Despite the chilling, imminent threat from the Shadows and Wispy Witches, not one of them regretted a second of their time in Samaria. During their brief stay in that amazing world they had come to love the Samarians as the Samarians had come to love them, they were each thinking along the same lines when Zowie voiced their thoughts out aloud. "Look guys, I don't know if we will die here, or if we will die back home, but we owe a lot to Tamarin and the others. Meekhi has been lovely to us and Ramulet has given Tom a lot of his valuable time. Mercy is just wonderful. The Samarians aren't just fighting for their lives, they are also fighting for *ours*. If the city is overrun and they lose, I'm sure Ogiin and his freak show aren't just going to let us three walk away. We owe them the same as they're giving us. These packages have got to be stuck onto those huge rattling trolls *by hand*. Why should they take all the risk? I'm not being brave, in fact, I'm crapping it! But I'm going to sneak out with some of these and try and give those trolls a taste of *our* world, and I'm not talking pepperoni pizzas!"

"I'm with you, Zee. Time to rock 'n' roll, I say," Thomas was game, "but lay off the pizza thing will ya, I'm getting really hungry!"

"You're always hungry, Tom, you big bloater! But yeah, let's do it," Lauren joked, "as you said, if those things get in here, we're brown bread anyway. What's the plan then, *lady* Zowie?"

Making mock-angry eyes at her, Zowie rubbed her chin as if deep in thought (a habit she had very quickly picked up from Meekhi), then she told her cousins of her bold, and precisely calculated strategy, "Well, I haven't really got a plan, I'm just thinking of quietly sneaking out of the eastern gate with horses, riding around Soledad to get near the trolls, then leaving the horses for our return trip and just legging it over to the western gates and getting stuck in. It's not really a very great plan, is it?"

"It's fine, let's just do it." Lauren wanted to start before she changed her mind.

Thomas' spirits were still high having conjured up the sticky bombs after being trumped by the girls and their bazookas, and he found the plan very exciting. "It's damned heroic, Zee! I dare say they'll want to do something similar themselves, so we'd better get stuck in quickly. There is *definitely* something very Samarian about you, apart from you being a complete nutter anyway. Let's go!"

"Oh give it a rest with the Samarian thing!" Zowie warned as each of them gathered up a bag of charges and began meandering innocently down the main street, nonchalantly heading for the east gate. In fact, the others were so busy dodging arrows, fighting off Venomeens, burning trolls, and watching out for Shadows that nobody would have noticed if the children had actually galloped through the city flat out on horseback.

Tamarin could see that the trolls had stopped using their clubs and had started ramming their massive shoulders into the main gate. The entire length of the wall was now starting to shake with every enormous impact. Guardsmen staggered under the blows, fighting to keep their footing as Soledad rocked under the ceaseless onslaught. Ramulet and Mercy had gathered more men and were doing their utmost to reinforce the rapidly weakening defences by bracing them with heavy oak cross members, a strenuous task in daylight but almost impossible in the dark with the trolls constantly battering away, making secure placement of the beams a hit and miss affair. Tamarin and Meekhi hurried back and forth along the battlements, giving orders and bolstering morale whilst hacking at any bulbous white fingers that crept up into view. A glowing head appeared suddenly over the parapet and Meekhi aimed a ferocious kick at it. Her booted foot kicked the Venomeen's fangs down its throat but became stuck in its mouth. She neatly lopped off the top half of the bloodsucker's head, freeing her foot and sending the body over the side. She moved on, unperturbed. 'The Flame of Dragonia' was easily visible in the dark, bursting into life every time Tamarin brought it to bear against the enemy. Every so often a flare would soar, streaking high into the sky above the city and leaving a trail of thick, acrid smoke in its wake. Then it would fall slowly—illuminating the gathered mass that was Ogiin's creed, before sinking into the stream of black arrows pouring into the city, and being obliterated by them. Tamarin had ordered men to keep a wary eye to the north and south of the city. If Ogiin had his hoards spread around the city to encircle it, then the Samarians would be trapped and under siege. He prayed the sheer arrogance of Ogiin would lead him to continue with his frontal assault in the belief that his followers, knowing he became stronger with every kill they made, would soon overcome by weight of numbers and brute force.

Imo—ever vigilant, was the first to spot the three small figures creeping along. They were hugging the wall and moving towards the trolls battering the west gate. The stout little guardsman called across to Ramulet. "Captain! Whom have you instructed beyond the gate? I see three bearing our mark, approaching from east to west, close to the wall!"

Ramulet raced up the steps and peered over. "I have given no such orders for anyone to be outside of these walls, Imo, it would be suicide. Fetch the king, quickly. ARCHERS! Keep these three shadowy figures in your sights!"

Imo pelted along the thick wooden boards, head bowed to dodge the hail of arrows. He returned with a troubled-looking Tamarin. The king took a quick glance over the wall and saw the trio moving stealthily forward.

"I know not who they may be, but I know they are assured of death at the gate. They must..."

"Tamarin, on your right!" Ramulet shouted in alarm.

Tamarin ducked immediately to his left and rolled away, springing back to his feet to see a Shadow hovering near where he had stood only a second ago. He moved with such speed and precision that no one could say when, exactly, he had drawn his sword, or even when it had begun to swoop down. It just appeared, buried deep in that robed head. In a blinding flash, the Shadow was no more. Only a thick, nauseating odour remained. Then, that very second, a huge explosion ripped the night apart, making everyone jump. Lumarr and Bestwin were calling out, "It's the young ones! They have killed a troll, alone, and without escort, they are beyond the gate!"

Tamarin and Meekhi, Ramulet and Mercy, positioned themselves just above the children below, and launched themselves from the heights. Black capes fluttering, the four of them sailed earthward with their weapons readied in their hands. With four, soft, successive thuds, they landed with perfect grace to see a sight they would not have ever dreamed of seeing. The young girls were actually attacking the still-burning trolls with their swords. They appeared nimble on their feet and the skills gifted to them by Hi-light were much in evidence. Thomas was ducking and diving, carrying three sticky bundles—the fuses already alight and glowing in the dark as he tried to get close to the trolls whilst avoiding their deadly tails. Tamarin quickly saw their plan—the girls were to provide distraction whilst the boy endeavoured to slap his sticky bums against the beasts. The trolls were lost to their hunger, forgetting their given task at the sudden appearance of human children—a delicacy so rare it was on a par with Samarian females. Their bright pink nostrils flared from under stony scales at the scent, and they grabbed at the children clumsily, roaring in frustration as they whipped by them with astonishing agility. Tamarin called up to his archers, "Men! Keep the Venomeen scum at bay!"

The deadly bowmen concentrated their fire around the children to prevent the suddenly excited Venomeens from aiding their troll allies. Many of the saggy-skinned bloodsuckers tried to reach the young trio, hoping to claim an unexpected prize, but were immediately cut down by the men above. Large, still-smoking chunks of the troll the children had previously blown up were strewn everywhere. The area was well lit by the countless torches burning fiercely along the cities defences, but in the darkness, beyond their limited reach, lay a seething carpet of Venomeens, their bloated bodies luminescent in the shifting light of the falling flares.

The Samarians rushed to the aid of the valiant young warriors from another world. Whilst each found their sword all but useless against the rocky giants, Tamarin discovered, with great pleasure, that his magical sword could penetrate their thick armour. But because of their sheer size and their monstrous whipping tails, he found it impossible to deal a fatal blow. His constant stabbing and harrowing did, however, cause them to forget the children momentarily, focusing on the Samarians now attacking them. The warriors were constantly ducking to avoid the trolls' swinging clubs, simultaneously dodging the gigantic paws that grabbed at them from all directions. The ground shook every time a club missed them and slammed into the sand. Then Thomas shouted out, "It's done! Get away from them, quick!"

The embattled group retreated so as to have the wall at their backs, shrinking away from the trolls who seemed to think they had won. Cruel smirks cracked out across their faces as they licked around their ugly mouths in anticipation of warm flesh laced with blood for their supper. Then, one after another, each of them exploded. Another roar of delight from up on the battlements sailed out across the desert and even the creeping Venomeens withdrew a fraction. Other scaly monsters, livid at the spectacular demise of more of their own kind, began stomping towards the city from out of the dark. Infuriated and incensed with rage, they did not wait for the Venomeens to move aside, preferring to crush anything that got in their way. The agonised screaming of the trampled could be heard by all and was mimicked by the guardsmen manning the wall, taunting Ogiin's creed. Thomas knelt down and carefully emptied a bag of sticky packages. He lit the fuses and passed some to Ramulet. The captain took them, his respect for the young warrior standing before him increased. The courage and valour of these young ones was not only commendable, it was of the truly selfless nature that is seen so very rarely, even over centuries of time.

Meekhi touched flame to yet another fuse. She had had an idea. As the lead troll came within range, she ran straight at it and hurled the sticky, tar-smeared packet, at the beast. It slammed onto the creature's chest, and stuck there. The troll did not seem to notice the sizzling addition to its many existing bumps and protrusions. It began assaulting her with its deadly club-tail and flailing fists. Taking her lead, the others followed Meekhi's example. Thomas' aim was a little less than true and his package sailed straight over an oncoming troll and into the darkness. The others faired far better, and all of the oncoming trolls were soon carrying a little extra weight. More of the brutes would soon appear and to chance their luck further would be folly indeed. Mercy grabbed up the remaining bags of charges—of which only a few remained, and called to Meekhi; "My lady! 'Tis time to take our leave! My lord! A rope?"

Zowie told them of the horses they had waiting nearby and they broke fast away from the slow moving trolls. The Samarians swung themselves up into the saddles easily, hoisting the children up behind them. It was only when they arrived back in the city that they realised that Ramulet was missing. They had escaped two on each horse, but there had been only three horses and seven people. *Where was Ramulet?* Meekhi was the first on the wall above the main western gate to see him being hauled up on a rope by Bestwin and Lumarr. The others arrived seconds later to watch the captain 'walking' up the wall whilst hanging onto the rope. Arrows peppered the area around him, but, miraculously, he seemed as yet unharmed. Then the trolls below him began exploding. Deep, deafening explosions, echoed out across the desert, the sky lighting up a bright orange every time another one was blown to smithereens. Dense palls of smoke, heavy with the smell of gunpowder and burnt troll, hung poisonously in the air. The percussion blasts from the explosions had Ramulet swinging on the rope like an ape. Guardsmen rushed to help the Westonians heave him up, but not before a huge slimy ball of steaming intestines slammed into him, leaving him covered in a grisly, greasy, gruesome mess.

The sudden, unexpected defeat of the rock trolls had the Venomeens running for the cover of darkness to regroup and await Ogiin's next command. Everybody in Soledad was grateful of the chance to catch their breath. The odd arrow would be fired into the city when the Venomeens thought they had an easy target, otherwise an uneasy lull settled on the besieged city. The children were exhausted. The girls had suffered minor cuts and bruises during their brave foray into the night and Meekhi tended to these as Ramulet was led away to get cleaned up by Mercy—the fair-haired warrior pinching her nose shut as she led him gingerly by the hand.

The Samarians applauded the children, and Tamarin spoke to them; "My friends, your bravery, courage, and loyalty, leave me speechless. I offer you all my respect and gratitude for both—your skills, and your intimate knowledge of sticky bums."

"Aaaargh, it's *bombs* not bums, sort it out!" The girls corrected Tamarin once more, still cracking up.

"I don't know, girls," Thomas told them, "out there I think those trolls definitely met a sticky end, from our bums, or otherwise."

Zowie faked offence, "You are so utterly gross."

Lauren was laughing, proud of her brother's achievement, "Revolting boy!" Their ears were ringing. The sudden calm after the constant pounding of the trolls and the enormous explosions felt more than a little eerie. For now at least, Ogiin's fiendish hordes seemed to have retreated to lick their wounds, and, no doubt, conceive some new devilish plan. A handful of the sticky bombs remained and Tamarin thought them an excellent weapon should the enemy deploy their siege towers the next day. Only two bombs were left within easy reach of the western gate, and the rest were safely stored away to prevent any errant spark from the flares from causing problems. The gates needed immediate repairs and a work party was formed for this task. Lumarr and Bestwin would watch over the men as they opened the gates a fraction during this break in battle and made good the damage inflicted upon them.

Tamarin and Meekhi were taking a cool drink of water, sharing precious seconds under the velvety night sky when Mercy came running with Ramulet in hot pursuit. Her face ashen as if she had just seen a ghost, she stood directly before them, and in a voice brimming with anger and sorrow, she sobbed, "The Shadows…we have seen four of our own, dead, horrible, cruel deaths, Shadows… lurking within the city."

Meekhi and Tamarin looked at each other with eyes that barely disguised their fears. An enemy as potent as the Shadows, as hard to kill, appearing in their midst was a devastating, but not unexpected, blow. Once again, wielding torches, the people of Sitivia moved apprehensively in tight groups throughout the city of Soledad. The men at the gates worked feverishly to complete the repairs. A clutch of Venomeens that had not retreated with the main body suddenly charged at the workers out of nowhere, hoping to get into the city through the open gate and wreak havoc from within. But it was a futile attempt—the massive warhammers of the Westonians swung into action in a flash, smashing the life out of the bloodsuckers, splattering their flabby bodies, their skulls flattened to pulp in the sand. One of them attempted to escape back into the darkness, but a dozen arrows from above put paid to his cowardly plans. Lumarr and Bestwin bravely left the safety of the gate and took a few steps out into the desert, wanting to be sure no more of Ogiin's scum lingered close by. They found nothing and withdrew, once more serving as eagle-eyed sentries.

Tamarin, with Meekhi and the children in tow, patrolled the city with the 'Flame of Dragonia' in his hand. It was unlikely another Shadow would risk itself by appearing near him, yet, simply because he *was* the *king*, he was a prized target, and hoped to draw their attentions. Sadly, and much to the horror of all, especially the children, now and again they would find the dried up corpse of an unfortunate Samarian—the face contorted, twisted in agony just as it had been when the very life-spirit was drawn from it. The repaired gates were closed and sealed again at last. Imo tripled the guards at the eastern gate to prevent unwelcome entry, but also to prevent his new young friends from taking any more foolhardy risks.

Cries of alarm had Ramulet looking out to the west, at first he thought the dense smoke from the sticky bombs still lingered, then, he thought a cloud had settled on the desert, but realisation dawned swiftly, and was not welcome. Venomeens were approaching the fortress of Soledad en masse, creeping forward with shields raised over their heads, their ranks swollen by Hoary Hags. The icy bodies of the withered crones were so cold that it was they that had chilled the warm night air. So much so, that it appeared as if a freezing mist loomed ahead. Soledad was once more subjected to a deluge of arrows. Tamarin's mind raced. "Do not break from your groups!" he roared out, "Stay together, and keep your eyes and ears open! We have beaten them back once, and shall do so again, in the name of the Great Dragon, STAND FAST!"

Out of earshot of the others, Meekhi whispered secretively in his ear, "Tamarin, we cannot hold the wall and brace the gate whilst these robed ghouls may twist the dagger of death at our backs. We must beat back this new assault quickly, so as to keep our people as safe as possible from the evil that is now already *within* the city." Even as she spoke, a blood curdling scream was heard from deep in the heart of Soledad. A sudden, horrible, and helpless end for yet another Samarian.

Tamarin made a decision and took a gamble, he ordered his archers to considerably reduce their efforts, but not cease firing entirely. He wanted to give the impression that his people were tired, dead, or out of ammunition. As the rate of fire waned, the approaching hoard seemed to gather confidence and pace, swarming towards the city across the open ground. Tamarin tossed a sticky bomb to Imo and took the other for himself. He and the guardsman lit the fuses, and waited. The Venomeens and hags began to mass at the gate, crowding right along the foot of the wall. Just as the fuses were seconds from the charge, they lobbed their deadly parcels into the middle of the gathered throng. A blinding flash, followed by a deafening 'BOOM!' filled the night, echoing throughout the city and causing windows to rattle. The bulk of the enemy at the gate were blown to oblivion, those that survived were picked off from the wall as they ran screaming and screeching in panic back into the darkness. The arrows inbound for Soledad and her occupants ceased to fall.

The entire city heaved a huge sigh of relief, as far as the eye could see there was no enemy in sight, but how many times could Ogiin's scourge be repelled when daylight was still such a long way away.

"I suggest, Sire," Ramulet put to Tamarin, "that even Ogiin is not aware of the might of the weapons of the British Army. The devastation caused by the sticky bums may well confuse that cold-hearted demon, buying us precious time. But most, we need the daylight to return, in the dark our people are being killed mercilessly, murdered, with no chance to defend themselves."

"I pray you are right about buying time, captain, it is a commodity in short supply to us, but one Ogiin has to spare." Tamarin confessed, "There is no more left for us to do but wait, our options have been depleted to none, and only behind these high walls can we have any say in what transpires. There can be no further action on our part other than protecting the lives of those in the city, at least until dawn lifts the dread of Shadows. We must await the hand that fate deals us next, for at this moment we are not in a position to deal any card of our own."

Mercy came up to him, her laboured breathing a sign of her many exertions that night. Her hair was a shocking unkempt mane giving her the semblance of an angry lioness. "Come quickly, my lord, something strange is happening in the Throne Room."

"By my sword!" cursed Tamarin, "Nary a moment to think."

He followed her to the Throne Room as requested, where Meekhi, the Westonians, and the children, already stood. Nothing out of the ordinary was at first apparent, so he asked them curtly, "What? Why have I been summoned from my vital position at the wall?"

Mercy pointed at the statues standing either side of the throne. It took a few seconds to register because he could not believe what was happening right before his own eyes. The constant effort of keeping Ogiin's vermin from entering the city had taken everyone's undivided attention and no one had noticed that Soledad, herself, had now returned wholly to her former self. There was not a black statue anywhere in sight, and the city shone, her lustre restored in the light of five thousand torches. A rainbow of colour once more coursed through her veins as she eagerly breathed in the sweet breath of life denied her for so long.

Tamarin eyed the figures beside the throne, the fingers of each beginning to twitch and move. The quick-witted king immediately dispatched Mercy to gather runners, to tell the people of Sitivia to be grouped near the awakening statues of Soledad—no statue was to be left unattended and at the mercy of the Shadows.

The statues in the Throne Room wore the black mantles of The Royal Guards, men that had been in the service of King

Darcinian when Ogiin had sown his seed of poison in the bowels of the city and black stone had taken sway, until now. The children were completely absorbed in the rapid transformation of the stone statues. They stood gawping at the ancient guardsmen, their eyes popping out of their heads.

The figures had all the colour and vitality of a living soul, their hair moved in the light breeze blowing through open doors. Their eyes had been open and vigilant when the curse had overcome them, and they were open now. So it gave everyone a shock (Meekhi and Lauren squealed out aloud), when one of them suddenly turned his head and looked at the onlookers. He bowed to Tamarin, "My king, I have slept too long, the flesh was stone but my soul did not sleep, my lifeless eyes did see all—though there was little to see for so many a year, and my ears did hear all, and what I have heard pains me greatly. My heart grieves that your great father is departed from the shores of this world, but now *you* are king, and my sword is yours. I have slept from one war in one time to the same war in another time. Shall we now make this war the last war, my lord, king, and consign Ogiin, finally, and forever, to the underworld!"

The man tried to move forward, but limbs stiffened over centuries failed him and he was about to fall when many friendly hands grabbed him and sat him on the throne. His friend, too, was now awake. All over the city cheering could be heard as more and more of the ancient Samarians drank once more the heady elixir of life.

The ranks of the defenders began to swell quickly and the guardsmen high up on the wall looked down to see the city beginning to fill up with her native inhabitants. Men and women of yesteryear, warriors all, arose from their accursed slumber, joyously greeting their brethren of today. Vengeance was high on their list of priorities and they could not wait to face Ogiin and his filthy creed in open battle. Tamarin and Meekhi, genuinely delighted at the tripling in size of the force at their command, and the ending of Ogiin's curse of stone, outwardly showed only exuberance, but were privately very concerned. So many people crammed together into one city were sitting ducks for Shadows and Wispy Witches alike. Tamarin told Ramulet and Meekhi, "It is, in part, a blessing that the people of Soledad were fully at war when they became darkened unto stone. They have awoken with their warrior hearts hungry for blood and their minds already on a war footing. But their thinking is still slow and confused, and I, for one, am not surprised given their heinous ordeal of suffering. This grogginess makes them more vulnerable than those of us from Sitivia to the fiends that lurk in the darkness."

"Tamarin," Meekhi told him, "if we can but maintain our numbers this night, we can drive hard into Ogiin's forces at first light without hindrance from his night dwellers. Our ranks are swollen threefold by friends from the past. If we could then but crush them in the daylight, our work the following night would be so much the easier."

Ramulet approved, "An excellent plan."

Tamarin took a deep breath, "My mind was thinking as yours, my love. The sticky bums of the young ones have allowed our walls to be left unmolested for n…"

"Not again!" Exclaimed Meekhi, "My lord, you really must correct yourself, the young ones have explained to me the very improper meaning of the word 'bums' in their world."

"Oh, really?" Tamarin was obviously a little embarrassed at having to be corrected yet *again*, "I will pay more attention in future, and gratitude for informing me of this. One would not want to mistakenly offend our newfound friends, they having been such a godsend. But yes—a counter attack by day in heavy numbers could well break Ogiin's foul ranks. But first, before day comes, we must survive this night of ghosts in the darkness. Devils or demons, whatever they may be, it is essential they are not able to run riot in this city, every one of us must guard his neighbour, especially those rousing from their long sleep, only thus can we avoid the mass murder of our people."

CHAPTER NINETEEN

THE SILENT CITY FINDS HER VOICE

There had been no further attacks made against them for over two hours and the dutiful soldiers had not seen any movement as far as they could see. But the evil hordes of Ogiin were not far away, hidden in the night his legions of darkness smothered the sands of Samaria, the sentries could feel it, sensing their cold blood-hungry presence. The odd arrow would drop, spent, onto the city streets from time to time, or clatter noisily as it tumbled harmlessly down the tiles of a roof. Soledad—packed full as she was, still had streets devoid of people, the defenders avoiding those solitary arrows by moving only when it was absolutely necessary, flitting from place to place in tight groups with eyes peeled and torches held high. An uncomfortable mood hung over Soledad. Though the sticky bombs of the 'British Army' had—as Ramulet had predicted, dissuaded the black hordes from attempting another frontal assault, there was an entirely different breed of enemy now lurking within the city. Shadows had been seen in numerous locations, appearing and disappearing like the scavenging ghosts they were. Having been caught unawares by those phantom fiends, horrifying corpses began to appear here and there. Tamarin was made distraught by these killings. 'The Flame of Dragonia' was never anywhere near where these spectres made their gruesome kills. Perhaps they were now wise to the nature of his sword after the earlier events in Sitivia, and later, in the defence of Soledad. He took a scant break from his duties to visit his injured, be-winged, friends. When he entered the great hall, he was struck dumb by the miraculous changes that had taken place in his absence. Restored to its former glory the hall was nothing less than breathtaking, the vibrant colours and timeless beauty such a stark contrast to when they had first arrived in the city, but the hall, though truly a vision in full, glowing colour, was not the cause of his being rooted to the spot, spellbound. It was, in fact, the statue of the silver dragon that stood staring at him. It seemed to reflect the flickering flames of the burning torches, causing it to appear as if all the colours of the universe were flowing through its sleek, silvery, hide. The glowing ruby eyes, as big as war shields, twinkled brightly, crimson bursts flashing deep within their depths, hinting at an entire secret cosmos existing somewhere inside. Filled with awe, he had been stopped dead in his tracks. Bending to one knee, his magical sword standing before him, he asked of the Great Dragon; "My lord, the gates of Soledad remain closed, but the gates of hell remain open. I must serve my people and the people of my father's time. I cannot fail them. Yet daybreak is so far and Ogiin's phantoms are so close. My Samarians, *your* Samarians, are falling without ever raising a sword. Great Lord, there is no honour in such a death. I beseech you—show me a way to the devil, Himself. I wield the sword of legend that carries your own sacred flame. I will face Ogiin, for my people, for Samaria…, and for her that is my true heart. I ask only that you watch over those you deem worthy, and allow me to face this tyrant. I would give my all for this realm that I cherish in your name. The just must prevail."

The statue remained a cold, impartial, tower of stone. No answers would be found here, but still, a voice *did* speak. A voice weak with pain yet full of power, full of love, and born of faith, "My king," came the low horsy voice of Rordorr, "you are not king because you are the son of Darcinian, and he was not king because he carried his father's blood in his veins. You are king because The Source saw you fit for this purpose. The Dragons of Light are but the instruments of a greater power, as are you, as are we all. Have faith, lord king. You would not have been born a king without good reason. I am sure that that reason will soon be made known to you, and I believe you will serve your purpose well. I am grateful that I have been able to play some small part in aiding you in this cause, I..."

Rordorr drifted away once more into troubled sleep. Tamarin stroked the faces of the sleeping brothers and bade Babel continue in her care of them. He reached up and placed a hand on the lower chest of the nearby dragon, closing his eyes; "If ever there was one of faith that is deserving of the mercy of your good grace more than any other, then it is that miserable, incessantly complaining old horse that lies dieing at your feet. The only one thing he has always remained positive about is his faith... *in you*." Donning the mantle of leadership over his brave young shoulders once more, he marched back to his awaiting people.

He was greeted by the sight of a group of men led by Imo, running blazing torches over the outer frame of the gates. He did not have to ask why. Wispy tentacles of ruddy smoke were trying to enter the city. Thin smoky fronds were attempting to slither through unseen, snaking silently through gaps and crevices, shrinking back suddenly when repelled by the burning heat. Tamarin took Ramulet and Meekhi to one side, "I think Ogiin has the same game plan as us, but in reverse order. If he can greatly reduce our numbers by night, then his daylight army can overrun the city with lesser resistance. We can not allow this to happen, we must somehow hold fast against his nocturnal vultures."

The others concurred but, like him, had no new gambit to offer. The sentries continued to report no movement and the population continued to keep searching in all directions for Shadows. Croaking cackles were heard now and then, dotted about the city here and there. Despite the valiant efforts of everyone within the wall, the hags had finally breached Soledad, and could now hunt at will with the Shadows. Keeping them at bay had been a hopeless task, better to try and stop air from entering, though air, at least, hath no sinister intent, nor is its purpose set by evil incarnate. Some claimed to have seen smoky shapes wafting along the streets, disappearing into buildings when spotted and pursued. The hags posed a serious and deadly threat, yes, but not one that was insurmountable. Dangerous as they were, at least a man had a fighting chance against a Wispy Witch if he was armed with fire. There was no such weapon available against the Shadows bar the king's own blade.

The ranks of the guardsmen had been well swollen by the awakening of their brothers-in-arms, and these 'extra' men patrolled the city—protecting the populace whilst searching for the enemy. Sheer brute force had faltered, then failed, against the mighty walls of Soledad, and it seemed as if Ogiin's creed were now attempting stealth and guile, knowing the Samarians must be exhausted and longing for sleep. Despite the tireless efforts of Tamarin and his men, the number of those killed by Shadows kept rising. He ordered the featherweight corpses be removed to a single, secure, place. There would be time for farewells later, but, for now, the remainder of the people must not be made any more anxious by such gruesome sights.

He and Ramulet were walking back to the gates to see how Imo was fairing, when, suddenly, a Shadow appeared next to him out of nowhere. Dull red orbs could be seen just under the rim of the cowl before it shot into the air above him. He had no time to defend himself, even as guardsmen began running to his aid the blanket of death was already falling fast. Ramulet had only time to shout; "ROLL!" Then, instinctively, he slashed at the descending devil with the new sword gifted him by the king. Just as his gleaming black triblade had made contact with the falling death, Tamarin had thrown himself down, and to the left. Ramulet was as surprised as anyone when he felt his sword strike not a ghost but something quite tangible and solid. Blue ice crackled forth from the hilt and right along the length of the primary blade. The Shadow was instantly frozen—falling to the ground and shattering into tiny fragments which began to thaw and disappear immediately. Tamarin sprang to his feet to see Ramulet standing shocked, his eyes fixed disbelievingly on his sword. He jerked him out of his trance and told him; "Well, you certainly are full of surprises, captain, my gratitude for this one, and the countless many before it. It seems another magical blade has come to our aid, though I cannot explain it. Explanations enough later, we can not be positioned together until daybreak. Your blade protects half the city, mine the other. I will remain in this half, you take some men and do what it is the duty of us all to do."

"I will indeed, Sire." Ramulet headed for the other side of the city leaving Tamarin to ponder the miracle of this icy blade that was fated to fall into Ramulet's hands. Perhaps it did have his name written all over it after all.

Having witnessed the incredible power of Ramulet's new sword Tamarin thought immediately of his beloved Meekhi, and the fact that she could avail herself of any such magical weapons, he could not leave her so vulnerable. Heading for the Throne Room, he sent for her and the young ones. They arrived quickly once summoned and he was relieved to see them all well and safe. He was busy discussing his plans for a daylight attack against Ogiin when Lauren spotted an old, gnarled hand, reaching in through an open window. The air around it chilled and froze as it moved, and, despite her screamed warning, the Hoary Hag managed to touch a soldier on his shoulder. The man froze instantly, falling dead to the floor. Tamarin stormed outside to see a tall, haggard, old crone, cackling through a one-toothed grin. Large icy warts and weeping pustules covered her revolting bare body. He was momentarily shocked by her obscene appearance, and she cooed at him in her gravely voice; "Oooh…such a pretty boy you are… King of Samaria you are." Hooking a crooked finger, she urged him, "Come here my pretty king, let me touch your warm, royal, flesh…"

Tamarin's sword flashed, but even before it fell upon its intended victim, Lauren had put two arrows in the witch and Meekhi's own blade arrived at her neck half a second before his own. The Hag's head rolled into the gutter, and she began to liquefy. Tamarin's smile was all the thanks the women needed as he began barking orders to the gathered guardsmen; "Secure the city! This filth cannot enter as a phantom does. We have overlooked a window, a door, or a gateway! Seal everything. Do not drop your guard for a second, Curses! Soledad is infested with this vermin! I will not have them enter here! Do you hear me, men! *I will not have them enter*! Hunt them down and cut off their heads. *Kill them all*!"

The king's commands were followed to the letter, but it was still a ghastly night. Everyone was on tenterhooks, not knowing what would appear next, or where it would manifest itself. The glorious Samarian evening was poisoned with the gratified cackles of Wispy Witches and Hoary Hags as yet another poor soul succumbed to their black desires. Shadows silently took a heavy toll on the population. The guardsmen found it impossible to keep everyone safe whilst manning the battlements against any possible attack. Tamarin and Ramulet managed to destroy but a handful of Shadows, although that, in itself, was a considerable feat and did much for morale. Ogiin's creed became more brazen and prolific as the night passed—perhaps trying to maximise the harm they could inflict before the suns rose. The Hoary Hags and Wispy Witches suffered heavily at the willing hands of the warriors, Lumarr and Bestwin hunting them down with a vengeance, glad, at last, to deal out some just retribution. The Westonians had the ingenious idea of dipping their scimitars in oil and setting them ablaze, creating a weapon capable of dispatching either breed of witch. The guardsmen copied them immediately and not many of the crones survived that night in the city. In the far distance, finally, two paper-thin cracks of light began to appear in opposite directions, penning in the horizon. Dawn was coming, and the besieged, haunted defenders of Soledad thought the tiny slivers of light the most beautiful sunrise of their long lives.

The duel suns seemed to be climbing faster today, as if eager to bring a halt to the atrocities being committed in their absence. But their revealing rays brought forth a sobering sight. In the cool thin light of early morning, it soon became apparent that Ogiin's ghouls and witches had served their master only too well. The number of dead in the city was far greater than they could have imagined. The ancients defending Soledad had born the brunt of the losses. Still groggy and unfocused from their suffering under the curse, they had been the easiest prey for the enemy. Gruesome corpses, shrivelled in agony, littered the city, and perhaps only half of the recently awakened had survived those murderous midnight hours. The 'occupying' people of Sitivia had also suffered losses, but nowhere near so great in number. Guardsmen and soldiers collected the dead at Tamarin's command. They were laid out respectfully, out in the open, away from the centre. Meekhi was particularly upset at their number. "It's just too sad, and just so unfair. They suffered in silence for so long, only to be awakened momentarily, to then be slaughtered like so much cattle. Should I see that devil, Ogiin, I swear, by The Dragon! I shall tear out his black heart with my own bare hands!"

Tamarin, quite shook up himself at the loss of so many, so many that had known his father, wrapped her first in his powerful arms to soothe her sad heart, and then in his cloak to warm her against the slight morning chill. They stood thus, high above the city gates, comforting and loving each other. He whispered to her softly; "My lady, my love, my beautiful angel. I am of the opinion that Ogiin *has* no heart. Perhaps those that have departed from this world in the night would say—better to have lived again for a day and died as a man, then to have lived forever in bondage and suffering as stone. The suns are rising, Meekhi, and a new day dawns not just for them, but for us, for Samaria. Our ranks are swollen with many seasoned warriors. Today we shall exact a heavy price upon the filth that dares to soil our shores. Take heart, dear heart, the war is never won or lost until the final battle is fought, and we are far from that finality as yet, today we will drench the sands with the blood of our enemies. I wish that you carry the 'Flame of Dragonia' henceforth, it would ease my mind, my love."

She squeezed him tightly, absorbing both his warmth, and his strength of resolve. "No, Tamarin. It is the sword of kings, and *you* are my king of kings, you must wield the blade forged by Chjandi, the people need to see it in your hands, and so do I. Fear not for me, my hankering for vengeance be so great, it will keep my heart beating so I may witness your parting of Ogiin's head from his body."

They tightened their embrace, melting into one another, each noting they felt the chill no more. The children had been climbing up the ladder to talk with them, but upon seeing the tender embrace in which they were locked, they held back, silently retracing their steps to the ground below. They were soon joined by the Westonians, Imo, Ramulet, and Mercy. All of them stood looking up at Tamarin and Meekhi, and the sight of the royal couple sharing such a true love was a truly encouraging one.

Lumarr told the people in his booming baritone, "Samarians! You who have fought, endured, and survived the worst of Ogiin's creed, do not weep for those that are lost, but, rather, rejoice for those who have been found! You have been delivered from the night by him that now stands embracing your queen, him that embraces you *all* with his tenderness, and his truth! It is he that will lead you to final victory this new born day, join me now and pay due homage to your king. King Tamarin—*Lord of Samaria!*"

The wise old Westonian raised his sword in salute to the couple standing watch on the heights, silhouetted against the clear morning sky, and the entire city did the same. Blades raised high with pride, the crowds cheered, clapping and applauding the king and queen until the pair turned around to face their people. Meekhi stood holding Tamarin's hand as he spoke to his loyal subjects; "My friends," his strong, confident, young voice, travelled easily from his elevated position, falling upon his people like a warm, reassuring blanket, "today we are a new people, for today we are joined by those we lost so long ago. Soledad is no longer The Silent City! Today she has a new voice, and this voice overflows with defiance in the face of her enemies. In the face of all enemies of Samaria! This day, two cities have become one. Today, my good and loyal subjects, we will take this war to Ogiin, and to those of his vile creed, and we will wreak a vengeance as has never been wrought before! Our triblades were not forged for the cutting of corn! Our faith is not born of *defeat*, but of glorious victories beyond the counting! Go now—in the safe arms of the day, take water and food. Take short rest, and make keen your blades. For soon, we ride against the dark tide!"

The air was filled with deafening cheers, riotous applause gripping the city as Tamarin's fervor and courage steadied the hearts of his people. When this eventually subsided they gradually melted away into the city to do his bidding. Ramulet approached, his face was grave. They were soon joined by Mercy and the children, clambering up to sit along the battlements whilst Imo and the Westonians went to fetch food and water.

Exhausted, no one spoke, each lost to his, or her, own private thoughts, until Ramulet broke the silence, "We have three hundred horses at best, Sire. Not one of the ancient flying horses of Soledad survived the night. Those accursed Shadows waited for them to move, taking them from a height beyond the reach of our blades, our arrows harmless to their unearthly coil. Despite every effort our men could not protect the horses from the grey ghosts. Foot soldiers we have aplenty, but there are many hellhounds beyond these walls. Our men would be easy prey if caught out in the open. I am very uneasy as to the extent of Ogiin's true powers. The most potent weapons in our arsenal are the swords you retrieved from beneath this sacred city, and our faith. I suggest if Ogiin be seen, then you and I confront him and finish him. This is my take of our stock. Does anyone think otherwise, or offer sound alternative?"

They sat rubbing at their chins, pondering the situation, the children shocked to find themselve's imitating the others exactly in their very Samarian trait. Meekhi was of the opinion that foot soldiers could move forward in close support of the horsemen, fighting in tight hedgehog formations, but this idea was dismissed as the sheer speed and brute force of the hellhounds would have them in the rear of the Samarian forces before they could form up. The Westonians returned, and to everyone's pleasant surprise, they brought with them a large pot of beef stew, Imo hauling the fresh water. A piping hot savoury meal was just what was needed, and the cooks amongst the guardsmen had been busy in the kitchens working their own brand of culinary magic. Sentries kept a wary eye as the nourishing meal revitalised the population. The children had never tasted such a delicious stew, Lauren taking down the recipe from Imo and tucking it away safely inside her cloak.

Many ideas on how to tackle Ogiin's massed ranks were put forward, but all were cast aside as too risky. They could ill afford to lose more horses, the might of Tamarin's army resting mainly with his horsemen. The enemy was so great in number that a simple, straightforward, frontal assault would be suicidal, and it was impossible to outflank them with the limited resources at hand. But the clock was ticking and another dreadful night filled with the spectre of Shadows was but a finite number of hours away. The frustration began to tell as the small gathering sat high amongst the ramparts argued as to the best course of action. Zowie eventually broke the deadlock, surprising everyone by asking; "What would they attack with first? I mean... I don't know what I'm talking about, but I have an idea—it's probably crap anyway, but it might work, I think, or, it might not. But what would they attack with first? Trolls, maybe? What??"

Lumarr searched deep into the eyes of the young warrior before answering her question. "Hellhounds, they are to Ogiin as Heavy Horse is to us. The trolls are too slow for a first strike. Yes, it would be Hellhounds. He sent them first long ago, and he would send them first again, to smash through our forward lines and cause havoc in the rear as his bloodsuckers poured into the breaches in our ranks. I have seen this happen."

"Well...," she suggested nervously with them all staring at her, "what if you mounted the Wraths on carts, or, on wagons? I mean... to trap those stinking great hounds? Lure them into attacking with a feint, and then... our guys chip off...err... I mean *run out of the way*, and you can shoot them with the mobile Wraths. No soldiers trapped out in the open, and the Wraths able to manoeuvre at will? That could work, couldn't it?"

Suddenly she felt very foolish, what did she know of warfare? Especially warfare her own world had never seen the likes of. She elected to stare at her boot-clad feet whilst discreetly kicking at Thomas as this was more his thing and she expected support from that quarter. But to her surprise, as yet no one had discounted the idea. It was almost possible to hear their minds working overtime, whirring away tirelessly, weighing up pros against cons. Everyone looked up hopefully when Tamarin muttered, "Mmm, uh, yes... I see." But he fell silent again, and they continued to think as time marched on. Then he spoke, his words more precise, "A feint, yes, a false charge by the horsemen, to be withdrawn once pursued by those abominable hounds, and as yet safe from Venomeen arrows. Would not Thomas' 'Firewall' be effective in greeting the hellhounds?"

"Yes!" Thomas cried enthusiastically, "What's more, you could mount a few of those Wraths on flat carts too, as Zowie suggested, then, you will have mobile artillery! So if any hellhounds escape the 'Firewall' you can still take them down from the carts! Brill'! Sounds like a plan to me, you two are really on the ball!"

Tamarin could not help noticing that there was no ball under either his feet or Zowie's, but he bit his tongue, the children's strange language was, at times, still beyond him.

It was the only half-feasible plan on offer, and so was adopted quickly. It was still very early in the day but preparations for the counter attack were well underway. Four-wheeled carts were cut down to two wheels, for faster steering and increased manoeuvrability as Thomas put it, and the deadly crossbows were mounted on them. These newly formed chariots then had long curved blades attached to the wheel hubs, meant to take the legs of any vermin foolish enough to get close. The rotating blades had been Zowie's idea, and Lauren told her she would even pay for the therapist back home, as long as Zowie promised to attend the appointments. Men slaved in smithies to produce a stockpile of spears for the Wrath of Amaris. The lost lord, it seemed, despite his long absence, would still play his part in the coming battle by proxy through his Wrath. Regular soldiers and Royal Guardsmen, alike, sharpened their swords, filling quivers to bursting point and testing bow strings. The children—feeling a little useless at this point, went to visit the horses in the great hall.

Both the brothers were awake, though Rordorr was only semi-conscious. The girls knelt on the floor talking to him even though they were unsure whether or not he could hear, or understand, them. Thomas sat cross-legged, as was his usual manner, having a conversation with Faradorr. The children stroked their faces and Babel made up a light mash to be spoon fed to them. Faradorr was speaking of Rordorr's home far away in the foothills of a Samarian mountain range. He lived there with Eronell, his wife. Faradorr stopped talking when his brother stirred and began to mutter and mumble. They strained to hear him, finally catching his coma-induced words. "Take my brother and leave this great hall, and remember to take his wooden leg, I believe it lies close to the door. Fear not for me, for when the hall is destroyed the dragon will fall, crushing my skull and ending my suffering. My life is of no consequence, it truly matters not. I can see the rats have eaten away my wings already. Soon I will feel them nibbling at my ears and chewing on my tail. I always knew this would be my final fate. Strangely, I've always been friendly to their kind. Never trust a rat, my friends, never..."

Thomas, angry at hearing this enormous horse (that he had grown particularly fond of) uttering such defeatist gibberish, grabbed him by his huge muzzle with both hands, staring sternly into the beautiful animal's eyes, "You talk so much crap, Rordorr, you really do, the dragon fall? Crush your skull?? I'll tell you something—you miserable old sod, since I've been in Samaria I've learned a lot, and seen things I'd never imagined existed, but *now*? Now I believe in the Great Dragon *too*. Tamarin and Meekhi, all of you, have so much faith in The Dragons of Light, and I'm just so gutted that I will never meet one. What I'd give just to see one! The Dragon will NEVER fall, Rordorr, but your big, thick skull might well get cracked open, by me!"

Before drifting back to his haunted sleep the gigantic horse responded; "So, you are gutted. So sad, a tragic waste of years yet unspent, years you will never live to see. The wounds of war strike deep, even upon our youngest warriors. Take your own life, my good friend, a stomach wound can take days to kill and your suffering will be too terrible for..."

"Great! Now he wants me to top myself!" Thomas was fuming, "You try and help the big lump, and he suggests... *suicide*! That's it! I give up."

Babel rested her furry blue paw gently on his shoulder, telling him in her soft, soothing, elfish voice, "Never give up. A believer, a man of true faith, never gives up. Your words, other than those of the king, are the first to which mighty Rordorr has responded at any length. Take heart in this."

The she-elf was aware of the boy's fears of losing his amazing, but always so miserable, new friend—the horse. His emotions were betrayed by the tears loitering threateningly in the corners of his eyes as he watched over Rordorr, the girls also equally overwhelmed by concern. Their love for the horses forced Babel to hold Solipop closer to her, knowing the worst was yet to come.

The Samarians were ready for the second great battle for the city of Soledad. Tamarin and Meekhi strode into the great hall with determined expressions and purpose in their stride. The young ones would have to make their own choices as to their role in the forthcoming confrontation, if they chose to play any part at all, for the Samarians freewill was one of the great cornerstones of their faith. Tamarin told the children that Samaria would ride out and confront her enemy face to face, if she proved victorious, then praise be to the Great Dragon, if not, then they would destroy as much of Ogiin's creed as possible before nightfall, then falling back to the city to endure another night of his ghastly ghosts, before attacking again the next day, if enough survived. Should this become a war of attrition, then they may well face annihilation within a week, they could not sustain losses at the rate they had suffered the previous night. Daylight victories needed to be substantial and decisive, or all would be lost in the dark. What did the young ones intend to do? He and Meekhi urged them to remain in Soledad. She told them that their presence in battle would distract the men, thus possibly putting them in harm's way. The children said they would meet them in two minutes time at the west gate with their answer. When the Samarians had left, Lauren said, "What a load of rubbish! They wouldn't be distracted by us, they just want us out of harm's way, safe and sound, here, in Soledad. Nuts to that! I want a piece of that lot outside the city, and I think I've damn well earned it. Fair enough—we don't want to be tripping them up or getting in their way, but from what we've seen out in the desert, I think there's enough of Ogiin's creed for all of us."

"Way to go," agreed Thomas, "I'm with you on that one, we've earned the right to fight. I'm really in an arse-kicking mood and I want Ogiin to feel the benefit of that! Anyway, what are the Samarians without their ninja knight."

"Lauren's right—Tamarin is talking cobblers." Zowie, as ever, was direct, "We're as much a part of this as they are. If we hadn't created a dream then this nightmare wouldn't have been born in balance. That loser, Ogiin, needs a proper sorting out, it's true. What a prat he must be, eh? You've only to look at history, in any world, and you'll see all these wannabe tyrant types get their teeth kicked in. But Ogiin, he's already had one really good pasting courtesy of the Great Dragon, and *that*, guys, is exactly why we are going to *remain* in Soledad when the others leave."

"What! Why, no way." The Shortwaters were as confused as they now looked.

"Because," She whispered, wiggling her eyebrows up and down, "I have a cunning plan."

Relieved, they grinned back at her conspiratorially, "*Cool.*"

The first column of horses was waiting at the gates with Tamarin and Meekhi at the head. Mercy and Ramulet were behind them with the line streaming out astern, hundreds of men astride mighty war-horses, ready to take the fight to the foe. Further back still was the unmistakeable sound of countless boots marching, the foot soldiers making ready for action. The Westonians sat atop their mounts independent of the neat Samarian formations, their enormous war hammers far too unwieldy to fit into anything so precise. Imo's horse galloped up and down the ranks, the guardsman checking on the battle readiness of the men. Chjandi once told Darcinian—"If you fail to prepare, you prepare to fail." This ethos had become a byword in Samarian life, passed down from generation to generation, and today of all days, Imo would see it followed to the last letter. The children approached Meekhi and told her of their decision to stay. She looked relieved, telling them it was a wise and caring choice that they had made. When she told Tamarin of their intentions he saluted them with 'The Flame of Dragonia' and they returned the salute knowing full well they harboured secret plans.

Tamarin dismounted and sprang up the steps, standing once more above the gates with his sword raised. A sudden hush fell over the assembled warriors at the sight of the king. He raised his legendary sword even higher towards the heavens, "My people, friends, now we go to war, and, some of us, to our deaths. This is something we all know only too well, yet, still, here we stand as free men, ready to do our duty, to uphold our honour. The forces of darkness are assembled against us, and I will not deceive you, we are outnumbered beyond the counting and face a challenge more terrible than any Samarian has ever faced before! But we will not be deterred! Nor will we be made afraid! We, the people of the dragon, the keepers of the faith, we remain undaunted because the spirit of Chjandi is always with us. Beyond the massed Venomeens lies their puppet master, the heartless creature—Ogiin. It is this devil we must seek out and destroy. You know as well as I, should we fail in this duty that fate has charged us with, if we falter at the altar of self sacrifice, if we lose faith for but a second! The bloodsucking tide will swallow us whole. If that were to come to pass then not one free, living soul would remain! Our mothers, our sisters, our children, will all be consumed by the void, consigned to become no more than livestock, kept for the feeding of the black hordes, or a worse fate still at the hands of Ogiin. When our people are spent the tyrant will turn his greedy gaze elsewhere, for his avarice knows no bounds. Ride now for me, for Samaria, and for freedom! Today we take no prisoners! There will be no surrender! We will know not the meaning of compassion, nor claim any knowledge of mercy. Today, we must slaughter without thought like the savages we face! We will pile their rotting corpses so high they will blot out the very suns! Are you with me, my brave Samarians!"

A thundering roar rose from the waiting warriors as they beat their swords against their shields. Men and women alike raised their blades in salute,

"Samaria, and the king! Samaria, and the king!"

The heavy, battle-scarred gates of Soledad, opened wide, and with the dragon fluttering on streaming banners, Tamarin and Meekhi led the column out of the city into the fast-warming sands of the desert.

The children waved their farewells as the horses passed by them, some of the men and women nodding their heads respectfully in acknowledgement. Then came the foot soldiers, tramping past noisily as the children eased away, slyly slipping away quietly towards the great hall, only to then double back and make for the east gate. On their way there they stopped at the stables, where Zowie had noticed some mules tethered earlier. They quietly unhitched the pack mules and led them away unchallenged—sentries were now sparse in number and far more concerned about the danger of any attempt to *enter* Soledad rather than to leave. They pried open the gates as quietly as they could, leading the plodding animals out by the nose. Zowie asked Lauren to keep watch on them as she sneaked back into the city with Thomas, he being the physically strongest of them. She had not had the time to explain her plan but the Shortwaters trusted her implicitly, she had always shown great leadership qualities and had never let them down yet. Lauren felt a little nervous loitering outside the wall with three mules, but the others poked their heads out from the gates after a few minutes to make sure the coast was clear. Thomas was carrying two heavy looking sacks, and Zowie a third.

"Supplies?" queried a curious Lauren.

"Sort of," Zowie explained, "there are five of Thomas' sticky bombs in each sack. No point in wasting them I thought. Ogiin, whoever, and whatever, he may be, is the source of all the crap that is happening to the Samarians. Dad, creating a dream and doing his 'test run' with the super models, allowed this Ogiin character his *nightmare* to restore balance—one chosen dream, one chosen nightmare. Why then, are *we* in Samaria? It's blatantly not a dream, is it guys? I've been thinking about what Meekhi told us in the Green Room about people being where they need to be. We are here for a specific reason, I think. Us not being here would mean no bazookas, no sticky bombs, right? We're here to help reset things back to their natural order, I really feel that. I know from now on, no matter what happens, even if we somehow make it back to our own world, I will always be a Samarian. Don't you feel it too?"

The Shortwaters looked at each other as if truly seeing each other for the first time. The three of them swished their cloaks, stroking the hilts of their swords, or, in Lauren's case—the silky smooth glossiness of her bow. They looked deep into each others eyes, "Yes—always Samarian." The Shortwaters pledged with sincerity.

"Fantastic!" Zowie was pleased, "So, we are Samarian, and we have sticky bombs, which are a lot more pleasant than Tamarin's version! Anyway, I bet Ogiin never had one of these babies stuffed up his…, his…*whatever!* So that's my plan, well… not literally, because that is simply just *too* gross, but if we can spot him whilst Tamarin and Co' are keeping him and his scumbags busy, we can get these bombs onto him directly, and blow his bloody nightmare apart! Dodgy but daring, what do you reckon?"

Thomas chuckled, "Dodgy is my middle name."

"Should've been your *first* name." his sister told him, adding, "Ok, Zee, if you two are game, then so am I, but I hope we can get the job done quickly, because if we have to leg it we won't get anywhere fast on these tired old mules. I think they were used to haul a big load here from Sitivia, and I think they think they're still hauling it!"

"From the look of them," joked Thomas, "they probably dragged Sitivia here!"

"Don't be mean, Tom." Zowie berated him before his sister had the chance, "Anyway, shush now, we've got to get over into that slack between the dunes—where Tamarin and Meekhi attacked from earlier.

Leading the reluctant mules forward, silver dragons blazing bright on their backs in the scorching heat, the intrepid young warriors began walking to the high dunes, aiming for the deep hollow in between. The sentries spotted them when they emerged from the blind spot in which they had been standing. Calling down to them some of the men urged them to return to the safety of the city, but the children turned, and looking up, faced them. Smiling, they raised their weapons in salute, and then continued on their course. The men did not pursue them but the guards at the east gate had a very large flea put in their ears by their commander. Tamarin had left strict orders that Soledad remain sealed, so sealed she would remain, aside from the parting of the young ones from another world.

Ogiin's army of ghouls, witches, hags, and hellhounds, had retreated further into the desert than had been first assumed. But Tamarin was not one to be fooled so easily, he knew this was because Ogiin wanted to thin out the Samarians by forcing them to over extend themselves, leaving themselves far more vulnerable to any outflanking manoeuvre and causing them to fight further away from the safety of Soledad's sturdy defences. Not too far into the distance he could see a long sinister line in the shimmering heat. It extended to the left and right as far as the eye could see. "Surely," he thought, "every single evil creature ever to walk the earth must have heeded Ogiin's call, and hell must be a lonely place today." He looked over his own brave soldiers, and despite their fearless commitment to the task that lay ahead, he knew, deep in his heart of hearts, that their numbers were still woefully low given the enormity of the massed ranks ahead. The only chance of winning this war was to destroy as many of the dark horde as was possible in quick order. If enough were destroyed it may allow him an opportunity to face Ogiin, Himself. Tamarin held no fears, he had no qualms about facing him in one-to-one combat, but he had studied his history and was very aware of the dark power that Ogiin's spirit possessed. Even if he could challenge him with Ramulet's mysterious sword allied with his own 'Flame of Dragonia', the outcome was most likely to fall in Ogiin's favour. After all, the master of dark deeds had fought, and mortally wounded, the Great Dragon, almost winning the day.

The heat was building in the air like a hot sticky glue, a thick gum that weighed down the chest and numbed the throat. As the suns rose ever higher on their daily trek, every breath became a laboured affair for men and horses alike. Tamarin and Meekhi knew they had to strike against Ogiin's creed immediately, before their people waned, becoming weary from heat exhaustion. Battledress was far from ideal for such prolonged periods and the men already had beads of sweat running down their faces. Soledad could still be seen quite clearly to the rear when they began to form up. The horsemen stood with their steeds snorting and stamping at the front. A thin line behind them masked off the "Firewall'. Outriders flanked the column—galloping up and down its length, maintaining a tight formation. Scouts scanned to left and right for any possible threat hiding there. The Samarians made an impressive sight as their silver chainmail gleamed from under black capes in the bright sunlight, bright battle colours waving proudly from atop pikes and lances. The foot soldiers made ready for action as the horsemen began steadily moving out towards the enemy, gradually gathering pace, the men on foot falling behind them far sooner than would normally be the case.

A great hysterical furore arose from the swaying mass lieing ahead. Meekhi kept apace with Tamarin, her eyes focused on the closing horde but her heart remaining locked on him as he rode beside her. She was adamant no one, and no thing, would harm her man that day. Tamarin had hoped the release of the hellhounds would precede the firing of arrows but he and Lumarr had overlooked a crucial point—the Venomeens' arrows would not kill, or even harm, the hellhounds, so they could be released directly into a volley, setting about the Samarians without fear of being injured by their own kind. Fortunately, the Royal Guardsmen—being Samaria's elite warriors, had some tricks of their own up their sleeves. As the sky darkened when a flurry of black shafts came whizzing at them, the riders pulled their cloaks tight about them, wrapping their bodies and raising the hoods to cover their heads. These most prized of all garments, given only to the most worthy of warriors, were woven from a fabric that was almost impervious to arrows. The missiles rained down and the pained grunts of those unlucky enough to be hit in the hands, or worse still, the face, were unsettling, but, on the whole, the riders sustained minor losses. A pair of horses fell immediately, still mounted riders scooping up those that had fallen from their saddles as they passed by. Tamarin dared not commit to a headlong charge as keeping the correct distance from the 'Firewall' was critical. He began thinking about abandoning the plan rather than exposing his limited number of horsemen to the full fury of the enemy. But then, and for the first time it was to his great pleasure, the shrieking wails of the hounds electrified the air. Meekhi saw the ever swelling tide ahead begin to sway and move, familiar black shapes bursting forth and hurtling towards them. They could not turn and flee straight away or their trap would be discovered too soon. Tamarin discreetly slowed his horsemen whilst continuing on a direct course towards the closing mass of fur and fangs. Even in the baking desert heat the ear piercing cries from the approaching monsters caused his skin to prickle. He took a quick glance, noting the equally grim expressions on all the faces around him, all, bar Meekhi, who shot him a warm smile. The horses were hesitant, reluctant to continue further toward those gaping jaws, but they were pressed forth all the same. It was then, as the opposing armies closed upon each other, that Tamarin felt his heart stop. There were far too many of Ogiin's creatures. The closer he got the further he could see, and the full extent of his enemy was a devastating sight. He had never dreamt that hellhounds still existed in such numbers. The 'Firewall' could not possibly destroy so many. He had to save his people and even as those enormous bared fangs became visible to the eye, he ordered his horsemen to turn about, and retreat. Where had so many of those damnable hounds come from? From what bottomless well of evil had that accursed tyrant dredged up such a multitude of minions! Where had they lain in wait all these many years without discovery? Against such odds he measured scant chance of any victory, but surrender was beyond contemplation and they charged back over the same ground, his mind racing to find answers to seemingly impossible questions.

The hellhounds had the scent and had not seen such a feast for an eternity. Now they craved satisfaction for that age old hunger. With black tongues lolling wetly from their ferocious jaws, they thundered along after the horsemen, eager for that first, firm bite, into ripe, tender, flesh. The riders, themselves, tore along the sand, each hoping to rejoin his comrades in one piece. Arrows poured into their backs, but the special fabric of their capes served them well, the deadly black shafts mostly failing to pierce it. The impenetrable weave did a good job of protecting their horses too, but the hellhounds seemed to be outpacing them. Their gigantic leaps were bringing them closer and closer to the tail end of the fleeing men with every passing second, and the desert shook with the sound of the chase, the men manning the 'Firewall' feeling the ground vibrating under their feet.

Climbing aboard her mule, Zowie yelled, "Sounds like it's all happening out there! We need to hurry up!"
"Yeah, it sounds really awful. I hope everyone's ok. I think we should take a quick peek, just to get our bearings." Lauren didn't much care for the sounds made by the hellhounds at all, "I want to get stuck in as soon as possible, or I'm going to need to have to wee. Nerves..."
They persuaded their tired grey mules up the high bank of sand until they could see out across the desert. They saw the horsemen in full flight with the hellhounds in hot pursuit and rapidly closing the gap. Their hearts fell as one when it became obvious the 'Firewall' could never deal with so many of the fearsome beasts. Zowie looked at them, a deep, faraway light, shining in her eyes. "You know what?" She asked them, "What's the point in trying to get to Ogiin if those stinking great hounds have already destroyed Tamarin's army? Maybe even killed him, and Meekhi, too? Those Royal Guards are well hard, but the Wraths need time to re-arm and the hellhounds aren't going to sit and wait for that, now, are they? I know it's a stupid thing to do, but I'm going to use my sticky bombs *now*, and try and help Tamarin deal with those bloody great hounds. I don't know how we are going to take out

that scumbag—Ogiin, afterwards, so I'm just going to have to do what the Samarians do, and put my faith in the Great Dragon—Chjandi. Are you two game? I think it's the best help we can give right now."

Thomas was definitely game. "Yeah, like I'm going to let you go out there alone, it's going to be a pant filler for sure, but I'm coming with you, in for a penny, in for a pound, sis'?"

"Need you ask? I'm in, but, Zowie, you're going to owe us *both* new pants all round, and no dodgy 'off the market' ones either, I'm talking proper lush designer jobbies."

Zowie agreed to the future purchasing of new underwear, "That's a deal then."

At last the horses were out of range of the Venomeen archers. It was stifling under a hood in that desert and Tamarin lowered his to allow cooling air to his sweltering face. He looked across at Meekhi, making certain she was still beside him and unharmed. Mercifully, she was, and remained without injury. Further out across the sands he could make out what appeared to be three mules being ridden by riders in Samarian battledress. They were coming flat-out towards his position as fast as the mules could cover ground. A mirage caused by the rising temperatures no doubt. He had no time for such bizarre visions right now as the last of his men could hear the deadly snapping of jaws at their backs. Meekhi also saw the mules heading for her and she recognised whom it was mounted aboard them, time would reveal their intentions and purpose soon enough. A wry smile marked her face. The bold hearts, and boundless courage, of these young ones were a marvel to her.

The horses finally began passing friendly faces, streaking past on either side of the most forward element of foot soldiers. These spread out, forming a wider line behind which the horses could run on, and began to move towards the brutes bearing down on them. Patiently they waited, barely able to breathe, their hearts beating deafeningly in their ears. The air was alive with the almost tangible tension of impending battle. The hellhounds, their mammoth paws pounding along the hot surface of the desert, were only twenty feet away, when Tamarin roared, "NOW!"

The men forming the frontline dived to the ground and the first row of Wraths let loose their fury. The long spears sailed through the air, ripped through fur, flesh, and bone, the momentum of the charging monsters driving the stakes home even deeper. The front runners fell as they ran, some stumbled over their own forelegs—their bodies bowling over and over. Yet more were reared up by the force of impact and fell back into the path of others. The rest of them—eyes blazing in fury and brimming with bloodlust, leapt over their own, blinded to all save making a kill. But these too were brought down as row after row of bowmen released the deadly potency of Thomas' 'Firewall'. But despite the enormous black corpses beginning to mount up, the most rearward of the beasts had changed course so as to circumvent the certain death awaiting them at the centre, and attack the Samarians in the rear.

The men saw what was happening, and knowing it would be difficult to get a clear shot from amongst their own, those with loaded crossbows disbanded the 'Firewall' so as to be able to shoot freely at will. Swords drawn, Tamarin and Ramulet rallied them together, preparing them for the onslaught of the hellhounds that had bypassed the frontline and would be hitting them in seconds. Meekhi was standing ready with the men in the front ranks when Mercy joined her. She had been staring hard into the far distance, and now turned to her friend, "Mercy, look yonder and inform the king of what you see there. Today, my dear, true friend, the courageous heart of our people will be tested beyond any limit. The suns shine so brightly upon us, the day is bursting, so full of light, yet I fear we are about to be buried under darkness."

Following Meekhi's eyes, Mercy could not believe her own, Ogiin's creed were moving forward as one enormous body. The Venomeens were waving their swords and shields in the air as they moved, their ranks swollen by the misty ice-figures of Hoary Hags. Their master had seen fit to keep some rock trolls in reserve too. She pulled back her long golden mane and stored it in a tight ponytail. Watching her queen staring steadfastly at the approaching tide, she told her as she wheeled her horse about to go in search of Tamarin with her news, "Meekhi, the Great Dragon is with us. We will abide, and, we will conquer. In days soon to come you and I, together, shall drink mead, a *lot* of mead, and talk of this day triumphantly as we bathe away the memory of such things in the Emerald River. Even Ogiin cannot save poor Ramulet from becoming my husband!"

Meekhi was laughing out aloud as Mercy's dappled grey charger took off in the direction of the king. Mercy's steadfast loyalty was a steadying staff indeed, but as her horse disappeared from view, Meekhi bade the Great Dragon bless her and Ramulet, that they may survive beyond today to know happier times.

The hellhounds ploughed into the Samarians as would a brutal desert storm. Men were hurled aside like leaves in a gale, others were crushed underfoot, some, still reeling from the impact as if hit by a battering ram, slashed at the wailing monsters with their triblades, driving them deep whenever they could. The loud, horribly feminine screams, coming from such decidedly *unfeminine* creatures, were shockingly unnerving, and some were forced to cover their ears with their hands, trying to block them out. The brutes did not pause for a second, seizing their opportunity, they took big, bloody bites out of the near-deafened men. Tamarin, mindful of Mercy's further alarming news, tried time and again to get close to one of the rampaging monsters. His horse, wedged within a compress of men, made it difficult to manoeuvre, and despite his valiant efforts, Lady Luck it seemed chose not to favour him. Ramulet had faired better, managing to drive the black-mirrored blade of his sword directly through the eye of one of the snarling beasts. As he had retracted the weapon the creature had suddenly stood rock still, cracks forming along the entire length of its body, tracking quickly to its head. It then turned to ice in an instant, and when the blade was rammed into its frozen belly it crumbled to pieces, melting quickly into the hot sand beneath. But now Ramulet was also struggling to get close to another of them as they turned and twisted amongst the men, savaging everything within their reach.

Tamarin's keen mind was still racing. He knew his brave warriors would eventually overcome the crazed creatures, but if this did not happen quickly, the hellhounds would reduce their numbers gravely, and already they were too few to challenge the black flood rolling towards them at such impossible speed. Lost to his quandaries, he was taken completely by surprise when he was told of the children approaching on mules. Not able take a minute's absence from his duty, he told the messenger to ride out and meet them, bringing them hither. He knew the young ones well enough by now to know that this was no chance visit to the battlefield. The messenger returned in short order, "Sticky bums, my lord, the young warriors have brought you their sticky bums."

"The word is *bombs*, not *bums*." Tamarin told him, unable to hide his immense gratitude from the watching children.

Gathering Meekhi and Mercy together, he handed out the messy bundles. The children were watching and he told them; "I am very happy to have you come to our aid once more. We have sore need of the British Army, and, in due course, an alliance must be formed between our two great lands. Samaria will be honoured to know a nation such as yours as friend. Let us put end to Ogiin and his creed, then your queen must come and drink, dine, and dance with us, under the stars! She must be a warrior mightier than most!"

The children chuckled, envisaging their queen partying with the likes of Meekhi and Mercy. But, being true patriots, they had to say something in response, Zowie piping up, "Yes, you're right, a true warrior... *in her own right*, I'm sure she'd be very pleased to make your acquaintance."

Lauren was cracking up and just couldn't stop, "Going to be dancing on the tables with HRH, are we?"

Zowie gave her a stern look, "Oi! behave yourself, don't be nasty, HRH is pure legend."

The threesome carrying the fizzing explosives made for the hellhounds. If it was not possible to reach one of them in person, then the bombs were passed from hand-to-hand until a brave soul was close enough to the deed, slapping the sticky mess onto the creature's fur. As soon as the bomb was attached, they fell away fast—encircling the beast, taunting it, trying to keep it in one place until it exploded. Lumarr and Bestwin, pounding at a hellhound's face with their enormous hammers, managed to force it to jump into the middle of a pack of its own kind. Bloody devastation ensued, and once more a grisly hail of guts and gore thumped down upon the warriors, the men cheering at the gruesome visceral downpour. But their jubilation was soon cut short when Tamarin ordered them to, "Turn about!"

CHAPTER TWENTY

THE RANIN RETURN

Venomeens ploughed forward, unstoppable, their excited, unearthly clucking drowning out all else as they surged across the desert. Hoary Hags also cranked awkwardly over the sands, unceremoniously carried along by the surrounding tide of pale, sagging flesh. Their haggard old frames crabbed forward at a shockingly fast pace, long, gangly, arms, outstretched before them, eager to place their withered hands on the living, inviting them to join with the dead. For those watching, the surreal sight of their bared icy forms streaking towards them under the glare of the suns was enough to send a tremor through many a sword hand. But never *more* than a brief tremor as the men steeled themselves, the involuntary shake quelled instantly by iron discipline. Adding to their sense of impending disaster, they could see that Wispy Witches would, unexpectedly, join the fray this day. Normally cowardly predators of the night, claiming sudden kills by stealth, today they would endure the discomfort of daylight to know the rewards that came of pleasing Ogiin. Behind them, the surviving trolls lumbered onward—seeking to wreak a terrible vengeance for the destruction of so many of their own. Trolls of both evil breeds were in evidence—mono-eyed Rock Trolls moving clumsily alongside their black-and-hairy, two-eyed cousins from the mountains. Only the Shadows remained amiss, they, and their dark lord—Ogiin. Most surely, he, his hounds having already caused such havoc amidst the Samarians, could not be far behind his legions.

Ramulet and Mercy were having a last ditch discussion with Tamarin and Meekhi. The children listened in as Imo and the Westonians marshalled the men. It was pointless now to try and cull enemy numbers. The hellhounds had caused catastrophic damage and had it not been for the timely intervention of the children and their sticky bombs, it was doubtful if anyone could have expected to make it back to the city alive. The plan had to change. Archers were brought to the fore to try and stave off, or, at least slow down, the enemy's advance. The plan now consisted of reaching Soledad alive. It was a simple plan. A plan based purely on survival, because the Samarians, finally fully aware of the impossible challenge facing them, were in full retreat.

Bestwin and Lumarr chose to linger close to the archers at what had been the frontline, and was now the rearguard, allowing the others to make for the safety of the city. The Westonians were still livid at Dorinn's failings and treachery. Guilt, though unjustified, needled at them as might a prickly thorn, and they were determined to delay Ogiin's slithering scum as long as possible in an attempt to save as many lives as they could. But they knew well that none can the shape the destiny of another. Fate was at play upon this battlefield—her most preferred stage, dealing out her hands as she deemed fit, doling out life and death with each throw of her weighted dice. Before long they were joined by Tamarin and Meekhi, who, in turn, were followed by the children and Mercy. Ramulet arrived next with Imo. Gathered together amidst the surrounding chaos of war, they listened closely when Tamarin spoke; "The speed at which the black tide spreads over our sands is too great for any successful retreat. We cannot outrun Ogiin's creed unless we sacrifice those that are on foot. Suffice to say we will never abandon our own, so that is not an option. The walls of Soledad simply cannot be reached in time, so, we have two choices. We die like cowards, fleeing from the enemy with arrows in our backs and Venomeen fangs buried deep in our throats, or, we die like that which we are—Samarians, Westonians, and these great warriors of the *British Army,* fighting to the finish, not once thinking of surrender, never trading freedom for tyranny, or allowing a fate worse than death to befall our women. I will take the latter choice, because, for me, there is no other. Each of you, and the assembled army, will make your own decisions, I can ask no man to give his life, for it is by freewill, the cornerstone of Chjandi's teachings, that Samaria was born, and by that belief she will endure, or fall. But do not dally in your musing. We have but precious minutes."

Meekhi reached out, gripping his arm by the bicep. "Whether I live or die, my lord, it is of no consequence. I am here, beside you, I am where I was born to be. I would not wish to be anywhere else, not now, not ever."

Bestwin allowed Lumarr, being the senior, to respond. "We are ready, come what may. These old Westonian blades are the same steel that stood by Darcinian, they will now stand firm with you, today, and all days. Your friendship has proven faultless, you record of honourable alliance unblemished, if Samaria should fall, then we Westonians fall with her, if she rises triumphant and victorious, our cheers shall be deemed loudest of all. The games are afoot, lord, king, let us play them out to the end, side-by-side."

Ramulet, too, was resolute. "I am Captain of the Royal Guards. My sword belongs to my king."

"You've gotta be in it, to win it." Lauren offered thinly on behalf of 'The British Army'.

"Quite so," Mercy agreed, ruffling the girl's hair.

Imo, having no woman to call his own, lived happily in the love shared by the brotherhood of the Royal Guards. He was still smarting from the loss of dear friends and was determined their sacrifices would not go to waste. Looking from face to face in turn, he said his piece, "I shall tell the men to make ready for our greatest hour, not a one will give an inch of ground to Ogiin or his creed, I swear it! Samarian unto death, we stand or fall united under the banner of the Great Dragon. My blade, its craving now unchained, lusts for Ogiin's blood, it's thirst be so great, it would swallow up rivers until it savours that which flows within his veins. Have no fears, the men know your resolve to be as unmoveable as the mountains. Whatever course we take under you, we will prevail. I shall return shortly to await your further commands, my lord."

From up high on the battlements the remaining guards watched their king turning his retreating men once more to face the pursueing hoard. It was certain death. If the enemy had consisted of armed men alone, he would still be vastly outnumbered. But this was no army of men, but, rather, an army of darkness. An unimaginable swarm of unnatural creatures, of monsters forged in hell, possessed of powers that no mere mortal could hope to match. The sentries could see their brave, beautiful queen, rallying her forces, her sword, bloodied in battle, still gleamed bright in her hand, the dragon emblazoned so proudly upon her back defiant, her faith unfazed by such hopeless odds. Her horse moved here, there, everywhere! Galloping from post-to-post, galvanising her people, Meekhi was proving to be the true warrior-queen the nation had always trusted her to be. The baking sands of Samaria her home, she moved upon them without so much as a glance at the ocean of evil about to swamp her. Her majesty unquestionable, her sovereignty absolute, she was the epitome of leadership. The men knew she would not only defend every last square inch of this barren desert, but every single grain of sand that lay upon it. The harsh, searing landscape had been called many things by many people, but the Samarians called it home. Home is where the heart is, and her heart belonged to the king.

Not many had remained in the city after the army rode out, for Samarians were a warrior race, each one capable of defending their faith and their freedom. Most had left with the king to do battle. Now, Soledad—empty for so long, felt once again forlorn, deserted as her few remaining inhabitants gathered up arms and marched out across the blazing desert to join with their brothers. If this was to be their last stand, then it would be the stand that stood tallest in the annals of history.

Tamarin and Meekhi sat in the middle of the front row with their friends fanning out to the left and right. Meekhi fondled the vial glowing at the base of her throat, wanting the memory of the moment of when she had received it to be vivid in her mind if this day became her last. Tamarin's hand rested reassuringly on her thigh, the occasional light squeeze still causing her pulse to quicken as it had always done. They would wait until the enemy was almost upon them before commencing their last charge. Not wanting the horsemen to leave the foot soldiers adrift and exposed, the final assault would have to well timed, the riders would smash into the enemy causing their lines to break, those behind them exploiting that advantage as best they could. To a man, each had it in his mind to survive as long as was possible, with or without injury, killing as many of Ogiin's vermin as could be killed before the inevitable came to pass. These unholy invaders would be made to pay the heaviest price this day and this one thought united them all to that one purpose.

Tamarin asked Meekhi to stay by his side. She lifted the small vial from her neck and kissed it, her eyes all the reply he needed. Ramulet and Mercy were sharing these few precious seconds together, he told her; "My lady, forgive my past ignorance. I have not paid heed to the most important of my duties, fool that I am. Were I to have again the time that is now lost, we would have been wed long since. May the Great Dragon see fit to allow this lowly soldier the joy of your presence in years yet to come, for be it so, you will not find me lacking again, I swear it!"

"Do not despair, my love," She replied with a bright, genuine smile, on her angelic face, "have faith. I have told Meekhi—even the dark, wretched soul of Ogiin, cannot save you from my hand. Be assured, my beloved Ramulet—I am no deceitful liar, nor a conjuror of falsehoods such as that witch, *that wanton harlot*—Teritee. You *will* marry me, or face me… in combat."

Ramulet emulated a not entirely false shudder at the thought of facing her in battle.

The children were sitting three abreast in their saddles to the left of Meekhi. Lauren was in the middle, "I'm *totally* crapping house bricks, *breeze blocks* in fact, but if I could wake up safe at home in the Dreampod right now, I wouldn't. I really need to see this through, even if it kills me—which it probably will. How are you two feeling? Are you ok with this? You've gotta be crapping it like me, yeah?"

Zowie was indeed in the same frame of mind. "Yes, I'm the same as you, Lauren, house bricks, breeze blocks, and a couple of bags of cement too, I think! But whatever happens in the rest of my life, if I have a life after today, it'll never measure up to this. It has occurred to me that we might have died in the Dreampod, *you know*, gone to heaven and all that, good fighting evil, I mean that could be possible, right? I mean Samaria is exactly how I imagine heaven should be, and Ogiin is evil incarnate."

Faking a yawn, Thomas predictably tryied to lighten the mood, "Don't know about you two, but I've suddenly got a craving for a garlic-chicken kebab."

The suns were half eclipsed and Ogiin's forces only minutes from the warriors awaiting them. The men stood firm despite the apprehension churning away in their gut. They could see the bared fangs of the Venomeens quite clearly at that short, rapidly decreasing, distance, and many a man instinctively placed a hand over his neck, as if protecting his blood from being plundered. The suns did their utmost in their reduced state to bring brightness and splendour to those facing darkness and horror down below. Swords shone, and armour gleamed. Horses whinnied anxiously, stamping on nervous, impatient, hooves. A gusting wind picked up, lofting the proud banners so that they streamed out, the dragons fluttering bravely for all to see. Tamarin's voice sounded throughout the desert. "Steady! Steady! Make ready!"

Razor-sharp lances were lowered, ready to skewer the foe, pikes, deadly and lethal, were brought to bear, eager to impale any daring to challenge their purpose, arrows were pulled tight on strings as taut as steel, and the Wrath of Amaris, evident in abundance, prepared for its final acts of violence in the name of its creator. Tamarin raised 'The Flame of Dragonia' up high for all to see, dazzling those that caught sight of it. Light danced along its length, the suns blessing the mythical blade with many kisses from the heavens. His black charger reared up as the wind snatched up his cloak about him, and pointing his sword at the oncoming Venomeens, he gave the command. "In the name of the Great Dragon, attack!"

Hundreds of silver arrows sailed over him from the rear, climbing steadily toward the coupled orbs in the sky, before hurtling down into the front ranks of the enemy. They fell in scores, but the fallen were replaced even before they hit the ground. Tamarin's horse was in full stride as he hunkered down beside it, eyes focused ahead. Beside him, the others also charged headlong into battle. Foot soldiers raced along behind the horsemen with blades readied and shields braced, pounding through sands that offered unusually good footing, as if Samaria, herself, were bending a knee to their victory. The riders too close now, the archers ceased their barrage, and the Venomeens raised shields and lowered thick, long stakes, then, Tamarin's horse smashed into the wall of pale flesh and fangs. The sound of steel-on-steel filled the air as the leading Venomeens were cut to ribbons by the horsemen. Cutting, slashing, stabbing, kicking, punching—Meekhi kept herself at Tamarin's back. The sheer momentum of the overwhelming hordes had engulfed the Samarians. Horsemen and foot soldiers alike were surrounded on all sides. In an instant they were fighting for their lives and the children formed the 'hedgehog' position which they had learned of in Soledad. In the midst of the teeming chaos they protected each other, striking down anything that came close. The Samarians were no strangers to battle and had had the foresight to dip their arrows in pitch. Many archers carried smouldering lanterns lashed on at the hip, enabling them to send fiery death to Wispy Witches whenever the opportunity arose. But a dull, resounding, 'Boom-Boom-Boom' warned that the trolls would soon be amongst them, their thick hides as impervious to arrow points as they were to the edge of a sword.

Tamarin knew it was impossible to maintain this intense level of combat for long. The constant drain on one's inner energy took its toll very quickly, survival drawing on every ounce of strength from every fibre in one's being. They would tire fast against this tireless foe, and the trolls were coming, unstoppable, near-invincible, giants, that would tear his people apart. There remained no more weapons of the young ones' making to be used against them. Amidst the pandemonium of battle it would be impossible to get in position to strike between the scales. Had the foe been lesser, or if he had had a greater force, the battle would be more widespread, and they may have been able to tackle them if able to manoeuvre, but squeezed as they were on all sides, it was a deluded fantasy, a distraction best dismissed. Incensed at the futility of the battle forced upon him and the needless loss of his people, he was slaughtering the enemy by the dozen. But dozens meant little when the enemy numbered in the thousands. His sword dripping with black blood and blazing with its inner flame, he was constantly aware of Meekhi fighting alongside him, and many a Venomeen reaching out to snatch the queen as the most coveted, and fertile, prize for Ogiin, was sliced asunder by the 'The Flame of Dragonia'.

Ramulet was leaving a long trail of frozen, fast-melting Venomeens behind him. The captain had known this battle to be doomed from the onset. "But it was to be their most shining moment in all history," he thought, as he severed limb after limb from the enemy. If Samaria fell, the dark tide would eventually engulf that entire world, the evil of Ogiin then fanning out across the universe to consume all other worlds, until the light of life was snuffed out everywhere. Man's right to be born free and pursue his dreams would be replaced by the everlasting nightmare of tyranny. Ramulet could see his warriors bravely battling not just against the enemy, but against fatigue. The women waned first, succumbing to exhaustion in that terrible heat, their fallen figures not seeing life for long after as the ravenous Venomeens pounced on them, sucking them dry of blood in seconds. It was galling seeing the fiends even attempting to devour the remains, tearing away flesh as if it were strips of wet parchment, raising their faces to gulp it down. The battleground was a scene from the very heart of hell itself. The awful sights, the foul smells, the heartbreaking sounds of such suffering, spurred the Samarians into summoning up every last ounce of energy to try and crush this armada of evil.

An enormous grey arm, covered in scaly armour, lashed out across a group of men, slamming into them like a brick wall and brushing them aside as if they were weightless mannequins. Their broken bodies were immediately pounced upon, the Venomeens sinking their bared fangs deep into their throats, stealing away lives that had only minutes remaining in their mortal coils. Guardsmen armed with lances, pikes, and all manner of long-reaching weapons, tried to get to them, but those that succeeded found it impossible to concentrate whilst fighting off Venomeens and avoiding the probing hands of the Hoary Hags. The crones were ever-present, hovering just behind the bloodsuckers, awaiting their moment to reach out and strike with a simple deadly touch. The constant cackling of the witches put test to many a man's resolve, distracting them, unnerving and unsettling their discipline. Such was the nature and tact of Ogiin's creed, to harass, shock, and frighten, until one made a fatal mistake, let one's guard lapse but for a second, and the murderous throng would be upon you.

Neither Tamarin nor his companions had expected the presence of yet more rock trolls. They had been thought to be near extinction, and so many had been destroyed by the weapons of the British Army. Ogiin, it seemed, was full of unpleasant surprises. Tamarin's people fought on in vain. Their lives were being lost for no measurable gain, it was impossible to deal a telling blow against so vast an enemy, a foe combining so many different threats within its arsenal. They had been fighting so hard, and for so long, but had made no discernible mark on the enemy. Carving a way through to Ogiin was a feat beyond their capabilities. All had been given but nought had been gained, it now seemed wiser for them to gain time within Soledad if retreat could save even a few, lick their wounds there, and form some new stratagem, if any existed to be had. Riders could be sent to neighbouring lands, warning them of Ogiin's advances whilst the oldest citadel of Samaria delayed his unholy host, buying precious time for other nations to make preparations for their own survival. Tamarin was crestfallen, thwarted at every turn he raged in frustration, feeling shame at not leading as his great father once had. He signalled his men, and the retreat was sounded. The first blaring call went out to the foot soldiers, so that they may have a chance to escape to the city, then, a little later, to the horsemen.

"For once, just *once!*" he thought to himself, "Something must *surely* go in our favour? Can we not even retreat successfully!?"

Those fighting on foot made for Soledad and those on horseback prevented the enemy from giving chase. The horses could easily outrun the waddling Venomeens and hobbling hags, so a few extra minutes of time for the fleeing soldiers to escape could be bought without too much sacrifice. Satisfied that they were well on their way, Tamarin ordered the full retreat, a single, crystal clear, horn, sounding it out to all. But none of his horsemen turned about in response. The children stared at each other, puzzled. Tamarin grabbed Meekhi's hand, his eyes searching hers. Even the enemy froze at the other sound that everyone, apart from the king, had heard. There it was again, a trick of the wind, perhaps. He ordered the retreat be sounded again, the small bugle trumpeting out his command for the second time. This time, just as the guardsmen made to turn about, the other sound came again, closer this time. Closer, and clearer, it was—The Call of Comrades, the signal Samarians sounded to declare their arrival, and, their aid. The deep bass sounded yet again. Unmistakeable! It was most certainly The Call of Comrades, but from where, by whom? Tamarin's army, once more in full retreat, turned their heads to their right and saw a sight not ever seen before by any of them save the very eldest. Lumarr turned to face Tamarin, his eyes blinking bright with hope, and informed him with great joy, "It would appear, my lord, king, that the *Ranin*... have returned home."

Tamarin slowed so quickly, his mount barely had time to respond, stumbling over its own legs and almost pitching him from the saddle. He wheeled the horse around, his riders clustering about him. The men almost at the city saw them stop and turn, the king facing the enemy. Parched with thirst and drained from fighting they overcame limbs reluctant to move, and began heading back. The temperatures had risen to the point where the stifling heat had become intolerable, many shedding any unnecessary items as they trampled, sweating and breathless, across the unforgiving sand. They left a long trail of discarded debris behind them, stark and ominous against the desert. Ogiin's legions shrieked and howled at the men just beyond their reach, but they ceased in their pursuit, their great momentum winding down, faltering, and, finally, petering out. Now, instead of giving chase, they were staring in shock to their right, just as the horsemen were doing to their left.

The suns broke free of each other abruptly, their sudden combined brilliance lighting up wave-after-wave of blue cloaks on the heights below them, capes that bore the eternal symbol of Samaria—the rampant silver dragon. Long dark hair, streaked liberally with the silvering of time, draped the mighty shoulders of hundreds of Samaria's most powerful, and deadliest, knights. Their horses, the *Mercerin*, looked down from above, pawing at the sand with their steel-blue hooves. The long, single spike protruding from their foreheads was of a matching shade and it was lowered for battle, with eyes of the same colour flashing angrily at the scene laid out before them. The sight of so many Ranin, mounted upon row-after-row of the pure white Mercerin, was more than anyone below could have hoped for, striking fear deep into the hearts of Ogiin's creed. Long silk banners adorned with the dragon danced excitedly atop silver lances, swords and shields winked like jewels in the sunlight, and, with deadly intent in their eyes, the Ranin eyed the filth amassed before the city.

Tamarin could not believe his own dumb luck, "They must have seen the flames I sent skyward yesterday by a chance mistake. Certainly I did not expect anyone to heed the ancient call, nor, if truth be told, did I know if a single Ranin still survived after these many long years. Yet there they now stand, as bold as you please, and as welcome as ever any Samarian could ever be."

The Ranin eased their Mercerin over the soft ridge and down the steep sand, pouring from the heights, heading for the men standing between Soledad and Ogiin's creed. The incredible size of the fabled unicorns—the Mercerin, dwarfed even the likes of Rordorr, and their pace was simply breathtaking as they moved across ground like the wind. One could not hear one's own thoughts as the pounding of their heavy hooves beat out a steady drum roll upon the desert. The riders aboard them were experienced men, battle-hardened knights that knew only duty. They had served Samaria well, carrying her proclamation of freedom and justice to faraway lands for years beyond the counting. Toppling would-be tyrants, serving the meek, feeding the needy, and protecting those less able, they had travelled far and wide bound by their oath, and now their presence humbled even Ramulet. Many of them had longed to see Samaria once more, to know the heart warming hospitality of home, to sit in peace and reflect with those who shared their faith. But a Ranin cannot return unless summoned, and the skies had remained devoid of any such invitation. When Samaria had called at long last they had come without hesitation, for, as everyone knows—there is no place like home. They carried their banners aloft with a pride so infectious, it spread across the desert like a glorious beacon of hope, lifting the spirits of the king and his people long before the Mercerin were lining up before him. The children looked on with leaping hearts, the magnificence of the Ranin and the beauty of their Mercerin was just too much to take in. Thomas, beside himself with excitement muttered the simple truth, "*Living legends.*"

Tamarin composed himself as the mighty white unicorns began gathering in front of him, tossing their heads and shaking out their manes before bowing at their rider's bidding. The Ranin saw the delicate silver band, the dragon at its fore, that encircled his brow. He was the new Lord of Samaria and *they* were now his, forever loyal, knights. One of the eldest of the men clad in blue capes spoke. His many years did not detract from his air of deadly capability, honour dripping from him as rain might pour from a steep roof, characteristics he shared with each of the others. His voice, brimming with sentiment and filled with reverence, remained humble despite his obvious power, "We saw the signal, my lord, king. We, the elders amongst us, served under Darcinian, since those far off times many more have joined our cause, and now, we are here to serve you. I saw the waves of evil ebb away long ago, leaving our shores free to shine in the sun, but it seems the dark tide has risen once more, risen to again threaten the people of the Great Dragon." He turned to Meekhi upon noticing her tiny sliver of a crown, and saluted, "It is good to see the rarest, most vibrant and spellbinding, of all jewels, still adorn the throne beside the king, my lady."

Meekhi bowed her head in gracious gratitude at the high compliment paid her, but waited for Tamarin to speak first, as was his right, "My noble and most loyal of knights, your return was undreamed of, and yet, it is a dream come true. Dreams and nightmares appear to be the order of the day in these trying times. I lit the old signal by mere chance, a mistake I am very happy to have made. I had not the remotest thought that our wandering knights—so long since departed, would heed the call, or even yet exist to see it. You are at once most welcome, and sorely needed."

"It is fitting, then, that we are summonsed, and thus returned, Sire." The obvious leader amongst the Ranin replied, "Each of us was born but a babe-in-arms on this sacred soil, and now, at last, we can die as knights-at-arms, in war, or in peace, in Samaria. We are home, and here will we remain until we make the final journey to join with the spirit of the Great Dragon amongst the stars. As ever we served your father before you, we serve you now. Your Ranin await your command."

There was no time for lengthy explanations. Ogiin's forces were gathering themselves again after their initial fright upon seeing the Ranin on the heights. Meekhi quickly told the Ranin knights of the situation whilst Tamarin formed a new battle plan. The Ranin added an enormously powerful punch to the beleaguered Samarians. Royal Guardsmen achieved the status of Ranin purely on their martial prowess and their unquestioning devotion to the king. The Mercerin were deceptive in their beauty, those long, sleek horns, gleaming blue under the suns, could penetrate any armour or shield. These fighting unicorns were well versed in the art of trampling evil-doers the world over. The combination of Ranin and Mercerin, was deadly, hence they normally travelled as only one rider and one horse. United under the banner of Samaria as they now stood, they could prove to be the undoing of Ogiin's army of ghouls. Now, at last, the Samarians had a real fighting chance to win the battle and destroy the enemy. Tamarin would use exactly the same tactic as before because it would not be expected. The horsemen—this time led by the Ranin, would charge and penetrate the enemy centre with a view to ploughing through to Ogiin. Tamarin and Ramulet—riding at the head of them, would engage him, and, with The Dragon's blessing, defeat him. The Ranin, perhaps only five hundred in number, were eager to win their spurs in this new conflict, and a small group volunteered to break from the main thrust of the attack and take the battle to the trolls. They did not fear the icy hags, their mystical mounts were immune to that deadly touch, and those magical blue horns would kill any hag as easily as the flame within the king's own blade.

The children were struggling to contain their excitement. Unicorns! They simply could not believe their luck. Who hasn't dreamed of seeing such a wonderful, fantastical, glorious animal? Despite the danger ever present on the battlefield, the unicorns seemed to impart a feeling of fearlessness upon all about them, their very presence a font of courage. Zowie asked one of them if she could stroke it, but was told by the Ranin sat in the saddle that the Mercerin did not speak. She could, however, touch the gleaming white coat. Both of the girls leapt at the chance, stroking and petting the exquisitely soft hide until the palms of their hands were at once polished, and dirty. They were totally captivated by the Mercerin's big, deep blue eyes, in which bright sparks seemed to dance constantly. Water had been rushed up from Soledad for the far-travelled Ranin and their mighty steeds. The battle weary defenders of the city took the opportunity to ease their own croaking throats as they watched the Knights water their mounts before, themselves, drinking from the same buckets.

With hope restoked, the Samarians formed up to challenge Ogiin's claim to universal rule. Newfound confidence coursed through their veins as they made ready. They knew the haunted night would surely come again, leaving even the mighty Ranin at the mercy of the Shadows, and that was why this war must be won... *today*.

CHAPTER TWENTY ONE

THE DRAGON SPEAKS

Rordorr's half conscious eyes parted open. His mind was adrift on a raft of Babel's medications and the pain from his wounds was still excruciating. He raised his head from the cushions that had been placed beneath it, and tried to look around. The Benijays could not be seen anywhere, (they had gone to the wall to observe the arrival of the Ranin when the horses had been fast asleep). Then his eyes fell on the snoozing form of his brother. The sickly Rordorr had to blink several times to be sure of what he was seeing, but his eyes were not deceiving him—Faradorr was engulfed in flames. He felt his hope for his brother draining away from his heart, the blush of life fading from his own cheeks at the sight, and then he realised that he, too, was ablaze. Yet he felt no pain from the blue flames that danced all over him. In fact, he felt less pain than before from his wounds. The burning horse began talking out aloud to himself. "Ah yes, too far burned now to feel a thing. Myself, and poor, dear, Faradorr, reduced to no more than a roast dinner for those damnable Venomeens. I hope they choke on us. No doubt, even now, Solipop and Babel are being boiled alive for dessert. Kind, brave little elves—they tried so hard. The desert must be awash with our dead, the sands as red as wine from their slaughter. So ends the time of Rordorr, I pray my beloved Eronell has escaped to..."

"SILENCE!" a rich, fiery voice, commanded the horse.

He ceased his ranting immediately. The Voice spoke again in its warm, wise, infinitely powerful tongue of fire. "Rordorr, you are truly the most miserable of horses. The most miserable of *all* animals! A well of misery so deep none could fathom its depths! Yet, some would say you are the most worthy of the greatest of gifts—the gift of life, and that, of love. So you shall have them, for they have been asked of me by your king on your behalf. *Do you know me*, you whining fool of a horse?"

Rordorr, still not convinced that he was not hallucinating in his final death throes, craned his neck to look about, even though his heart knew exactly where The Voice had come from. His eyes settled on the silver statue of The Great Dragon. Only it was no longer a life sized statue, it was *alive*. An intense kaleidoscope of colours, matched only by those within the vial at Meekhi's throat, flowed through the smooth, flat, silver scales in elegant waves. Pin pricks of every conceivable colour danced and twinkled deep inside the majestic body. It lowered its head from far above to face the now trembling horse. Chjandi, the greatest dragon to ever exist, and lord of The Dragons of Light, asked the cringing animal again in a deliberately low tone, "Do... you... know... *Me*?"

"Yes...YES!" Rordorr stammered, "You are Chjandi—the Great Dragon. I am just a simple horse. I thought you were dead, my lord. NOT *actually* dead...I mean... you were...err, you were not *here* anymore! You had gone somewhere else."

"Be at peace, Rordorr," Chjandi told him, "Love never dies, it is always everywhere. You have but to see it to know it, as I see it in you."

Rordorr, seeing the flames receding from his own body as they also diminished from his brother, staggered to his feet as Faradorr awoke.

"You see it in *me*? My lord, I am just an honest horse who knows his duty, honours his king, and reveres his queen. My brother *Farador,* on the other hand, is an exceptional horse! He's much smarter than me, as sharp as an eagle and braver than any horse I know. A shame he will die so young, he..."

The Great Dragon lifted a mighty forearm and Rordorr clamped his jaw shut tight. Chjandi told the horses in a tender, more paternal tone, "I have bathed you in the light of love, and the flames of life, be well. You have each earned your due time in this life, be sure to earn it in the next. Now, I have long unattended affairs to settle."

As he moved his great limbs to flex them, Faradorr could not resist asking him, "My lord, please forgive my bad manners, but I have a question—if I may ask it of you, please?"

"Ask then, little brother." Chjandi's voice was as warming as a mug of hot, milky cocoa, on a chilly winter's day.

"How did you come back to life in a statue?"

The red ruby eyes of the enormous dragon narrowed, so as to focus solely on the inquisitive horse standing below it. "I can not have come back, if I did not ever leave, Faradorr. Time should teach us all to prepare for the unexpected. My spirit, that is to say, a beat of my heart, has resided within what you have deemed a statue since its creation, a long time before your last great war. I am always with my heart, so I have remained within it too. Now it is I, and I, am it. In the mists of history past I placed another part of myself—a lick of my flame, within the sword your king now bears into battle. If the flame of my life and the spirit of my love were ever reunited—I would again return. It is the prophecy written on the very blade of which I speak:

> *A dragon's flame burns within,*
> *And when that flame makes my heart sing,*
> *then you shall know why I was made,*
> *and your darkest foe shall soon lay slain.*

"Your King—this bold young Tamarin, did inadvertently strike my tail with his flaming sword when he sought to light a torch to aid a child. The result is what you see before you. Rest here, my winged brothers. You have done your duty, now it is time that I did mine, for it is long overdue."

The horses did not dare to say another word. They just stood watching the dazzling dragon prepare itself in readiness to leave the great hall of Soledad through the wide-open dome.

Samaria

The children were in the saddle, lined up alongside Tamarin. This time they felt far more confident because they could see Mercerin dotted amongst the front rows, snorting and tossing their heads, their riders brandishing triblades forged in ancient fires long ago. Lauren had her bow in hand, her brother watching her—thinking how much she had changed, and wondering if he, too, looked as mature and composed as his sister. Zowie was running a wet stone along the edges of her sword, when Lauren told her, "You're actually looking forward to this, aren't you, Zee! I can see it on your face, you're gagging for it, I don't believe it, talk about mad axe murderer, all these years and I never realised just what a psycho you are. But the weird thing is I think we're all up for it here but *you*, you're wanting to do some really bad damage."

"*Actually*, I am!" Zowie replied honestly, "I can't deny it. This Ogiin really deserves what he's going to get, he started all this nasty crap and look how many good innocent people have been hurt. If we have to be here, and I'm really *glad* that I am, then I'm going to make every second count. After all, it's our wish for a dream that awoke Mr Maggot-Face Ogiin. As Ramulet often says—*kill them all*. I totally agree with him, it's a great philosophy, and there really is no other way you know. There's no problem if there's no problem, eh, so let's kill 'em all! I can see exactly why he was made Captain."

"As can I." added Mercy, sitting close by on her charger.

Lauren looked at them both in turn and grinned. "There's something very wrong with you two, so very twisted, very, very, twisted, indeed."

Naturally, Thomas had to have his say, "Not as twisted as me, sis', I'm more twisted than a twisted thing, even after it's been twisted some more!"

Mercy chose to ignore that which she could not understand, instead borrowing Zowie's stone to edge her blade.

Lumarr and Bestwin came thundering up to Tamarin. "My lord, we two shall keep some of those trolls at bay alongside the Ranin. These hammers can shatter boulders, and will crush at least one stony skull today."

He nodded his approval as Ramulet organised the horsemen, Imo forming up the men on foot. All this was done swiftly and smoothly, so when, at last, the enemy began moving forward, all that could be done had been done. Tamarin raised his sword, spurred his horse, and led the charge.

The Mercerin moved like lightening, outpacing the other horses in seconds. They tore into Ogiin's ranks as if they did not exist, obliterating their frontlines, slicing through as if parting corn. The hysterical screaming of a hag ripped through the dry desert air when a Mercerin speared her cold heart, tossing her melting form to one side as it ploughed on. The Ranin cut a deep swathe into the Venomeens and witches before the rest of the Samarians arrived in force. The battle for survival was on. A Venomeen drove his sword into Zowie's horse at the chest, she being thrown from her saddle. Mercy scooped her up, only to then have her own steed injured, both riders then being forced to fight on foot. Swords slicing the air they fought like enraged tigresses, surrounding themselves with the dead and dieing of Ogiin's creed. Lauren and Thomas had also been brought down from their saddles, and were fighting back to back. Avoiding the Venomeens lunging for them with their deadly jaws, they slammed their shields into their faces. The Ranin were hunting down the witches. One after another the obscene crones were howling their own death knell as sleek blue horns pierced cold black hearts. Ramulet was using his magical sword to good effect on the Hoary Hags, most of whom were desperately trying to find sanctuary amongst the teeming Venomeens. Open battle was not the usual hunting ground of any witch and they were there only at Ogiin's inexorable bidding. They preferred to snatch their prey with cowardly stealth in the dark of night, exposed out in the open under the blazing suns, they struggled to deny the Samarians their deadly intent.

Tamarin and Meekhi worked as a team. Circling as they moved, they found Venomeens and witches alike too afraid to face 'The Flame of Dragonia', allowing them to slaughter them mercilessly as, in desperation, they sought to escape death by fiery steel, scrambling over each other to avoid those eager flames.

A resounding, 'CRUNCH! CRUNCH!' told everyone that Bestwin and Lumarr were using their enormous war hammers precisely as promised. A towering brute of a Rock Troll could be seen grabbing at thin air and pounding the ground with its fists, trying to pulverise the deceptively agile Westonians who were battering away at it in turn. Big chunks of its stony hide flew off with each blow amidst a shower of sparks, but it was by no means defeated as yet. Its spiky club-tail hovered menacingly, scorpion-like, poised to land a fatal blow in an instant. Its snarling, brimming over with rage from the beast's core, could be heard by all across the battlefield.The aged lords pummelled away at the ponderous creature, relentlessly landing blow after devasating blow, but it just refused to keel over, the pounding hammers serving only to infuriate it further.

A pair of the dim witted trolls had been lured away from the centre by Ranin taunting and teasing them. They were swinging their tails and smashing their fists at the blue cloaked knights as the Ranin sought to drive a blade home between their tightly stacked scales. One of the trolls was caught completely unawares when a Ranin unexpectedly charged it head on. It spread out its overly long, apelike arms, ready to ensnare the knight, but his Mercerin reared up onto its hind legs, and using all the full might of its enormous frame, the unicorn rammed its deadly horn deep into the troll's chest. With an anguished roar that echoed over and over, the grey colossus crashed to the ground, sending a large cloud of filthy dust shooting up around it. The Ranin swooped in, half a dozen triblades finding their mark under the troll's scales. It died howling like a pained wolf—much to the delight of the Samarians and the horror of its own kind. The killing of the seemingly invincible troll spurred the warriors into ever more blood letting against Ogiin's creed. Samarians were being lost too, but Ogiin's vast land armada was fast shrinking in number and the remainder of it was only too aware of this fact. The Samarians—bolstered so dramatically by the returned Ranin, were now very much on the offensive and

Ogiin's own creed seemed to be shying away from the vengeful warriors, shrinking back towards the west.

Out of nowhere, and without warning, the air suddenly filled with swarms of flies. With thick, black, bulbous bodies, the disgusting insects were everywhere, the dreadful drone of their furious buzzing drowning out even the sounds of battle. They crawled all over the faces of the men and women, clogging the hair of the living and filling the open wounds of the dead. It became difficult to see past the clouds of insects and the Samarians were forced to squint, tightly screwing up their eyes and covering their noses to prevent the horribly fat bugs from crawling in. The baking desert resembled a scene from some biblical plague as the flies caused mayhem amongst Tamarin's people.

Ogiin's army seemed to relish this arrival of disease infested vermin. The hags cackled once more trilling their tongues with excitement as a terrible hissing furore arose from the Venomeens. Ogiin's creed broke free from the entangled chaos of war and retreated back, leaving the Samarians face to face with them, separated only by a narrow strip of blood stained sand. Tamarin rallied his people to him. Now was the time to strike, to finish this blight of darkness that had dared to run rife within his realm. At the head of his horsemen, he was about to initiate another charge when the enemy ranks began to part, directly ahead of him. A clear corridor appeared in their midst, and, at the far end, stood a lone figure. It was tall, far taller than Tamarin, and big, bigger even than Lumarr. A flat, cold, emotionless evil, emanated from the distant entity and washed over the Samarians like the cold, clammy hand of death itself. Ogiin.

Having feasted upon the ebbing life of so many dead and dieing, the demonic warlord had recovered much of his former physical self, an outward appearance some might now even call starkly handsome, albeit with a cruel, detached air. His hair, long once more, was of a dark russet hue. The skin appeared translucent, as white as the whitest porcelain. His features were fine and chiselled. He wore somber black leather battledress, and carried a single-bladed sword thrice the measure of any triblade. But now his eyes were of their true nature—flat discs of a bleak blue that would flash red every few seconds. The swarming clouds of flies rose as one from the weary warriors and spiralled directly towards the motionless figure. Lauren, appalled at the sight, vomited when the insects streamed up into the nostrils of Ogiin's nose. In no more than a single revolting minute, the entire crawling mass had disappeared inside him. His eyelids closed and he began to walk through the corridor of evil under his command. There was a boast of supreme confidence about him, an arrogance born of his fearsome reputation as *the dragon slayer*. He was only forty feet from Tamarin when he stopped and opened his eyes. Now, they were bright scarlet, blood red, with no pupils. His sinisterly glowing orbs did not move, staring ahead like those of some grotesque, monstrous doll. The wailing and clucking of his puppets had reached a crescendo when the puppet master raised a hand, and silence fell upon the desert. After the roar of battle it was deafening, ominous, brimful with foreboding.

Tamarin eased himself down from his horse and faced him, "Ogiin! Sucker of souls, and foulest of all filth, face ME! I shall cast you down to the lowest pit in hell, an abyss from which you will never escape. This is *my* realm, *my* kingdom, *my* Samaria! As long as one Samarian breathes life, you shall never abide here!"

Before speaking, Ogiin closed half the distance. The sound that came was beyond cold, more frozen than the blackest ice, flat, carrying no emotion. It wavered neither in note nor in tone. His voice was the voice of death, haling from beyond the pale, and it left no doubt as to his terrible intent. "No Samarian will remain breathing, save, perhaps, your queen. I *shall* abide here forever, harvesting her pleasures at my leisure. Your heroes have failed you and darkness now descends on your very existence. You have no future, puny weaklings that you are, and your pathetic history will not be remembered beyond today. This land will be burned to the ground, as was Dragonia, and I shall build my reign of darkness over the ashes of your Dragons of Light. I am not one to be challenged by mere mortals such as you. Die now, and do so quickly—an entire universe of souls awaits my feasting upon it."

The Samarians looked to their king as the children reeled under the sting of the venom in Ogiin's words. Tamarin stepped forward, moving towards Ogiin, it was the only course left to take. He knew Ramulet was right behind him and he had very strictly ordered Meekhi to hold back. As the warlord and the Samarians approached each other, guardsmen and Ranin poured into the breach, filling the corridor of death, packing it tight, holding back the black masses for fear of a treacherous attack upon the king. Ogiin's creed cackled and clucked, buzzing with excitement, certain of the imminent destruction of Samaria. The children, despite Meekhi's pleas to stay back, had stayed close to Tamarin, edging along in his wake.

Ogiin moved slowly, confidently, smirking as he handled his monster of a sword with such obvious ease. Its tip curved cruelly, jagged, vicious-looking, barbs running along one edge of the blade. The two men pounced as one, but Ogiin was too fast. He side stepped Tamarin's strike easily as his fist found Ramulet's face. The captain was thrown back with such violence he felt sure his neck must surely be broken. Mercy raced to help him, finding his neck to be swollen and bruised, but, miraculously, still intact. He staggered to his feet as a furious Mercy charged at Ogiin, only to find the flat of his blade slam into her midriff, dropping her instantly to the ground, struggling to find breath. Thomas and Lauren ran to her aid as Ramulet, his head spinning, weaved unsteadily towards Tamarin. The king was fighting sword-to-sword with the would-be tyrant in a savage flurry of blows. Flames streaked and blazed from 'The Flame of Dragonia' but Ogiin remained calm, manoeuvring his own blade with only one hand as if casually fencing for sport with a young novice. Ramulet, his nose broken, and bleeding profusely, joined battle once more. This time he and Tamarin tackled Ogiin from opposite directions, causing the warlord to divide his attentions and thus, perhaps, expose any weakness. But much to Ramulet's angst, Ogiin employed his dark magic to produce a deadly, duel-headed battleaxe, in his free hand, a weapon he used to fend off the captain with ease. Meekhi, predictably enough, had completely ignored Tamarin's command to hold back, and was helping the Shortwaters pull Mercy out of harm's way. The fair haired warrior was still struggling to fill her lungs with vital oxygen, and, by the agonising pain in her side, she knew she had suffered at least one cracked rib. Ogiin seemed tireless, smiling as if he was only toying with Tamarin and Ramulet by way of amusement. But this was no game to either of the Samarians and with a dazzling display of speed and courage, Tamarin finally managed to step inside of his enormous blade, 'The Flame of Dragonia' scorching a sizzling trail across his pale face. The wound did not bleed, but a long black gash appeared—stark against the deathly white skin, running right to left from forehead to chin. Ogiin's red eyes glowed brighter, and swatting the legendary blade aside like a child's play stick, he grabbed the young king by the throat. Ramulet seized the opportunity, sliding through the sand beneath Tamarin's dangling feet and driving his blade up and home, deep into Ogiin's belly. The warlord tossed Tamarin to one side as Ramulet regained his feet. To the shocked horror of the gathered Samarians, he calmly pulled the sword out of his own body whilst Ramulet was still pushing hard on the hilt. He hoisted the blade and the captain aloft, wielding the weapon by the blade with both hands. Its kiss of frozen death had not had any effect on the grinning demon. Meekhi, too, saw her chance, and pelting forward, she rammed her sword right through his neck. She could not believe her own eyes when he turned and smiled at her with the weapon still protruding either side of his throat. Holding Ramulet high in the air dangling from his own blade, he kicked out at her. The tremendous force of the blow sent Meekhi sailing through the air, landing hard amidst her people. Upon seeing their beloved queen assaulted in such a vicious manner the Samarians made for Ogiin en masse, but were immediately overrun by his gloating throng. Tamarin knew it would prove fatal for them all were they to become entrapped in the midst of such a vast number. He called for his people to break free before the corridor engulfed them and reform beyond the reach of the enemy.

Tired, wounded, and in complete disarray, they fell back, their dwindling force regrouping to face the countless ranks assembled against them. When the enemy had begun to fall earlier, the Samarians had caught a fleeting glimpse of victory, a tiny window in which to turn the tables. But Ogiin's appearance had settled his minions, calming their nerves and resurrecting their confidence. Tamarin had learned, with great sadness, that even his magical sword could not harm this superhuman adversary. He did not know what to do next, all options had been exploited and had failed, so he chose do what he knew how to do well—continue to fight whilst breath remained. The men, tattered and torn, took up weapons and remounted their horses. As if it were a cruel game devised to repeatedly tease and humiliate, the horde of hideous horrors parted once more to reveal Ogiin standing at the further end as if he had not a care in the world. But, sickeningly, he had somehow captured one of the Mercerin, her Ranin rider lieing butchered at his feet as he gripped the beautiful mare by the horn. The animal, forever loyal to her rider, bucked and kicked, futilely attempting to crush her captor. The Samarians looked on, helpless, as her noble head was raised forcefully by the horn and that monster sank his teeth into her pure white throat. Her eyes flashed wildly as her blood drained away from her, big red spurts spattering over Ogiin's face. He revelled in the sensation of her immense power now mingling with his own. Throwing her dead body to the ground when he was done, he raised his face so the Samarians could see him clearly, and raising his arms high above him with fists clenched, he began roaring with laughter as the blood trickled down his chest. The sound was terrifying, but it paled into insignificance when they saw what happened next. He began to grow, becoming almost twice the stature he had been, but worse, much worse, he began to sprout wings. Aghast, they watched a large pair of feathered wings erupt from the charred stumps on his back. They were enormous, a dark purple, streaked with the crimson of his killings. The death of the unicorn, the draining of her life, had given the demon the means by which to fully regenerate, become complete, and regain all that he had once lost. He was once more the Ogiin of old, lord of nightmares, and any chance of overcoming him now seemed but a vain, fast fleeting fantasy.

Tamarin, knowing all was lost, was seconds from launching his horse at him one final time when Ogiin's eyes met his own. Something in that devil's glare made him stay his hand, holding back his men when Ogiin began to open his mouth. Wider and wider it opened until all one could do was to stare in abject horror as his lower jaw began to move down his chest. Soon his mouth was open so wide it could have held the heads of three large men. An emotionless pair of eyes continued to stare at the Samarians as he tipped his head right back. His laughter filled the air, another swarm of filth shooting skywards from his gaping jaws. Meekhi recognised the insects immediately—they were the same as those encountered in the Desert of Iret—where they had poured from the cooking pot. She warned Tamarin of the danger—of how the disgusting beetles burrowed their way inside their victims, devouring them from within. The Samarians were neither prepared or equipped to deal with anything of this appalling nature. The children looked at each other with hopeless expressions on their faces. Ogiin's army cheered and jeered as the clattering swarm hovering high above dived down towards the assembled warriors. A fury of arrows sailed harmlessly through the dense black cloud, ineffective against such small targets. There was no possible defence against this airborne plague. The evil swarm made a horrible crackling sound as it neared. It was almost upon them, ready to swamp the hapless warriors when a voice of iron rang out across the desert, the suns seeming to shy a little in deference when it roared, "NO."

The voice was as old as time and as commanding as the hands of fate. It was both soothing and calm, yet shattering in its magnificent majesty, its authority absolute. It had boomed out from the direction of Soledad, and as the Samarians craned their necks to find the source, a blast of searing blue flame tore across the sky from the city and smote the deadly plague of Ogiin's making. The vile insects floated down to earth as burnt ash, not a one remaining aloft.

Ogiin's eyes flashed red again. He looked beyond the horsemen to see a magnificent dragon flying directly at him from Soledad.

Its body emanated light of all colours and was far more dazzling than the two suns that now appeared to be dancing at its arrival. The Samarians roared, unable to believe what their own eyes were telling them. Their whooping and clapping of hands could be heard by the few gatekeepers remaining in the city. Men and women bowed their heads in honour of the mighty dragon sailing majestically over them. The children did the same whilst keeping one eye firmly fixed on this most mythical, and mighty, of all creatures. Zowie whispered excitedly to her cousins, "Ogiin's in the craphouse *now*, that's for sure."

The Great Dragon landed with serene grace between Tamarin of Samaria and the would-be invaders. Ogiin drew his brutal sword once more. The blade was forged from dragon scales, scales taken from the Dragons of Light that he had slain in history. He stared Chjandi directly in the eyes, and in a voice apparently unperturbed, he hissed, "YOU!"

The sparkling ruby eyes of the dragon glowed with the unimaginable power burning deep within them. He spoke, his flame-red voice calm, but unquestionably threatening; "Forsake your arms. Disband this unholy host. Take your leave to the darkest corner of the darkest world, swear to abide there, and there alone, and you may yet live. But, Ogiin, know this—I am Chjandi, sworn guardian of The Sacred Lights, protector of The Essence of Love, and friend to the Samarian Nation. If you do not submit forthwith to my demands without condition, you and yours shall perish this day, becoming as one with the sands, you are so much less than you were, vile tyrant, and I, I am so much *more* than I ever was."

Ogiin looked to the left, and then to the right, only to see his much vaunted army of darkness shrinking back from the deadly dragon in their midst, and the still-potent army of fearless warriors standing behind it. He glared back at Chjandi and the Great Dragon met his cold gaze unflinchingly. "Today," came Ogiin's voice, "I shall forge myself a new blade from your pathetic hide! Less than I was? You underestimate me yet again. I have sipped the nectar of the white unicorn and am reborn beyond my imaginings! You cannot know the power I feel coursing through my veins for you know nothing of absolute power. I thought you long dead, Chjandi, but it is good that you live still, for I will wreak such a vengeance upon you, you will wish you had remained but a memory."

The master of darkness came straight at the dragon with his sword held high. His feet were barely skimming the ground as his newfound wings began easily lofting his heft. He was met by a blazing torrent of flame that blasted him right back along the path he had created through his own creed. As he was rocketed away, Chjandi followed after him with slow, deliberate steps between the two walls of the enemy. Not a single hand or weapon was raised against the Great Dragon, and upon seeing him pursue Ogiin, Tamarin cried out; "Samarians! In the name of the Great Dragon! Strike now!"

For the last and final time, the remnants of his army clashed against Ogiin's creed. Lauren compensated for her earlier embarrassing upheaval by shooting a troll through the eye, her prized bow proving more effective than others. It was then finished off by Ranin and their Mercerin. The last of the trolls fell to Mercy and Meekhi, both making great use of their recently acquired scale-penetrating techniques. The horsemen and the children chased after what was left of the invading plague of darkness. Ogiin's creed had lost the will to fight after the arrival of Chjandi, and they were in full flight. Their soft, fleshy bodies offered no resistance to Samarian steel as the panic stricken vermin bolted, helter skelter, in all directions, trying desperately to escape. They were pursued and cut down without mercy until their former legions resembled no more than a horrific scene from some nightmarish slaughterhouse. The odd straggler could be seen here and there, heading for Dizbaar with determined riders in hot pursuit. Meekhi started jumping up and down on the dead troll, shaking her head violently, screaming obscenities at it that I still refuse to put into print.

Ogiin rose to his feet as Chjandi approached him. He dusted off the sand from his battledress and faced the dragon. "It would seem the might of your vaunted flames has waned over these many years. I remain unharmed and the cringing carrion running for the borders are of no consequence, they have served their purpose in my resurrection. I will deal with them after I tear off your head!"

He leapt forward with a shocking burst of speed, grappling with the dragon as they rolled over and over in the sand, each looking to gain the upper hand. Ogiin's massive fists pummelled away at Chjandi's head as the dragon sought to bring his talons to bear, each avoided the other's face for each knew the other's mouth held deadly dangers within. The Samarians moved well back, they knew such a battle was not for their meddling with. Darkness and Light ripped, tore, and gouged at each other, head smashing into head many a time. Ogiin gripped the dragon's wing, trying to tear at it, but Chjandi lashed out with a massive hind leg, hurling him away. Ogiin was on his feet in flash, already airborne when the blast of dragon's flame arrived where he had been standing half a second before, smelting the sand into glass. The creature—Ogiin, continued to gain height, his monstrous wings, driven by the power of his countless kills, carried him higher and higher until he was but a small speck silhouetted against the eastern sun. He began to dive at Chjandi at such a speed he was just an ever growing blur. The Great Dragon launched into the air, climbing as furiously as Ogiin was descending, his lips curled, teeth bared, and wings swept back. The pair met with such tremendous impact, that both were blasted from the sky, crashing heavily in the sand, and staggering groggily to their feet. Ogiin opened wide his pit of a mouth and from it spewed forth bright green insects with bulging yellow eyes. They were conical in shape, and like so many poison darts, they peppered the dragon's chest. The children gasped when they saw that the pointed tips had penetrated the dragon's scales and the vermin were now spinning, drilling their way through the dragon's thick armour. Chjandi shielded himself from the next blast of filth by using his mighty wings as shields. The insects burst on impact when hitting the sturdier scales of a dragon's wings. The silver dragon lowered its head behind its wings and blasted a fury of fire along its own body, the inferno incinerating the bugs in an instant. Ogiin pounced, his sword ready to strike at Chjandi's neck, but the dragon's stature belied his pace. Turning in an instant, his enormous tail lashed out, striking Ogiin square in the face in mid air, sending him tumbling head-over-heels in the sand. The dragon faced him. "Enough! Be not a fool, you accursed wretch, even a life as low as yours is born of The Source. Force me not to snuff out your black candle. I will not ask you to yield again."

"Ha! It is you that would do well to yield! Swear allegiance to my cause and I will let you live, as my pet! You can serve to bring me an endless feast of maidens for my delectation. Otherwise, oh sole survivor of a long since vanquished race, you will die, now!"

Ogiin soared once more into the heavens, hovering menacingly above the dragon with the flap-flapping of his enormous wings filling the air, his hellhole of a mouth beginning to open wide once more. Chjandi looked about him. "Stand back, good people of true faith, it is time to put end to this mockery of life."

The Great Dragon spread his wings and raised his head to face the tyrant in the sky. His body began a slight trembling as it began heating up. The colours flowing within started to fuse together, getting brighter and brighter until it was almost impossible to look upon him. The lord of the Dragons of Light reared up on his mighty rear haunches just as he beamed brighter than the suns, and a river of white-hot flame streamed from his gaping jaws. The scorching blast hit Ogiin square in the mouth, a river of pain flooding down his throat. The Samarians were forced to shield their eyes from the blinding light pouring from Chjandi as he bathed the entire landscape with his glow, the light of truth dimming even the suns. Ogiin, a stunned expression on his face, burst into flames in the sky. His wings beat furiously, but, they, too, were soon consumed by the flames burning within him. With a last roar of rage, and burned beyond recognition, he plummeted to the ground at breakneck speed. He lay writhing in the sand with smoke pouring from him when the Great Dragon approached. The suns were almost out of each others sight and a cool northerly wind, almost too shy to show itself before The Dragon, tentatively soothed the once blistering desert. Chjandi's glare had reduced, ceasing to beam so brilliantly.

"So, you think you have won?" Ogiin choked, grey wisps rising from his mouth, "Look up and you will see the darkness is returning again, as it always does, as it always will. One day will dawn a black day, night followed by night, a reign of eternal darkness. You cannot prevent this, oh lover of light."

When Chjandi took another step towards him, the smouldering Ogiin began to shake and tremble. Thomas commenting, "Look at him now, girls, he's filling his pants! He's squeezing cheese, I reckon."

Zowie wasn't convinced, "I don't think so, Tom. From what we've heard he's not easily made afraid. Takes some pluck to take on a dragon, I'd stay back if I were you, I think he's up to something dodgy."

Sure enough, a black mist appeared, enveloping Ogiin so as to completely obscure him from view in the fading light. Strange growling sounds came from within it as if a thousand wolves were fighting over some small morsel. Chjandi spread out his dazzling silver wings, forcing everyone to move to the rear of him. He spoke to the black haze before him. "It does not have to be this way. Take heed, you cannot win this day. Stop now, and still you can be spared. Take your true form, and you will be no more, oh servile son of evil."

A horrible loud crackling came from the mist and a pair of spiralled horns could be seen rising from it. They gleamed in the twilight of dusk, and appeared wet with blood. When the vapour eventually dispersed in the wind a gasp went up from every man, woman, and child, stood there. A true demon of the most terrifying countenance stood before the silver dragon. It was as tall as Chjandi, its body a dull grey, sparsely covered in thick black spines. Long curved claws, and those fearsome horns, added to the horror with their gaudy red hue. The creature had legs better suited to some giant reptile than any man, and a powerful forked tail snaked menacingly to the rear. It had large pointed ears and below its bull's nose was its mouth, awash with fangs the size of a fist. The only thing bearing any resemblance to Ogiin's former form were his eyes—lidless orbs still glowing with that same inner hate that simply refused to subside. It had feet with three hooked toes equiped with razor sharp talons. The two titans began to circle each other, Ogiin seething with fury, Chjandi calm, and composed. The Samarians moved well back, this was beyond anything they had ever known.

The demon appeared even more frightening in the gathering dusk and Lauren asked in a shaky voice, "Will Chjandi be alright?"

Tamarin placed a comforting hand on the shoulder of each of the young girls, "Fear not, my young friends. What we *see* is nothing, what we *feel* is everything. I feel the mighty dragon knows full well what he does. Oft times evil must show itself in its truest form so it may be seen for what it truly is, unmasked and thus revealed to the light, it can then be consigned unto the void for eternity. But to be destroyed, it must first be recognized, encountered, perhaps even *experienced*. Evil thrives on fear and we must not fear what we see, for what we see is not always the whole story. We must always remember that all life treads inexorably towards death—as The Source intended, and the dead, if remembered, are living still. It is by are our deeds that we are defined, not by haughty words or outward appearance, and if our deeds be worthy of memory, of leaving an honourable mark on history, we need not fear death. The Great Dragon is possessed of a wisdom I shall never know or fully understand. My lord—Chjandi, now deals the final hand of Ogiin's fate."

Ogiin stamped heavily in the sand, his tail curling and uncurling as it sought the perfect moment to strike. The silver dragon moved with grace, making small precise movements to keep him in check. Zowie noticed that Chjandi seemed to have a great sadness in his eyes, and she found herself weeping, though she couldn't say why. Another comforting hand was placed gently on her head, and when she looked up at Meekhi, she saw that she, too, was lost to her emotions.

In a flash, the demon leapt at the dragon, the pair crashing to the ground once more, snarling and grappling at each other. Ogiin's claws could not penetrate the dragon's scales and the pair wrestled in the dark as he tried to lance the dragon with his horns. Plumes of dust rose into the air, half obscuring the sight of them as two tremendous tails whipped the desert into a sandstorm. The beast that was Ogiin rained blow after blow upon the silver dragon, but had little effect, the blast of dragon's flame having sapped much of his strength. The dragon glowed in the twilight, the colours flowing through it seemingly getting brighter and brighter again, until, like a blinding beacon, it once more illuminated the entire landscape. The raging combatants broke free of each other and stepped back. Ogiin, offering no respite, lowered his head, trying to ram the dragon with his deadly horns. Chjandi reached out and grabbed them with his powerful talons, he glowed so intensely that everyone averted their eyes, and, in that second, he tore the horns from the demon's head and threw them aside. Ogiin roared accusingly at the darkening sky, as if the darkness itself should come to the aid of him that worshipped it most fervently, but the Samarian stars remained unmoved by his anguished pleas. In indescribable agony he backed away from the dragon and began to open his tortured mouth, the lips slyly parting further and further as he averted his gaze. But whatever new diabolical form of menace he intended to unleash, it was not to be. Chjandi released a storm of blue flame, the river of searing death engulfing him. He fell back into the sand, smoke rising from every pore. Yet *still* he staggered back to his feet. Livid with rage, and betrayed by his dark gods, he snarled at the Great Dragon in futile defiance. The multicoloured glow from the dragon reached such an intensity that it lit up not only the desert, but, also, the entire sky, a blinding blast of supernova heat issued forth, striking the oncoming Ogiin square in the chest and sending him flying amidst a gigantic fireball. The would-be tyrant was charred almost beyond recognition, but still he would not concede. Struggling for breath and with thin grey smoke pouring from his ruined mouth, he told the Great Dragon. "You, you cannot win. The dark is upon us as often as the day, but it is the dark that is the greater, look to the night sky and see the truth of what I say, lover of light, your days number but a few..."

"Perhaps, and perhaps not," Chjandi replied in a kindly, gentle tone, "but, for now, let us end your suffering, brother. It is indeed almost fully dark, and, within the folds of that very darkness, it is time for you to sleep the eternal sleep."

Ogiin, in unimagineable pain, and barely able to move his shattered body, finally nodded his head in approval. With the tenderness of a doting mother, the Great Dragon placed his massive jaws about Ogiin's neck, and, with eyes deeply pained with sorrow, put an end to his suffering, forever.

He carried Ogiin's remains far away from the battlefield, and with a final blast from his fiery breath, he gave him the respect, and honour, of a funeral pyre.

The desert was littered with dead. Friend and foe, alike, wrought an ugly landscape filled with broken and twisted corpses. The carnage left by war a woeful reminder of the pointless futility of such things. Tamarin and Meekhi stood in the midst of the smouldering aftermath holding each other close, even as Ramulet and Mercy did the same elsewhere. Imo was busy pulling teeth from a dead troll to form a necklace for himself as a keepsake. He had offered to bring Thomas an eyeball but the young warrior had declined his generosity. The children stared all about them, finally realising that the war was over—they had won, and they were stuck in a world from which they did not know how to return home. Suddenly they felt very homesick and longed for the smiling faces of their friends in their own world, and the loving embrace of their parents. They saw Chjandi land close to Tamarin and Meekhi, beginning a discreet conversation with them. They could have sworn they heard their own names mentioned but wouldn't dream of inquiring on such matters. An hour or so later, the Great Dragon soared skywards and out, over Soledad, his glowing shape soon indistinguishable from the thousands of stars shining around him. No one asked the royal couple what he had said, where he had gone, or if he would ever return. It was just plainly obvious that his conversation with them had been intensely private. None would venture to dare to violate that confidence.

The following days were, at first, sad, and mournful, despite the great victory and the final thwarting of Ogiin's lust for tyrannical dominion over all life. This was because so many funeral pyres littered the sands outside Soledad in honour of the fallen brave. Much further away, a very large wreaking mound also smouldered in flames, piled high with the corpses of Ogiin's creed. This was no honourable pyre but rather built in the interests of sanitation, giving some degree of satisfaction to the survivors of the great battle as they watched their former foe become as ash. But as is the case with any great war, the people began to come to terms with their losses sooner than expected, and also with the fact that they were the ones chosen to endure.

The city was cleaned up and the streets cleared, thousands of sooty, blackened torches were stowed safely away—there was no longer any need to fear the dark. Chjandi had assured Tamarin that the Shadows—spectral extensions of Ogiin that they were, had perished at exactly the same time that their master had expired. The enchanting underground lake of Solenia turned a dazzling green in hue, and its pure waters once more felt deliciously warm to the touch. The children were beside themselves in disbelief when the legion of fairy folk awoke and paid homage to Tamarin. The floor of the Throne Room appeared to be covered in the most fantastic, most mesmerizing, butterflies, when Hi-Light led her people there. They, along with everyone else that did not normally reside within the ancient walls of Soledad, remained in the city to witness and celebrate the joyous occasion of the marriage of The Captain of The Royal Guards, to Lady Mercy. The marriage was a grand occasion with much revelry, dancing, and singing, followed by a dazzling display of fireworks. Faradorr introduced Rordorr to the joys of beer, and then Rordorr fell asleep, missing entirely the fireworks display he had been so looking forward to. He was convinced that as he had slept the pungent fumes from the fireworks had penetrated his ears, swearing that his hearing was fast beginning to fail him as a direct result, and he could see smoke occasionally leaking from around his eyes. The following day the winged brothers left Soledad to return to their homes in the faraway mountains, where the wife of one, and the apple of the other's eyes, awaited them eagerly. There was many a tear shed at the departing of the flying horses, particularly by the children.

Tamarin and Meekhi were immeasurably grateful to Ramulet and Mercy for their brave, selfless parts in the battle. As a gift upon their marriage, Ramulet was promoted Lord of Soledad, and he and his beautiful young wife were given the cares, pleasures, and responsibilities of the city. When Tamarin and Meekhi were ready to return to Sitivia with her citizens, the children rode out with them to the coastal capital. On their journey back across the desert Meekhi pointed, crying out happily, "Look! The land lives! Samaria doth breathe deep her fullest breaths once more."

Their eyes followed the direction of her finger and saw that where the Desert of Iret had been a barren landscape full of lies, treachery, and pollution of the soul, now the most breathtaking trees and plants were shooting up from the ground, many of them showing silver veins. A heavenly scent wafted over to the riders from the blooming oasis ahead, carrying the innocent kiss of white jasmine mingled with the passionate, exotic embrace of sandalwood, rose, and desert-lilly. As far as the eye could see, flowers were bursting into life—breaking from their tight little buds and climbing ever upward from the rich black soil that nourished their roots. Tamarin looked over at his beautiful young queen sat atop her pure white charger. Her silken black tresses—freshly washed and scented, framed her delicate features perfectly, and those magnetic emerald eyes were looking back at him, as always. He told her, "My lady, the Gardens of Paradise are alive once more for us Samarians to know, and to cherish. Not a trace of that aged old hag—Teritee, remains in this land, nor within you, or in any of our people. No doubt, that repulsive witch that is wickedness personified will endeavour to survive somewhere else, but be assured she will never find refuge or sanctuary on Samarian soil again. The Royal Guards are instructed to finish her on sight, though I do not believe she will dare soil our sands again with her putrid presence."

Meekhi smiled happily, the entourage continueing on its way with the children bringing up the rear.

Sitivia awaited them with open arms and Meekhi wept openly with joy upon returning to her true home. The Royal Guards swept the city for any lingering vermin, but found none. The palace atop the cliffs was lovingly restored by the people in honour of their king and queen. Once they were sure Tamarin and Meekhi were once again safely ensconced in their royal home, both Bestwin and Lumarr took their leave. After warm, tearful, farewells, they left for the Western Worlds. Once there, they would protect the vacant throne until Queen Yasmina returned, or, if she did not, another arose worthy of that noble seat.

Tamarin and Meekhi were kept busy over the next few days putting their realm back to rights, so the children spent most of their time with Imo. The elves had chosen to leave Soledad and go back to their elfish lands. They had left with Babel leading a mule loaded down with gifts, and with Solipop weighed down with sacks of fresh, and dried, dates. His fur had been a sticky mess of date juice baking in the heat of two suns as he waved goodbye with his tail.

Imo showed the children all the amazing sights of the city and they helped him to repair The Talking Table. It was given a final polish with an abundance of beeswax, and everyone swore that, afterwards, the wise old face seemed to harbour the faintest hint of a smile. No one walked past the statue of The Great Dragon without feeling butterflies in their stomach. After all, who knew when it might begin to move!

The children were on the beach on the seaward side of the palace, below the cliffs. It had been nearly three weeks since the great battle of Soledad and they were getting very concerned as to what would happen next. Admittedly, all three would have happily lived out the rest of their lives in Samaria, but they loved their parents dearly and could not even imagine how hurt and upset they would be if their children never returned home. Not knowing what would happen next, they relied on the timer on the Dream Machine to time out, and hopefully draw them back home. They were practising archery and, as usual, Lauren was by far the best archer present. She was also a very good teacher and had improved upon the archery skills of the other two a hundredfold. They looked up at the muted sound of footfalls on the sand. It was Tamarin and Meekhi. He wore a splendid black silk cloak that boasted the silver dragon over his royal garb. Meekhi also looked resplendent in a cape matching her husband's, but under hers she wore a long dress that mimicked the green of her eyes exactly. The twosome looked as perfect a pairing as was ever made in any world. Meekhi was carrying something in her arms.

Upon reaching the children, she gave each of them a gift—it was a cloak, a cloak exactly the same as the ones draping the shoulders of the royal couple. The children were about to say, "Thanks, but there's really no need," (as any polite person would, and *should*), when Tamarin politely silenced them with a raised hand. His eyes were as full of respect as Meekhi's were brimming with emotion, "I must relieve you of your weapons, they shall rest in the great hall of Sitivia until you have need of them again." He told them.

"Oh!" came the surprised reply.

"Ok... of course." Zowie unbuckled the exquisite sword Meekhi had given her in what seemed an eternity ago, and handed it over.

Smiling weakly, Thomas passed over his weapon. "I will miss this beastie sword being on my belt."

Lauren couldn't hide her sadness as she gave Meekhi the gleaming black bow. "I love this bow. I will always love it."

With the greatest courtesy, Zowie asked, "I don't wish to appear rude, Tamarin, but lots of people carry their swords in Sitivia, are we having to give them back because we're foreign?"

"Foreign? No, little one, the three of you will never be foreigners here. Samaria is yours as much as mine, but..." He met her eyes with a look of warm affection, "I am reliably informed that young warriors such as the three of you cannot carry such weapons in... your homeland."

"But we're not in our homeland right now, are we?" Thomas, too, needed an explanation for having to surrender his sword.

Meekhi's green eyes twinkled excitedly in the sun, and she told them, "No, but you soon will be."

"What! *Home*, how!" Lauren felt a hot flush starting to break across her face.

Tamarin gestured out over the sea, "*There.*"

In the distance, low over the ocean, a silver streak surrounded by a rainbow of colour was bearing down on them at breathtaking speed, vaporising the water as it passed over it.

"Crikey!" Thomas shouted, "Samaria has got F-14's! Or is that a Navy Harrier?"

No one had a chance to answer, or berate, him, as a few seconds later the Great Dragon alighted on the beach. He approached the five people awaiting him. The children could not help feeling a little jittery. It was not everyday they met a dragon, let alone the lord of all dragons. His ruby eyes were filled with dancing flames and all the colours of the universe flowed through his mighty silver frame. He nodded sagely to Tamarin, and Tamarin bade the children kneel. They did so without hesitation. There and then, Tamarin asked Thomas if he would take the oath of knighthood, and Thomas did, rising a Samarian Knight. Meekhi asked Zowie and Lauren if they swore fealty to the Crown of Samaria, they did, and rose as Ladies of The Royal Court.

Much to their own surprise, the children suddenly found they did not feel like leaving Samaria at all. But they had learned much from the Samarians. They knew what must be, must be. They simply had to put their full faith in the Great Dragon. There were long lasting, tearful embraces, followed by firm, lingering handshakes. Tamarin shook Thomas by the forearm and saluted him with 'The Flame of Dragonia', the boy bowing his head in return. When the beautiful queen kissed his forehead, he felt sure he would just melt into the sand. Tamarin bade fond farewells to the girls, kissing them on their foreheads too, with hopes of meeting again one day. He and Meekhi reluctantly stepped back from the young trio.

The Great Dragon lowered his head to face the children. In his gloriously rich, velvet voice, he asked them, "So, you would have a dream of your own choosing and creation, would you?"

Zowie, having the benefit of that elusive gift we call hindsight, replied, "Oh blimey, no! We didn't know what would happen. My dad is a really good, kind, man. If there really *is* anything Samarian about me at all, it's *him*."

"Well said, young Zowie," Chjandi told her, "an unselfish answer, for the benefit of another. Tell your father—this machine must never breathe again. I will be watching. I see no malice in you young ones, nor in the trees from which you have sprouted. I shall return you to your own world."

"Please! Before we go—Mr Great Dragon, please can you tell us—will Samaria be ok now? Will Tamarin, Meekhi, and everyone else, be safe from that maniac Ogiin and his dodgy crew?" Zowie had asked Chjandi what all three of them were wondering.

The Great Dragon tilted his huge majestic head to one side, pausing for a second before answering the question that had been asked of him. "Little ones, during the day we look to the sun and see daylight. We see blue skies and we are happy, safe within the warmth afforded us at that time. At night, we look to the skies and see the millions of stars, a multitude of worlds beyond our ken. We see little points of light in the heavens, but we too often fail to see that which is right before our eyes—The Dark. Look between the lights and see which is the greater? The darkness, or, the lights? It is fortunate indeed that such little light can hold back so much darkness. As we cannot reduce the all encompassing veil of darkness, we must always aspire to brighten the lights."

The children understood Chjandi perfectly, and after asking consent from Tamarin, Meekhi rushed forward and placed her little vial of colours about Zowie's neck. "Bring it back, Zowie, we will be waiting for it, and, *for all of you*."

She had shocked Zowie with the priceless gift, leaving her speechless. The Great Dragon spoke again, "You have served and honoured my people well, little ones! Now we shall honour *you*. You had a dream of flying, yes? Would you care to fly now on the back of A *DRAGON!*"

"Definitely yes!" they cheered excitedly as Chjandi lowered a tremendous forearm so they might clamber onto his back, sitting between his enormous silver wings.

The children waved furiously, bidding their farewells to the royal couple standing on the beach. The Samarians raised their swords in salute as Chjandi—the greatest of all of The Dragons of Light, soared high into the air. The dragon of myth and legend sailed effortlessly across Samaria, and the children, their silken cloaks blowing about them in the wind, watched as they passed over Sitivia, the Gardens of Paradise, the desert, Soledad, and then along the mighty Emerald River. Tears streamed down their faces, at both—the leaving of this beautiful, magical land, but also, at the prospect of *home*. The wind played musically about their faces, making their eyes stream even the more. They could smell the exotic, heady scents of Samaria, rising up from below, and the dragon felt so warm and safe under them. They held on tight and watched the hypnotic array of colours flowing constantly under their hands.

The Pink Mountain loomed ahead and they wondered how exactly they were to get home. When they were almost at the mouth of the mountain of dreams, Chjandi spoke to them. "Be at peace, little ones. The friendship and love you have found, and that which has found you, is a bond not easily broken. Remember—love shines well in the light, but burns the brighter in the dark. Now, you can, at last, fly. Or at least you can…FALL!"

With the deepest, most wholesome laugh the children had ever heard, the Great Dragon shot over the centre of the crater, and turned upside down. They plummeted earthwards, screaming as the dragon roared with fiery laughter.

They opened their eyes cautiously, expecting to find themselves with broken bones aplenty. But there was no pain, and there were no broken bones. They squinted, shaking their heads. There, through the clear sphere, stood Dug, Jack, and Lilley, drinking cups of tea.

"We're back! We're ok! We are back!" The children screamed and yelled at their parents. There was a very precise click as the intercom was switched on, and they heard Dug's voice, "Calm down, you noisy lot! We can't see you yet! The timer has only just buzzed. Wait for the Black Light to dissipate, then, I'll open the door."

The trio lay back in the super-comfy chairs, what would they tell their parents? No one would ever believe them. They knew they had to tell the truth (as children, *and* adults, should always do), but also knew they would look complete idiots.

The adults watched as the black Dreampod interior began to lighten. It was as if a silent, invisible vacuum was sucking the darkness from the glass globe. Then, in an instant, full vision was restored, and Lilly's mug of tea crashed to the floor. Dug raced to the door to then have an excited Zowie leap on him, hugging him for all she was worth. The Shortwaters did the same with Jack and Lilly. Zowie kissed her dad's face over and over, overjoyed to see him again, feeling that unconditional embrace of love that only a father can bestow upon a daughter. Thomas and Lauren looked to Zowie to explain their adventure as it was her father's machine that had to be dismantled.

"You will never believe us, dad, but you really, *really*, must!" She told him.

"Oh, I think we *might* believe you." He replied calmly, messing up her hair.

"*You might?*" Zowie was puzzled, "Why might you?"

"*Because*," Lilly butted in, "You didn't look like *that* when you got into the Dreampod."

The children only then realised they were still wearing their Samarian clothing, including the silk cloaks bearing the silver crest of the Great Dragon. Given the undeniable evidence of the clothing, and Thomas' little scar on his arm, the parents had no choice but to believe them. Dug immediately unplugged everything from the Dreampod and vowed to dismantle it the following day. To avoid any padded cells or unnecessary investigations, the six of them swore secrecy on the whole matter. Dug, Lilly, and Jack, were only too grateful that the children had returned unharmed from their bizarre, fantastical adventure. They would all have to go the doctor's for a general check-up of course, just to be sure all was as it should be. This did not please the children much, but it was a small price to pay.

The adults spent all day discussing what had happened to the youngsters, so the children went outside for some fresh air. Fumbling in the folds of her Samarian clothing, Lauren found the little piece of the Pink Mountain she had taken when they first arrived in that far off world. She showed the others, and all at once they looked up at the imposing figure of the silver dragon that formed the fountain. Lauren passed the piece of glowing pink crystal to Zowie, and the three of them stood before the dragon. The maidens were still bathing in the water, 'warmed' by the dragon's breath, the fibre optic wizardry illuminating the lithe, female figures, in a rainbow of colours. Zowie stepped forward and searched about to try and find the source of the lighting. She found it was coming from a hole at the rear of the pool in which the maidens bathed. The other two nodded approval, and she placed the small glowing piece of Samaria deep inside that hole. Stepping back, the three of them knelt on one knee, Zowie being in the middle. She looked up at the statue—thinking of the Great Dragon and their Samarian friends. "Forgive us, Great Dragon of Light, we did not mean to steal from your people, or from you. We return to you what is yours. We were, and will always remain, your loyal friends. We have faith."

They got back to their feet, and as they walked away they did not notice more colours appearing, shining even brighter in the waters of the fountain. Zowie did, however, feel a fleeting burst of heat in the vial at the base of her neck. She put it down to wishful thinking.

THE END...

EPILOGUE

Dorinn smiled smugly to himself, confident he had made good his escape. Who were these clowns—Lumarr and Bestwin, to think they could depose *him*! He would deal with them in due course. Did they think he did not have friends and allies? He would reach Dizbaar shortly, and be warmly welcomed by Nazmeer—the iron-willed ruler of that land. From there, he would plot his revenge on the Westonian traitors, and upon that pathetic boy-king of Samaria—Tamarin.

The desert heat had sapped away any remaining strength he had, but, he thought, at least he had had the good sense to drink all the water he had stolen from Soledad, rather than sharing it with the horse that was rapidly expiring beneath him. Looking ahead, he thought he could see movement and assumed it must be a mirage. Yet the closer he got, the more he became convinced that the vision was indeed real. A beautiful young woman was trudging haphazard across the baking sands. She was staggering in all directions, often falling on her face, then struggling to regain her feet in the loose sand. A victim of severe sunstroke at best, she wore a threadbare earthen-coloured robe that could barely hold itself together. Despite her exhausted and grimy state, her obvious womanly charms were in full view of the lecherous Dorinn as he sidled up beside her. She looked up with cold blue eyes, brushing aside her filthy hair. It was long, russet, reaching just past her shoulders, and coarse, almost wiry. Most of her makeshift dress had long since shredded and her semi-nudity caused Dorinn to stare like the scoundrel he was. She pleaded with him to save her from the severe and hostile terrain, swearing to forever serve him in every conceivable way if he did. Clutching at his leg with a surprisingly strong grip, she told him that if he would but spare her life and carry her away from the punishing torment of the blazing suns, she would become his loyal slave, bringing to him delights he had never imagined possible. The desert-weary beauty gave her name as—Anntillee.

Dorinn knew his tired and haggard horse would most surely die carrying *two* to the borders of Dizbaar, but what did that matter? After all, now he would not only have the hospitality of Nazmeer, but a healthy young wench to warm his cot at night. He reached out to haul the woman up behind him. It didn't bother him in the least when he noticed her left hand had two fingers missing.